NEIL GAIMAN

AMERICAN GODS

HEADLINE

First published in Great Britain in 2001 by HEADLINE BOOK PUBLISHING

First published in paperback in Great Britain in 2002 by HEADLINE BOOK PUBLISHING

First published in Great Britain in this paperback edition in 2005 by REVIEW
An imprint of HEADLINE BOOK PUBLISHING

This edition published in 2017 by HEADLINE PUBLISHING GROUP

6

'The Monarch of the Glen' taken from *Fragile Things*,
first published in 2006 by HEADLINE REVIEW

We gratefully acknowledge the following for granting us
permission to use their material in this book:

Excerpt from 'The Witch of Coos' from 'Two Witches' from *The Poetry of Robert Frost*,
edited by Edward Connery Latham, © 1951 Robert Frost, copyright 1923, 1969 by
Henry Holt and Co. Reprinted by permission of Henry Holt and Co., LLC. 'Tango Til
They're Sore' by Tom Waits. Copyright © 1985 Jalma Music. Used by permission.
All rights reserved. 'Old Friends' music and lyrics by Stephen Sondheim, © 1981 Rilting
Music, Inc. All rights reserved. Used by permission. Warner Bros. Publications US Inc.,
Miami, FL 33014. 'In the Dark With You' by Greg Brown. Copyright © 1985
Brown/Feldman Music, Hacklebarney Music/ASCAP. Used by permission. All rights
reserved. The lines from 'in Just—', copyright 1923, 1951, © 1991 Trustees for the
E. E. Cummings Trust. Copyright © 1976 George James Firmage, from *Complete Poems:
1904–1962* by E. E. Cummings, edited by George J. Firmage. Used by permission of
Liveright Publishing Corp. 'Don't let me be Misunderstood' by Bennie Benjamin, Sol
Marcus and Gloria Caldwell, © 1964 Bennie Benjamin Music Inc., © renewed, assigned
to WB Music Corp., Bennie Benjamin Music, Inc. and Chris-N-Jen Music. All rights o/b/o
Bennie Benjamin Music Inc. administered by Chappell & Co. All rights reserved. Used by
permission. Warner Bros. Publications US Inc., Miami, FL 33014. Excerpt from 'The
Second Coming' reprinted with the permission of Scribner, a division of Simon & Schuster
Inc., from *The Poems of W. B. Yeats: A New Edition*, edited by Richard J. Finneran.
Copyright © 1924 Macmillan Publishing Company; copyright renewed © 1952 Bertha
Georgie Yeats. (Every effort has been made to locate and contact the copyright owners
of material reproduced in this book. Omissions brought to our attention will be
corrected in subsequent editions.)

ISBN 978 1 4722 4554 0 (B format)
ISBN 978 1 4722 4908 1 (A format)

Typeset in ZapfEllipt by Avon DataSet Ltd, Bidford on Avon

Printed and bound by CPI Group (UK) Ltd, Croydon, CR0 4YY

Headline's policy is to use papers that are natural, renewable and recyclable products and
made from wood grown in sustainable forests. The logging and manufacturing processes
are expected to conform to the environmental regulations of the country of origin.

HEADLINE PUBLISHING GROUP
An Hachette UK Company
Carmelite House
50 Victoria Embankment
London EC4Y 0DZ

www.headline.co.uk
www.hachette.co.uk

Praise for Neil Gaiman

'Gaiman is god in the universe of story' Stephen Fry

'A very fine and imaginative writer' *The Sunday Times*

'Fantasy rooted in the darkest corners of reality' *Independent on Sunday*

'Gaiman is a master of fear, and he understands the nature of fairytales' A S Byatt, *Guardian*

'Gaiman's achievement is to make the fantasy world seem true' *The Times*

'In prose that dances and dazzles, Gaiman describes the indescribable' Susanna Clarke

'One of the best fabulists of our age' *Financial Times*

'Gaiman is, simply put, a treasure-house of story, and we are lucky to have him' Stephen King

'His mind is a dark, fathomless ocean, and every time I sink into it, this world fades, replaced by one far more terrible and beautiful in which I will happily drown' *New York Times Book Review*

'A rich imagination . . . and an ability to tackle large themes' Philip Pullman

'He's the master of fantasy and realism twisted together' Hugo Rifkind, *Spectator*

'A power that defies explanation' *Sunday Express*

'Neil Gaiman is a star. He constructs stories like some demented cook might make a wedding cake, building layer upon layer, including all kinds of sweet and sour in the mix' Clive Barker

By Neil Gaiman and published by Headline

The View From The Cheap Seats
Trigger Warning
The Ocean at the End of the Lane
Fragile Things
Anansi Boys
American Gods
Stardust
Smoke and Mirrors
Neverwhere

How the Marquis Got His Coat Back
(*a* Neverwhere *short story*)

Illustrated editions

American Gods
Anansi Boys
The Monarch of the Glen
Black Dog
(*illustrated by Daniel Egnéus*)

Neverwhere
(*illustrated by Chris Riddell*)

The Truth is a Cave in the Black Mountains
(*illustrated by Eddie Campbell*)

How to Talk to Girls at Parties
(*adaptation and artwork by Fábio Moon and Gabriel Bá*)

Troll Bridge
(*adaptation and artwork by Colleen Doran*)

Forbidden Brides of the Faceless Slaves in the Secret House
of the Night of Dread Desire
(*adaptation and artwork by Shane Oakley*)

MirrorMask: The Illustrated Film Script
(*with Dave McKean*)

For absent friends – Kathy Acker and
Roger Zelazny, and all points between

Caveat, and Warning for Travelers

This is a work of fiction, not a guidebook. While the geography of the United States of America in this tale is not entirely imaginary – many of the landmarks in this book can be visited, paths can be followed, ways can be mapped – I have taken liberties. Fewer liberties than you might imagine, but liberties nonetheless.

Permission has neither been asked nor given for the use of real places in this story when they appear: I expect that the owners of Rock City or the House on the Rock, and the hunters who own the motel in the centre of America are as perplexed as anyone would be to find their properties here.

I have obscured the location of several of the places in this book: the town of Lakeside, for example, and the farm with the ash-tree an hour south of Blacksburg. You may look for them if you wish. You might even find them. Furthermore, it goes without saying that all of the people, living, dead and otherwise in this story are fictional or used in a fictional context. Only the gods are real.

One question that has always intrigued me is what happens to demonic beings when immigrants move from their homelands. Irish-Americans remember the fairies, Norwegian-Americans the *nisser*, Greek-Americans the *vrykólakas*, but only in relation to events remembered in the Old Country. When I once asked why such demons are not seen in America, my informants giggled confusedly and said, 'They're scared to pass the ocean, it's too far,' pointing out that Christ and the apostles never came to America.

Richard Dorson, 'A Theory for American Folklore', *American Folklore and the Historian*, (University of Chicago Press, 1971)

Introduction to This Text

The book you're holding is slightly different from the version of the book that was previously published.

I wrote *American Gods* over a couple of years between 1999 and 2001. I wanted it to be a number of things. I wanted to write a book that was big and odd and meandering, and I did. I finished it, eventually, and I handed it in, taking a certain amount of comfort in the old saying that a novel can best be defined as a long piece of prose with something wrong with it, and I was fairly sure that I'd written one of those. My editor was concerned that the book was slightly too big and too meandering (she didn't mind it being too odd), and she wanted me to trim it, and I did. I suspect her instincts may have been right, for the book was very successful – it sold many copies, and it was given a number of awards including the Nebula and the Hugo awards (for, primarily, SF), the Bram Stoker award (for horror), the Locus award (for fantasy), demonstrating that it may have been a fairly odd novel and that even if it was popular nobody was quite certain which box it belonged in. And, of course, that people liked it.

Two of the people who liked it were Pete Atkins and Peter

Schneider, the partners in Hill House, Publishers, a small press book publisher, who, a few years later, arranged with the book's US publishers to do a small press edition of *American Gods*. As they told me about the wonderful treats they had planned for the limited edition – something they planned to be a miracle of the book-maker's art – I began feeling more and more uncomfortable with the text that they would be using.

Would they, I enquired rather diffidently, be willing to use my original, untrimmed text?

As it turned out, they would.

And then it became more complicated, as I realized that, of course, *after* I had trimmed *American Gods*, I had made other editorial corrections and changes, many of which were for the better. So the only way someone could create a definitive *American Gods* text would be by comparing my final, unedited version with my final edited version, and then with the final printed version (because I had cheerfully scrawled changes on the galley proofs, and just as cheerfully not actually bothered to keep track of them), and then making a number of judgement calls.

It was going to be an enormous amount of work. So I did the only sane thing under the circumstances that I could do: I sent several enormous computer files and two copies of the book (the English and the American editions) to Pete Atkins, along with my list of errors and typos I'd noticed since the book was published, and I asked him to sort it out. He did, excellently. Then I took the manuscript that Pete had prepared and went through it myself, fixing things and tidying and sometimes restoring cuts I'd made for a reason that wasn't just making it a bit shorter, to come up with a final version of the text that I was perfectly happy with, given that a novel is always, at least for the author, a long piece of prose with something wrong with it.

Hill House published it in a very nice (and expensive) limited edition of about 750 copies (described as 'a miracle of the book-maker's art' and not by them this time). They sent the books out along with free 'reader's copies' so the person who had bought the book could read the expanded text without worrying about getting jam stains on any of the pages.

When Headline Books decided it was time to reissue all my novels in this extremely elegant uniform edition, they enquired whether it would be possible to add anything to any of the books, as extra value for the readers – interviews and suchlike. In the case of *American Gods*, I had an entire book that I wanted people to read. This version of *American Gods* is about twelve thousand words longer than the one that won all the awards, and it's the version of which I'm the most proud.

I'm grateful that Headline were willing to publish the expanded version of the book, and I would particularly like to thank Pete Atkins for his help in the preparation of this manuscript.

On a plane to Singapore, 3 July, 2005

Part One
SHADOWS

Chapter One

The boundaries of our country, sir? Why sir, onto the north we are bounded by the Aurora Borealis, on the east we are bounded by the rising sun, on the south we are bounded by the procession of the Equinoxes, and on the west by the Day of Judgement.

– The American Joe Miller's Jest Book

Shadow had done three years in prison. He was big enough, and looked don't-fuck-with-me enough that his biggest problem was killing time. So he kept himself in shape, and taught himself coin tricks, and thought a lot about how much he loved his wife.

The best thing – in Shadow's opinion, perhaps the only good thing – about being in prison was a feeling of relief. The feeling that he'd plunged as low as he could plunge and he'd hit bottom. He didn't worry that the man was going to get him, because the man had got him. He did not awake in prison with a feeling of dread; he was no longer scared of what tomorrow might bring, because yesterday had brought it.

It did not matter, Shadow decided, if you had done what

you had been convicted of or not. In his experience everyone
he met in prison was aggrieved about something: there was
always something the authorities had got wrong, something
they said you did when you didn't – or you didn't do quite
like they said you did. What was important was that they
had got you.

He had noticed it in the first few days, when everything,
from the slang to the bad food, was new. Despite the misery
and the utter skin-crawling horror of incarceration, he was
breathing relief.

Shadow tried not to talk too much. Somewhere around the
middle of year two he mentioned his theory to Low Key
Lyesmith, his cell-mate.

Low Key, who was a grifter from Minnesota, smiled his
scarred smile. 'Yeah,' he said. 'That's true. It's even better
when you've been sentenced to death. That's when you
remember the jokes about the guys who kicked their boots
off as the noose flipped around their necks, because their
friends always told them they'd die with their boots on.'

'Is that a joke?' asked Shadow.

'Damn right. Gallows humor. Best kind there is – bang, the
worst has happened. You get a few days for it to sink in, then
you're riding the cart on your way to do the dance on
nothing.'

'When did they last hang a man in this state?' asked
Shadow.

'How the hell should I know?' Lyesmith kept his orange-
blond hair pretty much shaved. You could see the lines of his
skull. 'Tell you what, though. This country started going to
hell when they stopped hanging folks. No gallows dirt. No
gallows deals.'

Shadow shrugged. He could see nothing romantic in a
death sentence.

If you didn't have a death sentence, he decided, then
prison was, at best, only a temporary reprieve from life, for
two reasons. First, life creeps back into prison. There are

always places to go further down, even when you've been taken off the board; life goes on, even if it's life under a microscope or life in a cage. And second, if you just hang in there, some day they're going to have to let you out.

In the beginning it was too far away for Shadow to focus on. Then it became a distant beam of hope, and he learned how to tell himself 'this too shall pass' when the prison shit went down, as prison shit always did. One day the magic door would open and he'd walk through it. So he marked off the days on his *Songbirds of North America* calendar, which was the only calendar they sold in the prison commissary, and the sun went down and he didn't see it and the sun came up and he didn't see it. He practiced coin tricks from a book he found in the wasteland of the prison library; and he worked out; and he made lists in his head of what he'd do when he got out of prison.

Shadow's lists got shorter and shorter. After two years he had it down to three things.

First, he was going to take a bath. A real, long, serious soak, in a tub with bubbles in. Maybe read the paper, maybe not. Some days he thought one way, some days the other.

Second he was going to towel himself off, put on a robe. Maybe slippers. He liked the idea of slippers. If he smoked he would be smoking a pipe about now, but he didn't smoke. He would pick up his wife in his arms ('Puppy,' she would squeal in mock horror and real delight, 'what are you *doing*?'). He would carry her into the bedroom, and close the door. They'd call out for pizzas if they got hungry.

Third, after he and Laura had come out of the bedroom, maybe a couple of days later, he was going to keep his head down and stay out of trouble for the rest of his life.

'And then you'll be happy?' asked Low Key Lyesmith. That day they were working in the prison shop, assembling bird-feeders, which was barely more interesting than stamping out license plates.

'Call no man happy,' said Shadow, 'until he is dead.'

'Herodotus,' said Low Key. 'Hey. You're learning.'

'Who the fuck's Herodotus?' asked the Iceman, slotting together the sides of a birdfeeder, and passing it to Shadow, who bolted and screwed it tight.

'Dead Greek,' said Shadow.

'My last girlfriend was Greek,' said the Iceman. 'The shit her family ate. You would not believe. Like rice wrapped in leaves. Shit like that.'

The Iceman was the same size and shape as a Coke machine, with blue eyes and hair so blonde it was almost white. He had beaten the crap out of some guy who had made the mistake of copping a feel off his girlfriend in the bar where she danced and the Iceman bounced. The guy's friends had called the police, who arrested the Iceman and ran a check on him which revealed that the Iceman had walked from a work-release program eighteen months earlier.

'So what was I supposed to do?' asked the Iceman, aggrieved, when he had told Shadow the whole sad tale. "I'd told him she was my girlfriend. Was I supposed to let him disrespect me like that? Was I? I mean, he had his hands all over her.'

Shadow had said something meaningless like 'You tell 'em,' and left it at that. One thing he had learned early, you do your own time in prison. You don't do anyone else's time for them.

Keep your head down. Do your own time.

Lyesmith had loaned Shadow a battered paperback copy of Herodotus's *Histories* several months earlier. 'It's not boring. It's cool,' he said, when Shadow protested that he didn't read books. 'Read it first, then tell me it's cool.'

Shadow had made a face, but he had started to read, and had found himself hooked against his will.

'Greeks,' said the Iceman, with disgust. 'And it ain't true what they say about them, neither. I tried giving it to my girlfriend in the ass, she almost clawed my eyes out.'

Lyesmith was transferred one day, without warning. He left Shadow his copy of Herodotus with several actual coins hidden in the pages: two quarters, a penny, and a nickel. Coins were contraband: you can sharpen the edges against a stone, slice open someone's face in a fight. Shadow didn't want a weapon; Shadow just wanted something to do with his hands.

Shadow was not superstitious. He did not believe in anything he could not see. Still, he could feel disaster hovering above the prison in those final weeks, just as he had felt it in the days before the robbery. There was a hollowness in the pit of his stomach which he told himself was simply a fear of going back to the world on the outside. But he could not be sure. He was more paranoid than usual, and in prison usual is very, and is a survival skill. Shadow became more quiet, more shadowy, than ever. He found himself watching the body language of the guards, of the other inmates, searching for a clue to the bad thing that was going to happen, as he was certain that it would.

A month before he was due to be released, Shadow sat in a chilly office, facing a short man with a port-wine birthmark on his forehead. They sat across a dook from each other; the man had Shadow's file open in front of him, and was holding a ballpoint pen. The end of the pen was badly chewed.

'You cold, Shadow?'

'Yes,' said Shadow. 'A little.'

The man shrugged. 'That's the system,' he said. 'Furnaces don't go on until December the first. Then they go off March the first. I don't make the rules.' Social niceties done with, he ran his forefinger down the sheet of paper stapled to the inside left of the folder. 'You're thirty-two years old?'

'Yes, sir.'

'You look younger.'

'Clean living.'

'Says here you've been a model inmate.'

'I learned my lesson, sir.'

'Did you? Did you really?' He looked at Shadow intently, the birthmark on his forehead lowering. Shadow thought about telling the man some of his theories about prison, but he said nothing. He nodded, instead, and concentrated on appearing properly remorseful.

'Says here you've got a wife, Shadow.'

'Her name's Laura.'

'How's everything there?'

'Pretty good. She got kind of mad at me when I was arrested. But she's come down to see me as much as she could – it's a long way to travel. We write and I call her when I can.'

'What does your wife do?'

'She's a travel agent. Sends people all over the world.'

'How'd you meet her?'

Shadow could not decide why the man was asking. He considered telling him it was none of his business, then said, 'She was my best buddy's wife's best friend. They set us up on a blind date. We hit it off.'

'And you've got a job waiting for you?'

'Yessir. My buddy, Robbie, the one I just told you about, he owns the Muscle Farm, the place I used to train. He says my old job is waiting for me.'

An eyebrow raised. 'Really?'

'Says he figures I'll be a big draw. Bring back some old timers, and pull in the tough crowd who want to be tougher.'

The man seemed satisfied. He chewed the end of his ballpoint pen, then turned over the sheet of paper.

'How do you feel about your offense?'

Shadow shrugged. 'I was stupid,' he said, and meant it.

The man with the birthmark sighed. He ticked off a number of items on a checklist. Then he riffled through the papers in Shadow's file. 'How're you getting home from here?' he asked. 'Greyhound?'

'Flying home. It's good to have a wife who's a travel agent.'

The man frowned, and the birthmark creased. 'She sent you a ticket?'

'Didn't need to. Just sent me a confirmation number. Electronic ticket. All I have to do is turn up at the airport in a month and show 'em my ID, and I'm outta here.'

The man nodded, scribbled one final note, then he closed the file and put down the ballpoint pen. Two pale hands rested on the gray desk like pink animals. He brought his hands close together, made a steeple of his forefingers, and stared at Shadow with watery hazel eyes.

'You're lucky,' he said. 'You have someone to go back to, you got a job waiting. You can put all this behind you. You got a second chance. Make the most of it.'

The man did not offer to shake Shadow's hand as he rose to leave, nor did Shadow expect him to.

The last week was the worst. In some ways it was worse than the whole three years put together. Shadow wondered if it was the weather: oppressive, still and cold. It felt as if a storm was on the way, but the storm never came. He had the jitters and the heebie-jeebies, a feeling deep in his stomach that something was entirely wrong. In the exercise yard the wind gusted. Shadow imagined that he could smell snow on the air.

He called his wife collect. Shadow knew that MCI whacked a three-dollar surcharge on every call made from a prison phone. That was why operators are always real polite to people calling from prisons, Shadow had decided: they knew that he paid their wages.

'Something feels weird,' he told Laura. That wasn't the first thing he said to her. The first thing was 'I love you,' because it's a good thing to say if you can mean it, and Shadow did.

'Hello,' said Laura. 'I love you too. What feels weird?'

'I don't know,' he said. 'Maybe the weather. It feels like if we could only get a storm, everything would be okay.'

'It's nice here,' she said. 'The last of the leaves haven't

quite fallen. If we don't get a storm, you'll be able to see them when you get home.'

'Five days,' said Shadow.

'A hundred and twenty hours, and then you come home,' she said.

'Everything okay there? Nothing wrong?'

'Everything's fine. I'm seeing Robbie tonight. We're planning your surprise welcome-home party.'

'Surprise party?'

'Of course. You don't know anything about it, do you?'

'Not a thing.'

'That's my husband,' she said. Shadow realized that he was smiling. He had been inside for three years, but she could still make him smile.

'Love you, babes,' said Shadow.

'Love you, puppy,' said Laura.

Shadow put down the phone.

When they got married Laura told Shadow that she wanted a puppy, but their landlord had pointed out they weren't allowed pets under the terms of their lease. 'Hey,' Shadow had said, 'I'll be your puppy. What do you want me to do? Chew your slippers? Piss on the kitchen floor? Lick your nose? Sniff your crotch? I bet there's nothing a puppy can do I can't do!' And he picked her up as if she weighed nothing at all, and began to lick her nose while she giggled and shrieked, and then he carried her to the bed.

In the food hall Sam Fetisher sidled over to Shadow and smiled, showing his old teeth. He sat down beside Shadow and began to eat his macaroni and cheese.

'We got to talk,' said Sam Fetisher.

Sam Fetisher was one of the blackest men that Shadow had ever seen. He might have been sixty. He might have been eighty. Then again, Shadow had met thirty-year-old crack heads who looked older than Sam Fetisher.

'Mm?' said Shadow.

'Storm's on the way,' said Sam.

'Feels like it,' said Shadow. 'Maybe it'll snow soon.'

'Not that kind of storm. Bigger storms than that coming. I tell you, boy, you're better off in here than out on the street when the big storm comes.'

'Done my time,' said Shadow. 'Friday, I'm gone.'

Sam Fetisher stared at Shadow. 'Where you from?' he asked.

'Eagle Point. Indiana.'

'You're a lying fuck,' said Sam Fetisher. 'I mean originally. Where are your folks from?'

'Chicago,' said Shadow. His mother had lived in Chicago as a girl, and she had died there, half a lifetime ago.

'Like I said. Big storm coming. Keep your head down, Shadow-boy. It's like . . . what do they call those things continents ride around on? Some kind of plates?'

'Tectonic plates?' Shadow hazarded.

'That's it. Tectonic plates. It's like when they go riding, when North America goes skidding into South America, you don't want to be in the middle. You dig me?'

'Not even a little.'

One brown eye closed in a slow wink. 'Hell, don't say I didn't warn you,' said Sam Fetisher, and he spooned a trembling lump of orange Jell-O into his mouth.

'I won't.'

Shadow spent the night half-awake, drifting in and out of sleep, listening to his new cell-mate grunt and snore in the bunk below him. Several cells away a man whined and howled and sobbed like an animal, and from time to time someone would scream at him to shut the fuck up. Shadow tried not to hear. He let the empty minutes wash over him, lonely and slow.

Two days to go. Forty-eight hours, starting with oatmeal and prison coffee, and a guard named Wilson who tapped Shadow harder than he had to on the shoulder and said, 'Shadow? This way.'

Shadow checked his conscience. It was quiet, which did

not, he had observed, in a prison, mean that he was not in
deep shit. The two men walked more or less side by side, feet
echoing on metal and concrete.

Shadow tasted fear in the back of his throat, bitter as old
coffee. The bad thing was happening . . .

There was a voice in the back of his head whispering that
they were going to slap another year onto his sentence, drop
him into solitary, cut off his hands, cut off his head. He told
himself he was being stupid, but his heart was pounding fit
to burst out of his chest.

'I don't get you, Shadow,' said Wilson, as they walked.

'What's not to get, sir?'

'You. You're too fucking quiet. Too polite. You wait like the
old guys, but you're what? Twenty-five? Twenty-eight?'

'Thirty-two, sir.'

'And what are you? A spic? A gypsy?'

'Not that I know of, sir. Maybe.'

'Maybe you got nigger blood in you. You got nigger blood
in you, Shadow?'

'Could be, sir.' Shadow stood tall and looked straight
ahead, and concentrated on not allowing himself to be riled
by this man.

'Yeah? Well, all I know is, you fucking spook me.' Wilson
had sandy blond hair and a sandy blond face and a sandy
blond smile. 'You leaving us soon.'

'Hope so, sir.'

'You'll be back. I can see it in your eyes. You're a fuckup,
Shadow. Now, if I had my way, none of you assholes would
ever get out. We'd drop you in the hole and forget you.'

Oubliettes, thought Shadow, and he said nothing. It was a
survival thing: he didn't answer back, didn't say anything
about job security for prison guards, debate the nature of
repentance, rehabilitation, or rates of recidivism. He didn't
say anything funny or clever, and, to be on the safe side,
when he was talking to a prison official, whenever possible,
he didn't say anything at all. Speak when you're spoken to.

Do your own time. Get out. Get home. Have a long hot bath. Tell Laura you love her. Rebuild a life.

They walked through a couple of checkpoints. Wilson showed his ID each time. Up a set of stairs, and they were standing outside the Prison Warden's office. Shadow had never been there before, but he knew what it was. It had the prison warden's name – G. Patterson – on the door in black letters, and beside the door, a miniature traffic light.

The top light burned red.

Wilson pressed a button below the traffic light.

They stood there in silence for a couple of minutes. Shadow tried to tell himself that everything was all right, that on Friday morning he'd be on the plane up to Eagle Point, but he did not believe it himself.

The red light went out and the green light went on, and Wilson opened the door. They went inside.

Shadow had seen the warden a handful of times in the last three years. Once he had been showing a politician around; Shadow had not recognized the man. Once, during a lock-down, the warden had spoken to them in groups of a hundred, telling them that the prison was overcrowded, and that, since it would remain overcrowded, they had better get used to it. This was Shadow's first time up close to the man.

Up close, Patterson looked worse. His face was oblong, with gray hair cut into a military bristle cut. He smelled of Old Spice. Behind him was a shelf of books, each with the word Prison in the title; his desk was perfectly clean, empty but for a telephone and a tear-off-the-pages *Far Side* calendar. He had a hearing aid in his right ear.

'Please, sit down.'

Shadow sat down at the desk, noting the civility.

Wilson stood behind him.

The warden opened a desk drawer and took out a file, placed it on his desk.

'Says here you were sentenced to six years for aggravated

assault and battery. You've served three years. You were due to be released on Friday.'

Were? Shadow felt his stomach lurch inside him. He wondered how much longer he was going to have to serve – another year? Two years? All three? All he said was 'Yes, sir.'

The warden licked his lips. 'What did you say?'

'I said "Yes, sir".'

'Shadow, we're going to be releasing you later this afternoon. You'll be getting out a couple of days early.' The warden said this with no joy, as if he were intoning a death sentence. Shadow nodded, and he waited for the other shoe to drop. The warden looked down at the paper on his desk. 'This came from the Eagle Point Memorial Hospital . . . Your wife. She died in the early hours of this morning. It was an automobile accident. I'm sorry.'

Shadow nodded once more.

Wilson walked him back to his cell, not saying anything. He unlocked the cell door and let Shadow in. Then he said, 'It's like one of them good news, bad news jokes, isn't it? Good news, we're letting you out early, bad news, your wife is dead.' He laughed, as if it were genuinely funny.

Shadow said nothing at all.

***

Numbly, he packed up his possessions, gave several away. He left behind Low Key's *Herodotus* and the book of coin tricks, and, with a momentary pang, he abandoned the blank metal disks he had smuggled out of the workshop which had, until he had found Low Key's change in the book, served him for coins. There would be coins, real coins, on the outside. He shaved. He dressed in civilian clothes. He walked through door after door, knowing that he would never walk back through them again, feeling empty inside.

The rain had started to gust from the gray sky, a freezing rain. Pellets of ice stung Shadow's face, while the rain soaked the thin overcoat as they walked away from the prison building, toward the yellow ex-school bus that would take them to the nearest city.

By the time they got to the bus they were soaked. Eight of them were leaving, Shadow thought. Fifteen hundred still inside. He sat on the bus and shivered until the heaters started working, wondering what he was doing, where he was going now.

Ghost images filled his head, unbidden. In his imagination he was leaving another prison, long ago.

He had been imprisoned in a lightless garret room for far too long: his beard was wild and his hair was a tangle. The guards had walked him down a gray stone stairway and out into a plaza filled with brightly-colored things, with people and with objects. It was a market day and he was dazzled by the noise and the color, squinting at the sunlight that filled the square, smelling the salt-wet air and all the good things of the market, and on his left the sun glittered from the water . . .

The bus shuddered to a halt at a red light.

The wind howled about the bus, and the wipers slooshed heavily back and forth across the windshield, smearing the city into a red and yellow neon wetness. It was early afternoon, but it looked like night through the glass.

'Shit,' said the man in the seat behind Shadow, rubbing the condensation from the window with his hand, staring at a wet figure hurrying down the sidewalk. 'There's pussy out there.'

Shadow swallowed. It occurred to him that he had not cried yet – had in fact felt nothing at all. No tears. No sorrow. Nothing.

He found himself thinking about a guy named Johnnie Larch he'd shared a cell with when he'd first been put inside, who told Shadow how he'd once got out after five years behind bars, with $100 and a ticket to Seattle, where his sister lived.

Johnnie Larch had got to the airport, and he handed his ticket to the woman on the counter, and she asked to see his driver's license.

He showed it to her. It had expired a couple of years earlier. She told him it was not valid as ID. He told her it might not be valid as a driver's license, but it sure as hell was fine identification, and it had a photo of him on it, and his height and his weight, and damn it, who else did she think he was, if he wasn't him?

She said she'd thank him to keep his voice down.

He told her to give him a fucking boarding pass, or she was going to regret it, and that he wasn't going to be disrespected. You don't let people disrespect you in prison.

Then she pressed a button, and few moments later the airport security showed up, and they tried to persuade Johnnie Larch to leave the airport quietly, and he did not wish to leave, and there was something of an altercation.

The upshot of it all was that Johnnie Larch never actually made it to Seattle, and he spent the next couple of days in town in bars, and when his $100 was gone he held up a gas station with a toy gun for money to keep drinking, and the police finally picked him up for pissing in the street. Pretty soon he was back inside serving the rest of his sentence and a little extra for the gas station job.

And the moral of this story, according to Johnnie Larch, was this: don't piss off people who work in airports.

'Are you sure it's not something like "kinds of behavior that work in a specialized environment, such as a prison, can fail to work and in fact become harmful when used outside such an environment"?' said Shadow, when Johnnie Larch told him the story.

'No, listen to me, I'm *telling* you man,' said Johnnie Larch, 'don't piss off those bitches in airports.'

Shadow half-smiled at the memory. His own driver's license had several months still to go before it expired.

'Bus station! Everybody out!'

The building stank of piss and sour beer. Shadow climbed into a taxi and told the driver to take him to the airport. He told him that there was an extra five dollars if he could do it in silence. They made it in twenty minutes and the driver never said a word.

Then Shadow was stumbling through the brightly lit airport terminal. Shadow worried about the whole e-ticket business. He knew he had a ticket for a flight on Friday, but he didn't know if it would work today. Anything electronic seemed fundamentally magical to Shadow, and liable to evaporate at any moment. He liked things he could hold and touch.

Still, he had his wallet, back in his possession for the first time in three years, containing several expired credit cards and one Visa card which, he was pleasantly surprised to discover, didn't expire until the end of January. He had a reservation number. And, he realized, he had the certainty that once he got home everything would, somehow, be right once more. Laura would be fine again. Maybe it was some kind of scam to spring him a few days early. Or perhaps it was a simple mix-up: some other Laura Moon's body had been dragged from the highway wreckage.

Lightning flickered outside the airport, through the windows-walls. Shadow realized he was holding his breath, waiting for something. A distant boom of thunder. He exhaled.

A tired white woman stared at him from behind the counter.

'Hello,' said Shadow. *You're the first strange woman I've spoken to, in the flesh, in three years.* 'I've got an e-ticket number. I was supposed to be traveling on Friday but I have to go today. There was a death in my family.'

'Mm. I'm sorry to hear that.' She tapped at the keyboard, stared at the screen, tapped again. 'No problem. I've put you on the 3:30. It may be delayed, because of the storm, so keep an eye on the screens. Checking any baggage?'

He held up a shoulder bag. 'I don't need to check this, do I?'

'No,' she said. 'It's fine. Do you have any picture ID?'

Shadow showed her his driver's license. Then he assured her that no one had given him a bomb to take onto the plane, and she, in return, gave him a printed boarding pass. Then he passed through the metal detector while his bag went through the X-ray machine.

It was not a big airport, but the number of people wandering, just wandering, amazed him. He watched people put down bags casually, observed wallets stuffed into back pockets, saw purses put down, unwatched, under chairs. That was when he realized he was no longer in prison.

Thirty minutes to wait until boarding. Shadow bought a slice of pizza and burned his lip on the hot cheese. He took his change and went to the phones. Called Robbie at the Muscle Farm, but the machine answered.

'Hey Robbie,' said Shadow. 'They tell me that Laura's dead. They let me out early. I'm coming home.'

Then, because people do make mistakes, he'd seen it happen, he called home, and listened to Laura's voice.

'Hi,' she said. 'I'm not here or I can't come to the phone. Leave a message and I'll get back to you. And have a *good* day.'

Shadow couldn't bring himself to leave a message.

He sat in a plastic chair by the gate, and held his bag so tight he hurt his hand.

He was thinking about the first time he had ever seen Laura. He hadn't even known her name then. She was Audrey Burton's friend. He had been sitting with Robbie in a booth at Chi-Chi's, talking about something, probably how one of the other trainers had just announced she was opening her own dance studio, when Laura had walked in a pace or so behind Audrey, and Shadow had found himself staring. She had long, chestnut hair and eyes so blue Shadow mistakenly thought she was wearing tinted contact lenses.

She had ordered a strawberry daiquiri, and insisted that Shadow taste it, and laughed delightedly when he did.

Laura loved people to taste what she tasted.

He had kissed her goodnight, that night, and she had tasted of strawberry daiquiris, and he had never wanted to kiss anyone else again. A woman announced that his plane was boarding, and Shadow's row was the first to be called. He was in the very back, an empty seat beside him. The rain pattered continually against the side of the plane: he imagined small children tossing down dried peas by the handful from the skies.

As the plane took off he fell asleep.

Shadow was in a dark place, and the thing staring at him wore a buffalo's head, rank and furry with huge wet eyes. Its body was a man's body, oiled and slick.

'Changes are coming,' said the buffalo without moving its lips. 'There are certain decisions that will have to be made.'

Firelight flickered from wet cave walls.

'Where am I?' Shadow asked.

'In the Earth and under the Earth,' said the buffalo man. 'You are where the forgotten wait.' His eyes were liquid black marbles, and his voice was a rumble from beneath the world. He smelled like wet cow. 'Believe,' said the rumbling voice. 'If you are to survive, you must believe.'

'Believe what?' asked Shadow. 'What should I believe?'

He stared at Shadow, the buffalo man, and he drew himself up huge, and his eyes filled with fire. He opened his spit-flecked buffalo mouth and it was red inside with the flames that burned inside him, under the Earth.

'*Everything*,' roared the buffalo man.

The world tipped and spun, and Shadow was on the plane once more; but the tipping continued. In the front of the plane a woman screamed, half-heartedly.

Lightning burst in blinding flashes around the plane. The captain came on the intercom to tell them that he was going to try and gain some altitude, to get away from the storm.

The plane shook and shuddered, and Shadow wondered, coldly and idly, if he were going to die. It seemed possible, he decided, but unlikely. He stared out of the window and watched the lightning illuminate the horizon.

Then he dozed once more, and dreamed he was back in prison, and Low Key had whispered to him in the food line that someone had put out a contract on his life, but that Shadow could not find out who or why; and when he woke up they were coming in for a landing.

He stumbled off the plane, blinking and waking.

All airports, he had long ago decided, look very much the same. It doesn't actually matter where you are, you are in an airport: tiles and walkways and restrooms, gates and newsstands and fluorescent lights. This airport looked like an airport. The trouble is, this wasn't the airport he was going to. This was a big airport, with way too many people, and way too many gates.

The people had the glazed, beaten look you only see in airports and prisons. *If Hell is other people*, thought Shadow, *then Purgatory is airports.*

'Excuse me, ma'am?'

The woman looked at him over the clipboard. 'Yes?'

'What airport is this?'

She looked at him, puzzled, trying to decide whether or not he was joking, then she said, 'St Louis.'

'I thought this was the plane to Eagle Point.'

'It was. They redirected it here because of the storms. Didn't they make an announcement?'

'Probably. I fell asleep.'

'You'll need to talk to that man over there, in the red coat.'

The man was almost as tall as Shadow: he looked like the father from a seventies sitcom, and he tapped something into a computer and told Shadow to run – *run!* – to a gate on the far side of the terminal.

Shadow ran through the airport, but the doors were already closed as he got to the gate. He watched the plane pull away from the gate, through the plate glass. Then he explained his problem to the gate attendant (calmly, quietly, politely) and she sent him to a passenger assistance desk, where Shadow explained that he was on his way home after a long absence and his wife had just been killed in a road accident, and that it was vitally important that he went home *now*. He said nothing about prison.

The woman at the passenger assistance desk (short and brown, with a mole on the side of her nose) consulted with another woman and made a phone call ('Nope, that one's out. They've just cancelled it.') then she printed out another boarding card. 'This will get you there,' she told him. 'We'll call ahead to the gate and tell them you're coming.'

Shadow felt like a pea being flicked between three cups, or a card being shuffled through a deck. Again he ran through the airport, ending up near where he had gotten off in the first place.

A small man at the gate took his boarding pass. 'We've been waiting for you,' he confided, tearing off the stub of the boarding pass, with Shadow's seat assignment – 17-D – on it. Shadow hurried onto the plane, and they closed the door behind him.

He walked through first class – there were only four first class seats, three of which were occupied. The bearded man in a pale suit seated next to the unoccupied seat at the very front grinned at Shadow as he got onto the plane, then raised his wrist and tapped his watch as Shadow walked past.

Yeah, yeah, I'm making you late, thought Shadow. *Let that be the worst of your worries.*

The plane seemed pretty full, as he made his way down toward the back. Actually, Shadow quickly discovered, it was completely full, and there was a middle-aged woman sitting in seat 17-D. Shadow showed her his boarding card stub, and she showed him hers: they matched.

'Can you take your seat, please?' asked the flight attendant.

'No,' he said, 'I'm afraid I can't. This lady is sitting in it.'

She clicked her tongue and checked their boarding cards, then she led him back up to the front of the plane, and pointed him to the empty seat in first class. 'Looks like it's your lucky day,' she told him.

Shadow sat down. 'Can I bring you something to drink?' she asked him. 'We'll just have time before we take off. And I'm sure you need one after that.'

'I'd like a beer, please,' said Shadow. 'Whatever you've got.'

The flight attendant went away.

The man in the pale suit in the seat beside Shadow put out his arm and tapped his watch with his fingernail. It was a black Rolex. 'You're late,' said the man, and he grinned a huge grin with no warmth in it at all.

'Sorry?'

'I said, you're late.'

The flight attendant handed Shadow a glass of beer. He sipped it. For one moment, he wondered if the man were crazy, and then he decided he must have been referring to the plane, waiting for one last passenger.

'Sorry if I held you up,' he said, politely. 'You in a hurry?'

The plane backed away from the gate. The flight attendant came back and took away Shadow's beer, half-finished. The man in the pale suit grinned at her and said, 'Don't worry, I'll hold onto this tightly,' and she let him keep his glass of Jack Daniel's, protesting, weakly, that it violated airline regulations. ('Let me be the judge of that, m'dear.')

'Time is certainly of the essence,' said the man. 'But no, I am not in a hurry. I was merely concerned that you would not make the plane.'

'That was kind of you.'

The plane sat restlessly on the ground, engines throbbing, aching to be off.

'Kind my ass,' said the man in the pale suit. 'I've got a job for you, Shadow.'

A roar of engines. The little plane jerked forward into a take-off, pushing Shadow back into his seat. Then they were airborne, and the airport lights were falling away below them. Shadow looked at the man in the seat next to him.

His hair was a reddish-gray; his beard, little more than stubble, was grayish-red. He was smaller than Shadow, but he seemed to take up a hell of a lot of room. A craggy, square face with pale gray eyes. The suit looked expensive, and was the color of melted vanilla ice-cream. His tie was dark gray silk, and the tie-pin was a tree, worked in silver: trunk, branches, and deep roots.

He held his glass of Jack Daniels as they took off, and did not spill a drop.

'Aren't you going to ask me what kind of job?' he asked.

'How do you know who I am?"

The man chuckled. 'Oh, it's the easiest thing in the world to know what people call themselves. A little thought, a little luck, a little memory. Ask me what kind of job.'

'No,' said Shadow. The attendant brought him another glass of beer, and he sipped at it.

'Why not?'

'I'm going home. I've got a job waiting for me there. I don't want any other job.'

The man's craggy smile did not change, outwardly, but now he seemed, actually, amused. 'You don't have a job waiting for you at home,' he said. 'You have nothing waiting for you there. Meanwhile, I am offering you a perfectly legal job – good money, limited security, remarkable fringe benefits. Hell, if you live that long, I could throw in a pension plan. You think maybe you'd like one of them?'

Shadow said, 'You could have seen my name on my boarding pass. Or on the side of my bag.'

The man said nothing.

'Whoever you are,' said Shadow, 'you couldn't have known I was going to be on this plane. I didn't know I was going to be on this plane, and if my plane hadn't been diverted to St Louis, I wouldn't have been. My guess is you're a practical joker. Maybe you're hustling something. But I think maybe we'll have a better time if we end this conversation here.'

The man shrugged.

Shadow picked up the in-flight magazine. The little plane jerked and bumped through the sky, making it harder to concentrate. The words floated through his mind like soap bubbles, there as he read them, gone completely a moment later.

The man sat quietly in the seat beside him, sipping his Jack Daniels. His eyes were closed.

Shadow read the list of in-flight music channels available on transatlantic flights, and then he was looking at the map of the world with red lines on it that showed where the airline flew. Then he had finished reading the magazine, and, reluctantly, he closed the cover, and slipped it into the pocket on the wall.

The man opened his eyes. There was something strange about his eyes, Shadow thought. One of them was a darker gray than the other. He looked at Shadow. 'By the way,' he said, 'I was sorry to hear about your wife, Shadow. A great loss.'

Shadow nearly hit the man, then. Instead he took a deep breath. ('Like I said, don't piss off those bitches in airports,' said Johnnie Larch, in the back of his mind, 'or they'll haul your sorry ass back here before you can spit.') He counted to five.

'So was I,' he said.

The man shook his head. 'If it could but have been any other way,' he said, and sighed.

'She died in a car crash,' said Shadow. 'It's a fast way to go. Other ways could have been worse.'

The man shook his head, slowly. For a moment it seemed to Shadow as if the man was insubstantial; as if the plane had suddenly become more real, while his neighbor had become less so.

'Shadow,' he said. 'It's not a joke. It's not a trick. I can pay you better than any other job you'll find will pay you. You're an ex-con. There's not a long line of people elbowing each other out of the way to hire you.'

'Mister whoever-the-fuck you are,' said Shadow, just loud enough to be heard over the din of the engines, 'there isn't enough money in the world.'

The grin got bigger. Shadow found himself remembering a PBS show he had seen as a teenager, about chimpanzees. The show claimed that when apes and chimps smile it's only to bare their teeth in a grimace of hate or aggression or terror. When a chimp grins, it's a threat. This grin was one of those.

'Sure there's money enough. And there are also bonuses. Work for me, and I'll tell you things. There may be a little risk, of course, but if you survive you can have whatever your heart desires. You could be the next King of America. Now,' said the man, 'who else is going to pay you that well? Hmm?'

'Who are you?' asked Shadow.

'Ah, yes. The age of information – young lady, could you pour me another glass of Jack Daniel's? Easy on the ice, – not, of course, that there has ever been any other kind of age. Information and knowledge: these are currencies that have never gone out of style.'

'I said, who are you?'

'Let's see. Well, seeing that today certainly is my day – why don't you call me Wednesday? Mister Wednesday. Although given the weather, it might as well be Thursday, eh?'

'What's your real name?'

'Work for me long enough and well enough,' said the man in the pale suit, 'and I may even tell you that. There. Job offer. Think about it. No one expects you to say yes immediately, not knowing whether you're leaping into a piranha tank or a pit of bears. Take your time.' He closed his eyes and leaned back in his seat.

'I don't think so,' said Shadow. 'I don't like you. I don't want to work with you.'

'Like I say,' said the man, without opening his eyes, 'don't rush into it. Take your time.'

The plane landed with a bump, and a few passengers got off. Shadow looked out of the window: it was a little airport in the middle of nowhere, and there were still two little airports to go before Eagle Point. Shadow transferred his glance to the man in the pale suit – Mr Wednesday? He seemed to be asleep.

Shadow stood up, grabbed his bag, and stepped off the plane, down the steps onto the slick wet tarmac, walking at an even pace toward the lights of the terminal. A light rain spattered his face.

Before he went inside the airport building, he stopped, and turned, and watched. No one else got off the plane. The ground crew rolled the steps away, the door was closed, and it taxied off down the runway. Shadow stared at it until it took off, then he walked inside, to the Budget car rental desk, the only one open, and he rented what turned out, when he got to the parking lot, to be a small red Toyota.

Shadow unfolded the map they had given him. He spread it out on the passenger's seat. Eagle Point was about two hundred and fifty miles away, most of the journey on the freeway. He had not driven a car in three years.

The storms had passed, if they had come this far. It was cold and clear. Clouds scudded in front of the moon, and for a moment Shadow could not be certain whether it was the clouds or the moon that were moving.

He drove north for an hour and a half.

It was getting late. He was hungry, and when he realized how hungry he really was, he pulled off at the next exit, and drove into the town of Nottamun (Pop. 1301). He filled the gas-tank at the Amoco, and asked the bored woman at the cash register where the best bar in the area was – somewhere that he could get something to eat.

'Jack's Crocodile Bar,' she told him. 'It's west on County Road N.'

'Crocodile Bar?'

'Yeah. Jack says they add character.' She drew him a map on the back of a mauve flyer, which advertised a chicken roast to raise money for a young girl who needed a new kidney. 'He's got a couple of crocodiles, a snake, one a them big lizard things.'

'An iguana?'

'That's him.'

Through the town, over a bridge, on for a couple of miles, and he stopped at a low, rectangular building with an illuminated Pabst sign, and a Coca-Cola machine by the door.

The parking lot was half empty.Shadow parked the red Toyota and went inside.

The air was thick with smoke and 'Walking after Midnight' was playing on the jukebox. Shadow looked around for the crocodiles, but could not see them. He wondered if the woman in the gas station had been pulling his leg.

'What'll it be?' asked the bartender.

'You Jack?'

'It's Jack's night off. I'm Paul.'

'Hi, Paul. House beer, and a hamburger with all the trimmings. No fries.'

'Bowl of chili to start? Best chili in the state.'

'Sounds good,' said Shadow. 'Where's the rest room?'

The man pointed to a door in the corner of the bar. There was a stuffed alligator head mounted on the door. Shadow went through the door.

It was a clean, well-lit restroom. Shadow looked around the room first; force of habit. ('Remember, Shadow, you can't fight back when you're pissing,' Low Key said, low key as always, in the back of his head.) He took the urinal stall on the left. Then he unzipped his fly and pissed for an age, relaxing, feeling relief. He read the yellowing press clipping framed at eye-level, with a photo of Jack and two alligators.

There was a polite grunt from the urinal immediately to his right, although he had heard nobody come in.

The man in the pale suit was bigger standing than he had seemed sitting on the plane beside Shadow. He was almost Shadow's height, and Shadow was a big man. He was staring ahead of him. He finished pissing, shook off the last few drops, and zipped himself up.

Then he grinned, like a fox eating shit from a barbed wire fence. 'So,' said Mr Wednesday. 'You've had time to think, Shadow. Do you want a job?'

Somewhere in America

Los Angeles. 11:26 p.m.

In a dark red room – the color of the walls is close to that of raw liver – is a tall woman dressed cartoonishly in too-tight silk shorts, her breasts pulled up and pushed forward by the yellow blouse tied beneath them. Her black hair is piled high and knotted on top of her head. Standing beside her is a short man wearing an olive tee shirt and expensive blue jeans. He is holding, in his right hand, a wallet and a Nokia mobile phone with a red, white, and blue face-plate.

The red room contains a bed, upon which are white satin-style sheets and an ox-blood bedspread. At the foot of the bed is a small wooden table, upon which is a small stone statue of a woman with enormous hips, and a candleholder.

The woman hands the man a small red candle. 'Here,' she says. 'Light it.'

'Me?'

'Yes,' she says, 'If you want to have me.'

'I shoulda just got you to suck me off in the car.'

'Perhaps,' she says. 'Don't you want me?' Her hand runs up her body from thigh to breast, a gesture of presentation, as if she were demonstrating a new product.

Red silk scarves over the lamp in the corner of the room make the light red.

The man looks at her hungrily, then he takes the candle from her and pushes it into the candleholder. 'You got a light?'

She passes him a book of matches. He tears off a match, lights the wick: it flickers and then burns with a steady flame, which gives the illusion of motion to the faceless statue beside it, all hips and breasts.

'Put the money beneath the statue.'

'Fifty bucks.'

'Yes.'

'When I saw you first, on Sunset, I almost thought you were a man.'

'But I have these,' she says, unknotting the yellow blouse, freeing her breasts.

'So do a lot of guys, these days.'

She stretches and smiles. 'Yes,' she says. 'Now, come love me.'

He unbuttons his blue jeans, and removes his olive tee shirt. She massages his white shoulders with her brown fingers; then she turns him over, and begins to make love to him with her hands, and her fingers, and her tongue.

It seems to him that the lights in the red room have been dimmed, and the sole illumination comes from the candle, which burns with a bright flame.

'What's your name?' he asks her.

'Bilquis,' she tells him, raising her head. 'With a Q.'

'A what?'

'Never mind.'

He is gasping now. 'Let me fuck you,' he says. 'I have to fuck you.'

'Okay, hon,' she says. 'We'll do it. But will you do something for me, while you're doing it?'

'Hey,' he says, suddenly tetchy, '*I'm* paying *you*, you know.'

She straddles him, in one smooth movement, whispering, 'I know, honey, I know, you're paying me, and I mean, look at you, I should be paying you, I'm so lucky . . .'

He purses his lips, trying to show that her hooker talk is having no effect on him, he can't be taken; that she's a street whore for Chrissakes, while he's practically a *producer*, and he knows all about last-minute rip-offs, but she doesn't ask for money. Instead she says, 'Honey, while you're giving it to me, while you're pushing that big hard thing inside of me, will you *worship* me?'

'Will I what?'

She is rocking back and forth on him: the engorged head of his penis is being rubbed against the wet lips of her vulva.

'Will you call me goddess? Will you pray to me? Will you worship me with your body?'

He smiles. Is that what she wants? 'Sure,' he says. We've all got our kinks, at the end of the day. She reaches her hand between her legs and slips him inside her.

'Is that good, is it, goddess?' he asks, gasping.

'Worship me, honey,' says Bilquis, the hooker.

'Yes,' he says. 'I worship your breasts and your eyes and your cunt. I worship your thighs and your eyes and your cherry-red lips . . .'

'Yes . . .' she croons, riding him like a storm-tossed boat rides the waves.

'I worship your nipples, from which the milk of life flows. Your kiss is honey and your touch scorches like fire, and I worship it.' His words are becoming more rhythmic now, keeping pace with the thrust and roll of their bodies. 'Bring me your lust in the morning, and bring me relief and your blessing in the evening. Let me walk in dark places unharmed and let me come to you once more and sleep beside you and make love with you again. I worship you with everything that is within me, and everything inside my mind, with everywhere I've been and my dreams and my . . .' he breaks off, panting for breath. '. . . What are you *do*ing? That feels amazing. So amazing . . .' and he looks down at his hips, at the place where the two of them conjoin, but her forefinger touches his chin and pushes his head back, so he is looking only at her face and at the ceiling once again.

'Keep talking honey,' she says. 'Don't stop. Doesn't it feel good?'

'It feels better than anything has ever felt,' he tells her, meaning it as he says it. 'Your eyes are stars, burning in the, shit, the firmament, and your lips are gentle waves that lick the sand, and I worship them,' and now he's thrusting deeper and deeper inside her: he feels electric, as if his whole lower body has become sexually charged: priapic, engorged, blissful.

'Bring me your gift,' he mutters, no longer knowing what he is saying, 'your one true gift, and make me always this . . . always so . . . I pray . . . I . . .'

And then the pleasure crests into orgasm, blasting his mind into void, his head and self and entire beingness a perfect blank as he thrusts deeper into her and deeper still . . .

Eyes closed, spasming, he luxuriates in the moment; and then he feels a lurch, and it seems to him that he is hanging, head-down, although the pleasure continues.

He opens his eyes.

He thinks, grasping for thought and reason again, of birth, and wonders, without fear, in a moment of perfect postcoital clarity, whether what he sees is some kind of illusion.

This is what he sees:

He is inside her to the chest, and as he stares at this in disbelief and wonder she rests both hands upon his shoulders and puts gentle pressure on his body.

He slipslides further inside her.

'How are you doing this to me?' he asks, or he thinks he asks, but perhaps it is only in his head.

'You're doing it, honey,' she whispers. He feels the lips of her vulva tight around his upper chest and back, constricting and enveloping him. He wonders what this would look like to somebody watching them. He wonders why he is not scared. And then he knows.

'I worship you with my body,' he whispers, as she pushes him inside her. Her labia pull slickly across his face, and his eyes slip into darkness.

She stretches on the bed, like a huge cat, and then she yawns. 'Yes,' she says, 'You do.'

The Nokia phone plays a high, electrical transposition of the 'Ode to Joy'. She picks it up, and thumbs a key, and puts the telephone to her ear.

Her belly is flat, her labia small and closed. A sheen of sweat glistens on her forehead and on her upper lip.

'Yeah?' she says. And then she says, 'No, honey, he's not here. He's gone away.'

She turns the telephone off before she flops out on the bed in the dark red room, then she stretches once more, and she closes her eyes, and she sleeps.

Chapter Two

They took her to the cemet'ry
In a big ol' Cadillac
They took her to the cemet'ry
But they did not bring her back.

— Old Song

I have taken the Liberty,' said Mr Wednesday, washing his hands in the men's room of Jack's Crocodile Bar, 'of ordering food for myself, to be delivered to your table. We have much to discuss, after all.'

'I don't think so,' said Shadow. He dried his own hands on a paper towel and crumpled it, and dropped it into the bin.

'You need a job,' said Wednesday. 'People don't hire ex-cons. You folk make them uncomfortable.'

'I have a job waiting. A good job.'

'Would that be the job at the Muscle Farm?'

'Maybe,' said Shadow.

'Nope. You don't. Robbie Burton's dead. Without him the Muscle Farm's dead too.'

'You're a liar.'

'Of course. And a good one. The best you will ever meet.

But, I'm afraid, I'm not lying to you about this.' He reached into his pocket, produced a newspaper, much folded, and handed it to Shadow. 'Page seven,' he said. 'Come on back to the bar. You can read it at the table.'

Shadow pushed open the door, back into the bar. The air was blue with smoke, and the Dixie Cups were on the juke box singing 'Iko Iko'. Shadow smiled, slightly, in recognition of the old children's song.

The barman pointed to a table in the corner. There was a bowl of chili and a burger at one side of the table, a rare steak and a bowl of fries laid in the place across from it.

Look at my King all dressed in Red,
Iko Iko all day,
I bet you five dollars he'll kill you dead,
Jockamo-feena-nay

Shadow took his seat at the table. He put the newspaper down. 'I got out of prison this morning,' he said. 'This is my first meal as a free man. You won't object if I wait until after I've eaten to read your page seven?'

'Not in the slightest bit.'

Shadow ate his hamburger. It was better than prison hamburgers. The chili was good but, he decided, after a couple of mouthfuls, not the best in the state.

Laura made a great chili. She used lean-cut meat, dark kidney beans, carrots cut small, a bottle or so of dark beer, and freshly sliced hot peppers. She would let the chili cook for a while, then add red wine, lemon juice, and a pinch of fresh dill, and, finally, measure out and add her chili powders. On more than one occasion Shadow had tried to get her to show him how she made it: he would watch everything she did, from slicing the onions and dropping them into the olive oil at the bottom of the pot. He had even written down the sequence of events, ingredient by ingredient, and he had once made Laura's chili for himself on a weekend when she had been out of town. It had tasted okay – it was certainly edible, and he ate it, but it had not been Laura's chili.

The news item on page seven was the first account of his wife's death that Shadow had read. It felt strange, as if he were reading about someone in a story: how Laura Moon, whose age was given in the article as twenty-seven, and Robbie Burton, thirty-nine, were in Robbie's car on the interstate, when they swerved into the path of a thirty-two wheeler, which sideswiped them as it tried to change lanes and avoid them. The truck brushed Robbie's car and sent it spinning off the side of the road, where the car had hit a road sign, hard, and stopped spinning.

Rescue crews were on the scene in minutes. They pulled Robbie and Laura from the wreckage. They were both dead by the time they arrived at the hospital.

Shadow folded the newspaper up once more, and slid it back across the table, toward Wednesday, who was gorging himself on a steak so bloody and so blue it might never have been introduced to a kitchen flame.

'Here. Take it back,' said Shadow.

Robbie had been driving. He must have been drunk, although the newspaper account said nothing about this. Shadow found himself imagining Laura's face when she realized that Robbie was too drunk to drive. The scenario unfolded in Shadow's mind, and there was nothing he could do to stop it: Laura shouting at Robbie – shouting at him to pull off the road, then the thud of car against truck, and the steering wheel wrenching over . . .

. . . the car on the side of the road, broken glass glittering like ice and diamonds in the headlights, blood pooling in rubies on the road beside them. Two bodies, dead or soon-to-die, being carried from the wreck, or laid neatly by the side of the road.

'Well?' asked Mr Wednesday. He had finished his steak,

sliced and devoured it like a starving man. Now he was munching the french fries, spearing them with his fork.

'You're right,' said Shadow. 'I don't have a job.'

Shadow took a quarter from his pocket, tails up. He flicked it up in the air, knocking it against his finger as it left his hand to give it a wobble that made it look as if it were turning, caught it, slapped it down on the back of his hand.

'Call,' he said.

'Why?' asked Wednesday.

'I don't want to work for anyone with worse luck than me. Call.'

'Heads,' said Mr Wednesday.

'Sorry,' said Shadow, revealing the coin without even bothering to glance at it. 'It was tails. I rigged the toss.'

'Rigged games are the easiest ones to beat,' said Wednesday, wagging a square finger at Shadow. 'Take another look at the quarter.'

Shadow glanced down at it. The head was face up.

'I must have fumbled the toss,' he said, puzzled.

'You do yourself a disservice,' said Wednesday, and he grinned. 'I'm just a lucky, lucky guy.' Then he looked up. 'Well I never. Mad Sweeney. Will you have a drink with us?'

'Southern Comfort and Coke, straight up,' said a voice from behind Shadow.

'I'll go and talk to the barman,' said Wednesday. He stood up, and began to make his way toward the bar.

'Aren't you going to ask what I'm drinking?' called Shadow.

'I already know what you're drinking,' said Wednesday, and then he was standing by the bar. Patsy Cline started to sing 'Walking after Midnight' on the juke box again.

The man who had ordered Southern Comfort and Coke sat down beside Shadow. He had a short ginger-colored beard. He wore a denim jacket covered with bright sew-on patches, and under the jacket a stained white tee shirt. On the tee shirt was printed:

*IF YOU CAN'T EAT IT, DRINK IT, SMOKE IT OR SNORT
IT . . . THEN F*CK IT!*

He wore a baseball cap, on which was printed:

*THE ONLY WOMAN I HAVE EVER LOVED WAS ANOTHER
MAN'S WIFE . . . MY MOTHER!*

He opened a soft pack of Lucky Strikes with a dirty
thumbnail, took a cigarette, offered one to Shadow. Shadow
was about to take one, automatically – he did not smoke, but
a cigarette makes good barter material – when he realized
that he was no longer inside. You could buy cigarettes here
whenever you wanted. He shook his head.

'You working for our man then?' asked the bearded man.
He was not sober, although he was not yet drunk.

'It looks that way,' said Shadow.

The bearded man lit his cigarette. 'I'm a leprechaun,' he
said.

Shadow did not smile. 'Really?' he said. 'Shouldn't you be
drinking Guinness?'

'Stereotypes. You have to learn to think outside the box,'
said the bearded man. 'There's a lot more to Ireland than
Guinness.'

'You don't have an Irish accent.'

'I've been over here too fucken long.'

'So you *are* originally from Ireland?'

'I told you. I'm a leprechaun. We don't come from fucken
Moscow.'

'I guess not.'

Wednesday returned to the table, three drinks held easily
in his paw-like hands. 'Southern Comfort and Coke for you,
Mad Sweeney m'man, and a Jack Daniel's for me. And *this* is
for you, Shadow.'

'What is it?'

'Taste it.'

The drink was a tawny golden color. Shadow took a sip, tasting an odd blend of sour and sweet on his tongue. He could taste the alcohol underneath, and a strange blend of flavors. It reminded him a little of prison hooch, brewed in a garbage bag from rotten fruit and bread and sugar and water, but it was smoother, sweeter, infinitely stranger.

'Okay,' said Shadow. 'I tasted it. What was it?'

'Mead,' said Wednesday. 'Honey wine. The drink of heroes. The drink of the gods.'

Shadow took another tentative sip. Yes, he could taste the honey, he decided. That was one of the tastes. 'Tastes kinda like pickle juice,' he said. 'Sweet pickle juice wine.'

'Tastes like a drunken diabetic's piss,' agreed Wednesday. 'I hate the stuff.'

'Then why did you bring it for me?' asked Shadow, reasonably.

Wednesday stared at Shadow with his mismatched eyes. One of them, Shadow decided, was a glass eye, but he could not decide which one. 'I brought you mead to drink because it's traditional. And right now we need all the tradition we can get. It seals our bargain.'

'We haven't made a bargain.'

'Sure we have. You work for me. You protect me. You help me. You transport me from place to place. You investigate, from time to time – go places and ask questions for me. You run errands. In an emergency, but only in an emergency, you hurt people who need to be hurt. In the unlikely event of my death, you will hold my vigil. And in return I shall make sure that your needs are adequately taken care of.'

'He's hustling you,' said Mad Sweeney, rubbing his bristly ginger beard. 'He's a hustler.'

'Damn straight I'm a hustler,' said Wednesday. 'That's why I need someone to look out for my best interests.'

The song on the jukebox ended, and for a moment the bar fell quiet, every conversation at a lull.

'Someone once told me that you only get those everybody-shuts-up-at-once moments at twenty past or twenty to the hour,' said Shadow.

Sweeney pointed to the clock above the bar, held in the massive and indifferent jaws of a stuffed alligator head. The time was 11:20.

'There,' said Shadow. 'Damned if I know why that happens.'

'I know why,' said Wednesday.

'You going to share with the group?'

'I may tell you, one day, yes. Or I may not. Drink your mead.'

Shadow knocked the rest of the mead back in one long gulp. 'It might be better over ice,' he said.

'Or it might not,' said Wednesday. 'It's terrible stuff.'

'That it is,' agreed Mad Sweeney. 'You'll excuse me for a moment, gentlemen, but I find myself in deep and urgent need of a lengthy piss.' He stood up and walked away, an impossibly tall man. He had to be almost seven feet tall, decided Shadow.

A waitress wiped a cloth across the table and took their empty plates. She emptied Sweeney's ashtray, and asked if they would like to order any more drinks. Wednesday told her to bring the same again for everyone, although this time Shadow's mead was to be on the rocks.

'Anyway,' said Wednesday, 'that's what I need of you, if you're working for me. Which of course, you are.'

'That's what you want,' said Shadow. 'Would you like to know what I want?'

'Nothing could make me happier.'

The waitress brought the drink. Shadow sipped his mead on the rocks. The ice did not help – if anything it sharpened the sourness, and made the taste linger in the mouth after the mead was swallowed. However, Shadow consoled himself, it did not taste particularly alcoholic. He was not ready to be drunk. Not yet.

He took a deep breath.

'Okay,' said Shadow. 'My life, which for three years has been a long way from being the greatest life there has ever been, just took a distinct and sudden turn for the worse. Now there are a few things I need to do. I want to go to Laura's funeral. I want to say goodbye. After that, if you still need me, I want to start at five hundred dollars a week.' The figure was a stab in the dark, a made-up number. Wednesday's eyes revealed nothing. 'If we're happy working together, in six months' time you raise it to a thousand a week.'

He paused. It was the longest speech he'd made in years. 'You say you may need people to be hurt. Well, I'll hurt people if they're trying to hurt you. But I don't hurt people for fun or for profit. I won't go back to prison. Once was enough.'

'You won't have to,' said Wednesday.

'No,' said Shadow. 'I won't.' He finished the last of the mead. He wondered, suddenly, somewhere in the back of his head, whether the mead was responsible for loosening his tongue. But the words were coming out of him like the water spraying from a broken fire hydrant in summer, and he could not have stopped them if he had tried. 'I don't like you, Mister Wednesday, or whatever your real name may be. We are not friends. I don't know how you got off that plane without me seeing you, or how you trailed me here. But I'm impressed. You have class. And I'm at a loose end right now. You should know that when we're done, I'll be gone. And if you piss me off, I'll be gone too. Until then, I'll work for you.'

Wednesday grinned. His smiles were strange things, Shadow decided. They contained no shred of humor, no happiness, no mirth. Wednesday looked like he had learned to smile from a manual.

'Very good,' he said. 'Then we have a compact. And we are agreed.'

'What the hell,' said Shadow. Across the room, Mad Sweeney was feeding quarters into the juke box. Wednesday spat in his hand and extended it. Shadow shrugged. He spat in his own palm. They clasped hands. Wednesday began to squeeze. Shadow squeezed back. After a few seconds his hand began to hurt. Wednesday held the grip for another half-minute, and then he let go.

'Good,' he said. 'Good. Very good.' He smiled, a brief flash, and Shadow wondered if there had been real humor in that smile, actual pleasure. 'So, one last glass of evil, vile fucking mead to seal our deal, and then we are done.'

'It'll be a Southern Comfort and Coke for me,' said Sweeney, lurching back from the juke box.

The juke box began to play the Velvet Underground's 'Who Loves the Sun?' Shadow thought it a strange song to find on a juke box. It seemed very unlikely. But then, this whole evening had become increasingly unlikely.

Shadow took the quarter he had used for the coin-toss from the table, enjoying the sensation of a freshly milled coin against his fingers, producing it in his right hand between forefinger and thumb. He appeared to take it into his left hand in one smooth movement, while casually finger-palming it. He closed his left hand on the imaginary quarter. Then he took a second quarter in his right hand, between finger and thumb, and, as he pretended to drop that coin into the left hand, he let the palmed quarter fall into his right hand, striking the quarter he held there on the way. The chink confirmed the illusion that both coins were in his left hand, while they were now both held safely in his right.

'Coin tricks is it?' asked Sweeney, his chin raising, his scruffy beard bristling. 'Why, if it's coin tricks we're doing, watch this.'

He took a glass from the table, a glass that had once held mead, and he tipped the ice-cubes into the ashtray. Then he reached out and took a large coin, golden and shining, from the air. He dropped it into the glass. He took another gold coin from the air and tossed it into the glass, where it clinked against the first. He took a coin from the candle flame of a candle on the wall, another from his beard, a third from

Shadow's empty left hand, and dropped them, one by one, into the glass. Then he curled his fingers over the glass, and blew hard, and several more golden coins dropped into the glass from his hand. He tipped the glass of sticky coins into his jacket pocket, and then tapped the pocket to show, unmistakably, that it was empty.

'There,' he said. '*That's* a coin trick for you.'

Shadow, who had been watching closely throughout the impromptu performance, put his head on one side. 'We have to talk about that,' he said. 'I need to know how you did it.'

'I did it,' said Sweeney, with the air of one confiding a huge secret, 'with panache and style. That's how I did it.' He laughed, silently, rocking on his heels, his gappy teeth bared.

'Yes,' said Shadow. 'That is how you did it. You've got to teach me. All the ways of doing the Miser's Dream that I've read about you'd be hiding the coins in the hand that holds the glass, and dropping them in while you produce and vanish the coin in your right hand.'

'Sounds like a hell of a lot of work to me,' said Mad Sweeney. 'It's easier just to pick them out of the air.' He picked up his half-finished Southern Comfort and Coke, looked at it, and put it down on the table.

Wednesday stared at both of them as if he had just discovered new and previously unimagined life forms. Then he said, 'Mead for you, Shadow. I'll stick with Mister Jack Daniel's, and for the freeloading Irishman . . .?'

'A bottled beer, something dark for preference,' said Sweeney. 'Freeloader, is it?' He picked up what was left of his drink, and raised it to Wednesday in a toast. 'May the storm pass over us, and leave us hale and unharmed,' he said, and knocked the drink back.

'A fine toast,' said Wednesday. 'But it won't.'

Another mead was placed in front of Shadow.

'Do I have to drink this?' he asked, without enthusiasm.

'Yes, I'm afraid you do. It seals our deal. Third time's the charm, eh?'

'Shit,' said Shadow. He swallowed the mead in two large gulps. The pickled honey taste filled his mouth.

'There,' said Mr Wednesday. 'You're my man, now.'

'So,' said Sweeney, 'you want to know the trick of how it's done?'

'Yes,' said Shadow. 'Were you loading them in your sleeve?'

'They were never in my sleeve,' said Sweeney. He chortled to himself, rocking and bouncing as if he were a lanky, bearded, drunken volcano preparing to erupt with delight at his own brilliance. 'It's the simplest trick in the world. I'll fight you for it.'

Shadow shook his head. 'I'll pass.'

'Now *there's* a fine thing,' said Sweeney to the room. 'Old Wednesday gets himself a bodyguard, and the feller's too scared to put up his fists, even.'

'I won't fight you,' agreed Shadow.

Sweeney swayed and sweated. He fiddled with the peak of his baseball cap. Then he pulled one of his coins out of the air and placed it on the table. 'Real gold, if you were wondering,' said Sweeney. 'Win or lose – and you'll lose – it's yours if you fight me. A big fellow like you – who'd'a thought you'd be a fuckon coward?'

'He's already said he won't fight you,' said Wednesday. 'Go away, Mad Sweeney. Take your beer and leave us in peace.'

Sweeney took a step closer to Wednesday. 'Call me a freeloader, will you, you doomed old creature? You cold-blooded, heartless old tree-hanger.' His face was turning a deep, angry red.

Wednesday put out his hands, palms up, pacific. 'Foolishness, Sweeney. Watch where you put your words.'

Sweeney glared at him. Then he said, with the gravity of the very drunk, 'You've hired a coward. What would he do if I hurt you, do you think?'

Wednesday turned to Shadow. 'I've had enough of this,' he said. 'Deal with it.'

Shadow got to his feet and looked up into Mad Sweeney's face: how tall *was* the man? he wondered. 'You're bothering us,' he said. 'You're drunk. I think you ought to leave now.'

A slow smile spread over Sweeney's face. 'There, now,' he said. 'Like a little yapping dog, it's finally ready to fight. Hey, everybody,' he called to the room, 'there's going to be a lesson learned. Watch this!' He swung a huge fist at Shadow's face. Shadow jerked back: Sweeney's hand caught him beneath the right eye. He saw blotches of light, and felt pain.

And with that, the fight began.

Sweeney fought without style, without science, with nothing but enthusiasm for the fight itself: huge, barreling roundhouse blows that missed as often as they connected.

Shadow fought defensively, carefully, blocking Sweeney's blows or avoiding them. He became very aware of the audience around them. Tables were pulled out of the way with protesting groans, making a space for the men to spar. Shadow was aware at all times of Wednesday's eyes upon him, of Wednesday's humorless grin. It was a test, that was obvious, but what kind of a test?

In prison Shadow had learned there were two kinds of fights: *don't fuck with me* fights, where you made it as showy and impressive as you could, and private fights, *real* fights which were fast and hard and nasty, and always over in seconds.

'Hey, Sweeney,' said Shadow, breathless, 'why are we fighting?'

'For the joy of it,' said Sweeney, sober now, or at least, no longer visibly drunk. 'For the sheer unholy fucken delight of it. Can't you feel the joy in your own veins, rising like the sap in the springtime?' His lip was bleeding. So was Shadow's knuckle.

'So how'd you do the coin production?' asked Shadow. He swayed back and twisted, took a blow on his shoulder intended for his face.

'To tell the truth,' grunted Sweeney, 'I told you how I did it when first we spoke. But there's none so blind – ow! Good one! – as those who will not listen.'

Shadow jabbed at Sweeney, forcing him back into a table; empty glasses and ashtrays crashed to the floor. Shadow could have finished him off then. The man was defenseless, in no position to be able to do anything, sprawled back as he was.

Shadow glanced at Wednesday, who nodded. Shadow looked down at Mad Sweeney. 'Are we done?' he asked. Mad Sweeney hesitated, then nodded. Shadow let go of him, and took several steps backward. Sweeney, panting, pushed himself back up to a standing position.

'Not on yer ass!' he shouted. 'It ain't over till I say it is!' Then he grinned, and threw himself forward, swinging at Shadow. He stepped onto a fallen ice-cube, and his grin turned to open-mouthed dismay as his feet went out from under him, and he fell backward. The back of his head hit the barroom floor with a definite thud.

Shadow put his knee into Mad Sweeney's chest. 'For the second time, are we done fighting?' he asked.

'We may as well be, at that,' said Sweeney, raising his head from the floor, 'for the joy's gone out of me now, like the pee from a small boy in a swimming pool on a hot day.' And he spat the blood from his mouth and closed his eyes and began to snore, in deep and magnificent snores.

Somebody clapped Shadow on the back. Wednesday put a bottle of beer into his hand.

It tasted better than mead.

***

Shadow woke up stretched out in the back of a sedan car. The morning sun was dazzling, and his head hurt. He sat up awkwardly, rubbing his eyes.

Wednesday was driving. He was humming tunelessly as

he drove. He had a paper cup of coffee in the cup holder. They were heading along what looked like an interstate highway, with the cruise control set to an even sixty-five. The passenger seat was empty.

'How are you feeling, this fine morning?' asked Wednesday, without turning around.

'What happened to my car?' asked Shadow. 'It was a rental.'

'Mad Sweeney took it back for you. It was part of the deal the two of you cut last night.'

'Deal?'

'After the fight.'

'Fight?' He put one hand up and rubbed his cheek, and then he winced. Yes, there had been a fight. He remembered a tall man with a ginger beard, and the cheering and whooping of an appreciative audience. 'Who won?'

'You don't remember, eh?' Wednesday chuckled.

'Not so you'd notice,' said Shadow. Conversations from the night before began to jostle in his head uncomfortably. 'You got any more of that coffee?'

The big man reached beneath the passenger seat and passed back an unopened bottle of water. 'Here. You'll be dehydrated. This will help more than coffee, for the moment. We'll stop at the next gas station and get you some breakfast. You'll need to clean yourself up, too. You look like something the goat dragged in.'

'Cat dragged in,' said Shadow.

'Goat,' said Wednesday. 'Huge rank stinking goat with big teeth.'

Shadow unscrewed the top of the water and drank. Something clinked heavily in his jacket pocket. He put his hand into the pocket and pulled out a coin the size of a half dollar. It was heavy, and a deep yellow in color. It was also slightly sticky. Shadow palmed it in his right hand, classic palm, then produced it from between his third and fourth fingers. He front-palmed it, holding it between his first and his little finger, so it was invisible from behind, then slipped his two middle fingers under it, pivoting it smoothly into a back-palm. Then he dropped the coin back into his left hand, and he placed it into his pocket.

'What the hell was I drinking last night?' asked Shadow. The events of the night were crowding around him now, without shape, without sense, but he knew they were there.

Mr Wednesday spotted an exit sign promising a gas station, and he gunned the engine. 'You don't remember?'

'No.'

'You were drinking mead,' said Wednesday. He grinned a huge grin.

Mead.

Yes.

Shadow leaned back in the seat, and sucked down water from the bottle, and let the night before wash over him. Most of it, he remembered. Some of it, he didn't.

***

In the gas station Shadow bought a Clean-U-Up Kit, which contained a razor, a packet of shaving cream, a comb, and a disposable toothbrush packed with a tiny tube of toothpaste. Then he walked into the men's restroom and looked at himself in the mirror.

He had a bruise under one eye – when he prodded it, experimentally, with one finger, he found it hurt deeply, – and a swollen lower lip. His hair was a tangle, and he looked as if he had spent the first half of last night fighting and then the rest of the night fast asleep, fully dressed, in the back seat of a car. Tinny music played in the background: it took him some moments to identify it as the Beatles' 'Fool on the Hill'.

Shadow washed his face with the restroom's liquid soap, then he lathered his face and shaved. He wet his hair and combed it back. He brushed his teeth. Then he washed the last traces of the soap and the toothpaste from his face with lukewarm water. Stared back at his reflection: clean-shaven, but his eyes were still red and puffy. He looked older than he remembered.

He wondered what Laura would say when she saw him, and then he remembered that Laura wouldn't say anything ever again and he saw his face, in the mirror, tremble, but only for a moment.

He went out.

'I look like shit,' said Shadow.

'Of course you do,' agreed Wednesday.

Wednesday took an assortment of snack-food up to the cash register, and paid for that and their gas, changing his mind twice about whether he was doing it with plastic or with cash, to the irritation of the gum-chewing young lady behind the till. Shadow watched as Wednesday became increasingly flustered and apologetic. He seemed very old, suddenly. The girl gave him his cash back, and put the purchase on the card, and then gave him the card receipt and took his cash, then returned the cash and took a different card. Wednesday was obviously on the verge of tears, an old man made helpless by the implacable plastic march of the modern world.

Shadow checked out the pay-phone: an out-of-order sign hung on it.

They walked out of the warm gas station, and their breath steamed in the air.

'You want me to drive?' asked Shadow.

'Hell no,' said Wednesday.

The freeway slipped past them: browning grass meadows on each side of them. The trees were leafless and dead. Two black birds stared at them from a telegraph wire.

'Hey, Wednesday.'

'What?'

'The way I saw it in there, you never paid for the gas.'

'Oh?'

'The way I saw it, she wound up paying you for the

privilege of having you in her gas station. You think she's figured it out yet?'

'She never will.'

'So what are you? A two-bit con artist?'

Wednesday nodded. 'Yes,' he said. 'I suppose I am. Among other things.'

He swung out into the left lane to pass a truck. The sky was a bleak and uniform gray.

'It's going to snow,' said Shadow.

'Yes.'

'Sweeney. Did he actually show me how he did that trick with the gold coins?'

'Oh yes.'

'I can't remember.'

'It'll come back. It was a long night.'

Several small snowflakes brushed the windshield, melting in seconds.

'Your wife's body is on display at Wendell's Funeral Parlor at present,' said Wednesday. 'Then after lunch they will take her from there to the graveyard for the interment.'

'How do you know?'

'I called ahead while you were in the john. You know where Wendell's Funeral Parlor is?'

Shadow nodded. The snowflakes whirled and dizzied in front of them.

'This is our exit,' said Shadow. The car stole off the interstate, and past the cluster of motels to the north of Eagle Point.

Three years had passed. Yes. The Super-8 motel had gone, torn down: in its place was a Wendy's. There were more stoplights, unfamiliar storefronts. They drove downtown. Shadow asked Wednesday to slow as they drove past the Muscle Farm. CLOSED INDEFINITELY, said the hand-lettered sign on the door, DUE TO BEREAVEMENT.

Left on Main Street. Past a new tattoo parlor and the Armed Forces Recruitment Center, then the Burger King, and, familiar and unchanged, Olsen's Drug Store, then the yellow-brick facade of Wendell's Funeral Parlor. A neon sign in the front window said 'House of Rest.' Blank tombstones stood unchristened and uncarved in the window beneath the sign.

Wednesday pulled up in the parking lot.

'Do you want me to come in?' he asked.

'Not particularly.'

'Good.' The grin flashed, without humor. 'There's business I can be getting on with while you say your goodbyes. I'll get rooms for us at the Motel America. Meet me there when you're done.'

Shadow got out of the car, and watched it pull away. Then he walked in. The dimly lit corridor smelled of flowers and of furniture polish, with just the slightest tang of formaldehyde and rot beneath the surface. At the far end was the Chapel of Rest.

Shadow realized that he was palming the gold coin, moving it compulsively from a back palm to a front palm to a Downs palm, over and over. The weight was reassuring in his hand.

His wife's name was on a sheet of paper beside the door at the far end of the corridor. He walked into the Chapel of Rest. Shadow knew most of the people in the room: Laura's family, her workmates at the travel agency, several of her friends.

They all recognized him. He could see it in their faces. There were no smiles, though, no hellos.

At the end of the room was a small dais, and, on it, a cream-colored casket with several displays of flowers arranged about it: scarlets and yellows and whites and deep, bloody purples. He took a step forward. He could see Laura's body from where he was standing. He did not want to walk forward; he did not dare to walk away.

A man in a dark suit – Shadow guessed he worked at the funeral home – said, 'Sir? Would you like to sign the condolence and remembrance book?' and pointed him to a leather-bound book, open on a small lectern.

He wrote SHADOW and the date in his precise hand-writing, then, slowly, he wrote (PUPPY) beside it, putting off walking toward the end of the room, where the people were, and the casket, and the thing in the cream casket that was no longer Laura.

A small woman walked in from the corridor, and hesi-tated. She was in her early thirties. Her hair was dark red, and her skirt and blouse and jacket were all a funereal and elegant black. She wore dark lipstick. *Widow's weeds*, thought Shadow, recognizing her: Audrey Burton, Robbie's wife.

Audrey was holding a sprig of violets, wrapped at the base with silver foil. It was the kind of thing a child would make in June, thought Shadow. But violets were out of season.

Audrey looked directly at Shadow, and there was no recognition in her eyes. Then she walked across the room, to Laura's casket. Shadow followed her.

Laura lay with her eyes closed, and her arms folded across her chest. She wore a conservative blue suit he did not recognize. Her long brown hair was out of her eyes. It was his Laura and it was not: her repose, he realized, was what was unnatural. Laura was always such a restless sleeper.

Audrey placed her sprig of summer violets on Laura's chest. Then she pursed her blackberry-colored lips, worked her mouth for a moment and spat, hard, onto Laura's dead face.

The spit caught Laura on the cheek, and began to drip down toward her ear.

Audrey was already walking toward the door. Shadow hurried after her.

'Audrey?' he said. This time she recognized him. He wondered if she were taking tranquilizers. Her voice was distant and detached.

'Shadow? Did you escape? Or did they let you out?'

'Let me out yesterday. I'm a free man,' said Shadow. 'What the hell was that all about?'

She stopped in the dark corridor. 'The violets? They were always her favorite flower. When we were girls we used to pick them together.'

'Not the violets.'

'Oh, *that*,' she said. She wiped a speck of something invisible from the corner of her mouth. 'Well, I would have thought that was obvious.'

'Not to me, Audrey.'

'They didn't tell you?' Her voice was calm, emotionless. 'Your wife died with my husband's cock in her mouth, Shadow.'

She turned away, walked out into the parking lot, and Shadow watched her leave.

He went back in to the funeral home. Someone had already wiped away the spit.

***

None of the people at the viewing were able to meet Shadow's eye. Those who came over and talked to him did so as little as they could, mumbled awkward commiserations and fled.

After lunch – Shadow ate at the Burger King – was the burial. Laura's cream-colored coffin was interred in the small non-denominational cemetery on the edge of town: unfenced, a hilly woodland meadow filled with black granite and white marble headstones.

He rode to the cemetery in the Wendells' hearse, with Laura's mother. Mrs McCabe seemed to feel that Laura's death was Shadow's fault. 'If you'd been here,' she said, 'this would never have happened. I don't know why she married you. I told her. Time and again, I told her. But they don't listen to their mothers, do they?' She stopped, looked more closely at Shadow's face. 'Have you been fighting?'

'Yes,' he said.

'Barbarian,' she said, then she set her mouth, raised her head so her chins quivered, and stared straight ahead of her.

To Shadow's surprise Audrey Burton was also at the funeral, standing toward the back. The short service ended, the casket was lowered into the cold ground. The people went away.

Shadow did not leave. He stood there with his hands in his pockets, shivering, staring at the hole in the ground.

Above him the sky was iron-gray, featureless and flat as a mirror. It continued to snow, erratically, in ghost-like tumbling flakes.

There was something he wanted to say to Laura, and he was prepared to wait until he knew what it was. The world slowly began to lose light and color. Shadow's feet were going numb, while his hands and face hurt from the cold. He burrowed his hands into his pockets for warmth, and his fingers closed about the gold coin.

He walked over to the grave.

'This is for you,' he said.

Several shovels of earth had been emptied onto the casket, but the hole was far from full. He threw the gold coin into the grave with Laura, then he pushed more earth into the hole, to hide the coin from acquisitive gravediggers. He brushed the earth from his hands, and said, 'Goodnight Laura.' Then he said 'I'm sorry.' He turned his face toward the lights of the town, and began to walk back into Eagle Point.

His motel was a good two miles away, but after spending three years in prison he was relishing the idea that he could simply walk and walk, forever if need be. He could keep walking north, and wind up in Alaska, or head south, to Mexico and beyond. He could walk to Patagonia, or to Tierra del Fuego. The Land of Fire. He tried to remember how it had got its name: he remembered reading as a boy of naked men, crouched by fires to keep warm . . .

A car drew up beside him. The window hummed down.

'You want a lift, Shadow?' asked Audrey Burton.

'No,' he said. 'And not from you.'

He continued to walk. Audrey drove beside him at three miles an hour. Snowflakes danced in the beams of her headlights.

'I thought she was my best friend,' said Audrey. 'We'd talk every day. When Robbie and I had a fight, she'd be the first one to know – we'd go down to Chi-Chi's for margaritas and to talk about what scumpots men can be. And all the time she was fucking him behind my back.'

'Please go away, Audrey.'

'I just want you to know I had good reason for what I did.'

He said nothing.

'Hey!' she shouted. 'Hey! I'm talking to you!"

Shadow turned. 'Do you want me to tell you that you were right when you spit in Laura's face? Do you want me to say it didn't hurt? Or that what you told me made me hate her more than I miss her? It's not going to happen, Audrey.'

She drove beside him for another minute, not saying anything. Then she said, 'So, how was prison, Shadow?'

'It was fine,' said Shadow. 'You would have felt right at home.'

She put her foot down on the gas then, making the engine roar, and drove on and away.

With the headlights gone, the world was dark. Twilight faded into night. Shadow kept expecting the act of walking to warm him, to spread warmth through his icy hands and feet. It didn't happen.

Back in prison, Low Key Lyesmith had once referred to the little prison cemetery out behind the infirmary as the Bone Orchard, and the image had taken root in Shadow's mind. That night he had dreamed of an orchard under the moonlight, of skeletal white trees, their branches ending in bony hands, their roots going deep down into the graves. There was fruit that grew upon the trees in the bone orchard, in his dream, and there was something very disturbing about the fruit in the dream, but on waking he could no longer remember what strange fruit grew on the trees, or why he found it so repellent.

Cars passed him. Shadow wished that there was a sidewalk. He tripped on something that he could not see in the dark and sprawled into the ditch on the side of the road, his right hand sinking into several inches of cold mud. He climbed to his feet and wiped his hands on the leg of his pants. He stood there, awkwardly. He had only enough time to observe that there was someone beside him before something wet was forced over his nose and mouth, and he tasted harsh, chemical fumes.

This time the ditch seemed warm and comforting.

* * *

Shadow's temples felt as if they had been reattached to the rest of his skull with roofing nails, and his vision was blurred.

His hands were bound behind his back with what felt like some kind of straps. He was in a car, sitting on leather upholstery. For a moment he wondered if there was something wrong with his depth perception and then he understood that, no, the other seat really *was* that far away.

There were people sitting beside him, but he could not turn to look at them.

The fat young man at the other end of the stretch limo took a can of diet Coke from the cocktail bar and popped it open. He wore a long black coat, made of some silky material, and he appeared barely out of his teens: a spattering of acne glistened on one cheek. He smiled when he saw that Shadow was awake.

'Hello, Shadow,' he said. 'Don't fuck with me.'

'Okay,' said Shadow. 'I won't. Can you drop me off at the Motel America, up by the interstate?'

'Hit him,' said the young man to the person on Shadow's left. A punch was delivered to Shadow's solar plexus, knocking the breath from him, doubling him over. He straightened up, slowly.

'I said don't fuck with me. That was fucking with me. Keep your answers short and to the point or I'll fucking kill you. Or maybe I won't kill you. Maybe I'll have the children break every bone in your fucking body. There are two hundred and six of them. So don't fuck with me.'

'Got it,' said Shadow.

The ceiling lights in the limo changed color from violet to blue then to green and to yellow.

'You're working for Wednesday,' said the young man.

'Yes,' said Shadow.

'What the fuck is he after? I mean, what's he doing here? He must have a plan. What's the game plan?'

'I started working for Mister Wednesday this morning,' said Shadow. 'I'm an errand boy. Maybe a driver, if he ever lets me drive. We've barely exchanged a dozen words.'

'You're saying you don't know?'

'I'm saying I don't know.'

The boy stared at him. He swigged some Coke from the can, belched, stared some more. 'Would you tell me if you did know?'

'Probably not,' admitted Shadow. 'As you say, I'm working for Mister Wednesday.'

The boy opened his jacket and took out a silver cigarette case from an inside pocket. He opened it, and offered a cigarette to Shadow. 'Smoke?'

Shadow thought about asking for his hands to be untied, but decided against it. 'No thank you,' he said.

The cigarette appeared to have been hand-rolled, and when the boy lit it, with a matte black Zippo lighter, the odor that filled the limo was not tobacco. It was not pot either, decided Shadow. It smelled a little like burning electrical parts.

The boy inhaled deeply, then held his breath. He let the smoke trickle out from his mouth, pulled it back into his nostrils. Shadow suspected that he had practiced that in front of a mirror for a while before doing it in public.

'If you've lied to me,' said the boy, as if from a long way away, 'I'll fucking kill you. You know that.'

'So you said.'

The boy took another long drag on his cigarette. The lights inside the limo transmuted from orange, to red, and back to purple. 'You say you're staying at the Motel America?' He tapped on the driver's window, behind him. The glass window lowered. 'Hey. Motel America, up by the interstate. We need to drop off our guest.'

The driver nodded, and the glass rose up again.

The glinting fiber-optic lights inside the limo continued to change, cycling through their set of dim colors. It seemed to Shadow that the boy's eyes were glinting too, the green of an antique computer monitor.

'You tell Wednesday this, man. You tell him he's history. He's forgotten. He's old. And he better accept it. Tell him that we are the future and we don't give a fuck about him or anyone like him. His time is over. Yes? You fucking tell him that, man. He has been consigned to the dumpster of history while people like me ride our limos down the superhighway of tomorrow.'

'I'll tell him,' said Shadow. He was beginning to feel light-headed. He hoped that he was not going to be sick.

'Tell him that we have fucking reprogrammed reality. Tell him that language is a virus and that religion is an operating system and that prayers are just so much fucking spam. Tell him that or I'll fucking kill you,' said the young man mildly, from the smoke.

'Got it,' said Shadow. 'You can let me out here. I can walk the rest of the way.'

The young man nodded. 'Good talking to you,' he said. The smoke had mellowed him. 'You should know that if we do fucking kill you then we'll just delete you. You got that? One click and you're overwritten with random ones and zeros. Undelete is not an option.' He tapped on the window behind him. 'He's getting off here,' he said. Then he turned back to Shadow, pointed to his cigarette. 'Synthetic toadskins,' he said. 'You know they can synthesize bufotenin now?'

The car stopped. The person to Shadow's right got out and held the door open for Shadow. Shadow climbed out awkwardly, his hands tied behind his back. He realized that he had not yet got a clear look at either of the people who had been in the back seat with him. He did not know if they were men or women, old or young.

Shadow's bonds were cut. The nylon strips fell to the tarmac. Shadow turned around. The inside of the car was now one writhing cloud of smoke in which two lights glinted, copper-colored, like the beautiful eyes of a toad. 'It's all about the dominant fucking paradigm, Shadow. Nothing else is important. And hey, sorry to hear about your old lady.'

The door closed, and the stretch limo drove off, quietly. Shadow was a couple of hundred yards away from his motel, and he walked there, breathing the cold air, past red and yellow and blue lights advertising every kind of fast food a man could imagine, as long as it was a hamburger; and he reached the Motel America without incident.

Chapter Three

'Every hour wounds. The last one kills.'

– Old saying

There was a thin young woman behind the counter at the Motel America. She told Shadow he had already been checked in by his friend, and gave him his rectangular plastic room key. She had pale blonde hair and a rodent-like quality to her face that was most apparent when she looked suspicious, and eased when she smiled. Most of the time she looked at Shadow, she looked suspicious. She refused to tell him Wednesday's room number, and insisted on telephoning Wednesday on the house phone to let him know his guest was here.

Wednesday came out of a room down the hall, and beckoned to Shadow.

'How was the funeral?' he asked.

'It's over,' said Shadow.

'That shitty, huh? You want to talk about it?'

'No,' said Shadow.

'Good.' Wednesday grinned. 'Too much talking these days. Talk talk talk. This country would get along much better if people learned how to suffer in silence. You hungry?'

'A little.'

'There's no food here. But you can order a pizza and they'll put it on the room.'

Wednesday led the way back to his room, which was across the hall from Shadow's. There were maps all over the room, unfolded, spread out on the bed, taped to the walls. Wednesday had drawn all over the maps in bright marking pens, fluorescent greens and painful pinks and vivid oranges.

'I got hijacked by a fat kid in a limo,' said Shadow. 'He says to tell you that you have been consigned to the dung heap of history while people like him ride in their limos down the superhighways of life. Something like that.'

'Little snot,' said Wednesday.

'You know him?'

Wednesday shrugged. 'I know who he is.' He sat down, heavily, on the room's only chair. 'They don't have a clue,' he said. 'They don't have a fucking clue. How much longer do you need to stay in town?'

'I don't know. Maybe another week. I guess I need to wrap up Laura's affairs. Take care of the apartment, get rid of her clothes, all that. It'll drive her mother nuts, but the woman deserves it.'

Wednesday nodded his huge head. 'Well, the sooner you're done, the sooner we can move out of Eagle Point. Goodnight.'

Shadow walked across the hall. His room was a duplicate of Wednesday's room, down to the print of a bloody sunset on the wall above the bed. He ordered a cheese and meatball pizza, then he ran a bath, pouring all the motel's little plastic bottles of shampoo into the water, making it foam.

He was too big to lie down in the bathtub, but he sat in it and luxuriated as best he could. Shadow had promised himself a bath when he got out of prison, and Shadow kept his promises.

The pizza arrived shortly after he got out of the bath, and Shadow ate it, washing it down with a can of root beer.

He turned on the television, and watched an episode of Jerry Springer he remembered from before he went to prison. The theme of the show was 'I want to be a prostitute' and several would-be whores, most of them female, were brought out, shouted at and hectored by the audience; then a gold-draped pimp came out and offered them employment in his stable, and an ex-hooker ran out and pleaded with them all to get real jobs. Shadow turned it off before Jerry got to his thought for the day.

Shadow lay in bed, thinking, *This is my first bed as a free man*, and the thought gave him less pleasure than he had imagined that it would. He left the drapes open, watched the lights of the cars and of the fast food joints through the window glass, comforted to know there was another world out there, one he could walk to any time he wanted.

Shadow could have been in his bed at home, he thought, in the apartment that he had shared with Laura – in the bed that he had shared with Laura. But the thought of being there without her, surrounded by her things, her scent, her life, was simply too painful . . .

Don't go there, thought Shadow. He decided to think about something else. He thought about coin tricks. Shadow knew that he did not have the personality to be a magician: he could not weave the stories that were so necessary for belief, nor did he wish to do card tricks, or produce paper flowers. But he liked to manipulate coins; he enjoyed the craft of it. He started to list the coin vanishes he had mastered, which reminded him of the coin he had tossed into Laura's grave, and then, in his head, Audrey was telling him that Laura had died with Robbie's cock in her mouth, and once again he felt a small hurt in his chest. In his heart.

Every hour wounds. The last one kills. Where had he heard that? He could no longer remember. He could feel, somewhere deep inside him, anger and pain building, a knot of tension at the base of his skull, a tightness at the temples. He breathed in through his nose, out through his mouth, forcing himself to let the tension go.

He thought of Wednesday's comment and smiled, despite himself: Shadow had heard too many people telling each other not to repress their feelings, to let their emotions out, let the pain go. Shadow thought there was a lot to be said for bottling up emotions. If you did it long enough and deep enough, he suspected, pretty soon you wouldn't feel anything at all.

Sleep took him then, without Shadow noticing.

He was walking . . .

He was walking through a room bigger than a city, and everywhere he looked there were statues and carvings and rough-hewn images. He was standing beside a statue of a woman-like thing: her naked breasts hung, flat and pendulous on her chest, around her waist was a chain of severed hands, both of her own hands held sharp knives, and, instead of a head, rising from her neck there were twin serpents, their bodies arched, facing each other, ready to attack. There was something profoundly disturbing about the statue, a deep and violent wrongness. Shadow backed away from it.

He began to walk through the hall. The carved eyes of those statues that had eyes seemed to follow his every step.

In his dream, he realized that each statue had a name burning on the floor in front of it. The man with the white hair, with a necklace of teeth about his neck, holding a drum, was *Leucotios*; the broad-hipped woman, with monsters dropping from the vast gash between her legs was *Hubur*; the ram-headed man holding the golden ball was *Hershef*.

A precise voice, fussy and exact, was speaking to him, in his dream, but he could see no one.

'These are gods who have been forgotten, and now might as well be dead. They can be found only in dry histories.

They are gone, all gone, but their names and their images remain with us.'

Shadow turned a corner, and knew himself to be in another room, even vaster than the first. It went on further than the eye could see. Close to him was the skull of a mammoth, polished and brown, and a hairy ochre cloak, being worn by a small woman with a deformed left hand. Next to that were three women, each carved from the same granite boulder, joined at the waist: their faces had an unfinished, hasty look to them, although their breasts and genitalia had been carved with elaborate care; and there was a flightless bird which Shadow did not recognize, twice his height, with a beak made for rending, like a vulture's, but with human arms: and on, and on.

The voice spoke once more, as if it were addressing a class, saying, 'These are the gods who have passed out of memory. Even their names are lost. The people who worshiped them are as forgotten as their gods. Their totems are long since broken and cast down. Their last priests died without passing on their secrets.

'Gods die. And when they truly die they are unmourned and unremembered. Ideas are more difficult to kill than people, but they can be killed, in the end.'

There was a whispering noise that began then to run through the hall, a low susurrus that caused Shadow, in his dream, to experience a chilling and inexplicable fear. An all-engulfing panic took him, there in the halls of the Gods whose very existence had been forgotten – octopus-faced gods and gods who were only mummified hands or falling rocks or forest fires . . .

Shadow woke with his heart jackhammering in his chest, his forehead clammy, entirely awake. The red numerals on the bedside clock told him the time was 1:03 a.m. The light of the Motel America sign outside shone through his bedroom window. Disoriented, Shadow got up and walked into the tiny motel bathroom. He pissed without turning on the lights, and returned to the bedroom. The dream was still fresh and vivid in his mind's eye, but he could not explain to himself why it had scared him so.

The light that came into the room from outside was not bright, but Shadow's eyes had become used to the dark. There was a woman sitting on the side of his bed.

He knew her. He would have known her in a crowd of a thousand, or of a hundred thousand. She sat straight on the side of his bed. She was still wearing the navy-blue suit they had buried her in.

Her voice was a whisper, but a familiar one. 'I guess,' said Laura, 'you're going to ask what I'm doing here.'

Shadow said nothing.

He sat down on the room's only chair, and, finally, asked, 'Babe? Is that you?'

'Yes,' she said. 'I'm cold, puppy.'

'You're dead, babe.'

'Yes,' she said. 'Yes. I am.' She patted the bed next to her. 'Come and sit by me,' she said.

'No,' said Shadow. 'I think I'll stay right here for now. We have some unresolved issues to address.'

'Like me being dead?'

'Possibly, but I was thinking more of how you died. You and Robbie.'

'Oh,' she said. 'That.'

Shadow could smell – or perhaps, he thought, he simply imagined that he smelled – an odor of rot, of flowers and preservatives. His wife – his ex-wife . . . no, he corrected himself, his *late* wife . . . sat on the bed and stared at him, unblinking.

'Puppy,' she said. 'Could you – do you think you could possibly get me – a cigarette?'

'I thought you gave them up.'

'I did,' she said. 'But I'm no longer concerned about the health risks. And I think it would calm my nerves. There's a machine in the lobby.'

Shadow pulled on his jeans and a tee shirt and went, barefoot, into the lobby. The night clerk was a middle-aged man, reading a book by John Grisham. Shadow bought a pack of Virginia Slims from the machine. He asked the night clerk for a book of matches.

The man stared at him, asked for his room number. Shadow told him. The man nodded. 'You're in a non-smoking room,' he said. 'You make sure you open the window, now.' He passed Shadow a book of matches and a plastic ashtray with the Motel America logo on it.

'Got it,' said Shadow.

He went back into his bedroom. He did not turn the light on. His wife was still on the bed. She had stretched out now, on top of his rumpled covers. Shadow opened the window and then passed her the cigarettes and the matches. Her fingers were cold. She lit a match and he saw that her nails, usually pristine, were battered and chewed, and there was mud under them.

Laura lit the cigarette, inhaled, blew out the match. She took another puff. 'I can't taste it,' she said. 'I don't think this is doing anything.'

'I'm sorry,' he said.

'Me too,' said Laura.

When she inhaled the cigarette tip glowed, and he was able to see her face.

'So,' she said. 'They let you out.'

'Yes.'

'How was prison?'

'Could have been worse.'

'Yes.' The tip of the cigarette glowed orange. 'I'm still grateful. I should never have got you mixed up in it.'

'Well,' he said, 'I agreed to do it. I could have said no.' He wondered why he wasn't scared of her: why a dream of a museum could leave him terrified, while he seemed to be coping with a walking corpse without fear.

'Yes,' she said. 'You could have. You big galoot.' Smoke

wreathed her face. She was very beautiful in the dim light.
'You want to know about me and Robbie?'

'Yes.' It was Laura, he realized. Living or dead, he couldn't
fear her.

She stubbed out the cigarette in the ashtray. 'You were in
prison,' she said. 'And I needed someone to talk to. I needed
a shoulder to cry on. You weren't there. I was upset.'

'I'm sorry.' Shadow realized something was different about
her voice, and he tried to figure out what it was.

'I know. So we'd meet for coffee. Talk about what we'd do
when you got out of prison. How good it would be to see you
again. He really liked you, you know. He was looking
forward to giving you back your old job.'

'Yes.'

'And then Audrey went to visit her sister for a week. This
was, oh, a year, thirteen months after you'd gone away.' Her
voice lacked expression; each word was flat and dull, like
pebbles dropped, one by one, into a deep well. 'Robbie came
over. We got drunk together. We did it on the floor of the
bedroom. It was good. It was really good.'

'I didn't need to hear that.'

'No? I'm sorry. It's harder to pick and choose when you're
dead. It's like a photograph, you know. It doesn't matter as
much.'

'It matters to me.'

Laura lit another cigarette. Her movements were fluid and
competent, not stiff. Shadow wondered, for a moment, if she
was dead at all. Perhaps this was some kind of elaborate
trick. 'Yes,' she said. 'I see that. Well, we carried on our affair
– although we didn't call it that, we did not call it anything –
for most of the last two years.'

'Were you going to leave me for him?'

'Why would I do that? You're my big bear. You're my
puppy. You did what you did for me. I waited three years for
you to come back to me. I love you.'

He stopped himself from saying *I love you, too*. He wasn't

going to say that. Not any more. 'So what happened the other night?'

'The night I was killed?'

'Yes.'

'Well, Robbie and I went out to talk about your welcome-back surprise party. It would have been so good. And I told him that we were done. Finished. That now that you were back that was the way it had to be.'

'Mm. Thank you, babe.'

'You're welcome, darling.' The ghost of a smile crossed her face. 'We got maudlin. It was sweet. We got stupid. I got very drunk. He didn't. He had to drive. We were driving home and I announced that I was going to give him a good-bye blowjob, one last time with feeling, and I unzipped his pants, and I did.'

'Big mistake.'

'Tell me about it. I knocked the gearshift with my shoulder, and then Robbie was trying to push me out of the way to put the car back in gear, and we were swerving, and there was a loud crunch and I remember the world started to roll and to spin, and I thought "I'm going to die." It was very dispassionate. I remember that. I wasn't scared. And then I don't remember anything more.'

There was a smell like burning plastic. It was the cigarette, Shadow realized: it had burned down to the filter. Laura did not seem to have noticed.

'What are you doing here, Laura?'

'Can't a wife come and see her husband?'

'You're dead. I went to your funeral this afternoon.'

'Yes.' She stopped talking, stared into nothing. Shadow stood up and walked over to her. He took the smoldering cigarette butt from her fingers and threw it out of the window.

'Well?'

Her eyes sought his. 'I don't know much more than I did when I was alive. Most of the stuff I know now that I didn't know then I can't put into words.'

'Normally people who die stay in their graves,' said Shadow.

'Do they? Do they really, puppy? I used to think they did too. Now I'm not so sure. Perhaps.' She climbed off the bed and walked over to the window. Her face, in the light of the motel sign, was as beautiful as it had ever been. The face of the woman he had gone to prison for.

His heart hurt in his chest as if someone had taken it in a fist and squeezed. 'Laura . . .?'

She did not look at him. 'You've gotten yourself mixed up in some bad things, Shadow. You're going to screw it up, if someone isn't there to watch out for you. I'm watching out for you. And thank you for my present.'

'What present?'

She reached into the pocket of her blouse, and pulled out the gold coin he had thrown into the grave earlier that day. There was still black dirt on it. 'I may have it put on a chain. It was very sweet of you.'

'You're welcome.'

She turned then and looked at him with eyes that seemed both to see and not to see him. 'I think there are several aspects of our marriage we're going to have to work on.'

'Babes,' he told her. 'You're dead.'

'That's one of those aspects, obviously.' She paused. 'Okay,' she said. 'I'm going now. It will be better if I go.' And, naturally and easily, she turned and put her hands on Shadow's shoulders, and went up on tiptoes to kiss him goodbye, as she had always kissed him goodbye.

Awkwardly he bent to kiss her on the cheek, but she moved her mouth as he did so and pushed her lips against his. Her breath smelled, faintly, of mothballs.

Laura's tongue flickered into Shadow's mouth. It was cold, and dry, and it tasted of cigarettes and of bile. If Shadow had had any doubts as to whether his wife was dead or not, they ended then.

He pulled back.

'I love you,' she said, simply. 'I'll be looking out for you.' She walked over to the motel room door. There was a strange taste in his mouth. 'Get some sleep, puppy,' she told him. 'And stay out of trouble.'

She opened the door to the hall. The fluorescent light in the hallway was not kind: beneath it, Laura looked dead, but then, it did that to everyone.

'You could have asked me to stay the night,' she said, in her cold-stone voice.

'I don't think I could,' said Shadow.

'You will, hon,' she said. 'Before all this is over. You will.' She turned away from him, and walked down the corridor.

Shadow looked out of the doorway. The night clerk kept on reading his John Grisham novel, and barely looked up as she walked past him. There was thick graveyard mud clinging to her shoes. And then she was gone.

Shadow breathed out, a slow sigh. His heart was pounding arrhythmically in his chest. He walked across the hall, and knocked on Wednesday's door. As he knocked he got the weirdest notion, that he was being buffeted by black wings, as if an enormous crow was flying through him, out into the hall and the world beyond.

Wednesday opened the door. He had a white motel towel wrapped around his waist, but was otherwise naked. 'What the hell do you want?' he asked.

'Something you should know,' said Shadow. 'Maybe it was a dream – but it wasn't – or maybe I inhaled some of the fat kid's synthetic toadskin smoke, or probably I'm just going mad . . .'

'Yeah, yeah. Spit it out,' said Wednesday. 'I'm kind of in the middle of something here.'

Shadow glanced into the room. He could see that there was someone in the bed, watching him. A sheet pulled up over small breasts. Pale blonde hair, something rattish about the face. The girl from the motel desk. He lowered his voice. 'I just saw my wife,' he said. 'She was in my room.'

'A ghost, you mean? You saw a ghost?'

'No. Not a ghost. She was solid. It was her. She's dead all right, but it wasn't any kind of a ghost. I touched her. She kissed me.'

'I see.' Wednesday darted a look at the woman in the bed. 'Be right back, m'dear,' he said.

They crossed the hall to Shadow's room. Wednesday turned on the lamps. He looked at the cigarette butt in the ashtray. He scratched his chest. His nipples were dark, old-man nipples, and his chest hair was grizzled. There was a white scar down one side of his torso. He sniffed the air. Then he shrugged.

'Okay,' he said. 'So your dead wife showed up. You scared?'

'A little.'

'Very wise. The dead always give me the screaming mimis. Anything else?'

'I'm ready to leave Eagle Point. Laura's mother can sort out the apartment, all that. She hates me anyway. I'm ready to go when you are.'

Wednesday smiled. 'Good news, my boy. We'll leave in the morning. Now, you should get some sleep. I have some scotch in my room, if you need help sleeping. Yes?'

'No. I'll be fine.'

'Then do not disturb me further. I have a long night ahead of me.'

'No sleep?' asked Shadow, smiling.

'I don't sleep. It's overrated. A bad habit I do my best to avoid – in company, wherever possible, and the young lady may go off the boil if I don't get back to her.'

'Good night,' said Shadow.

'Exactly,' said Wednesday, and he closed the door as he went out.

Shadow sat down on the bed. The smell of cigarettes and preservatives lingered in the air. He wished that he were mourning Laura: it seemed more appropriate than being troubled by her or, he admitted it to himself now that she had gone, just a little scared by her. It was time to mourn. He turned the lights out, and lay on the bed, and thought of Laura as she was before he went to prison. He remembered their marriage when they were young and happy and stupid and unable to keep their hands off each other.

It had been a very long time since Shadow had cried, so long he thought he had forgotten how. He had not even cried when his mother died. But he began to cry then, in painful, lurching sobs. He missed Laura and the days that were forever gone.

For the first time since he was a small boy, Shadow cried himself to sleep.

Coming to America

They navigated the green sea by the stars and by the shore, and when the shore was only a memory and the night sky was overcast and dark they navigated by faith, and they called on the all-father to bring them safely to land once more.

A bad journey they had of it, their fingers numb and with a shiver in their bones that not even wine could burn off. They would wake in the morning to see that the rime had frosted their beards, and, until the sun warmed them, they looked like old men, white-bearded before their time.

Teeth were loosening and eyes were deep-sunken in their sockets when they made landfall on the green land to the West. The men said, 'We are far, far from our homes and our hearths, far from the seas we know and the lands we love. Here on the edge of the world we will be forgotten by our gods.'

Their leader clambered to the top of a great rock, and he mocked them for their lack of faith. 'The all-father made the world,' he shouted. 'He built it with his hands from the shattered bones and the flesh of Ymir, his grandfather. He placed Ymir's brains in the sky as clouds, and his salt blood became the seas we crossed. If he made the world, do you not realize that he created this land as well? And if we die here as men, shall we not be received into his hall?'

And the men cheered and laughed. They set to, with a will, to build a hall out of split trees and mud, inside a small stockade of sharpened logs, although as far as they knew they were the only men in the new land.

On the day that the hall was finished there was a storm: the sky at midday became as dark as night, and the sky was rent with forks of white flame, and the thunder-crashes were so loud that the men were almost deafened by them, and the ship's cat they had brought with them for good fortune hid beneath their beached longboat. The storm was hard enough and vicious enough that the men laughed and clapped each other on the back, and they said 'The thunderer is here with us, in this distant land,' and they gave thanks, and rejoiced, and they drank until they were reeling.

In the smoky darkness of their hall, that night, the bard sang them the old songs. He sang of Odin, the all-father, who was sacrificed to himself as bravely and as nobly as others were sacrificed to him. He sang of the nine days that the all-father hung from the world-tree, his side pierced and dripping from the spear-point (at this point his song became, for a moment, a scream), and he sang them all the things the all-father had learned in his agony: nine names, and nine runes, and twice-nine charms. When he told them of the spear piercing Odin's side, the bard shrieked in pain, as the all-father himself had called out in his agony, and all the men shivered, imagining his pain.

They found the scraeling the following day, which was the all-father's own day. He was a small man, his long hair black as a crow's wing, his skin the color of rich red clay. He spoke in words none of them could understand, not even their bard, who had been on a ship that had sailed through the pillars of Hercules, and who could speak the trader's pidgin men spoke all across the Mediterranean. The stranger was dressed in feathers and in furs, and there were small bones braided into his long hair.

They led him into their encampment, and they gave him roasted meat to eat, and strong drink to quench his thirst. They laughed riotously at the man as he stumbled and sang, at the way his head rolled and lolled, and this on less than a drinking-horn of mead. They gave him more drink, and soon enough he lay beneath the table with his head curled under his arm.

Then they picked him up, a man at each shoulder, a man at each leg, carried him at shoulder height, the four men making him an eight-legged horse, and they carried him at the head of a procession to an ash tree on the hill overlooking the bay, where they put a rope around his neck and hung him high in the wind, their tribute to the all-father, the gallows lord. The screaling's body swung in the wind, his face blackening, his tongue protruding, his eyes popping, his penis hard enough to hang a leather helmet on, while the men cheered and shouted and laughed, proud to be sending their sacrifice to the Heavens.

And, the next day, when two huge ravens landed upon the screaling's corpse, one on each shoulder, and commenced to peck at its cheeks and eyes, the men knew their sacrifice had been accepted.

It was a long winter, and they were hungry, but they were cheered by the thought that, when spring came, they would send the boat back to the northlands, and it would bring settlers, and bring women. As the weather became colder, and the days became shorter, some of the men took to searching for the screaling village, hoping to find food, and women. They found nothing, save for the places where fires had been, where small encampments had been abandoned.

One mid-winter's day, when the sun was as distant and cold as a dull silver coin, they saw that the remains of the screaling's body had been removed from the ash-tree. That afternoon it began to snow, in huge, slow flakes.

The men from the northlands closed the gates of their encampment, retreated behind their wooden wall.

The scraeling war party fell upon them that night: five hundred men to thirty. They climbed the wall, and, over the following seven days they killed each of the thirty men, in thirty different ways. And the sailors were forgotten, by history and their people.

The wall they tore down, and the village they burned. The longboat, upside down and pulled high on the shingle, they also burned, hoping that the pale strangers had but one boat, and that by burning it they were ensuring that no other Northmen would come to their shores.

It was more than a hundred years before Leif the Fortunate, son of Erik the Red, rediscovered that land, which he would call Vineland. His gods were already waiting for him when he arrived: Tyr, one-handed, and gray Odin gallows-god, and Thor of the thunders.

They were there.

They were waiting.

Chapter Four

Let the Midnight Special
Shine its light on me
Let the Midnight Special
Shine its ever-lovin' light on me
                          – The Midnight Special, traditional

Shadow and Wednesday ate breakfast at a Country Kitchen across the street from their motel. It was eight in the morning, and the world was misty and chill.

'You still ready to leave Eagle Point?' asked Wednesday, at the breakfast bar. 'I have some calls to make, if you are. Friday today. Friday's a free day. A woman's day. Saturday tomorrow. Much to do on Saturday.'

'I'm ready,' said Shadow. 'Nothing keeping me here.'

Wednesday heaped his plate high with several kinds of breakfast meats. Shadow took some melon, a bagel, and a packet of cream cheese. They went and sat down in a booth.

'That was some dream you had last night,' said Wednesday.

'Yes,' said Shadow. 'It was.' Laura's muddy footprints had been visible on the motel carpet when he got up that morning, leading from his bedroom to the lobby and out the door.

'So,' said Wednesday. 'Why'd they call you Shadow?'

Shadow shrugged. 'It's a name,' he said. Outside the plate glass the world in the mist had become a pencil drawing executed in a dozen different grays with, here and there, a smudge of electric red or pure white. 'How'd you lose your eye?'

Wednesday shoveled half a dozen pieces of bacon into his mouth, chewed, wiped the fat from his lips with the back of his hand. 'Didn't lose it,' he said. 'I still know exactly where it is.'

'So what's the plan?'

Wednesday looked thoughtful. He ate several vivid pink slices of ham, picked a fragment of meat from his beard, dropped it onto his plate. 'Plan is as follows. On Saturday night, which, as I have already remarked, is tomorrow, we shall be meeting with a number of persons preeminent in their respective fields – do not let their demeanor intimidate you. We shall meet at one of the most important places in the entire country. Afterward we shall wine and dine them. There will be, at a guess, thirty or forty of them. Perhaps more. I need to enlist them in my current enterprise.'

'And where is the most important place in the country?'

'One of them, m'boy. I said one of them. Opinions are justifiably divided. I have sent word to my colleagues. We'll stop off in Chicago on the way, as I need to pick up some money. Entertaining, in the manner we shall need to entertain, will take more ready cash than I happen to have available. Then on to Madison.'

'I see.'

'No, you don't. But all will become clear in time.'

Wednesday paid and they left, walked back across the road to the motel parking lot. Wednesday tossed Shadow the car keys. He drove down to the freeway and out of town.

'You going to miss it?' asked Wednesday. He was sorting through a folder filled with maps.

'The town? No. Too many Laura memories. I didn't really

ever have a life here. I was never in one place too long as a
kid, and I didn't get here until I was in my twenties. So this
town is Laura's.'

'Let's hope she stays here,' said Wednesday.

'It was a dream,' said Shadow. 'Remember.'

'That's good,' said Wednesday. 'Healthy attitude to have.
Did you fuck her last night?'

Shadow took a breath. Then, 'That is none of your damn
business. And no.'

'Did you want to?'

Shadow said nothing at all. He drove north, toward
Chicago. Wednesday chuckled, and began to pore over his
maps, unfolding and refolding them, making occasional
notes on a yellow legal pad with a large silver ballpoint pen.

Eventually he was finished. He put his pen away, put the
folder on the back seat. 'The best thing about the states we're
heading for,' said Wednesday, 'Minnesota, Wisconsin, all
around there, is it has the kind of women I liked when I was
younger. Pale-skinned and blue-eyed, hair so fair it's almost
white, wine-colored lips, and round, full breasts with the
veins running through them like a good cheese.'

'Only when you were younger?' asked Shadow. 'Looked
like you were doing pretty good last night.'

'Yes.' Wednesday smiled. 'Would you like to know the
secret of my success?'

'You pay them?'

'Nothing so crude. No, the secret is charm. Pure and
simple.'

'Charm, huh? Well, like they say, you either got it or you
ain't.'

'Charms can be learnt,' said Wednesday.

'So where are we going?' asked Shadow.

'There's an old friend of mine we need to talk to. He's one
of the people who'll be coming to the get-together. Old man,
now. He's expecting us for dinner.'

They drove north and west, toward Chicago.

'Whatever's happening with Laura,' said Shadow, breaking the silence. 'Is it your fault? Did you make it happen?'

'No,' said Wednesday.

'Like the kid in the car asked me: would you tell me if it was?'

'I'm as puzzled as you are.'

Shadow tuned the radio to an oldies station, and listened to songs that were current before he was born. Bob Dylan sang about a hard rain that was going to fall, and Shadow wondered if that rain had fallen yet, or if it was something that was still going to happen. The road ahead of them was empty and the ice crystals on the asphalt glittered like diamonds in the morning sun.

He sang along, under his breath.

***

Chicago happened slowly, like a migraine. First they were driving through countryside, then, imperceptibly, the occasional town became a low suburban sprawl, and the sprawl became the city.

They parked outside a squat black brownstone. The sidewalk was clear of snow. They walked to the lobby. Wednesday pressed the top button on the gouged metal intercom box. Nothing happened. He pressed it again. Then, experimentally, he began to press the other buttons, for other tenants, with no response.

'It's dead,' said a gaunt old woman, coming down the steps. 'Doesn't work. We call the super, ask him when he going to fix, when he going to mend the heating, he does not care, goes to Arizona for the winter for his chest.' Her accent was thick, Eastern European, Shadow guessed.

Wednesday bowed low. 'Zorya, my dear, may I say how unutterably beautiful you look? A radiant creature. You have not aged.'

The old woman glared at him. 'He don't want to see you. I

don't want to see you neither. You bad news.'

'That's because I don't come if it isn't important.'

The woman sniffed. She carried an empty string shopping bag, and wore an old red coat, buttoned up to her chin, and, perched on her gray hair, a green velvet hat that was, in appearance, a little bit flowerpot, a little bit bread-loaf. She looked at Shadow suspiciously.

'Who is the big man?' she asked Wednesday. 'Another one of your murderers?'

'You do me a deep disservice, good lady. This gentleman is called Shadow. He is working for me, yes, but on your behalf. Shadow, may I introduce you to the lovely Miss Zorya Vechernyaya.'

'Good to meet you,' said Shadow.

Bird-like, the old woman peered up at him. 'Shadow,' she said. 'A good name. When the shadows are long, that is my time. And you are the long shadow.' She looked him up and down, then she smiled. 'You may kiss my hand,' she said, and extended a cold hand to him.

Shadow bent down and kissed her thin hand. She had a large amber ring on her middle finger.

'Good boy,' she said. 'I am going to buy groceries. You see, I am the only one of us who brings in any money. The other two cannot make money fortune-telling. This is because they only tell the truth, and the truth is not what people want to hear. It is a bad thing, and it troubles people, so they do not come back. But I can lie to them, tell them what they want to hear. I tell the pretty fortunes. So I bring home the bread. Do you think you will be here for supper?'

'I would hope so,' said Wednesday.

'Then you had better give me some money to buy more food,' she said. 'I am proud, but I am not stupid. The others are prouder than I am, and *he* is the proudest of all. So give me money and do not tell them that you give me money.'

Wednesday opened his wallet, and reached in. He took out

a twenty. Zorya Vechernyaya plucked it from his fingers, and waited. He took out another twenty and gave it to her.

'Is good,' she said. 'We will feed you like princes. Like we would feed our own father. Now, go up the stairs to the top. Zorya Utrennyaya is awake, but our other sister is still asleep, so do not be making too much noise, when you get to the top.'

Shadow and Wednesday climbed the dark stairs. The landing two stories up was half filled with black plastic garbage bags and it smelled of rotting vegetables.

'Are they gypsies?' asked Shadow.

'Zorya and her family? Not at all. They're not *Rom*. They're Russian. Slavs, I believe.'

'But she does fortune-telling.'

'Lots of people do fortune-telling. I dabble in it myself.' Wednesday was panting as they went up the final flight of stairs. 'I'm out of condition.'

The landing at the top of the stairs ended in a single door painted red, with a peephole in it.

Wednesday knocked at the door. There was no response. He knocked again, louder this time.

'Okay! Okay! I heard you! I heard you!' The sound of locks being undone, of bolts being pulled, the rattle of a chain. The red door opened a crack.

'Who is it?' A man's voice, old and cigarette-roughened.

'An old friend, Czernobog. With an associate.'

The door opened as far as the security chain would allow. Shadow could see a gray face, in the shadows, peering out at them. 'What do you want, Grimnir?'

'Initially, simply the pleasure of your company. And I have information to share. What's that phrase . . . oh yes. You may learn something to your advantage.'

The door opened all the way. The man in the dusty bathrobe was short, with iron-gray hair, and craggy features. He wore gray pinstripe pants, shiny from age, and slippers. He held an unfiltered cigarette with square-tipped fingers, sucking the tip while keeping it cupped in his fist – like a convict, thought Shadow, or a soldier. He extended his left hand to Wednesday. 'Welcome then, Grimnir.'

'They call me Wednesday these days,' he said, shaking the old man's hand.

A narrow smile; a flash of yellow teeth. 'Yes,' he said. 'Very funny. And this is?'

'This is my associate. Shadow, meet Mister Czernobog.'

'Well met,' said Czernobog. He shook Shadow's left hand with his own. His hands were rough and calloused, and the tips of his fingers were as yellow as if they had been dipped in iodine.

'How do you do, Mister Czernobog.'

'I do old. My guts ache, and my back hurts, and I cough my chest apart every morning.'

'Why you are standing at the door?' asked a woman's voice. Shadow looked over Czernobog's shoulder, at the old woman standing behind him. She was smaller and frailer than her sister, but her hair was long and still golden. 'I am Zorya Utrennyaya,' she said. 'You must not stand there in the hall. You must come in, go through to the sitting room, through there, I will bring you coffee, go, go in, through there.'

Through the doorway into an apartment that smelled like over-boiled cabbage and cat-box and unfiltered foreign cigarettes, and they were ushered through a tiny hallway past several closed doors to the sitting room at the far end of the corridor, and were seated on a huge old horsehair sofa, disturbing an elderly gray cat in the process, who stretched, stood up, and walked, stiffly, to a distant part of the sofa, where he lay down, warily stared at each of them in turn, then closed one eye and went back to sleep. Czernobog sat in an armchair across from them.

Zorya Utrennyaya found an empty ashtray and placed it beside Czernobog. 'How you want your coffee?' she asked her guests. 'Here we take it black as night, sweet as sin.'

'That'll be fine, ma'am,' said Shadow. He looked out of the window, at the buildings across the street.

Zorya Utrennyaya went out. Czernobog stared at her as she left. 'That's a good woman,' he said. 'Not like her sisters. One of them is a harpy, the other, all she does is sleep.' He put his slippered feet up on a long, low coffee table, a chess board inset in the middle, cigarette burns and mug rings on its surface.

'Is she your wife?' asked Shadow.

'She's nobody's wife.' The old man sat in silence for a moment, looking down at his rough hands. 'No. We are all relatives. We come over here together, long time ago.'

From the pocket of his bathrobe, Czernobog produced a pack of unfiltered cigarettes. Shadow did not recognize the brand. Wednesday pulled out a narrow gold lighter from the pocket of his pale suit, and lit the old man's cigarette. 'First we come to New York,' said Czernobog. 'All our countrymen go to New York. Then, we come out here, to Chicago. Everything got very bad. In the old country, they had nearly forgotten me. Here, I am a bad memory no one wants to remember. You know what I did when I got to Chicago?'

'No,' said Shadow.

'I get a job in the meat business. On the kill floor. When the steer comes up the ramp, I was a knocker. You know why we are called knockers? Is because we take the sledge-hammer and we *knock* the cow down with it. *Bam!* It takes strength in the arms. Yes? Then the shackler chains the beef up, hauls it up, then they cut the throat. They drain the blood first before they cut the head off. We were the strongest, the knockers.' He pushed up the sleeve of his bathrobe, flexed his upper arm to display the muscles still visible under the old skin. 'Is not just strong though. There was an art to it. To the blow. Otherwise the cow is just stunned, or angry. Then, in the fifties, they give us the bolt gun. You put it to the forehead, *bam! bam!* Now you think, anybody can kill. Not so.' He mimed putting a metal bolt through a cow's head. 'It still takes skill.' He smiled at the memory, displaying an iron-colored tooth.

'Don't tell them cow-killing stories.' Zorya Utrennyaya carried in their coffee on a red wooden tray. Small brightly-enameled cups filled with a brown liquid so dark it was almost black. She gave them each a cup, then sat beside Czernobog.

'Zorya Vechernyaya is doing shopping,' she said. 'She will be soon back.'

'We met her downstairs,' said Shadow. 'She says she tells fortunes.'

'Yes,' said her sister. 'In the twilight, that is the time for lies. I do not tell good lies, so I am a poor fortune-teller. And our sister, Zorya Polunochnaya, she can tell no lies at all.'

The coffee was even sweeter and stronger than Shadow had expected.

Shadow excused himself to use the bathroom – a cramped, closet-like room near the front door, hung with several brown-spotted framed photographs. It was early afternoon, but already the daylight was beginning to fade. He heard voices raised from down the hall. He washed his hands in icy-cold water with a sickly-smelling sliver of pink soap.

Czernobog was standing in the hall as Shadow came out.

'You bring trouble!' he was shouting. 'Nothing but trouble! I will not listen! You will get out of my house!'

Wednesday was still sitting on the sofa, sipping his coffee, stroking the gray cat. Zorya Utrennyaya stood on the thin carpet, one hand nervously twining in and out of her long yellow hair.

'Is there a problem?' asked Shadow.

'*He* is the problem!' shouted Czernobog. '*He* is! You tell him that there is nothing will make me help him! I want him to go! I want him out of here! Both of you go!'

'Please,' said Zorya Utrennyaya, 'please be quiet, you wake up Zorya Polunochnaya.'

'You are like him, you want me to join his madness!'

shouted Czernobog. He looked as if he was on the verge of tears. A pillar of ash tumbled from his cigarette onto the threadbare hall carpet.

Wednesday stood up, walked over to Czernobog. He rested his hand on Czernobog's shoulder. 'Listen,' he said, peaceably. 'Firstly, it's not madness. It's the only way. Secondly, everyone will be there. You would not want to be left out, would you?'

'You know who I am,' said Czernobog. 'You know what these hands have done. You want my brother, not me. And he's gone.'

A door in the hallway opened, and a sleepy female voice said, 'Is something wrong?'

'Nothing is wrong, my sister,' said Zorya Utrennyaya, 'Go back to sleep.' Then she turned to Czernobog. 'See? See what you do with all your shouting? You go back in there and sit down. Sit!' Czernobog looked as if he were about to protest; and then the fight went out of him. He looked frail, suddenly: frail, and lonely.

The three men went back into the shabby sitting room. There was a brown nicotine ring around that room that ended about a foot from the ceiling, like the tide-line in an old bathtub.

'It doesn't have to be for you,' said Wednesday to Czernobog, unfazed. 'If it is for your brother, it's for you as well. That's one place you dualistic types have it over the rest of us, eh?'

Czernobog said nothing.

'Talking of Bielebog, have you heard anything from him?'

Czernobog shook his head. Then he spoke, staring down at the threadbare carpet. 'None of us have heard of him. I am almost forgotten, but still, they remember me a little, here and in the old country.' He looked up at Shadow. 'Do you have a brother?'

'No,' said Shadow. 'Not that I know of.'

'I have a brother. They say, you put us together, we are like

one person, you know? When we are young, his hair, it is
very blond, very light, and people say, he is the good one.
And my hair it is very dark, darker than yours even, and
people say I am the rogue, you know? I am the bad one. And
now time passes, and my hair is gray. His hair, too, I think,
is gray. And you look at us, you would not know who was
light, who was dark.'

'Were you close?' asked Shadow.

'Close?' asked Czernobog. 'No. We were not close. How
could we be? We cared about such different things.'

There was a clatter from the end of the hall, and Zorya
Vechernyaya came in. 'Supper in one hour,' she said. Then
she went out.

Czernobog sighed. 'She thinks she is a good cook,' he said.
'She was brought up, there were servants to cook. Now, there
are no servants. There is nothing.'

'Not nothing,' said Wednesday. 'Never nothing.'

'You,' said Czernobog. 'I shall not listen to you.' He turned
to Shadow. 'Do you play checkers?' he asked.

'Yes,' said Shadow.

'Good. You shall play checkers with me,' he said, taking a
wooden box of pieces from the mantlepiece, and shaking
them out onto the table. 'I shall play black.'

Wednesday touched Shadow's arm. 'You don't have to do
this, you know,' he said.

'Not a problem. I want to,' said Shadow. Wednesday
shrugged, and picked up an old copy of the *Reader's Digest*
from a small pile of yellowing magazines on the window sill.

Czernobog's brown fingers finished arranging the pieces
on the squares, and the game began.

***

In the days that were to come, Shadow often found himself
remembering that game. Some nights he dreamed of it. His
flat, round pieces were the color of old, dirty wood,

nominally white. Czernobog's were a dull, faded black. Shadow was the first to move. In his dreams, there was no conversation as they played, just the loud click as the pieces were put down, or the hiss of wood against wood as they were slid from square to adjoining square.

For the first half dozen moves each of the men slipped pieces out onto the board, into the center, leaving the back rows untouched. There were pauses between the moves, long, chess-like pauses, while each man watched, and thought.

Shadow had played checkers in prison: it passed the time. He had played chess, too, but he was not temperamentally suited to chess. He did not like planning ahead. He preferred picking the perfect move for the moment. You could win in checkers like that, sometimes.

There was a click, as Czernobog picked up a black piece and jumped it over one of Shadow's white pieces, placing it on the square on the other side. The old man picked up Shadow's white piece and put it on the table at the side of the board.

'First blood. You have lost,' said Czernobog. 'The game is done.'

'No,' said Shadow. 'Game's got a long way to go yet.'

'Then would you care for a wager? A little side bet, to make it more interesting?'

'No,' said Wednesday, without looking up from a *Humor in Uniform* column. 'He wouldn't.'

'I am not playing with you, old man. I play with him. So, you want to bet on the game, Mister Shadow?'

'What were you two arguing about, before?' asked Shadow.

Czernobog raised a craggy eyebrow. 'Your master wants me to come with him. To help him with his nonsense. I would rather die.'

'You want to make a bet. Okay. If I win, you come with us.'

The old man pursed his lips. 'Perhaps,' he said. 'But only if you take my forfeit, when you lose.'

'And that is?'

There was no change in Czernobog's expression. 'If I win, I get to knock your brains out. With the sledgehammer. First you go down on your knees. Then I hit you a blow with it, so you don't get up again.' Shadow looked at the man's old face, trying to read him. He was not joking, Shadow was certain of that: there was a hunger there for something, for pain, or death or retribution.

Wednesday closed the *Reader's Digest*. 'This is getting ridiculous,' he said. 'I was wrong to come here. Shadow, we're leaving.' The gray cat, disturbed, got to its feet and leapt onto the table beside the checkers game. It stared at the pieces, then leapt down onto the floor and, tail held high, it stalked from the room.

'No,' said Shadow. He was not scared of dying. After all, it was not as if he had anything left to live for. 'It's fine. I accept. If you win the game, you get the chance to knock my brains out with one blow of your sledgehammer,' and he moved his next white piece to the adjoining square on the edge of the board.

Nothing more was said, but Wednesday did not pick up his *Reader's Digest* again. He watched the game with his glass eye and his true eye, with an expression that betrayed nothing.

Czernobog took another of Shadow's pieces. Shadow took two of Czernobog's. From the corridor came the smell of unfamiliar foods cooking. While not all of the smells were appetizing, Shadow realized suddenly how hungry he was.

The two men moved their pieces, black and white, turn and turnabout. A flurry of pieces taken, a blossoming of two-piece-high kings: no longer forced to move only forward on the board, a sideways slip at a time, the kings could move forward or back, which made them doubly dangerous. They had reached the furthest row, and could go where they wanted. Czernobog had three kings, Shadow had two.

Czernobog moved one of his kings around the board,

eliminating Shadow's remaining pieces, while using the other two kings to keep Shadow's pieces pinned down.

And then Czernobog made a fourth king, and returned down the board to Shadow's two kings, and, unsmiling, took them both. And that was that.

'So,' said Czernobog. 'I get to knock out your brains. And you will go on your knees willingly. Is good.' He reached out an old hand, and patted Shadow's arm with it.

'We've still got time before dinner's ready,' said Shadow. 'You want another game? Same terms?'

Czernobog lit another cigarette, from a kitchen box of matches. 'How can it be same terms? You want I should kill you twice?'

'Right now, you have one blow, that's all. You told me yourself that it's not just strength, it's skill too. This way, if you win this game, you get two blows to my head.'

Czernobog glowered. 'One blow, is all it takes, one blow. That is the art.' He patted his upper right arm, where the muscles were, with his left, scattering gray ash from the cigarette in his left hand.

'It's been a long time. If you've lost your skill you might simply bruise me. How long has it been since you swung a killing hammer in the stockyards? Thirty years? Forty?'

Czernobog said nothing. His closed mouth was a gray slash across his face. He tapped his fingers on the wooden table, drumming out a rhythm with them. Then he pushed the twenty-four checkers pieces back to their home squares on the board.

'Play,' he said. 'Again, you are light. I am dark.'

Shadow pushed his first piece out. Czernobog pushed one of his own pieces forward. And it occurred to Shadow that Czernobog was going to try to play the same game again, the one that he had just won, that this would be his limitation.

This time Shadow played recklessly. He snatched tiny opportunities, moved without thinking, without a pause to consider. And this time, as he played, Shadow smiled; and whenever Czernobog moved a piece, Shadow smiled wider.

Soon, Czernobog was slamming his pieces down as he moved them, banging them down on the wooden table so hard that the remaining pieces shivered on their black squares.

'There,' said Czernobog, taking one of Shadow's men with a crash, slamming the black piece down. 'There. What do you say to that?'

Shadow said nothing: he simply smiled, and jumped the piece that Czernobog had put down, and another, and another, and a fourth, clearing the center of the board of black pieces. He took a white piece from the pile beside the board and kinged his man.

After that, it was just a mopping-up exercise: another handful of moves, and the game was done.

Shadow said, 'Best of three?'

Czernobog simply stared at him, his gray eyes like points of steel. And then he laughed, clapped his hands on Shadow's shoulders. 'I like you!' he exclaimed. 'You have balls.'

Then Zorya Utrennyaya put her head around the door to tell them that dinner was ready, and they should clear their game away, and put the tablecloth down on the table.

'We have no dining room,' she said, 'I am sorry. We eat in here.'

Serving dishes were placed on the table. Each of the diners was given a small painted tray on which was some tarnished cutlery, to place on his or her lap.

Zorya Vechernyaya took five wooden bowls and placed an unpeeled boiled potato in each, then ladled in a healthy serving of a ferociously crimson borscht. She plopped a spoonful of white sour cream in, and handed the bowls to each of them.

'I thought there were six of us,' said Shadow.

'Zorya Polunochnaya is still asleep,' said Zorya Vechernyaya. 'We keep her food in the refrigerator. When she wakes, she will eat.'

The borscht was vinegary, and tasted like pickled beets. The boiled potato was mealy.

The next course was a leathery pot-roast, accompanied by greens of some description – although they had been boiled so long and so thoroughly that they were no longer, by any stretch of the imagination, greens, and were in fact well on their way to becoming *browns*.

Then there were cabbage leaves stuffed with ground meat and rice, cabbage leaves of such a toughness that they were almost impossible to cut without spattering ground meat and rice all over the carpet. Shadow pushed his around his plate.

'We played checkers,' said Czernobog, hacking himself another lump of pot roast. 'The young man and me. He won a game, I won a game. Because he won a game, I have agreed to go with him and Wednesday, and help them in their madness. And because I won a game, when this is all done, I get to kill the young man, with a blow of a hammer.'

The two Zoryas nodded gravely. 'Such a pity,' said Zorya Vechernyaya. 'In my fortune for you, I should have said you would have a long life and a happy one, with many children.'

'That is why you are a good fortune teller,' said Zorya Utrennyaya. She looked sleepy, as if it were an effort for her to be up so late. 'You tell the best lies.'

It was a long meal, and at the end of it, Shadow was still hungry. Prison food had been pretty bad, and prison food was better than this.

'Good food,' said Wednesday, who had cleaned his plate with every evidence of enjoyment. 'I thank you ladies. And now, I am afraid that it is incumbent upon us to ask you to recommend to us a fine hotel in the neighborhood.'

Zorya Vechernyaya looked offended at this. 'Why should you go to a hotel?' she said. 'We are not your friends?'

'I couldn't put you to any trouble . . .' said Wednesday.

'Is no trouble,' said Zorya Utrennyaya, one hand playing with her incongruously golden hair, and she yawned.

'*You* can sleep in Bielebog's room,' said Zorya Vechernyaya, pointing to Wednesday. 'Is empty. And for you, young man, I make up a bed on sofa. You will be more comfortable than in feather bed. I swear.'

'That would be really kind of you,' said Wednesday. 'We accept.'

'And you pay me only no more than what you pay for hotel,' said Zorya Vechernyaya, with a triumphant toss of her head. 'A hundred dollars.'

'Thirty,' said Wednesday.

'Fifty.'

'Thirty-five.'

'Forty-five.'

'Forty.'

'Is good. Forty-five dollar.' Zorya Vechernyaya reached across the table and shook Wednesday's hand. Then she began to clean the pots off the table. Zorya Utrennyaya yawned so hugely Shadow worried that she might dislocate her jaw, and announced that she was going to bed before she fell asleep with her head in the pie, and she said goodnight to them all.

Shadow helped Zorya Vechernyaya to take the plates and dishes into the little kitchen. To his surprise there was an elderly dishwashing machine beneath the sink, and he filled it. Zorya Vechernyaya looked over his shoulder, tutted, and removed the wooden borscht-bowls. 'Those, in the sink,' she told him.

'Sorry.'

'Is not to worry. Now, back in there, we have pie,' she said, and she took the pie from the oven.

The pie – it was an apple pie – had been bought in a store and oven-warmed, and was very, very good indeed. The four of them ate it with ice-cream, and then Zorya Vechernyaya made everyone go out of the sitting room, and made up a very fine-looking bed on the sofa for Shadow.

Wednesday spoke to Shadow as they stood in the corridor.

'What you did in there, with the checkers game,' he said.
'Yes?'

'That was good. Very, very stupid of you. But good. Sleep
safe.'

Shadow brushed his teeth and washed his face in the cold
water of the little bathroom, and then walked back down the
hall to the sitting room, turned out the light, and was asleep
before his head touched the pillow.

* * *

There were explosions in Shadow's dream: he was driving a
truck through a mine-field, and bombs were going off on
each side of him. The windshield shattered and he felt warm
blood running down his face.

Someone was shooting at him.

A bullet punctured his lung, a bullet shattered his spine,
another hit his shoulder. He felt each bullet strike. He
collapsed across the steering wheel.

The last explosion ended in darkness.

I must be dreaming, thought Shadow, alone in the
darkness. *I think I just died.* He remembered hearing and
believing, as a child, that if you died in your dreams, you
would die in real life. He did not feel dead. He opened his
eyes, experimentally.

There was a woman in the little sitting room, standing
against the window, with her back to him. His heart missed
a half-beat, and he said, 'Laura?'

She turned, framed by the moonlight. 'I'm sorry,' she said.
'I did not mean to wake you.' She had a soft, eastern-
European accent. 'I will go.'

'No, it's okay,' said Shadow. 'You didn't wake me. I had a
dream.'

'Yes,' she said. 'You were crying out, and moaning. Part of
me wanted to wake you, but I thought, no, I should leave
him.'

Her hair was pale and colorless in the moon's thin light. She wore a thin white cotton nightgown, with a high, lace neck, and a hem that swept the ground. Shadow sat up, entirely awake. 'You are Zorya Polu . . .,' he hesitated. 'The sister who was asleep.'

'I am Zorya Polunochnaya, yes. And you are called Shadow, yes? That was what Zorya Vechernyaya told me, when I woke.'

'Yes. What were you looking at, out there?'

She looked at him, then she beckoned him to join her by the window. She turned her back while he pulled on his jeans. He walked over to her. It seemed a long walk, for such a small room.

He could not tell her age. Her skin was unlined, her eyes were dark, her lashes were long, her hair was to her waist, and white. The moonlight drained colors into ghosts of themselves. She was taller than either of her sisters.

She pointed up into the night sky. 'I was looking at that,' she said, pointing to the Big Dipper. 'See?'

'Ursa Major,' he said. 'The Great Bear.'

'That is one way of looking at it,' she said. 'But it is not the way from where I come from. I am going to sit on the roof. Would you like to come with me?'

'I guess,' said Shadow.

'Is good,' she said.

She lifted the window and clambered, barefoot, out onto the fire escape. A freezing wind blew through the window. Something was bothering Shadow, but he did not know what it was; he hesitated, then pulled on his sweater, shoes, and socks and followed her out onto the rusting fire escape. She was waiting for him. His breath steamed in the chilly air. He watched her bare feet pad up the icy metal steps, and followed her up to the roof.

The wind gusted cold, flattening her nightgown against her body, and Shadow became uncomfortably aware that Zorya Polunochnaya was wearing nothing at all underneath.

'You don't mind the cold?' he said, as they reached the top of the fire escape, and the wind whipped his words away.

'Sorry?'

She bent her face close to his. Her breath was sweet.

'I said, doesn't the cold bother you?'

In reply, she held up a finger: *wait.* She stepped, lightly, over the side of the building and onto the flat roof. Shadow stepped over a little more clumsily, and followed her across the roof, to the shadow of the water-tower. There was a wooden bench waiting for them there, and she sat down on it, and he sat down beside her.

The water-tower acted as a windbreak, for which Shadow was grateful. The lights of the city smudged the sky with yellow, swallowing half the stars he had been able to see from the open country. Still, he could see the Big Dipper and the North Star, and he found the three stars of Orion's belt, which allowed him to see Orion, which he always saw as a man running to kick a football –

'No,' she said. 'The cold does not bother me. This time is my time: I could no more feel uncomfortable in the night than a fish could feel uncomfortable in the deep water.'

'You must like the night,' said Shadow, wishing that he had said something wiser, more profound.

'My sisters are of their times. Zorya Utrennyaya is of the dawn. In the old country she would wake to open the gates, and let our father drive his – um, I forget the word, like a car but with horses?'

'Chariot?'

'His chariot. Our father would ride it out. And Zorya Vechernyaya, she would open the gates for him at dusk, when he returned to us.'

'And you?'

She paused. Her lips were full, but very pale. 'I never saw our father. I was asleep.'

'Is it a medical condition?'

She did not answer. The shrug, if she shrugged, was

imperceptible. 'So. You wanted to know what I was looking at.'

'The Big Dipper.'

She raised an arm to point to it, and the wind flattened her nightgown against her body. Her nipples, every goose-bump on the areolae, were visible momentarily, dark against the white cotton. Shadow shivered.

'Odin's Wain, they call it. And the Great Bear. Where we come from, we believe that is a, a thing, a, not a god, but like a god, a bad thing, chained up in those stars. If it escapes, it will eat the whole of everything. And there are three sisters who must watch the sky, all the day, all the night. If he escapes, the thing in the stars, the world is over. *Pf!*, like that.'

'And people believe that?'

'They did. A long time ago.'

'And you were looking to see if you could see the monster in the stars?'

'Something like that. Yes.'

He smiled. If it were not for the cold, he decided, he would have thought he was dreaming. Everything felt so much like a dream.

'Can I ask how old you are? Your sisters seem so much older.'

She nodded her head. 'I am the youngest. Zorya Utrennyaya was born in the morning, and Zorya Vechernyaya was born in the evening, and I was born at midnight. I am the midnight sister: Zorya Polunochnaya. Are you married?'

'My wife is dead. She died last week in a car accident. It was her funeral yesterday.'

'I'm so sorry.'

'She came to see me last night.' It was not hard to say, in the darkness and the moonlight; it was not as unthinkable as it was by daylight.

'Did you ask her what she wanted?'

'No. Not really.'

'Perhaps you should. It is the wisest thing to ask the dead. Sometimes they will tell you. Zorya Vechernyaya tells me that you played checkers with Czernobog.'

'Yes. He won the right to knock in my skull with a sledge.'

'In the old days, they would take people up to the top of the mountains. To the high places. They would smash the back of their skulls with a rock. For Czernobog.'

Shadow glanced about. No, they were alone on the roof.

Zorya Polunochnaya laughed. 'Silly, he is not here. And you won a game also. He may not strike his blow until this is all over. He said he would not. And you will know. Like the cows he killed. They always know, first. Otherwise, what is the point?'

'I feel,' Shadow told her, 'like I'm in a world with its own sense of logic. Its own rules. Like when you're in a dream, and you know there are rules you mustn't break, but you don't know what they are or what they mean. I have no idea what we're talking about, or what happened today, or pretty much anything since I got out of jail. I'm just going along with it, you know?'

'I know,' she said. She held his hand, with a hand that was icy cold. 'You were given protection once, but you lost it already. You gave it away. You had the sun in your hand. And that is life itself. All I can give you is much weaker protection. The daughter, not the father. But all helps. Yes?' Her white hair blew about her face in the chilly wind, and Shadow knew that it was time to go back inside.

'Do I have to fight you? Or play checkers?' he asked.

'You do not even have to kiss me,' she told him. 'Just take the moon.'

'How?'

'Take the moon.'

'I don't understand.'

'Watch,' said Zorya Polunochnaya. She raised her left hand and held it in front of the moon, so that her forefinger and thumb seemed to be grasping it. Then, in one smooth movement, she plucked at it. For a moment, it looked like she had taken the moon from the sky, but then Shadow saw that the moon shone still, and Zorya Polunochnaya opened her hand to display a silver Liberty-head dollar resting between finger and thumb.

'That was beautifully done,' said Shadow. 'I didn't see you palm it. And I don't know how you did that last bit.'

'I did not palm it,' she said. 'I took it. And now I give it you, to keep safe. Here. Don't give this one away.'

She placed it in his right hand and closed his fingers around it. The coin was cold in his hand. Zorya Polunochnaya leaned forward, and closed his eyes with her fingers, and kissed him, lightly, once upon each eyelid.

***

Shadow awoke on the sofa, fully dressed. A narrow shaft of sunlight streamed in through the window, making the dust-motes dance.

He got out of bed, and walked over to the window. The room seemed much smaller in the daylight.

The thing that had been troubling him since last night came into focus as he looked out and down and across the street. There was no fire escape outside this window: no balcony, no rusting metal steps.

Still, held tight in the palm of his hand, bright and shiny as the day it had been minted, was a 1922 Liberty-head silver dollar.

'Oh. You're up,' said Wednesday, putting his head around the door. 'That's good. You want coffee? We're going to rob a bank.'

Coming to America

1721

The important thing to understand about American history, *wrote Mr Ibis, in his leather-bound journal*, is that it is fictional, a charcoal-sketched simplicity for the children, or the easily bored. For the most part it is uninspected, unimagined, unthought, a representation of the thing, and not the thing itself. It is a fine fiction, *he continued, pausing to dip his pen in the inkwell, and to collect his thoughts, and to continue*, that America was founded by pilgrims, seeking the freedom to believe as they wished, that they came to the Americas, spread and bred and filled the empty land.

In truth, the American colonies were as much a dumping ground as an escape, a forgetting place. In the days where you could be hanged in London from Tyburn's triple-crowned tree for the theft of twelve pennies, the Americas became a symbol of clemency, of a second chance. But the conditions of transportation were such that, for some, it was easier to take the leap from the leafless and dance on nothing until the dancing was done. Transportation it was called: for five years, for ten years, for life. That was the sentence.

You were sold to a captain, and would ride in his ship, crowded tight as a slaver's, to the colonies or to the West Indies; off the boat the captain would sell you on as an indentured servant to one who would take the cost of your skin out in your labor until the years of your indenture were done. But at least you were not waiting to hang in an English prison (for in those days prisons were places where you stayed until you were freed, transported, or hanged: you were not sentenced there for a term), and you were free to make the best of your new world. You were also free to bribe a sea-captain to return you to England before the terms of your transportation were over and done. People did. And if the authorities caught you returning from transportation – if an old enemy, or an old friend with a score to settle, saw you and peached on you, – then you were hanged without a blink.

I am reminded, *he continued, after a short pause, during which he refilled the inkwell on his desk from the bottle of umber ink from the closet, dipped his pen once more*, of the life of Essie Tregowan, who came from a chilly little cliff-top village in Cornwall, in the Southwest of England, where her family had lived from time out of mind. Her father was a fisherman, and it was rumored that he was one of the wreckers – those who would hang their lamps high on the dangerous coast when the storm winds were high, luring ships onto the rocks, for the goods on shipboard. Essie's mother was in service as a cook at the squire's house, and, at the age of twelve, Essie began to work there, in the scullery. She was a thin little thing, with wide brown eyes and dark brown hair; and she was not a hard worker but was forever slipping off and away to listen to stories and tales, if there was anyone who would tell them: tales of the piskies and the spriggans, of the black dogs of the moors and the seal-women of the Channel. And, though the squire laughed at such things, the kitchen-folk always put out a china saucer of the creamiest milk at night, put it outside the kitchen door, for the piskies.

Several years passed, and Essie was no longer a thin little thing: now she curved and billowed like the swell of the green sea, and her brown eyes laughed, and her chestnut hair tossed and curled. Essie's eyes lighted on Bartholomew, the squire's eighteen-year old son, home from Rugby, and she went at night to the standing stone on the edge of the woodland, and she put some bread that Bartholomew had been eating but had left unfinished on the stone, wrapped in a cut strand of her own hair. And on the very next day Bartholomew came and talked to her, and looked on her approvingly with his own eyes, the dangerous blue of a sky when a storm is coming, while she was cleaning out the grate in his bedroom.

He had such dangerous eyes, said Essie Tregowan.

Soon enough Bartholomew went up to Oxford, and, when Essie's condition became apparent, she was dismissed. But the babe was stillborn, and, as a favor to Essie's mother, who was a very fine cook, the squire's wife prevailed upon her husband to return the former maiden to her former position in the scullery.

But Essie's love for Bartholomew had turned to hatred for his family, and, within the year she took for her new beau a man from a neighboring village, with a bad reputation, who went by the name of Josiah Horner. And one night, when the family slept, Essie arose in the night and unbolted the side door, to let her lover in. He rifled the house while the family slept on.

Suspicion immediately fell upon someone in the house, for it was apparent that someone must have opened the door (which the squire's wife distinctly remembered having bolted herself) and someone must have known where the squire kept his silver plate, and the drawer in which he kept his coins and his promissory notes. Still, Essie, by resolutely denying everything, was convicted of nothing until Master Josiah Horner was caught, in a chandler's in Exeter, passing one of the squire's notes. The squire identified it as his, and Horner and Essie went to trial.

Horner was convicted at the local assizes, and was, as the

slang of the time so cruelly and so casually had it, *turned off*, but the judge took pity on Essie, because of her age or her chestnut hair, and he sentenced her to seven years' transportation. She was to be transported on a ship called the Neptune, under the command of one Captain Clarke. So Essie went to the Carolinas; and on the way she conceived an alliance with the selfsame captain, and prevailed upon him to return her to England with him, as his wife, and to take her to his mother's house in London, where no man knew her. The journey back, when the human cargo had been exchanged for cotton and tobacco, was a peaceful time, and a happy one, for the captain and his new bride, who were as two lovebirds or courting butterflies, unable to cease from touching each other or giving each other little gifts and endearments.

When they reached London, Captain Clarke lodged Essie with his mother, who treated her in all ways as her son's new wife. Eight weeks later, the Neptune set sail again, and the pretty young bride with the chestnut hair waved her husband goodbye from dockside. Then she returned to her mother-in-law's house, where, the old woman being absent, Essie helped herself to a length of silk, several gold coins, and a silver pot in which the old woman kept her buttons, and pocketing these things Essie vanished into the stews of London.

Over the following two years Essie became an accomplished shoplifter, her wide skirts capable of concealing a multitude of sins, consisting chiefly of stolen bolts of silk and lace, and she lived life to the full. Essie gave thanks for her escapes from her vicissitudes to all the creatures that she had been told of as a child, to the piskies (whose influence, she was certain, extended as far as London), and she would put a wooden bowl of milk on a window-ledge each night, although her friends laughed at her; but she had the last laugh, as her friends got the pox or the clap and Essie remained in the peak of health.

She was a year shy of her twentieth birthday when fate
dealt her an ill-blow: she sat in the Crossed Forks Inn off
Fleet Street, in Bell Yard, when she saw a young man enter
and seat himself near the fire-place, fresh down from the
University. 'Oho! A pigeon ripe for the plucking,' thinks
Essie to herself, and she sits next to him, and tells him what
a fine young man he is, and with one hand she begins to
stroke his knee, while her other hand, more carefully, goes in
search of his pocket-watch. And then he looked her full in
the face, and her heart leapt and sank as eyes the dangerous
blue of the summer sky before a storm gazed back into hers,
and Master Bartholomew said her name.

She was taken to Newgate and charged with returning
from transportation. Found guilty, Essie shocked no one by
pleading her belly, although the town matrons, who assessed
such claims (which were usually spurious) were surprised
when they were forced to agree that Essie was indeed with
child; although who the father was, Essie declined to say.

Her sentence of death was once more commuted to
transportation, this time for life.

She rode out this time on The Sea-Maiden. There were
two hundred transportees on that ship, packed into the hold
like so many fat hogs on their way to market. Fluxes and
fevers ran rampant; there was scarcely room to sit, let alone
to lie down; a woman died in childbirth in the back of the
hold, and, the people being pushed in too tightly to pass her
body forward, she and the infant were forced out of a small
porthole in the back, directly into the choppy gray sea. Essie
was eight months gone, and it was a wonder she kept the
baby, but keep it she did.

In her life ever after she would have nightmares of her
time in that hold, and she would wake up screaming with
the taste and stench of the place in her throat.

The Sea-Maiden landed at Norfolk in Virginia, and Essie's
indenture was bought by a 'small planter", a tobacco farmer
named John Richardson, for his wife had died of the

childbirth fever a week after giving birth to his daughter, and he had need of a wet-nurse and a maid of all work upon his smallholding.

So Essie's baby boy, whom she called Anthony, after, she said, her late husband his father (knowing there was none there to contradict her, and perhaps she had known an Anthony once), sucked at Essie's breast alongside of Phyllida Richardson, and her employer's child always got first suck, so she grew into a healthy child, tall and strong, while Essie's son grew weak and rickety on what was left.

And along with the milk, the children as they grew drank Essie's tales: of the knockers and the blue-caps who live down the mines; of the Bucca, the tricksiest spirit of the land, much more dangerous than the red-headed, snub-nosed piskies, for whom the first fish of the catch was always left upon the shingle, and for whom a fresh-baked loaf of bread was left in the field, at reaping time, to ensure a fine harvest; she told them of the apple-tree men – old apple trees who talked when they had a mind, and who needed to be placated with the first cider of the crop, which was poured onto their roots as the year turned, if they were to give you a fine crop for the next year. She told them, in her mellifluous Cornish drawl, which trees they should be wary of, in the old rhyme:

> *Elm, he do brood*
> *And Oak, he do hate,*
> *But the willow-man goes walking,*
> *If you stays out late.*

She told them all these things, and they believed, because she believed.

The farm prospered, and Essie Tregowan placed a china saucer of milk outside the back door, each night, for the piskies. And after eight months John Richardson came a-knocking quietly on Essie's bedroom door, and asked her for

favors of the kind a woman shows a man, and Essie told him
how shocked and hurt she was, a poor widow-woman, and
an indentured servant no better than a slave, to be asked to
prostitute herself for a man whom she had had so much
respect for – and an indentured servant could not marry, so
how he could even think to torment an indentured
transportee girl so she could not bring herself to think – and
her nut-brown eyes filled with tears, such that Richardson
found himself apologizing to her, and the upshot of it was
that John Richardson wound up, in that corridor, of that hot
summer's night, going down on one knee to Essie Tregowan
and proposing an end to her indenture and offering his hand
in marriage. Now, although she accepted him, she would
not sleep a night with him until it was legal, whereupon she
moved from the little room in the attic to the master
bedroom in the front of the house; and if some of Farmer
Richardson's friends and their wives cut him when next
they saw him in town, many more of them were of the
opinion that the new Mistress Richardson was a damn fine
looking woman, and that Johnnie Richardson had done
quite well for himself.

Within a year, she was delivered of another child, another
boy, but as blonde as his father and his half-sister, and they
named him John, after his father.

The three children went to the local church to hear the
traveling preacher on Sundays, and they went to the little
school to learn their letters and their numbers with the
children of the other small farmers; while Essie also made
sure they knew the mysteries of the piskies, which were the
most important mysteries there were: red-headed men, with
eyes and clothes as green as a river, with turned-up noses,
funny, squinting men who would, if they got a mind to, turn
you and twist you and lead you out of your way, unless you
had salt in your pocket, or a little bread. When the children
went off to school, they each of them carried a little salt in
one pocket, a little bread in the other, the old symbols of life

and the earth, to make sure they came safely home once more, and they always did.

The children grew in the lush Virginia hills, grew tall and strong (although Anthony, her first son, was always weaker, paler, more prone to disease and bad airs) and the Richardsons were happy; and Essie loved her husband as best she could. They had been married a decade when John Richardson developed a toothache so bad it made him fall from his horse. They took him to the nearest town, where his tooth was pulled; but it was too late, and the blood-poisoning carried him off, black-faced and groaning, and they buried him beneath his favorite willow tree.

The widow Richardson was left the farm to manage until Richardson's two children were of age: she managed the indentured servants and the slaves, and brought in the tobacco crop, year in, year out; she poured cider on the roots of the apple trees on New Year's Eve, and placed a loaf of new-baked bread in the fields at harvest-time, and she always left a saucer of milk at the back door. The farm flourished, and the widow Richardson gained a reputation as a hard bargainer, but one whose crop was always good, and who never sold shoddy for better merchandise.

So all went well for another ten years; but after that was a bad year, for Anthony, her son, slew Johnnie, his half-brother, in a furious quarrel over the future of the farm and the disposition of Phyllida's hand; and some said he had not meant to kill his brother, and that it was a foolish blow that struck too deep, and some said otherwise. Anthony fled, leaving Essie to bury her youngest son beside his father. Now, some said Anthony fled to Boston, and some said he went south, to Florida, and his mother was of the opinion that he had taken ship to England, to enlist in George's army and fight the rebel Scots. But with both sons gone the farm was an empty place, and a sad one, and Phyllida pined and plained as if her heart had been broken, while nothing that her stepmother could say or do would put a smile back on her lips again.

But heartbroken or not, they needed a man about the farm, and so Phyllida married Harry Soames, a ship's carpenter by profession, who had tired of the sea and who dreamed of a life on land on a farm like the Lincolnshire farm upon which he had grown up. And although the Richardson's farm was little enough like that, Harry Soames found correspondences enough to make him happy. Five children were born to Phyllida and Harry, three of whom lived.

The widow Richardson missed her sons, and she missed her husband, although he was now little more than a memory of a fair man who treated her kindly. Phyllida's children would come to Essie for tales, and she would tell them of the Black Dog of the Moors, and of Raw-Head and Bloody-Bones, or the Apple Tree Man, but they were not interested; they only wanted tales of Jack – Jack up the Beanstalk, or Jack Giant-killer, or Jack and his Cat and the King. She loved those children as if they were her own flesh and blood, although sometimes she would call them by the names of those long dead.

It was May, and she took her chair out into the kitchen garden, to pick peas and to shuck them in the sunlight, for even in the lush heat of Virginia the cold had entered her bones as the frost had entered her hair, and a little warmth was a fine thing.

As the widow Richardson shucked the peas with her old hands, she got to thinking about how fine it would be to walk once more on the moors and the salty cliffs of her native Cornwall, and she thought of sitting on the shingle as a little girl, waiting for her father's boat to return from the gray seas. Her hands, blue-knuckled and clumsy, opened the pea-pods, forced the full peas into one bowl, while she dropped the empty pea-pods onto her aproned lap. And then she found herself remembering, as she had not remembered for a long time, a life well lost: how she had twitched purses and

filched silks with her clever fingers; and now she remembers
the warden of Newgate telling her that it will be a good
twelve weeks before her case would be heard, and that she
could escape the gallows if she could plead her belly, and
what a pretty thing she was – and how she had turned to the
wall and bravely lifted her skirts, hating herself and hating
him, but knowing he was right; and the feel of the life,
quickening inside her that meant that she could cheat death
for a little longer . . .

'Essie Tregowan?' said the stranger.

The widow Richardson looked up, shading her eyes in the
May sunshine. 'Do I know you?' she asked. She had not
heard him approach.

The man was dressed all in green: dusty green trews,
green jacket, and a dark green coat. His hair was a carroty
red, and he grinned at her all lopsided. There was something
about the man that made her happy to look at him, and
something else that whispered of danger. 'You might say that
you know me,' he said.

He squinted down at her, and she squinted right back up
at him, searching his moon-face for a clue to his identity. He
looked as young as one of her own grandchildren, yet he had
called her by her old name, and there was a burr in his voice
she knew from her childhood, from the rocks and the moors
of her home.

'You're a Cornishman?' she asked.

'That I am, a Cousin Jack,' said the red-haired man, 'Or
rather, that I was, but now I'm here in this new world, where
nobody puts out ale or milk for an honest fellow, or a loaf of
bread come harvest time.'

The old woman steadied the bowl of peas upon her lap. 'If
you're who I think you are,' she said, 'then I've no quarrel
with you.' In the house, she could hear Phyllida grumbling
to the housekeeper.

'Nor I with you,' said the red-haired fellow, a little sadly,
'although it was you that brought me here, you and a few like

you, into this land with no time for magic and no place for piskies and such folk.'

'You've done me many a good turn,' she said.

'Good and ill,' said the squinting stranger. 'We're like the wind. We blows both ways.'

Essie nodded.

'Will you take my hand, Essie Tregowan?' And he reached out a hand to her. Freckled it was, and although Essie's eyesight was going she could see each orange hair on the back of his hand, glowing golden in the afternoon sunlight. She bit her lip. Then, hesitantly, she placed her blue-knotted hand in his.

She was still warm when they found her, although the life had fled her body and only half the peas were shelled.

Chapter Five

Madam Life's a piece in bloom
Death goes dogging everywhere:
She's the tenant of the room,
He's the ruffian on the stair.
  – W.E. Henley, *Madam Life's a Piece in Bloom*

O nly Zorya Utrennyaya was awake to say goodbye to them, that Saturday morning. She took Wednesday's forty-five dollars and insisted on writing him out a receipt for it in wide, looping handwriting, on the back of an expired soft-drink coupon. She looked quite doll-like in the morning light, with her old face carefully made-up and her golden hair piled high upon her head.

Wednesday kissed her hand. 'Thank you for your hospitality, dear lady,' he said. 'You and your lovely sisters remain as radiant as the sky itself.'

'You are a bad old man,' she told him, and shook a finger at him. Then she hugged him. 'Keep safe,' she instructed him. 'I would not like to hear that you were gone for good.'

'It would distress me equally, my dear.'

She shook hands with Shadow. 'Zorya Polunochnaya

thinks very highly of you,' she said. 'I also.'

'Thank you,' said Shadow. 'Thanks for the dinner.'

She raised an eyebrow at him. 'You liked? You must come again.'

Wednesday and Shadow walked down the stairs. Shadow put his hands in his jacket pocket. The silver dollar was cold in his hand. It was bigger and heavier than any coins he'd used so far. He classic-palmed it, let his hand hang by his side naturally, then straightened his hand as the coin slipped down to a front-palm position. It felt natural there, held between his forefinger and his little finger by the slightest of pressure.

'Smoothly done,' said Wednesday.

'I'm just learning,' said Shadow. 'I can do a lot of the technical stuff. The hardest part is making people look at the wrong hand.'

'Is that so?'

'Yes,' said Shadow. 'It's called misdirection.' He slipped his middle fingers under the coin, pushing it into a back palm, and fumbled his grip on it, ever-so-slightly. The coin dropped from his hand to the stairwell with a clatter and bounced down half a flight of stairs. Wednesday reached down and picked it up.

'You cannot afford to be careless with people's gifts,' said Wednesday. 'Something like this, you need to hang onto it. Don't go throwing it about.' He examined the coin, looking first at the eagle side, then at the face of Liberty on the obverse. 'Ah, Lady Liberty. Beautiful, is she not?' He tossed the coin to Shadow, who picked it from the air, did a slide vanish – seeming to drop it into his left hand while actually keeping it in his right – and then appeared to pocket it with his left hand. The coin sat in the palm of his right hand, in plain view. It felt comforting there.

'Lady Liberty,' said Wednesday. 'Like so many of the gods that Americans hold dear, a foreigner. In this case, a French-woman, although, in deference to American sensibilities, the

French covered up her magnificent bosom on that statue they presented to New York. Liberty,' he continued, wrinkling his nose at the used condom that lay on the bottom flight of steps, toeing it to the side of the stairs with distaste – 'Someone could slip on that. Break their necks,' he muttered, interrupting himself. 'Like a banana peel, only with bad taste and irony thrown in.' He pushed open the door, and the sunlight hit them. The world outside was colder than it had looked from indoors: Shadow wondered if there was more snow to come. 'Liberty,' boomed Wednesday, as they walked to his car, 'is a bitch who must be bedded on a mattress of corpses.'

'Yeah?' said Shadow.

'Quoting,' said Wednesday. 'Quoting someone French. That's who they have a statue to, in their New York harbor: a bitch, who liked to be fucked on the refuse from the tumbril. Hold your torch as high as you want to, m'dear, there's still rats in your dress and cold jism dripping down your leg.' He unlocked the car, and pointed Shadow to the passenger seat.

'I think she's beautiful,' said Shadow, holding the coin up close. Liberty's silver face reminded him a little of Zorya Polunochnaya.

'That,' said Wednesday, driving off, 'is the eternal folly of man. To be chasing after the sweet flesh, without realizing that it is simply a pretty cover for the bones. Worm food. At night, you're rubbing yourself against worm food. No offense meant.'

Shadow had never seen Wednesday quite so expansive. His new boss, he decided, went through phases of extroversion followed by periods of intense quiet. 'So you aren't American?' asked Shadow.

'Nobody's American,' said Wednesday. 'Not originally. That's my point.' He checked his watch. 'We still have several hours to kill before the banks close. Good job last night with Czernobog, by the way. I would have closed him on coming eventually, but you enlisted him more wholeheartedly than ever I could have.'

'Only because he gets to kill me afterward.'

'Not necessarily. As you yourself so wisely pointed out, he's old, and the killing stroke might merely leave you, well, paralyzed for life, say. A hopeless invalid. So you have much to look forward to, should Mister Czernobog survive the coming difficulties.'

'And there is some question about this?' said Shadow, echoing Wednesday's manner, then hating himself for it.

'Fuck yes,' said Wednesday. He pulled up in the parking lot of a bank. 'This,' he said, 'is the bank I shall be robbing. They don't close for another few hours. Let's go in and say hello.'

He gestured to Shadow. Reluctantly, Shadow got out of the car and followed Wednesday in. If the old man was going to do something stupid, Shadow could see no reason why his face should be on the camera; still, Shadow followed him into the bank.

'Deposit forms, Ma'am?' said Wednesday to the lone teller.

'Over there.'

'Very good. And if I were to need to make a night deposit . . .?'

'Same forms.' She smiled at him. 'You know where the night deposit slot is, hon? Left out the main door, it's on the wall.'

'My thanks.'

Wednesday picked up several deposit forms. He grinned a goodbye at the teller, and he and Shadow walked out.

Wednesday stood there on the sidewalk for a moment, scratching his beard meditatively. Then he walked over to the ATM machine, and to the night safe, set in the side of the wall and inspected them. He led Shadow across the road to the supermarket, where he bought a chocolate fudge Popsicle for himself, and a cup of hot chocolate for Shadow. There was a payphone set in the wall of the entry way, as you went in, below a notice board with rooms to rent, and puppies and kittens in need of good homes. Wednesday wrote down the telephone number of the payphone. They crossed the road once more. 'What we need,' said Wednesday, suddenly, 'is snow. A good, driving, irritating snow. Think "snow" for me, will you?'

'Huh?'

'Concentrate on making those clouds – the ones over there, in the west, – making them bigger and darker. Think gray skies and driving winds coming down from the arctic. Think snow.'

'I don't think it will do any good.'

'Nonsense. If nothing else, it will keep your mind occupied,' said Wednesday, unlocking the car. 'Kinko's next. Hurry up.'

Snow, thought Shadow, in the passenger seat, sipping his hot chocolate. *Huge, dizzying, clumps and clusters of snow falling through the air, patches of white against an iron-gray sky, snow that touches your tongue with cold and winter, that kisses your face with its hesitant touch before freezing you to death. Twelve cotton-candy inches of snow, creating a fairy-tale world, making everything unrecognizably beautiful . . .*

Wednesday was talking to him.

'I'm sorry?' said Shadow.

'I said we're here,' said Wednesday. 'You were somewhere else.'

'I was thinking about snow,' said Shadow.

In Kinko's, Wednesday set about photocopying the deposit slips from the bank. He had the clerk instant print him two sets of ten business cards. Shadow's head had begun to ache, and there was an uncomfortable feeling between his shoulder blades; he wondered if he had slept on it wrong, if it was an awkward legacy of the night before's sofa.

Wednesday sat at the computer terminal, composing a letter, and, with the clerk's help, making several large-sized signs.

Snow, thought Shadow. *High in the atmosphere, perfect,*

tiny crystals that form about a minute piece of dust, each a lace-like work of unique, six-sided fractal art. And the snow crystals clump together into flakes as they fall, covering Chicago in their white plenty, inch upon inch . . .

'Here,' said Wednesday. He handed Shadow a cup of Kinko's coffee, a half-dissolved lump of non-dairy creamer powder floating on the top. 'I think that's enough, don't you?'

'Enough what?'

'Enough snow. Don't want to immobilize the city, do we?'

The sky was a uniform battleship gray. Snow was coming. Yes.

'I didn't really do that?' said Shadow. 'I mean, I didn't. Did I?'

'Drink the coffee,' said Wednesday. 'It's foul stuff, but it will ease the headache.' Then he said, 'Good work.'

Wednesday paid the Kinko's clerk, and he carried his signs and letters and cards outside to the car. He opened the trunk of his car, put the papers in a large black metal case of the kind carried by payroll guards, and closed the trunk. He passed Shadow a business card.

'Who,' said Shadow, 'is A. Haddock, Director of Security, A1 Security Services?'

'You are.'

'A. Haddock?'

'Yes.'

'What does the A. stand for?'

'Alfredo? Alphonse? Augustine? Ambrose? Your call entirely.'

'Oh. I see.'

'I'm James O'Gorman,' said Wednesday. 'Jimmy to my friends. See? I've got a card too.'

They got back in the car. Wednesday said, 'If you can think "A. Haddock", as well as you thought "snow", we should have plenty of lovely money with which to wine and dine my friends of tonight.'

'And if we're in jail by this evening?'

'Then my friends will just have to make do without us.'

'I'm not going back to prison.'

'You won't be.'

'I thought we had agreed that I wouldn't be doing anything illegal.'

'You aren't. Possibly aiding and abetting, a little conspiracy to commit, followed of course by receiving stolen money, but trust me, you'll come out of this smelling like a rose.'

'Is that before or after your elderly Slavic Charles Atlas crushes my skull with one blow?'

'His eyesight's going,' said Wednesday reassuringly. 'He'll probably miss you entirely. Now, we still have a little time to kill – the bank closes at midday on Saturdays, after all. Would you like lunch?'

'Yes,' said Shadow. 'I'm starving.'

'I know just the place,' said Wednesday. He hummed as he drove, some cheerful song that Shadow could not identify. Snowflakes began to fall, just as Shadow had imagined them, and he felt strangely proud. He knew, rationally, that he had nothing to do with the snow, just as he knew the silver dollar he carried in his pocket was not, and never had been the moon. But still . . .

They stopped outside a large shed-like building. A sign said that the All-U-Can-Eat lunch buffet was $4.99. 'I love this place,' said Wednesday.

'Good food?' asked Shadow.

'Not particularly,' said Wednesday. 'But the ambience is unmissable.'

The ambience that Wednesday loved, it turned out, once lunch had been eaten – Shadow had the fried chicken, and enjoyed it – was the business that took up the rear of the shed: it was, the hanging flag across the center of the room announced, a Bankrupt and Liquidated Stock Clearance Depot.

Wednesday went out to the car, and reappeared with a small suitcase, which he took into the men's room. Shadow figured he'd learn soon enough what Wednesday was up to, whether he wanted to or not, and so he prowled the liquidation aisles, staring at the things for sale: Boxes of coffee 'for use in airline filters only', Teenage Mutant Ninja Turtle toys and Xena: Warrior Princess harem dolls, teddy bears that played patriotic tunes on the xylophone when plugged in, and other teddy bears that played seasonal songs on the xylophone when plugged in, cans of processed meat, galoshes and sundry overshoes, marshmallows, Bill Clinton presidential wristwatches, artificial miniature Christmas trees, salt and pepper shakers in the shapes of animals, body parts, fruit and nuns, and, Shadow's favorite, a 'just add real carrot' snowman kit, with plastic coal eyes, a corncob pipe, and a plastic hat.

Shadow thought about how you made the moon seem to come out of the sky and become a silver dollar, and what made a woman get out of her grave and walk across town to talk to you.

'Isn't it a wonderful place?' asked Wednesday when he came out of the men's room. His hands were still wet, and he was drying them off on a handkerchief. 'They're out of paper towels in there,' he said. He had changed his clothes. He was now wearing a dark blue jacket, with matching trousers, a blue knit tie, a thick blue sweater, a white shirt, and black shoes. He looked like a security guard, and Shadow said so.

'What can I possibly say to that, young man,' said Wednesday, picking up a box of floating plastic aquarium fish (*'they'll never fade – and you'll never have to feed them!!'*), 'other than to congratulate you on your perspicacity. How about Arthur Haddock? Arthur's a good name.'

'Too mundane.'

'Well, you'll think of something. There. Let us return to town. We should be in perfect time for our bank robbery, and then I shall have a little spending money.'

'Most people,' said Shadow, 'would simply take it from the ATM.'

'Which is, oddly enough, more or less exactly what I was planning to do.'

Wednesday parked the car in the supermarket lot across the street from the bank. From the trunk of the car Wednesday brought out the metal case and a clipboard, and a pair of handcuffs. He handcuffed the case to his left wrist. He attached the other end of the cuff to the metal case's handle. The snow continued to fall. Then he put a peaked blue cap on, and velcroed a patch to the breast pocket of his jacket. 'A1 Security' was written on the cap and the patch. He put the deposit slips on his clipboard. Then he slouched. He looked like a retired beat cop, and appeared somehow to have gained himself a paunch.

'Now,' he said, 'you do a little shopping in the food store, then hang out by the phone. If anyone asks, you're waiting for a call from your girlfriend, whose car has broken down.'

'So why's she calling me there?'

'How the hell should you know?'

Wednesday put on a pair of faded pink earmuffs. He closed the trunk. Snowflakes settled on his dark blue cap, and on his earmuffs.

'How do I look?' he asked.

'Ludicrous,' said Shadow.

'Ludicrous?'

'Or goofy, maybe,' said Shadow.

'Mm. Goofy and ludicrous. That's good.' Wednesday smiled. The ear-muffs made him appear, at the same time, reassuring, amusing, and, ultimately, loveable. He strode across the street and walked along the block to the bank building, while Shadow walked into the supermarket hall and watched.

Wednesday taped a large red *Out of Order* notice to the ATM. He put a red ribbon across the night deposit slot, and he taped a photocopied sign up above it. Shadow read it with amusement.

FOR YOUR CONVENIENCE it said WE ARE WORKING

TO MAKE ONGOING IMPROVEMENT'S. WE APOLOGIZE
FOR THE TEMPORARY INCONVENIENCE.

Then Wednesday turned around and faced the street. He
looked cold and put-upon.

A young woman came over to use the ATM. Wednesday
shook his head, explained that it was out of order. She
cursed, apologized for cursing, and ran off.

A car drew up, and a man got out holding a small gray
sack and a key. Shadow watched as Wednesday apologized
to the man, then made him sign the clipboard, checked his
deposit slip, painstakingly wrote him out a receipt and
puzzled over which copy to keep, and, finally, opened his big
black metal case and put the man's sack inside.

The man shivered in the snow, stamping his feet, waiting
for the old security guard to be done with this administrative
nonsense, so he could leave his takings and get out of the
cold and be on his way, then he took his receipt and got back
into his warm car and drove off.

Wednesday walked across the street carrying the metal
case, and bought himself a coffee at the supermarket.

'Afternoon, young man,' he said, with an avuncular
chuckle, as he passed Shadow. 'Cold enough for you?'

He walked back across the street, and took gray sacks and
envelopes from people coming to deposit their earnings or
their takings on this Saturday afternoon, a fine old security
man in his funny pink earmuffs.

Shadow bought some things to read – *Turkey Hunting*,
People, and because the cover picture of Bigfoot was so endear-
ing, the *Weekly World News* – and stared out of the window.

'Anything I can do to help?' asked a middle aged black man
with a white moustache. He seemed to be the manager.

'Thanks, man, but no. I'm waiting for a phone call. My
girlfriend's car broke down.'

'Probably the battery,' said the man. 'People forget those
things only last three, maybe four years. It's not like they cost
a fortune.'

'Tell me about it,' said Shadow.

'Hang in there, big guy,' said the manager, and he went back into the supermarket.

The snow had turned the street scene into the interior of a snowglobe, perfect in all its details.

Shadow watched, impressed. Unable to hear the conversations across the street, he felt it was like watching a fine silent movie performance, all pantomime and expression: the old security guard was gruff, earnest – a little bumbling perhaps, but enormously well-meaning. Everyone who gave him their money walked away a little happier from having met him.

And then the cops drew up outside the bank, and Shadow's heart sank. Wednesday tipped his cap to them and ambled over to the police car. He said his Hellos and shook hands through the open window, and nodded, then hunted through his pockets until he found a business card and a letter, and passed them through the window of the car. Then he sipped his coffee.

The telephone rang. Shadow picked up the hand piece and did his best to sound bored. 'A1 Security Services,' he said.

'Can I speak to A. Haddock?' asked the cop across the street.

'This is Andy Haddock speaking,' said Shadow.

'Yeah, Mister Haddock, this is the police,' said the cop in the car across the street. 'You've got a man at the First Illinois Bank on the corner of Market and Second.'

'Uh, yeah. That's right. Jimmy O'Gorman. And what seems to be the problem, officer? Jim behaving himself? He's not been drinking?'

'No problem, sir. Your man is just fine, sir. Just wanted to make certain everything was in order.'

'You tell Jim that if he's caught drinking again, officer, he's fired. You got that? Out of a job. Out on his ass. We have zero tolerance at A1 Security.'

'I really don't think it's really my place to tell him that, sir. He's doing a fine job. We're just concerned because something like this really ought to be done by two personnel. It's risky, having one unarmed guard dealing with such large amounts of money.'

'Tell me about it. Or more to the point, you tell those cheapskates down at the First Illinois about it. These are my men I'm putting on the line, officer. Good men. Men like you.' Shadow found himself warming to this identity. He could feel himself becoming Andy Haddock, chewed cheap cigar in his ashtray, a stack of paperwork to get to this Saturday afternoon, a home in Schaumburg and a mistress in a little apartment on Lake Shore Drive. 'Y'know, you sound like a bright young man, officer, uh . . .'

'Myerson.'

'Officer Myerson. You need a little weekend work, or you wind up leaving the force, any reason, you give us a call. We always need good men. You got my card?'

'Yes sir.'

'You hang onto it,' said Andy Haddock. 'You call me.'

The police car drove off, and Wednesday shuffled through the snow to deal with the small line of people who were waiting to give him their money.

'She okay?' asked the manager, putting his head around the door. 'Your girlfriend?'

'It was the battery,' said Shadow. 'Now I just got to wait.'

'Women,' said the manager. 'I hope yours is worth waiting for.'

Winter darkness descended, the afternoon slowly graying into night. Lights went on. More people gave Wednesday their money. Suddenly, as if at some signal Shadow could not see, Wednesday walked over to the wall, removed the *Out of Order* signs, and trudged across the slushy road, heading for the car park. Shadow waited a minute, then followed him.

Wednesday was sitting in the back of the car. He had

opened the metal case and was methodically laying every-thing he had been given out on the back seat in neat piles.

'Drive,' he said. 'We're heading for the First Illinois Bank over on State Street.'

'Repeat performance?' asked Shadow. 'Isn't that kind of pushing your luck?'

'Not at all,' said Wednesday. 'We're going to do a little banking.'

While Shadow drove, Wednesday sat in the back seat and removed the bills from the deposit bags in handfuls, leaving the checks and the credit card slips, and taking the cash from some, although not all, of the envelopes. He dropped the cash back into the metal case. Shadow pulled up outside the bank, stopping the car about fifty yards down the road, well out of camera range. Wednesday got out of the car, and pushed the envelopes through the night deposit slot. Then he opened the night safe, and dropped in the gray bags. He closed it again.

He climbed into the passenger seat. 'You're heading for I-90,' said Wednesday. 'Follow the signs west for Madison.'

Shadow began to drive.

Wednesday looked back at the bank they were leaving. 'There, my boy,' he said, cheerfully, 'that will confuse every-thing. Now, to get the really big money, you need to do that at about 4:30 on a Sunday morning, when the clubs and the bars drop off their Saturday night's takings. Hit the right bank, the right guy making the drop off – they tend to pick them big and honest, and sometimes have a couple of bouncers accompany them, but they aren't necessarily smart – and you can walk away with a quarter of a million dollars for an evening's work.'

'If it's that easy,' said Shadow, 'how come everybody doesn't do it?'

'It's not an entirely risk-free occupation,' said Wednesday, 'especially not at 4:30 in the morning.'

'You mean the cops are more suspicious at 4:30 in the morning?'

'Not at all. But the bouncers are. And things can get awkward.'

He flicked through a sheaf of fifties, added a smaller stack of twenties, weighed them in his hand, then passed them over to Shadow. 'Here,' he said. 'Your first week's wages.'

Shadow pocketed the money without counting it. 'So, that's what you do?' he asked. 'To make money?'

'Rarely. Only when a great deal of cash is needed fast. On the whole, I make my money from people who never know they've been taken, and who never complain, and who will frequently line up to be taken when I come back that way again.'

'That Sweeney guy said you were a hustler.'

'He was right. But that is the least of what I am. And the least of what I need you for, Shadow.'

***

Snow spun through their headlights and into the windshield as they drove through the darkness. The effect was almost hypnotic.

'This is the only country in the world,' said Wednesday, into the stillness, 'that worries about what it is.'

'What?'

'The rest of them know what they are. No one ever needs to go searching for the heart of Norway. Or looks for the soul of Mozambique. They know what they are.'

'And . . .?'

'Just thinking out loud.'

'So you've been to lots of other countries, then?'

Wednesday said nothing. Shadow glanced at him. 'No,' said Wednesday, with a sigh. 'No. I never have.'

They stopped for gas, and Wednesday went into the restroom in his security guard jacket and his suitcase, and came out in a crisp, pale suit, brown shoes, and a knee-length brown coat that looked like it might be Italian.

'So when we get to Madison, what then?'

'Take Highway 14 west to Spring Green. We'll be meeting everyone at a place called the House on the Rock. You been there?'

'No,' said Shadow. 'But I've seen the signs.'

The signs for the House on the Rock were all around that part of the world: oblique, ambiguous signs all across Illinois and Minnesota and Wisconsin, probably as far away as Iowa, Shadow suspected, signs alerting you to the existence of the House on the Rock. Shadow had seen the signs, and wondered about them. Did the House balance perilously upon the Rock? What was so interesting about the Rock? About the House? He had given it a passing thought, but then forgotten it. Shadow was not in the habit of visiting roadside attractions.

They drove past the capital dome of Madison, another perfect snow globe scene in the falling snow, and then they were off the interstate, and driving down country roads. After almost an hour of driving through towns with names like Black Earth, they turned down a narrow driveway, past several enormous, snow-dusted flower pots entwined with lizard-like dragons. The tree-lined parking lot was almost empty.

'They'll be closing soon,' said Wednesday.

'So what is this place?' asked Shadow, as they walked through the parking lot toward a low, unimpressive wooden building.

'This is a roadside attraction,' said Wednesday. 'One of the finest. Which means it is a place of power.'

'Come again?'

'It's perfectly simple,' said Wednesday. 'In other countries, over the years, people recognized the places of power. Sometimes it would be a natural formation, sometimes, it would just be a place that was, somehow, special. They knew that something important was happening there, that there was some focusing point, some channel, some window to the Immanent. And so they would build temples, or cathedrals, or erect stone circles, or . . . well, you get the idea.'

'There are churches all across the States, though,' said Shadow.

'In every town. Sometimes on every block. And about as significant, in this context, as dentists' offices. No, in the USA, people still get the call, or some of them, and they feel themselves being called to from the transcendent void, and they respond to it by building a model out of beer bottles of somewhere they've never visited, or by erecting a gigantic bat-house in some part of the country that bats have traditionally declined to visit. Roadside attractions: people feel themselves being pulled to places where, in other parts of the world, they would recognize that part of themselves that is truly transcendent, and buy a hot dog and walk around, feeling satisfied on a level they cannot truly describe, and profoundly dissatisfied on a level beneath that.'

'You have some pretty whacked-out theories,' said Shadow.

'Nothing theoretical about it, young man,' said Wednesday. 'You should have figured that out by now.'

There was only one ticket window open. 'We stop selling tickets in half an hour,' said the girl. 'It takes at least two hours to walk around, you see.'

Wednesday paid for their tickets in cash.

'Where's the rock?' asked Shadow.

'Under the house,' said Wednesday.

'Where's the house?'

Wednesday put his finger to his lips, and they walked forward. Farther in, a player piano was playing something that was intended to have been Ravel's *Bolero*. The place seemed to be a geometrically reconfigured 1960s bachelor pad, with open stonework, pile carpeting, and magnificently ugly mushroom-shaped stained glass lampshades. Up a winding staircase to another room, filled with knick-knacks.

'They say this was built by Frank Lloyd Wright's evil twin,' said Wednesday. 'Frank Lloyd Wrong.' He chuckled at his joke.

'I saw that on a tee shirt,' said Shadow.

Up and down more stairs, and now they were in a long, long room, made of glass, that protruded, needle-like, out over the leafless black-and-white countryside hundreds of feet below them. Shadow stood and watched the snow tumble and spin.

'This is the House on the Rock?' he asked, puzzled.

'More or less. This is the Infinity Room, part of the actual house, although a late addition. But no, my young friend, we have not scratched the tiniest surface of what the house has to offer.'

'So according to your theory,' said Shadow, 'Walt Disney World would be the holiest place in America.'

Wednesday frowned, and stroked his beard. 'Walt Disney bought some orange groves in the middle of Florida and built a tourist town on them. No magic there of any kind, although I think there might be something real in the original Disneyland. There may be some power there, although twisted, and hard to access. There's definitely nothing out of the ordinary about Disney World. But some parts of Florida are filled with real magic. You just have to keep your eyes open. Ah, for the mermaids of Weeki Wachee . . . Follow me, this way.'

Everywhere was the sound of music: jangling, awkward, music, ever-so slightly off the beat and out of time. Wednesday took a five dollar bill and put it into a change machine, receiving a handful of brass-colored metal coins in return. He tossed one to Shadow, who caught it, and, realizing that a small boy was watching him, held it up between forefinger and thumb and vanished it. The small boy ran over to his mother, who was inspecting one of the ubiquitous Santa Clauses – over 6000 on display! the signs said – and he tugged, urgently at the hem of her coat.

Shadow followed Wednesday outside briefly, and then followed the signs to the Streets of Yesterday.

'Forty years ago Alex Jordan – his face is on the token you have palmed in your right hand, Shadow – began to build a house on a high jut of rock in a field he did not own, and even he could not have told you why. And people came to see him build it – the curious, and the puzzled, and those who were neither and who could not honestly have told you why they came. So he did what any sensible American male of his generation would do: he began to charge them money – nothing much. A nickel each, perhaps. Or a quarter. And he continued building, and the people kept coming.

'So he took those quarters and nickels and made something even bigger and stranger. He built these warehouses on the land beneath the house, and filled them with things for people to see, and then the people came to see them. Millions of people come here every year.'

'Why?'

But Wednesday simply smiled, and they walked into the dimly lit, tree-lined Streets of Yesterday. Prim-lipped Victorian china dolls stared in profusion through dusty store windows, like so-many props from respectable horror films. Cobblestones under their feet, the darkness of a roof above their heads, jangling mechanical music in the background. They passed a glass box of broken puppets, and an overgrown golden music box in a glass case. They passed the dentist's and the drugstore ('Restore potency! Use O'Leary's Magnetical belt!').

At the end of the street was a large glass box with a female mannequin inside it, dressed as a gypsy fortune teller.

'Now,' boomed Wednesday, over the mechanical music, 'at the start of any quest or enterprise it behooves us to consult the Norns. So let us designate this Sybil our *Urd*, eh?' He dropped a brass-colored House on the Rock coin into the slot. With jagged, mechanical motions, the gypsy lifted her arm and lowered it once more. A slip of paper chunked out of the slot.

Wednesday took it, read it, grunted, folded it up, and put it in his pocket.

'Aren't you going to show it to me? I'll show you mine,' said Shadow.

'A man's fortune is his own affair,' said Wednesday, stiffly. 'I would not ask to see yours.'

Shadow put his own coin in the slot. He took his slip of paper. He read it.

> EVERY ENDING IS A NEW BEGINNING.
> YOUR LUCKY NUMBER IS NONE.
> YOUR LUCKY COLOR IS DEAD.
> Motto:
> LIKE FATHER, LIKE SON.

Shadow made a face. He folded the fortune up and put it in his inside pocket.

They went further in, down a red corridor, past rooms filled with empty chairs upon which rested violins and violas and cellos which played themselves, or seemed to, when fed a coin. Keys depressed, cymbals crashed, pipes blew compressed air into clarinets and oboes. Shadow observed, with a wry amusement, that the bows of the stringed instruments, played by mechanical arms, never actually touched the strings, which were often loose or missing. He wondered whether all the sounds he heard were made by wind and percussion, or whether there were tapes as well.

They had walked for what felt like several miles when they came to a room called The Mikado, one wall of which was a nineteenth-century pseudo-Oriental nightmare, in which beetle-browed mechanical drummers banged cymbals and drums while staring out from their dragon-encrusted lair. Currently, they were majestically torturing Saint-Saëns' *Danse Macabre*.

Czernobog sat on a bench in the wall facing the Mikado machine, tapping out the time with his fingers. Pipes fluted, bells jangled.

Wednesday sat next to him. Shadow decided to remain standing. Czernobog extended his left hand, shook Wednesday's, shook Shadow's. 'Well met,' he said. Then he sat back, apparently enjoying the music.

The *Danse Macabre* came to a tempestuous and discordant end. That all the artificial instruments were ever-so-slightly out of tune added to the otherworldliness of the place. A new piece began.

'How was your bank robbery?' asked Czernobog. 'It went well?' He stood, reluctant to leave the Mikado and its thundering, jangling music.

'Slick as a snake in a barrel of butter,' said Wednesday.

'I get a pension from the slaughterhouse,' said Czernobog. 'I do not ask for more.'

'It won't last forever,' said Wednesday. 'Nothing does.'

More corridors, more musical machines. Shadow became aware that they were not following the path through the rooms intended for tourists, but seemed to be following a different route of Wednesday's own devising. They were going down a slope, and Shadow, confused, wondered if they had already been that way.

Czernobog grasped Shadow's arm. 'Quickly, come here,' he said, pulling him over to a large glass box by a wall. It contained a diorama of a tramp asleep in a churchyard in front of a church door. THE DRUNKARD'S DREAM said the label, which explained that it was a nineteenth-century penny-in-the-slot machine, originally from an English railway station. The coin slot had been modified to take the brass House on the Rock coins.

'Put in the money,' said Czernobog.

'Why?' asked Shadow.

'You must see. I show you.'

Shadow inserted his coin. The drunk in the graveyard raised his bottle to his lips. One of the gravestones flipped over, revealing a grasping corpse; a headstone turned around, flowers replaced by a grinning skull. A wraith appeared on the right of the church, while on the left of the church *something* with a half-glimpsed pointed, unsettlingly bird-like face, a pale, Boschian nightmare, glided smoothly from a headstone into the shadows and was gone. Then the church door opened, a priest came out, and the ghosts, haunts, and corpses vanished, and only the priest and the drunk were left alone in the graveyard. The priest looked down at the drunk disdainfully, and backed through the open door, which closed behind him, leaving the drunk on his own.

The clockwork story was deeply unsettling. Much more unsettling, thought Shadow, than clockwork has any right to be.

'You know why I show that to you?' asked Czernobog.

'No.'

'That is the world as it is. That is the real world. It is there, in that box.'

They wandered through a blood-colored room filled with old theatrical organs, huge organ pipes, and what appeared to be enormous copper brewing vats, liberated from a brewery.

'Where are we going?' asked Shadow.

'The carousel,' said Czernobog.

'But we've passed signs to the carousel a dozen times already.'

'He goes his way. We travel a spiral. The quickest way is sometimes the longest.'

Shadow's feet were beginning to hurt, and he found this sentiment to be extremely unlikely.

A mechanical machine played *Octopus's Garden* in a room that went up for many stories, the center of which was filled entirely with a replica of a great black whale-like beast, with a life-sized replica of a boat in its vast fiberglass mouth. They passed on from there to a Travel Hall, where they saw the car covered with tiles, and the functioning Rube Goldberg chicken device and the rusting Burma Shave ads on the wall.

Life is Hard
It's Toil and Trouble
Keep your Jawline
Free from Stubble
Burma Shave

read one, and

He undertook to overtake
The road was on a bend
From now on the Undertaker
Is his only friend
Burma Shave

and they were at the bottom of a ramp now, with an ice-cream shop in front of them. It was nominally open, but the girl washing down the surfaces had a closed look on her face, so they walked past it into the pizzeria-cafeteria, empty but for an elderly black man wearing a bright check suit and canary-yellow gloves. He was a small man, the kind of little old man who looked as if the passing of the years had shrunk him, eating an enormous, many-scooped ice-cream sundae, drinking a supersized mug of coffee. A black cigarillo was burning in the ashtray in front of him.

'Three coffees,' said Wednesday to Shadow. He went to the rest room.

Shadow bought the coffees and took them over to Czernobog, who was sitting with the old black man, and was smoking a cigarette surreptitiously, as if he were scared of being caught. The other man, happily toying with his sundae, mostly ignored his cigarillo, but as Shadow approached he picked it up, inhaled deeply, and blew two smoke rings – first one large one, then another, smaller one, which passed neatly through the first – and he grinned, as if he were astonishingly pleased with himself.

'Shadow, this is Mister Nancy,' said Czernobog.

The old man got to his feet, and thrust out his yellow-gloved right hand. 'Good to meet you,' he said with a dazzling smile. 'I know who you must be. You're working for the old one-eye bastard, aren't you?' There was a faint twang in his voice, a hint of a patois that might have been West Indian.

'I work for Mister Wednesday,' said Shadow. 'Yes. Please, sit down.'

Czernobog inhaled on his cigarette.

'I think,' he pronounced, gloomily, 'that our kind, we like the cigarettes so much because they remind us of the offerings that once they burned for us, the smoke rising up as they sought our approval or our favor.'

'They never gave me nothin' like that,' said Nancy. 'Best I could hope for was a pile of fruit to eat, maybe curried goat, something slow and cold and tall to drink, and a big old high-titty woman to keep me company.' He grinned white teeth, and winked at Shadow.

'These days,' said Czernobog, his expression unchanged, 'we have nothing.'

'Well, I don't get anywhere near as much fruit as I used to,' said Mr Nancy, his eyes shining. 'But there still ain't nothing out there in the world for my money that can beat a big old high-titty woman. Some folk you talk to, they say it's the booty you got to inspect at first, but I'm here to tell you that it's the titties that still crank my engine on a cold morning.' Nancy began to laugh, a wheezing, rattling, good-natured laugh, and Shadow found himself liking the old man despite himself.

Wednesday returned from the rest room, and shook hands

with Nancy. 'Shadow, you want something to eat? A slice of pizza? Or a sandwich?'

'I'm not hungry,' said Shadow.

'Let me tell you somethin',' said Mr Nancy. 'It can be a long time between meals. Someone offers you food, you say yes. I'm no longer young as I was, but I can tell you this, you never say no to the opportunity to piss, to eat, or to get half an hour's shut-eye. You follow me?'

'Yes. But I'm really not hungry.'

'You're a big one,' said Nancy, staring into Shadow's light-gray eyes with his old eyes the color of mahogany, 'a tall drink of water, but I got to tell you, you don't look too bright. I got a son, stupid as a man who bought his stupid at a two-for-one sale, and you remind me of him.'

'If you don't mind, I'll take that as a compliment,' said Shadow.

'Being called dumb as a man who slept late the mornin' they handed out brains?'

'Being compared to a member of your family.'

Mr Nancy stubbed out his cigarillo, then he flicked an imaginary speck of ash off his yellow gloves. 'You may not be the worst choice old one-eye could have made, come to that.' He looked up at Wednesday. 'You got any idea how many of us there's goin' to be here tonight?'

'I sent the message out to everyone I could find,' said Wednesday. 'Obviously not everyone is going to be able to come. And some of them,' with a pointed look at Czernobog, 'might not want to. But I think we can confidently expect several dozen of us. And the word will travel.'

They made their way past a display of suits of armor ('Victorian fake,' pronounced Wednesday as they passed the glassed-in display, 'modern fake, twelfth century helm on a seventeenth-century reproduction, fifteenth century left gauntlet . . .') and then Wednesday pushed through an exit door, circled them around the outside of the building ('I can't be doin' with all these ins and outs,' said Nancy, 'I'm not as

young as I used to be, and I come from warmer climes,')
along a covered walkway, in through another exit door, and
they were in the Carousel room.

Calliope music played: a Strauss waltz, stirring and
occasionally discordant. The wall as they entered was hung
with antique carousel horses, hundreds of them, some in
need of a lick of paint, others in need of a good dusting;
above them hung dozens of winged angels constructed
rather obviously from female store window mannequins;
some of them bared their sexless breasts; some had lost their
wigs and stared baldly and blindly down from the darkness.

And then there was the carousel.

A sign proclaimed it was the largest in the world, said how
much it weighed, how many thousand light bulbs were to be
found in the chandeliers that hung from it in gothic
profusion, and forbade anyone from climbing on it or from
riding on the animals.

And such animals! Shadow stared, impressed in spite of
himself, at the hundreds of full-sized creatures who circled
on the platform of the carousel. Real creatures, imaginary
creatures, and transformations of the two: each creature was
different – he saw mermaid and merman, centaur and
unicorn, elephants (one huge, one tiny), bulldog, frog and
phoenix, zebra, tiger, manticore and basilisk, swans pulling
a carriage, a white ox, a fox, twin walruses, even a sea
serpent, all of them brightly colored and more than real: each
rode the platform as the waltz came to an end and a new
waltz began. The carousel did not even slow down.

'What's it for?' asked Shadow. 'I mean, okay, world's
biggest, hundreds of animals, thousands of light bulbs, and
it goes around all the time, and no one ever rides it.'

'It's not there to be ridden, not by people,' said Wednesday.
'It's there to be admired. It's there to *be*.'

'Like a prayer wheel goin' round and round,' said Mr
Nancy. 'Accumulating power.'

'So where are we meeting everyone?' asked Shadow. 'I

thought you said that we were meeting them here. But the place is empty.'

Wednesday grinned his scary grin. 'Shadow,' he said. 'You're asking too many questions. You're paid not to ask questions.'

'Sorry.'

'Now, stand over here and help us up,' said Wednesday, and he walked over to the platform on one side, with a description of the carousel on it, and a warning that the carousel was not to be ridden.

Shadow thought of saying something, but instead he helped them, one by one, up onto the ledge. Wednesday seemed profoundly heavy, Czernobog climbed up himself, only using Shadow's shoulder to steady himself, Nancy seemed to weigh nothing at all. Each of the old men climbed out onto the ledge, and then, with a step and a hop, they walked out onto the circling carousel platform.

'Well?' barked Wednesday. 'Aren't you coming?'

Shadow, not without a certain amount of hesitation, and a hasty look around for any House on the Rock personnel who might be watching, swung himself up onto the ledge beside the World's Largest Carousel. Shadow was puzzled to realize that he was far more concerned with breaking the rules by climbing onto the carousel than he had been aiding and abetting this afternoon's bank robbery.

Each of the old men selected a mount. Wednesday climbed onto a golden wolf. Czernobog climbed onto an armored centaur, its face hidden by a metal helmet. Nancy, chuckling, slithered up onto the back of an enormous, leaping lion, captured by the sculptor mid-roar. He patted the side of the lion. The Strauss waltz carried them around, majestically.

Wednesday was smiling, and Nancy was laughing delightedly, an old man's cackle, and even the dour Czernobog seemed to be enjoying himself. Shadow felt as if a weight were suddenly lifted from his back: three old men were enjoying themselves, riding the world's biggest carousel. So what if they did get thrown out of the place? Wasn't it worth it, worth anything, to say that you had ridden on the world's biggest carousel? Wasn't it worth it to have traveled on one of those glorious monsters?

Shadow inspected a bulldog, and a mer-creature, and an elephant with a golden howdah, and then he climbed on the back of a creature with an eagle's head and the body of a tiger, and held on tight.

The rhythm of the Blue Danube waltz rippled and rang and sang in his head, the lights of a thousand chandeliers glinted and prismed, and for a heartbeat Shadow was a child again, and all it took to make him happy was to ride the carousel: he stayed perfectly still, riding his eagle-tiger at the center of everything, and the world revolved around him.

Shadow heard himself laugh, over the sound of the music. He was happy. It was as if the last thirty six hours had never happened, as if the last three years had not happened, as if his life had evaporated into the daydream of a small child, riding the carousel in Golden Gate Park in San Francisco, on his first trip back to the States, a marathon journey by ship and by car, his mother standing there, watching him proudly, and himself sucking his melting popsicle, holding on tightly, hoping that the music would never stop, the carousel would never slow, the ride would never end. He was going around and around and around again . . .

Then the lights went out, and Shadow saw the gods.

Chapter Six

Wide open and unguarded stand our gates,
And through them passes a wild motley throng —
Men from Volga and Tartar steppes,
Featureless figures from the Hoang-Ho,
Malayan, Scythian, Teuton, Kelt and Slav,
Flying the Old World's poverty and scorn;
These bringing with them unknown gods and rites,
Those, tiger passions, here to stretch their claws.
In street and alley what strange tongues are loud,
Accents of menace alien to our air,
Voices that once the Tower of Babel knew!
  – Thomas Bailey Aldrich, 'The Unguarded Gates', 1882

One moment Shadow was riding the World's Largest Carousel, holding onto his eagle-headed tiger, and then the red and white lights of the carousel stretched and shivered and went out, and he was falling through an ocean of stars, while the mechanical waltz was replaced by a pounding rhythmic roll and crash, as of cymbals or the breakers on the shores of a far ocean.

The only light was starlight, but it illuminated everything

with a cold clarity. Beneath him his mount stretched, and padded, its warm fur under his left hand, its feathers beneath his right.

'It's a good ride, isn't it?' The voice came from behind him, in his ears and in his mind.

Shadow turned, slowly, streaming images of himself as he moved, frozen moments, each him captured in a fraction of a second, every tiny movement lasting for an infinite period. The images that reached his mind made no sense: it was like seeing the world through the multifaceted jeweled eyes of a dragonfly, but each facet saw something completely different, and he was unable to combine the things he was seeing, or thought he was seeing, into a whole that made any sense.

He was looking at Mr Nancy, an old black man with a pencil moustache, in his check sports jacket and his lemon-yellow gloves, riding a carousel lion as it rose and lowered, high in the air; and, at the same time, in the same place, he saw a jeweled spider as high as a horse, its eyes an emerald nebula, strutting, staring down at him; and simultaneously he was looking at an extraordinarily tall man with teak-colored skin and three sets of arms, wearing a flowing ostrich-feather headdress, his face painted with red stripes, riding an irritated golden lion, two of his six hands holding on tightly to the beast's mane; and he was also seeing a young black boy, dressed in rags, his left foot all swollen and crawling with black flies; and last of all, and behind all these things, Shadow was looking at a tiny brown spider, hiding under a withered ochre leaf.

Shadow saw all these things, and he knew they were the same thing.

'If you don't close your mouth,' said the many things that were Mr Nancy, 'somethin's goin' to fly in there.'

Shadow closed his mouth and swallowed, hard.

There was a wooden hall on a hill, a mile or so from them. They were trotting toward the hall, their mounts' hooves and feet padding noiselessly on the dry sand at the sea's edge.

Czernobog trotted up on his centaur. He tapped the human arm of his mount. 'None of this is truly happening,' he said to Shadow. He sounded miserable. 'Is all in your head. Best not to think of it.'

Shadow saw a gray-haired old East-European immigrant, with a shabby raincoat and one iron-colored tooth, true. But he also saw a squat black thing, darker than the darkness that surrounded them, its eyes two burning coals; and he saw a prince, with long flowing black hair, and long black moustaches, blood on his hands and his face, riding, naked but for a bear-skin over his shoulder, on a creature half-man, half-beast, his face and torso blue-tattooed with swirls and spirals.

'Who are you?' asked Shadow. 'What are you?'

Their mounts padded along the shore. Waves broke and crashed implacably on the night beach.

Wednesday guided his wolf – now a huge and charcoal-gray beast with green eyes – over to Shadow. Shadow's mount caracoled away from it, and Shadow stroked its neck and told it not to be afraid. Its tiger tail swished, aggressively. It occurred to Shadow that there was another wolf, a twin to the one that Wednesday was riding, keeping pace with them in the sand dunes, just a moment out of sight.

'Do you know me, Shadow?' said Wednesday. He rode his wolf with his head high. His right eye glittered and flashed, his left eye was dull. He wore a cloak, with a deep, monk-like cowl, and his face stared out from the shadows. 'I told you I would tell you my names. This is what they call me. I am called Glad-of-War, Grim, Raider, and Third. I am One-eyed. I am called Highest, and True-Guesser. I am Grimnir, and I am the Hooded One. I am All-Father, and I am Gondlir Wand-bearer. I have as many names as there are winds, as many titles as there are ways to die. My ravens are Thought and Memory; my wolves are Freki and Geri; my horse is the gallows.' Two ghostly-gray ravens, like transparent skins of birds, landed on Wednesday's shoulders, pushed their beaks *into* the side of Wednesday's head as if tasting his mind, and flapped out into the world once more.

What should I believe? thought Shadow, and the voice came back to him from somewhere deep beneath the world, in a bass rumble: *Believe everything*.

'Odin?' said Shadow, and the wind whipped the word from his lips.

'Odin,' whispered Wednesday, and the crash of the breakers on the beach of skulls was not loud enough to drown that whisper. 'Odin,' said Wednesday, tasting the sound of the words in his mouth. 'Odin,' said Wednesday, his voice a triumphant shout which echoed from horizon to horizon. His name swelled and grew and filled the world like the pounding of blood in Shadow's ears.

And then, as in a dream, they were no longer riding toward a distant hall. They were already there, and their mounts were tied in the shelter beside the hall.

The hall was huge but primitive. The roof was thatched, the walls were wooden. There was a fire burning in the center of the hall, and the smoke stung Shadow's eyes.

'We should have done this in my mind, not in his,' muttered Mr Nancy to Shadow. 'It would have been warmer there.'

'We're in his mind?'

'More or less. This is Valaskjalf. It's his old hall.'

Shadow was relieved to see that Nancy was now once more an old man wearing yellow gloves, although his shadow shook and shivered and changed in the flames of the fire, and what it changed into was not always entirely human.

There were wooden benches against the walls, and, sitting on them or standing beside them, perhaps ten people. They kept their distance from each other: a mixed lot, who included a dark-skinned, matronly woman in a red sari, several shabby-looking businessmen, and others, too close to the fire for Shadow to be able to make them out.

'Where are they?' whispered Wednesday fiercely, to Nancy. 'Well? Where are they? There should be scores of us here. Dozens!"

'You did all the inviting,' said Nancy. 'I think it's a wonder you got as many here as you did. You think I should tell a story, to start things off?'

Wednesday shook his head. 'Out of the question.'

'They don't look very friendly,' said Nancy. 'A story's a good way of gettin' someone on your side. And you don't have a bard to sing to them.'

'No stories,' said Wednesday. 'Not now. Later, there will be time for stories. Not now.'

'No stories. Right. I'll just be the warm-up man.' And Mr Nancy strode out into the firelight with an easy smile.

'I know what you are all thinking,' he said. 'You are thinking, What is Compé Anansi doing, coming out to talk to you all, when the All-Father called you all here, just like he called me here? Well, you know, sometimes people need reminding of things. I look around when I come in, and I thought, where's the rest of us? But then I thought, just because we are few and they are many, we are weak, and they are powerful, it does not mean that we are lost.

'You know, one time I saw Tiger down at the waterhole: he had the biggest testicles of any animal, and the sharpest claws, and two front teeth as long as knives and as sharp as blades. And I said to him, Brother Tiger, you go for a swim, I'll look after your balls for you. He was so proud of his balls. So he got into the waterhole for a swim, and I put his balls on, and left him my own little spider-balls. And then, you know what I did? I ran away, fast as my legs would take me.

'I didn't stop till I got to the next town. And I saw Old Monkey there. You lookin' mighty fine, Anansi, said Old Monkey. I said to him, You know what they all singin' in the town over there? What are they singin'? he asks me. They

singin' the funniest song, I told him. Then I did a dance, and
I sings,

> *Tiger's balls, yeah,*
> *I ate Tiger's balls*
> *Now ain't nobody gonna stop me ever at all*
> *Nobody put me up against the big black wall*
> *'Cos I ate that Tiger's testimonials*
> *I ate Tiger's balls.*

'Old Monkey he laughs fit to bust, holding his side and
shakin', and stampin', then he starts singin' *Tiger's Balls, I ate
tiger's balls*, snappin' his fingers, spinnin' around on his two
feet. That's a fine song, he says, I'm going to sing it to all my
friends. You do that, I tell him, and I head back to the
waterhole.

'There's Tiger, down by the waterhole, walking up and
down, with his tail switchin' and swishin' and his ears and
the fur on his neck up as far as they can go, and he's snappin'
at every insect comes by with his huge old saber-teeth, and
his eyes flashin' orange fire. He looks mean and scary and
big, but danglin' between his legs, there's the littlest balls in
the littlest blackest most wrinkledy ball-sack you ever did
see.

'Hey, Anansi, he says, when he sees me. You were
supposed to be guarding my balls while I went swimming.
But when I got out of the swimming hole, there was nothing
on the side of the bank but these little black shriveled-up
good-for-nothing spider balls I'm wearing.

'I done my best, I tells him, but it was those monkeys, they
come by and eat your balls all up, and when I tell them off,
then they pulled off my own little balls. And I was so
ashamed I ran away.

'You a liar, Anansi, says Tiger. I'm going to eat your
liver. But then he hears the monkeys coming from their
town to the waterhole. A dozen happy monkeys, boppin'

down the path, clickin' their fingers and singin' as loud as
they could sing,

> Tiger's balls, yeah,
> I ate Tiger's balls
> Now ain't nobody gonna stop me ever at all
> Nobody put me up against the big black wall
> 'Cos I ate that Tiger's testimonials
> I ate Tiger's balls.

'And Tiger, he growls, and he roars and he's off into the
forest after them, and the monkeys screech and head for the
highest trees. And I scratch my nice new big balls, and damn
they felt good hangin' between my skinny legs, and I walk on
home. And even today, Tiger keeps chasin' monkeys. So you
all remember: just because you're small, doesn't mean you
got no power.'

Mr Nancy smiled, and bowed his head, and spread his
hands, accepting the applause and laughter like a pro, and
then he turned and walked back to where Shadow and
Czernobog were standing.

'I thought I said no stories,' said Wednesday.

'You call that a story?' said Nancy. 'I barely cleared my
throat. Just warmed them up for you. Go knock them dead.'

Wednesday walked out into the firelight, a big old man
with a glass eye in a brown suit and an old Armani coat. He
stood there, looking at the people on the wooden benches,
saying nothing for longer than Shadow could believe
someone could comfortably say nothing. And, finally, he
spoke.

'You know me,' he said. 'You all know me. Some of you
have no cause to love me, and I'm not sure I can blame you
for that, but love me or not, you know me.'

There was a rustling, a stir among the people on the
benches.

'I've been here longer than most of you. Like the rest of

you, I figured we could get by on what we got. Not enough to make us happy, but enough to keep going.

'That may not be the case any more. There's a storm coming, and it's not a storm of our making.'

He paused. Now he stepped forward, and folded his arms across his chest.

'When the people came to America they brought us with them. They brought me, and Loki and Thor, Anansi and the Lion-God, Leprechauns and Cluracans and Banshees, Kubera and Frau Holle and Ashtaroth, and they brought you. We rode here in their minds, and we took root. We traveled with the settlers to the new lands across the ocean.

'The land is vast. Soon enough, our people abandoned us, remembered us only as creatures of the old land, as things that had not come with them to the new. Our true believers passed on, or stopped believing, and we were left, lost and scared and dispossessed, to get by on what little smidgens of worship or belief we could find. And to get by as best we could.

'So that's what we've done, gotten by, out on the edges of things, where no one was watching us too closely.

'We have, let us face it and admit it, little influence. We prey on them, and we take from them, and we get by; we strip and we whore and we drink too much; we pump gas and we steal and we cheat and we exist in the cracks at the edges of society. Old gods, here in this new land without gods.'

Wednesday paused. He looked from one to another of his listeners, grave and statesmanlike. They stared back at him impassively, their faces mask-like and unreadable. Wednesday cleared his throat, and he spat, hard into the fire. It flared and flamed, illuminating the inside of the hall.

'Now, as all of you will have had reason aplenty to discover for yourselves, there are new gods growing in America, clinging to growing knots of belief: gods of credit-card and freeway, of internet and telephone, of radio and hospital and television, gods of plastic and of beeper and of neon. Proud gods, fat and foolish creatures, puffed up with their own newness and importance.

'They are aware of us, and they fear us, and they hate us,' said Odin. 'You are fooling yourselves if you believe otherwise. They will destroy us, if they can. It is time for us to band together. It is time for us to act.'

An old woman stepped into the firelight. She wore a red sari, and on her forehead was a small dark blue jewel. She said, 'You called us here for this nonsense?' And then she snorted, a snort of mingled amusement and irritation.

Wednesday's brows lowered. 'I called you here, yes. But this is sense, Mama-ji, not nonsense. Even a child could see that.'

'So I am a child, am I?' She wagged a finger at him. 'I was old in Kalighat before you were dreamed of, you foolish man. I am a child? Then I *am* a child, for there is nothing in your foolish talk to see.'

Again, a moment of double-vision: Shadow saw the old woman, her dark face pinched with age and disapproval, but behind her he saw something huge, a naked woman with skin as black as a new leather jacket, and lips and tongue the bright red of arterial blood. Around her neck were skulls, and her many hands held knives, and swords, and severed heads.

'I did not call you a child, Mama-ji,' said Wednesday, peaceably. 'But it seems self-evident—'

'The only thing that seems self-evident,' said the old woman, pointing (as behind her, through her, above her, a black finger, sharp-taloned, pointed in echo), 'is your own desire for glory. We've lived in peace in this country for a long time. Some of us do better than others, I agree. I do well. Back in India, there is an incarnation of me who does much better, but so be it. I am not envious. I've watched the new ones rise, and I've watched them fall again.' Her hand fell to her side. Shadow saw that the others were looking at her: a mixture of expressions – respect, amusement, embarrassment – in their eyes. 'They worshiped the railroads here, only a blink of an eye ago. And now the iron gods are as forgotten as the emerald hunters . . .'

'Make your point, Mama-ji,' said Wednesday.

'My point?' Her nostrils flared. The corners of her mouth turned down. 'I – and I am *obviously* only a child – say that we wait. We do nothing. We don't know that they mean us harm.'

'And will you still counsel waiting when they come in the night and they kill you, or they take you away?'

Her expression was disdainful and amused: it was all in the lips and the eyebrows and the set of the nose. 'If they try such a thing,' she said, 'they will find me hard to catch, and harder still to kill.'

A squat young man sitting on the bench behind her hrrumphed for attention, then said, with a booming voice, 'All-Father, my people are comfortable. We make the best of what we have. If this war of yours goes against us, we could lose everything.'

Wednesday said, 'You have already lost everything. I am offering you the chance to take something back.'

The fire blazed high as he spoke, illuminating the faces of the audience.

I don't really believe, Shadow thought. *I don't believe any of this. Maybe I'm still fifteen. Mom's still alive and I haven't even met Laura yet. Everything that's happened so far has been some kind of especially vivid dream.* And yet he could not believe that either. All we have to believe with is our senses: the tools we use to perceive the world, our sight, our touch, our memory. If they lie to us, then nothing can be trusted. And even if we do not believe, then still we cannot travel in any other way than the road our senses show us; and we must walk that road to the end.

Then the fire burned out, and there was darkness in Valaskjalf, Odin's Hall.

'Now what?' whispered Shadow.

'Now we go back to the Carousel room,' muttered Mr Nancy, 'And old One-Eye buys us all dinner, greases some palms, kisses some babies, and no one says the Gee-word any more.'

'Gee-word?'

'*Gods*. What *were* you doin' the day they handed out brains, boy, anyway?'

'Someone was telling a story about stealing a tiger's balls, and I had to stop and find out how it ended.'

Mr Nancy chuckled.

'But nothing was resolved. Nobody agreed to anything.'

'He's working them slowly. He'll land 'em one at a time. You'll see. They'll come around in the end.'

Shadow could feel that a wind was coming up from somewhere, stirring his hair, touching his face, pulling at him.

They were standing in the room of the biggest carousel in the world, listening to the Emperor Waltz.

There was a group of people, tourists by the look of them, talking with Wednesday over at the other side of the room, by the wall covered with all the wooden carousel horses: as many people as there had been shadowy figures on Wednesday's Hall. 'Through here,' boomed Wednesday, and he led them through the only exit, formed to look like the gaping mouth of a huge monster, its sharp teeth ready to rend them all to slivers. He moved among them like a politician, cajoling, encouraging, smiling, gently disagreeing, pacifying.

'Did that happen?' asked Shadow.

'Did what happen, shit-for-brains?' asked Mr Nancy.

'The hall. The fire. Tiger balls. Riding the carousel.'

'Heck, nobody's allowed to ride the carousel. Didn't you see the signs? Now hush.'

The monster's mouth led to the Organ room, which puzzled Shadow – hadn't they already come through that way? It was no less strange the second time. Wednesday led them all up some stairs, past life-sized models of the four horsemen of the apocalypse hanging from the ceiling, and they followed the signs to an early exit.

Shadow and Nancy brought up the rear. And then they were out of the House on the Rock, walking past the gift store and heading back into the parking lot.

'Pity we had to leave before the end,' said Mr Nancy. 'I was kind of hoping to see the biggest artificial orchestra in the whole world.'

'I've seen it,' said Czernobog. 'It's not so much.'

***

The restaurant was a big and barn-like structure, ten minutes up the road. Wednesday had told each of his guests that tonight's dinner was on him, and had organized rides to the restaurant for any of them that didn't have their own transportation.

Shadow wondered how they had gotten to the House on the Rock without their own transportation, and how they were going to get away again, but he said nothing. It seemed the smartest thing to say.

Shadow had a carful of Wednesday's guests to ferry to the restaurant: the woman in the red sari sat in the front seat beside him. There were two men in the back seat: a peculiar-looking young man whose name Shadow had not properly caught, but thought might be Elvis, and another man, in a dark suit, who Shadow could not remember.

He had stood beside the man as he got into the car, had opened and closed the door for him, and was unable to remember anything about him. He turned around in the driver's seat and looked at him, carefully noting his face, his hair, his clothes, making certain he would know him if he met him again, and turned back to start the car, to find that the man had slipped from his mind. An impression of wealth was left behind, but nothing more.

I'm tired, thought Shadow. He glanced to his right and snuck a glance at the Indian woman. He noted the tiny silver necklace of skulls that circled her neck, her charm bracelet of heads and hands that jangled, like tiny bells, when she moved. There was a dark blue jewel on her forehead. She smelled of spices, of cardamom and nutmeg and flowers. Her hair was pepper-and-salt, and she smiled when she saw him look at her.

'You call me Mama-ji,' she said.

'I am Shadow, Mama-ji,' said Shadow.

'And what do you think of your employer's plans, Mister Shadow?'

He slowed, as a large black truck sped past, overtaking them with a spray of slush. 'I don't ask, he don't tell,' he said.

'If you ask me, he wants a last stand. He wants us to go out in a blaze of glory. That's what he wants. And we are old enough, or stupid enough, that maybe some of us will say yes.'

'It's not my job to ask questions, Mama-ji,' said Shadow. The inside of the car filled with her tinkling laughter.

The man in the back seat – not the peculiar young man, the other one – said something, and Shadow replied to him, but a moment later he was damned if he could remember what had been said.

The peculiar-looking young man had said nothing, but now he started to hum to himself, a deep, melodic, bass humming that made the interior of the car vibrate and rattle and buzz.

The peculiar-looking man was of average height, but of an odd shape: Shadow had heard of men who were barrel-chested before, but had no image to accompany the metaphor. This man was barrel-chested, and he had legs like, yes, like tree-trunks, and hands like, exactly, ham-hocks. He wore a black parka with a hood, several sweaters, thick dungarees, and, incongruously, in the winter and with those clothes, a pair of white tennis shoes, which were the same size and shape as shoe boxes. His fingers resembled sausages, with flat, squared-off fingertips.

'That's some hum you got,' said Shadow from the driver's seat.

'Sorry,' said the peculiar young man, in a deep, deep voice, embarrassed. He stopped humming.

'No, I enjoyed it,' said Shadow. 'Don't stop.'

The peculiar young man hesitated, then commenced to hum once more, his voice as deep and reverberant as before. This time there were words interspersed in the humming. 'Down down down,' he sang, so deeply that the windows rattled. 'Down down down, down down, down down.'

Christmas lights were draped across the eaves of every house and building that they drove past. They ranged from discrete golden lights that dripped twinkles to giant displays of snowmen and teddy bears and multicolored stars.

Shadow pulled up at the restaurant and he let his passengers off by the front door, then he got back into the car. He would park it at the back of the parking lot. He wanted to make the short walk back to the restaurant on his own, in the cold, to clear his head.

He parked the car beside a black truck. He wondered if it was the same one that had sped past him earlier.

He closed the car door, and stood there in the parking lot, his breath steaming.

Inside the restaurant, Shadow could imagine Wednesday already sitting all his guests down around a big table, working the room. Shadow wondered whether he had really had Kali in the front of his car, wondered what he had been driving in the back . . .

'Hey bud, you got a match?' said a voice that was half-familiar, and Shadow turned to apologize and say no, he didn't have a match, but the gun barrel hit him over the left eye, and he started to fall. He put out an arm to steady himself as he went down. Someone pushed something soft into his mouth, to stop him crying out, and taped it into position: easy, practiced moves, like a butcher gutting a chicken.

Shadow tried to shout, to warn Wednesday, to warn them all, but nothing came out of his mouth but a muffled noise.

'The quarry are all inside,' said the half-familiar voice. 'Everyone in position?' A crackle of a voice, half-audible through a radio. 'Let's move in and round them all up.'

'What about the big guy?' said another voice.

'Package him up, take him out,' said the first voice.

They put a bag-like hood over Shadow's head, and bound his wrists and ankles with tape, and put him in the back of a truck, and drove him away.

***

There were no windows in the tiny room in which they had locked Shadow. There was a plastic chair, a lightweight folding table, and a bucket with a cover on it, which served Shadow as a makeshift toilet. There was also a six foot-long strip of yellow foam on the floor, and a thin blanket with a long-since crusted brown stain in the center: blood or shit or food, Shadow didn't know and didn't care to investigate. There was a naked bulb behind a metal grill high in the room, but no light switch that Shadow had been able to find. The light was always on. There was no door handle on his side of the door.

He was hungry.

The first thing he had done, when the spooks had pushed him into the room, after they'd ripped off the tape from his ankles and wrists and mouth and left him alone, was to walk around the room and inspect it, carefully. He tapped the walls. They sounded dully metallic. There was a small ventilation grid at the top of the room. The door was soundly locked.

He was bleeding above the left eyebrow in a slow ooze. His head ached.

The floor was uncarpeted. He tapped it. It was made of the same metal as the walls.

He took the top off the bucket, pissed in it, and covered it once more. According to his watch only four hours had passed since the raid on the restaurant.

His wallet was gone, but they had left him his coins.

He sat on the chair, at the card-table. The table was covered with a cigarette-burned green baize. Shadow practiced appearing to push coins through the table. Then he took two quarters and made up a Pointless Coin Trick.

He concealed a quarter in his right palm, and openly displayed the other quarter in his left hand, between finger and thumb. Then he appeared to take the quarter from his left hand, while actually letting it drop back into his left hand. He opened his right hand to display the quarter that had been there all along.

The thing about coin manipulation was that it took all Shadow's head to do it; or rather, he could not do it if he was angry or upset, so the action of practicing an illusion, even one with no possible use – consider, he had expended an enormous amount of effort and skill to make it appear that he had moved a quarter from one hand to the other, something that it takes no skill whatever to do for real – calmed him, cleared his mind of turmoil and fear.

He began a trick even more pointless: a one-handed half-dollar to penny transformation, but with his two quarters. Each of the coins was alternately concealed and revealed as the trick progressed: he began with one quarter visible, held between the tips of his forefingers, the other hidden horizontally in the fork of his thumb, a Downs palm. He raised his hand to his mouth and blew on the coin, while slipping the visible quarter onto the tip of his third finger and pushing it into a classic palm, as the first two fingers took the hidden quarter out of the Downs palm and presented it. The effect was that he displayed a quarter in his hand, raised it to his mouth, blew on it, and lowered it again, displaying the same quarter all the while.

He did it over and over and over again.

He wondered if they were going to kill him, and his hand trembled, just a little, and one of the quarters dropped from his fingertip onto the stained green baize of the card table.

And then, because he just couldn't do it any more, he put the coins away, and took out the Liberty head dollar that Zorya Polunochnaya had given him, and held onto it tightly, and waited.

***

At three in the morning, by his watch, the spooks returned to interrogate him. Two men in dark suits, with dark hair and shiny black shoes. Spooks. One was square-jawed, wide-shouldered, had great hair, looked like he played football in high school, badly bitten fingernails, the other had a receding hairline, silver-rimmed round glasses, manicured nails. While they looked nothing alike, Shadow found himself suspecting that, on some level, possibly cellular, the two men were identical. They stood on each side of the card table, looking down at him.

'How long have you been working for Cargo, sir?' asked one.

'I don't know what that is,' said Shadow.

'He calls himself Wednesday. Grimm. Olfather. Old guy. You've been seen with him, sir.'

'I've been working for him for three days.'

'Don't lie to us, sir,' said the spook with the glasses.

'Okay,' said Shadow. 'I won't. But it's still three days.'

The clean-jawed spook reached down and twisted Shadow's ear between finger and thumb. He squeezed as he twisted. The pain was intense. 'We told you not to lie to us, sir,' he said, mildly. Then he let go.

Each of the spooks had a gun-bulge under his jacket.

Shadow did not try to retaliate. He pretended he was back in prison. *Do your own time*, thought Shadow. *Don't tell them anything they don't know already. Don't ask questions.*

'These are dangerous people you're palling around with, sir,' said the spook with glasses. 'You will be doing your country a service by turning state's evidence.' He smiled, sympathetically: *I'm the good cop*, said the smile.

'I see,' said Shadow.

'And if you don't want to help us, sir,' said the clean-jawed spook, 'you can see what we're like when we're not happy.' He hit Shadow an open handed blow across the stomach, knocking the breath from him. It wasn't torture, Shadow thought, just punctuation: *I'm the bad cop*. He retched.

'I would like to make you happy,' said Shadow, as soon as he could speak.

'All we ask is your cooperation, sir.'

'Can I ask . . .' gasped Shadow (*don't ask questions*, he thought, but it was too late, the words were already spoken), 'can I ask who I'll be cooperating with?'

'You want us to tell you our names?' asked the clean-jawed spook. 'You have to be out of your mind.'

'No, he's got a point,' said the spook with glasses. 'It may make it easier for him to relate to us.' He looked at Shadow and smiled like a man advertising toothpaste. 'Hi. I'm Mister Stone, sir. My colleague is Mister Wood.'

'Actually,' said Shadow, 'I meant, what agency are you with? CIA? FBI?'

Stone shook his head. 'Chee. It's not as easy as that, any more, sir. Things just aren't that simple.'

'The private sector,' said Wood, 'the public sector. You know. There's a lot of interplay these days.'

'But I can assure you,' said Stone, with another smiley smile, 'we are the good guys. Are you hungry, sir?' He reached into a pocket of his jacket, pulled out a Snickers bar. 'Here. A gift.'

'Thanks,' said Shadow. He unwrapped the Snickers bar and ate it.

'I guess you'd like something to drink with that. Coffee? Beer?'

'Water, please,' said Shadow.

Stone walked to the door, knocked on it. He said something to the guard on the other side of the door, who nodded and returned a minute later with a polystyrene cup filled with cold water.

'CIA,' said Wood. He shook his head, ruefully. 'Those bozos. Hey, Stone. I heard a new CIA joke. Okay: how can we be sure the CIA wasn't involved in the Kennedy assassination?'

'I don't know,' said Stone. 'How *can* we be sure?'

'He's dead, isn't he?' said Wood.

They both laughed.

'Feeling better now, sir?' asked Stone.

'I guess.'

'So why don't you tell us what happened this evening, sir?'

'We did some tourist stuff. Went to the House on the Rock. Went out for some food. You know the rest.'

Stone sighed, heavily. Wood shook his head, as if disappointed, and kicked Shadow in the kneecap. The pain was excruciating. Then Wood pushed a fist slowly into Shadow's back, just above the right kidney, and he twisted his fist, and the pain was worse for Shadow than the pain in his knee.

I'm bigger than either of them, he thought. *I can take them.* But they were armed; and even if he – somehow – killed or subdued them both, he'd still be locked in the cell with them. (But he'd have a gun. He'd have two guns.) (*No.*)

Wood was keeping his hands away from Shadow's face. No marks. Nothing permanent: just fists and feet on his torso and knees. It hurt, and Shadow clutched the Liberty dollar tight in the palm of his hand, and waited for it to be over.

And after far too long a time the beating ended.

'We'll see you in a couple of hours, sir,' said Stone. 'You

know, Woody really hated to have to do that. We're reasonable men. Like I said, we are the good guys. You're on the wrong side. Meantime, why don't you try to get a little sleep?'

'You better start taking us seriously,' said Wood.

'Woody's got a point there, sir,' said Stone. 'Think about it.'

The door slammed closed behind them. Shadow wondered if they would turn out the light, but they didn't, and it blazed into the room like a cold eye. Shadow crawled across the floor to the yellow foam-rubber pad and climbed onto it, pulling the thin blanket over himself, and he closed his eyes, and he held onto nothing, and he held onto dreams.

Time passed.

He was fifteen again, and his mother was dying, and she was trying to tell him something very important, and he couldn't understand her. He moved in his sleep and a shaft of pain moved him from half-sleep to half-waking, and he winced.

Shadow shivered under the thin blanket. His right arm covered his eyes, blocking out the light of the bulb. He wondered whether Wednesday and the others were still at Liberty, if they were even still alive. He hoped that they were.

The silver dollar remained cold in his left hand. He could feel it there, as it had been during the beating. He wondered idly why it did not warm to his body temperature. Half-asleep, now, and half-delirious, the coin, and the idea of Liberty, and the moon, and Zorya Polunochnaya somehow became intertwined in one woven beam of silver light that shone from the depths to the heavens, and he rode the silver beam up and away from the pain and the heartache and the fear, away from the pain and, blessedly, back into dreams . . .

From far away he could hear some kind of noise, but it was too late to think about it: he belonged to sleep now.

A half-thought: he hoped it was not people coming to wake him up, to hit him or to shout at him. And then, he noticed with pleasure, he was really asleep, and no longer cold.

* * *

Somebody somewhere was shouting for help, in his dream or out of it.

Shadow rolled over on the foam rubber, finding new places that hurt as he rolled, hoping that he had not woken fully and relieved to find sleep was enfolding him once more.

Someone was shaking his shoulder.

He wanted to ask them not to wake him, to let him sleep and leave him be, but it came out as a grunt.

'Puppy?' said Laura. 'You have to wake up. Please wake up, hon.'

And there was a moment's gentle relief. He had had such a strange dream, of prisons and con-men and down-at-heel gods, and now Laura was waking him to tell him it was time for work, and perhaps there would be time enough before work to steal some coffee and a kiss, or more than a kiss; and he put out his hand to touch her.

Her flesh was cold as ice, and sticky.

Shadow opened his eyes.

'Where did all the blood come from?' he asked.

'Other people,' she said. 'It's not mine. I'm filled with formaldehyde, mixed with glycerin and lanolin.'

'Which other people?' he asked.

'The guards,' she said. 'It's okay. I killed them. You better move. I don't think I gave anyone a chance to raise the alarm. Take a coat from out there, or you'll freeze your butt off.'

'You killed them?'

She shrugged, and half-smiled, awkwardly. Her hands looked as if she had been finger-painting, composing a picture that had been executed solely in crimsons, and there were splashes and spatters on her face and clothes (the same blue suit in which she had been buried) that made Shadow think of Jackson Pollock, because it was less problematic to think of Jackson Pollock than to accept the alternative.

'It's easier to kill people, when you're dead yourself,' she told him. 'I mean, it's not such a big deal. You're not so prejudiced any more.'

'It's still a big deal to me,' said Shadow.

'You want to stay here until the morning crew come?' she said. 'You can if you like. I thought you'd like to get out of here.'

'They'll think I did it,' he said, stupidly.

'Maybe,' she said. 'Put on a coat, hon. You'll freeze.'

He walked out into the corridor. At the end of the corridor was a guardroom. In the guardroom were four dead men: three guards, and the man who had called himself Stone. His friend was nowhere to be seen. From the blood-colored skid-marks on the floor, two of them had been dragged into the guardroom, and dropped onto the floor.

His own coat was hanging from the coat rack. His wallet was still in the inside pocket, apparently untouched. Laura pulled open a couple of cardboard boxes, filled with candy bars.

The guards, now he could see them properly, were wearing dark camouflage uniforms, but there were no official tags on them, nothing to say for whom they were working. They might have been weekend duck hunters, dressed for the shoot.

Laura reached out her cold hand, and squeezed Shadow's hand in hers. She had the gold coin he had given her around her neck, on a golden chain.

'That looks nice,' he said.

'Thanks.' She smiled, prettily.

'What about the others,' he asked. 'Wednesday, and the rest of them? Where are they?' Laura passed him a handful of candy bars, and he filled his pockets with them.

'There wasn't anybody else here. A lot of empty cells, and

one with you in it. Oh, and one of the men had gone into the cell down there to jack off with a magazine. He got such a shock.'

'You killed him while he was jerking himself off?'

She shrugged. 'I guess,' she said, uncomfortably. 'I was worried they were hurting you. Someone has to watch out for you, and I told you I would, didn't I? Here, take these.' They were chemical hand- and footwarmers: thin pads – you broke the seal and they heated up to a little above body temperature and stayed that way for hours. Shadow pocketed them.

'Look out for me. Yes,' he said, 'you did.'

She reached out a finger, stroked him above his left eyebrow. 'You're hurt,' she said.

'I'm okay,' he said.

He opened a metal door in the wall. It swung open slowly. There was a four-foot drop to the ground, and he swung himself down to what felt like gravel. He picked up Laura by the waist, swung her down, as he used to swing her, easily, without a second thought . . .

The moon came out from behind a thick cloud. It was low on the horizon, ready to set, but the light it cast onto the snow was enough to see by.

They had emerged from what turned out to be the black-painted metal car of a long freight train, parked or abandoned in a woodland siding. The series of cars went on as far as he could see, into the trees and away. Of course he had been on a train. He should have known.

'How the hell did you find me here?' he asked his dead wife.

She shook her head slowly, amused. 'You shine like a beacon in a dark world,' she told him. 'It wasn't that hard. Now,' she told him, 'you need to go. Just go. Go as far and as fast as you can. Don't use your credit cards and you should be fine.'

'Where should I go?'

She pushed a hand through her matted hair, flicking it back out of her eyes. 'The road's that way,' she told him. 'Do whatever you can. Steal a car if you have to. Go south.'

'Laura,' he said, and hesitated. 'Do you know what's going on? Do you know who these people are? Who did you kill?'

'Yeah,' she said. 'I think I do know.'

'I owe you,' said Shadow. 'I'd still be in there if it wasn't for you. I don't think they had anything good planned for me.'

'No,' she said. 'I don't think they did.'

They walked away from the empty train cars. Shadow wondered about the other trains he'd seen, blank window-less metal cars which went on for mile after mile hooting their lonely way through the night. His fingers closed around the Liberty dollar in his pocket, and he remembered Zorya Polunochnaya, and the way she had looked at him in the moonlight. *Did you ask her what she wanted? It is the wisest thing to ask the dead. Sometimes they will tell you.*

'Laura . . . What do you want?' he asked.

'You really want to know?'

'Yes. Please.'

Laura looked up at him with dead blue eyes. 'I want to be alive again,' she said. 'Not in this half-life. I want to be *really* alive. I want to feel my heart pumping in my chest again. I want to feel blood moving through me – hot, and salty, and real. It's weird, you don't think you can feel it, the blood, but believe me, when it stops flowing, you'll know.' She rubbed her eyes, smudging her face with red from the mess on her hands. 'Look, I don't know why this happened to me. But it's hard. You know why dead people only go out at night, puppy? Because it's easier to pass for real, in the dark. And I don't want to have to pass. I want to be alive.'

'I don't understand what you want me to do.'

'Make it happen, hon. You'll figure it out. I know you will.'

'Okay,' he said. 'I'll try. And if I do figure it out, how do I find you?'

But she was gone, and there was nothing left in the

woodland but a gentle gray in the sky to show him where east was, and on the bitter December wind a lonely wail that might have been the cry of the last night bird or the call of the first bird of dawn.

Shadow set his face to the south, and he began to walk.

Chapter Seven

*As the Hindu gods are 'immortal' only in a very particular
sense – for they are born and they die – they experience
most of the great human dilemmas and often seem to differ
from mortals in a few trivial details ... and from demons
even less. Yet they are regarded by the Hindus as a class of
beings by definition totally different from any other; they
are symbols in a way that no human being, however
'archetypal' his life story, can ever be. They are actors
playing parts that are real only for us; they are the masks
behind which we see our own faces.*

– Wendy Doniger O'Flaherty, Introduction, *HINDU MYTHS*
(Penguin Books, 1975)

S hadow had been walking south, or what he hoped was
more or less south, for several hours, heading along a
narrow and unmarked road through the woods somewhere in, he imagined, southern Wisconsin. Several jeeps
came down the road toward him at one point, headlights
blazing, and he ducked well back into the trees until they
had passed. The early morning mist hung at waist level. The
cars were black.

When, thirty minutes later, he heard the noise of distant
helicopters coming from the west, he struck out away from
the timber trail and into the woods. There were two
helicopters, and he lay, crouched in a hollow beneath a fallen
tree, and listened to them pass over. As they moved away, he
looked out and looked up, for one hasty glance at the gray
winter sky. He was satisfied to observe that the helicopters
were painted a matte black. He waited beneath the tree until
the noise of the helicopters was completely gone.

Under the trees the snow was little more than a dusting,
which crunched underfoot. He was deeply grateful for the
chemical hand and feet warmers, which kept his extremities
from freezing. Beyond that, he was numb: heart-numb,
mind-numb, soul-numb. And the numbness, he realized,
went a long way down, and a long way back.

So what do I want? he asked himself. He couldn't answer,
so he just kept on walking, a step at a time, on and on
through the woods. Trees looked familiar, moments of
landscape were perfectly *déjà-vu*ed. Could he be walking in
circles? Maybe he would just walk and walk and walk until
the warmers and the candy bars ran out and then sit down
and never get up again.

He reached a large stream, of the kind the locals called a
creek and pronounced a *crick*, and decided to follow it.
Streams led to rivers, rivers all led to the Mississippi, and if
he kept walking, or stole a boat or built a raft, eventually he'd
get to New Orleans, where it was warm, an idea which
seemed both comforting and unlikely.

There were no more helicopters. He had the feeling that
the ones that had passed overhead had been cleaning up the
mess at the freight train siding, not hunting for him,
otherwise they would have returned; there would have been
tracker dogs and sirens and the whole paraphernalia of
pursuit. Instead, there was nothing.

What did *he* want? Not to get caught. Not to get blamed for
the deaths of the men on the train. 'It wasn't me,' he heard

himself saying, 'it was my dead wife.' He could imagine the expressions on the faces of the law officers. Then people could argue about whether he was crazy or not while he went to the chair . . .

He wondered whether Wisconsin had the death penalty. He wondered whether that would matter. He wanted to understand what was going on – and to find out how it was all going to end. And finally, producing a half-rueful grin, he realized that most of all he wanted everything to be normal. He wanted never to have gone to prison, for Laura to still be alive, for none of this ever to have happened.

'I'm afraid that's not exactly an option, m'boy,' he thought to himself, in Wednesday's gruff voice, and he nodded agreement. *Not an option. You burned your bridges. So keep walking. Do your own time* . . .

A distant woodpecker drummed against a rotten log.

Shadow became aware of eyes on him: a handful of red cardinals stared at him from a skeletal elder bush, then returned to pecking at the clusters of black elderberries. They looked like the illustrations in the *Songbirds of North America* calendar. He heard the birds' video-arcade trills and zaps and whoops follow him along the side of the creek. Eventually, they faded away.

The dead fawn lay in a glade in the shadow of a hill, and a black bird the size of a small dog was picking at its side with a large, wicked, beak, rending and tearing gobbets of red meat from the corpse. Its eyes were gone, but its head was untouched, and white fawn-spots were visible on its rump. Shadow wondered how it had died.

The black bird cocked its head onto one side, and then said, in a voice like stones being struck, 'You shadow man.'

'I'm Shadow,' said Shadow. The bird hopped up onto the fawn's rump, raised its head, ruffled its crown and neck feathers. It was enormous and its eyes were black beads. There was something intimidating about a bird that size, this close.

'Says he will see you in Kay-ro,' tokked the raven. Shadow wondered which of Odin's ravens this was: Huginn or Muninn: Memory or Thought.

'Kay-ro?' he asked.

'In Egypt.'

'How am I going to go to Egypt?'

'Follow Mississippi. Go south. Find Jackal.'

'Look,' said Shadow, 'I don't want to seem like I'm . . . Jesus, look . . .' he paused. Regrouped. He was cold, standing in a wood, talking to a big black bird who was currently brunching on Bambi. 'Okay. What I'm trying to say is, I don't want mysteries.'

'Mysteries,' agreed the bird, helpfully.

'What I want is explanations. Jackal in Kay-ro. This does not help me. It's a line from a bad spy thriller.'

'Jackal. Friend. *Tok*. Kay-ro.'

'So you said. I'd like a little more information than that.'

The bird half-turned, and pulled another bloody strip of raw venison from the fawn's ribs. Then it flew off into the trees, the red strip dangling from its beak like a long, bloody worm.

'Hey! Can you at least get me back to a real road?' called Shadow.

The raven flew up and away. Shadow looked at the corpse of the baby deer. He decided that if he were a real woodsman, he would slice off a steak and grill it over a wood fire. Instead, he sat on a fallen tree and ate a Snickers bar and knew that he really wasn't a real woodsman.

The raven cawed from the edge of the clearing.

'You want me to follow you?' asked Shadow. 'Or has Timmy fallen down another well?' The bird cawed again, impatiently. Shadow started walking towards it. It waited until he was close, then flapped heavily into another tree, heading somewhat to the left of the way Shadow had originally been going.

'Hey,' said Shadow. 'Huginn or Muninn, or whoever you are.'

The bird turned, head tipped, suspiciously, on one side, and it stared at him with bright eyes.

'Say "Nevermore",' said Shadow.

'Fuck you,' said the raven. It said nothing else as they went through the woodland together, the raven in the lead and flying from tree to tree, the man stomping heavily through the undergrowth trying to catch up.

The sky was a uniform gray. It was almost midday.

In half an hour they reached a blacktop road on the edge of a town, and the raven flew back into the wood. Shadow observed a Culvers Frozen Custard Butterburgers sign, and, next to it, a gas station. He went into the Culvers, which was empty of customers. There was a keen young man with shaven head behind the cash register. Shadow ordered two butterburgers and french fries. Then he went into the rest room to clean up. He looked a real mess. He did an inventory of the contents of his pockets: ho had a few coins, including the silver Liberty dollar, a disposable toothbrush and toothpaste, three Snickers bars, five chemical heater pads, a wallet (with nothing more in it than his driver's license and a credit card – he wondered how much longer the credit card had to live?), and in the coat's inside pocket, a thousand dollars in fifties and twenties, his take from yesterday's bank job. He washed his face and hands in hot water, slicked down his dark hair, then went back into the restaurant and ate his burgers and fries, and drank his coffee.

He went back to the counter. 'You want frozen custard?' asked the keen young man.

'No. No thanks. Is there anywhere around here I could rent a car? My car died, back down the road a way.'

The young man scratched his head-stubble. 'Not around here, Mister. If your car died you could call triple-A. Or talk to the gas station next door about a tow.'

'A fine idea,' said Shadow. 'Thanks.'

He walked across the melting snow, from the Culvers parking lot to the gas station. He bought candy bars and beef jerky sticks and more chemical hand- and feet-warmers.

'Anywhere hereabouts I could rent a car?' he asked the woman behind the cash register. She was immensely plump, and bespectacled, and was delighted to have someone to talk to.

'Let me think,' she said. 'We're kind of out of the way here. They do that kind of thing over in Madison. Where you going?'

'Kay-ro,' he said. 'Wherever that is.'

'I know where that is,' she said. 'Hand me that map from that rack over there.' Shadow passed her a plastic-coated map of Illinois. She unfolded it, then pointed in triumph to the bottommost corner of the state. 'There it is.'

'Cairo?'

'That's how they pronounce the one in Egypt. The one in Little Egypt, they call that one *Kayro*. They got a Thebes down there, all sorts. My sister-in-law comes from Thebes. I asked her about the one in Egypt, she looked at me as if I had a screw loose.' The woman chuckled like a drain.

'Any pyramids?' The city was five hundred miles away, almost directly south.

'Not that they ever told me. They call it Little Egypt because back, oh, mebbe a hundred, hundred and fifty years back, there was a famine all over. Crops failed. But they didn't fail down there. So everyone went there to buy food. Like in the Bible. Joseph and the Technicolor Dreamcoat. Off we go to Egypt, bad-a-boom.'

'So if you were me, and you needed to get there, how would you go?' asked Shadow.

'Drive.'

'Car died a few miles down the road. It was a pieceashit if you'll pardon my language,' said Shadow.

'Pee-Oh-Esses,' she said. 'Yup. That's what my brother-in-law calls 'em. He buys and sells cars in a small way. He'll call me up, say Mattie, I just sold another Pee-Oh-Ess. Say, maybe he'd be interested in your old car. For scrap or something.'

'It belongs to my boss,' said Shadow, surprising himself with the fluency and ease of his lies. 'I need to call him, so he can come pick it up.' A thought struck him. 'Your brother-in-law, is he around here?'

'He's in Muscoda. Ten minutes south of here. Just over the river. Why?'

'Well, does he have a Pee-Oh-Ess he'd like to sell me for, mm, five, six hundred bucks?'

She smiled sweetly. 'Mister, he doesn't have a car on that back lot you couldn't buy with a full tank of gas for five hundred dollars. But don't you tell him I said so.'

'Would you call him?' asked Shadow.

'I'm way ahead of you,' she told him, and she picked up the phone. 'Hon? It's Mattie. You get over here this minute. I got a man here wants to buy a car.'

* * *

The piece of shit he chose was a 1983 Chevy Nova, which he bought, with a full tank of gas, for four hundred and fifty dollars. It had almost a quarter of a million miles on the clock, and smelled faintly of bourbon, tobacco, and more strongly of something that reminded Shadow of bananas. He couldn't tell what color it was, under the dirt and the snow. Still, of all the vehicles in Mattie's brother-in-law's back lot, it was the only one that looked like it might take him five hundred miles.

The deal was done in cash, and Mattie's brother-in-law never asked for Shadow's name or social security number or for anything except the money.

Shadow drove west, then south, with five hundred and fifty dollars in his pocket, keeping off the interstate. The piece of shit had a radio, but nothing happened when he turned it on. A sign said he'd left Wisconsin and was now in Illinois. He passed a strip mining works, huge blue arc lights burning in the dim midwinter daylight.

He stopped and ate lunch at a place called Mom's, catching them just before they closed for the afternoon. The food was okay.

Each town he passed through had an extra sign up beside the sign telling him that he was now entering Our Town (pop.720). The extra sign announced that the town's Under-14s team was the third runner-up in the interstate Hundred-Yard Sprint, or that the town was the home of the Illinois Girl's Under 16s Wrestling semifinalist.

He drove on, head nodding, feeling more drained and exhausted with every minute that passed. He ran a stoplight, and was nearly sideswiped by a woman in a Dodge. As soon as he got out into open country he pulled off onto an empty tractor path on the side of the road, and he parked by a snow-spotted stubbly field in which a slow procession of fat black wild turkeys walked like a line of mourners; he turned off the engine, stretched out in the back seat, and fell asleep.

Darkness; a sensation of falling – as if he were tumbling down a great hole, like Alice. He fell for a hundred years into darkness. Faces passed him, swimming out of the black, then each face was ripped up and away before he could touch it . . .

Abruptly, and without transition, he was not falling. Now he was in a cave, and he was no longer alone. Shadow stared into familiar eyes: huge, liquid black eyes. They blinked.

Under the earth: yes. He remembered this place. The stink of wet cow. Firelight flickered on the wet cave walls, illuminating the buffalo head, the man's body, skin the color of brick clay.

'Can't you people leave me be?' asked Shadow. 'I just want to sleep.'

The buffalo man nodded, slowly. His lips did not move, but a voice in Shadow's head said, 'Where are you going, Shadow?'

'Cairo.'

'Why?'

'Where else have I got to go? It's where Wednesday wants me to go. I drank his mead.' In Shadow's dream, with the power of dream-logic behind it, the obligation seemed unarguable: he drank Wednesday's mead three times, and sealed the pact – what other choice of action did he have?

The buffalo-headed man reached a hand into the fire, stirring the embers and the broken branches into a blaze. 'The storm is coming,' he said. Now there was ash on his hands, and he wiped it onto his hairless chest, leaving soot-black streaks.

'So you people keep telling me. Can I ask you a question?'

There was a pause. A fly settled on the furry forehead. The buffalo man flicked it away. 'Ask.'

'Is this true? Are these people really gods? It's all so,' he paused. Then he said, 'unlikely,' which was not exactly the word he had been going for but seemed to be the best he could do.

'What are gods?' asked the buffalo man.

'I don't know,' said Shadow.

There was a tapping, relentless and dull. Shadow waited for the buffalo man to say something more, to explain what gods were, to explain the whole tangled nightmare that his life seemed to have become. He was cold. The fire no longer burned.

Tap. Tap. Tap.

Shadow opened his eyes, and, groggily, sat up. He was freezing, and the sky outside the car was the deep luminescent purple that divides the dusk from the night.

Tap. Tap. Someone said 'Hey, Mister,' and Shadow turned his head. The someone was standing beside the car, no more than a darker shape against the darkling sky. Shadow reached out a hand and cranked down the window a few inches. He made several waking-up noises, and then he said 'Hi.'

'You all right? You sick? You been drinking?' The voice was high – a woman's or a boy's.

'I'm fine,' said Shadow. 'Hold on.' He opened the door, and got out, stretching his aching limbs and neck as he did so. Then he rubbed his hands together, to get the blood circulating and to warm them up.

'Whoa. You're pretty big.'

'That's what they tell me,' said Shadow. 'Who are you?'

'I'm Sam,' said the voice.

'Boy Sam or girl Sam?'

'Girl-Sam. I used to be Sammi with an i, and I'd do a smiley face over the i, but then I got completely sick of it because like absolutely everybody was doing it, so I stopped.'

'Okay, girl-Sam. You go over there, and look out at the road.'

'Why? Are you a crazed killer or something?'

'No,' said Shadow, 'I need to take a leak and I'd like just the smallest amount of privacy.'

'Oh. Right. Okay. Got it. No problem. I am so with you. I can't even pee if there's someone in the next stall. Major shy bladder syndrome.'

'Now, please.'

She walked to the far side of the car, and Shadow took a few steps closer to the field, unzipped his jeans, and pissed against a fencepost for a very long time. He walked back to the car. The last of the gloaming had become night.

'You still there?' he asked.

'Yes,' she said. 'You must have a bladder like Lake Erie. I think empires rose and fell in the time it took you to pee. I could hear it the whole time.'

'Thank you. Do you want something?'

'Well, I wanted to see if you were okay. I mean, if you were dead or something I would have called the cops. But the windows were kind of fogged up so I thought, well, he's probably still alive.'

'You live around here?'

'Nope. Hitchhiking down from Madison.'

'That's not safe.'

'I've done it five times a year for three years now. I'm still alive. Where are you headed?'

'I'm going as far as Cairo.'

'Thank you,' she said. 'I'm going to El Paso. Staying with my Aunt for the holidays.'

'I can't take you all the way,' said Shadow.

'Not El Paso, Texas. The other one, in Illinois. It's a few hours south. You know where you are now?'

'No,' said Shadow. 'I have no idea. Somewhere on Highway Fifty-Two?'

'The next town's Peru,' said Sam. 'Not the one in Peru. The one in Illinois. Let me smell you. Bend down.' Shadow bent down, and the girl sniffed his face. 'Okay. I don't smell booze. You can drive. Let's go.'

'What makes you think I'm giving you a ride?'

'Because I'm a damsel in distress,' she said, 'And you are a knight in whatever. A really dirty car. You know someone wrote *Wash Me!* on your rear windshield?' Shadow got into the car and opened the passenger door. The light that goes on in cars when the front door is opened did not go on in this car.

'No,' he said, 'I didn't.'

She climbed in. 'It was me,' she said. 'I wrote it. While there was still enough light to see.'

Shadow started the car, turned on the headlights, and headed back onto the road. 'Left,' said Sam helpfully. Shadow turned left, and he drove. After several minutes the heater started to work, and blessed warmth filled the car.

'You haven't said anything yet,' said Sam. 'Say something.'

'Are you human?' asked Shadow. 'An honest to goodness, born of man and woman, living breathing human being?'

'Sure,' she said.

'Okay. Just checking. So what would you like me to say?'

'Something to reassure me, at this point. I suddenly have that *oh shit I'm in the wrong car with a crazy man* feeling.'

'Yeah,' he said. 'I've had that one. What would you find reassuring?'

'Just tell me you're not an escaped convict or a mass murderer or something.'

He thought for a moment. 'You know, I'm really not.'

'You had to think about it though, didn't you?'

'Done my time. Never killed anybody.'

'Oh.'

They entered a small town, lit up by streetlights and blinking Christmas decorations, and Shadow glanced to his right. The girl had a tangle of short dark hair and a face that was both attractive and, he decided, faintly mannish: her features might have been chiseled out of rock. She was looking at him.

'What were you in prison for?'

'I hurt a couple of people real bad. I got angry.'

'Did they deserve it?'

Shadow thought for a moment. 'I thought so at the time.'

'Would you do it again?'

'Hell, no. I lost three years of my life in there.'

'Mm. You got Indian blood in you?'

'Not that I know of.'

'You looked like it, was all.'

'Sorry to disappoint you.'

'S'okay. You hungry?'

Shadow nodded. 'I could eat,' he said.

'There's a good place just past the next set of lights. Good food. Cheap, too.'

Shadow pulled up in the parking lot. They got out of the car. He didn't bother to lock it, although he pocketed the keys. He pulled out some coins to buy a newspaper. 'Can you afford to eat here?' he asked.

'Yeah,' she said, raising her chin. 'I can pay for myself.'

Shadow nodded. 'Tell you what. I'll toss you for it,' he said. 'Heads you pay for my dinner, tails, I pay for yours.'

'Let me see the coin first,' she said, suspiciously. 'I had an uncle had a double-headed quarter.'

She inspected it, satisfied herself there was nothing

strange about the quarter. Shadow placed the coin head up on his thumb and cheated the toss, so it wobbled and looked like it was spinning, then he caught it and flipped it over onto the back of his left hand, and uncovered it with his right, in front of her.

'Tails,' she said, happily. 'Dinner's on you.'

'Yup,' he said. 'You can't win them all.'

Shadow ordered the meatloaf, Sam ordered lasagna. Shadow flipped through the newspaper to see if there was anything in it about dead men in a freight train. There wasn't. The only story of interest was on the cover: crows in record numbers were infesting the town. Local farmers wanted to hang dead crows around the town on public buildings to frighten the others away; ornithologists said that it wouldn't work, that the living crows would simply eat the dead ones. The locals were implacable. 'When they see the corpses of their friends,' said a spokesman, 'they'll know that we don't want them here.'

The food was good, and it came mounded on steaming plates, more than any one person could eat.

'So what's in Cairo?' asked Sam, with her mouth full.

'No idea. I got a message from my boss saying he needs me down there.'

'What do you do?'

'I'm an errand boy.'

She smiled. 'Well,' she said, 'you aren't mafia, not looking like that and driving that piece of shit. Why does your car smell like bananas, anyway?'

He shrugged, carried on eating.

Sam narrowed her eyes. 'Maybe you're a banana smuggler,' she said. 'You haven't asked me what I do yet.'

'I figure you're at school.'

'UW Madison.'

'Where you are undoubtedly studying art history, women's studies, and probably casting your own bronzes. And you probably work in a coffee house to help cover the rent.'

She put down her fork, nostrils flaring, eyes wide. 'How the fuck did you do that?'

'What? Now you say, no, actually I'm studying Romance languages and ornithology.'

'So you're saying that was a lucky guess or something?'

'What was?'

She stared at him with dark eyes. 'You are one peculiar guy, Mister . . . I don't know your name.'

'They call me Shadow,' he said.

She twisted her mouth wryly, as if she were tasting something she disliked. She stopped talking, put her head down, finished her lasagna.

'Do you know why it's called Egypt?' asked Shadow, when Sam finished eating.

'Down Cairo way? Yeah. It's in the delta of the Ohio and the Mississippi. Like Cairo in Egypt, in the Nile delta.'

'That makes sense.'

She sat back in her chair, ordered coffee and chocolate cream pie, ran a hand through her black hair. 'You married, Mister Shadow?' And then, as he hesitated, 'Gee. I just asked another tricky question, didn't I?'

'They buried her on Thursday,' he said, picking his words with care. 'She was killed in a car crash.'

'Oh. God. Jesus. I'm sorry.'

'Me too.'

An awkward pause. 'My half-sister lost her kid, my nephew, end of last year. It's rough.'

'Yeah. It is. What did he die of?'

She sipped her coffee. 'We don't know. We don't even really know that he's dead. He just vanished. But he was only thirteen. It was the middle of last winter. My sister was pretty broken up about it.'

'Were there any, any clues?' He sounded like a TV cop. He tried again. 'Did they suspect foul play?' That sounded worse.

'They suspected my non-custodial asshole brother-in-law,

his father. Who was asshole enough to have stolen him away. Probably did. But this is in a little town in the North Woods. Lovely, sweet, pretty little town where no one ever locks their doors.' She sighed, shook her head. She held her coffee cup in both hands. Then she looked up at him, changing the subject. 'How did you know I cast bronzes?'

'Lucky guess. It was just something to say.'

'Are you sure you aren't part Indian?'

'Not that I know. It's possible. I never met my father. I guess my Ma would have told me if he was Native American, though. Maybe.'

Again the mouth-twist. Sam gave up half-way through her chocolate cream pie: the slice was half the size of her head. She pushed the plate across the table to Shadow. 'You want?' He smiled, said 'Sure,' and finished it off.

The waitress handed them the check, and Shadow paid.

'Thanks,' said Sam.

It was getting colder now. The car coughed a couple of times before it started. Shadow drove back onto the road, and kept going south. 'You ever read a guy named Herodotus?' he asked.

'Jesus. What?'

'Herodotus. You ever read his *Histories*?'

'You know,' she said, dreamily, 'I don't get it. I don't get how you talk, or the words you use or anything. One moment you're a big dumb guy, the next you're reading my friggin' mind, and the next we're talking about Herodotus. So no. I have not read Herodotus. I've heard about him. Maybe on NPR. Isn't he the one they call the father of lies?'

'I thought that was the Devil.'

'Yeah, him too. But they were talking about Herodotus saying there were giant ants and gryphons guarding gold mines, and how he made this stuff up.'

'I don't think so. He wrote what he'd been told. It's like, he's writing these histories. And they're mostly pretty good histories. Loads of weird little details – like, did you know, in

Egypt, if a particularly beautiful girl, or the wife of a lord or whatever died, they wouldn't send her to the embalmer for three days? They'd let her body spoil in the heat first.'

'Why? Oh, hold on. Okay, I think I know why. Oh, that's disgusting.'

'And there're battles in there, all sorts of normal things. And then there are the gods. Some guy is running back to report on the outcome of a battle and he's running and running, and he sees Pan in a glade. And Pan says "Tell them to build me a temple here". So he says okay, and runs the rest of the way back. And he reports the battle news, and then says, "Oh, and by the way, Pan wants you to build him a temple." It's really matter-of-fact, you know?'

'So there are stories with gods in. What are you trying to say? That these guys had hallucinations?'

'No,' said Shadow. 'That's not it.'

She chewed a hangnail. 'I read some book about brains,' she said. 'My roommate had it and she kept waving it around. It was like, how 5,000 years ago the lobes of the brain fused and before that people thought when the right lobe of the brain said anything it was the voice of some god telling them what to do. It's just brains.'

'I like my theory better,' said Shadow.

'What's your theory?'

'That back then people used to run into the gods from time to time.'

'Oh.' Silence: only the rattling of the car, the roar of the engine, the growling of the muffler – which did not sound healthy. Then, 'Do you think they're still there?'

'Where?'

'Greece. Egypt. The islands. Those places. Do you think if you walked where those people walked you'd see the gods?'

'Maybe. But I don't think people'd know that was what they'd seen.'

'I bet it's like space aliens,' she said. 'These days, people see space aliens. Back then they saw gods. Maybe the space aliens come from the right side of the brain.'

'I don't think the gods ever gave rectal probes,' said Shadow. 'And they didn't mutilate cattle themselves. They got people to do it for them.'

She chuckled. They drove in silence for a few minutes, and then she said, 'Hey, that reminds me of my favorite god story, from Comparative Religion 101. You want to hear it?'

'Sure,' said Shadow.

'Okay. This is one about Odin. The Norse god. You know? There was some Viking king on a Viking ship – this was back in the Viking times, obviously – and they were becalmed, so he says he'll sacrifice one of his men to Odin if Odin will send them a wind, and get them to land. Okay. The wind comes up, and they get to land. So, on land, they draw lots to figure out who gets sacrificed – and it's the king himself. Well, he's not happy about this, but they figure out that they can hang him in effigy and not hurt him. They take a calf's intestines and loop them loosely around the guy's neck, and they tie the other end to a thin branch, and they take a reed instead of a spear and poke him with it and go "Okay, you've been hung" – hanged? – whatever – "you've been sacrificed to Odin."'

The road curved: Another Town, pop. 300, home of the runner-up to the state under-12s speed-skating championship, two huge giant-economy sized funeral parlors on each side of the road, and how many funeral parlors do you need, Shadow wonders, when you only have three hundred people . . .?

'Okay. As soon as they say Odin's name, the reed transforms into a spear and stabs the guy in the side, the calf intestines become a thick rope, the branch becomes a bough of a tree, and the tree pulls up, and the ground drops away, and the king is left hanging there to die with a wound in his side and his face going black. End of story. White people have some fucked-up gods, Mister Shadow.'

'Yes,' said Shadow. 'You're not white?'

'I'm a Cherokee,' she said.

'Full-blooded?'

'Nope. Only four pints. My mom was white. My dad was a real reservation Indian. He came out this way, eventually married my mom, had me, then when they split he went back to Oklahoma.'

'He went back to the reservation?'

'No. He borrowed money and opened a Taco Bell knock-off called Taco Bill's. He does okay. He doesn't like me. Says I'm half-breed.'

'I'm sorry.'

'He's a jerk. I'm proud of my Indian blood. It helps pay my college tuition. Hell, one day it'll probably help get me a job, if I can't sell my bronzes.'

'There's always that,' said Shadow.

He stopped in El Paso, IL (pop. 2500) to let Sam out at a down-at-heel house on the edge of the town. A large wire-framed model of a reindeer covered in twinkling lights stood in the front yard. 'You want to come in?' she asked. 'My aunt would give you a coffee.'

'No,' he said. 'I've got to keep moving.'

She smiled at him, looking suddenly, and for the first time, vulnerable. She patted him on the arm. 'You're fucked up, Mister. But you're cool.'

'I believe that's what they call the human condition,' said Shadow. 'Thanks for the company.'

'No problem,' she said. 'If you see any gods on the road to Cairo, you make sure and say hi to them from me.' She got out of the car, and went to the door of the house. She pressed a doorbell and stood there at the door, without looking back. Shadow waited until the door was opened and she was safely inside before he put his foot down and headed back for the highway. He passed through Normal, and Bloomington, and Lawndale.

At eleven that night Shadow started shaking. He was just

entering Middletown. He decided he needed sleep, or just not to drive any longer, and he pulled up in front of a Night's Inn, paid thirty five dollars, cash in advance, for his ground floor room, and went into the bathroom. A sad cockroach lay on its back in the middle of the tiled floor. Shadow took a towel and cleaned off the inside of the tub with it, then ran a bath. In the main room he took off his clothes and put them on the bed. The bruises on his torso were dark and vivid. He sat in the bath, watching the color of the bathwater change. Then, naked, he washed his socks and briefs and tee shirt in the basin, wrung them out and hung them on the clothesline that pulled out from the wall above the bathtub. He left the cockroach where it was, out of respect for the dead.

Shadow climbed into the bed. He wondered about watching an adult movie, but the pay-per-view device by the phone needed a credit card and it was too risky. Then again, he was not convinced that it would make him feel any better to watch other people have sex that he wasn't having. He turned on the TV for company, pressed the Sleep button on the remote three times, which would make the TV set turn itself off automatically in forty-five minutes, by which time he figured he'd be fast asleep. It was a quarter to midnight.

The picture was motel-fuzzy, and the colors swam across the screen. He flipped from late show to late show in the televisual wasteland, unable to focus. Someone was demonstrating something that did something in the kitchen, and replaced a dozen other kitchen utensils, none of which Shadow possessed. *Flip*. A man in a suit explained that these were the end times and that Jesus – a four or five syllable word the way the man pronounced it – would make Shadow's business prosper and thrive if Shadow sent him money. *Flip*: an episode of *M*A*S*H* ended and a *Dick Van Dyke* episode began.

Shadow hadn't seen an episode of *The Dick Van Dyke Show* for years, but there was something comforting about the 1965 black-and-white world it painted, and he put the channel changer down beside the bed, and turned off the bedside light. He watched the show, eyes slowly closing, aware that something was odd. He had not seen many episodes of *The Dick Van Dyke Show*, so he was not surprised that it was an episode he could not remember seeing before. What he found strange was the tone.

All the regulars were concerned about Rob's drinking: he was missing days at work. They went to his home: he had locked himself in the bedroom, and had to be persuaded to come out: he was staggering drunk, but still pretty funny. His friends, played by Maury Amsterdam and Rose Marie, left after getting some good gags in. Then, when Rob's wife went to remonstrate with him, he hit her, hard, in the face. She sat down on the floor and began to cry, not in that famous Mary Tyler Moore wail, but in small, helpless sobs, hugging herself and whispering, 'Don't hit me, please, I'll do anything, just don't hit me any more.'

'What the fuck is this?' said Shadow, aloud.

The picture dissolved into phosphor-dot fuzz. When it came back, *The Dick Van Dyke Show* had, inexplicably, become *I Love Lucy*. Lucy was trying to persuade Ricky to let her replace their old icebox with a new refrigerator. When he left, however, she walked over to the couch and sat down, crossing her ankles, resting her hands in her lap, and staring out patiently in black and white across the years.

'Shadow?' she said. 'We need to talk.'

Shadow said nothing. She opened her purse and took out a cigarette, lit it with an expensive silver lighter, put the lighter away. 'I'm talking to you,' she said. 'Well?'

'This is crazy,' said Shadow.

'Like the rest of your life is sane? Give me a fucking break.'

'Whatever. Lucille Ball talking to me from the TV is weirder by several orders of magnitude than anything that's happened to me so far,' said Shadow.

'It's not Lucille Ball. It's Lucy Ricardo. And you know something – I'm not even her. It's just an easy way to look, given the context. That's all.' She shifted uncomfortably on the sofa.

'Who are you?' asked Shadow.

'Okay,' she said. 'Good question. I'm the idiot box. I'm the TV. I'm the all-seeing eye and the world of the cathode ray. I'm the boob tube. I'm the little shrine the family gathers to adore.'

'You're the television? Or someone in the television?'

'The TV's the altar. I'm what people are sacrificing to.'

'What do they sacrifice?' asked Shadow.

'Their time, mostly,' said Lucy. 'Sometimes each other.' She raised two fingers, blew imaginary gun smoke from the tips. Then she winked, a big old *I Love Lucy* wink.

'You're a god?' said Shadow.

Lucy smirked, and took a lady-like puff of her cigarette. 'You could say that,' she said.

'Sam says hi,' said Shadow.

'What? Who's Sam? What are you talking about?'

Shadow looked at his watch. It was twenty-five past twelve. 'Doesn't matter,' he said. 'So, Lucy-on-the-TV. What do we need to talk about? Too many people have needed to talk recently. Normally it ends with someone hitting me.'

The camera moved in for a close-up: Lucy looked concerned, her lips pursed. 'I hate that. I hate that people were hurting you, Shadow. I'd never do that, honey. No, I want to offer you a job.'

'Doing what?'

'Working for me. I'm really sorry. I heard about the trouble you had with the Spookshow, and I was impressed with how you dealt with it. Efficient, no-nonsense, effective. Who'd've thought you had it in you? They are really pissed.'

'Really?'

'They underestimated you, sweetheart. Not a mistake I'm going to make. I want you in my camp.' She stood up, walked toward the camera. 'Look at it like this, Shadow: we are the coming thing. We're shopping malls – your friends are crappy roadside attractions. Hell, we're online malls, while your friends are sitting by the side of the highway selling homegrown produce from a garden cart. No – they aren't even fruit sellers. Buggy whip vendors. Whalebone corset repairers. We are now and tomorrow. Your friends aren't even yesterday any more.'

It was a strangely familiar speech. Shadow asked, 'Did you ever meet a fat kid in a limo?'

She spread her hands and rolled her eyes comically, funny Lucy Ricardo washing her hands of a disaster. 'The technical boy? You met the technical boy? Look, he's a good kid. He's one of us. He's just not good with people he doesn't know. When you're working for us, you'll see how amazing he is.'

'And if I don't want to work for you, I-Love-Lucy?'

There was a knock on the door of Lucy's apartment, and Ricky's voice could be heard off-stage, asking Loo-cy what was *keep*in' her so long, they was due down at the club in the next scene; a flash of irritation touched Lucy's cartoonish face. 'Hell,' she said. 'Look, whatever the old guys are paying you, I can pay you double. Treble. A hundred times. Whatever they're giving you, I can give you so much more.' She smiled, a perfect, roguish, Lucy Ricardo smile. 'You name it, honey. What do you need?' She began to undo the buttons of her blouse. 'Hey,' she said. 'You ever wanted to see Lucy's tits?'

The screen went black. The sleep function had kicked in and the set turned itself off. Shadow looked at his watch: it was half past midnight. 'Not really,' said Shadow.

He rolled over in bed and closed his eyes. It occurred to him that the reason he liked Wednesday and Mr Nancy and the rest of them better than their opposition was pretty straight-forward: they might be dirty, and cheap, and their food might taste like shit, but at least they didn't speak in cliches.

And he would take a roadside attraction, no matter how cheap, how crooked, or how sad, over a shopping mall, any day.

***

Morning found Shadow back on the road, driving through a gently undulating brown landscape of winter grass and leafless trees. The last of the snow had vanished. He filled up the tank of the piece of shit in a town which was home to the runner-up of the State Women's Under Sixteens 300 meter dash, and, hoping that the dirt wasn't all that was holding it together, he ran the car through the gas station car wash, and was surprised to discover that the car was, when clean, against all reason, white, and pretty much free of rust. He drove on.

The sky was impossibly blue, and white industrial smoke rising from factory chimneys was frozen in the sky, like a photograph. A hawk launched itself from a dead tree and flew toward him, wings strobing in the sunlight like a series of stop-motion photographs.

At some point he found himself, somewhat to his surprise, heading into East St Louis. He attempted to avoid it and instead found himself driving through what appeared to be a red light district in an industrial park. Eighteen wheelers and huge rigs were parked outside buildings that looked like temporary warehouses, that claimed to be *24 Hour Nite Clubs* and, in one case, *The Best Peap Show in Town*. Shadow shook his head, and drove on. Laura had loved to dance, clothed or naked (and, on several memorable evenings, moving from one state to the other), and he had loved to watch her.

Lunch was a sandwich and a can of Coke in a town called Red Bud.

He passed a valley filled with the wreckage of thousands of yellow bulldozers, tractors and Caterpillars. He wondered if this was the bulldozers' graveyard, where the bulldozers went to die.

He drove past the Pop-a-Top Lounge. He drove through Chester ('Home of Popeye'). He noticed that the houses had started to gain pillars out front, that even the shabbiest, thinnest house now had its white pillars, proclaiming it, in someone's eyes, a mansion. He drove over a big, muddy river, and laughed out loud when he saw that the name of it, according to the sign, was the Big Muddy River. He saw a covering of brown kudzu over three winter-dead trees, twisting them into strange, almost human shapes: they could have been witches, three bent old crones ready to reveal his fortune.

He drove alongside the Mississippi. Shadow had never seen the Nile, but there was a blinding afternoon sun burning on the wide brown river which made him think of the muddy expanse of the Nile: not the Nile as it is now, but as it was long ago, flowing like an artery through the papyrus marshes, home to cobra and jackal and wild cow . . .

A road sign pointed to Thebes.

The road was built up about twelve feet, so he was driving above the marshes. Clumps and clusters of birds in flight were questing back and forth, black dots against the blue sky, moving in some kind of desperate Brownian motion.

In the late afternoon the sun began to lower, gilding the world in elf-light, a thick warm custardy light that made the world feel unearthly and more than real, and it was in this light that Shadow passed the sign telling him he was Now Entering Historical Cairo. He drove under a bridge and found himself in a small, port town. The imposing structure of the Cairo court house and the even more imposing Customs House looked like enormous freshly-baked cookies in the syrupy gold of the light at the end of the day.

He parked his car in a side street and walked to the embankment at the edge of a river, unsure whether he was gazing at the Ohio or the Mississippi. A small brown cat nosed and sprang among the trash cans at the back of a building, and the light made even the garbage magical.

A lone seagull was gliding along the river's edge, flipping a wing to correct itself as it went.

Shadow realized that he was not alone. A small girl, wearing old tennis shoes on her feet and a man's gray woolen sweater as a dress, was standing on the sidewalk, ten feet away from him, staring at him with the somber gravity of a six year old. Her hair was black, and straight, and long; her skin was as brown as the river.

He grinned at her. She stared back at him, defiantly.

There was a squeal and a yowl from the waterfront, and the little brown cat shot away from a spilled garbage can, pursued by a long-muzzled black dog. The cat scurried under a car.

'Hey,' said Shadow to the girl. 'You ever seen invisible powder before?'

She hesitated. Then she shook her head.

'Okay,' said Shadow. 'Well, watch this.' Shadow pulled out a quarter with his left hand, held it up, tilting it from one side to another, then appeared to toss it into his right hand, closing his hand hard on nothing, and putting the hand forward. 'Now,' he said, 'I just take some invisible powder from my pocket . . .' and he reached his left hand into his breast pocket, dropping the quarter into the pocket as he did so, '. . . and I sprinkle it on the hand with the coin . . .' and he mimed sprinkling, '. . . and look – now the quarter's invisible too.' He opened his empty right hand, and, in astonishment, his empty left hand as well.

The little girl just stared.

Shadow shrugged and put his hands back in his pockets, loading a quarter in one hand, a folded up five dollar bill in the other. He was going to produce them from the air, and then give the girl the five bucks: she looked like she needed it. 'Hey,' he said, 'We've got an audience.'

The black dog and the little brown cat were watching him as well, flanking the girl, looking up at him intently. The dog's huge ears were pricked up, giving it a comically alert expression. A crane-like man with gold-rimmed spectacles was coming up the sidewalk toward them, peering from side

to side as if he were looking for something. Shadow
wondered if he was the dog's owner.

'What did you think?' Shadow asked the dog, trying to put
the little girl at her ease. 'Was that cool?'

The black dog licked its long snout. Then it said, in a deep,
dry voice, 'I saw Harry Houdini once, and believe me, man,
you are no Harry Houdini.'

The little girl looked at the animals, she looked up at
Shadow, and then she ran off, her feet pounding the
sidewalk as if all the powers of hell were after her. The two
animals watched her go. The crane-like man had reached the
dog. He reached down and scratched its high, pointed ears.

'Come on,' said the man in the gold-rimmed spectacles to
the dog, 'It was only a coin trick. It's not like he was doing an
underwater escape.'

'Not yet,' said the dog. 'But he will.' The golden light was
done, and the gray of twilight had begun.

Shadow dropped the coin and the folded bill back into his
pocket. 'Okay,' he said. 'Which one of you is Jackal?'

'Use your eyes,' said the black dog with the long snout.
'This way.' It began to amble along the sidewalk, beside the
man in the gold-rimmed glasses, and, after a moment's
hesitation, Shadow followed them. The cat was nowhere to
be seen. They reached a large old building on a row of
boarded-up houses.

The sign beside the door said *Ibis and Jacquel. A family
firm. Funeral Parlor. Since 1863.*

'I'm Mister Ibis,' said the man in the gold-rimmed glasses.
'I think I should buy you a spot of supper. I'm afraid my
friend here has some work that needs doing.'

Somewhere in America

New York scares Salim, and so he clutches his sample case protectively with both hands, holding it to his chest. He is scared of black people, the way they stare at him, and he is scared of the Jews, the ones dressed all in black with hats and beards and side curls he can identify and how many others that he cannot?; he is scared of the sheer quantity of the people, all shapes and sizes of people, as they spill from their high, high, filthy buildings, onto the sidewalks; he is scared of the honking hullabaloo of the traffic, and he is even scared of the air, which smells both dirty and sweet, and nothing at all like the air of Oman.

Salim has been in New York, in America, for a week. Each day he visits two, perhaps three different offices, opens his sample case, shows them the copper trinkets, the rings and bottles and tiny flashlights, the models of the Empire State Building, the Statue of Liberty, the Eiffel Tower, gleaming in copper inside; each night he writes a fax to his brother-in-law, Fuad, at home in Muscat, telling him that he has taken no orders, or, on one happy day, that he had taken several orders (but, as Salim is painfully aware, not yet enough even to cover his airfare and hotel bill).

For reasons Salim does not understand, his brother-in-law's business partners have booked him into the Paramount Hotel on 46th Street. He finds it confusing, claustrophobic, expensive, alien.

Fuad is Salim's sister's husband. He is not a rich man, but he is the co-owner of a small trinket factory, making knick-knacks from copper, brooches and rings and bracelets and statues. Everything is made for export, to other Arab countries, to Europe, to America.

Salim has been working for Fuad for six months. Fuad scares him a little. The tone of Fuad's faxes is becoming harsher. In the evening, Salim sits in his hotel room, reading his Qur'an, telling himself that this will pass, that his stay in this strange world is limited and finite.

His brother in law gave him a thousand dollars for miscellaneous traveling expenses and the money, which seemed so huge a sum when first he saw it, is evaporating faster than Salim can believe. When he first arrived, scared of being seen as a cheap Arab, he tipped everyone, handing extra dollar bills to everyone he encountered; and then he decided that he was being taken advantage of, that perhaps they were even laughing at him, and he stopped tipping entirely.

On his first and only journey by subway he got lost and confused, and missed his appointment; now he takes taxis only when he has to, and the rest of the time he walks. He stumbles into overheated offices, his cheeks numb from the cold outside, sweating beneath his coat, shoes soaked by slush; and when the winds blow down the avenues (which run from north to south, as the streets run west to east, all so simple, and Salim always knows where to face Mecca) he feels a cold on his exposed skin that is so intense it is like being struck.

He never eats at the hotel (for while the hotel bill is being covered by Fuad's business partners, he must pay for his own food); instead he buys food at falafel houses and at little food stores, smuggles it up to the room beneath his coat for days before he realizes that no one cares. And even then he feels strange about carrying the bags of food into the dimly-lit elevators (Salim always has to bend and squint to find the button to press to take him to his floor) and up to the tiny white room in which he stays.

Salim is upset. The fax that was waiting for him when he woke this morning was curt, and alternately chiding, stern, and disappointed: Salim was letting them down – his sister, Fuad, Fuad's business partners, the Sultanate of Oman, the whole Arab world. Unless he was able to get the orders, Fuad would no longer consider it his obligation to employ Salim. They depended upon him. His hotel was too expensive. What was Salim doing with their money, living like a sultan in America? Salim read the fax in his room (which has always been too hot and stifling, so last night he opened a window, and was now too cold) and sat there for a time, his face frozen into an expression of complete misery.

Then Salim walks downtown, holding his sample case as if it contained diamonds and rubies, trudging through the cold for block after block until, on Broadway and 19th Street, he finds a squat building over a laundromat and walks up the stairs to the fourth floor, to the office of Panglobal Imports.

The office is dingy, but he knows that Panglobal handles almost half of the ornamental souvenirs that enter the US from the Far East. A real order, a significant order from Panglobal could redeem Salim's journey, could make the difference between failure and success, so Salim sits on an uncomfortable wooden chair in an outer office, his sample case balanced on his lap, staring at the middle-aged woman with her hair dyed too bright a red who sits behind the desk, blowing her nose on Kleenex after Kleenex. After she blows her nose she wipes it, and drops the Kleenex into the trash.

Salim got there at 10:30 a.m., half an hour before his appointment. Now he sits there, flushed and shivering, wondering if he is running a fever. The time ticks by so slowly.

Salim looks at his watch. Then he clears his throat.

The woman behind the desk glares at him. 'Yes?' she says. It sounds like *Yed*.

'It is 11:35,' says Salim.

The woman glances at the clock on the wall, and says 'Yed,' again. *Id id*.

'My appointment was for eleven,' says Salim with a placating smile.

'Mister Blanding knows you're here,' she tells him, reprovingly. *Bidter Bladdig dode you're here*.

Salim picks up an old copy of the *New York Post* from the table. He speaks English better than he reads it, and he puzzles his way through the stories like a man doing a crossword puzzle. He waits, a plump young man with the eyes of a hurt puppy, glancing from his watch to his newspaper to the clock on the wall.

At twelve-thirty several men come out from the inner office. They talk loudly, jabbering away to each other in American. One of them, a big, paunchy man, has a cigar, unlit, in his mouth. He glances at Salim as he comes out. He tells the woman behind the desk to try the juice of a lemon, and zinc, as his sister swears by zinc, and vitamin C. She promises him that she will, and gives him several envelopes. He pockets them and then he, and the other men, go out into the hall. The sound of their laughter disappears down the stairwell.

It is one o'clock. The woman behind the desk opens a drawer and takes out a brown paper bag, from which she removes several sandwiches, an apple, and a Milky Way. She also takes out a small plastic bottle of freshly-squeezed orange juice.

'Excuse me,' says Salim, 'but can you perhaps call Mister Blanding and tell him that I am still waiting?'

She looks up at him as if surprised to see that he is still there, as if they have not been sitting five feet apart for two and a half hours. 'He's at lunch,' she says. *He'd ad dudge*.

Salim knows, knows deep down in his gut that Blanding was the man with the unlit cigar. 'When will he be back?'

She shrugs, takes a bite of her sandwich. 'He's busy with

appointments for the rest of the day.' she says. *He'd biddy wid abboidmeds for the red ob the day.*

'Will he see me, then, when he comes back?' asks Salim.

She shrugs, and blows her nose.

Salim is hungry, increasingly so, and frustrated, and powerless.

At three o'clock the woman looks at him and says 'He wode be gubbig bag.'

'Excuse?'

'Bidder Bladdig. He wode be gubbig bag today.'

'Can I make an appointment for tomorrow?'

She wipes her nose. 'You hab to teddephode. Appoidbeds odly by teddephode.'

'I see,' says Salim. And then he smiles: a salesman, Fuad had told him many times before he left Muscat, is naked in America without his smile. 'Tomorrow I will telephone,' he says. He takes his sample case, and he walks down the many stairs to the street, where the freezing rain is turning to sleet. Salim contemplates the long, cold walk back to the 46th Street hotel, and the weight of the sample case, then he steps to the edge of the sidewalk and waves at every yellow cab that approaches, whether the light on top is on or off, and every cab drives past him.

One of them accelerates as it passes; a wheel dives into a water-filled pothole, spraying freezing muddy water over Salim's pants and coat. For a moment, he contemplates throwing himself in front of one of the lumbering cars, and then he realizes that his brother-in-law would be more concerned with the fate of the sample case than of Salim himself, and that he would bring grief to no one but his beloved sister, Fuad's wife (for he had always been a slight embarrassment to his father and mother, and his romantic encounters had always, of necessity, been both brief and relatively anonymous): also, he doubts that any of the cars is going fast enough actually to end his life.

A battered yellow taxi draws up beside him and, grateful

to be able to abandon his train of thought, Salim gets in.

The backseat is patched with gray duct tape; the half-open Plexiglas barrier is covered with notices warning him not to smoke, telling him how much to pay to the various airports. The recorded voice of somebody famous he has never heard of tells him to remember to wear his seatbelt.

'The Paramount Hotel, please,' says Salim.

The cab driver grunts, and pulls away from the curb, into the traffic. He is unshaven, and he wears a thick, dust-colored sweater, and black plastic sunglasses. The weather is gray, and night is falling: Salim wonders if the man has a problem with his eyes. The wipers smear the street scene into grays and smudged lights.

From nowhere, a truck pulls out in front of them, and the cab drivers swears in Arabic, by the beard of the prophet.

Salim stares at the name on the dashboard, but he cannot make it out from here. 'How long have you been driving a cab, my friend?' he asks the man, in Arabic.

'Ten years,' says the driver, in the same language. 'Where are you from?'

'Muscat,' says Salim. 'In Oman.'

'From Oman. I have been in Oman. It was a long time ago. Have you heard of the City of Ubar?' asks the taxi driver.

'Indeed I have,' says Salim. 'The Lost City of Towers. They found it in the desert five, ten years ago, I do not remember exactly. Were you with the expedition that excavated it?'

'Something like that. It was a good city,' says the taxi driver. 'On most nights there would be three, maybe four thousand people camped there: every traveler would rest at Ubar, and the music would play, and the wine would flow like water and the water would flow as well, which was why the city existed.'

'That is what I have heard,' says Salim. 'And it perished, what, a thousand years ago? Two thousand?'

The taxi driver says nothing. They are stopped at a red traffic light. The light turns green, but the taxi driver does not move, despite the immediate discordant blare of horns behind them. Hesitantly, Salim reaches through the hole in the Plexiglas and he touches the driver on the shoulder. The man's head jerks up, with a start, and he puts his foot down on the gas, lurching them across the intersection.

'Fuckshitfuckfuck,' he says, in English.

'You must be very tired, my friend,' says Salim.

'I have been driving this Allah-forgotten taxi for thirty hours,' says the driver. 'It is too much. Before that, I sleep for five hours, and I drove fourteen hours before that. We are shorthanded, before Christmas.'

'I hope you have made a lot of money,' says Salim.

The driver sighs. 'Not much. This morning I drove a man from 51st Street to Newark Airport. When we got there, he ran off into the airport, and I could not find him again. A fifty dollar fare gone, and I had to pay the tolls on the way back myself.'

Salim nods. 'I had to spend today waiting to see a man who will not see me. My brother-in-law hates me. I have been in America for a week, and it has done nothing but eat my money. I sell nothing.'

'What do you sell?'

'Shit,' says Salim. 'Worthless gewgaws and baubles and tourist trinkets. Horrible, cheap, foolish, ugly shit.'

The taxi driver wrenches the wheel to the right, swings around something, drives on. Salim wonders how he can see to drive, between the rain, the night, and the thick sunglasses.

'You try to sell shit?'

'Yes,' says Salim, thrilled and horrified that he has spoken the truth about his brother-in-law's samples.

'And they will not buy it?'

'No.'

'Strange. You look at the stores here, that is all they sell.'

Salim smiles nervously.

A truck is blocking the street in front of them: a red-faced cop standing in front of it waves and shouts and points them down the nearest street.

'We will go over to Eighth Avenue, come uptown that way,' says the taxi driver. They turn onto the street, where the traffic has stopped completely. There is a cacophony of horns, but the cars do not move.

The driver sways in his seat. His chin begins to descend to his chest, one, two, three times. Then he begins, gently, to snore. Salim reaches out to wake the man, hoping that he is doing the right thing. As he shakes his shoulder the driver moves, and Salim's hand brushes the man's face, knocking the man's sunglasses from his face onto his lap.

The taxi driver opens his eyes and reaches for, and replaces, the black plastic sunglasses, but it is too late. Salim has seen his eyes.

The car crawls forward in the rain. The numbers on the meter increase.

'Are you going to kill me?' asks Salim.

The taxi driver's lips are pressed together. Salim watches his face in the driver's mirror.

'No,' says the driver, very quietly.

The car stops again. The rain patters on the roof.

Salim begins to speak. 'My grandmother swore that she had seen an ifrit, or perhaps a marid, late one evening, on the edge of the desert. We told her that it was just a sandstorm, a little wind, but she said no, she saw its face, and its eyes, like yours, were burning flames.'

The driver smiles, but his eyes are hidden behind the black plastic glasses, and Salim cannot tell whether there is any humor in that smile or not. 'The grandmothers came here too,' he says.

'Are there many jinn in New York?' asks Salim.

'No. Not many of us.'

'There are the angels, and there are men, who Allah made from mud, and then there are the people of the fire, the jinn,' says Salim.

'People know nothing about my people here,' says the driver. 'They think we grant wishes. If I could grant wishes do you think I would be driving a cab?'

'I do not understand.'

The taxi driver seems gloomy. Salim watches his face in the mirror as he speaks, staring at the ifrit's dark lips.

'They believe that we grant wishes. Why do they believe that? I sleep in one stinking room in Brooklyn. I drive this taxi for any stinking freak who has the money to ride in it, and for some who don't. I drive them where they need to go, and sometimes they tip me. Sometimes they pay me.' His lower lip began to tremble. The ifrit seemed on edge. 'One of them shat on the back seat once. I had to clean it before I could take the cab back. How could he do that? I had to clean the wet shit from the seat. Is that right?'

Salim puts out a hand, pats the ifrit's shoulder. He can feel solid flesh through the wool of the sweater. The ifrit raises his hand from the wheel, rests it on Salim's hand for a moment.

Salim thinks of the desert then: red sands blow a duststorm through his thoughts, and the scarlet silks of the tents that surrounded the lost city of Ubar flap and billow through his mind.

They drive up Eighth Avenue.

'The old believe. They do not piss into holes, because the Prophet told them that jinn live in holes. They know that the angels throw flaming stars at us when we try to listen to their conversations. But even for the old, when they come to this country we are very, very far away. Back there, I did not have to drive a cab.'

'I am sorry,' says Salim.

'It is a bad time,' says the driver. 'A storm is coming. It scares me. I would do anything to get away.'

The two of them say nothing more on their way back to the hotel.

When Salim gets out of the cab he gives the ifrit a twenty

dollar bill, tells him to keep the change. Then, with a sudden burst of courage, he tells him his room number. The taxi driver says nothing in reply. A young woman clambers into the back of the cab, and it pulls out into the cold and the rain.

Six o'clock in the evening. Salim has not yet written the fax to his brother-in-law. He goes out into the rain, buys himself this night's kebab and french fries. It has only been a week, but he feels that he is becoming heavier, rounder, softening in this country of New York.

When he comes back to the hotel he is surprised to see the taxi driver standing in the lobby, hands deep into his pockets. He is staring at a display of black-and-white postcards. When he sees Salim he smiles, self-consciously. 'I called your room,' he says, 'but there was no answer. So I thought I would wait.'

Salim smiles also, and touches the man's arm. 'I am here,' he says.

Together they enter the dim, green-lit elevator, ascend to the fifth floor holding hands. The ifrit asks if he may use Salim's bathroom. 'I feel very dirty,' he says. Salim nods. He sits on the bed, which fills most of the small white room and listens to the sound of the shower running. Salim takes off his shoes, his socks, and then the rest of his clothes.

The taxi driver comes out of the shower, wet, with a towel wrapped about his mid-section. He is not wearing his sunglasses, and in the dim room his eyes burn with scarlet flames.

Salim blinks back tears. 'I wish you could see what I see,' he says.

'I do not grant wishes,' whispers the ifrit, dropping his towel and pushing Salim gently, but irresistibly, down onto the bed.

It is an hour or more before the ifrit comes, thrusting and grinding into Salim's mouth. Salim has already come twice in this time. The jinn's semen tastes strange, fiery, and it burns Salim's throat.

Salim goes to the bathroom, washes out his mouth. When he returns to the bedroom the taxi-driver is already asleep in the white bed, snoring peacefully. Salim climbs into the bed beside him, cuddles close to the ifrit, imagining the desert on his skin.

As he starts to fall asleep he realizes that he still has not written his fax to Fuad, and he feels guilty. Deep inside he feels empty and alone: he reaches out, rests his hand on the ifrit's tumescent cock and, comforted, he sleeps.

They wake in the small hours, moving against each other, and they make love again. At one point Salim realizes that he is crying, and the ifrit is kissing away his tears with burning lips. 'What is your name?' Salim asks the taxi driver.

'There is a name on my driving permit, but it is not mine,' the ifrit says.

Afterward, Salim could not remember where the sex had stopped and the dreams began.

When Salim wakes, the cold sun creeping into the white room, he is alone.

Also, he discovers, his sample case is gone, all the bottles and rings and souvenir copper flashlights, all gone, along with his suitcase, his wallet, his passport, and his air tickets back to Oman.

He finds a pair of jeans, the tee shirt, and the dust-colored woolen sweater discarded on the floor. Beneath them he finds a driver's license in the name of Ibrahim bin Irem, a taxi permit in the same name, and a ring of keys with an address written on a piece of paper attached to them in English. The photographs on the license and the permit ID do not look much like Salim, but then, they did not look much like the ifrit.

The telephone rings: it is the front desk calling to point out that Salim has already checked out, and his guest needs to leave soon so that they can service the room, to get it ready for another occupant.

'I do not grant wishes,' says Salim, tasting the way the

words shape themselves in his mouth.

He feels strangely light-headed as he dresses.

New York is very simple: the avenues run north to south, the streets run west to east. How hard can it be? he asks himself.

He tosses the car keys into the air and catches them. Then he puts on the black plastic sunglasses he found in a pocket of the jeans, and leaves the hotel room to go and look for his cab.

Chapter Eight

He said the dead had souls, but when I asked him
How that could be – I thought the dead were souls,
He broke my trance. Don't that make you suspicious
That there's something the dead are keeping back?
Yes, there's something the dead are keeping back.
                              – Robert Frost, *Two Witches*

The week before Christmas is often a quiet one in a funeral parlor, Shadow learned, over supper. Mr Ibis explained it to him. 'The lingering ones are holding on for one final Christmas,' said Mr Ibis, 'or even for New Year's, while the others, the ones for whom other people's jollity and celebration will prove too painful, have not yet been tipped over the edge by that last showing of *It's a Wonderful Life*, have not quite encountered the final straw, or should I say, the final *sprig of holly* that breaks not the camel's but the *reindeer's* back.' And he made a little noise as he said it, half smirk, half snort, which suggested that he had just uttered a well-honed phrase of which he was particularly fond.

Ibis and Jacquel was a small, family-owned funeral home:

one of the last truly independent funeral homes in the area, or so Mr Ibis maintained. 'Most fields of human merchandising value nationwide brand identities,' he said. Mr Ibis spoke in explanations: a gentle, earnest lecturing that put Shadow in mind of a college professor who used to work out at the Muscle Farm and who could not talk, could only discourse, expound, explain. Shadow had figured out within the first few minutes of meeting Mr Ibis that his expected part in any conversation with the funeral director was to say as little as possible. They were sitting in a small restaurant, two blocks from Ibis and Jacquel's Funeral Home. Shadow's supper consisted of an all-day full breakfast – it came with hush puppies – while Mr Ibis picked and pecked at a slice of coffee cake. 'This, I believe, is because people like to know what they are getting ahead of time. Thus McDonald's, Wal-Mart, F.W. Woolworth (of blessed memory): store-brands maintained and visible across the entire country. Wherever you go, you will get something that is, with small regional variations, the same.

'In the field of funeral homes, however, things are, perforce, different. You need to feel that you are getting small-town personal service from someone who has a calling to the profession. You want personal attention to you and your loved one in a time of great loss. You wish to know that your grief is happening on a local level, not on a national one. But in all branches of industry – and death is an industry, my young friend, make no mistake about that, – one makes one's money from operating in bulk, from buying in quantity, from centralizing one's operations. It's not pretty, but it's true. Trouble is, no one wants to know that their loved ones are traveling in a cooler-van to some big old converted warehouse where they may have twenty, fifty, a hundred cadavers on the go. No, sir. Folks want to think they're going to a family concern, somewhere they'll be treated with respect by someone who'll tip his hat to them if he sees them in the street.'

Mr Ibis wore a hat. It was a sober brown hat that matched his sober brown blazer and his sober brown face. Small gold-rimmed glasses perched on his nose. In Shadow's memory Mr Ibis was a short man; whenever he would stand beside him, Shadow would rediscover that Mr Ibis was well over six feet in height, with a crane-like stoop. Sitting opposite him now, across the shiny red table, Shadow found himself staring at the man's face.

'So when the big companies come in they buy the name of the company, they pay the funeral directors to stay on, they create the apparency of diversity. But that is merely the tip of the gravestone. In reality, they are as local as Burger King. Now, for our own reasons, we are truly an independent. We do all our own embalming, and it's the finest embalming in the country, although nobody knows it but us. We don't do cremations, though. We could make more money if we had our own cromatorium, but it goes against what we're good at. What my business partner says is, if the Lord gives you a talent or a skill, you have an obligation to use it as best you can. Don't you agree?'

'Sounds good to me,' said Shadow.

'The Lord gave my business partner dominion over the dead, just as he gave me skill with words. Fine things, words. I write books of tales, you know. Nothing literary. Just for my own amusement. Accounts of lives.' He paused. By the time Shadow realized that he should have asked if he might be allowed to read one, the moment had passed. 'Anyway, what we give them here is continuity: there's been an Ibis and Jacquel in business here for almost two hundred years. We weren't always funeral directors, though. We used to be morticians, and before that, undertakers.'

'And before that?'

'Well,' said Mr Ibis, smiling just a little smugly, 'we go back a very long way. Of course, it wasn't until after the war between the states that we found our niche here. That was when we became the funeral parlor for the colored folks hereabouts. Before that no one thought of us as colored – foreign maybe, exotic and dark, but not colored. Once the war was done, pretty soon, no one could remember a time when we weren't perceived as black. My business partner, he's always had darker skin than mine. It was an easy transition. Mostly you are what they think you are. It's just strange when they talk about African-Americans. Makes me think of the people from Punt, Ophir, Nubia. We never thought of ourselves as Africans – we were the people of the Nile.'

'So you were Egyptians,' said Shadow.

Mr Ibis pushed his lower lip upward, then let his head bob from side to side, as if it were on a spring, weighing the pluses and minuses, seeing things from both points of view. 'Well, yes and no. Egyptians makes me think of the folk who live there now. The ones who built their cities over our graveyards and palaces. Do they look like me?'

Shadow shrugged. He'd seen black guys who looked like Mr Ibis. He'd seen white guys with tans who looked like Mr Ibis.

'How's your coffee-cake?' asked the waitress, refilling their coffees.

'Best I ever had,' said Mr Ibis. 'You give my best to your ma.'

'I'll do that,' she said, and bustled away.

'You don't want to ask after the health of anyone, if you're a funeral director. They think maybe you're scouting for business,' said Mr Ibis, in an undertone. 'Shall we see if your room is ready?'

Their breath steamed in the night air. Christmas lights twinkled in the windows of the stores they passed. 'It's good of you, putting me up,' said Shadow. 'I appreciate it.'

'We owe your employer a number of favors. And Lord knows, we have the room. It's a big old house. There used to be more of us, you know. Now it's just the three of us. You won't be in the way.'

'Any idea how long I'm meant to stay with you?'

Mr Ibis shook his head. 'He didn't say. But we are happy to have you here, and we can find you work. If you are not squeamish. If you treat the dead with respect.'

'So,' asked Shadow, 'what are you people doing here in Cairo? Was it just the name or something?'

'No. Not at all. Actually this region takes its names from us, although people barely know it. It was a trading post back in the old days.'

'Frontier times?'

'You might call it that,' said Mr Ibis. '*Evening Mizz Simmons! And a Merry Christmas to you too!* The folk who brought me here came up the Mississippi a long time back.'

Shadow stopped in the street, and stared. 'Are you trying to tell me that ancient Egyptians came here to trade five thousand years ago?'

Mr Ibis said nothing, but he smirked loudly. Then he said, 'Three thousand five hundred and thirty years ago. Give or take.'

'Okay,' said Shadow. 'I'll buy it, I guess. What were they trading?'

'Not much,' said Mr Ibis. 'Animal skins. Some food. Copper from the mines in the upper peninsula. The whole thing was rather a disappointment. Not worth the effort. They stayed here long enough to believe in us, to sacrifice to us, and for a handful of the traders to die of fever and be buried here, leaving us behind them.' He stopped dead in the middle of the sidewalk, turned around slowly, arms extended. 'This country has been Grand Central Station for ten thousand years or more. You say to me, what about Columbus?'

'Sure,' said Shadow, obligingly. 'What about him?'

'Columbus did what people had been doing for thousands of years. There's nothing special about coming to America. I've been writing stories about it, from time to time.' They began to walk again.

'True stories?'

'Up to a point, yes. I'll let you read one or two, if you like. It's all there for anyone who has eyes to see it. Personally – and this is speaking as a subscriber to *Scientific American*, here – I feel very sorry for the professionals whenever they find another confusing skull, something that belonged to the wrong sort of people, or whenever they find statues or artifacts that confuse them – for they'll talk about the odd, but they won't talk about the impossible, which is where I feel sorry for them, for as soon as something becomes impossible it slipslides out of belief entirely, whether it's true or not. I mean, here's a skúll that shows the Ainu, the Japanese aboriginal race, were in America nine thousand years ago. Here's another that shows there were Polynesians in California nearly two thousand years later. And all the scientists mutter and puzzle over who's descended from whom, missing the point entirely. Heaven knows what'll happen if they ever actually find the Hopi emergence tunnels. That'll shake a few things up, you just wait.

'Did the Irish come to America in the dark ages, you ask me? Of course they did, and the Welsh, and the Vikings, while the Africans from the West Coast, – what in later days they called the slave coast or the ivory coast – they were trading with South America, and the Chinese visited Oregon a couple of times – they called it Fu Sang. The Basque established their secret sacred fishing grounds off the coast of Newfoundland twelve hundred years back. Now, I suppose you're going to say, but Mister Ibis, these people were primitives, they didn't have radio controls and vitamin pills and jet airplanes.'

Shadow hadn't said anything, and hadn't planned to say anything, but he felt it was required of him, so he said, 'Well, weren't they?' The last dead leaves of the autumn crackled underfoot, winter-crisp.

'The misconception is that men didn't travel long distances in boats before the days of Columbus. Yet New

Zealand and Tahiti and countless Pacific Islands were settled by people in boats whose navigation skills would have put Columbus to shame; and the wealth of Africa was from trading, although that was mostly to the East, to India and China. My people, the Nile folk, we discovered early on that a reed boat will take you around the world, if you have the patience and enough jars of sweet water. You see, the biggest problem with coming to America in the old days was that there wasn't a lot here that anyone wanted to trade, and it was much too far away.'

They had reached a large house, built in the style people called Queen Anne. Shadow wondered who Queen Anne was, and why she had been so fond of Addams-Family-style-houses. It was the only building on the block that wasn't locked up with boarded-over windows. They went through the gate and walked around the back of the building.

Through large double doors, which Mr Ibis unlocked with a key from his keychain, and they were in a large, unheated room, occupied by two people. They were a very tall, dark-skinned man, holding a large metal scalpel, and a dead girl in her late teens, lying on a long, porcelain object that resembled both a table and a sink.

There were several photographs of the dead girl pinned up on a corkboard on the wall above the body. She was smiling in one, a high school head shot. In another she was standing in a line with three other girls; they were wearing what might have been prom dresses, and her black hair was tied above her head in an intricate knotwork.

Cold on the porcelain, her hair was down, loose around her shoulders, and matted with dried blood.

'This is my partner, Mister Jacquel,' said Ibis.

'We met already,' said Jacquel. 'Forgive me if I don't shake hands.'

Shadow looked down at the girl on the table. 'What happened to her?' he asked.

'Poor taste in boyfriends,' said Jacquel.

'It's not always fatal,' said Mr Ibis, with a sigh. 'This time it was. He was drunk, and he had a knife, and she told him that she thought she was pregnant. He didn't believe it was his.'

'She was stabbed . . .' said Mr Jacquel, and he counted. There was a click as he stepped on a footswitch, turning on a small Dictaphone on a nearby table, 'five times. There are three knife wounds in the left anterior chest wall. The first is between the fourth and fifth intercostal spaces at the medial border of the left breast, two point two centimeters in length; the second and third are through the inferior portion of the left mid-breast penetrating at the sixth interspace, overlapping, and measuring three centimeters. There is one wound two centimeters long in the upper anterior left chest in the second interspace, and one wound five centimeters long and a maximum of one point six centimeters deep in the anteromedial left deltoid, a slashing injury. All the chest wounds are deep penetrating injuries. There are no other visible wounds externally.' He released pressure from the foot switch. Shadow noticed a small microphone dangling above the embalming table by its cord.

'So you're the coroner as well?' asked Shadow.

'Coroner's a political appointment around here,' said Ibis. 'His job is to kick the corpse. If it doesn't kick him back, he signs the death certificate. Jacquel's what they call a prosector. He works for the county Medical Examiner. He does autopsies, and saves tissue samples for analysis. He's already photographed her wounds.'

Jacquel ignored them. He took a big scalpel and made a deep incision in a large V which began at both collarbones and met at the bottom of her breastbone, and then he turned the V into a Y, another deep incision that continued from her breastbone to her pubis. He picked up what looked like a small, heavy chrome drill with a medallion-sized round saw blade at the business end. He turned it on, and cut through the ribs at both sides of her breastbone.

The girl opened like a purse.

Shadow suddenly was aware of a mild but unpleasantly penetrating, pungent, meaty smell.

'I thought it would smell worse,' said Shadow.

'She's pretty fresh,' said Jacquel. 'And the intestines weren't pierced, so it doesn't smell of shit.'

Shadow found himself looking away, not from revulsion, as he would have expected, but from a strange desire to give the girl some privacy. It would be hard to be nakeder than this open thing.

Jacquel tied off the intestines, glistening and snakelike in her belly, above the stomach and deep in the pelvis. He ran them through his fingers, foot after foot of them, described them as 'normal' to the microphone, put them in a bucket on the floor. He sucked all the blood out of her chest with a vacuum pump, and measured the volume. Then he inspected the inside of her chest. He said to the microphone, 'There are three lacerations in the pericardium, which is filled with clotted and liquefying blood.'

Jacquel grasped her heart, cut it at its top, turned it about in his hand, examining it. He stepped on his switch and said, 'There are two lacerations of the myocardium; a one point five centimeter laceration in the right ventricle and a one point eight centimeter laceration penetrating the left ventricle.'

Jacquel removed each lung. The left lung had been stabbed and was half collapsed. He weighed them, and the heart, and he photographed the wounds. From each lung he sliced a small piece of tissue, which he placed into a jar.

'Formaldehyde,' whispered Mr Ibis, helpfully.

Jacquel continued to talk to the microphone, describing what he was doing, what he saw, as he removed the girl's liver, the stomach, spleen, pancreas, both kidneys, the uterus and the ovaries.

He weighed each organ, reported them as normal and uninjured. From each organ he took a small slice and put it into a jar of formaldehyde.

From the heart, the liver, and from one of the kidneys, he cut an additional slice. These pieces he chewed, slowly, making them last, and ate while he worked.

Somehow it seemed to Shadow a good thing for him to do: respectful, not obscene.

'So you want to stay here with us for a spell?' said Jacquel, masticating the slice of the girl's heart.

'If you'll have me,' said Shadow.

'Certainly we'll have you,' said Mr Ibis. 'No reasons why not and plenty of reasons why. You'll be under our protection as long as you're here.'

'I hope you don't mind sleeping under the same roof as the dead,' said Jacquel

Shadow thought of the touch of Laura's lips, bitter and cold. 'No,' he said. 'Not as long as they stay dead, anyhow.'

Jacquel turned and looked at him with dark brown eyes as quizzical and cold as a desert dog's. 'They stay dead here,' was all he said.

'Seems to me,' said Shadow. 'Seems to me that the dead come back pretty easy.'

'Not at all,' said Ibis. 'Even zombies, they make them out of the living, you know. A little powder, a little chanting, a little push, and you have a zombie. They live, but they believe they are dead. But to truly bring the dead back to life, in their bodies. That takes power.' He hesitates, then, 'In the old land, in the old days, it was easier then.'

'You could bind the *ka* of a man to his body for five thousand years,' said Jacquel. 'Binding or loosing. But that was a long time ago.' He took all the organs that he had removed and replaced them, respectfully, in the body cavity. He replaced the intestines and the breastbone and pulled the skin edges near each other. Then he took a thick needle and thread and, with deft, quick strokes, he sewed it up, like a man stitching a baseball: the cadaver transformed from meat into girl once again.

'I need a beer,' said Jacquel. He pulled off his rubber gloves and dropped them into the bin. He dropped his dark brown overalls into a hamper. Then he took the cardboard tray of jars filled with little red and brown and purple slices of the organs. 'Coming?'

They walked up the back stairs to the kitchen. It was brown and white, a sober and respectable room that looked to Shadow as if it had last been decorated in 1920. There was a huge Kelvinator rattling to itself by one wall. Jacquel opened the Kelvinator door, put the plastic jars with their slivers of spleen, of kidney, of liver, of heart, inside. He took out three brown bottles. Ibis opened a glass-fronted cupboard, removed three tall glasses. Then he gestured for Shadow to sit down at the kitchen table.

Ibis poured the beer and passed a glass to Shadow, a glass to Jacquel. It was a fine beer, bitter and dark.

'Good beer,' said Shadow.

'We brew it ourselves,' said Ibis. 'In the old days the women did the brewing. They wore better brewers than we are. But now it is only the three of us here. Me, him, and her.' He gestured toward the small brown cat, fast asleep in a cat-basket in the corner of the room. 'There were more of us, in the beginning. But Set left us to explore, what, two hundred years ago? Must be, by now. We got a postcard from him from San Francisco in 1905, 1906. Then nothing. While poor Horus . . .' he trailed off, in a sigh, and shook his head.

'I still see him, on occasion,' said Jacquel. 'On my way to a pick up.' He sipped his beer.

'I'll work for my keep,' said Shadow. 'While I'm here. You tell me what you need doing, and I'll do it.'

'We'll find work for you,' agreed Jacquel.

The small brown cat opened her eyes and stretched to her feet. She padded across the kitchen floor and pushed at Shadow's boot with her head. He put down his left hand and scratched her forehead and the back of her ears and the scruff of her neck. She arched ecstatically, then sprang into his lap, pushed herself up against his chest, and touched her cold nose to his. Then she curled up in his lap and went back to sleep. He put his hand down to stroke her: her fur was soft, and she was warm and pleasant in his lap: she acted like she was in the safest place in the world, and Shadow felt comforted.

The beer left a pleasant buzz in Shadow's head.

'Your room is at the top of the stairs, by the bathroom,' said Jacquel. 'Your work clothes will be hanging in the closet – you'll see. You'll want to wash up and shave first, I guess.'

Shadow did. He showered standing in the cast iron tub and he shaved, very nervously, with a straight razor that Jacquel loaned him. It was obscenely sharp, and had a mother-of-pearl handle, and Shadow suspected it was usually used to give dead men their final shave. He had never used a straight razor before, but he did not cut himself. He washed off the shaving cream, looked at himself naked in the fly-specked bathroom mirror. He was bruised: fresh bruises on his chest and arms overlaying the fading bruises that Mad Sweeney had left him. He looked at his wet, black hair and the dark gray eyes which looked back mistrustfully from the mirror at him, looked at the marks on his coffee-colored skin.

And then, as if someone else were holding his hand, he raised the straight razor, placed it, blade open, against his throat.

It would be a way out, he thought. An easy way out. And if there's anyone who'd simply take it in their stride, who'd just clean up the mess and get on with things, it's the two guys sitting downstairs at the kitchen table drinking their beer. No more worries. No more Laura. No more mysteries and conspiracies. No more bad dreams. Just peace and quiet and rest forever. One clean slash, ear to ear. That's all it'll take.

He stood there with the razor against his throat. A tiny smudge of blood came from the place where the blade touched the skin. He had not even noticed a cut. See, he told himself, and he could almost hear the words being whispered in his ear. *It's painless. Too sharp to hurt. I'll be gone before I know it.*

Then the door to the bathroom swung open, just a few inches, enough for the little brown cat to put her head around the doorframe and 'Mrr?' up at him, curiously.

'Hey,' he said to the cat. 'I thought I locked that door.'

He closed the cut-throat razor, put it down on the side of the sink, dabbed at his tiny cut with a toilet paper swab. Then he wrapped a towel around his waist and went into the bedroom next door.

His bedroom, like the kitchen, seemed to have been decorated some time in the 1920s: there was a washstand and a pitcher beside the chest of drawers and mirror. The room itself smelled faintly musty, as if it were too infrequently aired, and the sheets of the bed seemed faintly damp when he touched them.

Someone had already laid out clothes for him on the bed: a black suit, white shirt, black tie, white undershirt and underpants, black socks. Black shoes sat on the worn Persian carpet beside the bed.

He dressed himself. The clothes were of good quality, although none of them were new. He wondered who they had belonged to. Was he wearing a dead man's socks? Would he be stepping into a dead man's shoes? Then he put the clothes on and looked at himself in the mirror. The clothes fit perfectly: there was not even the stretching around the chest, or the shortness in the arms he had expected. He adjusted the tie in the mirror and now it seemed to him that his reflection was smiling at him, sardonically. He scratched the side of his nose, was actually relieved when his reflection did the same.

Now it seemed inconceivable to him that he had ever thought of cutting his throat. His reflection continued to smile as he adjusted his tie.

'Hey,' he said to it. 'You know something that I don't?' and immediately felt foolish.

The door creaked open and the cat slipped between the doorpost and the door and padded across the room, then up on the windowsill. 'Hey,' he said to the cat. 'I did shut that door. I know I shut that door.' She looked at him, interested. Her eyes were dark yellow, the color of amber. Then she jumped down from the sill, onto the bed, where she wrapped herself into a curl of fur and went back to sleep, a circle of cat upon the old counterpane.

Shadow left the bedroom door open, so the cat could leave and the room air a little, and he walked downstairs. The stairs creaked and grumbled as he walked down them, protesting his weight, as if they just wanted to be left in peace.

'*Damn* you look good,' said Jacquel. He was waiting at the bottom of the stairs, and was now himself dressed in a black suit, similar to Shadow's. 'You ever driven a hearse?'

'No.'

'First time for everything, then,' said Jacquel. 'It's parked out front.'

***

An old woman had died. Her name had been Lila Goodchild. At Mr Jacquel's direction, Shadow carried the folded aluminum gurney up the narrow stairs to her bedroom and unfolded it next to her bed. He unfolded a translucent blue plastic body bag, laid it next to the dead woman on the bed, and unzipped it open. She wore a pink nightgown and a quilted robe. Shadow lifted her and wrapped her, fragile and almost weightless, in a blanket, and placed it onto the bag. He zipped the bag shut and put it on the gurney. While Shadow did this, Jacquel talked to a very old man who had, when she was alive, been married to Lila Goodchild. Or rather, Jacquel listened while the old man talked. As Shadow had zipped Mrs Goodchild away the old man had been explaining how ungrateful his children had been, and grandchildren too, though that wasn't their fault, that was their parents', the apple didn't fall far from the tree, and he thought he'd raised them better than that.

Shadow and Jacquel wheeled the loaded gurney to the narrow flight of stairs. The old man followed them, still talking, mostly about money, and greed, and ingratitude. He wore bedroom slippers. Shadow carried the heavier bottom end of the gurney down the stairs and out onto the street, then he wheeled it along the icy sidewalk to the hearse. Jacquel opened the hearse's rear door. Shadow hesitated, and Jacquel said 'Just push it on in there. The supports'll fold up out of the way.' Shadow pushed the gurney, and the supports snapped up, the wheels rotated, and the gurney rolled right on to the floor of the hearse. Jacquel showed him how to strap it in securely, and Shadow closed up the hearse while Jacquel listened to the old man who had been married to Lila Goodchild, unmindful of the cold, an old man in his slippers and his bathrobe out on the wintry sidewalk telling Jacquel how his children were vultures, no better than hovering vultures, waiting to take what little he and Lila had scraped together, and how the two of them had fled to St Louis, to Memphis, to Miami, and how they wound up in Cairo, and how relieved he was that Lila had not died in a nursing home, how scared he was that he would.

They walked the old man back into the house, up the stairs to his room. A small TV set droned from one corner of the couple's bedroom. As Shadow passed it he noticed that the newsreader was grinning and winking at him. When he was sure that no one was looking in his direction he gave the set the finger.

'They've got no money,' said Jacquel when they were back in the hearse. 'He'll come in to see Ibis tomorrow. He'll choose the cheapest funeral. Her friends will persuade him to do her right, give her a proper sendoff in the front room, I expect. But he'll grumble. Got no money. Nobody around here's got money these days. Anyway, he'll be dead in six months. A year at the outside.'

Snowflakes tumbled and drifted in front of the head-lights. The snow was coming south. Shadow said, 'Is he sick?'

'It ain't that. Women survive their men. Men – men like him – don't live long when their women are gone. You'll see – he'll just start wandering, all the familiar things are going to be gone with her. He gets tired and he fades and then he gives up and then he's gone. Maybe pneumonia will take him or maybe it'll be cancer, or maybe his heart will stop. Old age, and all the fight gone out of you. Then you die.'

Shadow thought. 'Hey, Jacquel?'

'Yeah.'

'Do you believe in the soul?' It wasn't quite the question he had been going to ask, and it took him by surprise to hear it coming from his mouth. He had intended to say something less direct, but there was nothing less direct that he could say.

'Depends. Back in my day, we had it all set up. You line up when you die, and you answer for your evil deeds and for your good deeds, and if your evil deeds outweighed a feather, we'd feed your soul and your heart to Ammet, the Eater of Souls.'

'He must have eaten a lot of people.'

'Not as many as you'd think. It was a really heavy feather. We had it made special. You had to be pretty damn evil to tip the scales on that baby. Stop here, that gas station. We'll put in a few gallons.'

The streets were quiet, in the way that streets only are when the first snow falls. 'It's going to be a white Christmas,' said Shadow as he pumped the gas.

'Yup. Shit. That boy was one lucky son of a virgin.'

'Jesus?'

'Lucky, lucky guy. He could fall in a cesspit and come up smelling like roses. Hell, it's not even his birthday, you know that? He took it from Mithras. You run into Mithras yet? Red cap. Nice kid.'

'No, I don't think so.'

'Well . . . I've never seen Mithras around here. He was an army brat. Maybe he's back in the Middle East, taking it easy, but I expect he's probably gone by now. It happens. One day every soldier in the empire has to shower in the blood of your sacrificial bull. The next they don't even remember your birthday.'

Swish went the windshield wipers, pushing the snow to the side, bunching the flakes up into knots and swirls of clear ice.

A traffic light turned momentarily yellow and then red, and Shadow put his foot on the brake. The hearse fish-tailed and swung around on the empty road before it stopped.

The light turned green. Shadow took the hearse up to ten miles per hour, which seemed enough on the slippery roads. It was perfectly happy cruising in second gear: he guessed it must have spent a lot of its time at that speed, holding up traffic.

'That's good,' said Jacquel. 'So, yeah, Jesus does pretty good over here. But I met a guy who said he saw him hitchhiking by the side of the road in Afghanistan and nobody was stopping to give him a ride. You know? It all depends on where you are.'

'I think a real storm's coming,' said Shadow. He was talking about the weather.

Jacquel, when, eventually, he began to answer, wasn't talking about the weather at all. 'You look at me and Ibis,' he said. 'We'll be out of business in a few years. We got savings put aside for the lean years, but the lean years have been here for a long while, and every year they just get leaner. Horus is crazy, really bugfuck crazy, spends all his

time as a hawk, eats road kill, what kind of a life is that?
You've seen Bast. And *we're* in better shape than most of
them. At least we've got a little belief to be going along
with. Most of the suckers out there have barely got that. It's
like the funeral business – the big guys are going to buy you
up one day, like it or not, because they're bigger and more
efficient and because they *work*. Fighting's not going to
change a damned thing, because we lost this particular
battle when we came to this green land a hundred years ago
or a thousand or ten thousand. We arrived and America just
didn't care that we'd arrived. So we get bought out, or we
press on, or we hit the road. So, yes. You're right. The
storm's coming.'

Shadow turned onto the street where the houses were, all
but one of them, dead, and their windows were blind and
boarded. 'Take the back alley,' said Jacquel.

He backed the hearse up until it was almost touching the
double doors at the rear of the house. Ibis opened the hearse,
and the mortuary doors, and Shadow unbuckled the gurney
and pulled it out. The wheeled supports rotated and dropped
as they cleared the bumper. He wheeled the gurney to the
embalming table. He picked up Lila Goodchild, cradling her
in her opaque bag like a sleeping child, and placed her
carefully on the table in the chilly mortuary, as if he were
afraid to wake her.

'You know, I have a transfer board' said Jacquel. 'You don't
have to carry her.'

'Ain't nothing,' said Shadow. He was starting to sound
more like Jacquel. 'I'm a big guy. It doesn't bother me.'

As a kid Shadow had been small for his age, all elbows
and knees. The only photograph of Shadow as a kid that
Laura had liked enough to frame showed a serious child with
unruly hair and dark eyes standing beside a table, laden high
with cakes and cookies. Shadow thought the picture might
have been taken at an embassy Christmas party, as he had
been dressed in a bowtie and his best clothes, as one might

dress a doll. He was looking solemnly out at the adult world that surrounded him.

They had moved too much, his mother and Shadow, first around Europe, from embassy to embassy, where his mother had worked as a communicator in the Foreign Service, transcribing and sending classified telegrams across the world, and then, when he was eight years old, back to the US, where his mother, now too sporadically sick to hold down a steady job, had moved from city to city restlessly spending a year here or a year there, temping when she was well enough. They never spent long enough in any place for Shadow to make friends, to feel at home, to relax. And Shadow had been a small child . . .

He had grown so fast. In the spring of his thirteenth year the local kids had been picking on him, goading him into fights they knew they could not fail to win and after which Shadow would run, angry and often weeping, to the boys' room to wash the mud or the blood from his face before anyone could see it. Then came summer, a long, magical, thirteenth summer, which he spent keeping out of the way of the bigger kids, swimming in the local pool, reading library books at poolside. At the start of the summer he could barely swim. By the end of August he was swimming length after length in an easy crawl, diving from the high board, ripening to a deep brown from the sun and the water. In September, he had returned to school to discover that the boys who had made him miserable were small, soft things no longer capable of upsetting him. The two who tried it were taught better manners, hard and fast and painfully, and Shadow found that he had redefined himself: he could no longer be a quiet kid, doing his best to remain unobtrusively at the back of things. He was too big for that, too obvious. By the end of the year he was on the swimming team and on the weight-lifting team, and the coach was courting him for the triathlon team. He liked being big and strong. It gave him an identity. He'd been a shy, quiet, bookish kid, and that had been painful; now he was a big dumb guy, and nobody expected him to be able to do anything more than move a sofa into the next room on his own.

Nobody until Laura, anyway.

* * *

Mr Ibis had prepared dinner: rice and boiled greens for himself and Mr Jacquel. 'I am not a meat eater,' he explained, 'While Jacquel gets all the meat he needs in the course of his work.' Beside Shadow's place was a carton of chicken pieces from KFC, and a bottle of beer.

There was more chicken than Shadow could eat, and he shared the leftovers with the cat, removing the skin and crusty coating then shredding the meat for her with his fingers.

'There was a guy in prison named Jackson,' said Shadow, as he ate, 'worked in the prison library. He told me that they changed the name from Kentucky Fried Chicken to KFC because they don't serve real chicken any more. It's become this genetically modified mutant thing, like a giant centipede with no head, just segment after segment of legs and breasts and wings. It's fed through nutrient tubes. This guy said the government wouldn't let them use the word *chicken* any more.'

Mr Ibis raised his eyebrows. 'You think that's true?'

'Nope. Now, my old cellmate, Low Key, he said they changed the name because the word *fried* had become a bad word. Maybe they wanted people to think that the chicken cooked itself.'

After dinner Jacquel excused himself and went down to the mortuary. Ibis went to his study to write. Shadow sat in the kitchen for a little longer, feeding fragments of chicken breast to the little brown cat, sipping his beer. When the beer and the chicken were gone, he washed up the plates and cutlery, put them on the rack to dry, and went upstairs.

He took a bath in the claw-footed bathtub, brushed his teeth with his disposable toothbrush and toothpaste. Tomorrow, he decided, he would buy a new toothbrush.

When he returned to the bedroom the little brown cat was once more asleep at the bottom of the bed, curled into a fur crescent. In the middle drawer of the vanity he found several pairs of striped cotton pajamas. They looked seventy years old, but smelled fresh, and he pulled on a pair which, like the black suit, fitted him as if they had been tailored for him.

There was a small stack of *Reader's Digests* on the little table beside the bed, none of them dated later than March 1960. Jackson, the library guy – the same one who had sworn to the truth of the Kentucky Fried Mutant Chicken Creature story, who had told him the story of the black freight trains that the government uses to haul political prisoners off to Secret Northern Californian Concentration Camps, moving across the country in the dead of the night, – Jackson had also told him that the CIA used the *Reador's Digest* as a front for their branch offices around the world. He said that every *Reader's Digest* office in every country was really CIA.

'A joke,' said the late Mr Wood, in Shadow's memory. 'How can we be certain the CIA weren't involved in the Kennedy assassination?'

Shadow cracked the window open a few inches – enough for fresh air to get in, enough for the cat to be able to get out onto the balcony outside.

He turned on the bedside lamp, climbed into bed and read for a little, trying to turn off his mind, to get the last few days out of his head, picking the dullest-looking articles in the dullest-looking *Digests*. He noticed he was falling asleep half way through *I Am John's Pancreas*. He barely had time enough to turn out the bedside light and put his head down on the pillow before his eyes closed for the night.

***

Later he was never able to recollect the sequences and details of that dream: attempts to remember it produced nothing more than a tangle of dark images, underexposed in the darkroom of his mind. There was a girl. He had met her somewhere, and now they were walking across a bridge. It spanned a small lake, in the middle of a town. The wind was ruffling the surface of the lake, making waves tipped with whitecaps, which seemed to Shadow to be tiny hands reaching for him.

– *Down there*, said the woman. She was wearing a leopard-print skirt which flapped and tossed in the wind, and the flesh between the top of her stockings and her skirt was creamy and soft and in his dream, on the bridge, before God and the world, Shadow went down to his knees in front of her, burying his head in her crotch, drinking in the intoxicating jungle female scent of her. He became aware, in his dream, of his erection in real life, a rigid, pounding, monstrous thing as painful in its hardness as the erections he'd had as a boy, when he was crashing into puberty with no idea of what the unprompted rigidities were, knowing only that they scared him.

He pulled away and looked upward, and still he could not see her face. But his mouth was seeking hers and her lips were soft against his, and his hands were cupping her breasts, and then they were running across the satin smooth-ness of her skin, pushing into and parting the furs that hid her waist, sliding into the wonderful cleft of her which warmed and wetted and parted for him, opening to his hand like a flower.

The woman purred against him ecstatically, her hand moving down to the hardness of him and squeezing it. He pushed the bed sheets away and rolled on top of her, his hand parting her thighs, her hand guiding him between her legs, where one thrust, one magical push . . .

Now he was back in his old prison cell with her, and he was kissing her deeply. She wrapped her arms tightly around him, clamped her legs about his legs to hold him tight, so he could not pull out, not even if he wanted to.

Never had he kissed lips so soft. He had not known that there were lips so soft in the whole world. Her tongue, though, was sandpaper-rough as it slipped against his.

– *Who are you*? he asked.

She made no answer, just pushed him onto his back and, in one lithe movement, straddled him and began to ride him. No, not to ride him: to insinuate herself against him in series of silken-smooth waves, each more powerful than the one before, strokes and beats and rhythms which crashed against his mind and his body just as the wind-waves on the lake splashed against the shore. Her nails were needle-sharp and they pierced his sides, raking them, but he felt no pain, only pleasure, everything was transmuted by some alchemy into moments of utter pleasure.

He struggled to find himself, struggled to talk, his head now filled with sand dunes and desert winds.

– *Who are you*? he asked again, gasping for the words.

She stared at him with eyes the color of dark amber, then lowered her mouth to his and kissed him with a passion, kissed him so completely and so deeply that there, on the bridge over the lake, in his prison cell, in the bed in the Cairo funeral home, he almost came. He rode the sensation like a kite riding a hurricane, willing it not to crest, not to explode, wanting it never to end. He pulled it under control. He had to warn her.

– *My wife, Laura. She will kill you*.

– *Not me*, she said.

A fragment of nonsense bubbled up from somewhere in his mind: in medieval days it was said that a woman on top during coitus would conceive a bishop. That was what they called it: trying for a bishop . . .

He wanted to know her name, but he dared not ask her a third time, and she pushed her chest against his, and he could feel the hard nubs of her nipples against his chest, and she was squeezing him, somehow squeezing him down there deep inside her and this time he could not ride it or surf it, this time it picked him up and spun and tumbled him away, and he was arching up, pushing into her as deeply as he could imagine, as if they were, in some way, part of the same creature, tasting, drinking, holding, wanting . . .

– *Let it happen*, she said, her voice a throaty feline growl. *Give it to me. Let it happen.*

And he came, spasming and dissolving, the back of his mind itself liquefying then sublimating slowly from one state to the next.

Somewhere in there, at the end of it, he took a breath, a clear draught of air he felt all the way down to the depths of his lungs, and he knew that he had been holding his breath for a long time now. Three years, at least. Perhaps even longer.

– *Now rest*, she said, and she kissed his eyelids with her soft lips. *Let it go. Let it all go.*

The sleep he slept after that was deep and dreamless and comforting, and Shadow dived deep and embraced it.

$* * *$

The light was strange. It was, he checked his watch, 6:45 a.m., and still dark outside, but the room was filled with a pale blue dimness. He climbed out of bed. He was certain that he had been wearing pajamas when he went to bed, but now he was naked, and the air was cold on his skin. He walked to the window and closed it.

There had been a snowstorm in the night: six inches had fallen, perhaps more. The corner of the town that Shadow could see from his window, dirty and rundown, had been transformed into somewhere clean and different: these houses were not abandoned and forgotten, they were frosted into elegance. The streets had vanished completely, lost beneath a white field of snow.

There was an idea that hovered at the edge of his perception. Something about *transience*. It flickered and was gone.

He could see as well as if it were full daylight.

In the mirror, Shadow noticed something strange. He stepped closer, and stared, puzzled. All his bruises had vanished. He touched his side, pressing firmly with his fingertips, feeling for one of the deep pains that told him he had encountered Mr Stone and Mr Wood, hunting for the greening blossoms of bruise that Mad Sweeney had gifted him with, and finding nothing. His face was clear and unmarked. His sides, however, and his back (he twisted to examine it) were scratched with what looked like claw marks.

He hadn't dreamed it, then. Not entirely.

Shadow opened the drawers, and put on what he found: an ancient pair of blue-denim Levis, a shirt, a thick blue sweater, and a black undertaker's coat he found hanging in the wardrobe at the back of the room. He wondered again who the clothes had belonged to.

He wore his own old shoes.

The house was still asleep. He crept through it, willing the floorboards not to creak, and then he was outside (out through the front door, not the mortuary, not this morning, not when he didn't have to), and he walked through the snow, his feet leaving deep prints in the virgin snow, his steps crunching as they pushed the soft snow deep onto the sidewalk. It was lighter out than it had seemed from inside the house, and the snow reflected the light from the sky.

After fifteen minutes walking, Shadow came to a bridge, with a big sign on the side of it warning him he was now leaving historical Cairo. A man stood under the bridge, tall and gangling, sucking on a cigarette and shivering continually. Shadow thought he recognized the man, but the light on the snow was playing tricks on his eyes, and he walked closer and closer in order to be sure. The man wore a patched denim jacket and a baseball cap.

And then, under the bridge in the winter darkness he was close enough to see the purple smudge of bruise around the man's eye, and he said, 'Good morning, Mad Sweeney.'

The world was so quiet. Not even cars disturbed the snowbound silence.

'Hey man,' said Mad Sweeney. He did not look up. The cigarette had been rolled by hand. Shadow wondered if the man was smoking a joint. No, the smell was tobacco.

'You keep hanging out under bridges, Mad Sweeney,' said Shadow, 'people gonna think you're a troll.'

This time Mad Sweeney looked up. Shadow could see the whites of his eyes all around his irises. The man looked scared. 'I was lookin' for you,' he said. 'You gotta help me, man. I fucked up bigtime.' He sucked on his hand-rolled cigarette, pulled it away from his mouth. The cigarette paper stuck to his lower lip, and the cigarette fell apart, spilling its contents onto his ginger beard and down the front of his filthy tee shirt. Mad Sweeney brushed it off, convulsively, with blackened hands, as if it were a dangerous insect.

'My resources are pretty much tapped out, Mad Sweeney,' said Shadow. 'But why don't you tell me what it is you need. You want me to get you a coffee?'

Mad Sweeney shook his head. He took out a tobacco pouch and papers from the pocket of his denim jacket and began to roll himself another cigarette. His beard bristled and his mouth moved as he did this, although no words were said aloud. He licked the adhesive side of the cigarette paper and rolled it between his fingers. The result looked only distantly like a cigarette. Then he said, ''M not a troll. Shit. Those bastards're fucken *mean*.'

'I know you're not a troll, Sweeney,' said Shadow, gently, hoping that he did not sound as if he were patronizing the man. 'How can I help you?'

Mad Sweeney flicked his Zippo, and the first inch of his cigarette flamed and then subsided to ash. 'You remember I showed you how to get a coin? You remember?'

'Yes,' said Shadow. He saw the gold coin in his mind's eye, watched it tumble into Laura's casket, saw it glitter around her neck. 'I remember.'

'You took the wrong coin, man.'

A car approached the gloom beneath the bridge, blinding them with its lights. It slowed as it passed them, then stopped, and a window slid down. 'Everything okay here, gentlemen?'

'Everything's just peachy thank you, officer,' said Shadow. 'Just out for a morning walk.'

'Okay now,' said the cop. He did not look as if he believed that everything was okay. He waited. Shadow put a hand on Mad Sweeney's shoulder, and walked him forward, out of town, away from the police car. He heard the window hum closed, but the car remained where it was.

Shadow walked. Mad Sweeney walked, and sometimes he staggered. They passed a sign saying 'Future City'. Shadow imagined a city of spires and Frank R. Paul towers, all gleaming in gentle primary colors, bubble domed air-cars flitting from tower to tower like glittering hoverflies. That was Future City and somehow Shadow didn't think it was ever going to be built in Cairo.

The police car cruised past them slowly, then turned, and went back into the city, accelerating down the snowy road.

'Now, why don't you tell me what's troubling you,' said Shadow.

'I did it like he said. I did it all like he said, but I gave you the wrong coin. It wasn't meant to be that coin. That's for royalty. You see? I shouldn't even have been able to take it. That's the coin you'd give to the King of America himself. Not some pissant bastard like you or me. And now I'm in big trouble. Just give me the coin back, man. You'll never see me again, if you do, I sweartofuckenBran, okay? I swear by the years I spent in the fuck'n trees.'

'You did it like who said, Sweeney?'

'Grimnir. The dude you call Wednesday. You know who he is? Who he really is?'

'Yeah. I guess.'

There was a panicked look in the Irishman's crazy blue eyes. 'It was nothing bad. Nothing you can – nothing bad. He just told me to be there at that bar and to pick a fight with you. He said he wanted to see what you were made of.'

'He tell you do anything else?'

Sweeney shivered and twitched; Shadow thought it was the cold for a moment, then knew where he'd seen that shuddering shiver before. In prison: it was a junkie shiver. Sweeney was in withdrawal from something, and Shadow would have been willing to bet it was heroin. A junkie leprechaun? Mad Sweeney pinched off the burning head of his cigarette, dropped it on the ground, put the unfinished yellowing rest of it into his pocket. He rubbed his filthy fingers together, breathed on them to try and rub warmth into them. His voice was a whine now, 'Listen, just give me the fucken coin, man. What do you want it for? Huh? Hey, you know there's more where that came from. I'll give you another, just as good. Hell, I'll give you a shitload, man.'

He took off his filthy baseball cap – then, with his right hand, he stroked the air, producing a large golden coin. He dropped it into his cap. And then he took another from a wisp of breath steam, and another, catching and grabbing them from the still morning air until the baseball cap was brimming with them and Sweeney was forced to hold it with both hands.

He extended the baseball cap filled with gold to Shadow. 'Here,' he said. 'Take them, man. Just give me back the coin I gave to you.' Shadow looked down at the cap, wondered how much its contents would be worth.

'Where am I going to spend those coins, Mad Sweeney?' Shadow asked. 'Are there a lot of places you can turn your gold into cash?'

He thought the Irishman was going to hit him for a moment, but the moment passed and Mad Sweeney just stood there, holding out his gold-filled cap with both hands like Oliver Twist. And then tears swelled in his blue eyes and began to spill down his cheeks. He took the cap and put it – now empty of everything except a greasy sweatband – back over his thinning scalp. 'You gotta, man,' he was saying. 'Didn't I show you how to do it? I showed you how to take coins from the hoard. I showed you where the hoard was. The treasure of the sun. Just give me that first coin back. It didn't belong to me.'

'I don't have it any more.'

Mad Sweeney's tears stopped, and spots of color appeared in his cheeks. 'You, you fucken—' he said, and then the words failed him and his mouth opened and closed, wordlessly.

'I'm telling you the truth,' said Shadow. 'I'm sorry. If I had it, I'd give it back to you. But I gave it away.'

Sweeney's filthy hands clamped on Shadow's shoulders, and the pale blue eyes stared into his. The tears had made streaks in the dirt on Mad Sweeney's face. 'Shit,' he said. Shadow could smell tobacco and stale beer and whiskey-sweat. 'You're telling the truth, you fucker. Gave it away and freely and of your own will. Damn your dark eyes, you gave it a-fucken-way.'

'I'm sorry.' Shadow remembered the whispering thump the coin had made as it landed in Laura's casket.

'Sorry or not, I'm damned and I'm doomed.' The tears were flowing once more, and clear snot began to run from the man's nose. His words dissolved, then, into syllables which never quite congealed together into words. 'Bah-bah-bah-bah-bah,' he said. 'Muh-muh-muh-muh-muh.' He wiped his nose and his eyes on his sleeves, muddying his face into strange patterns, wiping the snot all over his beard and moustache.

Shadow squeezed Mad Sweeney's upper arm in an awkward male gesture. *I'm here*, it said.

''Twere better I had never been conceived,' said Mad Sweeney, at length. Then he looked up. 'The fellow you gave it to. Would he give it back?'

'It's a woman. And I don't know where she is. But no, I don't believe she would.'

Sweeney sighed, mournfully. 'When I was but a young pup,' he said, 'there was a woman I met, under the stars, who let me play with her bubbies, and she told me my fortune. She told me that I would be undone and abandoned west of the sunrise, and that a dead woman's bauble would seal my fate. And I laughed and poured more barley wine and played with her bubbies some more, and I kissed her full on her pretty lips. Those were the good days – the first of the gray monks had not yet come to our land, nor had they ridden the green sea to westward. And now.' He stopped, mid-sentence. His head turned and he focused on Shadow. 'You shouldn't trust him,' he said, reproachfully.

'Who?'

'Wednesday. You mustn't trust him.'

'I don't have to trust him. I work for him.'

'Do you remember how to do it?'

'What?' Shadow felt he was having a conversation with half a dozen different people. The self-styled leprechaun sputtered and jumped from persona to persona, from theme to theme, as if the remaining clusters of brain cells were igniting, flaming, and then going out for good.

'The coins, man. The coins. I showed you, remember?' He raised two fingers to his face, stared at them, then pulled a gold coin from his mouth. He tossed the coin to Shadow, who stretched out a hand to catch it, but no coin reached him.

'I was drunk,' said Shadow. 'I don't remember.'

Sweeney stumbled across the road. It was light now and the world was white and gray. Shadow followed him. Sweeney walked in a long, loping stride, as if he were always falling, but his legs were there to stop him, to propel him into another stumble. When they reached the bridge, he held onto the bricks with one hand, and turned and said, 'You got a few bucks? I don't need much. Just enough for a ticket out of this place. Twenty bucks will do me fine. You got a twenty? Just a lousy twenty?'

'Where can you go on a twenty dollar bus-ticket?' asked Shadow.

'I can get out of here,' said Sweeney. 'I can get away before the storm hits. Away from a world in which opiates have become the religion of the masses. Away from.' He stopped, wiped his nose on the side of his hand, then wiped his hand on his sleeve.

Shadow reached into his jeans, pulled out a twenty and passed it to Sweeney. 'Here.'

Sweeney crumpled it up and pushed it deep into the breast pocket of his oil-stained denim jacket, under the sew-on patch showing two vultures on a dead branch and, barely legible beneath them, the words *Patience my ass! I'm going to kill something!* He nodded. 'That'll get me where I need to go,' he said.

He leaned against the brick, fumbled in his pockets until he found the unfinished stub of cigarette he had abandoned earlier. He lit it carefully, trying not to burn his fingers or his beard. 'I'll tell you something,' he said, as if he had said nothing that day. 'You're walking on gallows ground, and there's a hempen rope around your neck and a raven-bird on each shoulder, waiting for your eyes, and the gallows tree has deep roots, for it stretches from heaven to hell, and our world is only the branch from which the rope is swinging.' He stopped. 'I'll rest here a spell,' he said, crouching down, his back resting against the black brickwork.

'Good luck,' said Shadow.

'Hell, I'm fucked,' said Mad Sweeney. 'Whatever. Thanks.'

Shadow walked back toward the town. It was 8:00 a.m. and Cairo was waking like a tired beast. He glanced back to the bridge, and saw Sweeney's pale face, striped with tears and dirt, watching him go.

It was the last time Shadow saw Mad Sweeney alive.

* * *

The brief winter days leading up to Christmas were like moments of light between the winter darknesses, and they fled fast in the house of the dead.

It was the twenty-third of December, and Jacquel and Ibis's played host to a wake for Lila Goodchild. Bustling women filled the kitchen with tubs and with saucepans and with skillets and with Tupperware, and the deceased was laid out in her casket in the funeral home's front room with hothouse flowers around her. There was a table on the other side of the room laden high with coleslaw and beans and cornmeal hush puppies and chicken and ribs and black-eyed peas, and by mid-afternoon the house was filled with people weeping and laughing and shaking hands with the minister, everything being quietly organized and overseen by the sober-suited Messrs Jacquel and Ibis. The burial would be on the following morning.

When the telephone in the hall rang (it was Bakelite and black and had an honest-to-goodness rotary dial on the front) Mr Ibis answered. Then he took Shadow aside. 'That was the police,' he said. 'Can you make a pickup?'

'Sure.'

'Be discreet. Here.' He wrote down an address on a slip of paper, then passed it to Shadow, who read the address, written in perfect copperplate handwriting, and then folded it up and put it in his pocket. 'There'll be a police car,' Ibis added.

Shadow went out back and got the hearse. Both Mr Jacquel and Mr Ibis had made a point, individually, of explaining that, really, the hearse should only be used for funerals, and they had a van that they used to collect bodies, but the van was being repaired, had been for three weeks now, and could he be very careful with the hearse? Shadow drove carefully down the street. The snowplows had cleaned the roads by now, but he was comfortable driving slowly. It seemed right to go slow in a hearse, although he could barely remember the last time he had seen a hearse on the streets. Death had vanished from the streets of America, thought Shadow; now it happened in hospital rooms and in ambulances. We must not startle the living, thought Shadow. Mr Ibis had told him that they move the dead about in some hospitals on the lower level of apparently empty covered gurneys, the deceased traveling their own paths in their own covered ways.

A dark blue police cruiser was parked on a side street, and Shadow pulled up the hearse behind it. There were two cops inside the cruiser, drinking their coffee from thermos tops. They had the engine running to keep warm. Shadow tapped on the side window.

'Yeah?'

'I'm from the funeral home,' said Shadow.

'We're waiting for the medical examiner,' said the cop. Shadow wondered if it was the same man who had spoken to him under the bridge. The cop, who was black, got out of the car, leaving his colleague in the driver's seat, and walked Shadow back to a dumpster. Mad Sweeney was sitting in the snow beside the dumpster. There was an empty green bottle in his lap, a dusting of snow and ice on his face and baseball cap and shoulders. He didn't blink.

'Dead wino,' said the cop.

'Looks like it,' said Shadow.

'Don't touch anything yet,' said the cop. 'Medical examiner should be here any time now. You ask me, the guy drank himself into a stupor and froze his ass.'

'Yes,' agreed Shadow. 'That's certainly what it looks like.'

He squatted down and looked at the bottle in Mad Sweeney's lap. Jameson Irish whiskey: a twenty dollar ticket out of this place. A small green Nissan pulled up, and a harassed middle-aged man with sandy hair and a sandy moustache got out, walked over. He touched the corpse's neck. *He kicks the corpse*, thought Shadow, *and if it doesn't kick him back . . .*

'He's dead,' said the medical examiner. 'Any ID?'

'He's a John Doe,' said the cop.

The medical examiner looked at Shadow. 'You working for Jacquel and Ibis?' he asked.

'Yes,' said Shadow.

'Tell Jacquel to get dentals and prints for ID and identity photos. We don't need a post. He should just draw blood for toxicology. Got that? Do you want me to write it down for you?'

'No,' said Shadow. 'It's fine. I can remember.'

The man scowled fleetingly, then pulled a business card from his wallet, scribbled on it, and gave it to Shadow, saying, 'Give this to Jacquel.' Then the medical examiner said 'Merry Christmas' to everyone, and was on his way. The cops kept the empty bottle.

Shadow signed for the John Doe and put it on the gurney. The body was pretty stiff, and Shadow couldn't get it out of a sitting position. He fiddled with the gurney, and found out that he could prop up one end. He strapped John Doe, sitting, to the gurney and put him in the back of the hearse, facing forward. Might as well give him a good ride. He closed the rear curtains. Then he drove back to the funeral home.

The hearse was stopped at traffic lights – the same lights he'd fishtailed at, several nights earlier – when Shadow heard a voice croak, 'And it's a fine wake I'll be wanting, with the best of everything, and beautiful women shedding tears and their clothes in their distress, and brave men lamenting and telling fine tales of me in my great days.'

'You're dead, Mad Sweeney,' said Shadow. 'You take what you're given when you're dead.'

'Aye, that I shall,' sighed the dead man sitting in the back of the hearse. The junkie whine had vanished from his voice now, replaced with a resigned flatness, as if the words were being broadcast from a long, long way away, dead words being sent out on a dead frequency.

The light turned green and Shadow put his foot gently down on the gas.

'But give me a wake tonight, nonetheless,' said Mad Sweeney. 'Set me a place at table, and give me a stinking drunk wake tonight. You killed me, Shadow, you owe me that much.'

'I never killed you, Mad Sweeney,' said Shadow. *It's twenty dollars,* he thought, *for a ticket out of here.* 'It was the drink and the cold killed you, not me.'

There was no reply, and there was silence in the car for the rest of the journey. After he parked at the back, Shadow wheeled the gurney out of the hearse and into the mortuary. He manhandled Mad Sweeney onto the embalming table as if he were hauling a side of beef.

He covered the John Doe with a sheet and left him there, with the paperwork beside him. As he went up the back stairs he thought he heard a voice, quiet and muted, like a radio playing in a distant room, which said, 'And what would drink or cold be doing killing me, a leprechaun of the blood? No, it was you losing the little golden sun killed me, Shadow, killed me dead as sure as water's wet and days are long and a friend will always disappoint you in the end.'

Shadow wanted to point out to Mad Sweeney that that was a kind of bitter philosophy, but he suspected it was the being dead that made you bitter.

He went upstairs to the main house, where a number of middle-aged women were putting Saran wrap on casserole dishes, popping the Tupperware tops onto plastic pots of cooling fried potatoes and macaroni and cheese.

Mr Goodchild, the husband of the deceased, had Mr Ibis against a wall, and was telling him how he knew none of his children would come out to pay their respects to their mother. The apple don't fall far from the tree, he told anyone who would listen to him. The apple don't fall far from the tree.

***

That evening Shadow laid an extra place at the table. He put a glass at each place, and a bottle of Jameson Gold in the middle of the table. It was the most expensive Irish whiskey they sold at the liquor store. After they ate (a large platter of leftovers left for them by the middle-aged women) Shadow poured a generous tot into each glass – his, Ibis's, Jacquel's and Mad Sweeney's.

'So what if he's sitting on a gurney in the cellar,' said Shadow, as he poured, 'on his way to a pauper's grave. Tonight we'll toast him, and give him the wake he wanted.

Shadow raised his glass to the empty place at the table. 'I only met Mad Sweeney twice, alive,' he said. 'The first time I thought he was a world class jerk with the devil in him. The second time I thought he was a major fuckup and I gave him the money to kill himself. He showed me a coin trick I don't remember how to do, gave me some bruises, and claimed he was a leprechaun. Rest in peace, Mad Sweeney.' He sipped the whiskey, letting the smoky taste evaporate in his mouth. The other two drank, toasting the empty chair along with him.

Mr Ibis reached into an inside pocket and pulled out a notebook, which he flipped through until he found the appropriate page, and he read out a summarized version of Mad Sweeney's life.

According to Mr Ibis, Mad Sweeney had started his life as the guardian of a sacred rock in a small Irish glade, over three thousand years ago. Mr Ibis told them of Mad Sweeney's love affairs, his enmities, the madness that gave him his power ('a later version of the tale is still told, although the sacred nature, and the antiquity, of much of the verse has long been forgotten'), the worship and adoration in his own land that slowly transmuted into a guarded respect and then, finally into amusement; he told them the story of the girl from Bantry who came to the New

World, and who brought her belief in Mad Sweeney the leprechaun with her, for hadn't she seen him of a night, down by the pool, and hadn't he smiled at her and called her by her own true name? She had become a refugee, in the hold of a ship of people who had watched their potatoes turn to black sludge in the ground, who had watched friends and lovers die of hunger, who dreamed of a land of full stomachs. The girl from Bantry Bay dreamed, specifically, of a city where a girl would be able to earn enough to bring her family over to the New World. Many of the Irish coming in to America thought of themselves as Catholics, even if they knew nothing of the catechism, even if all they knew of religion was the Bean Sidhe, the banshee, who came to wail at the walls of a house where death soon would be, and Saint Bride, who was once Bridget of the two sisters (each of the three was a Brigid, each was the same woman), and tales of Finn, of Oísin, of Conan the Bald – even of the leprechauns, the little people (and was that not the biggest joke of the Irish, for the leprechauns in their day were the tallest of the mound folk) . . .

All this and more Mr Ibis told them in the kitchen that night. His shadow on the wall was stretched and bird-like, and as the whiskey flowed Shadow imagined it the head of a huge waterfowl, beak long and curved, and it was somewhere in the middle of the second glass that Mad Sweeney himself began to throw both details and irrelevancies into Ibis's narrative ('. . . such a girl she was, with breasts cream-colored and speckled with freckles, with the tips of them the rich reddish pink of the sunrise on a day when it'll be bucketing down before noon but glorious again by supper . . .') and then Sweeney was trying, with both hands, to explain the history of the gods in Ireland, wave after wave of them as they came in from Gaul and from Spain and from every damn place, each wave of them transforming the last gods into trolls and fairies and every damn creature until Holy Mother Church herself arrived and every god in Ireland was transformed into a fairy or a saint or a dead King without so much as a by-your-leave . . .

Mr Ibis polished his gold-rimmed spectacles and explained – enunciating even more clearly and precisely than usual, so Shadow knew he was drunk (his words, and the sweat that beaded on his forehead in that chilly house were the only indications of this) – with forefinger wagging, explained that he was an artist and that his tales should not be seen as literal constructs but as imaginative recreations, truer than the truth, and Mad Sweeney said 'I'll show you an imaginative recreation, my fist imaginatively recreating your fucken face for starters,' and Mr Jacquel bared his teeth and growled at Sweeney, the growl of a huge dog who's not looking for a fight but can always finish one by ripping out your throat, and Sweeney took the message and sat down and poured himself another glass of whiskey.

'Have you remembered how I do my little coin trick?' he asked Shadow with a grin.

'I have not.'

'If you can guess how I did it,' said Mad Sweeney, his lips purple, his blue eyes beclouded, 'I'll tell you if you get warm.'

'It's not a palm is it?' asked Shadow.

'It is not.'

'Is it a gadget of some kind? Something up your sleeve or elsewhere that shoots the coins up for you to catch? Or a coin on a wire that swings in front of and behind your hand?'

'It is not that neither. More whiskey, anybody?'

'I read in a book about a way of doing the miser's dream with latex covering the palm of your hand, making a skin-colored pouch for the coins to hide behind.'

'This is a sad wake for Great Sweeney who flew like a bird across all of Ireland and ate watercress in his madness: to be dead and unmourned save for a bird, a dog, and an idiot. No, it is not a pouch.'

'Well, that's pretty much it for ideas,' said Shadow. 'I

expect you just take them out of nowhere.' It was meant to be
sarcasm, but then he saw the expression on Sweeney's face.
'You *do*,' he said. 'You do take them from nowhere.'

'Well, not exactly nowhere,' said Mad Sweeney. 'But now
you're getting the idea. You take them from the hoard.'

'The hoard,' said Shadow, starting to remember. 'Yes.'

'You just have to hold it in your mind, and it's yours to
take from. The sun's treasure. It's there in those moments
when the world makes a rainbow. It's there in the moment of
eclipse and the moment of the storm.'

And he showed Shadow how to do the thing.

This time Shadow got it.

* * *

Shadow's head ached and pounded, and his tongue tasted
and felt like flypaper. He squinted at the glare of the daylight.
He had fallen asleep with his head on the kitchen table. He
was fully dressed, although he had at some point taken off
his black tie.

He walked downstairs, to the mortuary, and was relieved
but unsurprised to see that John Doe was still on the
embalming table. Shadow pried the empty bottle of Jameson
Gold from the corpse's rigor-mortised fingers, and threw it
away. He could hear someone moving about in the house
above.

Mr Wednesday was sitting at the kitchen table when
Shadow went upstairs. He was eating leftover potato salad
from a Tupperware container with a plastic spoon. He wore
a dark gray suit, a white shirt and a deep gray tie: the
morning sun glittered on the silver tie-pin in the shape of a
tree. He smiled at Shadow when he saw him.

'Ah, Shadow m'boy, good to see you're up. I thought you
were going to sleep forever.'

'Mad Sweeney's dead,' said Shadow.

'So I heard,' said Wednesday. 'A great pity. Of course it will come to all of us, in the end.' He jerked on an imaginary rope, somewhere on the level of his ear, and then jerked his neck to one side, tongue protruding, eyes bulging. As quick pantomimes went, it was disturbing. And then he let go of the rope and smiled his familiar grin. 'Would you like some potato salad?'

'I would not.' Shadow darted a look around the kitchen and out into the hall. 'Do you know where Ibis and Jacquel are?'

'Indeed I do. They are burying Mrs Lila Goodchild – something that they would probably have liked your help in doing, but I asked them not to wake you. You have a long drive ahead of you.'

'We're leaving?'

'Within the hour.'

'I should say goodbye.'

'Goodbyes are overrated. You'll see them again, I have no doubt, before this affair is done with.'

For the first time since that first night, Shadow observed, the small brown cat was curled up in her basket. She opened her incurious amber eyes and watched him go.

So Shadow left the house of the dead. Ice sheathed the winter-black bushes and trees as if they'd been insulated, made into dreams. The path was slippery.

Wednesday led the way to Shadow's white Chevy Nova, parked out on the road. It had been recently cleaned, and the Wisconsin plates had been removed, replaced with Minnesota plates. Wednesday's luggage was already stacked in the back seat. Wednesday unlocked the car with keys that were duplicates of the ones Shadow had in his own pocket.

'I'll drive,' said Wednesday. 'It'll be at least an hour before you're good for anything.'

They drove north, the Mississippi on their left, a wide silver stream beneath a gray sky. Shadow saw, perched on a leafless gray tree beside the road, a huge brown and white hawk, which stared down at them with mad eyes as they drove toward it, then took to the wing and rose in slow and powerful circles and, in moments, was out of sight.

Shadow realized it had only been a temporary reprieve, his time in the house of the dead; and already it was beginning to feel like something that happened to somebody else, a long time ago.

Part Two
MY AINSEL

Chapter Nine

'Not to mention mythic creatures in the rubble . . .'
— Wendy Cope, *A Policeman's Lot*

As they drove out of Illinois late that evening, Shadow asked Wednesday his first question. He saw the *Welcome to Wisconsin* sign, and said, 'So who were the bunch that grabbed me in the parking lot? Mister Wood and Mister Stone? Who were they?'

The lights of the car illuminated the winter landscape. Wednesday had decided that they were not to take freeways because he didn't 'know whose side the freeways were on,' so Shadow was sticking to back roads. He didn't mind. He wasn't even sure that Wednesday was crazy.

Wednesday grunted. 'Just spooks. Members of the opposition. Black hats.'

'I think,' said Shadow, 'that they think they're the white hats.'

'Of course they do. There's never been a true war that wasn't fought between two sets of people who were certain they were in the right. The really dangerous people believe that they are doing whatever they are doing solely and only because it is without question the right thing to do. And that is what makes them dangerous.'

'And *you*?' asked Shadow. 'Why are *you* doing what you're doing?'

'Because I want to,' said Wednesday. And then he grinned. 'So *that's* all right.'

Shadow said, 'How did you all get away? Or did you all get away?'

'We did,' said Wednesday. 'Although it was a close thing. If they'd not stopped to grab you, they might have taken the lot of us. It convinced several of the people who had been sitting on the fence that I might not be completely crazy.'

'So how did you get out?'

Wednesday shook his head. 'I don't pay you to ask questions,' he said. 'I've told you before.'

Shadow shrugged.

They spent the night in a Super 8 motel, south of La Crosse.

Christmas Day was spent on the road, driving north and east. The farmland became pine forest. The towns seemed to come farther and farther apart.

They ate their Christmas lunch late in the afternoon in a hall-like family restaurant in northern central Wisconsin. Shadow picked cheerlessly at the dry turkey, jam-sweet red lumps of cranberry sauce, tough-as-wood roasted potatoes and the violently green canned peas. From the way he attacked it, and the way he smacked his lips, Wednesday seemed to be enjoying the food. As the meal progressed he became positively expansive – talking, joking, and, whenever she came close enough, flirting with the waitress, a thin blonde girl who looked scarcely old enough to have dropped out of high school.

'Excuse me, m'dear, but might I trouble you for another cup of your delightful hot chocolate? And I trust you won't think me too forward if I say what a mightily fetching and becoming dress that is. Festive, yet classy.'

The waitress, who wore a bright red and green skirt edged with glittering silver tinsel, giggled and colored and smiled happily, and went off to get Wednesday another mug of hot chocolate.

'Fetching,' said Wednesday, thoughtfully, watching her go. 'Becoming,' he said. Shadow did not think he was talking about the dress. Wednesday shoveled the final slice of turkey into his mouth, flicked at his beard with his napkin, and pushed his plate forward. 'Aaah. Good.' He looked around him, at the family restaurant. In the background a tape of Christmas songs was playing: the little drummer boy had no gifts to bring, *parupapom-pom, rapappom pom, rapappom pom.*

'Some things may change,' said Wednesday, abruptly. 'People, however . . . people stay the same. Some grifts last forever, others are swallowed soon enough by time and by the world. My favorite grift of all is no longer practical. Still, a surprising number of grifts are timeless – the Spanish Prisoner, the Pigeon Drop, the Fawney Rig (that's the Pigeon Drop but with a gold ring instead of a wallet), the Fiddle Game . . .'

'I've never heard of the Fiddle Game,' said Shadow. 'I think I've heard of the others. My old cellmate said he'd actually done the Spanish Prisoner. He was a grifter.'

'Ah,' said Wednesday, and his left eye sparkled. 'The Fiddle Game was a fine and wonderful con. In its purest form it is a two man grift. It trades on cupidity and greed, as all great grifts do. You *can* always cheat an honest man, but it takes more work. So. We are in a hotel, or an inn, or a fine restaurant, and, dining there, we find a man – shabby, but shabby genteel, not down-at-heel but certainly down on his luck. We shall call him Abraham. And when the time comes to settle his bill – not a huge bill, you understand, fifty, seventy-five dollars – an embarrassment! Where is his wallet? Good Lord he must have left it at a friend's, not far away. He shall go and obtain his wallet forthwith! But here, mine host, says Abraham, take this old fiddle of mine for security. It's old, as you can see, but it's how I make my living.'

Wednesday's smile when he saw the waitress approaching was huge and predatory. 'Ah, the hot chocolate! Brought to me by my Christmas Angel! Tell me my dear, could I have some more of your delicious bread when you get a moment?'

The waitress – what was she, Shadow wondered: sixteen, seventeen? – looked at the floor and her cheeks flushed crimson. She put down the chocolate with shaking hands and retreated to the edge of the room, by the slowly rotating display of pies, where she stopped and stared at Wednesday. Then she slipped into the kitchen, to fetch Wednesday his bread.

'So. The violin – old, unquestionably, perhaps even a little battered – is placed away in its case, and our temporarily impecunious Abraham sets off in search of his wallet. But a well-dressed gentleman, only just done with his own dinner, has been observing this exchange, and now he approaches our host: could he, perchance, inspect the violin that honest Abraham left behind?

'Certainly he can. Our host hands it over, and the well-dressed man – let us call him Barrington – opens his mouth wide, then remembers himself and closes it, examines the violin reverentially, like a man who has been permitted into a holy sanctum to examine the bones of a prophet. "Why!" he says, "this is – it *must* be – no, it *cannot* be – but *yes*, there it is – my *lord*! But this is *unbelievable*!" and he points to the maker's mark, on a strip of browning paper inside the violin – but still, he says, even without it he would have known it by the color of the varnish, by the scroll, by the shape.

'Now Barrington reaches inside his pocket and produces an engraved business card, proclaiming him to be a preeminent dealer in rare and antique musical instruments. "So this violin is rare?" asks mine host. "Indeed it is," says Barrington, still admiring it with awe, "and worth in excess of a hundred thousand dollars, unless I miss my guess. Even as a dealer in such things I would pay fifty – no, seventy-five thousand dollars, good cash money for such an exquisite piece. I have a man on the west coast who would buy it tomorrow, sight unseen, with one telegram, and pay whatever I asked for it." And then he consults his watch, and his face falls. "My train—" he says. "I have scarcely enough time to catch my train! Good sir, when the owner of this inestimable instrument should return, please give him my card, for, alas, I must be away." And with that, Barrington leaves, a man who knows that time and the train wait for no man.

'Mine host examines the violin, curiosity mingling with cupidity in his veins, and a plan begins to bubble up through his mind. But the minutes go by, and Abraham does not return. And now it is late, and through the door, shabby but proud, comes our Abraham, our fiddle-player, and he holds in his hands a wallet, a wallet that has seen better days, a wallet that has never contained more than a hundred dollars on its best day, and from it he takes the money to pay for his meal or his stay, and he asks for the return of his violin.

'Mine host puts the fiddle in its case on the counter, and Abraham takes it like a mother cradling her child. "Tell me," says the host (with the engraved card of a man who'll pay fifty thousand dollars, good cash money, burning in his inside breast pocket) "how much is a violin like this worth? For my niece has a yearning on her to play the fiddle, and it's her birthday coming up in a week or so."

'"Sell this fiddle?" says Abraham. "I could never sell her. I've had her for twenty years I have, fiddled all over the country with her. And to tell the truth, she cost me all of five hundred dollars back when I bought her."

'Mine host keeps the smile from his face. "Five hundred dollars? What if I were to offer you a thousand dollars for it, here and now?"

'The fiddle player looks delighted, then crestfallen, and he says "But lordy, I'm a fiddle player sir, it's all I know how to do. This fiddle knows me and she loves me, and my fingers know her so well I could play an air upon her in the dark. Where will I find another that sounds so fine? A thousand dollars is good money, but this is my livelihood. Not a thousand dollars, not for five thousand."

'Mine host sees his profits shrinking, but this is business, and you must spend money to make money. "Eight thousand dollars," he says. "It's not worth that, but I've taken a fancy to it, and I do love and indulge my niece."

'Abraham is almost in tears at the thought of losing his beloved fiddle, but how can he say no to eight thousand dollars? – especially when mine host goes to the wall safe, and removes, not eight but *nine* thousand dollars, all neatly banded and ready to be slipped into the fiddle player's threadbare pocket. "You're a good man," he tells his host. "You're a saint! But you must swear to take care of my girl!" and, reluctantly, he hands over his violin.'

'But what if mine host simply hands over Barrington's card and tells Abraham that he's come into some good fortune?' asked Shadow.

'Then we're out the cost of two dinners,' said Wednesday. He wiped the remaining gravy and leftovers from his plate with a slice of bread, which he ate with lip-smacking relish.

'Let me see if I've got it straight,' said Shadow. 'So Abraham leaves, nine thousand dollars the richer, and in the parking lot by the train station he and Barrington meet up. They split the money, get into Barrington's Model-A Ford and head for the next town. I guess in the trunk of that car they must have a box filled with hundred-dollar violins.'

'I personally made it a point of honor never to pay more than five dollars for any of them,' said Wednesday. Then he turned to the hovering waitress. 'Now, my dear, regale us with your description of the sumptuous desserts available to us on this, our Lord's natal day.' He stared at her – it was almost a leer – as if nothing that she could offer him would

be as toothsome a morsel as herself. Shadow felt deeply
uncomfortable: it was like watching an old wolf stalking a
fawn too young to know that if it did not run, and run now,
it would wind up in a distant glade with its bones picked
clean by the ravens.

The girl blushed once more and told them that dessert was
apple pie, apple pie à la mode – 'That's with a scoop of
vanilla ice cream' – Christmas Cake, Christmas Cake à la
mode, or a red and green whipped pudding. Wednesday
stared into her eyes and told her that he would try the
Christmas Cake à la mode. Shadow passed.

'Now, as grifts go,' said Wednesday, 'the fiddle game goes
back three hundred years or more. And if you pick your
chicken correctly you could still play it tomorrow anywhere
in America.'

'I thought you said that your favorite grift was no longer
practical,' said Shadow.

'I did indeed. However, that is not my favorite. It was fine
and enjoyable, but not my favorite. No, my favorite was one
they called The Bishop Game. It had everything: excitement,
subterfuge, portability, surprise. Perhaps, I think from time
to time, perhaps with a little modification, it might . . .' he
thought for a moment, then shook his head. 'No. Its time has
passed. It is, let us say, 1920, in a city of medium to large size
– Chicago, perhaps, or New York, or Philadelphia. We are in
a jeweler's emporium. A man dressed as a clergyman – and
not just any clergyman, but a Bishop, in his purple, – enters
and picks out a necklace – a gorgeous and glorious
confection of diamonds and pearls, and pays for it with a
dozen of the crispest hundred dollar bills.

'There's a smudge of green ink on the topmost bill and the
store owner, apologetically but firmly, sends the stack of bills
to the bank on the corner to be checked. Soon enough, the
store clerk returns with the bills. The bank says they are
none of them counterfeit. The owner apologizes again, and
the bishop is most gracious, he well understands the

problem, there are such lawless and ungodly types in the world today, such immorality and lewdness abroad in the world – and shameless women, and now that the underworld has crawled out of the gutter and come to live on the screens of the picture palaces what more could anyone expect? And the necklace is placed in its case, and the store owner does his best not to ponder why a bishop of the church would be purchasing a twelve-hundred dollar diamond necklace, nor why he would be paying good cash money for it.

'The bishop bids him a hearty farewell, and walks out on the street, only for a heavy hand to descend on his shoulder. "Why Soapy, yez spalpeen, up to your old tricks are you?" and a broad beat cop with an honest Irish face walks the bishop back into the jewelry store.

'"Beggin' your pardon, but has this man just bought anything from you?" asks the cop. "Certainly not," says the bishop. "Tell him I have not." "Indeed he has," says the jeweler. "He bought a pearl and diamond necklace from me – paid for it in cash as well." "Would you have the bills available, sir?" asks the cop.

'So the jeweler takes the twelve hundred dollar bills from the cash register and hands them to the cop, who holds them up to the light and shakes his head in wonder. "Oh Soapy, Soapy," he says, "these are the finest that you've made yet! You're a craftsman, that you are!"

'A self-satisfied smile spreads across the bishop's face. "You can't prove nothing," says the bishop. "And the bank said that they were on the level. It's the real green stuff." "I'm sure they did," agrees the cop on the beat, "but I doubt that the bank had been warned that Soapy Sylvester was in town, nor of the quality of the hundred dollar bills he'd been passing in Denver and in St Louis." And with that he reaches into the bishop's pocket and pulls out the necklace. "Twelve hundred dollars worth of diamonds and pearls in exchange for fifty cents worth of paper and ink," says the policeman, who is obviously a philosopher at heart. "And passing yourself off as a man of the church. You should be ashamed," he says, as he claps the handcuffs on the bishop, who is obviously no bishop, and he marches him away, but not before he gives the jeweler a receipt for both the necklace and the twelve hundred counterfeit dollars. It's evidence, after all.'

'Was it really counterfeit?' asked Shadow.

'Of course not! Fresh banknotes, straight from the bank, only with a thumbprint and a smudge of green ink on a couple of them to make them a little more interesting.'

Shadow sipped his coffee. It was worse than prison coffee. 'So the cop was obviously no cop. And the necklace?'

'Evidence,' said Wednesday. He unscrewed the top from the salt-shaker, poured a little heap of salt on the table. 'But the jeweler gets a receipt, and assurance that he'll get the necklace straight back as soon as Soapy comes to trial. He is congratulated on being a good citizen, and he watches, proudly, already thinking of the tale he'll have to tell at the next meeting of the Oddfellows tomorrow night, as the policeman marches the man pretending to be a bishop out of the store, twelve hundred dollars in one pocket, a twelve hundred dollar diamond necklace in the other, on their way to a police station that'll never see hide nor hair of either of them.'

The waitress had returned to clear the table. 'Tell me my dear,' said Wednesday. 'Are you married?'

She shook her head.

'Astonishing that a young lady of such loveliness has not yet been snapped up.' He was doodling with his fingernail in the spilled salt, making squat, blocky rune-like shapes. The waitress stood passively beside him, reminding Shadow less of a fawn and more of a young rabbit caught in an eighteen-wheeler's headlights, frozen in fear and indecision.

Wednesday lowered his voice, so much so that Shadow, only across the table, could barely hear him. 'What time do you get off work?'

'Nine,' she said, and swallowed. 'Nine thirty latest.'

'And what is the finest motel in this area?'

'There's a Motel 6,' she said. 'It's not much.'

Wednesday touched the back of her hand, fleetingly, with the tips of his fingers, leaving crumbs of salt on her skin. She made no attempt to wipe them off. 'To us,' he said, his voice an almost inaudible rumble, 'it shall be a pleasure-palace.'

The waitress looked at him. She bit her thin lips, hesitated, then nodded and fled for the kitchen.

'C'mon,' said Shadow. 'She looks barely legal.'

'I've never been overly concerned about legality' Wednesday told him. 'Not as long as I get what I want. Sometimes the nights are long and cold. And I need her, not as an end in herself, but to wake me up a little. Even King David knew that there is one easy prescription to get warm blood flowing through an old frame: take one virgin, call me in the morning.'

Shadow caught himself wondering if the girl on night duty in the hotel back in Eagle Point had been a virgin. 'Don't you ever worry about disease?' he asked. 'What if you knock her up? What if she's got a brother?'

'No,' said Wednesday. 'I don't worry about diseases. I don't catch them. People like me avoid them. Unfortunately, for the most part people like me fire blanks, so there's not a great deal of interbreeding. It used to happen in the old days. Nowadays, it's possible, but so unlikely as to be almost unimaginable. So no worries there. And many girls have brothers, and fathers. Some even have husbands. It's not my problem. Ninety-nine times out of a hundred, I've left town already.'

'So we're staying here for the night?'

Wednesday rubbed his chin. 'I shall stay in the Motel 6,' he said. Then he put his hand into his coat pocket. He pulled out a front door key, bronze-colored, with a card tag attached on which was typed an address: *502 Northridge Rd, Apt #3*. 'You, on the other hand, have an apartment waiting for you, in a city far from here.' Wednesday closed his eyes for a moment. Then he opened them, gray and gleaming and fractionally mismatched, and he said 'The Greyhound bus will be coming through town in twenty minutes. It stops at the gas station. Here's your ticket.' He pulled out a folded bus ticket, passed it across the table. Shadow picked it up and looked at it.

'Who's Mike Ainsel?' he asked. That was the name on the ticket.

'You are. Happy Christmas.'

'And where's Lakeside?'

'Your happy home in the months to come. And now, because good things come in threes . . .' He took a small, gift-wrapped package from his pocket, pushed it across the table. It sat beside the ketchup bottle with the black smears of dried ketchup on the top. Shadow made no move to take it.

'Well?'

Reluctantly, Shadow tore open the red wrapping paper, to reveal a fawn-colored calf-skin wallet, shiny from use. It was obviously somebody's wallet. Inside the wallet was a driver's license with Shadow's photograph on it, in the name of Michael Ainsel, with a Milwaukee address, a MasterCard for M. Ainsel, and twenty crisp fifty dollar bills. Shadow closed the wallet, put it into an inside pocket.

'Thanks,' he said.

'Think of it as a Christmas bonus. Now, let me walk you down to the Greyhound. I shall wave to you as you ride the gray dog north.'

They walked outside the restaurant. Shadow found it hard to believe how much colder it had gotten in the last few hours. It felt too cold to snow, now. Aggressively cold. This was a bad winter.

'Hey. Wednesday. Both of the scams you were telling me about – the violin scam and the bishop one, the bishop and the cop –' he hesitated, trying to form his thought, to bring it into focus.

'What of them?'

Then he had it. 'They're both two-man scams. One guy on each side. Did you used to have a partner?' Shadow's breath came in clouds. He promised himself that when he got to Lakeside he would spend some of his Christmas bonus on the warmest, thickest winter coat that money could buy.

'Yes,' said Wednesday. 'Yes. I had a partner. A junior partner. But, alas, those days are gone. *There's* the gas station, and *there*, unless my eye deceives me, is the bus.' It was already signaling its turn into the parking lot. 'Your address is on the key,' said Wednesday. 'If anyone asks, I am your Uncle, and I shall be rejoicing in the unlikely name of Emerson Borson. Settle in, in Lakeside, nephew Ainsel. I'll come for you within the week. We shall be traveling together. Visiting the people I have to visit. In the meantime, keep your head down and stay out of trouble.'

'My car–?' said Shadow.

'I'll take good care of it. Have a good time in Lakeside,' said Wednesday. He thrust out his hand, and Shadow shook it. Wednesday's hand was colder than a corpse's.

'Jesus,' said Shadow. 'You're cold.'

'Then the sooner I am making the two-backed beast with the little hotsy-totsy lass from the restaurant in a back room of the Motel 6, the better.' And he reached out his other hand and squeezed Shadow's shoulder.

Shadow experienced a dizzying moment of double vision: he saw the grizzled man facing him, squeezing his shoulder, but he saw something else: so many winters, hundreds and hundreds of winters, and a gray man in a broad-brimmed hat walking from settlement to settlement, leaning on his staff, staring in through windows at the firelight at a joy and a burning life he would never be able to touch, never even be able to feel . . .

'Go,' said Wednesday, his voice a reassuring growl. 'All is well, and all is well, and all shall be well.'

Shadow showed his ticket to the driver. 'Hell of a day to be traveling,' she said. And then she added, with a certain grim satisfaction, 'Merry Christmas.'

The bus was almost empty. 'When will we get in to Lakeside?' asked Shadow.

'Two hours. Maybe a bit more,' said the driver. 'They say there's a cold snap coming.' She thumbed a switch and the doors closed with a hiss and a thump.

Shadow walked halfway down the mostly empty bus, put the seat back as far as it would go, and he started to think. The motion of the bus and the warmth combined to lull him, and before he was aware that he was becoming sleepy, he was asleep.

***

In the earth, and under the earth. The marks on the wall were the red of wet clay: hand prints, finger-marks and, here and there, crude representations of animals and people and birds.

The fire still burned and the buffalo man still sat on the other side of the fire, staring at Shadow with huge eyes, eyes like pools of dark mud. The buffalo lips, fringed with matted brown hair, did not move as the buffalo voice said, 'Well, Shadow? Do you believe yet?'

'I don't know,' said Shadow. His mouth had not moved either, he observed. Whatever words were passing between the two of them were not being spoken, not in any way that Shadow understood speech. 'Are you real?'

'Believe,' said the buffalo man.

'Are you . . .' Shadow hesitated, and then he asked, 'Are you a god too?'

The buffalo man reached one hand into the flames of the fire and he pulled out a burning brand. He held the brand in the middle. Blue and yellow flames licked his red hand, but they did not burn.

'This is not a land for gods,' said the buffalo man. But it

was not the buffalo man talking any more, Shadow knew, in his dream: it was the fire speaking, the crackling and the burning of the flame itself that spoke to Shadow in the dark place under the earth.

'This land was brought up from the depths of the ocean by a diver,' said the fire. 'It was spun from its own substance by a spider. It was shat by a raven. It is the body of a fallen father, whose bones are mountains, whose eyes are lakes.

'This is a land of dreams and fire,' said the flame.

The buffalo man put the brand back on the fire.

'Why are you telling me this stuff?' said Shadow. 'I'm not important. I'm not anything. I was an okay physical trainer, a really lousy small-time crook and maybe not so good a husband as I thought I was . . .' He trailed off.

'How do I help Laura?' Shadow asked the buffalo man. 'She wants to be alive again. I said I'd help her. I owe her that.'

The buffalo man said nothing. He pointed up with his soot-blackened palm facing Shadow, his index finger pointing toward the roof of the cave. Shadow's eyes followed. There was a thin, wintry light, coming from a tiny opening far above.

'Up there?' asked Shadow, wishing that one of his questions would be answered. 'I'm supposed to go up there?'

The dream took him then, the idea becoming the thing itself, and Shadow was crushed into the rock and earth. He was like a mole, trying to push through the earth, like a badger, climbing through the earth, like a groundhog, pushing the earth out of his way, like a bear, but the earth was too hard, too dense, and his breath was coming in gasps, and soon he could go no further, dig and climb no more, and he knew then that he would die, somewhere in the deep place beneath the world.

His own strength was not enough. His efforts became weaker. He knew that though his body was riding in a hot bus through cold woods if he stopped breathing here, beneath the world, he would stop breathing there as well, that even now his breath was coming in shallow panting gasps.

He struggled and he pushed, ever more weakly, each movement using precious air. He was trapped: could go no further, and could not return the way that he had come.

'Now bargain,' said a voice in his mind. It might have been his own voice. He could not tell.

'What do I have to bargain with?' Shadow asked. 'I have nothing.'

He could taste the clay now, thick and mud-gritty in his mouth; he could taste the sharp mineral tang of the rocks that surrounded him.

And then Shadow said, 'Except myself. I have myself, don't I?'

It seemed as if everything was holding its breath – not just Shadow, but the whole world under the earth, every worm, every crevice, every cavern, holding its breath.

'I offer myself,' he said.

The response was immediate. The rocks and the earth that had surrounded him began to push down on Shadow, squeezed him so hard that the last ounce of air in his lungs was crushed out of him. The pressure became pain, pushing him on every side, and he felt he was being mashed, a fern becoming coal. He reached the zenith of pain and hung there, cresting, knowing that he could take no more, that no one could take more than this, at that moment the spasm eased and Shadow could breathe again. The light above him had grown larger.

He was being pushed toward the surface.

As the next earth-spasm hit, Shadow tried to ride with it. This time he felt himself being pushed upward, the pressure of the earth pushing him out, expelling him, pushing him closer to the light. And then a moment for a breath.

The spasms took him and rocked him, each harder, each more painful than the one before it.

He rolled and writhed through the earth, and now his face was pushed against the opening, a gap in the rock scarcely larger than the span of his hand, through which a muted gray light came, and air, blessed air.

The pain, on that last awful contraction, was impossible to believe as he felt himself being squeezed, crushed and pushed through that unyielding rock gap, his bones shattering, his flesh becoming something shapeless and snake-like, and as his mouth and ruined head cleared the hole he began to scream, to scream in fear and pain.

He wondered, as he screamed, whether, back in the waking world, he was also screaming – if he were screaming in his sleep back on the darkened bus.

And as that final spasm ended Shadow was on the ground, his fingers clutching the red earth, grateful only that the pain was over and he could breathe once more, deep lungsfull of warm, evening air.

He pulled himself into a sitting position, wiped the earth from his face with his hand and looked up at the sky. It was twilight, a long, purple twilight, and the stars were coming out, one by one, stars so much brighter and more vivid than any stars he had ever seen or imagined.

'Soon,' said the crackling voice of the flame, coming from behind him, 'they will fall. Soon they will fall and the star people will meet the earth people. There will be heroes among them, and men who will slay monsters and bring knowledge, but none of them will be gods. This is a poor place for gods.'

A blast of air, shocking in its coldness, touched his face. It was like being doused in ice water. He could hear the driver's voice saying that they were in Pinewood, anyone who needed a cigarette or wanted to stretch their legs, we'll be stopping here for ten minutes then we'll be back on the road.

Shadow stumbled off the bus. They were parked outside another rural gas station, almost identical to the one they had left. The driver was helping a couple of teenage girls onto the bus, putting their suitcases away in the luggage compartment.

'Hey,' the driver said, when she saw Shadow. 'You're getting off at Lakeside, right?'

Shadow agreed, sleepily, that he was.

'Heck, that's a *good* town,' said the bus-driver. 'I think sometimes that if I were just going to pack it all in, I'd move to Lakeside. Prettiest town I've ever seen. You've lived there long?'

'My first visit.'

'You have a pasty at Mabel's for me, you hear?'

Shadow decided not to ask for clarification. 'Tell me,' said Shadow, 'was I talking in my sleep?'

'If you were, I didn't hear you.' She looked at her watch. 'Back on the bus. I'll call you when we get to Lakeside.'

The two girls – he doubted that either of them was much more than fourteen years old – who had got on in Pinewood were now in the seat in front of him. They were friends, Shadow decided, eavesdropping without meaning to, not sisters. One of them knew almost nothing about sex, but knew a lot about animals, helped out or spent a lot of time at some kind of animal shelter, while the other was not interested in animals, but, armed with a hundred tidbits gleaned from the internet and from daytime television, thought she knew a great deal about human sexuality. Shadow listened with a horrified and amused fascination to the one who thought she was wise in the ways of the world detail the precise mechanics of using Alka-Seltzer tablets to enhance oral sex.

He listened to both of them – the girl who liked animals, and the one who knew why Alka-Seltzer gave you more oral bang for your buck than, like, even Altoids – dishing the dirt on the current Miss Lakeside, who had, like, everybody knew, only gotten her greasy hands on the coronet and sash by flirtin' up to the judges.

Shadow started to tune them out, blanked everything

except the noise of the road, and now only fragments of conversation would come back every now and again.

Goldie is, like, such a good dog, and he was a purebred retriever, if only my dad would say okay, he wags his tail whenever he sees me.

It's Christmas, he has to let me use the snowmobile.

You can write your name with your tongue on the side of his thing.

I miss Sandy.

Yeah, I miss Sandy too.

Six inches tonight they said, but they just make it up, they make up the weather and nobody ever calls them on it . . .

And then the brakes of the bus were hissing and the driver was shouting 'Lakeside!' and the doors clunked open. Shadow followed the girls out into the floodlit parking lot of a video store and tanning salon that functioned, Shadow guessed, as Lakeside's Greyhound station. The air was dreadfully cold, but it was a fresh cold. It woke him up. He stared at the lights of the town to the south and the west, and pale expanse of a frozen lake to the east.

The girls were standing in the lot, stamping and blowing on their hands dramatically. One of them, the younger one, snuck a look at Shadow, smiled awkwardly when she realized that he had seen her do so.

'Merry Christmas,' said Shadow. It seemed like a safe thing to say.

'Yeah,' said the other girl, perhaps a year or so older than the first, 'Merry Christmas to you too.' She had carroty red hair and a snub nose covered with a hundred thousand freckles.

'Nice town you got here,' said Shadow.

'We like it,' said the younger one. She was the one who liked animals. She gave Shadow a shy grin, revealing blue rubber band braces stretching across her front teeth. 'You look like somebody,' she told him, gravely. 'Are you somebody's brother or somebody's son or something?'

'You are such a spaz, Alison,' said her friend. 'Everybody's somebody's son or brother or *something*.'

'That wasn't what I meant,' said Alison. Headlights framed them all for one brilliant white moment. Behind the headlights was a station wagon with a mother in it, and in moments it took the girls and their bags away, leaving Shadow standing alone in the parking lot.

'Young man? Anything I can do for you?' The old man was locking up the video store. He pocketed his keys. 'Store ain't open Christmas,' he told Shadow cheerfully. 'But I come down to meet the bus. Make sure everything was okay. Couldn't live with myself if some poor soul'd found 'emselves stranded on Christmas Day.' He was close enough that Shadow could see his face: old but contented, the face of a man who had sipped life's vinegar and found it, by and large, to be mostly whiskey, and good whiskey at that.

'Well, you could give me the number of the local taxi company,' said Shadow.

'I *could*,' said the old man, doubtfully, 'but Tom'll be in his bed this time of night, and even if you could rouse him you'll get no satisfaction – I saw him down at the Buck Stops Here earlier this evening, and he was very merry. Very merry indeed. Where is it you're aiming to go?'

Shadow showed him the address tag on the door key.

'Well,' he said, 'that's a ten, mebbe a twenty minute walk over the bridge and around. But it's no fun when it's this cold, and when you don't know where you're going it always seems longer – you ever notice that? First time takes forever, and then ever after it's over in a flash?'

'Yes,' said Shadow. 'I've never thought of it like that. But I guess it's true.'

The old man nodded. His face cracked into a grin. 'What the heck, it's Christmas. I'll run you over there in Tessie.'

'Tessie?' said Shadow, and then he said, 'I mean, thank you.'

'You're welcome.'

Shadow followed the old man to the road, where a huge old roadster was parked. It looked like something that gangsters might have been proud to drive in the Roaring Twenties, running boards and all. It was a deep dark color under the sodium lights that might have been red and might have been green. 'This is Tessie,' the old man said. 'Ain't she a beaut?' He patted her proprietorially, where the hood curved up and arched over the front nearside wheel.

'What make is she?' asked Shadow.

'She's a Wendt Phoenix. Wendt went under in 'thirty one, name was bought by Chrysler, but they never made any more Wendts. Harvey Wendt, who founded the company, was a local boy. Went out to California, killed himself in, oh, nineteen forty one, forty two. Great tragedy.'

The car smelled of leather and old cigarette smoke – not a fresh smell, but as if enough people had smoked enough cigarettes and cigars in the car over the years that the smell of burning tobacco had become part of the fabric of the car. The old man turned the key in the ignition and Tessie started first time.

'Tomorrow,' he told Shadow, 'she goes into the garage. I'll cover her with a dust sheet, and that's where she'll stay until spring. Truth of the matter is, I shouldn't be driving her right now, with the snow on the ground.'

'Doesn't she ride well in snow?'

'Rides just fine. It's the salt they put on the roads to melt the snow. Rusts these old beauties faster than you could believe. You want to go door to door, or would you like the moonlight grand tour of the town?'

'I don't want to trouble you—'

'It's no trouble. You get to be my age, you're grateful for the least wink of sleep. I'm lucky if I get five hours a night nowadays – wake up and my mind is just turning and turning. Where are my manners? My name's Hinzelmann. I'd say, call me Richie, but round here folks who know me just call me plain Hinzelmann. I'd shake your hand, but I need two hands to drive Tessie. She knows when I'm not paying attention.'

'Mike Ainsel,' said Shadow. 'Pleased to meet you, Hinzelmann.'

'So we'll go round the lake. Grand tour,' said Hinzelmann.

Main Street, which they were on, was a pretty street, even at night, and it looked old-fashioned in the best sense of the word – as if, for a hundred years, people had been caring for that street and they had not been in a hurry to lose anything they liked.

Hinzelmann pointed out the town's two restaurants as they passed them (a German restaurant and what he described as 'Greek, Norwegian, bit of everything, and a popover at every plate'); he pointed out the bakery and the bookstore ('What I say is, a town isn't a town without a bookstore. It may call itself a town, but unless it's got a bookstore, it knows it's not foolin' a soul.') He slowed Tessie as they passed the library so Shadow could get a good look at it. Antique gas lights flickered over the doorway – Hinzelmann proudly called Shadow's attention to them. 'Built in the 1870s by John Henning, local lumber baron. He wanted it called the Henning Memorial Library, but when he died they started calling it the Lakeside Library, and I guess it'll be the Lakeside Library now until the end of time. Isn't it a dream?' He couldn't have been prouder of it if he had built it himself. The building reminded Shadow of a castle, and he said so. 'That's right,' agreed Hinzelmann. 'Turrets and all. Henning wanted it to look like that on the outside. Inside they still have all the original pine shelving. Miriam Shultz wants to tear the insides out and modernize, but it's on the register of historic places, and there's not a damn thing she can do.'

They drove around the south side of the lake. The town circled the lake, which was a thirty foot drop below the level of the road. Shadow could see the patches of white ice dulling the surface of the lake with, here and there, a shiny patch of water reflecting the lights of the town.

'Looks like it's freezing over,' he said.

'It's been frozen over for a month now,' said Hinzelmann. 'The dull spots are snowdrifts and the shiny spots are ice. It froze just after Thanksgiving in one cold night, froze smooth as glass. You do much ice-fishing, Mister Ainsel?'

'Never.'

'Best thing a man can do. It's not the fish you catch, it's the peace of mind that you take home at the end of the day.'

'I'll remember that.' Shadow peered down at the lake through Tessie's window. 'Can you actually walk on it already?'

'You can walk on it. Drive on it too, but I wouldn't want to risk it yet. It's been cold up here for six weeks,' said Hinzelmann. 'But you also got to allow that things freeze harder and faster up here in northern Wisconsin than they do most anyplace else there is. I was out hunting once – hunting for deer, and this was oh, thirty, forty years back, and I shot at a buck, missed him and sent him running off through the woods – this was over across the north end of the lake, up near where you'll be living, Mike. Now he was the finest buck I ever did see, twenty point, big as a small horse, no lie. Now, I'm younger and feistier back then than I am now, and though it had started snowing before Halloween that year, now it was Thanksgiving and there was clean snow on the ground, fresh as anything, and I could see the buck's footprints. It looked to me like the big fellow was heading for the lake in a panic.

'Well, only a damn fool tries to run down a buck, but there am I, a damn fool, running after him, and there he is, standing in the lake, in oh, eight, nine inches of water, and he's just looking at me. That very moment, the sun goes behind a cloud, and the freeze comes – temperature must have fallen thirty degrees in ten minutes, not a word of a lie. And that old stag, he gets ready to run, and he can't move. He's frozen into the ice.

'Me, I just walk over to him slowly. You can see he wants to run, but he's iced in and it just isn't going to happen. But there's no way I can bring myself to shoot a defenseless critter when he can't get away – what kind of man would I be if I done that, heh? So I takes my shotgun and I fires off one shell, straight up into the air.

'Well the noise and the shock is enough to make that buck just about jump out of his skin, and seein' that his legs are iced in, that's just what he proceeds to do. He leaves his hide and his antlers stuck to the ice, while he charges back into the woods, pink as a newborn mouse and shivering fit to bust.

'I felt bad enough for that old buck that I talked the Lakeside Ladies Knitting Circle into making him something warm to wear all the winter, and they knitted him an all-over one piece woolen suit, so he wouldn't freeze to death. Course the joke was on us, because they knitted him a suit of bright orange wool so no hunter ever shot at it. Hunters in these parts wear orange at hunting season,' he added, helpfully. 'And if you think there's a word of a lie in that, I can prove it to you. I've got the antlers up on my rec room wall to this day.'

Shadow laughed, and the old man smiled the satisfied smile of a master craftsman. They pulled up outside a brick building with a large wooden deck, from which golden holiday lights hung and twinkled invitingly.

'That's Five-Oh-Two,' said Hinzelmann. 'Apartment three would be on the top floor, round the other side, overlooking the lake. There you go, Mike.'

'Thank you, Mister Hinzelmann. Can I give you anything toward gas?'

'Just Hinzelmann. And you don't owe me a penny. Merry Christmas from me and from Tessie.'

'Are you sure you won't accept anything?'

The old man scratched his chin. 'Tell you what,' he said. 'Sometime in the next week or so I'll come by and sell you some tickets. For our raffle. Charity. For now, young man, you can be getting on to bed.'

Shadow smiled. 'Merry Christmas, Hinzelmann,' he said.

The old man shook Shadow's hand with one red-knuckled hand. It felt as hard and as calloused as an oak branch. 'Now, you watch the path as you go up there, it's going to be slippery. I can see your door from here, at the side there, see it? I'll just wait in the car down here until you're safely inside. You just give me the thumbs up when you're in okay, and I'll drive off.'

He kept the Wendt idling until Shadow was safely up the wooden steps on the side of the house, and had opened the apartment door with his key. The door to the apartment swung open. Shadow made a thumbs-up sign and the old man in the Wendt – Tessie, thought Shadow, and the thought of a car with a name made him smile one more time – Hinzelmann and Tessie swung around and made their way back across the bridge.

Shadow shut the front door. The room was freezing. It smelled of people who had gone away to live other lives, and of all they had eaten and dreamed. He found the thermostat and cranked it up to 70 degrees. He went into the tiny kitchen, checked the drawers, opened the avocado-colored refrigerator, but it was empty. No surprise there. At least the fridge smelled clean inside, not musty.

There was a small bedroom with a bare mattress in it, beside the kitchen, next to an even tinier bathroom that was mostly shower stall. An aged cigarette butt floated in the toilet bowl, staining the water brown. Shadow flushed it away.

He found sheets and blankets in a closet, and made the bed. Then he took off his shoes, his jacket and his watch, and he climbed into the bed fully dressed, wondering how long it would take him to get warm.

The lights were off, and there was silence, mostly, nothing but the hum of the refrigerator, and somewhere in the building, a radio playing. He lay there in the darkness, wondering if he had slept himself out on the Greyhound, if the hunger and the cold and the new bed and the craziness of the last few weeks would combine to keep him awake that night.

In the stillness he heard something snap like a shot. A branch, he thought, or the ice. It was freezing out there.

He wondered how long he would have to wait until Wednesday came for him. A day? A week? However long he had, he knew he had to focus on something in the meantime. He would start to work out again, he decided, and practice his coin sleights and palms until he was smooth as anything (*practice all your tricks*, somebody whispered inside his head, in a voice that was not his own, *all of them but one, not the trick that poor dead Mad Sweeney showed you, dead of exposure and the cold and of being forgotten and surplus to requirements, not that trick. Oh not that one*).

But this *was* a good town. He could feel it.

He thought of his dream, if it had been a dream, that first night in Cairo. He thought of Zorya . . . what the hell was her name? The midnight sister. And then he thought of Laura . . .

It was as if thinking of her opened a window in his mind. He could see her. He could, somehow, see her.

She was in Eagle Point, in the backyard outside her mother's big house.

She stood in the cold, which she did not feel any more, or which she felt all the time, she stood outside the house that her mother had bought in 1989 with the insurance money after Laura's father, Harvey McCabe, had passed on, a heart attack while straining on the can, and she was staring in, her cold hands pressed against the glass, her breath not fogging it, not at all, watching her mother, and her sister and her sister's children and husband in from Texas, home for Christmas. Out in the darkness, that was where Laura was, unable not to look.

Tears prickled in Shadow's eyes, and he rolled over in his bed.

Wednesday, he thought, and with just a thought a window opened and he was watching from a corner of the room in the Motel 6, watching two figures thrusting and rolling in the semi-darkness.

He felt like a Peeping Tom, turned his thoughts away, willed them to come back to him. He could imagine huge black wings pounding through the night toward him, he could see the lake spread out below him as the wind blew down from the arctic, breathed its cold on the land forcing any remaining liquids to become solid, prying jack-frost fingers a hundred times colder than the fingers of any corpse.

Shadow's breath came shallowly now, and he was no longer cold. He could hear a wind rising, a bitter screaming around the house, and for a moment he thought he could hear words on the wind.

If he was going to be anywhere, he might as well be here, he thought, and then he slept.

Meanwhile. A Conversation.

*D*ingdong.

'Miz Crow?'

'Yes.'

'You are Samantha Black Crow?'

'Yes.'

'Do you mind if we ask you a few questions, Ma'am?'

'Yeah. I do, actually.'

'There's no need to take that attitude, Ma'am.'

'Are you cops? What are you?'

'My name is Town. My colleague here is Mister Road. We're investigating the disappearance of two of our associates.'

'What were their names?'

'I'm sorry.'

'Tell me their names. I want to know what they were called. Your associates. Tell me their names and maybe I'll help you.'

'. . . okay. Their names were Mister Stone, and Mister Wood. Now, can we ask you some questions?'

'Do you guys just see things and pick names? "Oh, you be Mister Sidewalk, he's Mister Carpet, say hello to Mister Airplane"?'

'Very funny, young lady. First question: we need to know if you've seen this man. Here. You can hold the photograph.'

'Whoa. Straight on and profile, with numbers on the bottom . . . and big. He's cute, though. What did he do?'

'He was mixed up in a small town bank robbery, as a driver, some years ago. His two colleagues decided to keep all the loot for themselves and ran out on him. He got angry. Found them. Came close to killing them with his hands. The state cut a deal with the men he hurt: they testified and got a suspended sentence, Shadow here got six years. He served three. You ask me, guys like that, they should just lock them up and throw away the key.'

'I've never heard anyone say that in real life, you know. Not out loud.'

'Say what, Miz Crow?'

'*Loot*. It's not a word you ever hear people say. Maybe in movies people say it. Not for real.'

'This isn't a movie, Miz Crow.'

'Black Crow. It's Miz Black Crow. My friends call me Sam.'

'Got it, Sam. Now about this man—'

'But you aren't my friends. You can call me Miz Black Crow.'

'Listen, you snotnosed little—'

'It's okay, Mister Road. Sam here – pardon, Ma'am, – I mean, Miz Black Crow wants to help us. She's a law abiding citizen.'

'Ma'am, we know you helped Shadow. You were seen with him, in a white Chevy Nova. He gave you a ride. He bought you dinner. Did he say anything that could help us in our investigation? Two of our best men have vanished.'

'I never met him.'

'You met him. Please don't make the mistake of thinking we're stupid. We aren't stupid.'

'Mm. I meet a lot of people. Maybe I met him and forgot already.'

'Ma'am, it really is to your advantage to cooperate with us.'

'Otherwise, you'll have to introduce me to your friends Mister Thumbscrews and Mister Pentothal?'

'Ma'am, you aren't making this any easier on yourself.'

'Gee. I'm sorry. Now, is there anything else? 'Cos I'm going to say "buh-bye now" and close the door and I figure you two are going to go and get into Mister Car and drive away.'

'Your lack of cooperation has been noted, ma'am.'

'Buh-bye now.'

Click.

'Sam? Who was that at the door?'

'Nobody interesting.'

Chapter Ten

I'll tell you all my secrets
But I lie about my past
So send me off to bed forever more
                    — Tom Waits, *Tango Till They're Sore*

A whole life in darkness, surrounded by filth, that was what Shadow dreamed, his first night in Lakeside. A child's life, long ago and far away, in a land across the ocean, in the lands where the sun rose. But this life contained no sunrises, only dimness by day and blindness by night.

Nobody spoke to him. He heard human voices, from outside, but he could understand human speech no better than he understood the howling of the owls or the yelps of dogs. He remembered, or thought he remembered, one night, half a lifetime ago, when one of the big people had entered, quietly, and had not cuffed him or fed him, but had picked him up to her breast and embraced him. She smelled good. She had made crooning noises. Hot drops of water had fallen from her face to his. He had been scared, and had wailed loudly in his fear.

She put him down on the straw, hurriedly, and left the hut,

fastening the door behind her.

He remembered that moment, and he treasured it, just as he remembered the sweetness of a cabbage-heart, the tart taste of plums, the crunch of apples, the greasy delight of roasted fish.

And now he saw the faces in the firelight, all of them looking at him as he was led out from the hut for the first time, which was the only time. So that was what people looked like. Raised in darkness, he had never seen faces. Everything was so new. So strange. The bonfire light hurt his eyes. They pulled on the rope around his neck, to lead him to the space between the two bonfires, where the man waited for him.

And when the first blade was raised in the firelight, what a cheer went up from the crowd and the child from the darkness began to laugh and laugh with them, in delight and in freedom.

And then the blade came down.

Shadow opened his eyes and realized that he was hungry and cold, in an apartment with a layer of ice clouding the inside of the window glass. His frozen breath, he thought. He got out of bed, pleased he did not have to get dressed. He scraped at a window with a fingernail as he passed, felt the ice collect under the nail, then melt to water.

He tried to remember his dream, but remembered nothing but misery and darkness.

He put on his shoes. He figured he would walk into the town center, walk over the bridge across the northern end of the lake, if he had the geography of the town right. He put on his thin jacket, remembering his promise to himself that he would buy himself a warm winter coat, opened the apartment door and stepped out onto the wooden deck. The cold took his breath away: he breathed in, and felt every hair in his nostrils freeze into rigidity. The deck gave him a fine view of the lake, irregular patches of gray surrounded by an expanse of white.

He wondered how cold it was. The cold snap had come,

that was for sure. It could not be much above zero, and it would not be a pleasant walk, but he was certain he could make it into town without too much trouble. What did Hinzelmann say last night – a ten minute walk? And Shadow was a big man. He would walk briskly and keep himself warm.

He set off south, heading for the bridge.

Soon he began to cough, a dry, thin cough, as the bitterly cold air touched his lungs. Soon his ears and face and lips hurt, and then his feet hurt. He thrust his ungloved hands deep into his coat pockets, clenched his fingers together trying to find some warmth. He found himself remembering Low Key Lyesmith's tall tales of the Minnesota winters – particularly the one about a hunter treed by a bear during a hard freeze who took out his dick and pissed an arching yellow stream of steaming urine that was already frozen hard before it hit the ground, then slid down the rock-hard frozen-piss-pole to freedom. A wry smile at the memory and another dry, painful cough.

Step after step after step. He glanced back. The apartment building was not as far away as he had expected.

This walk, he decided, was a mistake. But he was already three or four minutes from the apartment, and the bridge over the lake was in sight. It made as much sense to press on us to go home (and then what? Call a taxi on the dead phone? Wait for spring? He had no food in the apartment, he reminded himself).

He kept walking, revising his estimates of the temperature downward as he walked. Minus Ten? Minus Twenty? Minus forty, maybe, that strange point on the thermometer when Celsius and Fahrenheit say the same thing. Probably not that cold. But then there was wind chill, and the wind was now hard and steady and continuous, blowing over the lake, coming down from the Arctic across Canada.

He remembered, enviously, the chemical hand- and foot-warmers he had taken from the men in the black train. He guessed he must have left them in Cairo. He wished he had them now.

Ten more minutes of walking, he guessed, and the bridge seemed to be no nearer. He was too cold to shiver. His eyes hurt. This was not simply cold: this was science fiction. This was a story set on the dark side of Mercury, back when they thought Mercury had a dark side. This was somewhere out on rocky Pluto, where the sun is just another star, shining only a little more brightly in the darkness. This, thought Shadow, is just a hair away from the places where air comes in buckets and pours just like beer.

The occasional cars that roared past him seemed unreal: space ships, little freeze-dried packages of metal and glass, inhabited by people dressed more warmly than he was. An old song his mother had loved, *Walking in a Winter Wonderland*, began to run through his head, and he hummed it through closed lips, kept pace to it as he walked.

He had lost all sensation in his feet. He looked down at his black leather shoes, at the thin cotton socks, and began, seriously, to worry about frostbite.

This was beyond a joke. This had moved beyond foolishness, slipped over the line into genuine 24 karat Jesus-Christ-I-fucked-up-bigtime territory. His clothes might as well have been netting or lace: the wind blew through him, froze his bones and the marrow in his bones, froze the lashes of his eyes, froze the warm place under his balls, which were retreating into his pelvic cavity.

Keep walking, he told himself. *Keep walking. I can stop and drink a pail of air when I get home.* A Beatles song started in his head, and he adjusted his pace to match it. It was only when he got to the chorus that he realized that he was humming *Help*.

He was almost at the bridge now. Then he had to walk across it, and he would still be another ten minutes from the stores on the west of the lake – maybe a little more . . .

A dark car passed him, stopped, then reversed in a foggy

cloud of exhaust smoke and came to a halt beside him. A window slid down, and the haze and steam from the window mixed with the exhaust to form a dragon's breath that surrounded the car. 'Everything okay here?' said a cop inside.

Shadow's first, automatic instinct was to say *Yup, everything's just fine and jim-dandy thank you officer, nothing's happening here. Move on. Nothing to see.* But it was too late for that, and he started to say, 'I think I'm freezing. I was walking into Lakeside to buy food and clothes, but I underestimated the length of the walk,' – he was that far through the sentence in his head, when he realized that all that had come out was 'F-f-freezing,' and a chattering noise, and he said, 'So s-sorry. Cold. Sorry.'

The cop pulled open the back door of the car, and said, 'You get in there this moment and warm yourself up, okay?' Shadow climbed into the car gratefully, and he sat in the back and rubbed his hands together, trying not to worry about frostbitten toes. The cop got back in the driver's seat. Shadow stared at him through the metal grille. Shadow tried not to think about the last time he'd been in the back of a police car, or to notice that there were no door handles in the back, and to concentrate instead on rubbing life back into his hands. His face hurt and his red fingers hurt, and now, in the warmth, his toes were starting to hurt once more. That was, Shadow figured, a good sign.

The cop put the car in drive and moved off. 'You know, that was,' he said, not turning to look at Shadow, just talking a little louder, 'if you'll pardon me saying so, a real stupid thing to do. You didn't hear any of the weather advisories? It's minus thirty out there. God alone knows what the wind chill is, minus sixty, minus seventy, although I figure when you're down at minus thirty, wind chill's the least of your worries.'

'Thanks,' said Shadow. 'Thanks for stopping. Very, very grateful.'

'Woman in Rhinelander went out this morning to fill her

birdfeeder in her robe and carpet slippers and she froze, literally froze, to the sidewalk. She's in intensive care now. It was on the radio this morning. You're new in town.' It was almost a question, but the man knew the answer already.

'I came in on the Greyhound last night. Figured today I'd buy myself some warm clothes, food, and a car. Wasn't expecting this cold.'

'Yeah,' said the cop. 'It took me by surprise as well. I was too busy worrying about global warming. I'm Chad Mulligan. I'm the chief of police here in Lakeside.'

'Mike Ainsel.'

'Hi, Mike. Feeling any better?'

'A little, yes.'

'So where would you like me to take you first?'

Shadow put his hands down to the hot air stream, painful on his fingers, then he pulled them away. Let it happen in its own time. 'Can you just drop me off in the town center?'

'Wouldn't hear of it. Long as you don't need me to drive a getaway car for your bank robbery I'll happily take you wherever you need to go. Think of it as the town welcome wagon.'

'Where would you suggest we start?'

'You only moved in last night.'

'That's right.'

'You eaten breakfast yet?'

'Not yet.'

'Well, that seems like a heck of a good starting place to me,' said Mulligan.

They were over the bridge now, and entering the north-west side of the town. 'This is Main Street,' said Mulligan, 'and this,' he said, crossing Main Street and turning right, 'is the town square.'

Even in the winter the town square was impressive, but Shadow knew that this place was meant to be seen in summer: it would be a riot of color, of poppies and irises and flowers of every kind, and the clump of birch trees in one corner would be a green and silver bower. Now it was a gray place, beautiful in a skeletal way, the band shell empty, the fountain turned off for the winter, the brownstone city hall capped by white snow.

'. . . and this,' concluded Chad Mulligan, bringing the car to a stop outside a high glass-fronted old building on the west of the square, 'is Mabel's.'

He got out of the car, opened the passenger door for Shadow. The two men put their heads down against the cold and the wind, and hurried across the sidewalk and into a warm room, fragrant with the smells of new-baked bread, of pastry and soup and bacon.

The place was almost empty. Mulligan sat down at a table and Shadow sat opposite him. He suspected that Mulligan was doing this to get a feel for the stranger in town. Then again, the police chief might simply be what he appeared: friendly, helpful, good.

A woman bustled over to their table, not fat but *big*, a big woman in her sixties, her hair bottle-bronze.

'Hello, Chad,' she said. 'You'll want a hot chocolate while you're thinking.' She handed them two laminated menus.

'No cream on the top, though,' he agreed. 'Mabel knows me too well,' he said to Shadow. 'What'll it be, pal?'

'Hot chocolate sounds great,' said Shadow. 'And I'm happy to have the whipped cream on the top.'

'That's good,' said Mabel. 'Live dangerously, hon. Are you going to introduce me, Chad? Is this young man a new officer?'

'Not yet,' said Chad Mulligan, with a flash of white teeth. 'This is Mike Ainsel. He moved to Lakeside last night. Now, if you'll excuse me.' He got up, walked to the back of the room, through the door marked POINTERS. It was next to a door marked SETTERS.

'You're the new man in the apartment up on Northridge Road. The old Pilsen place. Oh yes,' she said, happily, 'I know *just* who you are. Hinzelmann was by this morning for his morning pasty, he told me all about you. You boys only having hot chocolate or you want to look at the breakfast menu?'

'Breakfast for me,' said Shadow. 'What's good?'

'Everything's good,' said Mabel. 'I make it. But this is the furthest south and east of the yoopie you can get pasties, and they are particularly good. Warming and filling too. My specialty.'

Shadow had no idea what a pasty was, but he said that would be fine, and in a few moments Mabel returned with a plate with what looked like a folded-over pie on it. The lower half was wrapped in a paper napkin. Shadow picked it up with the napkin and bit into it: it was warm and filled with meat, potatoes, carrots, onions. 'First pasty I've ever had,' he said. 'It's real good.'

'They're a yoopie thing,' she told him. 'Mostly you need to be at least up Ironwood way to get one. The Cornish men who came over to work the iron mines brought them over.'

'Yoopie?'

'Upper Peninsula. U.P. Yoopie. Where the Yoopers come from. It's the little chunk of Michigan to the northeast.'

The chief of police came back. He picked up the hot chocolate and slurped it. 'Mabel,' he said, 'are you forcing this nice young man to eat one of your pasties?'

'It's good,' said Shadow. It was, too – a savory delight wrapped in hot pastry.

'They go straight to the belly,' said Chad Mulligan, patting his own stomach. 'I warn you. Okay. So, you need a car?' With his parka off, he was revealed as a lanky man with a round, apple-belly gut on him. He looked harassed and competent, more like an engineer than a cop.

Shadow nodded, mouth full.

'Right. I made some calls. Justin Liebowitz's selling his jeep, wants four thousand dollars for it, will settle for three. The Gunthers have had their Toyota 4-Runner for sale for eight months, ugly sonofabitch, but at this point they'd probably pay you to take it out of their driveway. And if you don't care about ugly, it's got to be a great deal. I used the phone in the men's room, left a message for Missy Gunther down at Lakeside Realty, but she wasn't in yet, probably getting her hair done down at Sheila's.'

The pasty remained good as Shadow chewed his way through it. It was astonishingly filling. 'Stick-to-your-ribs food,' as his mother would have said. 'Sticks to your sides.'

'So,' said Chief of Police Chad Mulligan, wiping the hot chocolate foam from around his lips. 'I figure we stop off next at Henning's Farm and Home Supplies, get you a real winter wardrobe, swing by Dave's Finest Food, so you can fill your larder, then I'll drop you up by Lakeside Realty. If you can put down a thousand up front for the car they'll be happy, otherwise five hundred a month for four months should see them okay. It's an ugly car, like I said, but if the kid hadn't painted it purple it'd be a ten thousand dollar car, and reliable, and you'll need something like that to get around this winter, you ask me.'

'This is very good of you,' said Shadow. 'But shouldn't you be out catching criminals, not helping newcomers? Not that I'm complaining, you understand.'

Mabel chuckled. 'We all tell him that,' she said.

Mulligan shrugged. 'It's a good town,' he said, simply. 'Not much trouble. You'll always get someone speeding within city limits – which is a good thing, as traffic tickets pay my wages. Friday, Saturday nights you get some jerk who gets drunk and beats on a spouse – and that one can go both ways, believe me. Men and women. And I learned when I was on the force in Green Bay, I'd rather attend a bank robbery than a domestic in a big city. But out here things are quiet. They call me out when someone's locked their keys in their vehicle. Barking dogs. Every year there's a couple of High School kids caught with weed behind the bleachers. Biggest police case we've had here in five years was when Dan Schwartz got drunk and shot up his own trailer, then he went on the run, down Main Street, in his wheelchair, waving this darn shotgun, shouting that he would shoot anyone who got in his way, that no one would stop him from getting to the interstate. I think he was on his way to Washington to shoot the president. I still laugh whenever I think of Dan heading down the interstate in that wheelchair of his with the bumper sticker on the back. "My Juvenile Delinquent is Screwing Your Honor Student". You remember, Mabel?'

She nodded, lips pursed. She did not seem to find it as funny as Mulligan did.

'What did you do?' asked Shadow.

'I talked to him. He gave me the shotgun. Slept it off down at the jail. Dan's not a bad guy, he was just drunk and upset.'

Shadow paid for his own breakfast and, over Chad Mulligan's half-hearted protests, both hot chocolates.

Henning's Farm and Home was a warehouse-sized building on the south of the town that sold everything from tractors to toys (the toys, along with the Christmas ornaments, were already on sale). The store was bustling with post-Christmas shoppers. Shadow recognized the younger of the girls who had sat in front of him on the bus. She was trailing after her parents. He waved at her and she gave him a hesitant, blue-rubber-banded smile. Shadow wondered idly what she'd look like in ten years' time.

Probably as beautiful as the girl at the Henning's Farm and Home checkout counter, who scanned in his purchases with a chattering hand-held gun, capable, Shadow had no doubt, of ringing up a tractor if someone drove it through.

'Ten pairs of long underwear?' said the girl. 'Stocking up, huh?' She looked like a movie starlet.

Shadow felt fourteen again, and tongue-tied and foolish. He said nothing while she rang up the thermal boots, the gloves, the sweaters, and the goose-down-filled coat.

He had no wish to put the credit card that Wednesday had given him to the test, not with Chief of Police Mulligan standing helpfully beside him, so he paid for everything in cash. Then he took his bags into the men's restroom, and came out wearing many of his purchases.

'Looking good, big fella,' said Mulligan.

'At least I'm warm,' said Shadow, and outside, in the parking lot, although the wind burned cold on the skin of his face, the rest of him was warm enough. At Mulligan's invitation, he put his shopping bags in the back of the police car, and rode in the passenger seat, in the front.

'So, what do you do, Mister Ainsel?' asked the Chief of Police. 'Big guy like you. What's your profession, and will you be practicing it in Lakeside?'

Shadow's heart began to pound, but his voice was steady. 'I work for my uncle. He buys and sells stuff all over the country. I just do the heavy lifting.'

'Does he pay well?'

'I'm family. He knows I'm not going to rip him off, and I'm learning a little about the trade on the way. Until I figure out what it is I really want to do.' It was coming out of him with conviction, smooth as a snake. He knew everything about big Mike Ainsel in that moment, and he liked Mike Ainsel. Mike Ainsel had none of the problems that Shadow had. Ainsel had never been married. Mike Ainsel had never been interrogated on a freight train by Mr Wood and Mr Stone. Televisions did not speak to Mike Ainsel (*You want to see Lucy's tits*? asked a voice in his head.) Mike Ainsel didn't have bad dreams, or believe that there was a storm coming.

He filled his shopping basket at Dave's Finest Foods, doing what he thought of as a gas-station stop – milk, eggs, bread, apples, cheese, cookies. Just some food. He'd do a real one later. As Shadow moved around, Chad Mulligan said hello to people and introduced Shadow to them. 'This is Mike Ainsel, he's taken the empty apartment at the old Pilsen place. Up around the back,' he'd say. Shadow gave up trying to remember names. He just shook hands with people and smiled, sweating a little, uncomfortable in his insulated layers in the hot store.

Chad Mulligan drove Shadow across the street to Lakeside Realty. Missy Gunther, her hair freshly set and lacquered, did not need an introduction – she knew exactly who Mike Ainsel was. Why that nice Mr Borson, his Uncle Emerson, such a nice man, he'd been by, what, about six, eight weeks ago now, and rented the apartment up at the old Pilsen Place, and wasn't the view just to die for up there? Well, honey, just wait until the spring, and we're so lucky, so many of the lakes in this part of the world go bright green from the algae in the summer, it would turn your stomach, but our lake, well, come fourth of July you could still practically *drink* it, and Mr Borson had paid for a whole year's lease in advance, and as for the Toyota 4-Runner, she couldn't believe that Chad Mulligan still remembered it, and yes, she'd be delighted to get rid of it. Tell the truth, she'd pretty much resigned herself to giving it to Hinzelmann as this year's klunker and just taking the tax write-off, not that the car was a *klunker*, far from it, no it was her son's car before he went to school in Green Bay, and, well, he'd painted it purple one day and, ha-ha, she certainly hoped that Mike Ainsel liked purple, that was all she had to say, and if he didn't she wouldn't blame him . . .

Chief of Police Mulligan excused himself near the middle of this litany. 'Looks like they need me back at the office, good meeting you, Mike,' he said, and he moved Shadow's shopping bags into the back of Missy Gunther's station wagon.

Missy drove Shadow back to her place, where, in the drive, he saw an elderly SUV. The blown snow had bleached half of it to a blinding white, while the rest of it was painted the kind of drippy purple that someone would need to be very stoned, very often, to even begin to be able to find attractive.

Still, the car started up on the first try, and the heater worked, although it took almost ten minutes of running the engine with the heater on full before it even started to change the interior of the car from unbearably cold to merely chilly. While this was happening, Missy Gunther took Shadow into her kitchen – excuse the mess, but the little ones just leave their toys all over after Christmas and she just doesn't have the heart, would he care for some leftover turkey dinner? Last year they did goose but this year it was a big old turkey, well, coffee then, won't take a moment to brew a fresh pot – and Shadow took a large red toy car off a window seat and sat down, while Missy Gunther asked if he had met his neighbors yet, and Shadow confessed that he hadn't.

There were, he was informed, while the coffee dripped and brewed, four other inhabitants of his apartment building – back when it was the Pilsen place the Pilsens lived in the downstairs flat and rented out the upper two flats, now their apartment, that was the downstairs one and that was taken by a couple of young men, Mr Holz and Mr Neiman, they actually are a couple and when she said *couple* Mr Ainsel, Heavens, we have all kinds here, more than one kind of tree in the forest, although mostly those kind of people wind up in Madison or the Twin Cities, but truth to tell, nobody here gives it a second thought. They're in Key West for the winter, they'll be back in April, he'll meet them then. The thing about Lakeside is that it's a good town. Now next door to Mr Ainsel, that's Marguerite Olsen and her little boy, a sweet lady, sweet, sweet lady, but she's had a hard life, still sweet as pie, and she works for the Lakeside News. Not the most exciting newspaper in the world, but truth to tell Missy Gunther thought that was probably the way most folk around here liked it.

Oh, she said, and poured him coffee, she just wished that Mr Ainsel could see the town in the summer or late in the spring, when the lilacs and the apple and the cherry blossoms were out, she thought there was nothing like it for beauty, nothing like it anywhere in the world.

Shadow gave her a five hundred dollar deposit, and he

climbed up into the car and started to back it up, out of her front yard and onto the driveway proper. Missy Gunther tapped on his front window. 'This is for you,' she said. 'I nearly forgot.' She handed him a buff envelope. 'It's kind of a gag. We had them printed up a few years back. You don't have to look at it now.'

He thanked her, and drove, cautiously, back into the town. He took the road that ran around the lake. He wished he could see it in the spring, or the summer, or the fall: it would be very beautiful, he had no doubt of that.

In ten minutes he was home.

He parked the car out on the street and walked up the outside steps to his cold apartment. He unpacked his shopping, put the food into the cupboards and the fridge, and then he opened the envelope Missy Gunther had given him.

It contained a passport. Blue, laminated cover and, inside, a proclamation that *Michael Ainsel* (his name handwritten in Missy Gunther's precise handwriting) was a citizen of Lakeside. There was a map of the town on the next page. The rest of it was filled with discount coupons for various local stores.

'I think I may like it here,' said Shadow, aloud. He looked out of the icy window at the frozen lake. 'If it ever warms up.'

There was a bang at the front door at around 2:00 pm. Shadow had been practicing the Sucker Vanish with a quarter, tossing it from one hand to the other undetectably. His hands were cold enough and clumsy enough that he kept dropping the coin onto the table, and the knock at the door made him drop it again.

He went to the door and opened it.

A moment of pure fear: the man at the door wore a black mask which covered the lower half of his face. It was the kind of mask that a bank robber might wear on TV, or a serial killer from a cheap movie might wear to scare his victims. The top of the man's head was covered by a black knit cap.

Still, the man was smaller and slighter than Shadow, and he did not appear to be armed. And he wore a bright plaid coat, of the kind that serial killers normally avoid.

'Ih hihelhan,' said the visitor.

'Huh?'

The man pulled the mask downward, revealing Hinzelmann's cheerful face. 'I said, it's Hinzelmann. You know, I don't know what we did before they came up with these masks. Well, I do remember what we did. Thick knitted caps that went all around your face, and scarves and you don't want to know what else. I think it's a miracle what they come up with these days. I may be an old man, but I'm not going to grumble about progress, not me.'

He finished this speech by thrusting a basket at Shadow, filled high with local cheeses, bottles, jars, and several small salamis that proclaimed themselves to be venison summer sausage. 'Merry Day after Christmas,' he said. His nose and ears and cheeks were red as raspberries, mask or no mask. 'I hear you already ate a whole one of Mabel's pasties. Brought you a few things.'

'That's very kind of you,' said Shadow.

'Kind, nothing. I'm going to stick it to you next week for the raffle. The Chamber of Commerce runs it, and I run the Chamber of Commerce. Last year we raised almost seventeen thousand dollars for the children's ward of Lakeside Hospital.'

'Well, why don't you put me down for a ticket now?'

'It don't start until the day the klunker hits the ice,' said Hinzelmann. He looked out of Shadow's window toward the lake. 'Cold out there. Must have dropped fifty degrees last night.'

'It happened really fast,' agreed Shadow.

'We used to pray for freezes like this back in the old days,' said Hinzelmann. 'My daddy told me. When the settlers were first coming into these parts, farming people and lumber people, long before ever the mining people came out, although the mines never really happened in this county, which they could have done, for there's iron enough under there . . .'

'You'd pray for days like this?' interrupted Shadow.

'Well, yah, it was the only way the settlers survived back then. Weren't enough food for everyone, and you couldn't just go down to Dave's and fill up your shopping trolley in the old days, no sir. So my grampaw, he got to thinking, and when a really cold day like this come along he'd take my grammaw, and the kids, my uncle and my aunt and my daddy – he was the youngest – and the serving girl and the hired man, and he'd go down with them to the creek, give 'em a little rum-and-herbs drink, it was a recipe he'd got from the old country, then he'd pour creek water over them. Course they'd freeze in seconds, stiff and blue as so many popsicles. He'd haul them to a trench they'd already dug and filled with straw, and he'd stack 'em down there, one by one, like so much cordwood in the trench, and he'd pack straw around them, then he'd cover the top of the trench with two-b'-fours to keep the critters out – in those days there were wolves and bears and all sorts you never see any more around here, no hodags though, that's just a story about the hodags and I wouldn't ever stretch your credulity by telling you no stories, no sir, – he'd cover the trench with two-b'-fours and the next snowfall would cover it up completely, save for the flag he'd planted to show him where the trench was.

'Then my grampaw would ride through the winter in comfort and never have to worry about running out of food or out of fuel. And when he saw that the true spring was coming he'd go to the flag, and he'd dig his way down through the snow, and he'd move the two-b'-fours, and he'd carry them in one by one and set the family in front of the fire to thaw. Nobody ever minded except one of the hired men who lost half an ear to a family of mice who nibbled it off one time my grampaw didn't push those two-b'-fours all the way closed. Of course, in those days we had *real* winters. You could do that back then. These pussy winters we get nowadays it don't hardly get cold enough.'

'No?' asked Shadow. He was playing straight-man, and enjoying it enormously.

'Not since the winter of '49 and you'd be too young to remember that one. *That* was a winter. I see you bought yourself a vee-hicle.'

'Yup. What do you think?'

'Truth to tell, I never liked that Gunther boy. I had a trout stream down in the woods a way, on back of my property, way back, well it's town land but I'd put down stones in the river, made little pools and places where the trout liked to live. Caught me some beauties too – one fellow must have been pretty much thirty inches long, and that little Gunther so-an'-so he kicked down each of the pools and threatened to report me to the DNR. Now he's in Green Bay, and soon enough he'll be back here. If there were any justice in the world he'd've gone off into the world as a winter runaway, but nope, sticks like a cockleburr to a woolen vest.' He began to arrange the contents of Shadow's welcome basket on the counter. 'This is Katherine Powdermaker's crabapple jelly. She's been giving me a pot for Christmas for longer than you've been alive, and the sad truth is I've never opened a one. They're down in my basement, forty, fifty pots. Maybe I'll open one and discover that I like the stuff. Meantime, here's a pot for you. Maybe you'll like it.'

Shadow put the jar away in the fridge, along with the other presents that Hinzelmann had brought him. 'What's this?' he asked, holding up a tall, unlabelled bottle filled with a greenish buttery substance.

'Olive oil. That's how it looks when it gets this cold. Don't worry, it'll cook up fine.'

'Okay. What are winter runaways?'

'Mm.' The old man pushed his woolen cap above his ears, rubbed his temple with a pink forefinger. 'Well, it ain't unique to Lakeside – we're a good town, better than most, but we're not perfect. Some winters, well, maybe a kid gets a bit stir-crazy, when it gets so cold that you can't go out, and the snow's so dry that you can't make so much as a snowball without it crumbling away . . .'

'They run off?'

The old man nodded, gravely. 'I blame the television, showing all the kids things they'll never have – *Dallas* and *Dynasty* and *Beverley Hills* and *Hawaii Five-O*, all of that nonsense. I've not had a television since the fall of '83, except for a black and white set I keep in the closet for if folk come in from out of town and there's a big game on.'

'Can I get you anything, Hinzelmann?'

'Not coffee. Gives me heartburn. Just water.' Hinzelmann shook his head. 'Biggest problem in this part of the world is poverty. Not the poverty we had in the depression but something more in . . . what's the word, means it creeps in at the edges, like cock-a-roaches?'

'*Insidious*?'

'Yeah. Insidious. Logging's dead. Mining's dead. Tourists don't drive further north than the Dells, 'cept for a handful of hunters and some kids going to camp on the lakes – and they aren't spending their money in the towns.'

'Lakeside seems kind of prosperous, though.'

The old man's blue eyes blinked. 'And believe me, it takes a lot of work,' he said. 'Hard work. But this is a good town, and all the work all the people here put into it is worthwhile. Not that my family weren't poor as kids. Ask me how poor we was as kids.'

Shadow put on his straight-man face and said, 'How poor were you as kids, Mister Hinzelmann?'

'Just Hinzelmann, Mike. We were so poor that we couldn't afford a fire. Come New Year's Eve my father would suck on a peppermint, and us kids, we'd stand around with our hands outstretched, basking in the glow.'

Shadow made a rimshot noise. Hinzelmann put on his ski-mask and did up his huge plaid coat, pulled out his car keys from his pocket and then, last of all, pulled on his great gloves. 'You get too bored up here, you just come down to the store and ask for me. I'll show you my collection of hand-tied fishing flies. Bore you so much that getting back here will be a relief.' His voice was muffled, but audible.

'I'll do that,' said Shadow with a smile. 'How's Tessie?'

'Hibernating. She'll be out in the spring. You take care now, Mister Ainsel.' And he closed the door behind him as he left.

The apartment grew ever colder.

Shadow put on his coat and his gloves. Then he put on his boots. He could hardly see through the windows now for the ice on the inside of the panes which turned the view of the lake into an abstract image.

His breath was clouding in the air.

He went out of his apartment onto the wooden deck and knocked on the door next door. He heard a woman's voice shouting at someone to *for heaven's sake shut up and turn that television down* – a kid he thought, adults don't shout like that at other adults, not with that tone in their voice. The door opened and a tired woman with very long, very black hair was staring at him warily.

'Yes?'

'How do you do, Ma'am. I'm Mike Ainsel. I'm your next door neighbor.'

Her expression did not change, not by a hair. 'Yes?'

'Ma'am. It's freezing in my apartment. There's a little heat coming out of the grate, but it's not warming the place up, not at all.'

She looked him up and down, then a ghost of a smile touched the edges of her lips and she said, 'Come in, then. If you don't there'll be no heat in here, either.'

He stepped inside her apartment. Plastic, multicolored toys were strewn all over the floor. There were small heaps of torn Christmas wrapping paper by the wall. A small boy sat inches away from the television set, a video of the Disney

Hercules playing, an animated satyr stomping and shouting his way across the screen. Shadow kept his back to the TV set.

'Okay,' she said. 'This is what you do. First you seal the windows, you can buy the stuff down at Henning's, it's just like Saran Wrap but for windows. Tape it to windows, then if you want to get fancy you run a blow-dryer on it, it stays there the whole winter. That stops the heat leaving through the windows. Then you buy a space heater or two. The building's furnace is old, and it can't cope with the real cold. We've had some easy winters recently, I suppose we should be grateful.' Then she put out her hand. 'Marguerite Olsen.'

'Good to meet you,' said Shadow. He pulled off a glove and they shook hands. 'You know ma'am, I'd always thought of Olsens as being blonder than you.'

'My ex-husband was as blond as they came. Pink and blond. Couldn't tan at gunpoint.'

'Missy Gunther told me you write for the local paper.'

'Missy Gunther tells everybody everything. I don't see why we need a local paper with Missy Gunther around.' She nodded. 'Yes. Some news reporting here and there, but my editor writes most of the news. I write the nature column, the gardening column, an opinion column every Sunday and the News From The Community column which tells, in mind-numbing detail, who went to dinner with who for fifteen miles around. Or is that whom?'

'*Whom*,' said Shadow, before he could stop himself. 'It's the objective case.'

She looked at him with her black eyes, and Shadow experienced a moment of pure *déjà vu*. I've been here before, he thought.

No, she reminds me of someone.

'Anyway, that's how you heat up your apartment,' she said.

'Thank you,' said Shadow. 'When it's warm you and your little one must come over.'

'His name's Leon,' she said. 'Good meeting you, Mister . . .

I'm sorry . . .'

'Ainsel,' said Shadow. 'Mike Ainsel.'

'And what sort of a name is Ainsel?' she asked.

Shadow had no idea. 'My name,' he said. 'I'm afraid I was never very interested in family history.'

'Norwegian, maybe?' she said.

'We were never close,' he said. Then he remembered Uncle Emerson Borson, and added, 'on that side, anyway.'

**

By the time that Mr Wednesday arrived, Shadow had put clear plastic sheeting across all the windows and had one space heater running in the main room and one in the bedroom at the back. It was practically cozy.

'What the hell is that purple piece of shit you're driving?' asked Wednesday, by way of greeting.

'Well,' said Shadow, 'you drove off with my white piece of shit. Where is it, by the way?'

'I traded it in in Duluth,' said Wednesday. 'You can't be too careful. Don't worry – you'll get your share when all this is done.'

'What am I doing here?' asked Shadow. 'In Lakeside, I mean. Not in the world.'

Wednesday smiled his smile, the one that made Shadow want to hit him. 'You're living here because it's the last place they'll look for you. I can keep you out of sight here.'

'By *they* you mean the black hats?'

'Exactly. I'm afraid the House on the Rock is now out of bounds. It's a little difficult, but we'll cope. Now it's just stamping our feet and flag-waving, caracole and saunter until the action starts – a little later than any of us expected. I think they'll hold off until spring. Nothing big can happen until then.'

'How come?'

'Because they may babble on about micro milliseconds

and virtual worlds and paradigm shifts and what-have-you, but they still inhabit this planet and are still bound by the cycle of the year. These are the dead months. A victory in these months is a dead victory.'

'I have no idea what you're talking about,' said Shadow. That was not entirely true. He had a vague idea, and he hoped it was wrong.

'It's going to be a bad winter, and you and I are going to use our time as wisely as we can. We shall rally our troops and pick our battleground.'

'Okay,' said Shadow. He knew that Wednesday was telling him the truth, or a part of a truth. War was coming. No, that was not it: the war had already begun. The battle was coming. 'Mad Sweeney said that he was working for you when we met him that first night. He said that before he died.'

'And would I have wanted to employ someone who could not even best a sad case like that in a bar fight? But never fear, you've repaid my faith in you a dozen times over. Have you ever been to Las Vegas?'

'Las Vegas, Nevada?'

'That's the one.'

'No.'

'We're flying in there from Madison later tonight, on a gentleman's red-eye, a charter plane for High Rollers. I've convinced them that we should be on it.'

'Don't you ever get tired of lying?' asked Shadow. He said it gently, curiously.

'Not in the slightest. Anyway, it's true. We are playing for the highest stakes of all. It shouldn't take us more than a couple of hours to get to Madison, the roads are clear. So lock your door and turn off the heaters. It would be a terrible thing if you burned down the house in your absence.'

'Who are we going to see in Las Vegas?'

Wednesday told him.

Shadow turned off the heaters, packed some clothes into

an overnight bag, then turned back to Wednesday and said, 'Look, I feel kind of stupid. I know you just told me who we're going to see, but I dunno. I just had a brain-fart or something. It's gone. Who is it again?'

Wednesday told him once more.

This time Shadow almost had it. The name was there on the tip of his mind. He wished he'd been paying closer attention when Wednesday told him. He let it go.

'Who's driving?' he asked Wednesday.

'You are,' said Wednesday. They walked out of the house, down the wooden stairs and the icy path to where a black Lincoln town car was parked.

Shadow drove.

***

Entering the Casino one is beset at every side by invitation – invitations such that it would take a man of stone, heartless, mindlesss, and curiously devoid of avarice, to decline them. Listen: a machine gun rattle of silver coins as they tumble and spurt down into a slot machine tray and overflow onto monogrammed carpets is replaced by the siren clangor of the slots, the jangling, blippeting chorus swallowed by the huge room, muted to a comforting background chatter by the time one reaches the card tables, the distant sounds only loud enough to keep the adrenaline flowing through the gamblers' veins.

There is a secret that the casinos possess, a secret they hold and guard and prize, the holiest of their mysteries. For most people do not gamble to win money, after all, although that is what is advertised, sold, claimed and dreamed. But that is merely the easy lie that allows the gamblers to lie to themselves, the big lie that gets them through the enormous, ever-open, welcoming doors.

The secret is this: people gamble to lose money. They come to the casinos for the moment in which they feel alive, to ride the spinning wheel and turn with the cards and lose themselves, with the coins, in the slots. They want to know they matter. They may brag about the nights they won, the money they took from the casino, but they treasure, secretly treasure, the times they lost. It's a sacrifice, of sorts.

The money flows through the casino in an uninterrupted stream of green and silver, streaming from hand to hand, from gambler to croupier, to cashier, to the management, to security, finally ending up in the Holy of Holies, the innermost sanctum, the Counting Room. And it is here, in the counting room of this casino, that you come to rest, here, where the greenbacks are sorted, stacked, indexed, here in a space that is slowly becoming redundant as more and more of the money that flows through the casino is imaginary: an electrical sequence of ons and offs, sequences that flow down telephone lines.

In the Counting Room you see three men, counting money under the glassy stare of the cameras they can see, the insectile gazes of the tiny cameras they cannot see. During the course of one shift each of the men counts more money than he will see in all the pay packets of his life. Each man, when he sleeps, dreams of counting money, of stacks and paper bands and numbers which climb inevitably, which are sorted and lost. Each of the three men has idly wondered, not less than once a week, how to evade the casino's security systems and run off with as much money as he could haul; and, reluctantly, each man has inspected the dream and found it impractical, has settled for a steady paycheck, avoided the twin specters of prison and an unmarked grave.

And here, in the sanctum sanctorum, there are the three men who count the money, and there are the guards who watch and who bring money and take it away; and then there is another person. His charcoal-gray suit is immaculate, his hair is dark, he is clean-shaven, and his face, and his demeanor, are, in every sense, forgettable. None of the other men has even observed that he is there, or if they have noticed him, they have forgotten him on the instant.

As the shift ends the doors are opened, and the man in the charcoal suit leaves the room and walks, with the guards, through the corridors, their feet shushing along the monogrammed carpets. The money, in strong boxes, is wheeled to an interior loading bay, where it is loaded into armored cars. As the ramp door swings open, to allow the armored car out onto the early streets of Las Vegas, the man in the charcoal suit walks, unnoticed, through the doorway, and saunters up the ramp, out onto the sidewalk. He does not even glance up to see the imitation of New York on his left.

Las Vegas has become a child's picture book dream of a city – here a story-book castle, there a sphinx-flanked black pyramid beaming white light into the darkness as a landing beam for UFOs, and everywhere neon oracles and twisting screens predict happiness and good fortune, announce singers and comedians and magicians in residence or on their way, and the lights always flush and beckon and call. Once every hour a volcano erupts in light and flame. Once every hour a pirate ship sinks a man o' war.

The man in the charcoal suit ambles comfortably along the sidewalk, feeling the flow of the money through the town. In the summer the streets are baking, and each store doorway he passes breathes wintry A/C out into the sweaty warmth and chills the sweat on his face. Now, in the desert winter, there's a dry cold, which he appreciates. In his mind the movement of money forms a fine lattice-work, a three dimensional cat's-cradle of light and motion. What he finds attractive about this desert city is the speed of movement, the way the money moves from place to place and hand to hand: it's a rush for him, a high, and it pulls him like an addict to the street.

A taxi follows him slowly down the street, keeping its distance. He does not notice it; it does not occur to him to notice it: he is so rarely noticed himself that he finds the concept that he could be being followed almost inconceivable.

It's four in the morning, and he finds himself drawn to a

hotel and casino that has been out of style for thirty years, still running until tomorrow or six months from now when they'll implode it and knock it down and build a pleasure palace where it was, and forget it forever. Nobody knows him, nobody remembers him, but the lobby bar is tacky and quiet, and the air is blue with old cigarette smoke and someone's about to drop several million dollars on a poker game in a private room upstairs. The man in the charcoal suit settles himself in the bar several floors below the game, and is ignored by a waitress. A Muzak version of Why Can't He Be You? *is playing, almost subliminally. Five Elvis Presley impersonators, each man wearing a different colored jumpsuit, watch a late night rerun of a football game on the bar TV.*

A big man in a light gray suit sits at the man in the charcoal suit's table, and, noticing him even if she does not notice the man in the charcoal suit, the waitress, who is too thin to be pretty, too obviously anorectic to work Luxor or the Tropicana, and who is counting the minutes until she gets off work, comes straight over and smiles. He grins widely at her. 'You're looking a treat tonight, m'dear, a fine sight for these poor old eyes,' he says, and, scenting a large tip, she smiles broadly at him. The man in the light gray suit orders a Jack Daniel's for himself and a Laphroaig and water for the man in the charcoal suit sitting beside him.

'You know,' says the man in the light gray suit, when his drink arrives, 'the finest line of poetry ever uttered in the history of this whole damn country was said by Canada Bill Jones in 1853, in Baton Rouge, while he was being robbed blind in a crooked game of Faro. George Devol, who was, like Canada Bill, not a man who was averse to fleecing the odd sucker, drew Bill aside and asked him if he couldn't see that the game was crooked. And Canada Bill sighed, and shrugged his shoulders, and said "I know. But it's the only game in town." And he went back to the game.'

Dark eyes stare at the man in the light gray suit distrustfully. The man in the charcoal suit says something in reply. The man in the light suit, who has a graying reddish beard, shakes his head.

'Look,' he says, 'I'm sorry about what went down in Wisconsin. But I got you all out safely, didn't I? No one was hurt.'

The man in the dark suit sips his Laphroaig and water, savoring the marshy taste, the body-in-the-bog quality of the whiskey. He asks a question.

'I don't know. Everything's moving faster than I expected. Everyone's got a hard-on for the kid I hired to run errands – I've got him outside, waiting in the taxi. Are you still in?'

The man in the dark suit replies.

The bearded man shakes his head. 'She's not been seen for two hundred years. If she isn't dead she's taken herself out of the picture.'

Something else is said.

'Look,' says the bearded man, knocking back his Jack Daniel's. 'You come in, be there when we need you, and I'll take care of you. Whaddayou want? Soma? I can get you a bottle of Soma. The real stuff.'

The man in the dark suit stares. Then he nods his head, reluctantly, and makes a comment.

'Of course I am,' says the bearded man, smiling like a knife. 'What do you expect? But look at it this way: it's the only game in town.' He reaches out a paw-like hand and shakes the other man's well-manicured hand. Then he walks away.

The thin waitress comes over, puzzled: there's now only one man at the corner table, a sharply dressed man with dark hair in a charcoal-gray suit. 'You doing okay?' she asks. 'Is your friend coming back?'

The man with the dark hair sighs, and explains that his friend won't be coming back, and thus she won't be paid for her time, or for her trouble. And then, seeing the hurt in her eyes, and taking pity on her, he examines the golden threads in his mind, watches the matrix, follows the money until he spots a node, and tells her that if she's outside Treasure Island

*at six a.m., thirty minutes after she gets off work, she'll meet
an oncologist from Denver who will just have won $40,000 at
a craps table, and will need a mentor, a partner, someone to
help him dispose of it all in the 48 hours before he gets on the
plane home.*

*The words evaporate in the waitress's mind, but they leave
her happy. She sighs and notes that the guys in the corner
have done a runner, and have not even tipped her; and it
occurs to her that, instead of driving straight home when she
gets off shift, she's going to drive over to Treasure Island; but
she would never, if you asked her, be able to tell you why.*

***

'So who was that guy you were seeing?' asked Shadow as
they walked back down the Las Vegas concourse. There were
slot machines in the airport. Even at this time of the morning
people stood in front of them, feeding them coins. Shadow
wondered if there were those who never left the airport, who
got off their planes, walked along the jetway into the airport
building and stopped there, trapped by the spinning images
and the flashing lights; people who would stay in the airport
until they had fed their last quarter to the machines, and
then would turn around and get onto the plane back home.

He guessed it must have happened. He suspected that
there wasn't much that hadn't happened in Las Vegas at some
point or other. And America was so damn big that with so
many people there was always bound to be *somebody*.

And then he realized that he had zoned out just as
Wednesday had been telling him who the man in the dark
suit they had followed in the taxi had been, and he had
missed it.

'So he's in,' said Wednesday. 'It'll cost me a bottle of Soma,
though.'

'What's Soma?'

'It's a drink.' They walked onto the charter plane, empty

but for them and a trio of corporate big spenders who needed
to be back in Chicago by the start of the next business day.

Wednesday got comfortable, ordered himself a Jack
Daniel's. 'My kind of people see your kind of people . . .' he
hesitated. 'It's like bees and honey. Each bee makes only a
tiny, tiny drop of honey. It takes thousands of them, millions
perhaps, all working together to make the pot of honey you
have on your breakfast table. Now imagine that you could
eat nothing but honey. That's what it's like for my kind of
people . . . we feed on belief, on prayers, on love. It takes a
lot of people believing just the tiniest bit to sustain us. That's
what we need, instead of food. Belief.'

'And Soma is . . .'

'To take the analogy further, it's honey wine. Mead.' He
chuckled. 'It's a drink. Concentrated prayer and belief,
distilled into a potent liqueur.'

They were somewhere over Nebraska eating an unimpressive in-flight breakfast when Shadow said, 'My wife.'

'The dead one.'

'Laura. She doesn't want to be dead. She told me. After she
got me away from the guys on the train.'

'The action of a fine wife. Freeing you from durance vile
and murdering those who would have harmed you. You
should treasure her, Nephew Ainsel.'

'She wants to be really alive. Not one of the walking dead,
or whatever she is. She wants to live again. Can we do that?
Is that possible?'

Wednesday said nothing for long enough that Shadow
started to wonder if he had heard the question, or if he had,
possibly, fallen asleep with his eyes open. Then he said, staring
ahead of him as he talked, 'I know a charm that can cure pain
and sickness, and lift the grief from the heart of the grieving.

'I know a charm that will heal with a touch.

'I know a charm that will turn aside the weapons of an
enemy.

'I know another charm to free myself from all bonds and

locks.

'A fifth charm: I can catch a bullet in flight and take no harm from it.'

His words were quiet, urgent. Gone was the hectoring tone, gone was the grin. Wednesday spoke as if he were reciting the words of a religious ritual, as if he were speaking something dark and painful.

'A sixth: spells sent to hurt me will hurt only the sender.

'A seventh charm I know: I can quench a fire simply by looking at it.

'An eighth: if any man hates me, I can win his friendship.

'A ninth: I can sing the wind to sleep and calm a storm for long enough to bring a ship to shore.

'Those were the first nine charms I learned. Nine nights I hung on the bare tree, my side pierced with a spear's point. I swayed and blew in the cold winds and the hot winds, without food, without water, a sacrifice of myself to myself, and the worlds opened to me.

'For a tenth charm, I learned to dispel witches, to spin them around in the skies so that they will never find their way back to their own doors again.

'An eleventh: if I sing it when a battle rages it can take warriors through the tumult unscathed and unhurt, and bring them safely back to their hearth and their home.

'A twelfth charm I know: if I see a hanged man I can bring him down from the gallows to whisper to us all he remembers.

'A thirteenth: if I sprinkle water on a child's head, that child will not fall in battle.

'A fourteenth. I know the names of all the gods. Every damned one of them.

'A fifteenth: I have a dream of power, of glory, and of wisdom, and I can make people believe my dreams.'

His voice was so low now that Shadow had to strain to hear it over the plane's engine noise.

'A sixteenth charm I know: if I need love I can turn the

mind and heart of any woman.

'A seventeenth, that no woman I want will ever want another.

'And I know an eighteenth charm, and that charm is the greatest of all, and that charm I can tell to no man, for a secret that no one knows but you is the most powerful secret there can ever be.'

He sighed, and then stopped talking.

Shadow could feel his skin crawl. It was as if he had just seen a door open to another place, somewhere worlds away where hanged men blew in the wind at every crossroads, where witches shrieked overhead in the night.

'Laura,' was all he said.

Wednesday turned his head, stared into Shadow's pale gray eyes with his own. 'I can't make her live again,' he said. 'I don't even know why she isn't as dead as she ought to be.'

'I think I did it,' said Shadow. 'It was my fault.'

Wednesday raised a bushy eyebrow.

'Mad Sweeney gave me a golden coin, back when he showed me how to do that trick. From what he said, he gave me the wrong coin. What he gave me was something more powerful than what he thought he was giving me. I passed it on to Laura.'

Wednesday grunted, lowered his chin to his chest, frowned. Then he sat back. 'That could do it,' he said. 'And no, I can't help you. What you do in your own time is your own affair, of course.'

'What,' asked Shadow, 'is that supposed to mean?'

'It means that I can't stop you from hunting eagle stones or thunderbirds. But I would infinitely prefer that you spend your days quietly sequestered in Lakeside, out of sight, and, I hope, out of mind. When things get hairy we'll need all hands to the wheel.'

He looked very old as he said this, and fragile, and his skin seemed almost transparent, and the flesh beneath was gray.

Shadow wanted, wanted very much, to reach out and put

his hand over Wednesday's gray hand. He wanted to tell him that everything would be okay – something that Shadow did not feel, but that he knew had to be said. There were men in black trains out there. There was a fat kid in a stretch limo and there were people in the television who did not mean them well.

He did not touch Wednesday. He did not say anything.

Later, he wondered if he could have changed things, if that gesture would have done any good, if it could have averted any of the harm that was to come. He told himself it wouldn't. He knew it wouldn't. But still, afterward, he wished that, just for a moment on that slow flight home, he had touched Wednesday's hand.

***

The brief winter daylight was already fading when Wednesday dropped Shadow outside his apartment. The freezing temperature when Shadow opened the car door felt even more science fictional when compared to Las Vegas.

'Don't get into any trouble,' said Wednesday. 'Keep your head below the parapet. Make no waves.'

'All at the same time?'

'Don't get smart with me, m'boy. You can keep out of sight in Lakeside. I pulled in a big favor to keep you here, safe and sound. If you were in a city they'd get your scent in minutes.'

'I'll stay put and keep out of trouble.' Shadow meant it as he said it. He'd had a lifetime of trouble and he was ready to let it go forever. 'When are you coming back?' he asked.

'Soon,' said Wednesday, and he gunned the Lincoln's engine, slid up the window and drove off into the frigid night.

Chapter Eleven

'Three may keep a secret, if two of them are dead.'
— Ben Franklin, *Poor Richard's Almanack*

Three cold days passed. The thermometer never made it up to the zero mark, not even at midday. Shadow wondered how people had survived this weather in the days before electricity, before thermal face masks and lightweight thermal underwear, before easy travel.

He was down at the Video, Tanning, Bait, and Tackle store, being shown Hinzelmann's hand-tied trout flies. They were more interesting than he had expected: colorful fakes of life, made of feather and thread, each with a hook hidden inside it.

He asked Hinzelmann.

'For real?' asked Hinzelmann.

'For real,' said Shadow.

'Well,' said the older man. 'Sometimes they didn't survive it, and they died. Leaky chimneys and badly ventilated stoves and ranges killed as many people as the cold. But those days were hard – they'd spend the summer and the fall laying up the food and the firewood for the winter. The worst thing of all was the madness. I heard on the radio, they were saying how it was to do with the sunlight, how there isn't enough of it in the winter. My daddy, he said folk just went stir crazy – winter madness they called it. Lakeside always had it easy, but some of the other towns around here, they had it hard. There was a saying still had currency when I was a kid, that if the serving girl hadn't tried to kill you by February she hadn't any backbone.

'Storybooks were like gold-dust – anything you could read was treasured, back before the town had a lending library. When my grampaw got sent a story book from his brother in Bavaria, all the Germans in town met up in the town hall to hear him read it, and the Finns and the Irish and the rest of them, they'd make the Germans tell them the stories.

'Twenty miles south of here, in Jibway, they found a woman walking mother-naked in the winter with a dead babe at her breast, and she'd not suffer them to take it from her.' He shook his head meditatively, closed the fly cabinet with a click. 'Bad business. You want a video rental card? Eventually they'll open a Blockbusters here, and then we'll soon be out of business. But for now we got a pretty fair selection.'

Shadow reminded Hinzelmann that he had no television and no VCR. He enjoyed Hinzelmann's company – the reminiscences, the tall tales, the goblin grin of the old man. It could make things awkward between them were Shadow to admit that television had made him uncomfortable ever since it had started to talk to him.

Hinzelmann fished in a drawer, and took out a tin box – by the look of it, it had once been a Christmas Box, of the kind that contained chocolates or cookies: a mottled Santa Claus, holding a tray of Coca-Cola bottles, beamed up from its lid. Hinzelmann eased off the metal top of the box, revealing a notebook and books of blank tickets, and said, 'How many you want me to put you down for?'

'How many of what?'

'Klunker tickets. She'll go out onto the ice today, so we've started selling tickets. Each ticket is ten dollars, five for forty, ten for seventy five. One ticket buys you five minutes. Of course we can't promise it'll go down in your five minutes, but the person who's closest stands to win five hundred bucks, and if it goes down in your five minutes, you win a thousand dollars. The earlier you buy your tickets, the more times aren't spoken for. You want to see the info sheet?'

'Sure.'

Hinzelmann handed Shadow a photocopied sheet. The klunker was an old car with its engine and fuel tank removed, which would be parked out on the ice for the winter. Sometime in the spring the lake ice would melt, and when it was too thin to bear the car's weight the car would fall into the lake. The earliest the klunker had ever tumbled into the lake was February the twenty-seventh ('That was the winter of 1998, I don't think you could rightly call that a winter at all,') the latest was May the First ('That was 1950. Seemed that year that the only way that winter would end was if somebody hammered a stake through its heart.') The beginning of April appeared to be the most common time for the car to sink – normally in mid-afternoon.

All of the mid-afternoons in April had already gone, marked off in Hinzelmann's lined notebook. Shadow bought a 25 minute period on the morning of March the 23rd, from 9:00 a.m. to 9: 25 a.m.. He handed Hinzelmann forty dollars.

'I just wish everybody in town was as easy a sell as you are,' said Hinzelmann.

'It's a thank-you for that ride you gave me that first night I was in town.'

'No, Mike,' said Hinzelmann. 'It's for the children.' For a moment he looked serious, with no trace of impishness on his creased old face. 'Come down this afternoon, you can lend a hand pushing the klunker out onto the lake.'

He passed Shadow five blue cards, each with a date and

time written on it in Hinzelmann's old-fashioned hand-writing, then entered the details of each in his notebook.

'Hinzelmann,' asked Shadow. 'Have you ever heard of eagle stones?'

'Up north of Rhinelander? Nope, that's Eagle River. Can't say I have.'

'How about thunderbirds?'

'Well, there was the Thunderbird Framing Gallery up on 5th Street, but that closed down. I'm not helping, am I?'

'Nope.'

'Tell you what, why don't you go look at the library. Good people, although they may be kind of distracted by the library sale on this week. I showed you where the library was, didn't I?'

Shadow nodded, and said so long. He wished he'd thought of the library himself. He got into the purple 4-Runner and drove south on Main Street, following the lake around to the southernmost point, until he reached the castle-like building which housed the city library. He walked inside. A sign pointed to the basement: LIBRARY SALE, it said. The library proper was on the ground floor, and he stamped the snow off his boots and went in.

A forbidding woman with pursed, crimson-colored lips asked him pointedly if she could help him.

'I suppose I need a library card,' he said. 'And I want to know all about thunderbirds.'

The woman had him fill out a form, then she told him it would take a week until he could be issued with his card. Shadow wondered if they spent the week sending out inquiries to ensure that he was not wanted in any other libraries across America for failure to return library books.

He had known a man in prison who had been imprisoned for stealing library books.

'Sounds kind of rough,' said Shadow, when the man told him why he was inside.

'Half a million dollars worth of books,' said the man,

proudly. His name was Gary McGuire. 'Mostly rare and antique books from libraries and universities. They found a whole storage locker filled with books from floor to ceiling. Open and shut case.'

'Why did you take them?' asked Shadow.

'I wanted them,' said Gary.

'Jesus. Half a million dollars worth of books.'

Gary flashed him a grin, lowered his voice and said, 'That was just in the storage locker they *found*. They never found the garage in San Clemente with the *really* good stuff in it.'

Gary had died in prison, when what the infirmary had told him was just a malingering, feeling-lousy kind of day turned out to be a ruptured appendix. Now, here in the Lakeside library, Shadow found himself thinking about a garage in San Clemente with box after box of rare, strange and beautiful books in it rotting away, all of them browning and wilting and being eaten by mold and insects in the darkness, waiting for someone who would never come to set them free.

Native American Beliefs and Traditions were on a single shelf in one castle-like turret. Shadow pulled down some books and sat in the window seat. In several minutes he had learned that thunderbirds were mythical gigantic birds who lived on mountaintops, who brought the lightning and who flapped their wings to make the thunder. There were some tribes, he read, who believed that the thunderbirds had made the world. Another half hour's reading did not turn up anything more, and he could find no mention of eagle stones anywhere in the books' indexes.

Shadow was putting the last of the books back on the shelf when he became aware of someone staring at him. Someone small and grave was peeking at him from around the heavy shelves. As he turned to look, the face vanished. He turned his back on the boy, then glanced around to see that he was being watched once more.

In his pocket was the Liberty dollar. He took it out of his

pocket, held it up in his right hand, making sure the boy could see it. He finger-palmed it into his left hand, displayed both hands empty, raised his left hand to his mouth and coughed once, letting the coin tumble from his left hand into his right.

The boy looked at him wide-eyed and scampered away, returning a few moments later, dragging an unsmiling Marguerite Olsen, who looked at Shadow suspiciously and said, 'Hello Mister Ainsel. Leon says you were doing magic for him.'

'Just a little prestidigitation, Ma'am.'

'Please don't,' she said.

'I'm sorry. I was just trying to entertain him.'

She shook her head, tautly. *Drop it*. Shadow dropped it. He said, 'I never did say thank you for your advice about heating the apartment. It's warm as toast in there right now.'

'That's good.' Her icy expression had not begun to thaw.

'It's a lovely library,' said Shadow.

'It's a beautiful building. But the city needs something more efficient and less beautiful. You going to the library sale downstairs?'

'I wasn't planning on it.'

'Well, you should. It's for a good cause. Makes money for new books, cleans out shelf space, and it's raising money to put in computers for the children's section. But the sooner we get a whole new library built, the better.'

'I'll make a point of getting down there.'

'Head out into the hall and then go downstairs. Good seeing you, Mister Ainsel.'

'Call me Mike,' he said.

She said nothing, just took Leon's hand and walked the boy over to the children's section.

'But mom,' Shadow heard Leon say, 'It wasn't *pressed igitation*. It wasn't. I *saw* it vanish and then it fell out of his nose. I saw it.'

An oil portrait of Abraham Lincoln gazed down from the

wall at him. Shadow walked down the marble and oak steps to the library basement, through a door into a large room filled with tables, each table covered with books of all kinds, indiscriminately assorted and promiscuously arranged: paperbacks and hardcovers, fiction and non-fiction, periodicals and encyclopedias all side by side upon the tables, spines up or spines out.

Shadow wandered to the back of the room where there was a table covered with old-looking leather-bound books, each with a library catalog number painted in white on the spine. 'You're the first person over in that corner all day,' said the man sitting by the stack of empty boxes and bags and the small, open, metal cashbox. 'Mostly folk just take the thrillers and the children's books and the Harlequin Romances. Jenny Kerton, Danielle Steel, all that.' The man was reading Agatha Christie's *The Murder of Roger Ackroyd*. 'Everything on the tables is fifty cents a book, or you can take three for a dollar.'

Shadow thanked him and continued to browse. He found a copy of Herodotus's *Histories* bound in peeling brown leather. It made him think of the paperback copy he had left behind in prison. There was a book called *Perplexing Parlour Illusions*, which looked like it might have some coin effects. He carried both the books over to the man with the cashbox.

'Buy one more, it's still a dollar,' said the man. 'And if you take another book away, you'll be doing us a favor. We need the shelf-space.'

Shadow walked back to the old leather-bound books. He decided to liberate the book that was least likely to be bought by anyone else, and found himself unable to decide between *Common Diseases of the Urinary Tract with Illustrations by a Medical Doctor* and *Minutes of the Lakeside City Council 1872–1884*. He looked at the illustrations in the medical book and decided that somewhere in the town there was a teenage boy who could use the book to gross out his friends. He took the *Minutes* to the man on the door who took his dollar and put all the books into a Dave's Finest Food brown paper sack.

Shadow left the library. He had a clear view of the lake, all the way to the north-eastern corner. He could even see his apartment building, a small brown box on the bank up past the bridge. And there were men on the ice near the bridge, four or five of them, pushing a dark green car into the center of the white lake.

'March the 23rd,' Shadow said to the lake, under his breath. '9:00 a.m. to 9: 25 a.m.' He wondered if the lake or the klunker could hear him – and if they would pay any attention to him, even if they could. He doubted it. In Shadow's world, luck, the good kind, was something that other people had, not him.

The wind blew bitter against his face.

Officer Chad Mulligan was waiting outside Shadow's apartment when he got back. Shadow's heart began to pound when he saw the police car, to relax a little when he observed that the policeman was doing paperwork in the front seat.

He walked over to the car, carrying his paper sack of books.

Mulligan lowered his window. 'Library sale?' he said.

'Yes.'

'I bought a box of Robert Ludlum books there two, three years back. Keep meaning to read them. My cousin swears by the guy. These days I figure if I ever get marooned on a desert island and I got my box of Robert Ludlum books with me, I can catch up on my reading.'

'Something particular I can do for you, Chief?'

'Not a damn thing, pal. Thought I'd stop by and see how you were settling in. You remember that Chinese saying, you save a man's life, you're responsible for him. Well, I'm not saying I saved your life last week. But I still thought I should check in. How's the Gunther Purple-mobile doing?'

'Good,' said Shadow. 'It's good. Running fine.'

'Pleased to hear it.'

'I saw my next-door neighbor in the library,' said Shadow. 'Miz Olsen. I was wondering . . .'

'What crawled up her butt and died?'

'If you want to put it like that.'

'Long story. You want to ride along for a spell, and I'll tell you all about it.'

Shadow thought about it for a moment. 'Okay,' he said. He got into the car, sat in the front passenger seat. Mulligan drove north of town. Then he turned off his lights and parked beside the road.

'Darren Olsen met Marge at U.W. Stevens Point and he brought her back north to Lakeside. She was a journalism major. He was studying, shit, hotel management, something like that. When they got here, jaws dropped. This was, what, thirteen, fourteen years ago. She was so beautiful . . . that black hair . . .,' he paused. 'Darren managed the Motel America over in Camden, twenty miles west of here. Except nobody ever seemed to want to stop in Camden and eventually the motel closed. They had two boys. At that time Sandy was eleven. The little one – Leon is it? – was just a babe in arms.

'Darren Olsen wasn't a brave man. He'd been a good high school football player, but that was the last time he was flying high. Whatever. He couldn't find the courage to tell Margie that he'd lost his job. So for a month, maybe for two months, he'd drive off early in the morning, come home late in the evening complaining about the hard day he'd had at the motel.'

'What was he doing?' asked Shadow.

'Mm. Couldn't say for certain. I reckon he was driving up to Ironwood, maybe down to Green Bay. Guess he started out as a job hunter. Pretty soon he was drinking the time away, getting stoned, more than probably meeting the occasional working girl for a little instant gratification. He could have been gambling. What I do know for certain is that he emptied

out their joint account in about ten weeks. It was only a
matter of time before Margie figured out – there we go!"

He swung the car out, flicked on the siren and the lights,
and scared the daylights out of a small man with Iowa plates
who had just come down the hill at seventy.

The rogue Iowan ticketed, Mulligan returned to his story.

'Where was I? Okay. So Margie kicks him out, sues for
divorce. It turned into a vicious custody battle. That's what
they call 'em when they get into *People* magazine. Vicious
Custody Battle. Always makes me think of lawyers with
knives and assault weapons and brass knuckles. She got the
kids. Darren got visitation rights and precious little else.
Now, back then Leon was pretty small. Sandy was older, a
good kid, the kind of boy who worships his daddy. Wouldn't
let Margie say nothing bad about him. They lost the house –
had a nice place down on Daniel's Road. She moved into the
apartments. He left town. Came back every few months to
make everybody miserable.

'This went on for a few years. He'd come back, spend
money on the kids, leave Margie in tears. Most of us just
started wishing he'd never come back at all. His mom and
pop had moved to Florida when they retired, said they
couldn't take another Wisconsin winter. So last year he came
out, said he wanted to take the boys to Florida for Christmas.
Margie said not a hope, told him to get lost. It got pretty
unpleasant – at one point I had to go over there. Domestic
dispute. By the time I got there Darren was standing in the
front yard shouting stuff, the boys were barely holding it
together, Margie was crying.

'I told Darren he was shaping up for a night in the cells. I
thought for a moment he was going to hit me, but he was
sober enough not to do that. I gave him a ride down to the
trailer park south of town, told him to shape up. That he'd
hurt her enough . . . Next day he left town.'

'Two weeks later, Sandy vanished. Didn't get onto the
school bus. Told his best friend that he'd be seeing his dad

soon, that Darren was bringing him a specially cool present to make up for having missed Christmas in Florida. Nobody's seen him since. Non-custodial kidnappings are the hardest. It's tough to find a kid who doesn't want to be found, y'see?'

Shadow said that he did. He saw something else as well. Chad Mulligan was in love with Marguerite Olsen himself. He wondered if the man knew how obvious it was.

Mulligan pulled out once more, lights flashing, and pulled over some teenagers doing sixty. He didn't ticket them, 'just put the fear of God in them'.

***

That evening Shadow sat at the kitchen table trying to figure out how to transform a silver dollar into a penny. It was a trick he had found in *Perplexing Parlour Illusions* but the instructions were infuriating, unhelpful, and vague. Phrases like 'then vanish the penny in the usual way,' occurred every sentence or so. In this context, Shadow wondered, what was 'the usual way?' A French drop? Sleeving it? Shouting 'Oh my god, look out! – a mountain lion!' and dropping the coin into his side pocket while the audience's attention was diverted?

He tossed his silver dollar into the air, caught it, remembering the moon and the woman who gave it to him, then he attempted the illusion. It didn't seem to work. He walked into the bathroom and tried it in front of the mirror, and confirmed that he was right. The trick as written simply didn't work. He sighed, dropped the coins in his pocket and sat down on the couch. He spread the cheap throw rug over his legs and flipped open the *Minutes of the Lakeside Council 1872-1884*. The type, in two columns, was so small as to be almost unreadable. He flipped through the book, looking at the reproductions of the photographs of the period, at the several incarnations of the Lakeside City Council therein: long side-whiskers and clay pipes and battered hats and shiny hats, worn with faces which were, many of them, peculiarly familiar. He was unsurprised to see that the portly secretary of the 1882 city council was a Patrick Mulligan: shave him, make him lose 20 pounds and he'd be a dead ringer for Chad Mulligan, his – what, great-great-grandson? He wondered if Hinzelmann's pioneer grandfather was in the photographs, but it did not appear that he had been city council material. Shadow thought he had seen a reference to a Hinzelmann in the text, while flipping from photograph to photograph, but it eluded him when he leafed back for it, and the tiny type made Shadow's eyes ache.

He put the book down on his chest and realized his head was nodding. It would be foolish to fall asleep on the couch, he decided, soberly. The bedroom was only a few feet away. On the other hand, the bedroom and the bed would still be there in five minutes, and anyway, he was not going to go to sleep, only to close his eyes for a moment . . .

Darkness roared.

He stood on an open plain. Beside him was the place from which he had once emerged, from which the earth had squeezed him. Stars were still falling from the sky and each star that touched the red earth became a man or a woman. The men had long black hair and high cheekbones. The women all looked like Marguerite Olsen. These were the star people.

They looked at him with dark, proud eyes.

'Tell me about the thunderbirds,' said Shadow. 'Please. It's not for me. It's for my wife.'

One by one they turned their backs on him, and as he lost their faces they were gone, one with the landscape. But the last of them, her hair streaked white on dark gray, pointed before she turned away, pointed into the wine-colored sky.

'Ask them yourself,' she said. Summer lightning flickered, momentarily illuminating the landscape from horizon to horizon.

There were high rocks near him, peaks and spires of

sandstone, and Shadow began to climb the nearest. The spire was the color of old ivory. He grabbed at a handhold, and felt it slice into his hand. It's bone, thought Shadow. Not stone. It's old dry bone.

But it was a dream, and in dreams, sometimes, you have no choices: either there are no decisions to be made, or they were made for you long before ever the dream began. Shadow continued to climb, pulling himself up. His hands hurt. Bone popped and crushed and fragmented under his bare feet, cutting them painfully. The wind tugged at him, and he pressed himself to the spire, and he continued to climb the tower.

It was made of only one kind of bone, he realized, repeated over and over. Each of the bones was dry and ball-like. For a moment he had imagined they might be old yellow shells or the eggs of some dreadful bird. But another flare of lightning told him differently: they had holes for eyes, and they had teeth, which grinned without humor.

Somewhere birds were calling. Rain spattered his face.

He was hundreds of feet above the ground, clinging to the side of the tower of skulls, while flashes of lightning burned in the wings of the shadowy birds who circled the spire – enormous black, condor-like birds, each with a ruff of white at its neck. They were huge, graceful, awful birds, and the beats of their wings crashed like thunder on the night air.

They were circling the spire.

They must be fifteen, twenty feet from wingtip to wingtip, thought Shadow.

Then the first bird swung out of its glide toward him, blue lightning crackling in its wings. He pushed himself into a crevice of skulls, hollow eye-holes stared at him, a clutter of ivory teeth smiled at him, but he kept climbing, pulling himself up the mountain of skulls, every sharp edge cutting into his skin, feeling revulsion and terror and awe.

Another bird came at him, and one hand-sized talon sank into his arm.

He reached out and tried to grasp a feather from its wing. If he returned to his tribe without a thunderbird's feather he would be disgraced, he would never be a man, but the bird pulled up, so that he could not grasp even one feather. The thunderbird loosened its grip and swung back onto the wind. Shadow continued to climb.

There must be a thousand skulls, thought Shadow. A thousand thousand. And not all of them are human. He stood at last on the top of the spire, the great birds, the thunderbirds, circling him slowly, navigating the gusts of the storm with tiny flicks of their wings.

He heard a voice, the voice of the buffalo man, calling to him on the wind, telling him who the skulls belonged to . . .

The tower began to tumble, and the biggest bird, its eyes the blinding blue-white of forked lightning, plummeted down toward him in a rush of thunder, and Shadow was falling, tumbling down the tower of skulls . . .

The telephone shrilled. Shadow had not even known that it was connected. Groggy, shaken, he picked it up.

'What the fuck,' shouted Wednesday, angrier than Shadow had ever heard him, 'What the almighty flying fuck do you think you are playing at?'

'I was asleep,' said Shadow into the receiver, stupidly.

'What do you think is the fucking point of stashing you in a hiding place like Lakeside, if you're going to raise such a ruckus that not even a dead man could miss it?'

'I dreamed of thunderbirds . . .' said Shadow. 'And a tower. Skulls . . .' It seemed to him very important to recount his dream.

'I know what you were dreaming. Everybody damn well knows what you were dreaming. Christ almighty. What's the point in hiding you, if you're going to start to fucking advertise?

'Look . . .' said Wednesday. Shadow thought he was about to start shouting again, but instead he said, 'A tower of skulls, you say?'

'Yes,' said Shadow.

There was a pause at the other end of the telephone. 'I'll be there in the morning,' said Wednesday. It sounded like the anger had died down. 'We're going to San Francisco. The flowers in your hair are optional.' And the line went dead.

Shadow put the telephone down on the carpet, and sat up, stiffly. It was six a.m. and still night-dark outside. He got up from the sofa, shivering. He could hear the wind as it screamed across the frozen lake. And he could hear somebody nearby, crying, only the thickness of a wall away. He was certain it was Marguerite Olsen, and her sobbing was insistent and low and heart-breaking.

Shadow walked into the bathroom and pissed, then went into his bedroom and closed the door, blocking off the sound of the crying woman. Outside the wind howled and wailed as if it, too, was seeking for a lost child, and he slept no more that night.

* * *

San Francisco in January was unseasonably warm, warm enough that the sweat prickled on the back of Shadow's neck. Wednesday was wearing a deep blue suit, and a pair of gold-rimmed spectacles that made him look like an entertainment lawyer.

They were walking along Haight Street. The street people and the hustlers and the moochers watched them go by, and no one shook a paper cup of change at them, no one asked them for anything at all.

Wednesday's jaw was set. Shadow had seen immediately that the man was still angry, and had asked no questions when the black Lincoln town car had pulled up outside the apartment that morning. They had not talked on the way to the airport. He had been relieved that Wednesday was in first class and he was back in coach.

Now it was late in the afternoon. Shadow, who had not

been in San Francisco since he was a boy, who had only seen
it since then as a background to movies, was astonished at
how familiar it was, how colorful and unique the wooden
houses, how steep the hills, how very much it didn't feel like
anywhere else.

'It's almost hard to believe that this is in the same country
as Lakeside,' he said.

Wednesday glared at him. Then he said, 'It's not. San
Francisco isn't in the same country as Lakeside any more
than New Orleans is in the same country as New York or
Miami is in the same country as Minneapolis.'

'Is that so?' said Shadow, mildly.

'Indeed it is. They may share certain cultural signifiers –
money, a federal government, entertainment – it's the same
land, obviously – but the only things that give it the illusion
of being one country are the greenback, *The Tonight Show*,
and McDonald's.' They were approaching a park at the end
of the road. 'Be nice to the lady we are visiting. But not too
nice.'

'I'll be cool,' said Shadow.

They stepped onto the grass.

A young girl, no older than fourteen, her hair dyed green
and orange and pink, stared at them as they went by. She sat
beside a dog, a mongrel, with a piece of string for a collar and
a leash. She looked hungrier than the dog did. The dog
yapped at them, then wagged its tail.

Shadow gave the girl a dollar bill. She stared at it as if she
was not sure what it was. 'Buy dog food with it,' Shadow
suggested. She nodded, and smiled.

'Let me put it bluntly,' said Wednesday. 'You must be very
cautious around the lady we are visiting. She might take a
fancy to you, and that would be bad.'

'Is she your girlfriend or something?'

'Not for all the little plastic toys in China,' said
Wednesday, agreeably. His anger seemed to have dissipated,
or perhaps to have been invested for the future. Shadow

suspected that anger was the engine that made Wednesday run.

There was a woman sitting on the grass, under a tree, with a paper tablecloth spread in front of her, and a variety of Tupperware dishes on the cloth.

She was – not fat, no, far from fat: what she was, a word that Shadow had never had cause to use until now, was *curvaceous*. Her hair was so fair that it was white, the kind of platinum blonde tresses that should have belonged to a long-dead movie starlet, her lips were painted crimson, and she looked to be somewhere between twenty-five and fifty.

As they reached her she was selecting from a plate of devilled eggs. She looked up as Wednesday approached her, and put down the egg she had chosen, and wiped her hand. 'Hello, you old fraud,' she said, but she smiled as she said it, and Wednesday bowed low, took her hand and raised it to his lips.

He said, 'You look divine.'

'How the hell else should I look?' she demanded, sweetly. 'Anyway, you're a liar. New Orleans was *such* a mistake – I put on, what, thirty pounds there? I swear. I knew I had to leave when I started to waddle. The tops of my thighs rub together when I walk now, can you believe that?' This last was addressed to Shadow. He had no idea what to say in reply, and felt a hot flush suffuse his face. The woman laughed delightedly. 'He's *blushing*! Wednesday my sweet, you brought me a *blusher*. How perfectly wonderful of you. What's he called?'

'This is Shadow,' said Wednesday. He seemed to be enjoying Shadow's discomfort. 'Shadow, say hello to Easter.'

Shadow said something that might have been Hello, and the woman smiled at him again. He felt like he was caught in headlights – the blinding kind that poachers use to freeze deer before they shoot them. He could smell her perfume from where he was standing, an intoxicating mixture of jasmine and honeysuckle, of sweet milk and female skin.

'So, how's tricks?' asked Wednesday.

The woman – Easter – laughed a deep and throaty laugh, full-bodied and joyous. How could you not like someone who laughed like that? 'Everything's fine,' she said. 'How about you, you old wolf?'

'I was hoping to enlist your assistance.'

'Wasting your time.'

'At least hear me out before dismissing me.'

'No point. Don't even bother.'

She looked at Shadow. 'Please, sit down here and help yourself to some of this food. Here, take a plate and pile it high. It's all good. Eggs, roast chicken, chicken curry, chicken salad, and over here is lapin – rabbit, actually, but cold rabbit is a delight, and in that bowl over there is the jugged hare, well, why don't I just fill a plate for you?' And she did, taking a plastic plate and piling it high with foods and passing it to him. Then she looked at Wednesday. 'Are you eating?' she asked.

'I am at your disposal, my dear,' said Wednesday.

'You,' she told him, 'are so full of shit it's a wonder your eyes don't turn brown.' She passed him an empty plate. 'Help yourself,' she said.

The afternoon sun at her back burned her hair into a platinum aura. 'Shadow,' she said, chewing a chicken leg with gusto. 'That's a sweet name. Why do they call you Shadow?'

Shadow licked his lips to moisten them. 'When I was a kid,' he said. 'We lived, my mother and I, we were, I mean, she was, well, like a secretary, at a bunch of US Embassies, we went from city to city all over northern Europe. Then she got sick and had to take early retirement and we came back to the States. I never knew what to say to the other kids, so I'd just find adults and follow them around, not saying anything. I just needed the company, I guess. I don't know. I was a small kid.'

'You grew,' she said.

'Yes,' said Shadow. 'I grew.'

She turned back to Wednesday, who was spooning down a bowl of what looked like cold gumbo. 'Is this the boy who's got everybody so upset?'

'You heard?'

'I keep my ears pricked up,' she said. Then to Shadow, 'You keep out of their way. There are too many secret societies out there, and they have no loyalties and no love. Commercial, independent, government, they're all in the same boat. They range from the barely competent to the deeply dangerous. Hey, old wolf, I heard a joke you'd like the other day. How do you know the CIA weren't involved in the Kennedy assassination?'

'I've heard it,' said Wednesday.

'Pity.' She turned her attention back to Shadow. 'But the spookshow, the ones you met, they're something else. They exist because everyone knows they must exist.' She drained a paper cup of something that looked like white wine, and then she got to her feet. 'Shadow's a good name,' she said. 'I want a Mochaccino. Come on.'

She began to walk away. 'What about the food?' asked Wednesday. 'You can't just leave it here.'

She smiled at him, and pointed to the girl sitting by the dog, and then extended her arms to take in the Haight and the world. 'Let it feed them,' she said, and she walked, with Wednesday and Shadow trailing behind her.

'Remember,' she said to Wednesday, as they walked, '*I'm* rich. I'm doing just peachy. Why should I help you?'

'You're one of us,' he said. 'You're as forgotten and as unloved and unremembered as any of us. It's pretty clear whose side you should be on.'

They reached a sidewalk coffee house, went inside, sat down. There was only one waitress, who wore her eyebrow ring as a mark of caste, and a woman making coffee behind the counter. The waitress advanced upon them, smiling automatically, sat them down, took their orders.

Easter put her slim hand on the back of Wednesday's square gray hand. 'I'm telling you,' she said, 'I'm doing *fine*. On my festival days they still feast on eggs and rabbits, on candy and on flesh, to represent rebirth and copulation. They wear flowers in their bonnets and they give each other flowers. They do it in my name. More and more of them every year. In *my* name, old wolf.'

'And you wax fat and affluent on their worship and their love?' he said, dryly.

'Don't be an asshole.' Suddenly she sounded very tired. She sipped her Mochaccino.

'Serious question, m'dear. Certainly I would agree that millions upon millions of them give each other tokens in your name, and that they still practice all the rites of your festival, even down to hunting for hidden eggs. But how many of them know who you are? Eh? Excuse me miss?' This to their waitress.

She said, 'You need another espresso?'

'No, my dear. I was just wondering if you could solve a little argument we were having over here. My friend and I were disagreeing over what the word "Easter" means. Would you happen to know?'

The girl stared at him as if green toads had begun to push their way between his lips. Then she said, 'I don't know about any of that Christian stuff. I'm a pagan.'

The woman behind the counter said, 'I think it's like Latin or something for "Christ Has Risen" maybe.'

'Really?' said Wednesday.

'Yeah, sure,' said the woman. 'Easter. Just like the sun rises in the east, you know.'

'The risen son. Of course – a most logical supposition.' The woman smiled and returned to her coffee grinder. Wednesday looked up at their waitress. 'I think I *shall* have another espresso, if you do not mind. And tell me, as a pagan, who do *you* worship?'

'Worship?'

'That's right. I imagine you must have a pretty wide-open field. So to whom do you set up your household altar? To whom do you bow down? To whom do you pray at dawn and at dusk?'

Her lips described several shapes without saying anything before she said, 'The female principle. It's an empowerment thing. You know.'

'Indeed. And this female principle of yours. Does she have a name?'

'She's the goddess within us all,' said the girl with the eyebrow ring, color rising to her cheek. 'She doesn't need a name.'

'Ah,' said Wednesday, with a wide monkey grin, 'so do you have mighty bacchanals in her honor? Do you drink blood wine under the full moon, while scarlet candles burn in silver candle holders? Do you step naked into the sea-foam, chanting ecstatically to your nameless goddess while the waves lick at your legs, lapping your thighs like the tongues of a thousand leopards?'

'You're making fun of me,' she said. 'We don't do any of that stuff you were saying.' She took a deep breath. Shadow suspected she was counting to ten. 'Any more coffees here? Another Mochaccino for you ma'am?' Her smile was a lot like the one she had greeted them with when they had entered.

They shook their heads, and the waitress turned to greet another customer.

'There,' said Wednesday, 'is one who "*does not have the faith and will not have the fun*". Chesterton. Pagan indeed. So. Shall we go out onto the street, Easter my dear, and repeat the exercise? Find out how many passers-by know that their Easter festival takes its name from Eostre of the Dawn? Let's see — I have it. We shall ask a hundred people. For every one that knows the truth, you may cut off one of my fingers, and when I run out of them, toes; for every twenty who don't know you spend a night making love to

me. And the odds are certainly in your favor here – this is
San Francisco, after all. There are heathens and pagans and
Wiccans aplenty on these precipitous streets.'

Her green eyes looked at Wednesday. They were, Shadow
decided, the exact same color as a leaf in spring with the sun
shining through it. She said nothing.

'We *could* try it,' continued Wednesday. 'But I would end
up with ten fingers, ten toes, and five nights in your bed. So
don't tell me they worship you and keep your festival day.
They mouth your name, but it has no meaning to them.
Nothing at all.'

Tears stood out in her eyes. 'I know that,' she said, quietly.
'I'm not a fool.'

'No,' said Wednesday. 'You're not.'

He's pushed her too far, thought Shadow.

Wednesday looked down, ashamed. 'I'm sorry,' he said.
Shadow could hear the real sincerity in his voice. 'We *need*
you. We need your energy. We need your power. Will you
fight beside us when the storm comes?'

She hesitated. She had a chain of blue forget-me-nots
tattooed around her left wrist.

'Yes,' she said, after a while. 'I guess I will.'

Wednesday kissed his finger, touched it to her cheek.
Then he called their waitress over and paid for their coffees,
counting out the money carefully, folding it over with the
check and presenting it to her.

As she walked away, Shadow said, 'Ma'am? Excuse me? I
think you dropped this.' He picked up a ten dollar bill from
the floor.

'No,' she said, looking at the wrapped bills in her hand.

'I saw it fall, ma'am,' said Shadow, politely. 'You should
count them.'

She counted the money in her hand, looked puzzled and
said, 'Jesus. You're right. I'm sorry.' She took the ten dollar
bill from Shadow, and walked away.

Easter walked out onto the sidewalk with them. The light

was just starting to fade. She nodded to Wednesday, then she touched Shadow's hand and said, 'What did you dream about, last night?'

'Thunderbirds,' he said. 'A mountain of skulls.'

She nodded. 'And do you know whose skulls they were?'

'There was a voice,' he said. 'In my dream. It told me.'

She nodded and waited.

He said, 'It said they were mine. Old skulls of mine. Thousands and thousands of them.'

She looked at Wednesday, and said, 'I think this one's a keeper.' She smiled her bright smile. Then she patted Shadow's arm and walked away down the sidewalk. He watched her go, trying – and failing – not to think of her thighs rubbing together as she walked.

In the taxi on the way to the airport, Wednesday turned to Shadow. 'What the hell was that business with the ten dollars about?'

'You shortchanged her. It comes out of her wages if she's short.'

'What the hell do you care?' Wednesday seemed genuinely irate.

Shadow thought for a moment. Then he said, 'Well, I wouldn't want anyone to do it to me. She hadn't done anything wrong.'

'No?' Wednesday stared off into the middle-distance, and said, 'When she was seven years old she shut a kitten in a closet. She listened to it mew for several days. When it ceased to mew, she took it out of the closet, put it into a shoebox, and buried it in the back yard. She wanted to bury something. She consistently steals from everywhere she works. Small amounts, usually. Last year she visited her grandmother in the nursing home to which the old woman is confined. She took an antique gold watch from her grandmother's bedside table, and then went prowling through several of the other rooms, stealing small quantities of money and personal effects from the twilight folk in their golden years. When she got home she did not know what to do with her spoils, scared someone would come after her, so she threw everything away except the cash.'

'I get the idea,' said Shadow.

'She also has asymptomatic gonorrhea,' said Wednesday. 'She suspects she might be infected but does nothing about it. When her last boyfriend accused her of having given him a disease she was hurt, offended, and refused to see him again.'

'This isn't necessary,' said Shadow. 'I said I get the idea. You could do this to anyone, couldn't you? Tell me bad things about them.'

'Of course,' agreed Wednesday. 'They all do the same things. They may think their sins are original, but for the most part they are petty and repetitive.'

'And that makes it okay for you to steal ten bucks from her?'

Wednesday paid the taxi and the two men walked into the airport, wandered up to their gate. Boarding had not yet begun. Wednesday said, 'What the hell *else* can I do? They don't sacrifice rams or bulls to me. They don't send me the souls of killers and slaves, gallows-hung and raven-picked. *They* made me. *They* forgot me. Now I take a little back from them. Isn't that fair?'

'My mom used to say, *Life isn't fair,*' said Shadow.

'Of course she did,' said Wednesday. 'It's one of those things that moms say, right up there with *if all your friends jumped off a cliff would you do it too?*'

'You stiffed that girl for ten bucks, I slipped her ten bucks,' said Shadow, doggedly. 'It was the right thing to do, and I did it.'

Someone announced that their plane was boarding. Wednesday stood up. 'May your choices always be so clear,' he said, and once again, he sounded totally sincere.

It's true what they say, thought Shadow. *If you can fake sincerity, you've got it made.*

***

The cold snap was easing when Wednesday dropped Shadow off, in the small hours of the morning. It was still obscenely cold in Lakeside, but it was no longer impossibly cold. The lighted sign on the side of the M&I Bank flashed alternately 3:30 a.m. and −5° F as they drove through the town.

It was 9:30 a.m. when Chief of Police Chad Mulligan knocked on the apartment door and asked Shadow if he knew a girl named Alison McGovern.

'I don't think so,' said Shadow, sleepily.

'This is her picture,' said Mulligan. It was a high school photograph. Shadow recognized the person in the picture immediately: the girl with the blue rubber band braces on her teeth, the one who had been learning all about the oral uses of Alka Seltzer from her friend.

'Oh yeah. Okay. She was on the bus when I came into town.'

'Where were you yesterday, Mister Ainsel?'

Shadow felt his world begin to spin away from him. He knew he had nothing to feel guilty about (*you're a parole-violating felon living under an assumed name*, whispered a calm voice in his mind. *Isn't that enough?*)

'San Francisco,' he said. 'California. Helping my uncle transport a four poster bed.'

'You got any way of proving it? Ticket stubs? Anything like that?'

'Sure.' He had both his boarding pass stubs in his back pocket, pulled them out. 'What's going on?'

Chad Mulligan examined the boarding passes. 'Alison McGovern's vanished. She helped out up at the Lakeside Humane Society. Feed animals, walk dogs. She'd come out for a few hours after school. One of those animal kids. So. Dolly Knopf, who runs the Humane Society, she'd always run her home when they closed up for the night. Yesterday Alison never got there.'

'She's vanished.'

'Yup. Her parents called us last night. Silly kid used to hitchhike up to the Humane Society. It's out on County W, pretty isolated. Her parents told her not to, but this isn't the kind of place where things happen . . . people here don't lock their doors, you know? And you can't tell kids. So, look at the photo again.'

Alison McGovern was smiling. The rubber bands on her teeth in the photograph were red, not blue.

'You can honestly say you didn't kidnap her, rape her, murder her, anything like that?'

'I was in San Francisco. And I wouldn't do that shit.'

'That was what I figured, pal. So you want to come help us look for her?'

'Me?'

'You. We've had the K-9 guys out this morning – nothing so far.' He sighed. 'Heck, Mike. I just hope she turns up in the Twin Cities with some dopey boyfriend.'

'You think it's likely?'

'I think it's possible. You want to join the hunting party?'

Shadow remembered seeing the girl in Henning's Farm and Home Supplies, the flash of a shy blue-braced smile, how beautiful he had known she was going to be one day. 'I'll come,' he said.

There were two dozen men and women waiting in the lobby of the fire station. Shadow recognized Hinzelmann, and several other faces looked familiar. There were several police officers, dressed in blue, and some men and women from the Lumber County Sheriff's department, dressed in brown.

Chad Mulligan told them what Alison was wearing when she vanished (a scarlet snow-suit, green gloves, blue woolen hat under the hood of her snowsuit) and divided the volunteers into groups of three. Shadow, Hinzelmann, and a man named Brogan comprised one of the groups. They were reminded how short the daylight period was, told that if, god forbid, they found Alison's body they were not repeat not to disturb anything, just to radio back for help, but that if she was alive they were to keep her warm until help came.

They were dropped off out on County W.

Hinzelmann, Brogan and Shadow walked along the edge of a frozen creek. Each group of three had been issued a small hand-held walkie-talkie before they left.

The cloud cover was low, and the world was gray. No snow had fallen in the last 36 hours. Footprints stood out in the glittering crust of the crisp snow.

Brogan looked like a retired army colonel, with his slim moustache and white temples. He drove them, told Shadow he was a retired High School Principal. 'I took early retirement when I saw I wasn't getting any younger. These days I still teach a little, do the school play – that was always the high point of the year anyhow – and now I hunt a little and have a cabin down on Pike Lake, spend too much time there.' As they set out Brogan said, 'On the one hand, I hope we find her. On the other, if she's going to be found, I'd be very grateful if it was someone else who got to find her, and not us. You know what I mean?'

Shadow knew exactly what he meant.

The three men did not talk much. They walked, looking for a red snowsuit, or green gloves, or a blue hat, or a white body. Now and again Brogan, who had the walkie-talkie, would check in with Chad Mulligan.

At lunchtime they sat with the rest of the search party on a commandeered school bus and ate hot dogs and drank hot soup. Someone pointed out a red-tailed hawk in a bare tree, and someone else said that it looked more like a falcon, but it flew away and the argument was abandoned.

Hinzelmann told them a story about his grandfather's trumpet, and how he tried playing it during a cold snap, and the weather was so cold outside by the barn, where his grandfather had gone to practice, that no music came out.

'Then after he came inside he put the trumpet down by the

woodstove to thaw. Well, the family're all in bed that night and suddenly the unfrozen tunes start coming out of that trumpet. Scared my grandmother so much she nearly had kittens.'

The afternoon was endless, unfruitful, and depressing. The daylight faded slowly: distances collapsed and the world turned indigo and the wind blew cold enough to burn the skin on your face. When it was too dark to continue, Mulligan radioed to them to call it off for the evening, and they were picked up and driven back to the fire station.

In the block next to the fire station was the Buck Stops Here Tavern, and that was where most of the searchers wound up. They were exhausted and dispirited, talking to each other of the bald eagle that had circled them, how cold it had become, how more than likely Alison would show up in a day or so, no idea of how much trouble she'd caused everyone.

'You shouldn't think badly of the town because of this,' said Brogan. 'It is a good town.'

'Lakeside,' said a trim woman whose name Shadow had forgotten, if ever they'd been introduced, 'is the best town in the North Woods. You know how many people are unemployed in Lakeside?'

'No,' said Shadow.

'Less than twenty,' she said. 'There's over five thousand people live in and around this town. We may not be rich, but everyone's working. It's not like the mining towns up in the northeast – most of them are ghost towns now. There were farming towns that were killed by the falling cost of milk, or the low price of hogs. You know what the biggest cause of unnatural death is among farmers in the Midwest?'

'Suicide?' Shadow hazarded.

She looked almost disappointed. 'Yeah. That's it. They kill themselves.' She shook her head. Then she continued, 'There are too many towns hereabouts that only exist for the hunters and the vacationers, towns that just take their money and send them home with their trophies and their bug bites. Then there are the company towns, where everything's just hunky-dory until Wal-Mart relocates their distribution center or 3M stops manufacturing CD cases there or whatever and suddenly there's a boatload of folks who can't pay their mortgages. I'm sorry, I didn't catch your name.'

'Ainsel,' said Shadow. 'Mike Ainsel.' The beer he was drinking was a local brew, made with spring water. It was good.

'I'm Callie Knopf,' she said. 'Dolly's sister.' Her face was still ruddy from the cold. 'So what I'm saying is that Lakeside's lucky. We've got a little of everything here – farm, light industry, tourism, crafts. Good schools.'

Shadow looked at her in puzzlement. There was something empty at the bottom of all her words. It was as if he were listening to a salesman, a good salesman, who believed in his product, but still wanted to make sure you wont home with all the brushes or the full set of encyclopedias. Perhaps she could see it in his face. She said 'I'm sorry. When you love something you just don't want to stop talking about it. What do you do Mister Ainsel?'

'Heavy lifting,' said Shadow. 'My uncle buys and sells antiques all over the country. He uses me to move big, heavy things. Without breaking them too badly. It's a good job, but not steady work.' A black cat, the bar mascot, wound between Shadow's legs, rubbing its forehead on his boot. It leapt up beside him onto the bench and went to sleep.

'At least you get to travel,' said Brogan. 'You do anything else?'

'You got eight quarters on you?' asked Shadow. Brogan fumbled for his change. He found five quarters, pushed them across the table to Shadow. Callie Knopf produced another three quarters. 'And a nickel,' said Shadow, pulling one from his own pocket. 'We'll need that as a marker.'

He laid out the coins, four in one row, five in the other.

Then, with scarcely a fumble, he did the Coins Through the Table, appearing to drop half the coins through the wood of the table, from his left hand into his right.

After that, he put the nickel away, divided the quarters into two piles of four. He took all eight coins in his right hand, an empty water glass in his left, covered the glass with a napkin and appeared to make the coins vanish from his right hand and land in the glass beneath the napkin with an audible clink. Finally, he opened his right hand to show it was empty, then swept the napkin away to show the coins in the glass.

He returned their coins – three to Callie, five to Brogan – then took a quarter back from Brogan's hand, leaving four coins. He blew on it, and it was a penny, which he gave to Brogan, who counted his quarters and was dumbfounded to find that he still had all five in his hand.

'You're a Houdini,' cackled Hinzelmann in delight. 'That's what you are!"

'Just an amateur,' said Shadow. 'I've got a long way to go.' Still, he felt a smidgen of pride. It had, he realized, been his first adult audience.

He stopped at the food store on the way home to buy a carton of milk. The ginger-haired girl on the checkout counter looked familiar, and her eyes were red-rimmed from crying. Her face was one big freckle.

'I know you,' said Shadow. 'You're – ' and he was about to say the Alka Seltzer girl, but bit it back and finished, 'You're Alison's friend. From the bus. I hope she's going to be okay.'

She sniffed and nodded. 'Me too.' She blew her nose on a tissue, hard, and pushed it back into her sleeve.

Her badge said '*Hi! I'm SOPHIE! Ask ME how YOU can lose 20 lbs. in 30 days!*'

'I spent today looking for her. No luck yet.'

Sophie nodded, blinked back tears. She waved the milk carton in front of a scanner and it chirped its price at them. Shadow passed her two dollars.

'I'm leaving this fucking town,' said the girl in a sudden, choked voice. 'I'm going to live with my mom in Ashland. Alison's gone. Sandy Olsen went last year. Jo Ming the year before that. What if it's me next year?'

'I thought Sandy Olsen was taken by his father.'

'Yes,' said the girl, bitterly. 'I'm sure he was. And Jo Ming went out to California, and Sarah Lindquist got lost on a trail hike and they never found her. Whatever. I want to go to Ashland.'

She took a deep breath and held it for a moment. Then she smiled at him. There was nothing insincere about that smile. It was just the smile of someone who knew that it was her job to smile when she gave someone their change, and as she put Shadow's change and receipt into his hand she told him to have a nice day. Then she turned to the woman with the full shopping cart behind him and began to unload-and-scan. A boy no older than Sophie sauntered over to bag the groceries.

Shadow took his milk and drove away, past the gas station and the klunker on the ice, and over the bridge and home.

Coming to America

1778

There was a girl, and her uncle sold her, *wrote Mr Ibis in his perfect copper-plate handwriting.*
That is the tale; the rest is detail.

There are stories that are true, in which each individual's tale is unique and tragic, and the worst of the tragedy is that we have heard it before, and we cannot allow ourselves to feel it too deeply. We build a shell around it like an oyster dealing with a painful particle of grit, coating it with smooth pearl layers in order to cope. This is how we walk and talk and function, day in, day out, immune to others' pain and loss. If it were to touch us it would cripple us or make saints of us; but, for the most part, it does not touch us. We cannot allow it to.

Tonight, as you eat, reflect if you can: there are children starving in the world, starving in numbers larger than the mind can easily hold, up in the big numbers where an error of a million here, a million there, can be forgiven. It may be uncomfortable for you to reflect upon this or it may not, but still, you will eat.

There are accounts which, if we open our hearts to them will cut us too deeply. Look – here is a good man, good by his own lights and the lights of his friends: he is faithful and true to his wife, he adores and lavishes attention on his little children, he cares about his country, he does his job punctiliously, as best he can. So, efficiently and good-naturedly, he exterminates Jews: he appreciates the music that plays in the background to pacify them; he advises the Jews not to forget their identification numbers as they go into the showers – many people, he tells them, forget their numbers, and take the wrong clothes, when they come out of the showers. This calms the Jews: there will be life, they assure themselves, after the showers. And they are wrong. Our man supervises the detail taking the bodies to the ovens; and if there is anything he feels bad about, it is that he still allows the gassing of vermin to affect him. Were he a truly good man, he knows, he would feel nothing but joy, as the earth is cleansed of its pests.

Leave him; he cuts too deep. He is too close to us and it hurts.

Women and men, the old and the young of them: there are so many of them, and so many of their stories are tragedies with griefs too deep to be contained, but holding here and there tiny joys, snatched from the darkness like flowers picked by a fallen traveler from the side of a cliff.

There was a girl, and her uncle sold her. Put like that it seems so simple.

No man, proclaimed Donne, *is an Island*, and he was wrong. If we were not islands, we would be lost, drowned in each other's tragedies. We are insulated (a word that means, literally, remember, *made into an island*) from the tragedy of others, by our island nature, and by the repetitive shape and form of the stories. We know the shape, and the shape does not change. There was a human being who was born, lived, and then, by some means or other, died. There. You may fill in the details from your own experience. As unoriginal as any other tale, as unique as any other life. Lives are snowflakes – unique in detail, forming patterns we have seen before, but as like one another as peas in a pod (and have you ever looked at peas in a pod? I mean, really *looked* at them?

There's not a chance you'd mistake one for another, after a minute's close inspection.)

We need individual stories. Without individuals we see only numbers: a thousand dead, a hundred thousand dead, 'casualties may rise to a million'. With individual stories, the statistics become people – but even that is a lie, for the people continue to suffer in numbers that themselves are numbing and meaningless. *Look*, see the child's swollen, swollen belly, and the flies that crawl at the corners of his eyes, his skeletal limbs: will it make it easier for you to know his name, his age, his dreams, his fears? To see him from the inside? And if it does, are we not doing a disservice to his sister, who lies in the searing dust beside him, a distorted, distended caricature of a human child. And there, if we feel for them, are they now more important to us than a thousand other children touched by the same famine, a thousand other young lives who will soon be food for the flies' own myriad squirming children?

We draw our lines around these moments of pain, and remain upon our islands, and they cannot hurt us. They are covered with a smooth, safe, nacreous layer to let them slip, pearl-like, from our souls without real pain.

Fiction allows us to slide into these other heads, these other places, and look out through other eyes. And then in the tale we stop before we die, or we die vicariously and unharmed, and in the world beyond the tale we turn the page or close the book, and we resume our lives.

A life, which is, like any other, unlike any other.

And anyway, the simple truth is this: *there was a girl and her uncle sold her.*

This is what they used to say, where the girl came from: no man may be certain who fathered a child, but the mother, ah, that you could be certain of. Lineage and property was something that moved in the matrilineal line, but power remained in the hands of the men: a man had complete ownership of his sister's children.

There was a war in that place, and it was a small war, no more than a skirmish between the men of two rival villages. It was almost an argument. One village won the argument, one village lost it.

Life as a commodity, people as possessions. Enslavement had been part of the culture of those parts for thousands of years. The Arab slavers had destroyed the last of the great kingdoms of East Africa, while the West African nations had destroyed each other.

There was nothing untoward or unusual about their uncle selling the twins, although twins were considered magical beings, and their uncle was scared of them, scared enough that he did not tell them that they were to be sold in case they harmed his shadow and killed him. They were twelve years old. She was called Wututu, the messenger bird; he was called Agasu, the name of a dead king. They were healthy children, and, because they were twins, male and female, they were told many things about the gods, and because they were twins they listened to the things that they were told, and they remembered.

Their uncle was a fat and lazy man. If he had owned more cattle, perhaps he would have given up one of his cattle instead of the children, but he did not. He sold the twins. Enough of him: he shall not enter further into this narrative. We follow the twins.

They were marched, with several other slaves taken or sold in the war, for a dozen miles to a small outpost. Here they were traded, and the twins, along with thirteen others were bought by six men with spears and knives who marched them to the west, toward the sea, and then for many miles along the coast. There were fifteen slaves now altogether, their hands loosely bound, tied neck to neck.

Wututu asked her brother Agasu what would happen to them.

'I do not know,' he said. Agasu was a boy who smiled often: his teeth were white and perfect, and he showed them as he grinned, his happy smiles making Wututu happy in her turn. He was not smiling now. Instead he tried to show bravery for his sister, his head back and shoulders spread, as proud, as menacing, as comical as a puppy with its hackles raised.

The man in the line behind Wututu, his cheeks scarred, said, 'They will sell us to the white devils, who will take us to their home across the water.'

'And what will they do to us there?' demanded Wututu.

The man said nothing.

'Well?' asked Wututu. Agasu tried to dart a glance over his shoulder. They were not allowed to talk or sing as they walked.

'It is possible they will eat us,' said the man. 'That is what I have been told. That is why they need so many slaves. It is because they are always hungry.'

Wututu began to cry as she walked. Agasu said, 'Do not cry, my sister. They will not eat you. I shall protect you. Our gods will protect you.'

But Wututu continued to cry, walking with a heavy heart, feeling pain and anger and fear as only a child can feel it: raw and overwhelming. She was unable to tell Agasu that she was not worried about the white devils eating her. She would survive, she was certain of it. She cried because she was scared that they would eat her brother, and she was not certain that she could protect him.

They reached a trading post, and they were kept there for ten days. In the morning of the tenth day they were taken from the hut in which they had been imprisoned (it had become very crowded in the final days, as men arrived from far away, some of them from hundreds of miles, bringing their own strings and skeins of slaves). They were marched to the harbor, and Wututu saw the ship that was to take them away.

Her first thought was how big a ship it was, her second that it was too small for all of them to fit inside. It sat lightly

on the water. The ship's boat came back and forth, ferrying
the captives to the ship where they were manacled and
arranged in low decks by sailors, some of whom were brick-
red or tan skinned, with strange pointy noses and beards that
made them look like beasts. Several of the sailors looked like
her own people, like the men who had marched her to the
coast. The men and the women and the children were
separated, forced into different areas on the slave deck.
There were too many slaves for the ship to hold easily, so
another dozen men were chained up on the deck in the open,
beneath the places where the crew would sling their
hammocks.

Wututu was put in with the children, not with the women;
and she was not chained, merely locked in. Agasu, her
brother, was forced in with the men, in chains, packed like
herrings. It stank under that deck, although the crew had
scrubbed it down since their last cargo. It was a stink that
had entered the wood: the smell of fear and bile and diarrhea
and death, of fever and madness and hate. Wututu sat in the
hot hold with the other children. She could feel the children
on each side of her sweating. A wave tumbled a small boy
into her, hard, and he apologized in a tongue that Wututu did
not recognize. She tried to smile at him in the semi-darkness.

The ship set sail. Now it rode heavy in the water.

Wututu wondered about the place the white men came
from (although none of them were truly white: sea-burned
and sunburned they were, and their skins were dark). Were
they so short of food that they had to send all the way to her
land for people to eat? Or was it that she was to be a delicacy,
a rare treat for a people who had eaten so many things that
only black-skinned flesh in their cook pots made their
mouths water?

On the second day out of port the ship hit a squall, not a
bad one, but the ship's decks lurched and tumbled, and the
smell of vomit joined the mixed smells of urine and liquid
feces and fear-sweat. Rain poured down on them in

bucketloads from the air gratings set in the ceiling of the slave deck.

A week into the voyage, and well out of sight of land, the slaves were allowed out of irons. They were warned that any disobedience, any trouble, and they would be punished more than they had ever imagined.

In the morning the captives were fed beans and ship's biscuits, and a mouthful each of vinegared lime juice, harsh enough that their faces would twist, and they would cough and splutter, and some of them would moan and wail as the lime juice was spooned out. They could not spit it out, though: if they were caught spitting or dribbling it out they were lashed or beaten.

The night brought them salted beef. It tasted unpleasant, and there was a rainbow sheen to the gray surface of the meat. That was at the start of the voyage. As the voyage continued, the meat grew worse.

When they could, Wututu and Agasu would huddle together, talking of their mother and their home and their playfellows. Sometimes Wututu would tell Agasu the stories their mother had told them, like those of Elegba, the trickiest of the gods, who was Great Mawu's eyes and ears in the world, who took messages to Mawu and brought back Mawu's replies.

In the evenings, to while away the monotony of the voyage, the sailors would make the slaves sing for them and dance the dances of their native lands.

Wututu was lucky that she had been put in with the children. The children were packed in tightly and ignored; the women were not always so fortunate. On some slave ships the female slaves were raped repeatedly and continually by the crew, simply as an unspoken perquisite of the voyage. This was not one of those ships, which is not to say that there were no rapes.

A hundred men, women and children died on that voyage and were dropped over the side; and some of the captives who were dropped over the side had not yet died, but the green chill of the ocean cooled their final fever and they went down flailing, choking, lost.

Wututu and Agasu were traveling on a Dutch ship, but they did not know this, and it might as easily have been British, or Portuguese, or Spanish, or French.

The black crewmen on the ship, their skins even darker than Wututu's, told the captives where to go, what to do, when to dance. One morning Wututu caught one of the black guards staring at her. When she was eating, the man came over to her and stared down at her, without saying anything.

'Why do you do this?' she asked the man. 'Why do you serve the white devils?'

He grinned at her as if her question was the funniest thing he ever had heard. Then he leaned over, so his lips were almost brushing her ears, so his hot breath on her ear made her suddenly feel sick. 'If you were older,' he told her, 'I would make you scream with happiness from my penis. Perhaps I will do it tonight. I have seen how well you dance.'

She looked at him with her nut-brown eyes and she said, unflinching, smiling even, 'If you put it in me down there I will bite it off with my teeth down there. I am a witch girl, and I have very sharp teeth down there.' She took pleasure in watching his expression change. He said nothing and walked away.

The words had come out of her mouth, but they had not been her words: she had not thought them or made them. No, she realized, those were the words of Elegba the trickster. Mawu had made the world and then, thanks to Elegba's trickery, had lost interest in it. It was Elegba of the clever ways and the iron-hard erection who had spoken through her, who had ridden her for a moment, and that night before she slept she gave thanks to Elegba.

Several of the captives refused to eat. They were whipped until they put food into their mouths and swallowed, although the whipping was severe enough that two men died of it. Still, no one else on the ship tried to starve themselves to freedom. A man and a woman tried to kill themselves by leaping over the side. The woman succeeded. The man was rescued and he was tied to the mast and lashed for the better part of a day, until his back ran with blood, and he was left there as the day became night. He was given no food to eat, and nothing to drink but his own piss. By the third day he was raving, and his head had swollen and grown soft, like an old melon. When he stopped raving they threw him over the side. Also, for five days following the escape attempt the captives were returned to their manacles and chains.

It was a long journey and a bad one for the captives, and it was not pleasant for the crew, although they had learned to harden their hearts to the business, and pretended to themselves that they were no more than farmers, taking their livestock to the market.

They made harbor on a pleasant, balmy day in Bridgetown, Barbados, and the captives were carried from the ship to the shore in low boats sent out from the dock, and taken to the market square where they were, by dint of a certain amount of shouting, and blows from cudgels, arranged into lines. A whistle blew, and the market square filled with men, poking, prodding, red-faced men, shouting, inspecting, calling, appraising, grumbling.

Wututu and Agasu were separated then. It happened so fast – a big man forced open Agasu's mouth, looked at his teeth, felt his arm muscles, nodded, and two other men hauled Agasu away. He did not fight them. He looked at Wututu and called, 'Be brave,' to her. She nodded, and then her vision smeared and blurred with tears, and she wailed. Together they were twins, magical, powerful. Apart they were two children in pain.

She never saw him again but once, and never in life.

This is what happened to Agasu. First they took him to a seasoning farm, where they whipped him daily for the things he did and didn't do, they taught him a smattering of English and they gave him the name of Inky Jack, for the darkness of his skin. When he ran away they hunted him down with dogs and brought him back, and cut off a toe with a chisel, to teach him a lesson he would not forget. He would have starved himself to death, but when he refused to eat his front teeth were broken and thin gruel was forced into his mouth, until he had no choice but to swallow or to choke.

Even in those times they preferred slaves born into captivity to those brought over from Africa. The free-born slaves tried to run, or they tried to die, and either way, there went the profits.

When Inky Jack was sixteen he was sold, with several other slaves, to a sugar plantation on St Domingue. They called him Hyacinth, the big, broken-toothed slave. He met an old woman from his own village on that plantation – she had been a house slave before her fingers became too gnarled and arthritic – who told him that the whites intentionally split up captives from the same towns and villages and regions, to avoid insurrection and revolts. They did not like it when slaves spoke to each other in their own languages.

Hyacinth learned some French, and was taught a few of the teachings of the Catholic Church. Each day he cut sugar-cane from well before the sun rose until after the sun had set.

He fathered several children. He went with the other slaves, in the small hours of the night, to the woods, although it was forbidden, to dance the Calinda, to sing to Damballa-Wedo, the serpent god, in the form of a black snake. He sang to Elegba, to Ogu, Shango, Zaka, and to many others, all the gods the captives had brought with them to the island, brought in their minds and their secret hearts.

The slaves on the sugar plantations of St Domingue rarely lived more than a decade. The free time they were given – two hours in the heat of noon, and five hours in the dark of the night (from eleven until four) – was also the only time they had to grow and tend the food they would eat (for they were not fed by their masters, merely given small plots of land to cultivate, with which to feed themselves), and it was also the time they had to sleep and to dream. Even so, they would take that time and they would gather and dance, and sing and worship. The soil of St Domingue was a fertile soil and the gods of Dahomey and the Congo and the Niger put down thick roots there and grew lush and huge and deep, and they promised freedom to those who worshiped them at night in the groves.

Hyacinth was twenty-five years of age when a spider bit the back of his right hand. The bite became infected and the flesh on the back of his hand was necrotic: soon enough his whole arm was swollen and purple, and the hand stank. It throbbed and it burned.

They gave him crude rum to drink, and they heated the blade of a machete in the fire until it glowed red and white. They cut his arm off at the shoulder with a saw, and they cauterized it with the burning blade. He lay in a fever for a week. Then he returned to work

The one-armed slave called Hyacinth took part in the slave revolt of 1791.

Elegba himself took possession of Hyacinth in the grove, riding him as a white man rode a horse, and spoke through him. He remembered little of what was said, but the others who were with him told him that he had promised them freedom from their captivity. He remembered only his erection, rod-like and painful; and raising both hands – the one he had, and the one he no longer possessed – to the moon.

A pig was killed, and the men and the women of that plantation drank the hot blood of the pig, pledging themselves and binding themselves into a brotherhood. They swore that they were an army of freedom, pledged themselves once more to the gods of all the lands from which they had been dragged as plunder.

'If we die in battle with the whites,' they told each other, 'we will be reborn in Africa, in our homes, in our own tribes.'

There was another Hyacinth in the uprising, so they now called Agasu by the name of Big One-Arm. He fought, he worshiped, he sacrificed, he planned. He saw his friends and his lovers killed, and he kept fighting.

They fought for twelve years, a maddening, bloody struggle with the plantation owners, with the troops brought over from France. They fought, and they kept fighting, and, impossibly, they won.

On January the First, 1804, the independence of St Domingue, soon to be known to the world as the Republic of Haiti, was declared. Big One Arm did not live to see it. He had died in August, 1802, bayoneted by a French soldier.

At the precise moment of the death of Big One-Arm (who had once been called Hyacinth, and before that, Inky Jack, and who was forever in his heart Agasu,) his sister, whom he had known as Wututu, who had been called Mary on her first plantation in the Carolinas, and Daisy when she had become a house slave, and Sukey when she was sold to the Lavere family down the river to New Orleans, felt the cold bayonet slide between her ribs and started to scream and weep uncontrollably. Her twin daughters woke and began to howl. They were cream-and-coffee colored, her new babies, not like the black children she had borne when she was on the plantation and little more than a girl herself – children she had not seen since they were fifteen and ten years old. The middle girl had been dead for a year, when she was sold away from them.

Sukey had been whipped many times since she had come ashore – once, salt had been rubbed into the wounds, on another occasion she had been whipped so hard and for so long that she could not sit, or allow anything to touch her back, for several days. She had been raped several times when younger: by black men who had been ordered to share her wooden palette, and by white men. She had been chained. She had not wept then, though. Since her brother had been taken from her she had only wept once. It was in

North Carolina, when she had seen the food for the slave children and the dogs poured into the same trough, and she had seen her little children scrabbling with the dogs for the scraps. She saw that happen one day – and she had seen it before, every day on that plantation, and she would see it again many times before she left – she saw it that one day and it broke her heart.

She had been beautiful for a while. Then the years of pain had taken their toll, and she was no longer beautiful. Her face was lined, and there was too much pain in those brown eyes.

Eleven years earlier, when she was twenty-five, her right arm had withered. None of the white folk had known what to make of it. The flesh seemed to melt from the bones, and now her right arm hung by her side, little more than a skeletal arm covered in skin, and almost immobile. After this she had become a house-slave.

The Casterton family, who had owned the plantation were impressed by her cooking and house skills, but Mrs. Casterton found the withered arm unsettling, and so she was sold to the Lavere family who were out for a year from Louisiana: M Lavere was a fat, cheerful man, who was in need of a cook and a maid of all work, and who was not in the slightest repulsed by the slave Daisy's withered arm. When, a year later, they returned to Louisiana, slave Sukey went with them.

In New Orleans the women came to her, and the men also, to buy cures and love charms and little fetishes, black folks, yes, of course, but white folks too. The Lavere family turned a blind eye to it. Perhaps they enjoyed the prestige of having a slave who was feared and respected. They would not, however, sell her her freedom.

Sukey went into the Bayou late at night, and she danced the Calinda and the Bamboula. Like the dancers of St Domingue and the dancers of her native land, the dancers in the bayou had a black snake as their *voudon*; even so, the

gods of her homeland and of the other African nations did
not possess her people as they had possessed her brother and
the folk of St Domingue. She would still invoke them and
call their names, to beg them for favors.

She listened when the white folk spoke of the revolt in St
Domingo (as they called it), and how it was doomed to fail –
'Think of it! A cannibal land!' – and then she observed that
they no longer spoke of it.

Soon, it seemed to her that they pretended that there never
had been a place called St Domingo, and as for Haiti, the
word was never mentioned. It was as if the whole American
nation had decided that they could, by an effort of will,
command a good-sized Caribbean island to no longer exist
merely by willing it so.

A generation of Lavere children grew up under Sukey's
watchful eye. The youngest, unable to say 'Sukey' as a child,
had called her Mama Zouzou, and the name had stuck. Now
the year was 1821, and Sukey was in her mid-fifties. She
looked much older.

She knew more of the secrets than old Sanité Dédé, who
sold candies in front of the Cabildo, more than Marie
Saloppé, who called herself the voodoo queen: both were
free women of color, while Mama Zouzou was a slave, and
would die a slave, or so her master had said.

The young woman who came to her to find what had
happened to her husband styled herself the Widow Paris.
She was high-breasted and young and proud. She had
African blood in her, and European blood, and Indian blood.
Her skin was reddish, her hair was a gleaming black. Her
eyes were black and haughty. Her husband, Jacques Paris,
was, perhaps, dead. He was three-quarters white as these
things were calculated, and the bastard of a once-proud
family, one of the many immigrants who had fled from St
Domingo, and as freeborn as his striking young wife.

'My Jacques. Is he dead?' asked the Widow Paris. She was
a hairdresser who went from home to home, arranging the

coiffures of the elegant ladies of New Orleans before their
demanding social engagements.

Mama Zouzou consulted the bones, then shook her head.
'He is with a white woman, somewhere north of here,' she
said. 'A white woman with golden hair. He is alive.' This was
not magic. It was common knowledge in New Orleans just
with whom Jacques Paris had run off, and the color of her
hair.

Mama Zouzou was surprised to realize that the Widow
Paris did not already know that Jacques was sticking his
quadroon little *pipi* into a pink-skinned girl up in Colfax
every night that he was not so drunk he could use it for
nothing better than pissing. Perhaps she did know. Perhaps
she had another reason for coming.

The Widow Paris came to see the old slave woman one or
two times a week. After a month she brought gifts for the old
woman: hair ribbons, and a seed-cake, and a black rooster.

'Mama Zouzou,' said the girl, 'It is time for you to teach me
what you know.'

'Yes,' said Mama Zouzou, who knew which way the wind
blew. And besides, the Widow Paris had confessed that she
had been born with webbed toes, which meant that she was
a twin and she had killed her twin in the womb. What choice
did Mama Zouzou have?

She taught the girl that two nutmegs hung upon a string
around the neck until the string breaks will cure heart
murmurs, while a pigeon that has never flown, cut open and
laid on the patient's head, will draw a fever. She showed her
how to make a wishing bag, a small leather bag containing
thirteen pennies, nine cotton seeds and the bristles of a black
hog, and how to rub the bag to make wishes come true.

The Widow Paris learned everything that Mama Zouzou
told her. She had no real interest in the gods, though. Not
really. Her interests were in the practicalities. She was
delighted to learn that if you dip a live frog in honey and
place it in an ants' nest, then, when the bones are cleaned

and white, a close examination will reveal a flat, heart-shaped bone, and another with a hook on it: the bone with the hook on it must be hooked onto the garment of the one you wish to love you, while the heart-shaped bone must be kept safely (for if it is lost, your loved one will turn on you like an angry dog). Infallibly, if you do this, the one you love will be yours.

She learned that dried snake powder, placed in the face powder of an enemy will produce blindness, and that an enemy can be made to drown herself by taking a piece of her underwear, turning it inside out, and burying it at midnight under a brick.

Mama Zouzou showed the Widow Paris the World Wonder Root, the great and the little roots of John the Conqueror, she showed her Dragon's Blood, and Valerian and Five-Finger Grass. She showed her how to brew waste-away tea, and follow-me-water and faire-Shingo water.

All these things and more Mama Zouzou showed the Widow Paris. Still, it was disappointing for the old woman. She did her best to teach her the hidden truths, the deep knowledge, to tell her of Elegba, of Mawu, of Aido-Hwedo the voudon serpent, and the rest, but the Widow Paris (I shall now tell you the name she was born with, and the name she later made famous: it was Marie Laveau. But this was not the great Marie Laveau, the one you have heard of, this was her mother, who eventually became the Widow Glapion) she had no interest in the gods of the distant land. If St Domingo had been a lush black earth for the African gods to grow in, this land, with its corn and its melons, its crawfish and its cotton, was barren and infertile.

'She does not want to know,' complains Mama Zouzou to Clémentine, her confidant, who took in the washing for many of the houses in that district, washing their curtains and coverlets. Clémentine had a blossom of burns on her cheek, and one of her children had been scalded to death when a copper overturned.

'Then do not teach her,' says Clémentine.

'I teach her, but she does not see what is valuable – all she sees is what she can do with it. I give her diamonds, but she cares only for pretty glass. I give her a demi-bouteille of the best claret and she drinks river-water. I give her quail and she wishes to eat only rat.'

'Then why do you persist?' asks Clémentine.

Mama Zouzou shrugs her thin shoulders, causing her withered arm to shake.

She cannot answer. She could say that she teaches because she is grateful to be alive, and she is: she has seen too many die. She could say that she dreams that one day the slaves will rise, as they rose (and were defeated) in LaPlace, but that she knows in her heart that without the gods of Africa they will never overcome their white captors, will never return to their homelands.

When she woke that terrible night almost twenty years earlier, and felt the cold stool between her ribs, that was when Mama Zouzou's life had ended. Now she was someone who did not live, who simply hated. If you asked her about the hate she would have been unable to tell you about a twelve year old girl on a stinking ship: that had scabbed over in her mind – there had been too many whippings and beatings, too many nights in manacles, too many partings, too much pain. She could have told you about her son, though, and how his thumb had been cut off when their master discovered the boy was able to read and to write. She could have told you of her daughter, twelve years old and already eight months pregnant by an overseer, and how they dug a hole in the red earth to take her daughter's pregnant belly, and then they whipped her until her back had bled. Despite the carefully dug hole, her daughter had lost her baby and her life on a Sunday morning, when all the white folks were in church . . .

Too much pain.

'Worship them,' Mama Zouzou told the young Widow

Paris in the Bayou, one hour after midnight. They were both naked to the waist, sweating in the humid night, their skins given accents by the white moonlight.

The Widow Paris's husband Jacques (whose own death, three years later, would have several remarkable features) had told Marie a little about the gods of St Domingo, but she did not care. Power came from the rituals, not from the gods.

Together Mama Zouzou and the Widow Paris crooned and stamped and keened in the swamp. They were singing in the blacksnakes, the free woman of color and the slave woman with the withered arm.

'There is more to it than just, you prosper, your enemies fail,' said Mama Zouzou.

Many of the words of the ceremonies, words she knew once, words her brother had also known, these words had fled from her memory. She told pretty Marie Laveau that the words did not matter, only the tunes and the beats, and there, singing and tapping in the blacksnakes, in the swamp, she has an odd vision. She sees the beats of the songs, the Calinda beat, the Bamboula beat, all the rhythms of equatorial Africa spreading slowly across this midnight land until the whole country shivers and swings to the beats of the old gods whose realms she had left. And even that, she understands somehow, in the swamp, even that will not be enough.

She turns to pretty Marie and sees herself through Marie's eyes, a black-skinned old woman, her face lined, her bony arm hanging limply by her side, her eyes the eyes of one who has seen her children fight in the trough for food from the dogs. She saw herself, and she knew then for the first time the revulsion and the fear the younger woman had for her.

Then she laughed, and crouched, and picked up in her good hand a blacksnake as tall as a sapling and as thick as a ship's rope.

'Here,' she said, 'Here will be our *voudon*.'

She dropped the unresisting snake into a basket that yellow Marie was carrying.

And then, in the moonlight, the second sight possessed her for a final time, and she saw her brother Agasu, not the twelve-year-old boy she had last seen in the Bridgeport market so long ago, but a huge man, bald and grinning with broken teeth, his back lined with deep scars. In one hand he held a machete-knife. His right arm was barely a stump.

She reached out her own good left hand.

'Stay, stay a while,' she whispered. 'I will be there. I will be with you soon.'

And Marie Paris thought the old woman was speaking to her.

Chapter Twelve

America has invested her religion as well as her morality in sound income-paying securities. She has adopted the unassailable position of a nation blessed because it deserves to be blessed; and her sons, whatever other theologies they may affect or disregard, subscribe unreservedly to this national creed.

— Agnes Repplier, *Times and Tendencies*

Shadow drove west, across Wisconsin and Minnesota and into North Dakota, where the snow-covered hills looked like huge sleeping buffalo, and he and Wednesday saw nothing but nothing and plenty of it for mile after mile. They went south, then, into South Dakota, heading for reservation country.

Wednesday had traded in the Lincoln town car, which Shadow had liked driving, for a lumbering and ancient Winnebago, which smelled non-specifically but pervasively and unmistakably of male cat, and which he didn't enjoy driving at all.

As they passed their first signpost for Mount Rushmore, still several hundred miles away, Wednesday grunted. 'Now that,' he said, 'is a holy place.'

Shadow had thought Wednesday was asleep. He said, 'I know it used to be sacred to the Indians.'

'It's a holy place,' said Wednesday. 'That's the American Way – they need to give people an excuse to come and worship. These days, people can't just go and see a mountain. Thus, Mister Gutzon Borglum's tremendous presidential faces. Once they were carved, permission was granted, and now the people drive out in their multitudes to see something in the flesh that they've already seen on a thousand postcards.'

'I knew a guy once. He did weight training at the Muscle Farm, years back. He said that the Dakota Indians, the young men climb up the mountain, then form death-defying human chains off the heads, just so that the guy at the end of the chain can piss on the president's nose.'

Wednesday guffawed. 'Oh, fine! Very fine! Is any specific president the particular butt of their ire?'

Shadow shrugged. 'He never said.'

Miles vanished beneath the wheels of the Winnebago. Shadow began to imagine that he was staying still while the American landscape moved past them at a steady sixty-seven miles per hour. A wintry mist fogged the edges of things.

It was midday on the second day of the drive, and they were almost there. Shadow, who had been thinking, said, 'A girl vanished from Lakeside last week. When we were in San Francisco.'

'Mm?' Wednesday sounded barely interested.

'Kid named Alison McGovern. She's not the first kid to vanish there. There have been others. They go in the wintertime.'

Wednesday furrowed his brow. 'It is a tragedy, is it not? The little faces on the milk-cartons – although I can't remember the last time I saw a kid on a milk-carton – and on the walls of freeway rest areas. *Have you seen me?* they ask. A deeply existential question at the best of times. *Have you seen me?* Pull off at the next exit.'

Shadow thought he heard a helicopter pass overhead, but the clouds were too low to see anything.

'Why did you pick Lakeside?' asked Shadow.

'I told you. It's a nice quiet place to hide you away. You're off the board there, under the radar.'

'*Why?*'

'Because that's the way it is. Now hang a left,' said Wednesday.

Shadow turned left.

'There's something wrong,' said Wednesday. 'Fuck. Jesus fucking Christ on a bicycle. Slow down, but don't stop.'

'Care to elaborate?'

'Trouble. Do you know any alternative routes?'

'Not really. This is my first time in South Dakota,' said Shadow. 'Also I don't know where we're going.'

On the other side of the hill something flashed redly, smudged by the mist.

'Roadblock,' said Wednesday. He pushed his hand deeply into first one pocket of his suit then another, searching for something.

'I can stop and turn around. If we had a jeep I'd go off-road, but the Winnebago's just going to tip if I try and drive her across that ditch.'

'We can't turn. They're behind us as well,' said Wednesday. 'Take your speed down to ten, fifteen miles per hour.'

Shadow glanced into the mirror. There were headlights behind them, under a mile back. 'Are you sure about this?' he asked.

Wednesday snorted. 'Sure as eggs is eggs,' he said. 'As the turkey-farmer said when he hatched his first turtle. Ah, success!' and from the bottom of a pocket he produced a small piece of white chalk.

He started to scratch with the chalk on the dashboard of the camper, making marks as if he were solving an algebraic puzzle – or perhaps, Shadow thought, as if he were a hobo,

scratching long messages to the other hobos in hobo code –
*bad dog here, dangerous town, nice woman, soft jail in which
to overnight* . . .

'Okay,' said Wednesday. 'Now increase your speed to
thirty. And don't slow down from that.'

One of the cars behind them turned on its lights and siren
and accelerated toward them. 'Do not slow down,' repeated
Wednesday. 'They just want us to slow before we get to the
roadblock.' *Scratch. Scratch. Scratch.*

They crested the hill. The roadblock was less than a
quarter of a mile away. Twelve cars arranged across the road,
and on the side of the road, police cars, and several big black
SUVs.

'There,' said Wednesday, and he put his chalk away. The
dashboard of the Winnebago was now covered with rune-
like scratchings.

The car with the siren was just behind them. It had slowed
to their speed, and an amplified voice was shouting, 'Pull
over!' Shadow looked at Wednesday.

'Turn right,' said Wednesday. 'Just pull off the road.'

'I can't take this thing off-road. We'll tip.'

'It'll be fine. Take a right. Now!'

Shadow pulled the wheel down with his right hand, and
the Winnebago lurched and jolted. For a moment he thought
he had been correct, that the camper was going to tip, and
then the world through the windshield dissolved and
shimmered, like the reflection in a clear pool when the wind
brushes the surface, and the Dakotas stretched and shifted.

The clouds and the mist and the snow and the day were
gone.

Now there were stars overhead, hanging like frozen spears
of light, stabbing the night sky.

'Park here,' said Wednesday. 'We can walk the rest of the
way.'

Shadow turned off the engine. He went into the back of
the Winnebago, pulled on his coat, his Sorel winter boots,

and his gloves. Then he climbed out of the vehicle and waited. 'Okay,' he said. 'Let's go.'

Wednesday looked at him with amusement and something else – irritation perhaps. Or pride. 'Why don't you argue?' asked Wednesday. 'Why don't you exclaim that it's all impossible? Why the hell do you just do what I say and take it all so fucking calmly?'

'Because you're not paying me to ask questions,' said Shadow. And then he said, realizing the truth as the words came out of his mouth, 'Anyway, nothing's really surprised me since Laura.'

'Since she came back from the dead?'

'Since I learned she was screwing Robbie. That one hurt. Everything else just sits on the surface. Where are we going now?'

Wednesday pointed, and they began to walk. The ground beneath their feet was rock of some kind, slick and volcanic, occasionally glassy. The air was chilly, but not winter-cold. They sidestepped their way awkwardly down a hill. There was a rough path, and they followed it. Shadow looked down to the bottom of the hill, and realized that what he was looking at was impossible.

'What the hell is that?' asked Shadow, but Wednesday touched his finger to his lips, shook his head sharply. Silence.

It looked like a mechanical spider, blue metal, glittering LED lights, and it was the size of a tractor. It squatted at the bottom of the hill. Beyond it were an assortment of bones, each with a flame beside it little bigger than a candle-flame, flickering.

Wednesday gestured for Shadow to keep his distance from these objects. Shadow took an extra step to the side to make sure he kept his distance, which was a mistake on that glassy path, as his ankle twisted and he tumbled down the slope as if he had been dropped, rolling and slipping and bouncing. He grabbed at a rock as he went past, and the obsidian snag ripped his leather glove as if it were paper.

He came to rest at the bottom of the hill, between the mechanical spider and the bones.

He put a hand down to push himself to his feet, and found himself touching what appeared to be a thighbone with the palm of his hand, and he was . . .

. . . standing in the daylight, smoking a cigarette, and looking at his watch. There were cars all around him, some empty, some not. He was wishing he had not had that last cup off coffee, for he dearly needed a piss, and it was starting to become uncomfortable.

One of the local law enforcement people came over to him, a big man with frost in his walrus moustache. He had already forgotten the man's name.

'I don't know how we could have lost them,' says Local Law Enforcement, apologetic and puzzled.

'It was an optical illusion,' he replies. 'You get them in freak weather conditions. The mist. It was a mirage. They were driving down some other road. We thought they were on this one.'

Local Law Enforcement looks disappointed. 'Oh. I thought it was maybe like an X-Files kinda thing,' he says.

'Nothing so exciting, I'm afraid.' He suffers from occasional hemorrhoids and his ass has just started itching in the way that signals that a flare-up is coming. He wants to be back inside the Beltway. He wishes there was a tree to go and stand behind: the urge to piss is getting worse. He drops the cigarette and steps on it.

Local Law Enforcement walks over to one of the police cars and says something to the driver. They both shake their heads.

He wonders if he should simply grit his teeth, try to imagine that he is in Maui with no one else around, and piss against the rear wheel of the car. He wishes he weren't so utterly pee-shy, and he thinks maybe he can hold it in for longer but he finds himself remembering a newspaper clipping that someone had tacked up in the lounge in his frat house, thirty years before: the cautionary tale of an old man who had been on a long bus ride with a busted rest-room, who had held it in, and, at the end of his journey, needed to be catheterized in order ever to piss again . . .

That was ridiculous. He isn't that old. He is going to celebrate his fiftieth birthday in April, and his waterworks work just fine. Everything works just fine.

He pulls out his telephone, touches the menu, pages down, and finds the address entry marked 'Laundry' which had amused him so much when he typed it in – a reference to *The Man from UNCLE*, and as he looks at it he realizes that it's not from that at all, that was a tailor's, he's thinking of *Get Smart*, and he still feels weird and slightly embarrassed after all these years about not realizing it was a comedy when he was a kid, and just wanting a shoephone . . .

A woman's voice on the phone. 'Yes?'

'This is Mister Town, for Mister World.'

'Hold please. I'll see if he's available.'

There is silence. Town crosses his legs, tugs his belt higher on his belly – *got* to lose these last ten pounds – and away from his bladder. Then an urbane voice says, 'Hello, Mister Town.'

'We lost them,' says Town. He feels a knot of frustration in his gut: these were the bastards, the lousy dirty sons of bitches who killed Woody and Stone, for Chrissakes. Good men. Good men. He badly wants to fuck Mrs Wood, but knows it's still too soon after Woody's death to make a move, so he is taking her out for dinner every couple of weeks, an investment in the future, she's just grateful for the attention . . .

'How?'

'I don't know. We set up a roadblock, there was nowhere they could have gone and they went there anyway.'

'Just another one of life's little mysteries. Not to worry. Have you calmed the locals?'

'Told 'em it was an optical illusion.'

'They buy it?'

'Probably.'

There was something very familiar about Mr World's voice
– which was a strange thing to think, he'd been working for
him directly for two years now, spoken to him every day, of
course there was something familiar about his voice.

'They'll be far away by now.'

'Should we send people down to the rez to intercept
them?'

'Not worth the aggravation. Too many jurisdictional
issues, and there are only so many strings we can pull in a
morning. We have plenty of time. Just get back here. I've got
my hands full at this end trying to organize the policy
meeting.'

'Trouble?'

'It's a pissing contest. I've proposed that we have it out
here. The techies want it in Austin, or maybe San Jose, the
players want it in Hollywood, the intangibles want it on Wall
Street. Everybody wants it in their own back yard. Nobody's
going to give.'

'You need me to do anything?'

'Not yet. I'll growl at some of them, stroke others. You
know the routine.'

'Yes, sir.'

'Carry on, Town.'

The connection is broken.

Town thinks he should have had a SWAT team to pick off
that fucking Winnebago, or land-mines on the road, or a
tactical friggin' nukuler device, that would have showed
those bastards they meant business. It was like Mr World had
once said to him, *We are writing the future in Letters of Fire*
and Mr Town thinks that Jesus Christ if he doesn't piss now
he'll lose a kidney, it'll just burst, and it was like his Pop had
said when they were on long journeys, when Town was a
kid, out on the interstate, his Pop would always say 'My back
teeth are afloat,' and Mr Town could hear that voice even

now, that sharp Yankee accent saying 'I got to take a leak soon. My back teeth are afloat' . . .

. . . and it was then that Shadow felt a hand opening his own hand, prising it open one finger at a time, off the thighbone it was clutching. He no longer needed to urinate; that was someone else. He was standing under the stars on a glassy rock plain, and the bone was down on the ground beside the other bones.

Wednesday made the signal for silence again. Then he began to walk, and Shadow followed.

There was a creak from the mechanical spider, and Wednesday froze. Shadow stopped and waited with him. Green lights flickered and ran up and along its side in clusters. Shadow tried not to breathe too loudly.

He thought about what had just happened. It had been like looking through a window into someone else's mind. And then he thought, *Mr World. It was me who thought his voice sounded familiar. That was my thought, not Town's. That was why that seemed so strange*. He tried to identify the voice in his mind, to put it into the category in which it belonged, but it eluded him.

It'll come to me, thought Shadow. *Sooner or later, it'll come to me*.

The green lights went blue, then red, then faded to a dull red, and the spider settled down on its metallic haunches. Wednesday began to walk forward, a lonely figure beneath the stars, in a broad-brimmed hat, his frayed dark cloak gusting randomly in the nowhere wind, his staff tapping on the glassy rock floor.

When the metallic spider was only a distant glint in the starlight, far back on the plain, Wednesday said, 'It should be safe to speak, now.'

'Where are we?'

'Behind the scenes,' said Wednesday.

'Sorry?'

'Think of it as being behind the scenes. Like in a theatre or something. I just pulled us out of the audience and now we're walking about backstage. It's a shortcut.'

'When I touched that bone, I was in the mind of a guy named Town. He's with that spookshow. He hates us.'

'Yes.'

'He's got a boss named Mister World. He reminds me of someone, but I don't know who. I was looking into Town's head – or maybe I was in his head. I'm not certain.'

'Do they know where we're headed?'

'I think they're calling off the hunt right now. They didn't want to follow us to the reservation. Are we going to a reservation?'

'Maybe.' Wednesday leaned on his staff for a moment, then continued to walk.

'What was that spider thing?'

'A pattern manifestation. A search engine.'

'Are they dangerous?'

'You only get to be my age by assuming the worst.'

Shadow smiled. 'And how old would that be?'

'Old as my tongue,' said Wednesday. 'And a few months older than my teeth.'

'You play your cards so close to your chest,' said Shadow, 'that I'm not even sure that they're really cards at all.'

Wednesday only grunted.

Each hill they came to was harder to climb.

Shadow began to feel headachy. There was a pounding quality to the starlight, something that resonated with the pulse in his temples and his chest. At the bottom of the next hill he stumbled, opened his mouth to say something and, without warning, he vomited.

Wednesday reached into an inside pocket, and produced a small hipflask. 'Take a sip of this,' he said. 'Only a sip.'

The liquid was pungent, and it evaporated in his mouth like a good brandy, although it did not taste like alcohol. Wednesday took the flask away, and pocketed it. 'It's not good for the audience to find themselves walking about backstage. That's why you're feeling sick. We need to hurry to get you out of here.'

They walked faster – Wednesday at a solid trudge, Shadow stumbling from time to time, but feeling better for the drink, which left his mouth tasting of orange peel, of rosemary oil and peppermint and cloves.

Wednesday took his arm. 'There,' he said, pointing to two identical hillocks of frozen rock-glass to their left. 'Walk between those two mounds. Walk beside me.'

They walked, and the cold air and bright daylight smashed into Shadow's face at the same time. He stopped, closed his eyes, dazzled and light-blinded, then, shading his eyes with his hand, he opened them once more.

They were standing half-way up a gentle hill. The mist had gone, the day was sunny and chill, the sky was a perfect blue. At the bottom of the hill was a gravel road, and a red station wagon bounced along it like a child's toy car. A gust of wood smoke stung Shadow's face, making his eyes tear. The smoke came from a building nearby, which looked as if someone had picked up a mobile home and dropped it on the side of the hill thirty years ago. It was much repaired, patched, and, in places, added onto: Shadow was certain that the galvanized tin chimney, from which the wood smoke was coming, was not part of the original structure.

As they reached the door it opened, and a middle-aged man with dark skin, sharp eyes and a mouth like a knife-slash looked down at them and said, 'Eyah, I heard that there were two white men on their way to see me. Two whites in a Winnebago. And I heard that they got lost, like white men always get lost if they don't put up their signs everywhere. And now look at these two sorry beasts at the door. You know you're on Lakota land?' His hair was gray, and long.

'Since when were you Lakota, you old fraud?' said Wednesday. He was wearing a coat and a flap-eared cap, and already it seemed to Shadow unlikely that only a few moments ago under the stars he had been wearing a broad-

brimmed hat and a tattered cloak. 'So, Whiskey Jack. You sad
bastard. I'm starving, and my friend here just threw up his
breakfast. Are you going to invite us in?'

Whiskey Jack scratched an armpit. He was wearing blue
jeans and an undershirt the gray of his hair. He wore
moccasins, and he seemed not to notice the cold. Then he
said, 'I like it here. Come in, white men who lost their
Winnebago.'

There was more wood smoke in the air inside the trailer,
and there was another man in there, sitting at a table. The
man wore stained buckskins, and was barefoot. His skin was
the color of bark.

Wednesday seemed delighted. 'Well,' he said, 'it seems our
delay was fortuitous. Whiskey Jack and Apple Johnny. Two
birds with one stone.'

The man at the table, Apple Johnny, stared at Wednesday,
then he reached down a hand to his crotch, cupped it and
said, 'Wrong again. I jes' checked and I got both of my stones,
jes' where they oughta be.' He looked up at Shadow, raised
his hand, palm out. 'I'm John Chapman. You don't mind
anything your boss says about me. He's an asshole. Always
was an asshole. Always goin' to be an asshole. Some people
is jes' assholes, and that's an end of it.'

'Mike Ainsel,' said Shadow.

Chapman rubbed his stubbly chin. 'Ainsel,' he said. 'That's
not a name. But it'll do at a pinch. What do they call you?'

'Shadow.'

'I'll call you Shadow, then. Hey, Whiskey Jack,' – but it
wasn't really *Whiskey Jack* he was saying, Shadow realized.
Too many syllables – 'how's the food looking?'

Whiskey Jack took a wooden spoon and lifted the lid off a
black iron pot, bubbling away on the range of the wood
burning stove. 'It's ready for eating,' he said.

He took four plastic bowls and spooned the contents of the
pot into the bowls, put them down on the table. Then he
opened the door, stepped out into the snow, and pulled a

plastic gallon jug from the snow bank. He brought it inside, and poured four large glasses of a cloudy yellow-brown liquid, which he put beside each bowl. Last of all, he found four spoons. He sat down at the table with the other men.

Wednesday raised his glass suspiciously. 'Looks like piss,' he said.

'You still drinking that stuff?' asked Whiskey Jack. 'You white men are crazy. This is better.' Then, to Shadow, 'The stew is mostly wild turkey. John here brought the applejack.'

'It's a soft apple cider,' said John Chapman. 'I never believed in hard liquor. Makes men mad.'

The stew was delicious, and it was very good apple cider. Shadow forced himself to slow down, to chew his food, not to gulp it, but he was more hungry than he would have believed. He helped himself to a second bowl of the stew and a second glass of the cider.

'Damo Rumor says that you've been out talking to all manner of folk, offering them all manner of things. Says you're takin' the old folks on the war path,' said John Chapman. Shadow and Whiskey Jack were washing up, putting the leftover stew into Tupperware bowls. Whiskey Jack put the bowls into the snowdrifts outside his front door, and put a milk crate on top of the place he'd pushed them, so he could find them again.

'I think that's a fair and judicious summary of events,' said Wednesday.

'They will win,' said Whiskey Jack flatly. 'They won already. You lost already. Like the white man and my people. They won. And when they lost, they made treaties. Then they broke the treaties. And they won again. I'm not fighting for another lost cause.'

'And it's no use you lookin' at me,' said John Chapman, 'for even if I fought for you – which'n I won't – I'm no use to you. Mangy rat-tailed bastards jes' picked me off and clean forgot me.' He stopped. Then he said, 'Paul Bunyan.' He shook his head slowly and he said it again. '*Paul Bunyan*.' Shadow had

never heard two such innocuous words made to sound so
damning.

'Paul Bunyan?' Shadow said. 'What did he ever do?'

'He took up head space,' said Whiskey Jack. He bummed a
cigarette from Wednesday and the two men sat and smoked.

'It's like the idiots who figure that hummingbirds worry
about their weight or tooth decay or some such nonsense,
maybe they just want to spare hummingbirds the evils of
sugar,' explained Wednesday. 'So they fill the hummingbird
feeders with fucking NutraSweet. The birds come to the
feeders and they drink it. Then they die, because their food
contains no calories even though their little tummies are full.
That's Paul Bunyan for you. Nobody ever told Paul Bunyan
stories. Nobody ever believed in Paul Bunyan. He came
staggering out of a New York ad agency in 1910 and filled the
nation's myth stomach with empty calories.'

'I like Paul Bunyan,' said Whiskey Jack. 'I went on his ride
at the Mall of America, few years back. You see big old Paul
Bunyan at the top then you come crashing down. Splash.
He's okay by me. I don't mind that he never existed, means
he never cut down any trees. Not as good as planting trees
though. That's better.'

'You said a mouthful,' said Johnny Chapman.

Wednesday blew a smoke ring. It hung in the air like
something from a Warner Brothers cartoon, dissipating
slowly in wisps and curls. 'Damn it, Whiskey Jack, that's not
the point and you know it.'

'I'm not going to help you,' said Whiskey Jack. 'When you
get your ass kicked, you can come back here and if I'm still
here I'll feed you again. You get the best food in the fall.'

Wednesday said, 'All the alternatives are worse.'

'You have no idea what the alternatives are,' said Whiskey
Jack. Then he looked at Shadow. 'You are hunting,' he said.
His voice was cigarette-roughened, and it resonated in that
space, smoky with leaking wood smoke and cigarettes.

'I'm working,' said Shadow.

Whiskey Jack shook his head. 'You are also hunting something,' he said. 'There is a debt that you wish to pay.'

Shadow thought of Laura's blue lips and the blood on her hands, and he nodded.

'Listen. Fox was here first, and his brother was the wolf. Fox said, people will live for ever. If they die they will not die for long. Wolf said, no, people will die, people must die, all things that live must die, or they will spread and cover the world, and eat all the salmon and the caribou and the buffalo, eat all the squash and all the corn. Now one day Wolf died, and he said to the fox, quick, bring me back to life. And Fox said, No, the dead must stay dead. You convinced me. And he wept as he said this. But he said it, and it was final. Now Wolf rules the world of the dead and Fox lives always under the sun and the moon, and he still mourns his brother.'

Wednesday said, 'If you won't play, you won't play. We'll be moving on.'

Whiskey Jack's face was impassive. 'I'm talking to this young man,' he said. 'You are beyond help. He is not.' He turned back to Shadow. 'You know, you cannot come to me here unless I wish it.'

Shadow realized that he did know this. 'Yes.'

'Tell me your dream,' said Whiskey Jack.

Shadow said, 'I was climbing a tower of skulls. There were huge birds flying around it. They had lightning in their wings. They were attacking me. The tower fell.'

'Everybody dreams,' said Wednesday. 'Can we hit the road?'

'Not everybody dreams of the Wakinyau, the thunder-birds,' said Whiskey Jack. 'We felt the echoes of it here.'

'I *told* you,' said Wednesday. 'Jesus.'

'There's a clutch of thunderbirds in West Virginia,' said Chapman, idly. 'A couple of hens and an old cock-bird at least. There's also a breeding pair in the land, they used to call it the State of Franklin, but old Ben never got his state, up between Kentucky and Tennessee. 'Course, there was never a great number of them, even at the best of times.'

Whiskey Jack reached out a hand the color of the red clay, and he touched Shadow's face, gently. His irises were light brown banded with dark brown, and in that face those eyes seemed luminous. 'Eyah,' he said. 'It's true. If you hunt the thunderbird you could bring your woman back. But she belongs to the wolf, in the dead places, not walking the land.'

'How do you *know*?' asked Shadow.

Whiskey Jack's lips did not move. 'What did the Buffalo tell you?'

'To believe.'

'Good advice. Are you going to follow it?'

'Kind of. I guess.' They were talking without words, without mouths, without sound. Shadow wondered if, for the other two men in the room, they were standing, unmoving, for a heartbeat or for a fraction of a heartbeat.

'When you find your tribe, come back and see me,' said Whiskey Jack. 'I can help.'

'I shall.'

Whiskey Jack lowered his hand. Then he turned to Wednesday. 'Are you going to fetch your Ho Chunk?'

'My what?'

'*Ho Chunk*. It's what the Winnebago call themselves.'

Wednesday shook his head. 'It's too risky. Retrieving it could be problematic. They'll be looking for it.'

'Is it stolen?'

Wednesday looked affronted. 'Not a bit of it. The papers are in the glove compartment.'

'And the keys?'

'I've got them,' said Shadow.

'My nephew, Harry Bluejay, has an '81 Buick. Why don't you give me the keys to your camper? You can take his car.'

Wednesday bristled. 'What kind of trade is that?'

Whiskey Jack shrugged. 'You know how hard it will be to bring back your camper from where you abandoned it? I'm doing you a favor. Take it or leave it. I don't care.' He closed his knife-wound mouth.

Wednesday looked angry, and then the anger became rue, and he said, 'Shadow, give the man the keys to the Winnebago.' Shadow passed the car keys to Whiskey Jack.

'Johnny,' said Whiskey Jack, 'will you take these men down to find Harry Bluejay? Tell him I said for him to give them his car.'

'Be my pleasure,' said John Chapman.

He got up and walked to the door, picked up a small Hessian sack sitting next to it, opened the door and walked outside. Shadow and Wednesday followed him. Whiskey Jack waited in the doorway. 'Hey,' he said to Wednesday. 'Don't come back here, you. You are not welcome.'

Wednesday extended his middle finger heavenward. 'Rotate on this,' he said politely.

They walked downhill through the snow, pushing their way through the drifts. Chapman walked in front, his bare feet red against the crust-topped snow. 'Aren't you cold?' asked Shadow.

'My wife was Choctaw,' said Chapman.

'And she taught you mystical ways to keep out the cold?'

'Nope. She thought I was crazy,' said Chapman. 'She used t'say, "Johnny, why don't you jes' put on boots?" The slope of the hill became steeper, and they were forced to stop talking. The three men stumbled and slipped on the snow, using the trunks of birch trees on the hillside to steady themselves, and to stop themselves from falling. When the ground became slightly more level, Chapman said, 'She's dead now, a'course. When she died I guess maybe I went a mite crazy. It could happen to anyone. It could happen to you.' He clapped Shadow on the arm. 'By Jesus and Jehosophat, you're a big man.'

'So they tell me,' said Shadow.

They trudged down that hill for about half an hour, until they reached the gravel road that wound around the base of it, and the three men began to walk along it, toward the cluster of buildings they had seen from high on the hill.

A car slowed and stopped. The woman driving it reached over, wound down the passenger window, and said 'You bozos need a ride?'

'You are very gracious, madam,' said Wednesday. 'We're looking for a Mister Harry Bluejay.'

'He'll be down at the rec hall,' said the woman. She was in her forties, Shadow guessed. 'Get in.'

They got in. Wednesday took the passenger seat, John Chapman and Shadow climbed into the back. Shadow's legs were too long to sit in the back comfortably, but he did the best he could. The car jolted forward, down the gravel road.

'So where did you three come from?' asked the driver.

'Just visiting with a friend,' said Wednesday.

'Lives on the hill back there,' said Shadow.

'What hill?' she asked.

Shadow looked back through the dusty rear window, looking back at the hill. But there was no high hill back there; nothing but clouds on the plains.

'Whiskey Jack,' he said.

'Ah,' she said. 'We call him Inktomi here. I think it's the same guy. My grandfather used to tell some pretty good stories about him. Of course, all the best of them were kind of dirty.' They hit a bump in the road, and the woman swore. 'You okay back there?'

'Yes ma'am,' said Johnny Chapman. He was holding on to the back seat with both hands.

'Rez roads,' she said. 'You get used to them.'

'Are they all like this?' asked Shadow.

'Pretty much,' said the woman. 'All the ones round here. And don't you go asking about all the money from casinos, because who in their right mind wants to come all the way out here to go to a casino? We don't see none of that money out here.'

'I'm sorry.'

'Don't be.' She changed gear with a crash and a groan. 'You know the white population all round here is falling? You go out there, you find ghost towns. How you going to keep them down on the farm, after they seen the world on their television screens? And it's not worth anyone's while to farm the Badlands anyhow. They took our lands, they settled here, now they're leaving. They go south. They go west. Maybe if we wait for enough of them to move to New York and Miami and LA we can take the whole of the middle back without a fight.'

'Good luck,' said Shadow.

They found Harry Bluejay in the rec hall, at the pool table, doing trick shots to impress a group of several girls. He had a blue jay tattooed on the back of his right hand, and multiple piercings in his right ear.

'Ho hoka, Harry Bluejay,' said John Chapman.

'Fuck off you crazy barefoot white ghost,' said Harry Bluejay, conversationally. 'You give me the creeps.'

There were older men at the far end of the room, some of them playing cards, some of them talking. There were other men, younger men of about Harry Bluejay's age, waiting for their turn at the pool table. It was a full-sized pool table, and a rip in the green baize on one side had been repaired with silver-gray duct tape.

'I got a message from your uncle,' said Chapman, unfazed. 'He says you're to give these two your car.'

There must have been thirty, maybe even forty people in that hall, and now they were every one of them looking intently at their playing cards, or their feet, or their fingernails, and pretending as hard as they could not to be listening.

'He's not my uncle.'

A cigarette-smoke fug hung over the hall like a cirrus cloud. Chapman smiled widely, displaying the worst set of teeth that Shadow had seen in a human mouth. 'You want to tell your uncle that? He says you're the only reason he stays among the Lakota.'

'Whiskey Jack says a lot of things,' said Harry Bluejay, petulantly. But he did not say Whiskey Jack either. It sounded almost the same, to Shadow's ear, but not quite: *Wisakedjak*, he thought. That's what they're saying. Not Whiskey Jack at all.

Shadow said, 'Yeah. And one of the things he said was that we're trading our Winnebago for your Buick.'

'I don't see a Winnebago.'

'He'll bring you the Winnebago,' said John Chapman. 'You know he will.'

Harry Bluejay attempted a trick shot and missed. His hand was not steady enough. 'I'm not the old fox's nephew,' said Harry Bluejay. 'I wish he wouldn't say that to people.'

'Better a live fox than a dead wolf,' said Wednesday, in a voice so deep it was almost a growl. 'Now, will you sell us your car?'

Harry Bluejay shivered, visibly and violently. 'Sure,' he said. 'Sure. I was only kidding. I kid a lot, me.' He put down the pool cue on the pool table, and took a thick jacket, pulling it out from a cluster of similar jackets hanging from pegs by the door. 'Let me get my shit out of the car first,' he said.

He kept darting glances at Wednesday, as if he were concerned that the older man were about to explode.

Harry Bluejay's car was parked a hundred yards away. As they walked toward it, they passed a small whitewashed Catholic church, and a fair-haired man in a priest's collar who stared at them from the doorway as they went past. He was sucking on a cigarette as if he did not enjoy smoking it.

'Good day to you, father!' called Johnny Chapman, but the man in the dog-collar made no reply; he crushed his cigarette under his heel, picked up the butt, and dropped it into the bin beside the door, and went inside.

'I told you not to give him those pamphlets last time you were here,' said Harry Bluejay.

'It is he that is in error, not me,' said Chapman. 'If he'd jes' read the Swedenborg I gave him he'd know that. It'd bring light into his life.'

Harry Bluejay's car was missing its side mirrors, and its tires were the baldest Shadow had ever seen: perfectly smooth black rubber. Harry Bluejay told them the car drank oil, but as long as you kept pouring oil in, it would just keep running forever, unless it stopped.

Harry Bluejay filled a black garbage bag with shit from the car (said shit including several screw-top bottles of cheap beer, unfinished, a small packet of cannabis resin wrapped in silver foil and badly hidden in the car's ashtray, a skunk-tail, two dozen country and western cassettes and a battered, yellowing copy of *Stranger in a Strange Land*). 'Sorry I was jerking your chain before,' said Harry Bluejay to Wednesday, passing him the car keys. 'You know when I'll get the Winnebago?'

'Ask your uncle. He's the fucking used car dealer,' growled Wednesday.

'Wisakedjak is *not* my uncle,' said Harry Bluejay. He took his black garbage bag and went into the nearest house, and closed the door behind him.

They dropped Johnny Chapman in Sioux Falls, outside a whole-food store.

Wednesday said nothing on the drive. He was brooding.

In a family restaurant just outside St Paul Shadow picked up a newspaper someone else had put down. He looked at it once, then again, then he showed it to Wednesday. Wednesday was in a black sulk, as he had been since they left Whiskey Jack's place.

'Look at that,' said Shadow.

Wednesday sighed, and looked down at the paper with an expression of pain, as if lowering his head hurt more than he could put into words. 'I am,' he said, 'delighted that the air-traffic controllers' dispute has been resolved without recourse to industrial action.'

'Not that,' said Shadow. 'Look. It says it's the fourteenth of February.'

'Happy Valentine's Day.'

'So we set out January the what, twentieth, twenty-first. I wasn't keeping track of the dates, but it was the third week of January. We were three days on the road, all told. So how is it the fourteenth of February?'

'Because we walked for almost a month,' said Wednesday. 'In the Badlands. Backstage.'

'Hell of a shortcut,' said Shadow.

Wednesday pushed the paper away. 'Fucking Johnny Appleseed, always going on about Paul Bunyan. In real life Chapman owned fourteen apple orchards. He farmed thousands of acres. Yes, he kept pace with the western frontier, but there's not a story out there about him with a word of truth in it, save that he went a little crazy once. But it doesn't matter. Like the newspapers used to say, if the truth isn't big enough, you print the legend. This country needs its legends. And even the legends don't believe it any more.'

'But you see it.'

'I'm a has-been. Who the fuck cares about me?'

Shadow said softly, 'You're a god.'

Wednesday looked at him sharply. He seemed to be about to say something, and then he slumped back in his seat, and looked down at the menu and said, 'So?'

'It's a good thing to be a god,' said Shadow.

'Is it?' asked Wednesday, and this time it was Shadow who looked away.

In a gas station twenty-five miles outside Lakeside, on the wall by the rest rooms, Shadow saw a home-made photo-copied notice: a black and white photo of Alison McGovern and the handwritten question *Have You Seen Me*? above it. Same yearbook photograph: smiling confidently, a girl with rubber band braces on her top teeth who wants to work with animals when she grows up. *Have you seen me?*

Shadow bought a Snickers bar, a bottle of water, and a

copy of the *Lakeside News*. The above-the-fold story, written by Marguerite Olsen, our Lakeside Reporter, showed a photograph of a boy and an older man, out on the frozen lake, standing by an outhouse-like ice-fishing shack, and between them they were holding a big fish. They were smiling. *Father and Son Catch Record Northern Pike. Full story inside.*

Wednesday was driving. He said, 'Read me anything interesting you find in the paper.'

Shadow looked carefully, and he turned the pages slowly, but he couldn't find anything.

Wednesday dropped him off in the driveway outside his apartment. A smoke-colored cat stared at him from the driveway, then fled when he bent to stroke it.

Shadow stopped on the wooden deck outside his apartment and looked out at the lake, dotted here and there with green and brown ice-fishing huts. Many of them had cars parked beside them. On the ice nearer the bridge sat the old green klunker, just as it had sat in the newspaper. 'March the 23rd,' said Shadow, encouragingly. 'Round 9:15 in the morning. You can do it.'

'Not a chance,' said a woman's voice. 'April third. Six p.m. That way the day warms up the ice.' Shadow smiled. Marguerite Olsen was wearing a ski suit. She was at the far end of the deck, refilling the bird feeder with white blocks of suet.

'I read your article in the *Lakeside News* on the Town Record Northern Pike.'

'Exciting, huh?'

'Well, educational, maybe.'

'I thought you weren't coming back to us,' she said. 'You were gone for a while, huh?'

'My uncle needed me,' said Shadow. 'The time kind of got away from us.'

She placed the last suet brick in its cage, and began to fill a net sock with thistle-seeds from a plastic milk-jug. Several goldfinches, olive in their winter coats, twitted impatiently from a nearby fir-tree.

'I didn't see anything in the paper about Alison McGovern.'

'There wasn't anything to report. She's still missing. There was a rumor that someone had seen her in Detroit, but it turned out to be a false alarm.'

'Poor kid.'

Marguerite Olsen screwed the top back onto the gallon jug. 'I hope she's dead,' she said, matter-of-factly.

Shadow was shocked. 'Why?'

'Because the alternatives are worse.'

The goldfinches hopped frantically from branch to branch of the fir tree, impatient for the people to be gone. A downy woodpecker joined them.

You aren't thinking about Alison, thought Shadow. *You're thinking of your son. You're thinking of Sandy.*

He remembered someone saying *I miss Sandy*. Who was that?

'Good talking to you,' he said.

'Yeah,' she said. 'You, too.'

* * *

February passed in a succession of short, gray days. Some days the snow fell, most days it didn't. The weather warmed up, and on the good days it got above freezing. Shadow stayed in his apartment until it began to feel like a prison cell, and then, on the days that Wednesday did not need him, he began to walk.

He would walk for much of the day, long trudges out of the town. He walked, alone, until he reached the national forest to the north and the west, or the corn fields and cow pastures to the south. He walked the Lumber County Wilderness Trail, and he walked along the old railroad tracks, and he walked the back roads. A couple of times he even walked along the frozen lake, from north to south. Sometimes he'd see locals or winter tourists or joggers, and he'd wave and say hi. Mostly he saw nobody at all, just crows and finches and, a few times, he spotted a hawk feasting on a road kill possum or raccoon. On one memorable occasion he watched an eagle snatch a silver fish from the middle of the White Pine River, the water frozen at the edges, but still rushing and flowing at the center. The fish wriggled and jerked in the eagle's talons, glittering in the midday sun; Shadow imagined the fish freeing itself and swimming off across the sky, and he smiled, grimly.

If he walked, he discovered, he did not have to think, and that was just the way he liked it; when he thought, his mind went to places he could not control, places that made him feel uncomfortable. Exhaustion was the best thing. When he was exhausted, his thoughts did not wander to Laura, or to the strange dreams, or to things that were not and could not be. He would return home from walking, and sleep without difficulty and without dreaming.

He ran into Police Chief Chad Mulligan in George's Barber Shop in the town square. Shadow always had high hopes for haircuts, but they never lived up to his expectations. After every haircut he always looked more or less the same, only with shorter hair. Chad, seated in the barber's chair beside Shadow's, seemed surprisingly concerned about his own appearance. When his haircut was finished he gazed grimly at his reflection, as if he were preparing to give it a speeding ticket.

'It looks good,' Shadow told him.

'Would it look good to you if you were a woman?'

'I guess.'

They went across the square to Mabel's together, ordered mugs of hot chocolate. Chad said, 'Hey. Mike. Have you ever thought about a career in law enforcement?'

Shadow shrugged. 'I can't say I have,' he said. 'Seems like there's a whole lot of things you got to know.'

Chad shook his head. 'You know the main part of police work, somewhere like this? It's just keeping your head. Something happens, somebody's screaming at you, screaming blue murder, you simply have to be able to say that you're sure that it's all a mistake, and you'll just sort it all out if they just step outside quietly. And you have to be able to mean it.'

'And then you sort it out?'

'Mostly, that's when you put handcuffs on them. But yeah, you do what you can to sort it out. Let me know if you want a job. We're hiring. And you're the kind of guy we want.'

'I'll keep that in mind, if the thing with my uncle falls through.'

They sipped their hot chocolate. Mulligan said, 'Say, Mike, what would you do if you had a cousin? Like a widow. And she started calling you?'

'Calling you how?'

'On the phone. Long distance. She lives out of state.' His cheeks crimsoned. 'I saw her last year at a family wedding, out in Oregon. She was married, back then, though, I mean, her husband was still alive, and she's family. Not a first cousin. Pretty distant.'

'You got a thing for her?'

Blush. 'I don't know about that.'

'Well then, put it another way. Does she have a thing for you?'

'Well, she's said a few things, on the phone. She's a very fine looking woman.'

'So . . . what are you going to do about it?'

'I could ask her out here. I could do that, couldn't I? She's kind of said she'd like to come up here.'

'You're both adults. I'd say go for it.'

Chad nodded, and blushed, and nodded again.

The telephone in Shadow's apartment was silent and dead. He thought about getting it connected, but could think of no one he wanted to call. Late one night he picked it up and listened, and was convinced that he could hear a wind blowing and a distant conversation between a group of people whose voices were too faint to distinguish. He said, 'Hello?' and 'Who's there?' but there was no reply, only a sudden silence and then the faraway sound of laughter, so faint he was not certain he was not imagining it.

***

Shadow made more journeys with Wednesday in the weeks that followed.

He waited in the kitchen of a Rhode Island cottage, and listened while Wednesday sat in a darkened bedroom and argued with a woman who would not get out of bed, nor would she let Wednesday or Shadow look at her face. In the refrigerator was a plastic bag filled with crickets, and another filled with the corpses of baby mice.

In a rock club in Seattle Shadow watched Wednesday shout his greeting, over the noise of the band, to a young woman with short red hair and blue-spiral tattoos. That talk must have gone well, for Wednesday came away from it grinning delightedly.

Five days later Shadow was waiting in the rental when Wednesday walked, scowling, from the lobby of an office building in Dallas. Wednesday slammed the car door when he got in, and sat there in silence, his face red with rage. He said, 'Drive.' Then he said, 'Fucking Albanians. Like anybody cares.'

Three days after that they flew to Boulder, where they had a pleasant lunch with five young Japanese women. It was a meal of pleasantries and politeness, and Shadow walked away from it unsure of whether anything had been agreed to or decided. Wednesday, though, seemed happy enough.

Shadow had begun to look forward to returning to Lakeside. There was a peace there, and a welcome, that he appreciated.

Each morning, when he was not away working for Wednesday, he would drive across the bridge to the town square. He would buy two pasties at Mabel's; he would eat one pasty then and there, and drink a coffee. If someone had left a newspaper out he would read it, although he was never interested enough in the news to purchase a newspaper himself.

He would pocket the second pasty, wrapped in its paper bag, and eat it for his lunch.

He was reading *USA Today* one morning when Mabel said, 'Hey, Mike. Where you going today?'

The sky was pale blue. The morning mist had left the trees covered with hoarfrost. 'I don't know,' said Shadow. 'Maybe I'll walk the wilderness trail again.'

She refilled his coffee. 'You ever gone east on County Q? It's kind of pretty out thataway. That's the little road that starts across from the carpet store on Twentieth Avenue.'

'No. Never have.'

'Well,' she said, 'it's kind of pretty.'

It was extremely pretty. Shadow parked his car at the edge of town, and walked along the side of the road, a winding, country road that curled around the hills to the east of the town. Each of the hills was covered with leafless maple trees, and bone-white birches, and dark firs and pines. There was no footpath, and Shadow walked along the middle of the road, making for the side whenever he heard a car.

At one point a small dark cat kept pace with him beside the road. It was the color of dirt, with white forepaws. He walked over to it. It did not run away.

'Hey, cat,' said Shadow, unselfconsciously.

The cat put its head on one side, looked up at him with emerald eyes. Then it hissed – not at him, but at something over on the side of the road, something he could not see.

'Easy,' said Shadow. The cat stalked away across the road, and vanished into a field of old unharvested corn.

Around the next bend in the road Shadow came upon a

tiny graveyard. The headstones were weathered, although
several of them had sprays of fresh flowers resting against
them. There was no wall about the graveyard, and no fence,
only low mulberry trees, planted at the margins, bent over
with ice and age. Shadow stepped over the piled-up ice and
slush at the side of the road. There were two stone gateposts
marking the entry to the graveyard, although there was no
gate between them. He walked into the graveyard between
the two posts.

. He wandered around the graveyard, looking at the
headstones. There were no inscriptions later than 1969. He
brushed the snow from a solid-looking granite angel, and he
leaned against it.

He took the paper bag from his pocket, and removed the
pasty from it. He broke off the top: it breathed a faint wisp of
steam into the wintry air. It smelled really good, too. He bit
into it.

Something rustled behind him. He thought for a moment
it was the cat, but then he smelled perfume, and under the
perfume, the scent of something rotten.

'Please don't look at me,' she said, from behind him.

'Hello, Laura,' said Shadow.

Her voice was hesitant, perhaps, he thought, even a little
scared. She said, 'Hello, puppy.'

He broke off some pasty. 'Would you like some?' he asked.

She was standing immediately behind him, now. 'No,' she
said. 'You eat it. I don't eat food any more.'

He ate his pasty. It was good. 'I want to look at you,' he
said.

'You won't like it,' she told him.

'Please?'

She stepped around the stone angel. Shadow looked at
her, in the daylight. Some things were different and some
things were the same. Her eyes had not changed, nor had the
crooked hopefulness of her smile. And she was, very
obviously, very dead. Shadow finished his pasty. He stood

up and tipped the crumbs out of the paper bag, then folded it up and put it back into his pocket.

The time he had spent in the funeral home in Cairo made it easier somehow for him to be in her presence. He did not know what to say to her.

Her cold hand sought his, and he squeezed it gently. He could feel his heart beating in his chest. He was scared, and what scared him was the normality of the moment. He felt so comfortable with her at his side that he would have been willing to stand there for ever.

'I miss you,' he admitted.

'I'm here,' she said.

'That's when I miss you most. When you're here. When you aren't here, when you're just a ghost from the past or a dream from another life, it's easier then.'

She squeezed his fingers.

'So,' he asked. 'How's death?'

'Hard,' she said. 'It just keeps going.'

She rested her head on his shoulder, and it almost undid him. He said, 'You want to walk for a bit?'

'Sure.' She smiled up at him, a nervous, crooked smile in a dead face.

They walked out of the little graveyard, and made their way back down the road, toward the town, hand in hand. 'Where have you been?' she asked.

'Here,' he said. 'Mostly.'

'Since Christmas,' she said, 'I kind of lost you. Sometimes I would know where you were, for a few hours, for a few days. You'd be all over. Then you'd fade away again.'

'I was in this town,' he said. 'Lakeside. It's a good little town.'

'Oh,' she said.

She no longer wore the blue dress in which she had been buried. Now she wore several sweaters, a long, dark, skirt, and high, burgundy boots. Shadow commented on them.

Laura ducked her head. She smiled. 'Aren't they great boots? I found them in this great shoe store in Chicago.'

'So what made you decide to come up from Chicago?'

'Oh, I've not been in Chicago for a while, puppy. I was heading south. The cold was bothering me. You'd think I'd welcome it. But it's something to do with being dead, I guess. You don't feel it as cold. You feel it as a sort of *nothing*, and when you're dead I guess the only thing that you're scared of is nothing. I was going to go to Texas. I planned to spend the winter in Galveston. I think I used to winter in Galveston, when I was a kid.'

'I don't think you did,' said Shadow. 'You've never mentioned it before.'

'No? Maybe it was someone else, then. I don't know. I remember seagulls – throwing bread in the air for seagulls, hundreds of them, the whole sky becoming nothing but seagulls as they flapped their wings and snatched the bread from the air.' She paused. 'If I didn't see it, I guess someone else did.'

A car came around the corner. The driver waved them hello. Shadow waved back. It felt wonderfully normal to walk with his wife.

'This feels good,' said Laura, as if she was reading his mind.

'Yes,' said Shadow.

'I'm pleased it feels good for you, too. When the call came I had to hurry back. I was barely into Texas.'

'Call?'

She looked up at him. Around her neck the gold coin glinted. 'It felt like a call,' she said. 'I started to think about you, about how much more fun I would have with you than down in Galveston. About how much I needed to see you. It was like a hunger.'

'You knew I was *here*, then?'

'Yes.' She stopped. She frowned, and her upper teeth pressed into her blue lower lip, biting it gently. She put her

head on one side and said, 'I did. Suddenly, I did. I thought
you were calling me, but it wasn't you, was it?'

'No.'

'You didn't want to see me.'

'It wasn't that.' He hesitated. 'No. I didn't want to see you.
It hurts too much.'

The snow crunched beneath their feet and it glittered
diamonds as the sunlight caught it.

'It must be hard,' said Laura, 'not being alive.'

'You mean it's hard for you to be dead? Look, I'm still
going to figure out how to bring you back, properly. I think
I'm on the right track—'

'No,' she said. 'I mean, I'm grateful. And I hope you really
can do it. I did a lot of bad stuff . . .' She shook her head. 'But
I was talking about you.'

'I'm alive,' said Shadow. 'I'm not dead. Remember?'

'You're not dead,' she said. 'But I'm not sure that you're
alive, either. Not really.'

This isn't the way this conversation goes, thought Shadow.
This isn't the way anything goes.

'I love you,' she said, dispassionately. 'You're my puppy.
But when you're really dead you get to see things clearer. It's
like there isn't anyone there. You know? You're like this big,
solid, man-shaped hole in the world.' She frowned. 'Even
when we were together. I loved being with you because you
adored me, and you would do anything for me. But
sometimes I'd go into a room and I wouldn't think there was
anybody in there. And I'd turn the light on, or I'd turn the
light off, and I'd realize that you were in there, sitting on
your own, not reading, not watching TV, not doing anything.'

She hugged him then, as if to take the sting from her
words, and she said, 'The best thing about Robbie was that
he was *somebody*. He was a jerk sometimes, and he could be
a joke, and he loved to have mirrors around when we made
love so he could watch himself fucking me, but he was alive,
puppy. He *wanted* things. He filled the space.' She stopped,

looked up at him, tipped her head a little to one side. 'I'm sorry. Did I hurt your feelings?'

He did not trust his voice not to betray him, so he simply shook his head.

'Good,' she said. 'That's good.'

They were approaching the rest area where he had parked his car. Shadow felt that he needed to say something: *I love you*, or *please don't go*, or *I'm sorry*. The kind of words you use to patch a conversation that had lurched, without warning, into the dark places. Instead he said, 'I'm not dead.'

'Maybe not,' she said. 'But are you sure you're alive?'

'Look at me,' he said.

'That's not an answer,' said his dead wife. 'You'll know it, when you are.'

'What now?' he said.

'Well,' she said, 'I've seen you now. I'm going south again.'

'Back to Texas?'

'Somewhere warm. I don't care.'

'I have to wait here,' said Shadow. 'Until my boss needs me.'

'That's not living,' said Laura. She sighed; and then she smiled, the same smile that had been able to tug at his heart no matter how many times he saw it. Every time she smiled at him had been the first time all over again.

'Will I see you again?'

She looked up at him and she stopped smiling. 'I guess so,' she said. 'In the end. Nothing's finished, yet, is it?'

'No,' he said. 'It's not.'

He went to put his arm around her, but she shook her head and pulled out of his reach. She sat down on the edge of a snow-covered picnic table, and she watched him drive away.

Interlude

The war had begun and nobody saw it. The storm was lowering and nobody knew it.

Wars are being fought all the time, with the world outside no more the wiser: the war on crime, the war on poverty, the war on drugs. This war was smaller than those, and huger, and more selective, but it was as real as any.

A falling girder in Manhattan closed a street for two days. It killed two pedestrians, an Arabic taxi-driver and the taxi-driver's passenger.

A truck-driver in Denver was found dead in his home. The murder instrument, a rubber-gripped claw-headed hammer, had been left on the floor beside his corpse. His face was untouched, but the back of his head was completely destroyed, and several words in a foreign alphabet were written on the bathroom mirror in brown lipstick.

In a postal sorting station in Phoenix, Arizona, a man went crazy, *went postal* as they said on the evening news, and shot Terry 'The Troll' Evensen, a morbidly obese, awkward man who lived alone in a trailer. Several other people in the sorting station were fired on, but only Evensen was killed. The man who fired the shots – first thought to be a disgruntled postal worker – was not caught, and was never identified.

'Frankly,' said Terry 'The Troll' Evensen's supervisor, on the News at Five, 'if anyone around here was gonna go postal, we would have figured it was gonna be the Troll.

Okay worker, but a weird guy. I mean, you never can tell, huh?'

That interview was cut when the segment was repeated, later that evening.

A community of nine anchorites in Montana were found dead. Reporters speculated that it was a mass suicide, but soon the cause of death was reported as carbon monoxide poisoning from an elderly furnace.

A lobster tank was smashed in the lobby of an Atlanta seafood restaurant.

A crypt was defiled in the Key West graveyard.

An Amtrak passenger train hit a UPS truck in Idaho, killing the driver of the truck. No passengers were seriously injured.

It was still a cold war at this stage, a phony war, nothing that could be truly won or lost.

The wind stirred the branches of the tree. Sparks flew from the fire. The storm was coming.

***

The Queen of Sheba, half-demon, they said, on her father's side, witch-woman, wise-woman and queen, who ruled Sheba when Sheba was the richest land there ever was, when its spices and its gems and scented woods were taken by boat and camel-back to the corners of the earth, who was worshiped even when she was alive, worshiped as a living goddess by the wisest of kings, stands on the sidewalk of Sunset Boulevard at 2:00 a.m. staring blankly out at the traffic like a slutty plastic bride on a black and neon wedding cake. She stands as if she owns the sidewalk and the night that surrounds her.

When someone looks straight at her, her lips move, as if she is talking to herself. When men in cars drive past her she makes eye-contact and she smiles. She ignores the men who walk past her on the sidewalk (it happens, people walk everywhere, even in West Hollywood); she ignores them, does her best to pretend that they are not there.

It's been a long night.

It's been a long week, and a long four thousand years.

She is proud that she owes nothing to anyone. The other girls on the street, they have pimps, they have habits, they have children, they have people who take what they make. Not her.

There is nothing holy left in her profession. Not any more.

A week ago the rains began in Los Angeles, slicking the streets into road accidents, crumbling the mud from the hillsides and toppling houses into canyons, washing the world into the gutters and storm drains, drowning the bums and the homeless camped down in the concrete channel of the river. When the rains come in Los Angeles they always take people by surprise.

Bilquis has spent the last week inside. Unable to stand on the sidewalk, she has curled up in her bed in the room the color of raw liver, listening to the rain pattering on the metal box of the window air-conditioner and placing personals on the Internet. She has left her invitations on adultfriend finder.com, LA-escorts.com, Classyhollywoodbabes.com, has given herself an anonymous e-mail address. She was proud of herself for negotiating the new territories, but remains nervous – she has spent a long time avoiding anything that might resemble a paper trail. She has never even taken a small ad in the back pages of the *LA Weekly*, preferring to pick out her own customers, to find by eye and smell and touch the ones who will worship her as she needs to be worshiped, the ones who will let her take them all the way . . .

And it occurs to her now, standing and shivering on the street corner (for the late February rains have left off, but the chill they brought with them remains) that she has a habit as bad as that of the smack whores and the crack whores, and this distresses her, and her lips begin to move again. If you

were close enough to her rubyred lips you would hear her
say,

*'I will rise now and go about the city in the streets, and in
the broad ways I will seek the one I love.'* She is whispering
that, and she whispers, *'I am my beloved's, and my beloved
is mine. He said, this stature of mine is like to a palm tree, and
my breasts like clusters of grapes. He said he would come to
me then. I am my beloved's and his desire is only toward me.'*

Bilquis hopes that the break in the rains will bring the
johns back. Most of the year she walks the two or three
blocks on Sunset, enjoying the cool LA nights. Once a month
she pays off a man named Sabbah, an officer in the LAPD,
who replaced another officer in the LAPD she used to pay
off, who had vanished. That man's name was Jerry LeBec,
and his disappearance had been a mystery to the LAPD. He
had become obsessed with Bilquis, had taken to following
her on foot, and one afternoon she woke, startled by a noise,
and opened the door to her apartment, and found Jerry LeBec
in civilian clothes kneeling and swaying on the worn carpet,
his head bowed, waiting for her to come out. The noise she
had heard was the noise of his head, thumping against her
door as he rocked back and forth on his knees.

She stroked his hair and told him to come inside, and later
she put his clothes into a black plastic garbage bag and
tossed them into a dumpster behind a hotel several blocks
away. His gun and his wallet she put into a grocery store bag.
She poured used coffee grounds and food waste on top of
them, folded the top of the bag and dropped it into a trash
can at a bus-stop.

She kept no souvenirs.

The orange night-sky glimmers to the west with distant
lightning, somewhere out to sea, and Bilquis knows that the
rain will be starting soon. She sighs. She does not want to be
caught in the rain. She will return to her apartment, she
decides, and take a bath, and shave her legs, it seems to her
she is always shaving her legs, and sleep.

'By night on my bed I sought him whom my soul loveth,' she whispers. *'Let him kiss me with the kisses of his mouth. My beloved is mine and I am his.'*

She begins to walk up a side-street, walking up the hillside to where her car is parked.

Headlights come up behind her, slowing as they approach her, and she turns her face to the street and smiles. The smile freezes when she sees the car is a white stretch limo. Men in stretch limos want to fuck in stretch limos, not in the privacy of Bilquis's shrine. Still, it might be an investment. Something for the future.

A tinted window hums down and Bilquis walks over to the limo, smiling. 'Hey, honey,' she says. 'You looking for something?'

'Sweet loving,' says a voice from the back of the stretch. She peers inside, as much as she can through the open window: she knows a girl who got into a stretch with five drunk football players and got hurt real bad, but there's only one john in there that she can see, and he looks kind of on the young side. He doesn't feel like a worshiper, but money, good money that's passed from his hand to hers, that's an energy in its own right – *baraka* they called it, once on a time, – which she can use and frankly these days, every little helps.

'How much?' he asks.

'Depends on what you want and how long you want it for,' she says. 'And whether you can afford it.' She can smell something smoky drifting out of the limo window. It smells like burning wires and overheating circuit boards. The door is pushed open from inside.

'I can pay for anything I want,' says the john. She leans into the car and looks around. There's nobody else in there, just the john, a puffy-faced kid who doesn't even look old enough to drink. Nobody else, so she gets in.

'Rich kid, huh?' she says.

'Richer than rich,' he tells her, edging along the leather seat towards her. He moves awkwardly. She smiles at him.

'Mm. Makes me hot, honey,' she tells him. 'You must be one of them dot coms I read about?'

He preens then, puffs like a bullfrog. 'Yeah. Among other things. I'm a technical boy.' The car moves off.

'So,' he says. 'Tell me, Bilquis, how much just to suck my cock?'

'What you call me?'

'Bilquis,' he says, again. And then he sings, in a voice not made for singing, '*You are an immaterial girl living in a material world.*' There is something rehearsed about his words, as if he's practiced this exchange in front of a mirror.

She stops smiling, and her face changes, becomes wiser, sharper, harder. 'What do you want?'

'I told you. Sweet loving.'

'I'll give you whatever you want,' she says. She needs to get out of the limo. It's moving too fast for her to throw herself from the car, she figures, but she'll do it if she can't talk her way out of this. Whatever's happening here, she doesn't like it.

'What I want. Yes.' He pauses. His tongue runs over his lips. 'I want a clean world. I want to own tomorrow. I want evolution, devolution, and revolution. I want to move our kind from the fringes of the slipstream to the higher ground of the mainstream. You people are underground. That's wrong. We need to take the spotlight and shine. Front and center. You people have been so far underground for so long you've lost the use of your eyes.'

'My name's Ayesha,' she says. 'I don't know what you're talking about. There's another girl on that corner, her name's Bilquis. We could go back to Sunset, you could have both of us . . .'

'Oh, Bilquis,' he says, and he sighs, theatrically. 'There's only so much belief to go around. They're reaching the end of what they can give us. The credibility gap.' And then he sings, once again, in his tuneless nasal voice, '*You are an analog girl, living in a digital world.*' The limo takes a corner too fast, and he tumbles across the seat into her. The driver of the car is hidden behind tinted glass. An irrational conviction strikes her, that nobody is driving the car, that the white limo is driving through Beverly Hills like Herbie the Love Bug, under its own power.

Then the john reaches out his hand and taps on the tinted glass.

The car slows, and before it has stopped moving Bilquis has pushed open the door and she half-jumps, half-falls out onto the blacktop. She's on a hillside road. To the left of her is a steep hill, to the right is a sheer drop. She starts to run down the road.

The limo sits there, unmoving.

It starts to rain, and her high heels slip and twist beneath her. She kicks them off and runs, soaked to the skin, looking for somewhere she can get off the road. She's scared. She has power, true, but it's hunger-magic, cunt-magic. It has kept her alive in this land for so long, true, but for everything else that's not simply living she uses her sharp eyes and her mind, her height and her presence.

There's a metal guard-rail at knee-height on her right, to stop cars from tumbling over the side of the hill, and now the rain is running down the hill-road turning it into a river, and the soles of her feet have started to bleed.

The lights of LA are spread out in front of her, a twinkling electrical map of an imaginary kingdom, the heavens laid out right here on earth, and she knows that all she needs to be safe is to get off the road.

I am black but comely, she mouths to the night and the rain. *I am the rose of Sharon, and the lily of the valleys. Stay me with flagons, comfort me with apples: for I am sick of love.*

A fork of lightning burns greenly across the night sky. She loses her footing, slides several feet, skinning her leg and elbow, and she is getting to her feet when she sees the lights of the car descending the hill toward her. It's coming down too fast for safety and she wonders whether to throw herself to the right, where it could crush her against the hillside, or the left, where she might tumble down the gully, and she runs across the road, intending to push herself up the wet earth, to climb, when the white stretch limo comes fishtailing down the slick hillside road, hell it must be doing eighty, maybe even aquaplaning on the surface of the road, and she's pushing her hands into a handful of weeds and earth, and she's going to get up and away, she knows, when the wet earth crumbles and she tumbles back down onto the road.

The car hits her with an impact that crumples the grille and tosses her into the air like a glove puppet. She lands on the road behind the limo, and the impact shatters her pelvis, fractures her skull. Cold rainwater runs over her face.

She begins to curse her killer: curse him silently, as she cannot move her lips. She curses him in waking and in sleeping, in living and in death. She curses him as only someone who is half-demon on her father's side can curse.

A car door slams. Someone approaches her. 'You were an analog girl,' he sings again, tunelessly, 'living in a digital world.' And then he says, 'You fucking madonnas. All you fucking madonnas.' He walks away.

The car door slams.

The limo reverses, and runs back over her, slowly, for the first time. Her bones crunch beneath the wheels. Then the limo comes back down the hill toward her.

When, finally, it drives away, down the hill, all it leaves behind on the road is the smeared red meat of road kill, barely recognizable as human, and soon even that will be washed away by the rain.

Interlude 2

H i, Samantha.'

'Mags? Is that you?'

'Who else? Leon said that Auntie Sammy called when I was in the shower.'

'We had a good talk. He's such a sweet kid.'

'Yeah. I think I'll keep him.'

A moment of discomfort for both of them, barely a crackle of a whisper over the telephone lines. Then, 'Sammy, how's school?'

'They're giving us a week off. Problem with the furnaces. How are things in your neck of the North Woods?'

'Well, I've got a new next-door neighbor. He does coin tricks. The *Lakeside News* letter column currently features a blistering debate on the potential rezoning of the town land down by the old cemetery on the southeast shore of the lake and yours truly has to write a strident editorial summarizing the paper's position on this without offending anybody or in fact giving anyone any idea what our position is.'

'Sounds like fun.'

'It's not. Alison McGovern vanished last week – Jilly and Stan McGovern's oldest. I don't think you met them. Nice kid. She babysat for Leon a few times.'

A mouth opens to say something, and it closes again, leaving whatever it was to say unsaid, and instead it says, 'That's awful.'

'Yes.'

'So . . .' and there's nothing to follow that with that isn't going to hurt, so she says, 'Is he cute?'

'Who?'

'The neighbor.'

'His name's Ainsel. Mike Ainsel. He's okay. Too young for me. Big guy, looks . . . what's the word. Begins with an M.'

'Mean? Moody? Magnificent? Married?'

A short laugh, then 'Yes, I guess he does look married. I mean, if there's a look that married men have, he kind of has it. But the word I was thinking of was Melancholy. He looks Melancholy.'

'And Mysterious?'

'Not particularly. When he moved in he seemed kinda helpless – he didn't even know to heat-seal the windows. These days he still looks like he doesn't know what he's doing here. When he's here – he's here, then he's gone again. I've seen him out walking from time to time. He's no trouble.'

'Maybe he's a bank robber.'

'Uh-huh. Just what I was thinking.'

'You were not. That was my idea. Listen, Mags, how are *you*? Are *you* okay?'

'Yeah.'

'Really?'

'No.'

A long pause then. 'I'm coming up to see you.'

'Sammy, no.'

'It'll be after the weekend before the furnaces are working and school starts again. It'll be fun. You can make up a bed on the couch for me. And invite the mysterious neighbor over for dinner one night.'

'Sam, you're matchmaking.'

'Who's matchmaking? After Claudine-the-bitch-from-hell, maybe I'm ready to go back to boys for a while. I met a nice strange boy when I hitchhiked down to El Paso for Christmas.'

'Oh. Look, Sam, you've got to stop hitchhiking.'

'How do you think I'm going to get to Lakeside?'

'Alison McGovern was hitchhiking. Even in a town like this, it's not safe. I'll wire you the money. You can take the bus.'

'I'll be fine.'

'*Sammy.*'

'Okay, Mags. Wire me the money if it'll let you sleep easier.'

'You know it will.'

'Okay, bossy big sister. Give Leon a hug and tell him Auntie Sammy's coming up and he's not to hide his toys in her bed this time.'

'I'll tell him. I don't promise it'll do any good.'

'So when should I expect you?'

'Tomorrow night. You don't have to meet me at the bus station – I'll ask Hinzelmann to run me over in Tessie.'

'Too late. Tessie's in mothballs for the winter. But Hinzelmann will give you a ride anyway. He likes you. You listen to his stories.'

'Maybe you should get Hinzelmann to write your editorial for you. Let's see. *On the Rezoning of the Land by the Old Cemetery, it so happens that in the winter of ought three my grampaw shot a stag down by the old cemetery by the lake. He was out of bullets, so he used a cherry-stone from the lunch my grandmama had packed for him. Creased the skull of the stag and it shot off like a bat out of heck. Two years later he was down that way and he sees this mighty buck with a spreading cherry tree growing between its antlers. Well, he shot it, and grandmama made cherry pies enough that they were still eating them come the next Fourth of July . . .*'

And they both laughed, then.

Interlude 3

Jacksonville Florida. 2:00 a.m.

T he sign says help wanted.'

'We're always hiring.'

'I can only work the night shift. Is that going to be a problem?'

'Shouldn't be. I can get you an application to fill out. You ever worked in a gas station before?'

'No. I figure, how hard can it be?'

'Well, it ain't rocket science, that's for sure.'

'I'm new here. I don't have a telephone. Waiting for them to put it in.'

'I surely know that one. I surely do. They just make you wait because they can. You know, ma'am, you don't mind my saying this, but you do not look well.'

'I know. It's a medical condition. Looks worse than it is. Nothing life-threatening.'

'Okay. You leave that application with me. We are really short handed on the late shift right now. Round here we call it the zombie shift. You do it too long, that's how you feel. Well now . . . is that *Larna*?'

'Laura.'

'Laura. Okay. Well, I hope you don't mind dealing with weirdos. Because they come out at night.'

'I'm sure they do. I can cope.'

Chapter Thirteen

Hey, old friend.
What do you say, old friend?
Make it okay, old friend,
Give an old friendship a break.
Why so grim? We're going on forever.
You, me, him—
Too many lives are at stake . . .

         – Stephen Sondheim, '*Old Friends*'

It was Saturday morning. Somebody knocked at Shadow's door. He had been brushing his teeth, so it took him a minute to answer it.

Marguerite Olsen was there. She did not come in, just stood there in the sunlight, looking serious. 'Mister Ainsel . . .?'

'Mike, please,' said Shadow.

'Mike, yes. Would you like to come over for dinner tonight? About six-ish? It won't be anything exciting, just spaghetti and meatballs.'

'Not a problem. I like spaghetti and meatballs.'

'Obviously, if you have any other plans . . .'

'I have no other plans.'

'Six o'clock.'

'Should I bring flowers?'

'If you must. But this is a social gesture. Not a romantic one.' She closed the door behind her.

He showered. He went for a short walk, down to the bridge and back. The sun was up, a tarnished quarter in the sky, and he was sweating in his coat by the time he got home. It had to be above freezing. He drove the 4-Runner down to Dave's and bought a bottle of wine. It was a twenty dollar bottle, which seemed to Shadow like some kind of guarantee of quality. He didn't know wines, but he figured that for twenty bucks it ought to taste good. He bought a Californian Cabernet, because Shadow had once seen a bumper sticker, back when he was younger and people still had bumper stickers on their cars, which said LIFE IS A CABERNET and it had made him laugh.

He bought a plant in a pot as a gift. Green leaves, no flowers. Nothing remotely romantic about that.

He bought a carton of milk, which he would never drink, and a selection of fruit, which he would never eat.

Then he drove over to Mabel's and bought a single lunchtime pasty. Mabel's face lit up when she saw him. 'Did Hinzelmann catch up with you?'

'I didn't know he was looking for me.'

'Yup. Wants to take you ice fishing. And Chad Mulligan wanted to know if I'd seen you around. His cousin's here from out of state. She's a widow. His second cousin, what we used to call kissing cousins. Such a sweetheart. You'll love her,' and she dropped the pasty into a brown paper bag, twisted the top of the bag over to keep the pasty warm.

Shadow drove the long way home, eating one-handed, the steaming pasty's pastry-crumbs tumbling onto his jeans and onto the floor of the 4-Runner. He passed the library on the south shore of the lake. It was a black and white town in the ice and the snow. Spring seemed unimaginably far away: the klunker would always sit on the ice, with the ice-fishing shelters and the pick-up trucks and the snowmobile tracks.

He reached his apartment, parked, walked up the drive, up the wooden steps to his apartment. The goldfinches and nuthatches on the birdfeeder hardly gave him a glance. He went inside. He watered the plant, wondered whether or not to put the wine into the refrigerator.

There was a lot of time to kill until six.

Shadow wished he could comfortably watch television once more. He wanted to be entertained, not to have to think, just to sit and let the sounds and the light wash over him. *Do you want to see Lucy's tits*? something with a Lucy voice whispered in his memory, and he shook his head, although there was no one there to see him.

He was nervous, he realized. This would be his first real social interaction with other people – normal people, not people in jail, not gods or culture heroes or dreams – since he was first arrested, over three years ago. He would have to make conversation, as Mike Ainsel.

He checked his watch. It was two-thirty. Marguerite Olsen had told him to be there at six. Did she mean six *exactly*? Should he be there a little early? A little late? He decided, eventually, to walk next door at five past six.

Shadow's telephone rang.

'Yeah?' he said.

'That's no way to answer the phone,' growled Wednesday.

'When I get my telephone connected I'll answer it politely,' said Shadow. 'Can I help you?'

'I don't know,' said Wednesday. There was a pause. Then he said, 'Organizing gods is like herding cats into straight lines. They don't take naturally to it.' There was a deadness, and an exhaustion, in Wednesday's voice that Shadow had never heard before.

'What's wrong?'

'It's hard. It's too fucking hard. I don't know if this is going to work. We might as well cut our throats. Just cut our own throats.'

'You mustn't talk like that.'

'Yeah. Right.'

'Well, if you do cut your throat,' said Shadow, trying to jolly Wednesday out of his darkness, 'maybe it wouldn't even hurt.'

'It would hurt. Even for my kind, pain still hurts. If you move and act in the material world, then the material world acts on you. Pain hurts, just as greed intoxicates and lust burns. We may not die easy and we sure as hell don't die well, but we can die. If we're still loved and remembered, something else a whole lot like us comes along and takes our place and the whole damn thing starts all over again. And if we're forgotten, we're done.'

Shadow did not know what to say. He said, 'So where are you calling from?'

'None of your goddamn business.'

'Are you drunk?'

'Not yet. I just keep thinking about Thor. You never knew him. Big guy, like you. Good hearted. Not bright, but he'd give you the goddamned shirt off his back if you asked him. And he killed himself. He put a gun in his mouth and blew his head off in Philadelphia in 1932. What kind of a way is that for a god to die?'

'I'm sorry.'

'You don't give two fucking cents, son. He was a whole lot like you. Big and dumb.' Wednesday stopped talking. He coughed.

'What's wrong?' said Shadow, for the second time.

'They got in touch.'

'Who did?'

'The opposition.'

'And?'

'They want to discuss a truce. Peace talks. Live and let fucking live.'

'So what happens now?'

'Now I go and drink bad coffee with the modern assholes in a Kansas City Masonic Hall.'

'Okay. You going to pick me up, or shall I meet you somewhere?'

'You stay there and you keep your head down. Don't get into any trouble. You hear me?'

'But—'

There was a click, and the line went dead and stayed dead. There was no dial tone, but then, there never was.

Nothing but time to kill. The conversation with Wednesday had left Shadow with a sense of disquiet. He got up, intending to go for a walk, but already the light was fading, and he sat back down again.

Shadow picked up the *Minutes of the Lakeside City Council 1872-1884* and turned the pages, his eyes scanning the tiny print, not actually reading it, occasionally stopping to scan something that caught his eye.

In July of 1874, Shadow learned, the City Council was concerned about the number of itinerant foreign loggers arriving in the town. An opera house was to be built on the corner of Third Street and Broadway. It was to be expected that the nuisances attendant to the damming of the Mill Creek would abate once the mill-pond had become a lake. The council authorized the payment of seventy dollars to Mr Samuel Samuels, and of eighty-five dollars to Mr Heikki Salminen, in compensation for their land and for the expenses incurred in moving their domiciles out of the area to be flooded.

It had never occurred to Shadow before that the lake was man-made. Why call a town Lakeside, when the lake had begun as a dammed mill-pond? He read on, to discover that a Mr Hinzelmann, originally of Hüdemuhlen in Bavaria, was in charge of the lake-building project, and that the city council had granted him the sum of $370 toward the project, any shortfall to be made up by public subscription. Shadow tore off a strip of a paper towel and placed it into the book as a bookmark. He could imagine Hinzelmann's pleasure in seeing the reference to his grandfather. He wondered if the old man knew that his family had been instrumental in building the lake. Shadow flipped forward through the book, scanning for more references to the lake-building project.

They had dedicated the lake in a ceremony in the spring of 1876, as a precursor to the town's centennial celebrations. A vote of thanks to Mr Hinzelmann was taken by the council.

Shadow checked his watch. It was five thirty. He went into the bathroom, shaved, combed his hair. He changed his clothes. Somehow the final fifteen minutes passed. He got the wine and the plant, and he walked next door.

The door opened as he knocked. Marguerite Olsen looked almost as nervous as he felt. She took the wine bottle and the potted plant, and said thank you. The television was on, *The Wizard of Oz* on video. It was still in sepia, and Dorothy was still in Kansas, sitting with her eyes closed in Professor Marvel's wagon as the old fraud pretended to read her mind, and the twister-wind that would tear her away from her life was approaching. Leon sat in front of the screen, playing with a toy fire truck. When he saw Shadow an expression of delight touched his face; he stood up and ran, tripping over his feet in his excitement, into a back bedroom, from which he emerged a moment later, triumphantly waving a quarter.

'Watch Mike Ainsel!' he shouted. Then closed both his hands and he pretended to take the coin into his right hand, which he opened wide. 'I made it disappear Mike Ainsel!"

'You did,' agreed Shadow. 'After we've eaten, if it's okay with your mom, I'll show you how to do it even smoother than that.'

'Do it now if you want,' said Marguerite. 'We're still waiting for Samantha. I sent her out for sour cream. I don't know what's taking her so long.'

And, as if that was her cue, footsteps sounded on the wooden deck, and somebody shouldered open the front door. Shadow did not recognize her at first, then she said 'I didn't know if you wanted the kind with calories or the kind that tastes like wallpaper paste so I went for the kind with calories,' and he knew her then: the girl from the road to Cairo.

'That's fine,' said Marguerite. 'Sam, this is my neighbor, Mike Ainsel. Mike, this is Samantha Black Crow, my sister.'

I don't know you, thought Shadow desperately. *You've never met me before. We're total strangers.* He tried to remember how he had thought *snow*, how easy and light that had been: this was desperate. He put out his hand and said 'Pleased to meetcha.'

She blinked, looked up at his face. A moment of puzzlement, then recognition entered her eyes and curved the corners of her mouth into a grin. 'Hello,' she said.

'I'll see how the food is doing,' said Marguerite, in the taut voice of someone who burns things in kitchens if they leave them alone and unwatched even for a moment.

Sam took off her puffy coat and her hat. 'So you're the melancholy but mysterious neighbor,' she said. 'Who'da thunk it?' She kept her voice down.

'And you,' he said, 'are girl Sam. Can we talk about this later?'

'If you promise to tell me what's going on.'

'Deal.'

Leon tugged at the leg of Shadow's pants. 'Will you show me now?' he asked, and held out his quarter.

'Okay,' said Shadow. 'But if I show you, you have to remember that a master magician never tells anyone how it's done.'

'I promise,' said Leon, gravely.

Shadow took the coin in his left hand, then moved Leon's right hand in, cupping it in his own hand, huge by comparison, showing him how to appear to take the coin in his right hand while actually leaving it in Shadow's left hand. Then he put the coin into Leon's left hand and made him repeat the movements on his own.

After several attempts the boy mastered the move. 'Now you know half of it,' said Shadow. 'Because the moves are only half of it. The other half is this: put your attention on the place where the coin *ought* to be. Look at it. Follow it with your eyes. If you act like it's in your right hand, no one will even look at your left hand, no matter how clumsy you are.'

Sam watched all this with her head tipped slightly on one side, saying nothing.

'Dinner!' called Marguerite, pushing her way in from the kitchen with a steaming bowl of spaghetti in her hands. 'Leon, go wash your hands.'

The food was good: crusty garlic bread, thick red sauce, good spicy meatballs. Shadow complimented Marguerite on it.

'Old family recipe,' she told him, 'from the Corsican side of thc family.'

'I thought you were Native American.'

'Dad's Cherokee,' said Sam. 'Mag's mom's father came from Corsica.' Sam was the only person in the room who was actually drinking the Cabernet. 'Dad left her when Mags was ten and he moved across town. Six months after that, I was born. Mom and Dad got married when the divorce came through and I think they tried to make it work for a while, and when I was ten he went away. I think he has a ten-year attention span.'

'Well, he's been out in Oklahoma for ten years,' said Marguerite.

'Now, *my* mom's family were European Jewish,' continued Sam, 'from one of those places that used to be communist and now are just chaos. I think she liked the idea of being married to a Cherokee. Fry bread and chopped liver.' Sam took another sip of the red wine.

'Her mom's a wild woman,' said Marguerite, semi-approvingly.

'You know where she is now?' asked Sam. Shadow shook

his head. 'She's in Australia. She met a guy on the Internet, who lived in Hobart. When they met in the flesh she decided he was actually kind of icky. But she really liked Tasmania. So she's living down there, with a woman's group, teaching them to batik cloth and things like that. Isn't that cool? At her age?'

Shadow agreed that it was, and helped himself to more meatballs. Sam told them how all the aboriginal natives of Tasmania had been wiped out by the British, and about the human chain they made across the island to catch them which trapped only an old man and a sick boy. She told him how the Tasmanian Tigers, the thylacines, had been killed by farmers, scared for their sheep, how the politicians in the 1930s noticed that the thylacines should be protected only after the last of them was dead. She finished her second glass of wine, poured her third.

'So, Mike,' said Sam, suddenly, her cheeks reddening, 'Tell us about your family. What are the Ainsels like?' She was smiling, and there was mischief in that smile.

'We're real dull,' said Shadow. 'None of us ever got as far as Tasmania. So you're at school in Madison. What's that like?'

'*You* know,' she said. 'I'm studying art history, women's studies, and casting my own bronzes.'

'When I grow up,' said Leon, 'I'm going to do magic. Poof. Will you teach me, Mike Ainsel?'

'Sure,' said Shadow. 'If your mom doesn't mind.'

Marguerite shrugged.

Sam said, 'After we've eaten, while you're putting Leon to bed, Mags, I think I'm going to get Mike to take me to the Buck Stops Here for an hour or so.'

Marguerite did not shrug. Her head moved, an eyebrow raised slightly.

'I think he's interesting,' said Sam. 'And we have lots to talk about.'

Marguerite looked at Shadow, who busied himself in

dabbing an imaginary blob of red sauce from his chin with a paper napkin. 'Well, you're grown-ups,' she said, in a tone of voice that did its best to imply that they weren't, and that even if they were they shouldn't be.

After dinner Shadow helped Sam with the washing up – he dried – and then he did a trick for Leon, counting pennies into Leon's palm: each time Leon opened his hand and counted them there was one less coin than he had counted in. And as for the final coin – 'Are you squeezing it? Tightly?' – when Leon opened his hand, he found it had transformed into a dime. Leon's plaintive cries of 'How'd you do that? Momma, how'd he do that?' followed him out into the hall.

Sam handed him his coat. 'Come on,' she said. Her cheeks were flushed from the wine.

Outside it was cold.

Shadow stopped in his apartment, tossed the *Minutes of the Lakeside City Council* into a plastic grocery bag and brought it along. Hinzelmann might be down at the Buck, and he wanted to show him the mention of his grandfather.

They walked down the drive side by side.

He opened the garage door, and she started to laugh. 'Omigod,' she said, when she saw the 4-Runner. 'Paul Gunther's car. You bought Paul Gunther's car. Omigod.'

Shadow opened the door for her. Then he went around and got in. 'You know the car?'

'When I came up here two or three years ago to stay with Mags. It was me that persuaded him to paint it purple.'

'Oh,' said Shadow. 'It's good to have someone to blame.'

He drove the car out onto the street. Got out and closed the garage door. Got back into the car. Sam was looking at him oddly as he got in, as if the confidence had begun to leak out of her. He put on his seatbelt, and she said, 'I'm scared. This was a stupid thing to do, wasn't it? Getting into a car with a psycho-killer.'

'I got you safe home last time,' said Shadow.

'You killed two men,' she said. 'You're wanted by the Feds.

And now I find out you're living under an assumed name next door to my sister. Unless Mike Ainsel is your real name?'

'No,' said Shadow, and he sighed. 'It's not.' He hated saying it. It was if he was letting go of something important, abandoning Mike Ainsel by denying him, as if he were taking his leave of a friend.

'Did you kill those men?'

'No.'

'They came to my house, and said we'd been seen together. And this guy showed me photographs of you. What was his name – Mister Hat? No. Mister Town. That was him. It was like *The Fugitive*. But I said I hadn't seen you.'

'Thank you.'

'So,' she said. 'Tell me what's going on. I'll keep your secrets if you keep mine.'

'I don't know any of yours,' said Shadow.

'Well, you know that it was my idea to paint this thing purple, thus forcing Paul Gunther to become such an object of scorn and derision for several counties around that he was forced to leave town entirely. We were kind of stoned,' she admitted.

'I doubt that bit of it's much of a secret,' said Shadow. 'Everyone in Lakeside must have known. It's a stoner sort of purple.'

And then she said, very quiet, very fast, 'If you're going to kill me please don't hurt me. I shouldn't have come here with you. I am so dumb. I am so fucking fucking dumb. I should have run away or called the cops when I first saw you. I can identify you. Jesus. I am so dumb.'

Shadow sighed. 'I've never killed anybody. Really. Now I'm going to take you to the Buck,' he said. 'Or if you give the word, I'll turn this car around and take you home. I'll buy you a drink, if you're actually old enough to drink, and I'll buy you a soda if you're not. Then I'll take you back to Marguerite, deliver you safe and sound, and hope you aren't going to call the cops.'

There was silence as they crossed the bridge.

'Who did kill those men?' she asked.

'You wouldn't believe me if I told you.'

'I *would*.' She sounded angry now. He wondered if bringing the wine to the dinner had been a wise idea. Life was certainly not a Cabernet right now.

'It's not easy to believe.'

'I,' she told him, 'can believe anything. You have no idea what I can believe.'

'Really?'

'I can believe things that are true and I can believe things that aren't true and I can believe things where nobody knows if they're true or not. I can believe in Santa Claus and the Easter Bunny and Marilyn Monroe and the Beatles and Elvis and Mister Ed. Listen – I believe that people are perfectible, that knowledge is infinite, that the world is run by secret banking cartels and is visited by aliens on a regular basis, nice ones that look like wrinkledy lemurs and bad ones who mutilate cattle and want our water and our women. I believe that the future sucks and I believe that the future rocks and I believe that one day White Buffalo woman is going to come back and kick everyone's ass. I believe that all men are just overgrown boys with deep problems communicating and that the decline in good sex in America is coincident with the decline in Drive-In Movie theatres from state to state. I believe that all politicians are unprincipled crooks and I still believe that they are better than the alternative. I believe that California is going to sink into the sea when the big one comes, while Florida is going to dissolve into madness and alligators and toxic waste. I believe that antibacterial soap is destroying our resistance to dirt and disease so that one day we'll all be wiped out by the common cold like the Martians in *War of the Worlds*. I believe that the greatest poets of the last century were Edith Sitwell and Don Marquis, that jade is dried dragon sperm, and that thousands of years ago in a former life I was a one-armed Siberian Shaman. I believe that

Mankind's destiny lies in the stars. I believe that candy really did taste better when I was a kid, that it's aerodynamically impossible for a bumblebee to fly, that light is a wave and a particle, that there's a cat in a box somewhere who's alive and dead at the same time (although if they don't ever open the box to feed it it'll eventually just be two different kinds of dead), and that there are stars in the universe billions of years older than the universe itself. I believe in a personal god who cares about me and worries and oversees everything I do. I believe in an impersonal god who set the universe in motion and went off to hang with her girlfriends and doesn't even know that I'm alive. I believe in an empty and godless universe of causal chaos, background noise and sheer blind luck. I believe that anyone who says that sex is overrated just hasn't done it properly. I believe that anyone who claims to know what's going on will lie about the little things too. I believe in absolute honesty and sensible social lies. I believe in a woman's right to choose, a baby's right to live, that while all human life is sacred there's nothing wrong with the death penalty if you can trust the legal system implicitly, and that no one but a moron would ever trust the legal system. I believe that life is a game, life is a cruel joke and that life is what happens when you're alive and that you might as well lie back and enjoy it.' She stopped, out of breath.

Shadow almost took his hands off the wheel to applaud. Instead he said, 'Okay. So if I tell you what I've learned you won't think that I'm a nut.'

'Maybe,' she said. 'Try me.'

'Would you believe that all the gods that people have ever imagined are still with us today?'

' . . . maybe.'

'And that there are new gods out there, gods of computers and telephones and whatever, and that they all seem to think there isn't room for them both in the world. And that some kind of war is kind of likely.'

'And these gods killed those two men?'

'No, my wife killed those two men.'

'I thought you said your wife was dead.'

'She is.'

'She killed them before she died, then?'

'After. Don't ask.'

She reached up a hand and flicked her hair from her forehead.

They pulled up on Main Street, outside The Buck Stops Here. The sign over the window showed a surprised looking stag standing on its hind legs holding a glass of beer. Shadow got out. He grabbed the bag with the book in it, and took the keys. He did not bother to lock the door. Nobody in Lakeside ever did.

'Why would they have a war?' asked Sam. 'It seems kind of redundant. What is there to win?'

'I don't know,' admitted Shadow.

'It's easier to believe in aliens than in gods,' said Sam. 'Maybe Mister Town and Mister Whatever were Men in Black, only the alien kind.'

'Maybe they were, at that,' said Shadow.

They were standing on the sidewalk outside the Buck Stops Here and Sam stopped. She looked up at Shadow, and her breath hung on the night air like a faint cloud. She said, 'Just tell me you're one of the good guys.'

'I can't,' said Shadow. 'I wish I could. But I'm doing my best.'

She looked up at him, and bit her lower lip. Then she nodded. 'Good enough,' she said. 'I won't turn you in. You can buy me a beer.'

Shadow pushed the door open for her, and they were hit by a blast of heat and music, enveloped by a cloud of warm air that smelled of beer and hamburgers. They went inside.

Sam waved at some friends. Shadow nodded to a handful of people whose faces – although not their names – he remembered from the day he had spent searching for Alison McGovern, or who he had met in Mabel's in the morning.

Chad Mulligan was standing at the bar, with his arm around the shoulders of a small woman – the kissing cousin, Shadow figured. He wondered what she looked like, but she had her back to him. Chad's hand raised in a mock salute when he saw Shadow. Shadow grinned, and waved back at him. Shadow looked around for Hinzelmann, but the old man did not seem to be there this evening. He spied a free table at the back and started walking toward it.

Then somebody began to scream.

It was a bad scream, a full-throated, seen-a-ghost hysterical scream, which silenced all conversation. Shadow looked around, certain somebody was being murdered, and then he realized that all the faces in the bar were turning toward him. Even the black cat, who slept in the window during the day, was standing up on top of the juke box with its tail high and its back arched and was staring at Shadow.

Time slowed.

'Get him!' shouted a woman's voice, parked on the verge of hysteria. 'Oh for god's sake, somebody stop him! Don't let him get away! Please!' it was a voice he knew.

Nobody moved. They stared at Shadow. He stared back at them.

Chad Mulligan stepped forward, walking through the people. The small woman walked behind him warily, her eyes wide, as if she was preparing to start screaming once more. Shadow knew her. Of course he knew her.

Chad was still holding his beer, which he put down on a nearby table. He said, 'Mike.'

Shadow said, 'Chad.'

Audrey Burton was a step behind Chad Mulligan. Her face was white, and there were tears in her eyes. She had been screaming. 'Shadow,' she said. 'You bastard. You murderous evil bastard.'

'Are you sure that you know this man, hon?' said Chad. He looked uncomfortable. It was obvious that he hoped that whatever was happening here was all some kind of case of mistaken identity, something that one day they might be able to laugh about.

Audrey Burton looked at him incredulously. 'Are you *crazy*? He worked for Robbie for *years*. His slutty wife was my best *friend*. He's wanted for *murder*. I had to answer *questions*. He's an escaped *convict*.' She was way over the top, her voice trembling with suppressed hysteria, sobbing out her words like a soap actress going for a daytime Emmy. *Kissing cousins*, thought Shadow, unimpressed.

Nobody in the bar said a word. Chad Mulligan looked up at Shadow. 'It's probably a mistake. I'm sure we can sort this all out,' he said, sensibly. Then he said, to the bar, 'It's all fine. Nothing to worry about. We can sort this out. Everything's fine.' Then, to Shadow. 'Let's step outside, Mike.' Quiet competence. Shadow was impressed.

'Sure,' said Shadow.

He felt a hand touch his hand, and he turned to see Sam staring at him. He smiled down at her as reassuringly as he could.

Sam looked at Shadow, then she looked around the bar at the faces staring at them. She said to Audrey Burton, 'I don't know who you are. But. You. Are. Such. A cunt.' Then she went up on tiptoes and pulled Shadow down to her, and kissed him hard on the lips, pushing her mouth against his for what felt to Shadow like several minutes, and might have been as long as five seconds in real, clock-ticking time.

It was a strange kiss, Shadow thought, as her lips pressed against his: it wasn't intended for him. It was for the other people in the bar, to let them know that she had picked sides. It was a flag-waving kiss. Even as she kissed him, he became certain that she didn't even like him – well, not like that.

Still, there was a tale he had read once, long ago, as a small boy: the story of a traveler who had slipped down a cliff, with man-eating tigers above him and a lethal fall below him, who managed to stop his fall halfway down the side of the cliff, holding on for dear life. There was a clump of strawberries beside him, and certain death above him and below. *What should he do*? went the question. And the reply was, *Eat the strawberries*.

The story had never made any sense to him as a boy. It did now.

So he closed his eyes, threw himself into the kiss and experienced nothing but Sam's lips and the softness of her skin against his, sweet as a wild strawberry.

'C'mon Mike,' said Chad Mulligan, firmly. 'Please. Let's take it outside.'

Sam pulled back. She licked her lips, and smiled, a smile that nearly reached her eyes. 'Not bad,' she said. 'You kiss good for a boy. Okay, go play outside.' Then she turned to Audrey Burton. 'But you,' she said, 'are still a cunt.'

Shadow tossed Sam his car keys. She caught them, one-handed. He walked through the bar, and stepped outside, followed by Chad Mulligan. A gentle snow had begun to fall, the flakes spinning down into the light of the neon bar sign. 'You want to talk about this?' asked Chad.

'Am I under arrest?' asked Shadow.

Audrey followed them out onto the sidewalk. She looked as if she were ready to start screaming again. She said, her voice trembling, 'He killed two men, Chad. The FBI came to my door. He's a psycho. I'll come down to the station with you, if you want.'

'You've caused enough trouble ma'am,' said Shadow. He sounded tired, even to himself. 'Please go away.'

'Chad? Did you hear that? He threatened me!' said Audrey.

'Get back inside, Audrey,' said Chad Mulligan. She looked as if she were about to argue, then she pressed her lips together so hard they went white, and went back into the bar.

'Would you like to comment on anything she said?' asked Chad Mulligan.

'I've never killed anyone,' said Shadow.

Chad nodded. 'I believe you,' he said. 'I'm sure we can deal with these allegations easily enough. It's probably nothing. I have to do this. You won't give me any trouble, will you Mike?'

'No trouble,' said Shadow. 'This is all a mistake.'

'Exactly,' said Chad. 'So I figure we ought to head down to my office and sort it all out there?'

'Am I under arrest?' asked Shadow, for the second time.

'Nope,' said Chad. 'Not unless you want to be. I figure, we go down to my office together, you come with me out of a sense of civic duty, and we do whatever we can to straighten all this out.'

Chad patted Shadow down, found no weapons. They got into Mulligan's car. Again Shadow sat in the back, looking out through the metal cage. He thought *SOS. Mayday. Help.* He tried to push Mulligan with his mind, as he'd once pushed a cop in Chicago – *this is your old friend Mike Ainsel. You saved his life. Don't you know how silly this is? Why don't you just drop the whole thing?*

'I figure it was good to get you out of there,' said Chad. 'All you needed was some loudmouth deciding that you were Alison McGovern's killer and we'd've had a lynch mob on our hands.'

'Point.'

'So you sure there's nothing you want to tell me?'

'Nope. Nothing to say.'

They pulled up outside the Lakeside police offices. The building, Chad said, as they pulled up outside it, actually belonged to the county sheriff's department. The local police had a few rooms in there. Pretty soon the county would build something modern. For now they had to make do with what they had.

They walked inside.

'Should I call a lawyer?' asked Shadow.

'You aren't accused of anything,' said Mulligan. 'Up to you.' They pushed through some swing doors. 'Take a seat over there.'

Shadow took a seat on the wooden chair with cigarette

burns on the side. He felt stupid and numb. There was small poster on the notice board, beside a large NO SMOKING sign: ENDANGERED MISSING it said. The photograph was Alison McGovern's.

There was a wooden table, with old copies of *Sports Illustrated* and *Newsweek* on it, with the place on the cover where an address label had been pasted cut neatly away. The light was bad. The paint on the wall was yellow, but it might once have been white.

After ten minutes Chad brought him a watery cup of vending machine hot chocolate. 'What's in the bag?' he asked. And it was only then that Shadow realized he was still holding the plastic bag containing the *Minutes of the Lakeside City Council*.

'Old book,' said Shadow. 'Your grandfather's picture's in here. Or great grandfather maybe.'

'Yeah?'

Shadow flipped through the book until he found the portrait of the town council, and he pointed to the man called Mulligan. Chad chuckled. 'If that don't beat all,' he said.

Minutes passed, and hours, in that room. Shadow read two of the *Sports Illustrated*s and he started the *Newsweek*. From time to time Chad would come through, checking to see if Shadow needed to use the restroom, once to offer him a ham roll and a small packet of potato chips.

'Thanks,' said Shadow, taking them. 'Am I under arrest?'

Chad sucked the air between his teeth. 'Well,' he said, 'We'll know pretty soon. It doesn't look like you came by the name Mike Ainsel legally. On the other hand, you can call yourself whatever you want in this state, if it's not for fraudulent purposes. You just hang loose.'

'Can I make a phone call?'

'Is it a local call?'

'Long distance.'

'It'll save money if I put it on my calling card, otherwise

you'll just be feeding ten bucks worth of quarters into that thing in the hall.'

Sure, thought Shadow. *And this way you'll know the number I dialed, and you'll probably be listening in on an extension.*

'That would be great,' said Shadow. They went into an empty office, next to Chad's. The light was slightly better in there. The number Shadow gave Chad to dial for him was that of a funeral home in Cairo, Illinois. Chad dialed it, handed Shadow the receiver. 'I'll leave you in here,' he said, and went out.

The telephone rang several times, then it was picked up.

'Jacquel and Ibis? Can I help you?'

'Hi. Mister Ibis, this is Mike Ainsel. I helped out there for a few days over Christmas.'

A moment's hesitation, then, 'Of course. Mike. How *are* you?'

'Not great, Mister Ibis. In a patch of trouble. About to be arrested. Hoping you'd seen my uncle about, or maybe you could get a message to him.'

'I can certainly ask around. Hold on, uh, Mike. There's someone here who wishes a word with you.'

The phone was passed to somebody, and then a smoky female voice said, 'Hi, honey. I miss you.'

He was certain he'd never heard that voice before. But he knew her. He was sure that he knew her . . .

Let it go, the smoky voice whispered in his mind, in a dream. *Let it all go.*

'Who's that girl you were kissing, hon? You trying to make me jealous?'

'We're just friends,' said Shadow. 'I think she was trying to prove a point. How did you know she kissed me?'

'I got eyes wherever my folk walk,' she said. 'You take care now, hon . . .' There was a moment of silence, then Mr Ibis came back on the line and said 'Mike?'

'Yes.'

'There's a problem getting hold of your uncle. He seems to be kind of tied up. But I'll try and get a message to your Aunt Nancy. Best of luck.' The line went dead.

Shadow sat down, expecting Chad to return. He sat in the empty office, wishing he had something to distract him. Reluctantly, he picked up the *Minutes* once more, opened it to somewhere in the middle of the book, and began to read.

An ordinance prohibiting expectoration on sidewalks and on the floors of public buildings, or throwing thereon tobacco in any form was introduced and passed, eight to four, in December of 1876.

Lemmi Hautala was twelve years old and had 'it was feared, wandered away in a fit of delirium' on December the 13th, 1876. 'A search being immediately effected, but impeded by the snows, which are blinding.' The council had voted unanimously to send the Hautala family their condolences.

The fire at Olsen's livery stables the following week was extinguished without any injury or loss of life, human or equine.

Shadow scanned the closely-printed columns. He found no further mention of Lemmi Hautala.

And then, on something slightly more than a whim, he flipped the pages forward to the winter of 1877. He found what he was looking for mentioned as an aside in the January minutes: Jessie Lovat, age not given, 'a Negro child' had vanished on the night of 28th of December. It was believed that she might have been 'abducted by traveling so-called pedlars, who were run out of town the previous week, having been discovered to be engaged in certain larcenous acts. They were said to be making for St Paul'. Telegrams had been sent to St Paul, but no results were reported. Condolences were not sent to the Lovat family.

Shadow was scanning the minutes of winter 1878 when Chad Mulligan knocked and entered, looking shamefaced, like a child bringing home a bad report card.

'Mister Ainsel,' he said. 'Mike. I'm truly sorry about this. I appreciate how easy you've been about all this. Personally, I like you. But that don't change anything, you know?'

Shadow said he knew.

'I got no choice in the matter,' said Chad, 'but to place you under arrest for violating your parole.' Then Police Chief Chad Mulligan read Shadow his rights. He filled out some paperwork. He took Shadow's prints. He walked him down the hall to the county jail, on the other side of the building.

There was a long counter and several doorways on one side of the room, two holding cells and a doorway on the other. One of the cells was occupied – a man slept on a cement bed under a thin blanket. The other was empty.

There was a sleepy-looking woman in a brown uniform behind the counter, watching Jay Leno on a small white portable television. She took the papers from Chad, and signed for Shadow. Chad hung around, filled in more papers. The woman came around the counter, patted Shadow down, took all his possessions – wallet, coins, front door key, book, watch – and put them on the counter, then gave him a plastic bag with orange clothes in and told him to go into the open cell and change into them. He could keep his own underwear and socks. He went in and changed into the orange clothes and the shower footwear. It stank evilly in there. The orange top he pulled over his head had LUMBER COUNTY JAIL written on the back, in large black letters.

The metal toilet in the cell had backed up, and was filled to the brim with a brown stew of liquid feces and sour, beerish urine.

Shadow came back out, gave the woman his clothes, which she put into the plastic bag with the rest of his possessions. She had him sign for them. Shadow signed for them as Mike Ainsel, although he found that he was already thinking of Mike Ainsel as someone he had liked well enough in the past but would no longer be seeing in the future. He had thumbed through the wallet before he handed it over. 'You take care of this,' he had said to the woman, 'My whole life is in here.' The woman took the wallet from him, and assured him that it would be safe with them. She asked Chad if that wasn't true, and Chad, looking up from the last of his paperwork, said Liz was telling the truth, they'd never lost a prisoner's possessions yet.

Shadow had slipped the four hundred-dollar bills that he had palmed from the wallet into his socks, when he had changed, along with the silver Liberty dollar he had palmed as he had emptied his pockets.

'Say,' Shadow asked, when he came out. 'Would it be okay if I finished reading the book?'

'Sorry, Mike. Rules are rules,' said Chad.

Liz put Shadow's possessions in a bag in the back room. Chad said he'd leave Shadow in Officer Bute's capable hands. Liz looked tired and unimpressed. Chad left. The telephone rang, and Liz – Officer Bute – answered it. 'Okay,' she said. 'Okay. No problem. Okay. No problem. Okay.' She put down the phone and made a face.

'Problem?' asked Shadow.

'Yes. Not really. Kinda. They're sending someone up from Milwaukee to collect you. Okay, do you have any history of medical problems, diabetes, anything like that?'

'No,' said Shadow. 'Nothing like that. Why is that a problem?'

'Because I got to keep you in here with me for three hours,' she said. 'And the cell over there–' she pointed to the cell by the door, with the sleeping man in it, 'that's occupied. He's on suicide watch. I shouldn't put you in with him. But it's not worth the trouble to sign you in to the county and then sign you out again.' She shook her head. 'And you don't want to go in there–' she pointed to the empty cell in which he'd changed his clothes, 'because the can is shot. It stinks in there, doesn't it?'

'Yes. It was gross.'

'It's common humanity, that's what it is. The sooner we get

into the new facilities, it can't be too soon for me. One of the women we had in yesterday must've flushed a tampon away. I tell 'em not to. We got bins for that. They clog the pipes. Every damn tampon down that john costs the county a hundred bucks in plumbers' fees. So, I can keep you out here, if I cuff you. Or you can go in the cell.' She looked at him. 'Your call,' she said.

'I'm not crazy about them,' he said. 'But I'll take the cuffs.'

She took a pair from her utility belt, then patted the semi-automatic in its holster, as if to remind him that it was there. 'Hands behind your back,' she said.

The cuffs were a tight fit: he had big wrists. Then she put hobbles on his ankles, and sat him down on a bench on the far side of the counter, against the wall. 'Now,' she said. 'You don't bother me, and I won't bother you.' She tilted the television so that he could see it.

'Thanks,' he said.

'When we get our new offices,' she said, 'there won't be none of this nonsense.'

The Tonight Show finished. Jay and his guests grinned the world good night. An episode of *Cheers* began. Shadow had never really watched *Cheers*. He had only ever seen one episode of it – the one where Coach's daughter comes to the bar – although he had seen that several times. Shadow had noticed that you only ever catch one episode of shows you don't watch, over and over, years apart; he thought it must be some kind of cosmic law.

Officer Liz Bute sat back in her chair. She was not obviously dozing, but she was by no means awake, so she did not notice when the gang at Cheers stopped talking and getting off one-liners and just started staring out of the screen at Shadow.

Diane, the blonde barmaid who fancied herself an intellectual, was the first to talk. 'Shadow,' she said. 'We were so *worried* about you. You'd fallen off the world. It's so good to see you again – albeit in bondage and orange *couture*.'

'What I figure, is, the thing to do,' pontificated bar-bore Cliff, 'is to escape in hunting season, when everybody's wearing orange anyway.'

Shadow said nothing.

'Ah, cat got your tongue, I see,' said Diane. 'Well, you've led us a merry chase!"

Shadow looked away. Officer Liz had begun, gently, to snore. Carla, the little waitress, snapped, 'Hey, jerk-wad! We interrupt this broadcast to show you something that's going to make you piss in your friggin' pants. You ready?'

The screen flickered and went black. The words 'LIVE FEED' pulsated in white at the bottom left of screen. A subdued female voice said, in voice-over, 'It's certainly not too late to change to the *winning* side. But you know, you *also* have the freedom to stay *just* where you are. That's what it means to *be* an American. *That's* the miracle of America. Freedom to believe means the freedom to believe the wrong thing, after all. Just as freedom of *speech* gives you the right to stay silent.'

The picture now showed a street scene. The camera lurched forward, in the manner of hand-held video cameras in real-life documentaries.

A man with thinning hair, a tan, and a faintly hangdog expression filled the frame. He was standing by a wall sipping a cup of coffee from a plastic cup. He looked into the camera and said, 'Terrorism is too easy a word to bandy about. It means that the real terrorists hide behind weasel-words, like *freedom fighter*, when they are murdering scum, pure and simple. It doesn't make our job any easier, but at least we know we're making a difference. We're risking our lives to make a difference.'

Shadow recognized the voice. He had been inside the man's head once. Mr Town sounded different from inside – his voice was deeper, more resonant – but there was no mistaking it.

The cameras pulled back to show that Mr Town was

standing outside a brick building on an American street. Above the door was a set-square and compass framing the letter G.

'In position,' said somebody off-screen.

'Let's see if the cameras *inside* the hall are working,' said the female voice-over voice. It was the kind of reassuring voice they use on commercials to try to sell you things only people as smart as you are going to take this opportunity to buy.

The words LIVE FEED continued to blink at the bottom left of the screen. Now the picture showed the interior of a small hall: the room was underlit. Two men sat at a table at the far end of the room. One of them had his back to the camera. The camera zoomed in to them awkwardly, in a series of jagged movements. For a moment they were out of focus, and then they became sharp once more. The man facing the camera got up and began to pace, like a bear on a chain. It was Wednesday. He looked as if, on some level, he was enjoying this. As they came into focus the sound came on with a pop.

The man with his back to the screen was saying, '– we are offering is the chance to end this, here and now, with no more bloodshed, no more aggression, no more pain, no more loss of life. Isn't that worth giving up a little?'

Wednesday stopped pacing and turned. His nostrils flared. 'First,' he growled, 'you have to understand that you are asking me to speak for all of us, for each and every individual in my position across this country. Which is manifestly nonsensical. They will do what they will do, and I have no say in it. Secondly, what on earth makes you think that I believe that you people are going to keep your word?'

The man with his back to the camera moved his head. 'You do yourself an injustice,' he said. 'Obviously you people have no leaders. But you're the one they listen to. They pay attention to you, Mister Cargo. And as for keeping my word, well, these preliminary talks are being filmed and broadcast live,' and he gestured back toward the camera. 'Some of your people are watching as we speak. Others will see videotapes. Others will be told, by those they trust. The camera does not lie.'

'Everybody lies,' said Wednesday.

Shadow recognized the voice of the man with his back to the camera. It was Mr World, the one who had spoken to Town on the cell phone while Shadow was in Town's head.

'You don't believe,' said Mr World, 'that we will keep our word?'

'I think your promises were made to be broken and your oaths to be forsworn. But *I* will keep *my* word.'

'Safe conduct is safe conduct,' said Mr World, 'and a flag of truce is what we agreed. I should tell you, by the way, that your young protégé is once more in our custody.'

Wednesday snorted. 'No,' he said. 'He's not.'

'We were discussing the ways to deal with the coming paradigm shift. We don't *have* to be enemies. Do we?'

Wednesday still seemed shaken. He said, 'I will do whatever is in my power . . .'

Shadow noticed something strange about the image of Wednesday on the television screen. A red glint burned on his left eye, the glass one. The eye burned with a scarlet light. The glint left a phosphor-dot after-image as he moved. Wednesday seemed unaware of it.

'It's a big country,' said Wednesday, marshaling his thoughts. He moved his head and the scarlet glitter-blur slipped to his cheek, a red laser-pointer dot. Then it edged up to his glass eye once more. 'There is room for—'

There was a bang, muted by the television speakers, and the side of Wednesday's head exploded. His body tumbled backward.

Mr World stood up, his back still to the camera, and walked out of shot.

'Let's see that again, in slow motion this time,' said the announcer's voice, reassuringly.

The words LIVE FEED became REPLAY. Slowly now the
red laser pointer traced its bead onto Wednesday's glass eye,
and once again the side of his face dissolved into a cloud of
blood. Freeze frame.

'Yes, it's still God's Own Country,' said the announcer, a
news reporter pronouncing the final tag line. 'The only
question is, which gods?'

Another voice – Shadow thought that it was Mr World's, it
had that same half-familiar quality – said, 'We now return
you to your regularly scheduled programming.'

On *Cheers* Coach assured his daughter that she was truly
beautiful, just like her mother.

The telephone rang, and officer Liz sat up with a start. She
picked it up. Said 'Okay. Okay. Yes. Okay, I'll be over there,'
put the phone down and got up from behind the counter. She
said to Shadow, 'Sorry. I'm going to have to put you in the
cell. Don't use the can. If you need to go, press the buzzer by
the door, and I'll come down as soon as I can and escort you
to the rest rooms out back. The Lafayette sheriffs'
department should be here to collect you soon.'

She removed the cuffs and the hobble, locked him into the
holding cell. The smell was worse, now that the door was
closed.

Shadow sat down on the concrete bed, slipped the Liberty
dollar from his sock and began moving it from finger to
palm, from position to position, from hand to hand, his only
aim to keep the coin from being seen by anyone who might
look in. He was passing the time. He was numb.

He missed Wednesday, then, sudden and deep. He missed
the man's confidence, his attitude. His conviction.

He opened his hand, looked down at Lady Liberty, a silver
profile. He closed his fingers over the coin, held it tightly. He
wondered if he'd get to be one of those guys who get life for
something he didn't do. If he even made it that far. From
what he'd seen of Mr World and Mr Town, they would have
little trouble pulling him out of the system. Perhaps he'd

suffer an unfortunate accident on the way to the next holding facility. He could be shot while making a break for it. It did not seem at all unlikely.

There was a stir of activity in the room on the other side of the glass. Officer Liz came back in. She pressed a button, a door that Shadow could not see opened, and a black deputy in a brown sheriff's uniform entered and walked briskly over to the desk.

Shadow slipped the dollar coin back into his sock, pushing it down toward his ankle.

The new deputy handed over some papers, Liz scanned them and signed. Chad Mulligan came in, said a few words to the new man, then he unlocked the cell door and came in.

'It stinks in here.'

'Tell me about it.'

'Okay. Folk are here to pick you up. Seems you're a matter of national security. You know that?'

'It'll make a great front page story for the *Lakeside News*,' said Shadow.

Chad looked at him without expression. 'That a drifter got picked up for parole violations? Not much of a story.'

'So that's the way it is?'

'That's what they tell me,' said Chad Mulligan. Shadow put his hands in front of him this time, and Chad cuffed him. Chad locked on the ankle hobbles, and a rod from the cuffs to the hobbles.

Shadow thought, *they'll take me outside. Maybe I can make a break for it, some kind of break for it, in hobbles and cuffs and lightweight orange clothes, out into the snow*, and even as he thought it he knew how stupid and hopeless it was.

Chad walked him out into the office. Liz had turned the TV off now. The black deputy looked him over. 'He's a big guy,' he said to Chad. Liz passed the new deputy the paper bag with Shadow's possessions in it, and he signed for it.

Chad looked at Shadow, then at the deputy. He said to the

deputy, quietly, but loudly enough for Shadow to hear, 'Look. I just want to say, I'm not comfortable with the way this is happening.'

The deputy nodded. His voice was deep, and cultured: the voice of a man who could as easily organize a press briefing as a massacre. 'You'll have to take it up with the appropriate authorities, sir. Our job is simply to bring him in.'

Chad made a sour face. He turned to Shadow. 'Okay,' said Chad. 'Through that door and into the sally port.'

'What?'

'Out there. Where the car is.'

Liz unlocked the doors. 'You make sure that orange uniform comes right back here,' she said to the deputy. 'The last felon we sent down to Lafayette, we never saw the uniform again. They cost the county money.' They walked Shadow out to the sally port, where a car was waiting. It wasn't a sheriff's department car. It was a black town car. Another deputy, a grizzled white guy with a moustache, stood by the car, smoking a cigarette. He crushed it out underfoot as they came close, and opened the back door for Shadow.

Shadow sat down, awkwardly, his movements hampered by the cuffs and the hobble. There was no grille between the back and the front of the car.

The two deputies climbed into the front of the car. The black deputy started the motor. They waited for the sally port door to open.

'Come on, come on,' said the black deputy, his fingers drumming against the steering wheel.

Chad Mulligan tapped on the side window. The white deputy glanced at the driver, then he lowered the window. 'This is wrong,' said Chad. 'I just wanted to say that.'

'Your comments have been noted, and will be conveyed to the appropriate authorities,' said the driver.

The doors to the outside world opened. The snow was still falling, dizzying into the car's headlights. The driver put his foot on the gas, and they were heading back down the street and onto Main Street.

'You heard about Wednesday?' said the driver. His voice sounded different, now, older, and familiar. 'He's dead.'

'Yeah. I know,' said Shadow. 'I saw it on TV.'

'Those fuckers,' said the white officer. It was the first thing he had said, and his voice was rough and accented and, like the driver's, it was a voice that Shadow knew. 'I tell you, they are fuckers, those fuckers.'

'Thanks for coming to get me,' said Shadow.

'Don't mention it,' said the driver. In the light of an oncoming car his face already looked older. He looked smaller, too. The last time Shadow had seen him he had been wearing lemon-yellow gloves and a check jacket. 'We were in Milwaukee. Still had to drive like demons when Ibis called.'

'You think we let them lock you up and send you to the chair, when I'm still waiting to break your head with my hammer?' asked the white deputy gloomily, fumbling in his pocket for a pack of cigarettes. His accent was East European.

'The real shit will hit the fan in an hour or less,' said Mr Nancy, looking more like himself with each moment, 'When they *really* turn up to collect you. We'll pull over before we get to Highway 53 and get you out of those shackles and back into your own clothes.' Czernobog held up a handcuff key and smiled.

'I like the moustache,' said Shadow. 'Suits you.'

Czernobog stroked it with a yellowed finger. 'Thank you.'

'Wednesday,' said Shadow. 'Is he really dead? This isn't some kind of trick is it?'

He realized that he had been holding on to some kind of hope, foolish though it was. But the expression on Nancy's face told him all he needed to know, and the hope was gone.

Coming to America

14,000 BC

Cold it was, and dark, when the vision came to her, for in the far north daylight was a gray dim time in the middle of the day that came, and went, and came again: an interlude between darknesses.

They were not a large tribe as these things were counted then: nomads of the Northern Plains. They had a god, who was the skull of a mammoth, and the hide of a mammoth fashioned into a rough cloak. *Nunyunnini* they called him. When they were not traveling, he rested on a wooden frame, at man height.

She was the holy woman of the tribe, the keeper of its secrets, and her name was Atsula, the fox. Atsula walked before the two tribesmen who carried their god on long poles, draped with bearskins, that it should not be seen by profane eyes, nor at times when it was not holy.

They roamed the tundra, with their tents. The finest of the tents was made of caribou-hide, and it was the holy tent, and there were four of them inside it: Atsula, the priestess, Gugwei, the tribal elder, Yanu, the war leader, and Kalanu, the scout. She called them there, the day after she had her vision.

Atsula scraped some lichen into the fire, then she threw in dried leaves with her withered left hand: they smoked, with an eye-stinging gray smoke, and gave off an odor that was sharp and strange. Then she took a wooden cup from the wooden platform, and she passed it to Gugwei. The cup was half-filled with a dark yellow liquid.

Atsula had found the *pungh* mushrooms – each with seven spots, only a true holy woman could find a seven-spotted mushroom – and had picked them at the dark of the moon, and dried them on a string of deer-cartilage.

Yesterday, before she slept, she had eaten the three dried mushroom caps. Her dreams had been confused and fearful things, of bright lights moving fast, of rock mountains filled with lights spearing upward like icicles. In the night she had woken, sweating, and needing to make water. She squatted over the wooden cup and filled it with her urine. Then she placed the cup outside the tent, in the snow, and returned to sleep.

When she woke, she picked the lumps of ice out from the wooden cup, as her mother had taught her, leaving a darker, more concentrated liquid behind.

It was this liquid she passed around the skin tent, first to Gugwei, then to Yanu and to Kalanu. Each of them took a large gulp of the liquid, then Atsula took the final draught. She swallowed it, and poured what was left on the ground in front of their god, a libation to Nunyunnini.

They sat in the smoky tent, waiting for their god to speak. Outside, in the darkness, the wind wailed and breathed.

Kalanu, the scout, was a woman who dressed and walked as a man: she had even taken Dalani, a fourteen year old maiden, to be her wife. Kalanu blinked her eyes tightly, then she got up and walked over to the mammoth skull. She pulled the mammoth-hide cloak over herself, and stood so her head was inside the mammoth-skull.

'There is evil in the land,' said Nunyunnini. 'Evil, such that if you stay here, in the land of your mothers and your mother's mothers, you shall all perish.'

The three listeners grunted.

'Is it the slavers? Or the great wolves?' asked Gugwei,

whose hair was long and white, and whose face was as wrinkled as the gray skin of a thorn tree.

'It is not the slavers,' said Nunyunnini, old stone-hide. 'It is not the great wolves.'

'Is it a famine? Is a famine coming?' asked Gugwei.

Nunyunnini was silent. Kalanu came out of the skull and waited with the rest of them.

Gugwei put on the mammoth-hide cloak and put his head inside the skull. 'It is not a famine as you know it,' said Nunyunnini, through Gugwei's mouth, 'although a famine will follow.'

'Then what is it?' asked Yanu. 'I am not afraid. I will stand against it. We have spears, and we have throwing rocks. Let a hundred mighty warriors come against us, still we shall prevail. We shall lead them into the marshes, and split their skulls with our rocks.'

'It is not a man thing,' said Nunyunnini, in Gugwei's old voice. 'It will come from the skies, and none of your spears or your rocks will protect you.'

'How can we protect ourselves?' asked Atsula. 'I have seen flames in the skies. I have heard a noise louder than ten thunderbolts. I have seen forests flattened and rivers boil.'

'Ai . . .,' said Nunyunnini, but he said no more. Gugwei came out of the skull, bending stiffly, for he was an old man, and his knuckles were swollen and knotted.

There was silence. Atsula threw more leaves on the fire, and the smoke made their eyes tear.

Then Yanu strode to the mammoth-head, put the cloak about his broad shoulders, put his head inside the skull. His voice boomed. 'You must journey,' said Nunyunnini. 'You must travel to sun-ward. Where the sun rises, there you will find a new land, where you will be safe. It will be a long journey: the moon will swell and empty, die and live, twice, and there will be slavers and beasts, but I shall guide you and keep you safe, if you travel toward the sunrise.'

Atsula spat on the mud of the floor, and said, 'No.' She could feel the god staring at her. 'No, she said. 'You are a bad god to tell us this. We will die. We will all die, and then who will be left to carry you from high place to high place, to raise your tent, to oil your great tusks with fat?'

The god said nothing. Atsula and Yanu exchanged places. Atsula's face stared out through the yellowed mammothbone.

'Atsula has no faith,' said Nunyunnini in Atsula's voice. 'Atsula shall die before the rest of you enter the new land, but the rest of you shall live. Trust me: there is a land to the East that is manless. This land shall be your land and the land of your children and your children's children, for seven generations, and seven sevens. But for Atsula's faithlessness, you would have kept it forever. In the morning, pack your tents and your possessions, and walk toward the sunrise.'

And Gugwei and Yanu and Kalanu bowed their heads and exclaimed at the power and wisdom of Nunyunnini.

The moon swelled and waned and swelled and waned once more. The people of the tribe walked east, toward the sunrise, struggling through the icy winds, which numbed their exposed skin. Nunyunnini had promised them truly: they lost no one from the tribe on the journey, save for a woman in childbirth, and women in childbirth belong to the moon, not to Nunyunnini.

They crossed the land-bridge.

Kalanu had left them at first light to scout the way. Now the sky was dark, and Kalanu had not returned, but the night sky was alive with lights, knotting and flickering and winding, flux and pulse, white and green and violet and red. Atsula and her people had seen the northern lights before, but they were still frightened by them, and this was a display like they had never seen before.

Kalanu returned to them, as the lights in the sky formed and flowed.

'Sometimes,' she said to Atsula, 'I feel that I could simply spread my arms and fall into the sky.'

'That is because you are a scout,' said Atsula, the priestess. 'When you die, you shall fall into the sky and become a star, to guide us as you guide us in life.'

'There are cliffs of ice to the east, high cliffs,' said Kalanu, her raven-black hair worn long, as a man would wear it. 'We can climb them, but it will take many days.'

'You shall lead us safely,' said Atsula. 'I shall die at the foot of the cliff, and that shall be the sacrifice that takes you into the new lands.'

To the west of them, back in the lands from which they had come, where the sun had set hours before, there was a flash of sickly yellow light, brighter than lightning, brighter than daylight: a burst of pure brilliance that forced the folk on the land bridge to cover their eyes and spit and exclaim. Children began to wail.

'That is the doom that Nunyunnini warned us of,' said Gugwei the old. 'Surely he is a wise god and a mighty one.'

'He is the best of all gods,' said Kalanu. 'In our new land we shall raise him up on high, and we shall polish his tusks and skull with fish oil and animal fat, and we shall tell our children, and our children's children, and our seventh children's children, that Nunyunnini is the mightiest of all gods, and shall never be forgotten.'

'Gods are great,' said Atsula, slowly, as if she were comprehending a great secret. 'But the heart is greater. For it is from our hearts they come, and to our hearts they shall return . . .'

And there is no telling how long she might have continued in this blasphemy, had it not been interrupted in a manner that brooked no argument.

The roar that erupted from the west was so loud that ears bled, that they could hear nothing for some time, temporarily blinded and deafened but alive, knowing that they were luckier than the tribes to the west of them.

'It is good,' said Atsula, but she could not hear the words inside her head.

Atsula died at the foot of the cliffs when the spring sun was at its zenith. She did not live to see the New World, and the tribe walked into those lands with no holy woman.

They scaled the cliffs, and they went south and west, until they found a valley with fresh water, and rivers that teemed with silver fish, and deer that had never seen man before, and were so tame it was necessary to spit and to apologize to their spirits before killing them.

Dalani gave birth to three boys, and some said that Kalanu had performed the final magic and could do the man-thing with her bride; while others said that old Gugwei was not too old to keep a young bride company when her husband was away; and certainly once Gugwei died, Dalani had no more children.

And the ice times came and the ice times went, and the people spread out across the land, and formed new tribes and chose new totems for themselves: ravens and foxes and ground sloths and great cats and buffalo, each a taboo beast that marked a tribe's identity, each beast a god.

The mammoths of the new lands were bigger, and slower, and more foolish than the mammoth of the Siberian plains, and the *pungh* mushrooms, with their seven spots, were not to be found in the new lands, and Nunyunnini did not speak to the tribe any longer.

And in the days of the grandchildren of Dalani and Kalanu's grandchildren, a band of warriors, members of a big and prosperous tribe, returning from a slaving expedition in the north to their home in the south, found the valley of the first people: they killed most of the men, and they took the women and many of the children captive.

One of the children, hoping for clemency, took them to a cave in the hills, in which they found a mammoth-skull, the tattered remnants of a mammoth-skin cloak, a wooden cup, and the preserved head of Atsula the oracle.

While some of the warriors of the new tribe were for taking the sacred objects away with them, stealing the gods of the First People and owning their power, others counseled against it, saying that they would bring nothing but ill-luck, and the malice of their own god (for these were the people of a raven tribe, and ravens are jealous gods).

So they threw the objects down the side of the hill, into a deep ravine, and took the survivors of the First People with them on their long journey south. And the raven tribes, and the fox tribes, grew more powerful in the land, and soon Nunyunnini was entirely forgot.

Part Three
THE MOMENT OF THE STORM

Chapter Fourteen

People are in the dark, they don't know what to do
I had a little lantern, oh but it got blown out too.
I'm reaching out my hand. I hope you are too.
I just want to be in the dark with you.
                              – Greg Brown, *'In the Dark with You'*

They changed cars at five in the morning, in Minneapolis, in the airport's long term parking lot. They drove to the top floor, where the parking building was open to the sky.

Shadow took the orange uniform and the handcuffs and leg hobbles, put them in the brown paper bag that had briefly held his possessions, folded the whole thing up and dropped it into a parking lot garbage can. They had been waiting for ten minutes when a barrel-chested short man came out of an airport door and walked over to them. He was eating a packet of Burger King french fries. Shadow recognized him immediately: he had sat in the back of the car when they had left the House on the Rock, and hummed so deeply the car had vibrated. He now sported a white-streaked winter beard he had not had when they had met at the House on the Rock.

The man wiped the grease from his hands onto his sweater, extended one huge hand to Shadow. 'I heard of the all-father's death,' he said. 'They will pay, and they will pay dearly.'

'Wednesday was your father?' asked Shadow.

'He was the all-father,' said the man. His deep voice caught in his throat. 'You tell them, tell them all, that when we are needed my people will be there.'

Czernobog picked at a flake of tobacco from between his teeth and spat it out onto the frozen slush. 'And how many of you is that? Ten? Twenty?'

The barrel-chested man's beard bristled. 'And aren't ten of us worth a hundred of them? Who would stand against even one of my folk, in a battle? But there are more of us than that, at the edge of the cities. There are a few in the mountains. Some in the Catskills, a few living in the carny towns in Florida. They keep their axes sharp. They will come if I call them.'

'You do that, Elvis,' said Mr Nancy. Shadow thought he said Elvis, anyway, but he couldn't be sure. Nancy had exchanged the deputy's uniform for a thick brown cardigan, corduroy trousers, and brown loafers. 'You call them. It's what the old bastard would have wanted.'

'They betrayed him. They killed him. I laughed at Wednesday, but I was wrong. None of us are safe any longer,' said the man who might have been named Elvis. 'But you can rely on us.' He gently patted Shadow on the back and almost sent him sprawling. It was like being gently patted on the back by a wrecking ball.

Czernobog had been looking around the parking lot. Now he said, 'You will pardon me asking, but our new vehicle is which?'

The barrel-chested man pointed. 'There she is,' he said.

Czernobog snorted. 'That?'

It was a 1970 VW bus. There was a rainbow decal in the rear window.

'It's a fine vehicle. And it's the last thing that they'll be expecting you to be driving. The last thing they'll be looking for.'

Czernobog walked around the vehicle. Then he started to cough, a lung-rumbling, old-man, five-in-the-morning, smoker's cough. He hawked, and spat, and put his hand to his chest, massaging away the pain. 'Yes. The last car they will suspect. So what happens when the police pull us over, looking for the hippies, and the dope? Eh? We are not here to ride the magic bus. We are to blend in.'

The bearded man unlocked the door of the bus. 'So they take a look at you, they see you aren't hippies, they wave you goodbye. It's the perfect disguise. And it's all I could find at no notice.'

Czernobog seemed to be ready to argue it further, but Mr Nancy intervened smoothly. 'Elvis, you come through for us. We are very grateful. Now, that car needs to get back to Chicago.'

'We'll leave it in Bloomington,' said the bearded man. 'The wolves will take care of it. Don't give it another thought.' He turned back to Shadow. 'Again, you have my sympathy and I share your pain. Good luck. And if the vigil falls to you, my admiration, and my sympathy.' He squeezed Shadow's hand in sympathy and in friendship with his own catcher's mitt fist. It hurt. 'You tell his corpse when you see it. Tell him that Alviss son of Vindalf will keep the faith.'

The VW bus smelled of patchouli, of old incense and rolling tobacco. There was a faded pink carpet glued to the floor and to the walls.

'Who was that?' asked Shadow, as he drove them down the ramp, grinding the gears.

'Just like he said, Alviss son of Vindalf. He's the king of the dwarfs. The biggest, mightiest, greatest of all the dwarf folk.'

'But he's not a dwarf,' pointed out Shadow. 'He's what, five eight? Five nine?'

'Which makes him a giant among dwarfs,' said Czernobog from behind him. 'Tallest dwarf in America.'

'What was that about the vigil?' asked Shadow.

The two old men said nothing. Shadow glanced to his right. Mr Nancy was staring out of the window.

'Well? He was talking about a vigil. You heard him.'

Czernobog spoke up from the back seat. 'You will not have to do it,' he said.

'Do what?'

'The vigil. He talks too much. All the dwarfs talk and talk and talk. And sing. All the time, sing, sing, sing. Is nothing to think of. Better you put it out of your mind.'

***

They drove south, keeping off the freeways ('We must assume,' said Mr Nancy, 'that they are in enemy hands. Or that they are perhaps enemy hands in their own right.') Driving south was like driving forward in time. The snows erased, slowly, and were completely gone by the following morning when the bus reached Kentucky. Winter was already over in Kentucky, and spring was on its way. Shadow began to wonder if there were some kind of equation to explain it – perhaps every fifty miles he drove south he was driving a day into the future.

He would have mentioned his idea to his passengers, but Mr Nancy was asleep in the passenger seat in the front, while Czernobog snored unceasingly in the back.

Time seemed a flexible construct at that moment, an illusion he was imagining as he drove. He found himself becoming painfully aware of birds and animals: he saw the crows on the side of the road, or in the bus's path, picking at road kill; flights of birds wheeled across the skies in patterns that almost made sense; cats stared at them from front lawns and fence-posts.

Czernobog snorted and woke, sitting up slowly. 'I dreamed a strange dream,' he said. 'I dreamed that I am truly Bielebog.

That forever the world imagines that there are two of us, the light god and the dark, but that now we are both old, I find it was only me all the time, giving them gifts, taking my gifts away.' He broke the filter from a Lucky Strike, put it between his lips and lit it with his lighter.

Shadow wound down his window.

'Aren't you worried about lung cancer?' he said.

'I *am* cancer,' said Czernobog. 'I do not frighten myself.' He chuckled, and then the chuckle became a wheeze and the wheeze turned into a cough.

Nancy spoke. 'Folk like us don't get cancer. We don't get arteriosclerosis or Parkinson's disease or syphilis. We're kind of hard to kill.'

'They killed Wednesday,' said Shadow.

He pulled over for gas, and then parked next door at a restaurant, for an early breakfast. As they entered, the payphone in the entrance began to jangle. They walked past it without answering it, and it stopped ringing.

They gave their orders to an elderly woman with a worried smile, who had been sitting reading a paperback copy of *What My Heart Meant* by Jenny Kerton. The telephone began to ring once more. The woman sighed, then walked back and over to the phone, picked it up, said 'Yes.' Then she looked back at the room, said, 'Yep. Looks like they are. You just hold the line now,' and walked over to Mr Nancy.

'It's for you,' she said.

'Okay,' said Mr Nancy. 'Now ma'am, you make sure those fries are real *crisp* now. Think burnt.' He walked over to the payphone.

'This is he,' he said.

'And what makes you think I'm dumb enough to trust you?' he said.

'I can find it,' he said. 'I know where it is.'

'Yes,' he said. 'We want it. You know we want it. And I know you want to get rid of it. So don't give me any shit.'

He put down the telephone, came back to the table.

'Who was it?' asked Shadow.

'Didn't say.'

'What did they want?'

'They were offerin' us a truce, while they hand over the body.'

'They lie,' said Czernobog. 'They want to lure us in, and then they will kill us. What they did to Wednesday. Is what I always used to do,' he added, with gloomy pride. 'Promise them anything, but do what you will.'

'It's on neutral territory,' said Nancy. 'Truly neutral.'

Czernobog chuckled. It sounded like a metal ball rattling in a dry skull. 'I used to say *that* also. Come to a neutral place, I would say, and then in the night we would rise up and kill them all. Those were the good days.'

Mr Nancy shrugged. He crunched down on his dark brown french fries, grinned his approval. 'Mm-mm. These are fine fries,' he said.

'We can't trust those people,' said Shadow.

'Listen, I'm older than you and I'm smarter than you and I'm better lookin' than you,' said Mr Nancy, thumping the bottom of the ketchup bottle, blobbing ketchup over his burnt fries. 'I can get more pussy in an afternoon than you'll get in a year. I can dance like an angel, fight like a cornered bear, plan better than a fox, sing like a nightingale . . .'

'And your point here is . . .?'

Nancy's brown eyes gazed into Shadow's. 'And they need to get rid of the body as much as we need to take it.'

Czernobog said, 'There is no such neutral place.'

'There's one,' said Mr Nancy. 'It's the center.'

Czernobog shook his head abruptly. 'No. They would not meet us there. They can do nothing to us, there. It is a bad place for all of us.'

'That's just why they've proposed to make the handover at the center.'

Czernobog seemed to think about this for a while. And then he said, 'Perhaps.'

'When we get back on the road,' said Shadow, 'you can drive. I need to sleep.'

* * *

Determining the exact center of anything can be problematic at best. With living things – people, for example, or continents – the problem becomes one of intangibles: What is the center of a man? What is the center of a dream? And in the case of the continental United States, should one count Alaska when one attempts to find the center? Or Hawaii?

As the Twentieth Century began, they made a huge model of the USA, the lower forty-eight states, out of cardboard, and to find the center they balanced it on a pin, until they found the single place it balanced.

Near as anyone could figure it out, the exact center of the continental United States was several miles from Lebanon, in Smith County, Kansas, on Johnny Grib's hog farm. By the 1930s, the people of Lebanon were all ready to put a monument up in the middle of the hog farm, but Johnny Grib said that he didn't want millions of tourists coming in and tramping all over and upsetting the hogs, and the locals figured he had a point, so they put the monument to the geographical center of the United States two miles north of the town. They built a park, and a stone monument to put in the park, and put a brass plaque to go on the monument to tell you that you were indeed looking at the exact geographic center of the United States of America. They blacktopped the road from the town to the little park, and, certain of the influx of tourists just waiting to come to Lebanon, they even built a motel by the monument. They brought in a little mobile chapel as well, and took off the wheels. Then they waited for the tourists and the holidaymakers to come: all the people who wanted to tell the world they'd been at the center of America, and marveled, and prayed.

The tourists did not come. Nobody came.

It's a sad little park, now, with a mobile church in it little bigger than an ice-fishing hut, a church that wouldn't fit a small funeral party, and a motel whose windows look like dead eyes.

'Which is why,' concluded Mr Nancy, as they drove into Humansville, Missouri (pop. 1084), 'the exact center of America is a tiny run-down park, an empty church, a pile of stones, and a derelict motel.'

'Hog farm,' said Czernobog. 'You just said that the real center of America was a hog farm.'

'This isn't about what is,' said Mr Nancy. 'It's about what people *think* is. It's all imaginary anyway. That's why it's important. People only fight over imaginary things.'

'My kind of people?' asked Shadow. 'Or your kind of people?'

Nancy said nothing. Czernobog made a noise that might have been a chuckle, might have been a snort.

Shadow tried to get comfortable in the back of the bus. He had slept a little, but only a little. He had a bad feeling in the pit of his stomach. Worse than the feeling he had had in prison, worse than the feeling he had had back when Laura had come to him and told him about the robbery. This was bad. The back of his neck prickled, he felt sick and, several times, in waves, he felt scared.

Mr Nancy pulled over in Humansville, parked outside a supermarket. Mr Nancy went inside, and Shadow followed him in. Czernobog waited in the parking lot, stretching his legs, smoking his cigarette.

There was a young fair-haired man, little more than a boy, restocking the breakfast cereal shelves.

'Hey,' said Mr Nancy.

'Hey,' said the young man. 'It's true, isn't it? They killed him?'

'Yes,' said Mr Nancy. 'They killed him.'

The young man banged several boxes of Cap'n Crunch

down on the shelf. 'They think they can crush us like cockroaches,' he said. He had an eruption of acne across one cheek and over his forehead. He had a silver bracelet high on one forearm. 'We don't crush that easy, do we?'

'No,' said Mr Nancy. 'We don't.'

'I'll be there, sir,' said the young man, his pale blue eyes blazing.

'I know you will, Gwydion,' said Mr Nancy.

Mr Nancy bought several large bottles of R.C. Cola, a six-pack of toilet paper, a pack of evil-looking black cigarillos, a bunch of bananas and a pack of Doublemint chewing gum. 'He's a good boy. Came over in the seventh century. Welsh.'

The bus meandered first to the west and then to the north. Spring faded back into the dead end of winter. Kansas was the cheerless gray of lonesome clouds, empty windows and lost hearts. Shadow had become adept at hunting for radio stations, negotiating between Mr Nancy, who liked talk radio and dance music, and Czernobog, who favored classical music, the gloomier the better, leavened with the more extreme evangelical religious stations. For himself, Shadow liked oldies stations.

Toward the end of the afternoon they stopped, at Czernobog's request, on the outskirts of Cherryvale, Kansas (pop. 2,464). Czernobog led them to a meadow outside the town. There were still traces of snow in the shadows of the trees, and the grass was the color of dirt.

'Wait here,' said Czernobog.

He walked, alone, to the center of the meadow. He stood there, in the winds of the end of February, for some time. At first he hung his head, then he began gesticulating.

'He looks like he's talking to someone,' said Shadow.

'Ghosts,' said Mr Nancy. 'They worshiped him here, over a hundred years ago. They made blood-sacrifice to him, libations spilled with the hammer. After a time, the townsfolk figured out why so many of the strangers who passed through the town didn't ever come back. This was where they hid some of the bodies.'

Czernobog came back from the middle of the field. His moustache seemed darker now, and there were streaks of black in his gray hair. He smiled, showing his iron tooth. 'I feel good, now. Ahh. Some things linger, and blood lingers longest.'

They walked back across the meadow to where they had parked the VW bus. Czernobog lit a cigarette, but did not cough. 'They did it with the hammer,' he said. 'Grimnir, he would talk of the gallows and the spear, but for me, it is one thing . . .' He reached out a nicotine-colored finger and tapped it, hard, in the center of Shadow's forehead.

'Please don't do that,' said Shadow, politely.

'*Please don't do that*,' mimicked Czernobog. 'One day I will take my hammer and do much worse than that to you, my friend, remember?'

'Yes,' said Shadow. 'But if you tap my head again, I'll break your hand.'

Czernobog snorted. Then he said, 'They should be grateful, the people here. There was such power raised. Even thirty years after they forced my people into hiding, this land, this very land, gave us the greatest movie star of all time. She was the greatest there ever was.'

'Judy Garland?' asked Shadow.

Czernobog shook his head curtly.

'He's talking about Louise Brooks,' said Mr Nancy.

Shadow decided not to ask who Louise Brooks was. Instead he said, 'So, look, when Wednesday went to talk to them, he did it under a truce.'

'Yes.'

'And now we're going to get Wednesday's body from them, as a truce.'

'Yes.'

'And we know that they want me dead or out of the way.'

'They want all of us dead,' said Nancy.

'So what I don't get is, why do we think they'll play fair this time, when they didn't for Wednesday.'

'That,' said Czernobog, over enunciating each word, as he would for a deaf foreign idiot child, 'is why we are meeting at the center. Is . . .' He frowned. 'What is the word for it? The opposite of sacred?'

'Profane,' said Shadow, without thinking.

'No,' said Czernobog. 'I mean, when a place is less sacred than any other place. Of negative sacredness. Places where they can build no temples. Places where people will not come, and will leave as soon as they can. Places where gods only walk if they are forced to.'

'I don't know,' said Shadow. 'I don't think there is a word for it.'

'All of America has it, a little,' said Czernobog. 'That is why we are not welcome here. But the center,' said Czernobog. 'The center is worst. Is like a mine field. We all tread too carefully there to dare break the truce.'

'I told you all this already,' said Mr Nancy.

'Whatever,' said Shadow.

They had reached the bus. Czernobog patted Shadow's upper arm. 'You don't worry,' he said, with gloomy reassurance. 'Nobody else is going to kill you. Nobody but me.'

***

Shadow found the center of America at evening that same day, before it was fully dark. It was on a slight hill to the northwest of Lebanon. He drove around the little hillside park, past the tiny mobile chapel and the stone monument, and when Shadow saw the one-story 1950s motel at the edge of the park his heart sank. There was a huge black car parked in front of it –a HumVee, which looked like a jeep reflected in a fun-house mirror, as squat and pointless and ugly as an armored car. There were no lights on in the building.

They parked beside the motel, and as they did so, a man in a chauffeur's uniform and cap walked out of the motel and was illuminated by the headlights of the bus. He touched his cap to them, politely, got into the HumVee, and drove off.

'Big car, tiny dick,' said Mr Nancy.

'Do you think they'll even have beds here?' asked Shadow. 'It's been days since I slept in a bed. This place looks like it's just waiting to be demolished.'

'It's owned by hunters from Texas,' said Mr Nancy. 'Come up here once a year. Damned if I know what they're huntin'. It stops the place being condemned and destroyed.'

They climbed out of the bus. Waiting for them in front of the motel was a woman Shadow did not recognize. She was perfectly made-up, perfectly coiffed. She reminded him of every newscaster he'd ever seen on morning television sitting in a studio that didn't really resemble a living room, smiling at the good morning crowd.

'Lovely to see you,' she said. 'Now, *you* must be Czernobog. I've heard a lot about you. And *you're* Anansi, always up to mischief, eh? You *jolly* old man. And you, you *must* be Shadow. You've certainly led us a merry chase, haven't *you*?' A hand took his, pressed it firmly; she looked him straight in the eye. 'I'm Media. Good to meet you. I hope we can get this evening's business done as *pleasantly* as possible.'

The main doors opened. 'Somehow, Toto,' said the fat kid Shadow had last seen sitting in a limo, 'I don't believe we're in Kansas any more.'

'We're in Kansas,' said Mr Nancy. 'I think we must have driven through most of it today. Damn but this place is flat.'

'This place has no lights, no power, and no hot water,' said the fat kid. 'And, no offense, you people really need the hot water. You just smell like you've been in that bus for a week.'

'I don't think there's *any* need to go there,' said the woman, smoothly. 'We're all friends here. Come on in. We'll show you to your rooms. *We* took the first four rooms. Your late friend is in the fifth. All the ones beyond room five are empty – you can take your pick. I'm afraid it's *not* the Four Seasons, but then, what *is*?'

She opened the door to the motel lobby for them. It smelled of mildew, of damp and dust and of decay.

There was a man sitting in the lobby, in the near darkness. 'You people hungry?' he asked.

'I can always eat,' said Mr Nancy.

'Driver's gone out for a sack of hamburgers,' said the man. 'He'll be back soon.' He looked up. It was too dark to see faces, but he said, 'Big guy. You're Shadow, huh? The asshole who killed Woody and Stone?'

'No,' said Shadow. 'That was someone else. And I know who you are.' He did. He had been inside the man's head. 'You're Town. Have you slept with Wood's widow yet?'

Mr Town fell off his chair. In a movie, it would have been funny; in real life it was simply clumsy. He stood up quickly, came toward Shadow. Shadow looked down at him, and said 'Don't start anything you're not prepared to finish.'

Mr Nancy rested his hand on Shadow's upper arm. 'Truce, remember?' he said. 'We're at the center.'

Mr Town turned away, leaned over to the counter and picked up three keys. 'You're down at the end of the hall,' he said. 'Here.'

He handed the keys to Mr Nancy and walked away, into the shadows of the corridor. They heard a motel room door open, and they heard it slam.

Mr Nancy passed a key to Shadow, another to Czernobog. 'Is there a flashlight on the bus?' asked Shadow.

'No,' said Mr Nancy. 'But it's just dark. You mustn't be afraid of the dark.'

'I'm not,' said Shadow. 'I'm afraid of the people in the dark.'

'Dark is good,' said Czernobog. He seemed to have no difficulty seeing where he was going, leading them down the darkened corridor, putting the keys into the locks without fumbling. 'I will be in room ten,' he told them. And then he said, 'Media. I think I have heard of her. Isn't she the one who killed her children?'

'Different woman,' said Mr Nancy. 'Same deal.'

Mr Nancy was in room eight, and Shadow opposite the two of them, in room nine. The room smelled damp, and dusty, and deserted. There was a bed-frame in there, with a mattress on it, but no sheets. A little light entered the room from the gloaming outside the window. Shadow sat down on the mattress, pulled off his shoes, and stretched out at full length. He had driven too much in the last few days.

Perhaps he slept.

***

He was walking.

A cold wind tugged at his clothes. The tiny snowflakes were little more than a crystalline dust which gusted and flurried in the wind.

There were trees, bare of leaves in the winter. There were high hills on each side of him. It was late on a winter's afternoon: the sky and the snow had attained the same deep shade of purple. Somewhere ahead of him – in this light, distances were impossible to judge – the flames of a bonfire flickered, yellow and orange.

A gray wolf padded through the snow before him.

Shadow stopped. The wolf stopped also, and turned, and waited. One of its eyes glinted yellowish-green. Shadow shrugged and walked toward the flames and the wolf ambled ahead of him.

The bonfire burned in the middle of a grove of trees. There must have been a hundred trees, planted in two rows. There were shapes hanging from the trees. At the end of the rows was a building that looked a little like an overturned boat. It was carved of wood, and it crawled with wooden creatures and wooden faces – dragons, gryphons, trolls and boars – all of them dancing in the flickering light of the fire.

The bonfire was so high, and burning so hard, that Shadow could barely approach it. The wolf seemed unfazed, and it padded around the crackling fire.

He waited for it to return, but in place of the wolf a man walked back around the fire. He was leaning on a tall stick.

'You are in Uppsala, in Sweden,' said the man, in a familiar, gravelly voice. 'About a thousand years ago.'

'Wednesday?' said Shadow.

The man who might have been Wednesday continued to talk, as if Shadow was not there. 'First every year, then, later, when the rot set in, and they became lax, every nine years, they would sacrifice here. A sacrifice of nines. Each day, for nine days, they would hang nine animals from trees in the grove. One of those animals was always a man.'

He strode away from the firelight, toward the trees, and Shadow followed him. As he approached the trees the shapes that hung from them trees resolved: legs and eyes and tongues and heads. Shadow shook his head: there was something about seeing a bull hanging by its neck from a tree that was darkly sad, and at the same time surreal enough almost to be funny. Shadow passed a hanging stag, a wolfhound, a brown bear, and a chestnut horse with a white mane, little bigger than a pony. The dog was still alive: every few seconds it would kick spasmodically, and it was making a strained whimpering noise, as it dangled from the rope.

The man he was following took his long stick, which Shadow realized now, as it moved, was actually a spear, and he slashed at the dog's stomach with it, in one knife-like cut downward. Steaming entrails tumbled onto the snow. 'I dedicate this death to Odin,' said the man, formally.

'It is only a gesture,' he said, turning back to Shadow. 'But gestures mean everything. The death of one dog symbolizes the death of all dogs. Nine men they gave to me, but they stood for all the men, all the blood, all the power. It just wasn't *enough. One day, the blood stopped flowing. Belief without blood only takes us so far. The blood must flow.'*

'I saw you die,' said Shadow.

'In the god business,' said the figure – and now Shadow was certain it was Wednesday, nobody else had that rasp, that deep cynical joy in words, 'it's not the death that matters. It's the opportunity for resurrection. And when the blood flows . . .' He gestured at the animals, at the people, hanging from the trees.

Shadow could not decide whether the dead humans they walked past were more or less horrifying than the animals: at least the humans had known the fate they were going to. There was a deep, boozy smell about the men that suggested that they had been allowed to anaesthetize themselves on their way to the gallows; while the animals would simply have been lynched, hauled up alive and terrified. The faces of the men looked so young: none of them was older than twenty.

'Who am I?' asked Shadow.

'You are a diversion,' said the man. 'You were an opportunity. You gave the whole affair an air of credibility I would have been hard put to deliver solo. Although both of us are committed enough to the affair to die for it. Eh?'

'Who are you?' asked Shadow.

'The hardest part is simply surviving,' said the man. The bonfire – and Shadow realized with a strange horror that it truly was a bone-fire: ribcages and fire-eyed skulls stared and stuck and jutted from the flames, sputtering trace-element colors into the night, greens and yellows and blues – was flaring and crackling and burning hotly. 'Three days on the tree, three days in the underworld, three days to find my way back.'

The flames sputtered and flamed too brightly for Shadow to look at directly. He looked down into the darkness beneath the trees.

There was no fire, no snow. There were no trees, no hanged bodies, no bloody spear.

***

A knock on the door – and now there was moonlight coming in the window. Shadow sat up with a start. 'Dinner's served,' said Media's voice.

Shadow put his shoes back on, walked over to the door, went out into the corridor. Someone had found some candles, and a dim yellow light illuminated the reception hall. The driver of the HumVee came in through the swing doors holding a cardboard tray and a paper sack. He wore a long black coat and a peaked chauffeur's cap.

'Sorry about the delay,' he said, hoarsely. 'I got everybody the same: a couple of burgers, large fries, large Coke, and apple pie. I'll eat mine out in the car.' He put the food down, then walked back outside. The smell of fast food filled the lobby. Shadow took the paper bag and passed out the food, the napkins, the packets of ketchup.

They ate in silence while the candles flickered and the burning wax hissed.

Shadow noticed that Town was glaring at him. He turned his chair a little, so his back was to the wall. Media ate her burger with a napkin poised by her lips to remove crumbs.

'Oh. Great. These burgers are nearly cold,' said the fat kid. He was still wearing his shades, which Shadow thought pointless and foolish, given the darkness of the room.

'Sorry about that. The guy had to drive a way to find them,' said Town. 'The nearest McDonald's is in Nebraska.'

They finished their lukewarm hamburgers and cold fries. The fat kid bit into his single-person apple-pie, and the filling spurted down his chin. Unexpectedly, the filling was still hot. 'Ow,' he said. He wiped at it with his hand, licking his fingers to get them clean. 'That stuff burns!' he said. 'Those pies are a class action suit waiting to fucking happen.'

Shadow realized he wanted to hit the kid. He'd wanted to hit him since the kid had his goons hurt him in the limo, after Laura's funeral. He knew it was not a wise thing to be

thinking, not here, not now. 'Can't we just take Wednesday's
body and get out of here?' he asked.

'Midnight,' said Mr Nancy and the fat kid, at the same
time.

'These things must be done according to the rules,' said
Czernobog. 'All things have rules.'

'Yeah,' said Shadow. 'But nobody tells me what they are.
You keep talking about the goddamn rules, I don't even know
what game you people are playing.'

'It's like breaking the street date,' said Media, brightly. 'You
know. When things are allowed to be on sale.'

Town said, 'I think the whole thing's a crock of shit. But if
their rules make them happy, then my agency is happy and
everybody's happy.' He slurped his Coke. 'Roll on midnight.
You take the body, you go away. We're all lovey-fucking-
dovey and we wave you goodbye. And then we can get on
with hunting you down like the rats you are.'

'Hey,' said the fat kid to Shadow. 'Reminds me. I told you
to tell your boss he was history. Did you ever tell him?'

'I told him,' said Shadow. 'And you know what he said to
me? He said to tell the little snot, if ever I saw him again, to
remember that today's future is tomorrow's yesterday.'
Wednesday had never said any such thing, but Shadow
delivered it as Wednesday would have done. These people
seemed to like clichés. The black sunglasses reflected the
flickering candle-flames back at him, like eyes.

The fat kid said, 'This place is such a fucking dump. No
power. Out of wireless range. I mean, when you got to be
wired, you're already back in the Stone Age.' He sucked the
last of his Coke through the straw, dropped the cup on the
table and walked away down the corridor.

Shadow reached over and placed the fat kid's garbage back
into the paper sack. 'I'm going to see the center of America,'
he announced. He got up and walked outside, into the night.
Mr Nancy followed him. They strolled together, across the
little park, saying nothing until they reached the stone

monument. The wind gusted at them, fitfully, first from one direction, then from another. 'So,' he said. 'Now what?'

The half-moon hung pale in the dark sky.

'Now,' said Nancy, 'you should go back to your room. Lock the door. You try to get some more sleep. At midnight they give us the body. And then we get the hell out of here. The center is not a stable place for anybody.'

'If you say so.'

Mr Nancy inhaled on his cigarillo. 'This should never have happened,' he said. 'None of this should have happened. Our kind of people, we are . . .' he waved the cigarillo about, as if using it to hunt for a word, then stabbing forward with it, '. . . *exclusive*. We're not social. Not even me. Not even Bacchus. Not for long. We walk by ourselves or we stay in our own little groups. We do not play well with others. We like to be adored and respected and worshiped – me, I like them to be tellin' tales about me, tales showing my cleverness. It's a fault, I know, but it's the way I am. We like to be big. Now, in these shabby days, we are small. The new gods rise and fall and rise again. But this is not a country that tolerates gods for long. Brahma creates, Vishnu preserves, Shiva destroys, and the ground is clear for Brahma to create once more.'

'So what are you saying?' asked Shadow. 'The fighting's over, now? The battle's done?'

Mr Nancy snorted. 'Are you out of your mind? They killed Wednesday. They killed him and they bragged about it. They spread the word. They've showed it on every channel to those with eyes to see it. No, Shadow. It's only just begun.'

He bent down at the foot of the stone monument, stubbed out his cigarillo on the earth, and left it there, like an offering.

'You used to make jokes,' said Shadow. 'You don't any more.'

'It's hard to find the jokes these days. Wednesday's dead. Are you comin' inside?'

'Soon.'

Nancy walked away, toward the motel. Shadow reached out his hand and touched the monument's stones. He dragged his big fingers across the cold brass plate. Then he turned and walked over to the tiny white church, walked through the open doorway, into the darkness. He sat down in the nearest pew and closed his eyes and lowered his head, and thought about Laura, and about Wednesday, and about being alive.

There was a click from behind him, and a scuff of shoe against earth. Shadow sat up, and turned. Someone stood just outside the open doorway, a dark shape against the stars. Moonlight glinted from something metal.

'You going to shoot me?' asked Shadow.

'Jesus – I wish,' said Mr Town. 'It's only for self defense. So, you're praying? Have they got you thinking that they're gods? They aren't gods.'

'I wasn't praying,' said Shadow. 'Just thinking.'

'The way I figure it,' said Town, 'they're mutations. Evolutionary experiments. A little hypnotic ability, a little hocus pocus, and they can make people believe anything. Nothing to write home about. That's all. They die like men, after all.'

'They always did,' said Shadow. He got up, and Town took a step back. Shadow walked out of the little chapel, and Mr Town kept his distance. 'Hey,' Shadow said. 'Do you know who Louise Brooks was?'

'Friend of yours?'

'Nope. She was a movie star from south of here.'

Town paused. 'Maybe she changed her name, and became Liz Taylor or Sharon Stone or someone,' he suggested, helpfully.

'Maybe.' Shadow started to walk back to the motel. Town kept pace with him.

'You should be back in prison,' said Mr Town. 'You should be on fucking death row.'

'I didn't kill your associates,' said Shadow. 'But I'll tell you something a guy once told me, back when I was in prison. Something I've never forgotten.'

'And that is?'

'There was only one guy in the whole bible Jesus ever personally promised a place with him in Paradise. Not Peter, not Paul, not any of those guys. He was a convicted thief, being executed. So don't knock the guys on death row. Maybe they know something you don't.'

The driver stood by the HumVee. 'G'night gentlemen,' he said, as they passed.

'Night,' said Mr Town. And then he said, to Shadow, 'I personally don't give a fuck about any of this. What I do, is what Mister World says. It's easier that way.'

Shadow walked down the corridor to room nine.

He unlocked the door, went inside. He said, 'Sorry. I thought this was my room.'

'It is,' said Media. 'I was waiting for you.' He could see her hair in the moonlight, and her pale face. She was sitting on his bed, primly.

'I'll find another room.'

'I won't be here for long,' she said. 'I just thought it might be an appropriate time to make you an *offer*.'

'Okay. Make the offer.'

'Relax,' she said. There was a smile in her voice. 'You have *such* a stick up your butt. Look, Wednesday's *dead*. You don't owe anyone anything. Throw in with us. Time to Come Over to the Winning Team.'

Shadow said nothing.

'We can make you *famous*, Shadow. We can give you power over what people believe and say and wear and dream. You want to be the next Cary Grant? We can make that *happen*. We can make you the next Beatles.'

'I think I preferred it when you were offering to show me Lucy's tits,' said Shadow. 'If that was you.'

'Ah,' she said.

'I need my room back. Good night.'

'And then of course,' she said, not moving, as if he had not spoken, 'we can turn it all around. We can make it bad for you. You could be a bad joke forever, Shadow. Or you could be remembered as a monster. You could be remembered forever, but as a Manson, a Hitler . . . how would you *like* that?'

'I'm sorry, ma'am, but I'm kind of tired,' said Shadow. 'I'd be grateful if you'd leave now.'

'I offered you the world,' she said. 'When you're dying in a gutter, you re*mem*ber that.'

'I'll make a point of it,' he said.

After she had gone her perfume lingered. He lay on the bare mattress and thought about Laura, but whatever he thought about – Laura playing Frisbee, Laura eating a root-beer float without a spoon, Laura giggling, showing off the exotic underwear she had bought when she attended a travel agents' convention in Anaheim – always morphed, in his mind, into Laura sucking Robbie's cock as a truck slammed them off the road and into oblivion. And then he heard her words, and they hurt every time.

You're not dead, said Laura in her quiet voice, in his head. *But I'm not sure that you're alive, either.*

There was a knock. Shadow got up and opened the door. It was the fat kid. 'Those hamburgers,' he said. 'They were just icky. Can you believe it? Fifty miles from McDonald's. I didn't think there was anywhere in the *world* that was fifty miles from McDonald's.'

'This place is turning into Grand Central Station,' said Shadow. 'Okay, so I guess you're here to offer me the freedom of the internet if I come over to your side of the fence. Right?'

The fat kid was shivering. 'No. You're already dead meat,' he said. 'You-you're a fucking illuminated gothic black letter manuscript. You couldn't be hypertext if you tried. I'm . . . I'm synaptic, while, while you're synoptic . . .' He smelled strange, Shadow realized. There was a guy in the cell across the way, whose name Shadow had never known. He had taken off all his clothes in the middle of the day and told everyone that he had been sent to take them away, the truly good ones, like him, in a silver space ship to a perfect place. That had been the last time Shadow had seen him. The fat kid smelled like that guy.

'Are you here for a reason?'

'Just wanted to talk,' said the fat kid. There was a whine in his voice. 'It's creepy in my room. That's all. It's *creepy* in there. Fifty miles to a McDonald's, can you believe that? Maybe I could stay in here with you.'

'What about your friends from the limo? The ones who hit me? Shouldn't you ask them to stay with you?'

'The children wouldn't operate out here. We're in a dead zone.'

Shadow said, 'It's a while until midnight, and it's longer to dawn. I think maybe you need rest. I know I do.'

The fat kid said nothing for a moment, then he nodded, and walked out of the room.

Shadow closed his door, and locked it with the key. He lay back on the mattress.

After a few moments the noise began. It took him a few moments to figure out what it had to be, then he unlocked his door and walked out into the hallway. It was the fat kid, now back in his own room. It sounded like he was throwing something huge against the walls of the room. From the sounds, Shadow guessed that what he was throwing was himself. 'It's just me!' he was sobbing. Or perhaps, 'It's just meat.' Shadow could not tell.

'Quiet!' came a bellow from Czernobog's room, down the hall.

Shadow walked down to the lobby and out of the motel. He was tired.

The driver still stood beside the HumVee, a dark shape in a peaked cap.

'Couldn't sleep, sir?' he asked.

'No,' said Shadow.

'Cigarette, sir?'

'No, thank you.'

'You don't mind if I do?'

'Go right ahead.'

The driver used a Bic disposable lighter, and it was in the yellow light of the flame that Shadow saw the man's face, actually saw it for the first time, and recognized him, and began to understand.

Shadow knew that thin face. He knew that there would be close-cropped orange hair beneath the black driver's cap, cut close to the scalp like the embers of a fire. He knew that when the man's lips smiled they would crease into a network of rough scars.

'You're looking good, big guy,' said the driver.

'Low Key?' Shadow stared at his old cell-mate warily.

Prison friendships are good things: they get you through bad places and through dark times. But a prison friendship ends at the prison gates, and a prison friend who reappears in your life is at best a mixed blessing.

'Jesus. Low Key Lyesmith,' said Shadow, and then he heard what he was saying and he understood. 'Loki,' he said. 'Loki Lie-Smith.'

'You're slow,' said Loki, 'but you get there in the end.' And his lips twisted into a crooked smile and embers danced in the shadows of his eyes.

***

They sat in Shadow's room in the abandoned motel, sitting on the bed, at opposite ends of the mattress. The sounds from the fat kid's room had pretty much stopped.

'You lied to me,' said Shadow.

'It's one of the things I'm good at,' said Loki. 'But you were lucky we were inside together. You would never have survived your first year without me.'

'You couldn't have walked out if you wanted?'

'It's easier just to do the time. You got to understand the god thing. It's not magic. Not exactly. It's about focus. It's about being you, but the you that people believe in. It's about being the concentrated, magnified, essence of you. It's about becoming thunder, or the power of a running horse, or wisdom. You take all the belief, all the prayers and they become a kind of certainty, something that lets you become bigger, cooler, more than human. You crystallize.' He paused. 'And then one day they forget about you, and they don't believe in you, and they don't sacrifice, and they don't care, and the next thing you know you're running a three card monte game on the corner of Broadway and 43rd.'

'Why were you in my cell?'

'Coincidence. Pure and simple. That was where they put me. You don't believe me? It's true.'

'And now you're a driver?'

'I do other stuff too.'

'Driving for the opposition.'

'If you want to call them that. It depends where you're standing. The way I figure it, I'm driving for the winning team.'

'But you and Wednesday, you were from the same, you're both—'

'Norse pantheon. We're both from the Norse pantheon. Is that what you're trying to say?'

'Yeah.'

'So?'

Shadow hesitated. 'You must have been friends. Once.'

'No. We were never friends. I'm not sorry he's dead. He was just holding the rest of us back. With him gone, the rest of them are going to have to face up to the facts: it's change or die, evolve or perish. I'm all for evolution – it's the old change or die game. He's dead. War's over.'

Shadow looked at him, puzzled. 'You aren't that stupid,' he said. 'You were always so sharp. Wednesday's death isn't going to end anything. It's just pushed all of the ones who were on the fence over the edge.'

'Mixing metaphors, Shadow. Bad habit.'

'Whatever,' said Shadow. 'It's still true. Jesus. His death did in an instant what he'd spent the last few months trying to do. It united them. It gave them something to believe in.'

'Perhaps.' Loki shrugged. 'As far as I know, the thinking on this side of the fence, was that with the troublemaker out of the way, the trouble would also be gone. It's not any of my business, though. I just drive.'

'So tell me,' said Shadow, 'why does everyone care about me? They act like I'm important. Why does it matter what I do.'

'You're an investment,' said Loki. 'You were important to us because you were important to Wednesday. As for the why of it . . . I don't think any of us know. He did. He's dead. Just another one of life's little mysteries.'

'I'm tired of mysteries.'

'Yeah? I think they add a kind of zest to the world. Like salt in a stew.'

'So you're their driver. You drive for all of them?'

'Whoever needs me,' said Loki. 'It's a living.'

He raised his wristwatch to his face, pressed a button: the dial glowed a gentle blue, which illuminated his face, giving it a haunting, haunted appearance. 'Five to midnight. Time,' said Loki. 'Time to light the candles. Say a few words about the dearly departed. Do the formalities. You coming?'

Shadow took a deep breath. 'I'm coming,' he said.

They walked down the dark motel corridor. 'I bought some candles for this, but there were plenty of old ones around too,' said Loki. 'Old stumps and stubs and candle-ends in the rooms, and in a box in a closet. I don't think I missed any. And I got a box of matches. You start lighting candles with a lighter, the end gets too hot.'

They reached room five.

'You want to come in?' asked Loki.

Shadow didn't want to enter that room. 'Okay,' he said. They went in.

Loki took a box of matches from his pocket, and thumb-nailed a match into flame. The momentary flare hurt Shadow's eyes. A candlewick flickered and caught. And another. Loki lit a new match, and continued to light candles: they were on the windowsills and on the headboard of the bed and on the sink in the corner of the room. They showed him the room by candlelight.

The bed had been hauled from its position against the wall into the middle of the motel room, leaving a foot or so of space between the bed and the wall on each side. There were sheets draped over the bed, old motel sheets, moth-holed and stained, which Loki must have found in a closet somewhere. On top of the sheets lay Wednesday, perfectly still.

He was fully dressed, in the pale suit he had been wearing when he was shot. The right side of his face was untouched, perfect, unmarred by blood. The left side of his face was a ragged mess, and the left shoulder and front of the suit was spattered with dark spots, a pointillist mess. His hands were at his side. The expression on that wreck of a face was far from peaceful: it looked hurt – a soul-hurt, a real down deep hurt, filled with hatred and anger and raw craziness. And, on some level, it looked satisfied.

Shadow imagined Mr Jacquel's practiced hands smoothing that hatred and pain away, rebuilding a face for Wednesday with mortician's wax and make-up, giving him a final peace and dignity that even death had denied him.

Still, the body seemed no smaller in death. It had not shrunk. And it still smelled faintly of Jack Daniel's.

The wind from the plains was rising: he could hear it howling around the old motel at the exact imaginary center of America. The candles on the window-sill guttered and flickered.

He could hear footsteps in the hallway. Someone knocked

on a door, called, 'Hurry up please, it's time,' and they began to shuffle in, heads lowered.

Town came in first, followed by Media and Mr Nancy and Czernobog. Last of all came the fat kid: he had fresh red bruises on his face, and his lips were moving all the time, as if he were reciting some words to himself, but he was making no sound. Shadow found himself feeling sorry for him.

Informally, without a word being spoken, they ranged themselves about the body, each an arm's length away from the next. The atmosphere in the room was religious – deeply religious, in a way that Shadow had never previously experienced. There was no sound but the howling of the wind and the crackling of the candles.

'We are come together, here in this godless place,' said Loki, 'to pass on the body of this individual to those who will dispose of it properly according to the rites. If anyone would like to say something, say it now.'

'Not me,' said Town. 'I never properly met the guy. And this whole thing makes me feel uncomfortable.'

Czernobog said, 'These actions will have consequences. You know that? This can only be the start of it all.'

The fat kid started to giggle, a high-pitched, girlish noise. He said, 'Okay. Okay I've got it.' And then, all on one note, he recited:

> *'Turning and turning in the widening gyre*
> *The falcon cannot hear the falconer;*
> *Things fall apart; the center cannot hold . . .'*

and then he broke off, his brow creasing. He said 'Shit. I used to know the whole thing,' and he rubbed his temples and made a face and was quiet.

And then they were all looking at Shadow. The wind was screaming now. He didn't know what to say. He said, 'This whole thing is pitiful. Half of you killed him or had a hand in his death. Now you're giving us his body. Great. He was an irascible old fuck but I drank his mead and I'm still working for him. That's all.'

Media said, 'In a world where people die every day, I think the *important* thing to remember is that for each moment of sorrow we get when people *leave* this world there's a corresponding moment of *joy* when a new baby comes into this world. That first wail is – well, it's *magic*, isn't it? Perhaps it's a *hard* thing to say, but joy and sorrow are like milk and cookies. *That's* how well they go together. I think we should all take a moment to meditate on that.'

And Mr Nancy cleared his throat and said, 'So. I got to say it, because nobody else here will. We are at the center of this place: a land that has no time for gods, and here at the center it has less time for us than anywhere. It is a no-man's land, a place of truce, and we observe our truces, here. We have no choice. So. You give us the body of our friend. We accept it. You will pay for this, murder for murder, blood for blood.'

Town said, 'Whatever. You could save yourselves a lot of time and effort by going back to your homes and shooting yourselves in the heads. Cut out the middle man.'

'Fuck you,' said Czernobog. 'Fuck you and fuck your mother and fuck the fucking horse you fucking rode in on. You will not even die in battle. No warrior will taste your blood. No one alive will take your life. You will die a soft, poor death. You will die with a kiss on your lips and a lie in your heart.'

'Leave it, old man,' said Town.

'*The blood-dimmed tide is loose*,' said the fat kid. 'I think that comes next.'

The wind howled.

'Okay,' said Loki. 'He's yours. We're done. Take the old bastard away.'

He made a gesture with his fingers, and Town, Media and the fat kid left the room. He smiled at Shadow. 'Call no man happy, huh, kid?' he said. And then he, too, walked away.

'What happens now?' asked Shadow.

'Now we wrap him up,' said Anansi. 'And we take him away from here.'

They wrapped the body in the motel sheets, wrapped it well in its impromptu shroud, so there was no body to be seen, and they could carry it. The two old men walked to each end of the body, but Shadow said, 'Let me see something,' and he bent his knees and slipped his arms around the white-sheeted figure, pushed him up and over his shoulder. He straightened his knees, until he was standing, more or less easily. 'Okay,' he said. 'I've got him. Let's put him into the back of the car.'

Czernobog looked as if he were about to argue, but he closed his mouth. He spat on his forefinger and thumb and began to snuff the candles between his fingertips. Shadow could hear them fizz as he walked from the darkening room.

Wednesday was heavy, but Shadow could cope, if he walked steadily. He had no choice. Wednesday's words were in his head with every step he took along the corridor, and he could taste the sour-sweetness of mead in the back of his throat. *You work for me. You protect me. You help me. You transport me from place to place. You investigate, from time to time – go places and ask questions for me. You run errands. In an emergency, but only in an emergency, you hurt people who need to be hurt. In the unlikely event of my death, you will hold my vigil . . .*

A deal was a deal, and this one was in his blood and in his bones.

Mr Nancy opened the motel lobby door for him, then hurried over and opened the back of the bus. The other four were already standing by their HumVee, watching them as if they could not wait to be off. Loki had put his driver's cap back on. The cold wind whipped at the sheets, tugged at Shadow as he walked.

He placed Wednesday down as gently as he could in the back of the bus.

Someone tapped him on the shoulder. He turned. Town

stood there with his hand out. He was holding something.

'Here,' said Mr Town, 'Mister World wanted you to have this.' It was a glass eye. There was a hairline crack down the middle of it, and a tiny chip gone from the front. 'We found it in the Masonic Hall, when we were cleaning up. Keep it for luck. God knows you'll need it.'

Shadow closed his hand around the eye. He wished he could come back with something smart and sharp and clever, but Town was already back at the HumVee, and climbing up into the car; and Shadow still couldn't think of anything clever to say.

***

Czernobog was the last person out of the motel. As he locked the building he watched the HumVee pull out of the park and head off down the blacktop. He put the key to the motel beneath a rock by the lobby door, and he shook his head. 'I should have eaten his heart,' he said to Shadow, conversationally. 'Not just cursed his death. He needs to be taught respect.' He climbed into the back of the bus.

'You ride shotgun,' said Mr Nancy to Shadow. 'I'll drive a while.'

He drove east.

***

Dawn found them in Princeton, Missouri. Shadow had not slept yet.

Nancy said, 'Anywhere you want us to drop you? If I were you, I'd rustle up some ID and head for Canada. Or Mexico.'

'I'm sticking with you guys,' said Shadow. 'It's what Wednesday would have wanted.'

'You aren't working for him any more. He's dead. Once we drop his body off, you are free to go.'

'And do what?'

'Keep out of the way, while the war is on. Like I say, you should leave the country,' said Nancy. He flipped his turn signal, and took a left.

'Hide yourself, for a little time,' said Czernobog. 'Then, when this is over, you will come back to me, and I will finish the whole thing. With my hammer.'

Shadow said, 'Where are we taking the body?'

'Virginia. There's a tree,' said Nancy.

'A world tree,' said Czernobog with gloomy satisfaction. 'We had one in my part of the world. But ours grew under the world, not above it.'

'We put him at the foot of the tree,' said Nancy. 'We leave him there. We let you go. We drive south. There's a battle. Blood is shed. Many die. The world changes, a little.'

'You don't want me at your battle? I'm pretty big. I'm good in a fight.'

Nancy turned his head to Shadow and smiled – the first real smile Shadow had seen on Mr Nancy's face since he had rescued Shadow from the Lumber County Jail. 'Most of this battle will be fought in a place you cannot go, and you cannot touch.'

'In the hearts and the minds of the people,' said Czernobog. 'Like at the big roundabout.'

'Huh?'

'The carousel,' said Mr Nancy.

'Oh,' said Shadow. 'Backstage. I got it. Like the desert with all the bones in.'

Mr Nancy raised his head. 'Backstage. Yes. Every time I figure you don't have enough sense to bring guts to a bear, you surprise me. That's right. Backstage. That's where the real battle will happen. Everything else will just be flash and thunder.'

'Tell me about the vigil,' said Shadow.

'Someone has to stay with the body. It's a tradition. One of our people will do it.'

'He wanted me to do it.'

'No,' said Czernobog. 'It will kill you. Bad, bad, bad idea.'

'Yeah? It'll kill me? To stay with his body?'

'It's what happens when the all-father dies,' said Mr Nancy. 'It wouldn't be true for me. When I die, I just want them to plant me somewhere warm. And then when pretty women walk over my grave I would grab their ankles, like in that movie.'

'I never saw that movie,' said Czernobog.

'Of course you did. It's right at the end. It's the high school movie. All the children going to the prom.'

Czernobog shook his head.

Shadow said, 'The film's called *Carrie*, Mister Czernobog. Okay, one of you tell me about the vigil.'

Nancy said, 'You tell him. I'm drivin'.'

'I never heard of no film called *Carrie*. You tell him.'

Nancy said, 'The person on the vigil – gets tied to the tree. Just like Wednesday was. And then they hang there for nine days and nine nights. No food, no water. All alone. At the end they cut the person down, and if they lived . . . well, it could happen. And Wednesday will have had his vigil.'

Czernobog said, 'Maybe Alviss will send us one of his people. A dwarf could survive it.'

'I'll do it,' said Shadow.

'No,' said Mr Nancy.

'Yes,' said Shadow.

The two old men were silent. Then Nancy said, 'Why?'

'Because it's the kind of thing a living person would do,' said Shadow.

'You are crazy,' said Czernobog.

'Maybe. But I'm going to hold Wednesday's vigil.'

When they stopped for gas Czernobog announced he felt sick, and wanted to ride in the front. Shadow didn't mind moving to the back of the bus. He could stretch out more, and sleep.

They drove on in silence. Shadow felt that he'd done

something very big and very strange, and he wasn't certain exactly what it was.

'Hey. Czernobog,' said Mr Nancy, after a while. 'You check out the technical boy back at the motel? He was not happy. He's been screwin' with something that screwed him right back. That's the biggest trouble with the new kids – they figure they know everythin', and you can't teach them nothin' but the hard way.'

'Good,' said Czernobog.

Shadow was stretched out full length on the seat in the back. He felt like two people, or more than two. There was part of him that felt gently exhilarated: he had done something. He had moved. It wouldn't have mattered if he hadn't wanted to live, but he did want to live, and that made all the difference. He hoped he would live through this, but he was willing to die, if that was what it took to be alive. And, for a moment he thought that the whole thing was funny, just the funniest thing in the world; and he wondered if Laura would appreciate the joke.

There was another part of him – maybe it was Mike Ainsel, he thought, vanished off into nothing at the press of a button in the Lakeside Police Department – who was still trying to figure it all out, trying to see the big picture.

'Hidden Indians,' he said out loud.

'What?' came Czernobog's irritated croak from the front seat.

'The pictures you'd get to color in as kids. "Can you see the hidden Indians in this picture? There are ten Indians in this picture, can you find them all?" And at first glance you could only see the waterfall and the rocks and the trees, then you see that if you just tip the picture on its side that shadow is an Indian . . .' He yawned.

'Sleep,' suggested Czernobog.

'But the big picture,' said Shadow. Then he slept, and dreamed of hidden Indians.

* * *

The tree was in Virginia. It was a long way away from anywhere, on the back of an old farm. To get to the farm they had had to drive for almost an hour south from Blacksburg, to drive on roads with names like Pennywinkle Branch and Rooster Spur. They got turned around twice and Mr Nancy and Czernobog both lost their tempers with Shadow and with each other.

They stopped to get directions at a tiny general store, set at the bottom of the hill in the place where the road forked. An old man came out of the back of the store and stared at them: he wore Oshkosh B'Gosh denim overalls and nothing else, not even shoes. Czernobog bought a pickled hog's foot from the huge jar of hogs' feet on the counter, and went outside to eat it on the deck, while Nancy and the man in the overalls took turns drawing each other maps on the back of napkins, marking off turnings and local landmarks.

They set off once more, with Mr Nancy driving, and they were there in ten minutes. A sign on the gate said ASH.

Shadow got out of the bus, and opened the gate. The bus drove through, jolting through the meadowland. Shadow closed the gate. He walked a little behind the bus, stretching his legs, jogging when the bus got too far in front of him, enjoying the sensation of moving his body.

He had lost all sense of time on the drive from Kansas. Had they been driving for two days? Three days? He did not know.

The body in the back of the bus did not seem to be rotting. He could smell it – a faint odor of Jack Daniel's, overlaid with something that might have been sour honey. But the smell was not unpleasant. From time to time he would take out the glass eye from his pocket and look at it: it was shattered deep inside, fractured from what he imagined was the impact of a bullet, but apart from a chip to one side of the iris the surface was unmarred. Shadow would run it through his hands, palming it, rolling it, pushing it along with his fingers. It was a ghastly souvenir, but oddly comforting: and he suspected that it would have amused Wednesday to know that his eye had wound up in Shadow's pocket.

The farmhouse was dark and shut up. The meadows were overgrown and seemed abandoned. The farm roof was crumbling at the back; it was covered in black plastic sheeting. They jolted over a ridge and Shadow saw the tree.

It was silver-gray and it was higher than the farmhouse. It was the most beautiful tree Shadow had ever seen: spectral and yet utterly real and almost perfectly symmetrical. It also looked instantly familiar: he wondered if he had dreamed it, then realized that no, he had seen it before, or a representation of it, many times. It was Wednesday's silver tie-pin.

The VW bus jolted and bumped across the meadow, and came to a stop about twenty feet from the trunk of the tree.

There were three women standing by the tree. At first glance Shadow thought that they were the Zorya, but he realized in moments that he was mistaken. They were three women he did not know. They looked tired and bored, as if they had been standing there for a long time. Each of them held a wooden ladder. The biggest one of them also carried a brown sack. They looked like a set of Russian dolls: a tall one – she was Shadow's height, or even taller – a middle-sized one, and a woman so short and hunched that at first glance Shadow wrongly supposed her to be a child. Still, they looked so much alike – something in the forehead, or the eyes, or the set of the chin – that Shadow was certain that the women must be sisters.

The smallest of the women dropped to a curtsy when the bus drew up. The other two just stared. They were sharing a cigarette, and they smoked it down to the filter before one of them stubbed it out against a root.

Czernobog opened the back of the bus and the biggest of the women pushed past him, and, easily as if it were a sack of flour, she lifted Wednesday's body out of the back and carried it to the tree. She laid it in front of the tree, put it down about ten feet from the trunk. She and her sisters unwrapped Wednesday's body. He looked worse by daylight than he had by candlelight in the motel room, and after one quick glance Shadow looked away. The women arranged his clothes, tidied his suit, then placed him at the corner of the sheet, and wound it around him once more.

Then the women came over to Shadow.

– *You are the one*? the biggest of them asked.

– *The one who will mourn the all-father*? asked the middle-sized one.

– *You have chosen to take the vigil*? asked the smallest.

Shadow nodded. Afterward, he was unable to remember whether he had actually heard their voices. Perhaps he had simply understood what they had meant from their looks and their eyes.

Mr Nancy, who had gone back to the house to use the bathroom, came walking back to the tree. He was smoking a cigarillo. He looked thoughtful.

'Shadow,' he called. 'You really don't have to do this. We can find somebody more suited. You ain't ready for this.'

'I'm doing it,' said Shadow, simply.

'You don't have to,' said Mr Nancy. 'You don't know what you're lettin' yourself in for.'

'It doesn't matter,' said Shadow.

'And if you die?' asked Mr Nancy. 'If it kills you?'

'Then,' said Shadow, 'it kills me.'

Mr Nancy flicked his cigarillo into the meadow, angrily. 'I said you had shit for brains, and you still have shit for brains. Can't see when somebody's tryin' to give you an out?'

'I'm sorry,' said Shadow. He didn't say anything else. Nancy walked back to the bus.

Czernobog walked over to Shadow. He did not look pleased. 'You must come through this alive,' he said. 'Come through this safely for me.' And then he tapped his knuckle gently against Shadow's forehead and said '*Bam!*' He squeezed Shadow's shoulder, patted his arm, and walked back to the bus.

The biggest woman, whose name seemed to be Urtha or Urder – Shadow could not repeat it back to her to her satisfaction – told him, in pantomime, to take off his clothes.

'All of them?'

The big woman shrugged. Shadow stripped to his briefs and tee shirt. The women propped the ladders against the tree. One of the ladders – it was painted by hand, with little flowers and leaves twining up the struts – they pointed out to him.

He climbed the nine steps. Then, at their urging, he stepped onto a low branch.

The middle woman tipped out the contents of the sack onto the meadow-grass. It was filled with a tangle of thin ropes, brown with age and dirt, and the woman began to sort them out into lengths, and to lay them carefully on the ground beside Wednesday's body.

They climbed their own ladders now, and they began to knot the ropes, intricate and elegant knots, and they wrapped the ropes first about the tree, and then about Shadow. Unembarrassed, like midwives or nurses or those who lay out corpses, they removed his tee shirt and briefs, then they bound him, never tightly, but firmly and finally. He was amazed at how comfortably the ropes and the knots bore his weight. The ropes went under his arms, between his legs, around his waist, his ankles, his chest, binding him to the tree.

The final rope was tied, loosely, about his neck. It was initially uncomfortable, but his weight was well distributed and none of the ropes cut his flesh.

His feet were five feet above the ground. The tree was leafless and huge, its branches black against the gray sky: its bark a smooth silvery gray.

They took the ladders away. There was a moment of panic

as he dropped a few inches, as all his weight was taken by the ropes. He made no sound.

He was entirely naked by that point.

The women placed the body, wrapped in its motel-sheet shroud, at the foot of the tree, and they left him there.

They left him there alone.

Chapter Fifteen

Hang me, O hang me, and I'll be dead and gone,
Hang me, O hang me, and I'll be dead and gone,
I wouldn't mind the hangin', it's bein' gone so long,
It's lyin' in the grave so long.

— Old Song

The first day that Shadow hung from the tree he experienced only discomfort, that edged slowly into pain and fear and, occasionally, an emotion that was somewhere between boredom and apathy: a gray acceptance, a waiting.

He hung.

The wind was still.

After several hours fleeting bursts of color started to explode across his vision in blossoms of crimson and gold, throbbing and pulsing with a life of their own.

The pain in his arms and legs became, by degrees, intolerable. If he relaxed them, let his body go slack and dangle, if he flopped forward, then the rope around his neck would take up the slack and the world would shimmer and swim. So he pushed himself back against the trunk of the tree. He could feel his heart laboring in his chest, a pounding arrhythmic tattoo as it pumped the blood through his body . . .

Emeralds and sapphires and rubies crystallized and burst in front of his eyes. His breath came in shallow gulps. The bark of the tree was rough against his back. The chill of the afternoon on his naked skin made him shiver, made his flesh prickle and goose.

It's easy, said someone in the back of his head. *There's a trick to it. Either you do it, or you die.*

It was a wise thing to have thought, he decided. He was pleased with it, and repeated it over and over in the back of his head, part mantra, part nursery rhyme, rattling along to the drumbeat of his heart.

It's easy, there's a trick to it, you do it or you die.
It's easy, there's a trick to it, you do it or you die.
It's easy, there's a trick to it, you do it or you die.
It's easy, there's a trick to it, you do it or you die.

Time passed. The chanting continued. He could hear it. Someone was repeating the words, only stopping when Shadow's mouth began to dry out, when his tongue turned dry and skin-like in his mouth. He pushed himself up and away from the tree with his feet, trying to support his weight in a way that would still allow him to fill his lungs.

He breathed until he could hold himself up no more, and then he fell back into the bonds, and hung from the tree.

When the chattering started – an angry, laughing chattering noise – he closed his mouth, concerned that it was he himself making it; but the noise continued. *It's the world laughing at me, then*, thought Shadow. His head lolled to one side. Something ran down the tree-trunk beside him, stopping beside his head. It chittered loudly in his ear, one word, which sounded a lot like 'ratatosk'. Shadow tried to repeat it, but his tongue stuck to the roof of his mouth. He turned, slowly, and stared into the gray-brown face and pointed ears of a squirrel.

In close up, he learned, a squirrel looks a lot less cute than it does from a distance. The creature was rat-like, and dangerous, not sweet or charming. And its teeth looked sharp. He hoped that it would not perceive him as a threat, or as a food source. He did not think that squirrels were carnivorous . . . but then, so many things he had not thought had turned out to be so . . .

He slept.

The pain woke him several times in the next few hours. It pulled him from a dark dream in which dead children rose and came to him, their eyes peeling, swollen pearls, and they reproached him for failing them and it pulled him from another dream, in which he was staring up at a mammoth, hairy and dark, as it lumbered toward him from the mist, but – *awake for a moment, a spider edging across his face, and he shook his head, dislodging or frightening it* – now the mammoth was an elephant-headed man, pot-bellied, one tusk broken, and he was riding toward Shadow on the back of a huge mouse. The elephant-headed man curled his trunk towards Shadow and said, 'If you had invoked me before you began this journey, perhaps some of your troubles might have been avoided.' Then the elephant took the mouse, which had, by some means that Shadow could not perceive, become tiny while not changing in size at all, and passed it from hand to hand to hand, fingers curling about it as the little brown creature scampered from palm to palm, and Shadow was not at all surprised when the elephant-headed god finally opened all four of his hands to reveal them perfectly empty. He shrugged arm after arm after arm in a peculiar fluid motion, and looked at Shadow, his face unreadable.

'It's in the trunk,' Shadow told the elephant man, who had seen the flickering tail vanish.

The elephant man nodded his huge head, and said, 'Yes.

In the trunk. You will forget many things. You will give many
things away. You will lose many things. But do not lose this,'
and then the rains began, and Shadow was awake once more.
He tumbled, shivering and wet, from deep sleep to
wakefulness in moments. The shivering intensified, until it
scared Shadow: he was shivering more violently than he had
ever imagined possible, a series of convulsive shudders
which built upon each other. He willed himself to stop
shaking, but still he shivered, his teeth banging together, his
limbs twitching and jerking beyond his control. There was
real pain there, too, a deep, knife-like pain that covered his
body with tiny, invisible wounds, intimate and unbearable.

* * *

He opened his mouth to catch the rain as it fell, moistening
his cracked lips and his dry tongue, wetting the ropes that
bound him to the trunk of the tree. There was a flash of
lightning so bright it felt like a blow to his eyes, transforming
the world into an intense panorama of image and after-
image. Then the thunder, a crack and a boom and a rumble,
and, as the thunder echoed, the rain redoubled. In the rain
and the night the shivering abated; the knife-blades were put
away. Shadow no longer felt the cold, or rather, he felt only
the cold, but the cold had now become part of himself, it
belonged to him and he belonged to it.

Shadow hung from the tree while the lightning flickered
and forked across the sky, and the thunder subsided into an
omnipresent rumbling, with occasional bangs and roars like
distant bombs exploding in the night, and the wind tugged at
Shadow, trying to pull him from the tree, flaying his skin,
cutting to the bone; and at the height of the storm – and
Shadow knew in his soul that the real storm had truly begun,
the true storm, and that now it was here there was nothing
any of them could do but ride it out: none of them, old gods
or new, spirits, powers, women or men . . .

A strange joy rose within Shadow then, and he started laughing, as the rain washed his naked skin and the lightning flashed and thunder rumbled so loudly that he could barely hear himself. He laughed and exulted.

He was alive. He had never felt like this. Ever.

If he died, he thought. If he died right now, here on the tree, it would be worth it to have had this one, perfect, mad moment.

'Hey!' he shouted, at the storm. 'Hey! It's me! I'm here!'

He trapped some water between his bare shoulder and the trunk of the tree, and he twisted his head over and drank the trapped rainwater, sucking and slurping at it, and he drank more and he laughed, laughed with joy and delight, not madness, until he could laugh no more, until he hung there, too exhausted to move.

At the foot of the tree, on the ground, the rain had made the sheet partly transparent, and had lifted it and pushed it forward so that Shadow could see Wednesday's dead hand, waxy and pale, and the shape of his head, and he thought of the shroud of Turin and he remembered the open girl on Jaquel's slab in Cairo, and then, as if to spite the cold, he observed that he was feeling warm and comfortable, and the bark of the tree felt soft, and he slept once more, and if he dreamed any dreams in the darkness this time he could not remember them.

* * *

By the following morning the pain was omnipresent. It was no longer local, not confined to the places where the ropes cut into his flesh, or where the bark scraped his skin. Now the pain was everywhere.

And he was hungry, with empty pangs down in the pit of him. His head was pounding. Sometimes he imagined that he had stopped breathing, that his heart had ceased to beat. Then he would hold his breath until he could hear his heart pounding an ocean in his ears and he was forced to suck air like a diver surfacing from the depths.

It seemed to him that the tree reached from hell to heaven, and that he had been hanging there forever. A brown hawk circled the tree, landed on a broken branch near to him, and then took to the wing, flying west.

The storm, which had abated at dawn, began to return as the day passed. Gray, roiling clouds stretched from horizon to horizon; a slow drizzle began to fall. The body at the base of the tree seemed to have become less, in its stained motel winding sheet, crumbling into itself like a sugar cake left in the rain.

Sometimes Shadow burned, sometimes he froze.

When the thunder started once more he imagined that he heard drums beating, kettledrums in the thunder and the thump of his heart, inside his head or outside, it did not matter.

He perceived the pain in colors: the red of a neon bar-sign, the green of a traffic light on a wet night, the blue of an empty video screen.

The squirrel dropped from the bark of the trunk onto Shadow's shoulder, sharp claws digging into his skin. 'Ratatosk!' it chattered. The tip of its nose touched his lips. 'Ratatosk.' It sprang back onto the tree.

His body was on fire with pins and needles, a pricking covering his whole body. The sensation was intolerable.

His life was laid out below him, on the motel sheet shroud: literally laid out, like the items at some Dada picnic, a surrealist tableau: he could see his mother's puzzled stare, the American embassy in Norway, Laura's eyes on their wedding day . . .

He chuckled through dry lips.

'What's so funny, puppy?' asked Laura.

'Our wedding day,' he said. 'You bribed the organist to change from playing the Wedding March to the theme-song from *Scooby-Doo* as you walked toward me down the aisle. Do you remember?'

'Of course I remember, darling. I would have made it too, if it wasn't for those meddling kids.'

'I loved you so much,' said Shadow.

He could feel her lips on his, and they were warm and wet and living, not cold and dead, so he knew that this was another hallucination. 'You aren't here, are you?' he asked.

'No,' she said. 'But you are calling me, for the last time. And I am coming.'

Breathing was harder now. The ropes cutting his flesh were an abstract concept, like free will or eternity.

'Sleep, puppy,' she said, although he thought it might have been his own voice he heard, and he slept.

***

The sun was a pewter coin in a leaden sky. Shadow was, he realized slowly, awake, and he was cold. But the part of him that understood that seemed very far away from the rest of him. Somewhere in the distance he was aware that his mouth and throat were burning, painful and cracked. Sometimes, in the daylight, he would see stars fall; other times he saw huge birds, the size of delivery trucks, flying toward him. Nothing reached him; nothing touched him.

'Ratatosk. Ratatosk.' The chattering had become a scolding.

The squirrel landed, heavily, with sharp claws, on his shoulder and stared into his face. He wondered if he were hallucinating: the animal was holding a walnut-shell, like a doll's house cup, in its front paws. The animal pressed the shell to Shadow's lips. Shadow felt the water, and, involuntarily, he sucked it in to his mouth, drinking from the tiny cup. He ran the water around his cracked lips, his dry tongue. He wet his mouth with it, and swallowed what was left, which was not much.

The squirrel leapt back to the tree, and ran down it, towards the roots, and then, in seconds, or minutes, or hours, Shadow could not tell which (all the clocks in his mind were broken, he thought, and their gears and cogs and springs were simply a jumble down there in the writhing grass), the squirrel returned with its walnut-shell cup, climbing carefully, and Shadow drank the water it brought to him.

The muddy-iron taste of the water filled his mouth, cooled his parched throat. It eased his fatigue and his madness.

By the third walnut-shell, he was no longer thirsty.

He began to struggle, then, pulling at the ropes, flailing his body, trying to get down, to get free, to get away. He moaned.

The knots were good. The ropes were strong, and they held, and soon he exhausted himself once more.

***

In his delirium, Shadow became the tree. Its roots went deep into the loam of the earth, deep down into time, into the hidden springs. He felt the spring of the woman called Urd, which is to say, *Past*. She was huge, a giantess, an underground mountain of a woman, and the waters she guarded were the waters of time. Other roots went to other places. Some of them were secret. Now, when he was thirsty, he pulled water from his roots, pulled them up into the body of his being.

He had a hundred arms which broke into a hundred thousand fingers, and all of his fingers reached up into the sky. The weight of the sky was heavy on his shoulders.

It was not that the discomfort was lessened, but the pain belonged to the figure hanging from the tree, rather than to the tree itself, and Shadow in his madness was now so much more than the man on the tree. He was the tree, and he was the wind rattling the bare branches of the world tree; he was the gray sky and the tumbling clouds; he was Ratatosk the squirrel running from the deepest roots to the highest branches; he was the mad-eyed hawk who sat on a broken branch at the top of the tree surveying the world; he was the worm in the heart of the tree.

The stars wheeled, and he passed his hundred hands over the glittering stars, palming them, switching them, vanishing them . . .

***

People were walking around beside him, in his mind or out of it. Some of the people he seemed to recognise, others were strangers.

'And what's a stranger but a friend you haven't met yet?' said someone to him, passing him a drink.

He took the drink, walked with the person down a light brown corridor. They were in a Spanish-style building, and they moved from adobe corridor to open courtyard to corridor once more, while the sun beat down on the water gardens and the fountains.

'It might be an enemy you've not met yet too,' said Shadow.

'Bleak, Shadow, very bleak,' said the man. Shadow sipped his drink. It was a brackish red wine.

'It's been a bleak few months,' said Shadow. 'It's been a bleak few years.'

The man was slender, tanned, of medium height, and he looked up at Shadow with a gentle, empathetic smile. 'How's the vigil going, Shadow?'

'The tree?' Shadow had forgotten that he was hanging from the silver tree. He wondered what else he had forgotten. 'It hurts.'

'Suffering is sometimes cleansing,' said the man. His clothes were casual, but expensive. 'It can purify.'

'It can also fuck you up,' said Shadow.

The man led Shadow into a vast office. There was no desk

in there, though. 'Have you thought about what it means to be a god?' asked the man. He had a beard and a baseball cap. 'It means you give up your mortal existence to become a meme: something that lives forever in people's minds, like the tune of a nursery rhyme. It means that everyone gets to recreate you in their own minds. You barely have your own identity any more. Instead, you're a thousand aspects of what people need you to be. And everyone wants something different from you. Nothing is fixed, nothing is stable.'

Shadow sat in a comfortable leather chair, by the window. The man sat on the enormous sofa. 'Great place you've got here,' said Shadow.

'Thanks. Be honest now, how's the wine?'

Shadow hesitated. 'Kind of sour, I'm afraid.'

'Sorry. That's the trouble with wine. Okay wine I can do easily, but good wine, let alone great wine . . . well, you've got weather, soil acidity, rainfall, even which side of a hill the grapes are grown. Don't get me started on vintages . . .'

'It's fine, really,' said Shadow, and he swallowed the rest of the wine in one long gulp. He could feel it burning in his empty stomach, feel the bubbles of drunkenness rising at the back of his head.

'And then this whole deal of new gods, old gods,' said his friend. 'You ask me, I welcome new gods. Bring them on. The god of the guns. The god of bombs. All the gods of ignorance and intolerance, of self-righteousness, idiocy and blame. All the stuff they try and land me with. Take a lot of the weight off my shoulders.' He sighed.

'But you're so successful,' said Shadow. 'Look at this place.' He gestured, indicating the paintings on the walls, the hardwood floor, the fountain in the courtyard below them.

His friend nodded. 'It has a cost,' he said. 'Like I said. You have to be all things to all people. Pretty soon, you're spread so thin you're hardly there at all. It's not good.'

He reached out one calloused hand – the fingers were etched with old chisel scars – and squeezed Shadow's hand.

'I know, I know. I should count my blessings. And one of those blessings is getting time just to meet you like this, and to talk. It's great that you were able to make it,' he said. 'Really great. Don't be a stranger now.'

'No. I'll just be a friend you've not met yet,' said Shadow.

'Funny guy,' said the man with the beard.

'Ratatosk, ratatosk,' chattered the squirrel in Shadow's ear. He could taste the bitter wine still, in his mouth and the back of his throat, and it was almost dark.

*   *   *

A moment of clarity, in the pain and the madness: Shadow felt himself surfacing. He knew it would not be for long. The morning sun was dazzling him. He closed his eyes, wishing he could shade them.

There was not long to go. He knew that, too.

When he opened his eyes, Shadow noticed that there was a young man in the tree with him.

His skin was dark brown. His forehead was high and his dark hair was tightly curled. He was sitting on a branch high above Shadow's head. Shadow could see him clearly by craning his head. And the man was mad. Shadow could see that at a glance.

'You're naked,' confided the madman, in a cracked voice. 'I'm naked, too.'

'I see that,' croaked Shadow.

The madman looked at him, then he nodded and twisted his head down and around, as if he were trying to remove a crick from his neck. Eventually he said, 'Do you know me?'

'No,' said Shadow.

'I know you. I watched you in Cairo. I watched you after. My sister likes you.'

'You are...' the name escaped him. Eats roadkill. Yes. 'You are Horus.'

The madman nodded. 'Horus,' he said. 'I am the falcon of

the morning, the hawk of the afternoon. I am the sun. As you
are the sun. And I know the true name of Ra. My mother told
me.'

'That's great,' said Shadow, politely.

The madman stared at the ground below them intently,
saying nothing. Then he dropped from the tree.

A hawk fell like a stone to the ground, pulled out of its
plummet into a swoop, beat its wings heavily and flew back
to the tree, a baby rabbit in its talons. It landed on a branch
closer to Shadow.

'Are you hungry?' asked the madman.

'No,' said Shadow. 'I guess I should be, but I'm not.'

'I'm hungry,' said the madman. He ate the rabbit rapidly,
pulling it apart, sucking, tearing, rending. As he finished
with them, he dropped the gnawed bones and the fur to the
ground. He walked further down the branch until he was
only an arm's length from Shadow. Then he peered at
Shadow unselfconsciously, inspecting him with care and
caution, from his feet to his head. There was rabbit-blood on
his chin and his chest, and he wiped it off with the back of
his hand.

Shadow felt he had to say something. 'Hey,' he said.

'Hey,' said the madman. He stood up on the branch,
turned away from Shadow and let a stream of dark urine
arc out into the meadow below. It went on for a long time.
When he had finished he crouched down again on the
branch.

'What do they call you?' asked Horus.

'Shadow,' said Shadow.

The madman nodded. 'You are the shadow. I am the light,'
he said. 'Everything that is, casts a shadow.' Then he said,
'They will fight soon. I was watching them as they started to
arrive. I was high in the sky, and none of them saw me,
although some of them have keen eyes.'

And then the madman said, 'You are dying. Aren't you?'

But Shadow could no longer speak. Everything was very

far away. A hawk took wing, and circled slowly upward, riding the updrafts into the morning.

***

Moonlight.

A cough shook Shadow's frame, a racking painful cough that stabbed his chest and his throat. He gagged for breath.

'Hey, puppy,' called a voice that he knew.

He looked down.

The moonlight burned whitely through the branches of the tree, bright as day, and there was a woman standing in the moonlight on the ground below him, her face a pale oval. The wind rattled in the branches of the tree.

'Hi, puppy,' she said.

He tried to speak, but he coughed instead, deep in his chest, for a long time.

'You know,' she said, helpfully, 'that doesn't sound good.'

He croaked, 'Hello Laura.'

She looked up at him with dead eyes, and she smiled.

'How did you find me?' he asked.

She was silent, for a while, in the moonlight. Then she said, 'You are the nearest thing I have to life. You are the only thing I have left, the only thing that isn't bleak and flat and gray. I could be blindfolded and dropped into the deepest ocean and I would know where to find you. I could be buried a hundred miles underground and I would know where you are.'

He looked down at the woman in the moonlight, and his eyes stung with tears.

'I'll cut you down,' she said, after a while. 'I spend too much time rescuing you, don't I?'

He coughed again. Then, 'No, leave me. I have to do this.'

She looked up at him, and shook her head. 'You're crazy,' she said. 'You're dying up there. Or you'll be crippled, if you aren't already.'

'Maybe,' he said. 'But I'm alive.'

'Yes,' she said, after a moment. 'I guess you are.'

'You told me,' he said. 'In the graveyard.'

'It seems like such a long time ago, puppy,' she said. Then she said, 'I feel better, here. It doesn't hurt as much. You know what I mean? But I'm so dry.'

The wind let up, and he could smell her now: a stink of rotten meat and sickness and decay, pervasive and unpleasant.

'I lost my job,' she said. 'It was a night job, but they said people had complained. I told them I was sick, and they said they didn't care. I'm so thirsty.'

'The women,' he told her. 'They have water. The house.'

'Puppy . . .' she sounded scared.

'Tell them . . . tell them I said to give you water . . .'

The white face stared up at him. 'I should go,' she told him. Then she hacked, and made a face, and spat a mass of something white onto the grass. It broke up when it hit the ground and wriggled away.

It was almost impossible to breathe. His chest felt heavy, and his head was swaying.

'Stay,' he said, in a breath that was almost a whisper, unsure whether or not she could hear him. 'Please don't go.' He started to cough. 'Stay the night.'

'I'll stop a while,' she said. And then, like a mother to a child she said, 'Nothing's gonna hurt you when I'm here. You know that?'

Shadow coughed once more. He closed his eyes – only for a moment, he thought, but when he opened them again the moon had set and he was alone.

***

A crashing and a pounding in his head, beyond the pain of migraine, beyond all pain. Everything dissolved into tiny butterflies which circled him like a multicolored dust storm and then evaporated into the night.

The white sheet wrapped about the body at the base of the tree flapped noisily in the morning wind.

The pounding eased. Everything slowed. There was nothing left to make him keep breathing. His heart ceased to beat in his chest.

The darkness that he entered this time was deep, and lit by a single star, and it was final.

Chapter Sixteen

'I know it's crooked. But it's the only game in town.'
— Canada Bill Jones

The tree was gone, and the world was gone, and the morning-gray sky above him was gone. The sky was now the color of midnight. There was a single cold star shining high above him, a blazing, twinkling light, and nothing else. He took a single step and almost tripped.

Shadow looked down. There were steps cut into the rock, going down, steps so huge that he could only imagine that giants had cut them and descended them a long time ago.

He clambered downward, half jumping, half vaulting from step to step. His body ached, but it was the ache of lack of use, not the tortured ache of a body that has hung on a tree until it was dead.

He observed, without surprise, that he was now fully dressed, in jeans and a white tee shirt. He was barefoot. He experienced a profound moment of *déjà vu*: this was what he had been wearing when he stood in Czernobog's apartment the night when Zorya Polunochnaya had come to him and told him about the constellation called Odin's Wain. She had taken the moon down from the sky for him.

He knew, suddenly, what would happen next. Zorya Polunochnaya would be there.

She was waiting for him at the bottom of the steps. There was no moon in the sky, but she was bathed in moonlight nonetheless: her white hair was moon-pale, and she wore the same lace-and-linen nightdress she had worn that night in Chicago.

She smiled when she saw him, and looked down, as if momentarily embarrassed. 'Hello,' she said.

'Hi,' said Shadow.

'How are you?'

'I don't know,' he said. 'I think this is maybe another strange dream on the tree. I've been having crazy dreams since I got out of prison.'

Her face was silvered by the moonlight (but no moon hung in that plum-black sky, and now, at the foot of the steps, even the single star was lost to view) and she looked both solemn and vulnerable. She said, 'All your questions can be answered, if that is what you want. But once you learn your answers, you can never unlearn them. You have to understand that.'

'I got it,' he said.

Beyond her, the path forked. He would have to decide which path to take, he knew that. But there was one thing he had to do first. He reached into the pocket of his jeans and was relieved when he felt the familiar weight of the coin at the bottom of the pocket. He eased it out, held it between finger and thumb: a 1922 Liberty dollar. 'This is yours,' he said.

He remembered then that his clothes were really at the foot of the tree. The women had placed his clothes in the canvas sack from which they had taken the ropes, and tied the end of the sack, and the biggest of the women had placed a heavy rock on it to stop it from blowing away. And so he knew that, in reality, the Liberty dollar was in a pocket in that sack, beneath the rock. But still, it was heavy in his hand, at the entrance to the underworld.

She took it from his palm with her slim fingers.

'Thank you. It bought you your liberty twice,' she said. 'And now it will light your way into dark places.'

She closed her hand around the dollar, then she reached up and placed it in the air, as high as she could reach. Then she let go of it. Shadow knew, then, that this was another dream, for instead of falling, the coin floated upward until it was a foot or so above Shadow's head. It was no longer a silver coin, though. Lady Liberty and her crown of spikes were gone. The face he saw on the coin was the indeterminate face of the moon in the summer sky, the face that was only visible until you stared at it, whereupon it would become dark seas and shapes on the moon's cratered surface, the pattern and the face replaced by shadows of pure randomness and chance.

Shadow could not decide whether he was looking at a moon the size of a dollar, a foot above his head; or whether he was looking at a moon the size of the Pacific Ocean, many thousands of miles away. Nor whether there was any difference between the two ideas. Perhaps it was all a matter of perspective. Perhaps it was all a matter of point of view.

He looked at the forking path ahead of him.

'Which path should I take?' he asked. 'Which one is safe?'

'Take one, and you cannot take the other,' she said. 'But neither path is safe. Which way would you walk – the way of hard truths or the way of fine lies?'

Shadow hesitated. 'Truths,' he said. 'I've come too far for more lies.'

She looked sad. 'There will be a price, then,' she said.

'I'll pay it. What's the price.'

'Your name,' she said. 'Your real name. You will have to give it to me.'

'How?'

'Like this,' she said. She reached a perfect hand toward his head. He felt her fingers brush his skin, then he felt them penetrate his skin, his skull, felt them push deep into his head. Something tickled, in his skull and all down his spine. She pulled her hand out of his head. A flame, like a candle-flame but burning with a clear magnesium-white luminance, was flickering on the tip of her forefinger.

'Is that my name?' he asked.

She closed her hand, and the light was gone. 'It was,' she said. She extended her hand, and pointed to the right-hand path. 'That way,' she said. 'For now.'

Nameless, Shadow walked down the right-hand path in the moonlight. When he turned around to thank her, he saw nothing but darkness. It seemed to him that he was deep under the ground, but when he looked up into the darkness above him he still saw the tiny moon.

He turned a corner.

If this was the afterlife, he thought, it was a lot like the House on the Rock: part diorama, part nightmare.

He was looking at himself in prison blues, in the warden's office, as the warden told him that Laura had died in a car crash. He saw the expression on his own face – he looked like a man who had been abandoned by the world. It hurt him to see it, the nakedness and the fear. He hurried on, pushed through the warden's gray office, and found himself looking at the VCR repair store on the outskirts of Eagle Point. Three years ago. Yes.

Inside the store, he knew, he was beating the living crap out of Larry Powers and B.J. West, bruising his knuckles in the process: pretty soon he would walk out of there, carrying a brown supermarket bag filled with twenty dollar bills. The money they could never prove he had taken: his share of the proceeds, and a little more, for they shouldn't have tried to rip him and Laura off like that. He was only the driver, but he had done his part, done everything that she had asked of him . . .

At the trial, nobody mentioned the bank robbery, although he was certain everybody wanted to. They couldn't prove a thing, as long as nobody was talking. And nobody was. The prosecutor was forced instead to stick to the bodily damage that Shadow had inflicted on Powers and West. He showed photographs of the two men on their arrival in the local hospital. Shadow barely defended himself in court; it was easier that way. Neither Powers nor West seemed able to remember what the fight had been about, but they each admitted that Shadow had been their assailant.

Nobody talked about the money.

Nobody even mentioned Laura, and that was all that Shadow had wanted.

Shadow wondered whether the path of comforting lies would have been a better one to walk. He walked away from that place, and followed the rock path down into what looked like a hospital room, a public hospital in Chicago and he felt the bile rise in his throat. He stopped. He did not want to look. He did not want to keep walking.

In the hospital bed his mother was dying again, as she'd died when he was sixteen, and, yes, here he was, a large, clumsy sixteen-year old with acne pocking his cream-and-coffee skin, sitting at her bedside, unable to look at her, reading a thick paperback book. Shadow wondered what the book was, and he walked around the hospital bed to inspect it more closely. He stood between the bed and the chair looking from the one to the other, the big boy hunched into his chair, his nose buried in *Gravity's Rainbow*, trying to escape from his mother's death into London during the blitz, the fictional madness of the book no escape and no excuse.

His mother's eyes were closed in a morphine peace: what she had thought was just another sickle-cell crisis, another bout of pain to be endured, had turned out, they had discovered, too late, to be lymphoma. There was a lemonish-gray tinge to her skin. She was in her early thirties, but she looked much older.

Shadow wanted to shake himself, the awkward boy that he once was, get him to hold her hand, talk to her, do *something* before she slips away, as he knows that she will. But he cannot touch himself, and he continues to read; and so his mother died while he sat in the chair next to her, reading a fat book.

After that he had more or less stopped reading. You could not trust fiction. What good were books, if they couldn't protect you from something like that?

Shadow walked away from the hospital room, down the winding corridor, deep into the bowels of the earth.

He sees his mother first and he cannot believe how young she is, not yet twenty-five he guesses, before her medical discharge and they're in their apartment, another embassy rental somewhere in Northern Europe, he looks around for something to give him a clue, and he's just a shrimp of a kid now, big pale-gray eyes and straight dark hair and skin that's neither one thing nor another. They are arguing. Shadow knows without hearing the words what they're arguing about: it was the only thing they quarreled about, after all.

– *Tell me about my father.*

– *He's dead. Don't ask about him.*

– *But who was he?*

– *Forget him. Dead and gone and you ain't missed nothing.*

– *I want to see a picture of him.*

– *I ain't got a picture*, she'd say and her voice would get quiet and fierce, and he knew that if he kept asking her questions she would shout, or even hit him, and he knew that he could not stop asking questions, so he turned away and walked on down the tunnel.

The path he followed twisted and wound and curled back on itself, and it put him in mind of snake-skins and intestines and of deep, deep tree roots. There was a pool to his left; he heard the *drip, drip* of water into it somewhere at the back of the tunnel, the falling water barely ruffling the mirrored surface of the pool. He dropped to his knees and drank, using his hand to bring the water to his lips. Then he walked on until he was standing in the floating disco-glitter patterns of a mirror-ball. It was like being in the exact center of the universe with all the stars and planets circling him, and he could not hear anything, not the music, nor the shouted conversations over the music, and now Shadow was staring at a woman who looked just like his mother never looked in all the years he knew her, she's little more than a child, after all . . .

And she is dancing.

Shadow found that he was completely unsurprised when he recognized the man who dances with her. He had not changed that much in thirty-three years.

She is drunk: Shadow could see that at a glance. She is not very drunk, but she is unused to drink, and in a week or so she will take a ship to Norway. They have been drinking margaritas, and she has salt on her lips and salt clinging to the back of her hand.

Wednesday is not wearing a suit and tie, but the pin in the shape of a silver tree he wears over the pocket of his shirt glitters and glints when the mirror-ball light catches it. He does not dance badly; they make a fine-looking couple, considering the difference in their ages. There is a lupine grace to his movements.

A slow dance. He pulls her close to him, and his paw-like hand curves around the seat of her skirt possessively, moving her closer to him. His other hand takes her chin, pushes it upward into his face, and the two of them kiss, there on the floor, as the glitter-ball lights circle them into the center of the universe.

Soon after, they leave. She sways against him, and he leads her from the dance hall.

Shadow buries his head in his hands, and does not follow them, unable or unwilling to witness his own conception.

The mirror lights were gone, and now the only illumination came from the tiny moon that burned high above his head.

He walked on. At a bend in the path he stopped for a moment, to catch his breath.

He felt a hand run gently up his back, and gentle fingers ruffle the hair on the back of his head.

'Hello, hon,' whispered a smoky female voice, over his shoulder.

'Hello,' he said, turning to face her.

She had brown hair and brown skin and her eyes were the deep golden-amber of good honey. Her pupils were vertical slits. 'Do I know you?' he asked, puzzled.

'Intimately,' she said, and she smiled. 'I used to sleep on your bed. And my people have been keeping their eyes on you, for me.' She turned to the path ahead of him, pointed to the three ways he could go. 'Okay,' she said. 'One way will make you wise. One way will make you whole. And one way will kill you.'

'I'm already dead, I think,' said Shadow. 'I died on the tree.'

She made a moue. 'There's dead,' she said, 'and there's dead, and there's dead. It's a relative thing.' Then she smiled again. 'I could make a joke about that, you know. Something about dead relatives.'

'No,' said Shadow. 'It's okay.'

'So,' she said. 'Which way do you want to go?'

'I don't know,' he admitted.

She tipped her head on one side, a perfectly feline gesture. Suddenly, Shadow knew exactly who she was, and where he knew her from. He felt himself beginning to blush. 'If you trust me,' said Bast, 'I can choose for you.'

'I trust you,' he said, without hesitation.

'Do you want to know what it's going to cost you?'

'I've already lost my name,' he told her.

'Names come and names go. Was it worth it?'

'Yes. Maybe. It wasn't easy. As revelations go, it was kind of personal.'

'All revelations are personal,' she said. 'That's why all revelations are suspect.'

'I don't understand.'

'No,' she said, 'you don't. I'll take your heart. We'll need it later,' and she reached her hand deep inside his chest, and she pulled it out with something ruby and pulsing held between her sharp fingernails. It was the color of pigeon's blood, and it was made of pure light. Rhythmically it expanded and contracted.

She closed her hand, and it was gone.

'Take the middle way,' she said.

Shadow hesitated. 'Are you really here?' he asked.

She tipped her head on one side, regarded him gravely, said nothing at all.

'What are you?' he asked. 'What are you people?'

She yawned, showing a perfect, dark-pink tongue. 'Think of us as symbols – we're the dream that humanity creates to make sense of the shadows on the cave wall. Now go on, keep moving. Your body is already growing cold. The fools are gathering on the mountain. The clock is ticking.'

Shadow nodded, and walked on.

The path was becoming slippery now. There was ice on the rock. Shadow stumbled and skidded as he walked down the rock path, toward the place where it divided, scraping his knuckles on a jut of rock at chest height. He edged forward as slowly as he could. The moon above him glittered through the ice-crystals in the air: there was a ring about the moon, a moonbow, diffusing the light. It was beautiful, but it made walking harder. The path was unreliable.

He reached the place where the path divided.

He looked at the first path with a feeling of recognition. It opened into a vast chamber, or a set of chambers, like a dark museum. He knew it already. He had been there once, although for several moments he was unable to remember where or when. He could hear the long echoes of tiny noises.

He could hear the noise that the dust makes as it settles. Then it came to him.

It was the Hall of Forgotten Gods. The place that he had dreamed of, that first night that Laura had come to him, in the motel, so long ago; the endless memorial hall to the gods that were forgotten, and the ones whose very existence had been lost.

He took a step backward.

He walked to the path on the far side, and looked ahead. There was a Disneyland quality to the corridor: black Plexiglas walls with lights set in them. The colored lights blinked and flashed in the illusion of order, for no particular reason, like the console lights on a television starship.

He could hear something there as well: a deep vibrating bass drone which Shadow could feel in the pit of his stomach.

He stopped and looked around. Neither way seemed right. Not any longer. He was done with paths. The middle way, the way the cat-woman had told him to walk, that was his way. He moved toward it.

The moon above him was beginning to fade: the edge of it was pinking and going into eclipse. The path was framed by a huge doorway.

There were no deals to make any more, no more bargains. There was nothing to do but enter. So Shadow walked through the doorway, in darkness. The air was warm, and it smelled of wet dust, like a city street after the summer's first rain.

He was not afraid.

Not any more. Fear had died on the tree, as Shadow had died. There was no fear left, no hatred, no pain. Nothing left but essence.

Something big splashed, quietly, in the distance, and the splash echoed into the vastness. He squinted, but could see nothing. It was too dark. And then, from the direction of the splashes, a ghost-light glimmered and the world took form:

he was in a cavern, and in front of him, mirror-smooth, was water.

The splashing noises came closer and the light became brighter, and Shadow waited on the shore. Soon enough a low, flat boat came into sight, a flickering white lantern burning at its raised prow, another reflected in the glassy black water several feet below it. The boat was being poled by a tall figure, and the splashing noise Shadow had heard was the sound of the pole being lifted and moved as it pushed the craft across the waters of the underground lake.

'Hello there!' called Shadow. Echoes of his words suddenly surrounded him: he could imagine that a whole chorus of people were welcoming him, and calling to him and each of them had his voice.

The person poling the boat made no reply.

The boat's pilot was tall, and very thin. He – if it was a he – wore an unadorned white robe, and the pale head that topped it was so utterly inhuman that Shadow was certain that it had to be a mask of some sort: it was a bird's head, small on a long neck, its beak long and high. Shadow was certain he had seen it before, this ghostly, bird-like figure. He grasped at the memory and then, disappointed, realized that he was picturing the clockwork penny-in-the-slot machine in the House on the Rock, and the pale, bird-like, half-glimpsed figure that glided out from behind the crypt for the drunkard's soul.

Water dripped and echoed from the pole and the prow, and the ship's wake rippled the glassy waters. The boat was made of reeds, bound and tied.

The boat came close to the shore. The pilot leaned on its pole. Its head turned slowly, until it was facing Shadow. 'Hello,' it said, without moving its long beak. The voice was male, and, like everything else in Shadow's afterlife so far, familiar. 'Come on board. You'll get your feet wet, I'm afraid, but there's not a thing can be done about that. These are old boats, and if I come in closer I could rip out the bottom.'

Shadow took off the shoes he had not been aware he was wearing, and stepped out into the water. It came half-way up his calves, and was, after the initial shock of wetness, surprisingly warm. He reached the boat, and the pilot put down a hand, and pulled him aboard. The reed boat rocked a little, and water splashed over the low sides of it, and then it steadied.

The pilot poled off away from the shore. Shadow stood there and watched, his pants-legs dripping.

'I know you,' he said to the creature at the prow.

'You do indeed,' said the boatman. The oil lamp which hung at the front of the boat burned more fitfully, and the smoke from the lamp made Shadow cough. 'You worked for me. I'm afraid we had to inter Lila Goodchild without you.' The voice was fussy and precise.

The smoke stung Shadow's eyes. He wiped the tears away with his hand, and, through the smoke, he thought he saw a tall man, in a suit, with gold-rimmed spectacles. The smoke cleared and the boatman was once more a half-human creature with the head of a river-bird.

'Mister Ibis?'

'Good to see you, Shadow,' said the creature, with Mr Ibis's voice. 'Do you know what a *psychopomp* is?'

Shadow thought he knew the word, but it had been a long time. He shook his head.

'It's a fancy term for an escort,' said Mr Ibis. 'We all have so many functions, so many ways of existing. In my own vision of myself, I am a scholar who lives quietly, and pens his little tales, and dreams about a past that may or may not ever have existed. And that is true, as far as it goes. But I am also, in one of my capacities, like so many of the people you have chosen to associate with, a psychopomp. I escort the living to the world of the dead.'

'I thought this was the world of the dead,' said Shadow.

'No. Not *per se*. It's more of a preliminary.'

The boat slipped and slid across the mirror-surface of the

underground pool. The bird-head of the creature at the prow stared ahead. And then Mr Ibis said, without moving its beak, 'You people talk about the living and the dead as if they were two mutually exclusive categories. As if you cannot have a river that is also a road, or a song that is also a color.'

'You can't,' said Shadow. 'Can you?' The echoes whispered his words back at him from across the pool.

'What you have to remember,' said Mr Ibis, testily, 'is that life and death are different sides of the same coin. Like the heads and tails of a quarter.'

'And if I had a double-headed quarter?'

'You don't. They only belong to fools, and gods.'

Shadow had a frisson, then, as they crossed the dark water. He imagined he could see the faces of children staring up at him reproachfully from beneath the water's glassy surface: their faces were waterlogged and softened, their blind eyes clouded. There was no wind in that underground cavern to disturb the black surface of the lake.

'So I'm dead,' said Shadow. He was getting used to the idea. 'Or I'm going to be dead.'

'We are on our way to the Hall of the Dead. I requested that I be the one to come for you.'

'Why?'

'I'm a psychopomp. I like you. You were a hard worker. Why not?'

'Because . . .' Shadow marshaled his thoughts. 'Because I never believed in you. Because I don't know much about Egyptian mythology. Because I didn't expect this. What happened to Saint Peter and the Pearly Gates?'

The long-beaked white head shook from side to side, gravely. 'It doesn't matter that you didn't believe in us,' said Mr Ibis. 'We believed in you.'

The boat touched bottom. Mr Ibis stepped off the side, into the pool, and told Shadow to do the same. Mr Ibis took a line from the prow of the boat, and passed Shadow the lantern to carry. It was in the shape of a crescent moon. They walked ashore, and Mr Ibis tied the boat to a metal ring set in the rock floor. Then he took the lamp from Shadow and walked swiftly forward, holding the lamp high as he walked, throwing vast shadows across the rock floor and the high rock walls.

'Are you scared?' asked Mr Ibis.

'Not really.'

'Well, try to cultivate the emotions of true awe and spiritual terror, as we walk. They are the appropriate feelings for the situation at hand.'

Shadow was not scared. He was interested, and apprehensive, but no more. He was not scared of the shifting darkness, nor of being dead, nor even of the dog-headed creature the size of a grain silo who stared at them as they approached. It growled, deep in its throat, and Shadow felt his neck-hairs prickle.

'Shadow,' it said. 'Now is the time of judgment.'

Shadow looked up the creature. 'Mister Jacquel?' he said.

The hands of Anubis came down, huge dark hands, and they picked Shadow up and brought him close.

The jackal head examined him with bright and glittering eyes; examined him as dispassionately as Mr Jacquel had examined the dead girl on the slab. Shadow knew that all his faults, all his failings, all his weaknesses were being taken out and weighed and measured; that he was, in some way, being dissected, and sliced, and tasted.

We do not always remember the things that do no credit to us. We justify them, cover them in bright lies or with the thick dust of forgetfulness. All of the things that Shadow had done in his life of which he was not proud, all the things he wished he had done otherwise or left undone, came at him then in a swirling storm of guilt and regret and shame, and he had nowhere to hide from them. He was as naked and as open as a corpse on a table, and dark Anubis the jackal god was his prosector and his prosecutor and his persecutor.

'Please,' said Shadow. 'Please stop.'

But the examination did not stop. Every lie he had ever told, every object he had stolen, every hurt he had inflicted on another person, all the little crimes and the tiny murders that make up the day, each of these things and more were extracted and held up to the light by the jackal-headed judge of the dead.

Shadow began to weep, painfully, in the palm of the dark god's hand. He was a tiny child again, as helpless and as powerless as he had ever been.

And then, without warning, it was over. Shadow panted, and sobbed, and snot streamed from his nose; he still felt helpless, but the hands placed him, carefully, almost tenderly, down on the rock floor.

'Who has his heart?' growled Anubis.

'I do,' purred a woman's voice. Shadow looked up. Bast was standing there beside the thing that was no longer Mr Ibis, and she held Shadow's heart in her right hand. It lit her face with a ruby light.

'Give it to me,' said Thoth, the ibis-headed god, and he took the heart in his hands, which were not human hands, and he glided forward.

Anubis placed a pair of golden scales in front of him.

'So is this where we find out what I get?' whispered Shadow to Bast. 'Heaven? Hell? Purgatory?'

'If the feather balances,' she said, 'you get to choose your own destination.'

'And if not?'

She shrugged, as if the subject made her uncomfortable. Then she said, 'Then we feed your heart and your soul to Ammet, the Eater of Souls . . .'

'Maybe,' he said. 'Maybe I can get some kind of a happy ending.'

'Not only are there no happy endings,' she told him. 'There aren't even any endings.'

On one of the pans of the scales, carefully, reverently, Anubis placed a feather.

Anubis put Shadow's heart on the other pan of the scales. Something moved in the shadows under the scale, something it made Shadow uncomfortable to examine too closely.

It was a heavy feather, but Shadow had a heavy heart, and the scales tipped and swung worryingly.

But they balanced, in the end, and the creature in the shadows skulked away, unsatisfied.

'So that's that,' said Bast, wistfully. 'Just another skull for the pile. It's a pity. I had hoped that you would do some good, in the current troubles. It's like watching a slow-motion car crash and being powerless to prevent it.'

'You won't be there?'

She shook her head. 'I don't like other people picking my battles for me,' she said.

There was silence then, in the vast hall of death, where it echoed of water and the dark.

Shadow said, 'So now I get to choose where I go next?'

'Choose,' said Thoth. 'Or we can choose for you.'

'No,' said Shadow. 'It's okay. It's my choice.'

'Well?' roared Anubis.

'I want to rest now,' said Shadow. 'That's what I want. I want nothing. No heaven, no hell, no anything. Just let it end.'

'You're certain?' asked Thoth.

'Yes,' said Shadow.

Mr Jacquel opened the last door for Shadow, and behind that door there was nothing. Not darkness. Not even oblivion. Only nothing.

Shadow accepted it, completely and without reservation, and he walked through the door into nothing with a strange fierce joy.

Chapter Seventeen

Everything is upon a great scale upon this continent. The rivers are immense, the climate violent in heat and cold, the prospects magnificent, the thunder and lightning tremendous. The disorders incident to the country make every constitution tremble. Our own blunders here, our misconduct, our losses, our disgraces, our ruin, are on a great scale.

— Lord Carlisle, to George Selwyn, 1778

The most important place in the southeastern United States is advertised on hundreds of aging barn-roofs across Georgia and Tennessee and up into Kentucky. On a winding road through a forest a driver will pass a rolling red barn, and see, painted on its roof

SEE ROCK CITY
THE EIGHTH WONDER OF THE WORLD

and on the roof of a tumbledown milking shed nearby, painted in white block letters,

SEE SEVEN STATES FROM ROCK CITY
THE WORLD'S WONDER

The driver is led by this to believe that Rock City is surely just around the nearest corner instead of being a day's drive away, on Lookout Mountain, a hair over the state line, in Georgia, just southwest of Chattanooga, Tennessee.

Lookout Mountain is not much of a mountain. It resembles an impossibly high and commanding hill, brown from a distance, green with trees and houses from up-close. The Chickamauga, a branch of the Cherokee, lived there when the white men came; they called the mountain Chattotonoogee, which has been translated as *the mountain that rises to a point.*

In the 1830s Andrew Jackson's Indian Relocation Act forced them all from their land – all the Choctaw and Chickamauga and Cherokee and Chickasaw – and US troops forced every one of them they could find and catch to walk over a thousand miles to the new Indian Territories in what would one day be Oklahoma, down the trail of tears: a cheerful gesture of casual genocide. Thousands of men, women, and children died on the way. When you've won, you've won, and nobody can argue with that.

For whoever controlled Lookout Mountain controlled the land; that was the legend. It was a sacred site, after all, and it was a high place. In the Civil War, the War Between the States, there was a battle there: the Battle Above the Clouds, that was the first day's fighting, and then the Union forces did the impossible, and, without orders, swept up Missionary Ridge and took it. The troops of General Grant won the day, and the North took Lookout Mountain and the North took the war.

There are tunnels and caves, some very old, beneath Lookout Mountain. For the most part they are blocked off now, although a local businessman excavated an underground waterfall, which he called Ruby Falls. It can be reached by elevator. It's a tourist attraction, although the biggest tourist attraction of all is at the top of Lookout Mountain. That is Rock City.

Rock City begins as an ornamental garden on a mountainside: its visitors walk a path that takes them through rocks, over rocks, between rocks. They throw corn into a deer enclosure, cross a hanging bridge and peer out through a quarter-a-throw binoculars at a view that promises them seven states on the rare sunny days when the air is perfectly clear. And from there, like a drop into some strange hell, the path takes the visitors, millions upon millions of them every year, down into caverns, where they stare at black-lit dolls arranged into nursery rhyme and fairy tale dioramas. When they leave, they leave bemused, uncertain of why they came, of what they have seen, of whether they had a good time or not.

***

They came to Lookout Mountain from all across the United States. They were not tourists. They came by car and they came by plane and by bus and by railroad and on foot. Some of them flew – they flew low, and they flew only in the dark of the night, but still, they flew. Several of them traveled their own ways beneath the earth. Many of them hitchhiked, cadging rides from nervous motorists or from truck drivers. Those who had cars or trucks would see the ones who had not walking beside the roads or at rest stations and in diners on the way, and, recognizing them for what they were, would offer them rides.

They arrived dust-stained and weary at the foot of Lookout Mountain. Looking up to the heights of the tree-covered slope they could see, or imagine that they could see, the paths and gardens and streams of Rock City.

They started arriving early in the morning. A second wave of them arrived at dusk. And for several days they simply kept coming.

A battered U-Haul truck pulled up, disgorging several travel-weary *vila* and *rusalka*, their make-up smudged, runs in their stockings, their expressions heavy-lidded and tired.

In a clump of trees at the bottom of the hill, an elderly *wampyr* offered a Marlboro to a huge naked ape-like creature covered with a tangle of orange fur. It accepted graciously, and they smoked in silence, side by side.

A Toyota Previa pulled up by the side of the road, and seven Chinese men and women got out of it. They looked, above all, clean, and they wore the kind of dark suits that, in some countries, are worn by minor government officials. One of them carried a clipboard, and he checked the inventory as they unloaded large golf-bags from the back of the car: the bags contained ornate swords with lacquer handles, and carved sticks, and mirrors. The weapons were distributed, checked off, signed for.

A once-famous comedian, believed to have died in the 1920s, climbed out of his rusting car, and proceeded to remove his clothing: his legs were goat-legs, and his tail was short and goatish.

Four Mexicans arrived, all smiles, their hair black and very shiny: they passed among themselves a beer bottle which they kept out of sight in a brown paper bag, its contents a bitter mixture of powdered chocolate, liquor, and blood.

A small, dark-bearded man with a dusty black derby on his head, curling *payess* at his temples, and a ragged fringed prayer shawl came to them walking across the fields. He was several feet in front of his companion, who was twice his height and was the blank gray color of good Polish clay: the word inscribed on his forehead meant *life*.

They kept coming. A cab drew up and several *Rakshasas*, the demons of the Indian subcontinent, climbed out and milled around, staring at the people at the bottom of the hill without speaking, until they found Mama-ji, her eyes closed, her lips moving in prayer. She was the only thing here that was familiar to them, but still, they hesitated to approach her, remembering old battles. Her hands rubbed the necklace of skulls about her neck. Her brown skin became slowly black, the glassy black of jet, of obsidian: her lips curled and her long white teeth were very sharp. She opened all her eyes, and beckoned the Rakshasas to her, and greeted them as she would have greeted her own children.

The storms of the last few days, to the north and the east, had done nothing to ease the feeling of pressure and discomfort in the air. Local weather forecasters had begun to warn of cells that might spawn tornados, of high pressure areas that did not move. It was warm by day there, but the nights were cold.

They clumped together in informal companies, banding together sometimes by nationality, by race, by temperament, even by species. They looked apprehensive. They looked tired.

Some of them were talking. There was laughter, on occasion, but it was muted and sporadic. Six-packs of beer were handed around.

Several local men and women came walking over the meadows, their bodies moving in unfamiliar ways: their voices, when they spoke, were the voices of the *Loa* who rode them: a tall, black man spoke in the voice of Papa Legba who opens the gates; while Baron Samedi, the Voudon lord of death, had taken over the body of a teenage Goth girl from Chattanooga, possibly because she possessed her own black silk top hat, which sat on her dark hair at a jaunty angle. She spoke in the Baron's own deep voice, smoked a cigar of enormous size, and commanded three of the *Gédé*, the Loa of the dead. The *Gédé* inhabited the bodies of three middle-aged brothers. They carried shotguns and told continual jokes of such astounding filthiness that only they were willing to laugh at them, which they did, raucously and repeatedly.

Two ageless Chickamauga women, in oil-stained blue jeans and battered leather jackets, walked around, watching the people and the preparations for battle. Sometimes they pointed and laughed; they did not intend to take part in the coming conflict.

The moon swelled and rose in the east, a day away from full. It seemed half as big as the sky as it rose, a deep reddish-orange, immediately above the hills. As it crossed the sky it seemed to shrink and pale until it hung high in the sky like a lantern.

There were so many of them waiting there, in the moonlight, at the foot of Lookout Mountain.

* * *

Laura was thirsty.

Sometimes living people burned steadily in her mind like candles and sometimes they flamed like torches. It made them easy to avoid, and it made them easy, on occasion, to find. Shadow had burned so strangely, with his own light, up on that tree.

She had chided him once, on that day when they had walked and held hands, for not being alive. She had hoped, perhaps, to see a spark of raw emotion, something that would show her that the man she had once been married to was a real man, a live one. And she had seen nothing at all.

She remembered walking beside him, wishing that he could understand what she was trying to say.

Now, dying on the tree, Shadow was utterly alive. She had watched him as the life had faded, and he had been focused and real. And he had asked her to stay with him, to stay the whole night. He had forgiven her . . . perhaps he had forgiven her. It did not matter. He had changed; that was all she knew.

Shadow had told her to go to the farmhouse, that they would give her water to drink there. There were no lights burning in the farm building, and she could feel nobody at home. But he had told her that they would care for her. She pushed against the door of the farmhouse and it opened, rusty hinges protesting the whole while.

Something moved in her left lung, something that pushed and squirmed and made her cough.

She found herself in a narrow hallway, her way almost blocked by a tall and dusty piano. The inside of the building smelled of old damp. She squeezed past the piano, pushed open a door and found herself in a dilapidated drawing room, filled with ramshackle furniture. An oil lamp burned on the mantelpiece. There was a coal fire burning in the fireplace beneath it, although she had neither seen nor smelled smoke outside the house. The coal fire did nothing to lift the chill she felt in that room, although, Laura was willing to concede, that might not be the fault of the room.

Death hurt Laura, although the hurt consisted mostly of absences, of things that were not there: a parching thirst that drained every cell of her, a cold in her bones that no heat could lift. Sometimes she would catch herself wondering whether the crisp and crackling flames of a pyre would warm her, or the soft brown blanket of the earth; whether the cold sea would quench her thirst . . .

The room, she realized, was not empty.

Three women sat on an elderly couch, as if they had come as a matched set in some outlandish artistic exhibition. The couch was upholstered in threadbare velvet, a faded brown that might, once, a hundred years ago, have been a bright canary yellow. The women were dressed in identical fog-gray skirts and sweaters. Their eyes were too deeply set, their skin the white of fresh bone. The one on the left of the sofa was a giantess, or almost, the one on the right was little more than a dwarf, and, between them, was a woman Laura was certain would be her own height. They followed her with their eyes as she entered the room, and they said nothing.

Laura had not known they would be there.

Something wriggled and fell in her nasal cavity. Laura fumbled in her sleeve for a tissue, and she blew her nose into it. She crumpled the tissue and flung it and its contents onto the coals of the fire, watched it crumple and blacken and become orange lace. She watched the maggots shrivel and brown and burn.

This done, she turned back to the women on the couch. They had not moved since she had entered, not a muscle, not a hair. They stared at her.

'Hello. Is this your farm?' she asked.

The largest of the women nodded. Her hands were very red, and her expression was impassive.

'Shadow – that's the guy hanging on the tree. He's my husband. He said I should tell you that he wants you to give me water.' Something large shifted in her bowels. It squirmed, and then was still.

The smallest woman nodded. She clambered off the couch. Her feet had not previously touched the floor. She scurried from the room.

Laura could hear doors opening and closing, through the farmhouse. Then, from outside, she could hear a series of loud creaks. Each was followed by a splash of water.

Soon enough, the small woman returned. She was carrying a brown earthenware jug of water. She put it down, carefully, on the table, and retreated to the couch. She pulled herself up, with a wriggle and a shiver, and was seated beside her sisters once again.

'Thank you.' Laura walked over to the table, looked around for a cup or a glass, but there was nothing like that to be seen. She picked up the jug. It was heavier than it looked. The water in it was perfectly clear.

She raised the jug to her lips and began to drink.

The water was colder than she had ever imagined liquid water could be. It froze her tongue and her teeth and her gullet. Still, she drank, unable to stop drinking, feeling the water freezing its way into her stomach, her bowels, her heart, her veins.

The water flowed into her. It was like drinking liquid ice.

She realized that the jug was empty and, surprised, she put it down on the table.

The women were observing her, dispassionately. Since her death, Laura had not thought in metaphors: things were, or they were not. But now, as she looked at the women on the sofa, she found herself thinking of juries, of scientists observing a laboratory animal.

She shook, suddenly and convulsively. She reached out a hand to the table to steady herself, but the table was slipping and lurching, and it almost avoided her grasp. As she put her hand on the table she began to vomit. She brought up bile and formalin, centipedes, and maggots. And then she felt herself starting to void, and to piss: stuff was being pushed violently, wetly, from her body. She would have screamed if she could; but then the dusty floorboards came up to meet her so fast and so hard that, had she been breathing, they would have knocked the breath from her body.

Time rushed over her and into her, swirling like a dust-devil. A thousand memories began to play at once: she was wet and stinking on the floor of the farmhouse; and she was lost in a department store the week before Christmas and her father was nowhere to be seen; and now she was sitting in the bar at Chi-Chi's, ordering a strawberry daiquiri and checking out her blind date, the big, grave man-child, and wondering how he kissed; and she was in the car as, sickeningly, it rolled and jolted, and Robbie was screaming at her until the metal post finally stopped the car, but not its contents, from moving . . .

The water of time, which comes from the spring of fate, Urd's Well, is not the water of life. Not quite. It feeds the roots of the world tree, though. And there is no other water like it.

When Laura woke in the empty farmhouse room, she was shivering, and her breath actually steamed in the morning air. There was a scrape on the back of her hand, and a smear of blood on the scrape, the red-orange of fresh blood.

And she knew where she had to go. She had drunk from the water of time, which comes from the spring of fate. She could see the mountain in her mind.

She licked the blood from the back of her hand, marveling at the film of saliva, and she began to walk.

* * *

It was a wet March day, and it was unseasonably cold, and the storms of the previous few days had lashed their way across the southern states, which meant that there were very few real tourists at Rock City on Lookout Mountain. The Christmas lights had been taken down, the summer visitors were yet to start arriving.

Still, there were a number of people there. There was even a tour bus that drew up that morning, releasing a dozen men and women with perfect tans and gleaming, reassuring smiles. They looked like news anchors, and one could almost imagine there was a phosphor-dot quality to them: they seemed to blur gently as they moved. A black HumVee was parked in the front lot of Rock City, near to Rocky the animatronic gnome.

The TV people walked intently through Rock City, stationing themselves near the balancing rock, where they talked to each other in pleasant, reasonable voices.

They were not the only visitors. If you had walked the paths of Rock City that day, you might have noticed people who looked like movie stars, and people who looked like aliens and a number of people who looked most of all like the idea of a person and nothing like the reality. You might have seen them, but most likely you would never have noticed them at all.

They came to Rock City in long limousines and in small sports cars and in oversized SUVs. Many of them wore the sunglasses of those who habitually wear sunglasses indoors and out, and do not willingly or comfortably remove them.

There were suntans and suits and shades and smiles and scowls. They came in all sizes and shapes, all ages and styles.

All they had in common was a look, a very specific look. It said, *you know me*; or perhaps, *you ought to know me*. An instant familiarity that was also a distance, a look, or an attitude – the confidence that the world existed for them, and that it welcomed them, and that they were adored.

The fat kid moved among them with the shuffle of one who, despite having no social skills, has still become successful beyond his dreams. His black coat flapped in the wind.

Something that stood beside the soft drink stand in Mother Goose Court coughed to attract his attention. It was massive, and scalpel-blades jutted from its face and its fingers. Its face was cancerous. 'It will be a mighty battle,' it told him, in a glutinous voice.

'It's not going to be a battle,' said the fat kid. 'All we're facing here is a fucking paradigm shift. It's a shakedown. Modalities like *battle* are so fucking Lao Tzu.'

The cancerous thing blinked at him. 'Waiting,' is all it said in reply.

'Whatever,' said the fat kid. Then, 'I'm looking for Mister World. You seen him?'

The thing scratched itself with a scalpel-blade, a tumorous lower lip pushed out in concentration. Then it nodded. 'Over there,' it said.

The fat kid walked away, without a thank you, in the direction indicated. The cancerous thing waited, saying nothing, until the kid was out of sight.

'It *will* be a battle,' said the cancerous thing to a woman whose face was smudged with phosphor-dots.

She nodded, and leaned closer to it. 'So how does that make you *feel*?' she asked, in a sympathetic voice.

It blinked, and then it began to tell her.

**

Town's Ford Explorer had a global positioning system, a little
silver box that listened to the satellites and whispered back
to the car its location, but he still got lost once he got south
of Blacksburg and onto the country roads: the roads he drove
seemed to bear little relationship to the tangle of lines on the
map on the screen. Eventually he stopped the car in a
country lane, wound down the window and asked a fat white
woman being pulled by a wolfhound on its early morning
walk for directions to Ashtree farm.

She nodded, and pointed and said something to him. He
could not understand what she had said, but he said thanks
a million and wound up the window and drove off in the
general direction she had indicated.

He kept going for another forty minutes, down country
road after country road, each of them promising, none of
them the road he sought. Town began to chew his lower lip.

'I'm too old for this shit,' he said aloud, relishing the
movie-star world-weariness of the line.

He was pushing fifty. Most of his working life had been
spent in a branch of government which went only by its
initials, and whether or not he had left his government job a
dozen years ago for employment by the private sector was a
matter of opinion: some days he thought one way, some days
another. Anyway, it was only when you got down to the joes
on the street that anyone seemed to assume there was a
difference.

He was on the verge of giving up on the farm when he
drove up a hill and saw the sign, hand painted, on the gate.
It said simply, as he had been told it would, ASH. He pulled
up the Ford Explorer, climbed out and untwisted the wire
that held the gate closed. He got back in the car and drove
through.

It was like cooking a frog, he thought. You put the frog in
the water, and then you turn on the heat. And by the time the

frog notices that there's anything wrong, it's already been cooked. The world in which he worked was all too weird. There was no solid ground beneath his feet; the water in the pot was bubbling fiercely.

When he'd been transferred to the Agency it had all seemed so simple. Now it was all so – not complex, he decided; merely bizarre. He had been sitting in Mr World's office at two that morning, and he had been told what he was to do. 'You got it?' said Mr World, handing him the knife in its dark leather sheath. 'Cut me a stick. It doesn't have to be longer than a couple of feet.'

'Affirmative,' he said. And then he said, 'Why do I have to do this, sir?'

'Because I tell you to,' said Mr World, flatly. 'Find the tree. Do the job. Meet me down in Chattanooga. Don't waste any time.'

'And what about the asshole?'

'Shadow? If you see him, just avoid him. Don't touch him. Don't even mess with him. I don't want you turning him into a martyr. There's no room for martyrs in the current game-plan.' He smiled then, his scarred smile. Mr World was easily amused. Mr Town had noticed this on several occasions. It had amused him to play chauffeur, in Kansas, after all.

'Look—'

'No martyrs, Town.'

And Town had nodded, and taken the knife in its sheath, and pushed the rage that welled up inside him down deep and away.

Mr Town's hatred of Shadow had become a part of him. As he was falling asleep he would see Shadow's solemn face, see that smile that wasn't a smile, the way Shadow had of smiling without smiling that made Town want to sink his fist into the man's gut, and even as he fell asleep he could feel his jaws squeeze together, his temples tense, his gullet burn.

He drove the Ford Explorer across the meadow, past an abandoned farmhouse. He crested a ridge and saw the tree.

He parked the car a little way past it, and turned off the engine. The clock on the dashboard said it was 6:38 a.m. He left the keys in the car, and walked toward the tree.

The tree was large; it seemed to exist on its own sense of scale. Town could not have said if it was fifty feet high or two hundred. Its bark was the gray of a fine silk scarf.

There was a naked man tied to the trunk a little way above the ground by a webwork of ropes, and there was something wrapped in a sheet at the foot of the tree. Town realized what it was as he passed it. He pushed at the sheet with his foot. Wednesday's ruined half-a-face stared out at him. He would have expected it to be alive with maggots and flies, but it was untouched by insects. It didn't even smell bad. It looked just as it had when he had taken it to the motel.

Town reached the tree. He walked a little way around the thick trunk, away from the sightless eyes of the farmhouse, then he unzipped his fly and pissed against the trunk of the tree. He did up his fly. He walked back over to the house, found a wooden extension ladder, carried it back to the tree. He leaned it carefully against the trunk. Then he climbed up it.

Shadow hung, limply, from the ropes that tied him to the tree. Town wondered if the man were still alive: his chest did not rise or fall. Dead or almost dead, it did not matter.

'Hello, asshole,' Town said, aloud. Shadow did not move.

Town reached the top of the ladder, and he pulled out the knife. He found a small branch which seemed to meet Mr World's specifications, and hacked at the base of it with the knife-blade, cutting it half-through, then breaking it off with his hand. It was about thirty inches long.

He put the knife back in its sheath. Then he started to climb back down the ladder. When he was opposite Shadow, he paused. 'God, I hate you,' he said. He wished he could just have taken out a gun and shot him, and he knew that he could not. And then he jabbed the stick in the air toward the hanging man, in a stabbing motion. It was an instinctive gesture, containing all the frustration and rage inside Town. He imagined that he was holding a spear and twisting it into Shadow's guts.

'Come on,' he said, aloud. 'Time to get moving.' Then he thought, *first sign of madness. Talking to yourself.* He climbed down a few more steps, then jumped the rest of the way to the ground. He looked at the stick he was holding, and felt like a small boy, holding his stick as a sword or a spear. *I could have cut a stick from any tree, he thought. It didn't have to be this tree. Who the fuck would have known?*

And he thought, *Mr World would have known.*

He carried the ladder back to the farmhouse. From the corner of his eye he thought he saw something move, and he looked in through the window, into the dark room filled with broken furniture, with the plaster peeling from the walls, and for a moment, in a half-dream, he imagined that he saw three women sitting in the dark parlor.

One of them was knitting. One of them was staring directly at him. One of them appeared to be asleep. The woman who was staring at him began to smile, a huge smile that seemed to split her face lengthwise, a smile that crossed from ear to ear. Then she raised a finger and touched it to her neck, and ran it gently from one side of her neck to the other.

That was what he thought he saw, all in a moment, in that empty room, which contained, he saw at a second glance, nothing more than old rotting furniture and fly-spotted prints and dry rot. There was nobody there at all.

He rubbed his eyes.

Town walked back to the brown Ford Explorer and climbed in. He tossed the stick onto the white leather of the passenger seat. He turned the key in the ignition. The dashboard clock said 6:37 a.m. Town frowned, and checked his wristwatch, which blinked that it was 13:58.

Great, he thought. *I was either up on that tree for eight hours, or for minus a minute.* That was what he thought, but what he believed was that both timepieces had, coincidentally, begun to misbehave.

On the tree, Shadow's body began to bleed. The wound was in his side. The blood that came from it was slow and thick and treacle-black.

He did not move. If he was sleeping, he did not wake.

***

Clouds covered the top of Lookout Mountain.

Easter sat some distance away from the crowd at the bottom of the mountain, watching the dawn over the hills to the east. She had a chain of blue forget-me-nots tattooed around her left wrist, and she rubbed them, absently, with her right thumb.

Another night had come and gone, and nothing. The folk were still coming, by ones and twos. The last night had brought several creatures from the southwest, including two young boys each the size of an apple tree, and something which she had only glimpsed, but which had looked like a disembodied head the size of a VW bug. They had disappeared into the trees at the base of the mountain.

Nobody bothered them. Nobody from the outside world even seemed to have noticed they were there: she imagined the tourists at Rock City staring down at them through their insert-a-quarter binoculars, staring straight at a ramshackle encampment of things and people at the foot of the mountain, and seeing nothing but trees and bushes and rocks.

She could smell the smoke from a cooking fire, a smell of burning bacon on the chilly dawn wind. Someone at the far end of the encampment began to play the harmonica, which made her, involuntarily, smile and shiver. She had a paperback book in her backpack, and she waited for the sky to become light enough for her to read.

There were two dots in the sky, immediately below the

clouds: a small one and a larger one. A spatter of rain brushed her face in the morning wind.

A barefoot girl came out from the encampment, walking toward her. She stopped beside a tree, hitched up her skirts, and squatted. When she had finished, Easter hailed her. The girl walked over.

'Good morning, lady,' she said. 'The battle will start soon now.' The tip of her pink tongue touched her scarlet lips. She had a black crow's wing tied with leather onto her shoulder, a crow's foot on a chain around her neck. Her arms were blue-tattooed with lines and patterns and intricate knots.

'How do you know?'

The girl grinned. 'I am Macha, of the Morrigan. When war comes, I can smell it in the air. I am a war goddess, and I say, blood shall be spilled this day.'

'Oh,' said Easter. 'Well. There you go.' She was watching the smaller dot in the sky as it tumbled down toward them, dropping like a rock.

'And we shall fight them, and we shall kill them, every one,' said the girl. 'And we shall take their heads as trophies, and the crows shall have their eyes and their corpses.' The dot had become a bird, its wings outstretched, riding the gusty morning winds above them.

Easter cocked her head on one side. 'Is that some hidden war goddess knowledge?' she asked. 'The whole "who's going to win" thing? Who gets whose head?'

'No,' said the girl. 'I can smell the battle, but that's all. But we'll win. Won't we? We *have* to. I saw what they did to the all-father. It's them or us.'

'Yeah,' said Easter. 'I suppose it is.'

The girl smiled again, in the half-light, and made her way back to the camp. Easter put her hand down and touched a green shoot which stabbed up from the earth like a knife blade. As she touched it it grew, and opened, and twisted, and changed, until she was resting her hand on a green tulip head. When the sun was high the flower would open.

Easter looked up at the hawk. 'Can I help you?' she said.

The hawk circled about fifteen feet above Easter's head, slowly, then it glided down to her, and landed on the ground nearby. It looked up at her with mad eyes.

'Hello, cutie,' she said. 'Now, what do you really look like, eh?'

The hawk hopped toward her, uncertainly, and then it was no longer a hawk, but a young man. He looked at her, and then looked down at the grass. 'You?' he said. His glance went everywhere, to the grass, to the sky, to the bushes. Not to her.

'Me,' she said. 'What about me?'

'You.' He stopped. He seemed to be trying to muster his thoughts; strange expressions flitted and swam across his face. *He spent too long a bird*, she thought. *He has forgotten how to be a man.* She waited patiently. Eventually, he said, 'Will you come with me?'

'Maybe. Where do you want me to go?'

'The man on the tree. He needs you. A ghost hurt, in his side. The blood came, then it stopped. I think he is dead.'

'There's a war on. I can't just go running away.'

The naked man said nothing, just moved from one foot to another as if he were uncertain of his weight, as if he were used to resting on the air or on a swaying branch, not on the solid and unchanging earth. Then he said, 'If he is gone forever, it is all over.'

'But the battle—'

'If he is lost, it will not matter who wins.' He looked like he needed a blanket, and a cup of sweet coffee, and someone to take him somewhere he could shiver and babble until he got his mind back. He held his arms stiffly against his sides.

'Where is this? Nearby?'

He stared at the tulip plant, and shook his head. 'Way away.'

'Well,' she said, 'I'm needed here. And I can't just leave. How do you expect me to get there? I can't fly, like you, you know.'

'No,' said Horus. 'You can't.' Then he looked up, gravely, and pointed to the other dot that circled them, as it dropped from the darkening clouds, growing in size. '*He* can.'

* * *

Another several hours' pointless driving, and by now Town hated the global positioning system almost as much as he hated Shadow. There was no passion in the hate, though. He had thought finding his way to the farm, to the great silver ash tree, had been hard; finding his way *away* from the farm was much harder. It did not seem to matter which road he took, which direction he drove down the narrow country lanes – the twisting Virginia back roads which must have begun, he was sure, as deer trails and cow paths – eventually he would find himself passing the farm once more, and the hand-painted sign, ASH.

This was crazy, wasn't it? He simply had to retrace his way, take a left turn for every right he had taken on his way here, a right turn for every left.

Only that was what he had done last time, and now here he was, back at the farm once more. There were heavy storm clouds coming in, it was getting dark fast, it felt like night, not morning, and he had a long drive ahead of him: he would never get to Chattanooga before afternoon at this rate.

His cell phone gave him only a *No Service* message. The fold-out map in the car's glove compartments showed the main roads, all the interstates and the real highways, but as far as it was concerned nothing else existed.

Nor was there anyone around that he could ask. The houses were set back from the roads; there were no welcoming lights. Now the fuel gauge was nudging Empty. He heard a rumble of distant thunder, and a single drop of rain splashed heavily onto his windshield.

So when Town saw the woman, walking along the side of the road, he found himself smiling, involuntarily. 'Thank

God,' he said, aloud, and he drew up beside her. He thumbed down her window. 'Ma'am? I'm sorry. I'm kind of lost. Can you tell me how to get to Highway 81 from here?'

She looked at him through the open passenger-side window and said, 'You know, I don't think I can explain it. But I can show you, if you like.' She was pale and her wet hair was long and dark.

'Climb in,' said Town. He didn't even hesitate. 'First thing, we need to buy some gas.'

'Thanks,' she said. 'I needed a ride.' She got in. Her eyes were astonishingly blue. 'There's a stick here, on the seat,' she said, puzzled.

'Just throw it in the back. Where are you heading?' he asked. 'Lady, if you can get me to a gas station, and back to a freeway, I'll take you all the way to your own front door.'

She said, 'Thank you. But I think I'm going further than you are. If you can get me to the freeway, that will be fine. Maybe a trucker will give me a ride.' And she smiled, a crooked, determined smile. It was the smile that did it.

'Ma'am,' he said, 'I can give you a finer ride than any trucker.' He could smell her perfume. It was heady and heavy, a cloying scent, like magnolias or lilacs, but he did not mind.

'I'm going to Georgia,' she said. 'It's a long way.'

'I'm going to Chattanooga. I'll take you as far as I can.'

'Mmm,' she said. 'What's your name?'

'They call me Mack,' said Mr Town. When he was talking to women in bars, he would sometimes follow that up with 'And the ones that know me really well call me Big Mack.' That could wait. They would have many hours in each other's company to get to know each other, after all. 'What's yours?'

'Laura,' she told him.

'Well, Laura,' he said, 'I'm sure we're going to be great friends.'

**

The fat kid found Mr World in the Rainbow Room – a walled section of the path, its window glass covered in clear plastic sheets of green and red and yellow film. He was walking impatiently from window to window, staring out, in turn, at a golden world, a red world, a green world. His hair was reddish-orange and close-cropped to his skull. He wore a Burberry raincoat.

The fat kid coughed. Mr World looked up.

'Excuse me? Mister World?'

'Yes? Is everything on schedule?'

The fat kid's mouth was dry. He licked his lips, and said, 'I've set up everything. I don't have confirmation on the choppers.'

'The helicopters will be here when we need them.'

'Good,' said the fat kid. 'Good.' He stood there, not saying anything, not going away. There was a bruise on his forehead.

After a while Mr World said, 'Is there anything else I can do for you?'

A pause. The boy swallowed and nodded. 'Something else,' he said. 'Yes.'

'Would you feel more comfortable discussing it in private?'

The boy nodded again.

Mr World walked with the kid back to his operations center: a damp cave containing a diorama of drunken pixies making moonshine with a still. A sign outside warned tourists away during renovations. The two men sat down on plastic chairs.

'How can I help you?' asked Mr World.

'Yes. Okay. Right, two things, Okay. One. What are we waiting for? And two. Two is harder. Look. We have the guns. Right. We have the firepower. They have fucking swords and knives and fucking hammers and stone axes. And like, tire irons. We have fucking *smart* bombs.'

'Which we will not be using,' pointed out the other man.

'I know that. You said that already. I know that. And that's doable. But. Look, ever since I did the job on that bitch in LA I've been . . .' He stopped, made a face, seemed unwilling to go on.

'You've been troubled?'

'Yes. Good word. *Troubled*. Yes. Like a home for troubled teens. Funny. Yes.'

'And what exactly is troubling you?'

'Well, we fight, we win.'

'And that is a source of trouble? I find it a matter of triumph and delight, myself.'

'But. They'll die out anyway. They are passenger pigeons and thylacines. Yes? Who cares? This way, it's going to be a bloodbath. If we just wait them out, we get the whole thing.'

'Ah.' Mr World nodded.

He was following. That was good. The fat kid said, 'Look, I'm not the only one who feels this way. I've checked with the crew at Radio Modern, and they're all for settling this peacefully; and the Intangibles are pretty much in favor of letting market forces take care of it. I'm being. You know. The voice of reason here.'

'You are indeed. Unfortunately, there is information you do not have.' The smile that followed was twisted and scarred.

The boy blinked. He said, 'Mister World? What happened to your lips?'

World sighed. 'The truth of the matter,' he said, 'is that somebody sewed them together. A long time ago.'

'Whoa,' said the fat kid. 'Serious *omertà* shit.'

'Yes. You want to know what we're waiting for? Why we didn't strike last night?'

The fat kid nodded. He was sweating, but it was a cold sweat.

'We didn't strike yet, because I'm waiting for a stick.'

'A stick?'

'That's right. A stick. And do you know what I'm going to do with the stick?'

A head shake. 'Okay. I'll bite. What?'

'I could tell you,' said Mr World, soberly. 'But then I'd have to kill you.' He winked, and the tension in the room evaporated.

The fat kid began to giggle, a low, snuffling laugh in the back of his throat and in his nose. 'Okay,' he said. '*Hee. Hee.* Okay. *Hee.* Got it. Message received on Planet Technical. Loud and clear. Ixnay on the Estionsquay.'

Mr World shook his head. He rested a hand on the fat kid's shoulder. 'Hey,' he said. 'You really want to know?'

'Sure.'

'Well,' said Mr World, 'seeing that we're friends, here's the answer: I'm going to take the stick, and I'm going to throw it over the armies as they come together. As I throw it, it will become a spear. And then, as the spear arcs over the battle, I'm going to shout "I dedicate this battle to Odin".'

'Huh?' said the fat kid. 'Why?'

'Power,' said Mr World. He scratched his chin. 'And food. A combination of the two. You see, the outcome of the battle is unimportant. What matters is the chaos, and the slaughter.'

'I don't get it.'

'Let me show you. It'll be just like this,' said Mr World, 'Watch!' He took the wooden-bladed hunter's knife from the pocket of his Burberry and, in one fluid movement, he slipped the blade of it into the soft flesh beneath the fat kid's chin, and pushed hard upward, toward the brain. 'I dedicate this death to Odin,' he said, as the knife sank in.

There was a leakage onto his hand of something that was not actually blood, and a sputtering sparking noise behind the fat kid's eyes. The smell on the air was that of burning insulation wire, as if somewhere a plug was overloading.

The fat kid's hand twitched spastically, and then he fell. The expression on his face was one of puzzlement, and misery. 'Look at him,' said Mr World, conversationally, to the air. 'He looks as if he just saw a sequence of zeroes and ones turn into a cluster of brightly colored birds, and then just fly away.'

There was no reply from the empty rock corridor.

Mr World shouldered the body as if it weighed very little, and he opened the pixie diorama and dropped the body beside the still, covering it with its long black raincoat. He would dispose of it that evening, he decided, and he grinned his scarred grin: hiding a body on a battlefield would almost be too easy. Nobody would ever notice. Nobody would care.

For a little while there was silence in that place. And then a gruff voice, which was not Mr World's cleared its throat in the shadows, and said, 'Good start.'

Chapter Eighteen

They tried to stand off the soldiers, but the men fired and killed them both. So the song's wrong about the jail, but that's put in for poetry. You can't always have things like they are in poetry. Poetry hain't what you'd call truth. There ain't room enough in the verses.

— A singer's commentary on 'The Ballad of Sam Bass'.
A Treasury of American Folklore

None of this can actually be happening. If it makes you more comfortable, you could simply think of it as metaphor. Religions are, by definition, metaphors, after all: God is a dream, a hope, a woman, an ironist, a father, a city, a house of many rooms, a watchmaker who left his prize chronometer in the desert, someone who loves you – even, perhaps, against all evidence, a celestial being whose only interest is to make sure your football team, army, business, or marriage thrives, prospers and triumphs over all opposition.

Religions are places to stand and look and act, vantage points from which to view the world.

So, none of this is happening. Such things could not occur

in this day and age. Never a word of it is literally true, although it all happened, and the next thing that happened, happened like this:

At the foot of Lookout Mountain, which is scarcely more than a very high hill, men and women were gathered around a small bonfire in the rain. They stood beneath the trees, which provided poor cover, and they were arguing.

The lady Kali, with her ink-black skin and white, sharp teeth, said, 'It is time.'

Anansi, with lemon-yellow gloves and silvering hair shook his head. 'We can wait,' he said. 'While we *can* wait, we *should* wait.'

There was a murmur of disagreement from the crowd.

'No, listen. He's right,' said an old man with iron-gray hair: Czernobog. He was holding a small sledgehammer, resting the head of it on his shoulder. 'They have the high ground. The weather is against us. This is madness, to begin this now.'

Something that looked a little like a wolf and a little more like a man, grunted and spat on the forest floor. 'When better to attack them, *dedushka*? Shall we wait until the weather clears, when they expect it? I say we go now. I say we move.'

'There are clouds, between us and them,' pointed out Isten of the Hungarians. He had a fine black moustache, a large, dusty black hat, and the grin of a man who makes his living selling aluminum siding and new roofs and gutters to senior citizens but who always leaves town the day after the checks clear whether the work is done or not.

A man in an elegant suit, who had until now said nothing, put his hands together, stepped into the firelight, and made his point succinctly and clearly. There were nods and mutters of agreement.

A voice came from one of three warrior-women who comprised the Morrigan, standing so close together in the shadows that they had become an arrangement of blue-tattooed limbs and dangling crow's wings. She said, 'It doesn't matter whether this is a good time or a bad time. This is *the* time. They have been killing us. They will continue to kill us, whether we fight or not. Perhaps we will triumph. Perhaps we will die. Better to die together, on the attack, like gods, than to die fleeing and singly, like rats in a cellar.'

Another murmur, this time one of deep agreement. She had said it for all of them. Now was the time.

'The first head is mine,' said a very tall Chinese man, with a rope of tiny skulls around his neck. He began to walk, slowly and intently, up the mountain, shouldering a staff with a curved blade at the end of it, like a silver moon.

* * *

Even Nothing cannot last forever.

He might have been there, been Nowhere, for ten minutes or for ten thousand years. It made no difference. Time was an idea for which he no longer had any need.

He could no longer remember his real name. He felt empty and cleansed, in that place that was not a place.

He was without form, and void.

He was nothing.

And into that nothing a voice said, 'Ho-hoka, cousin. We got to talk.'

And something that might once have been Shadow said, 'Whiskey Jack?'

'Yeah,' said Whiskey Jack, in the darkness. 'You are a hard man to hunt down, when you're dead. You didn't go to any of the places I figured. I had to look all over before I thought of checking here. Say, you ever find your tribe?'

Shadow remembered the man and the girl in the disco beneath the spinning mirror-ball. 'I guess I found my family. But no, I never found my tribe.'

'Sorry to have to disturb you.'

'No. You aren't sorry. Let me be. I got what I wanted. I'm done.'

'They are coming for you,' said Whiskey Jack. 'They are going to revive you.'

'But I'm done,' said Shadow. 'It was all over and done.'

'No such thing,' said Whiskey Jack. 'Never any such thing. We'll go to my place. You want a beer?'

He guessed he *would* like a beer, at that. 'Sure.'

'Get me one too. There's a cooler outside the door,' said Whiskey Jack, and he pointed. They were in his shack.

Shadow opened the door to the shack with hands it seemed to him he had not possessed moments before. There was a plastic cooler filled with chunks of river-ice out there, and, in the ice, a dozen cans of Budweiser. He pulled out a couple of cans of beer and then sat in the doorway and looked out over the valley.

They were at the top of a hill, near a waterfall, swollen with melting snow and run-off. It fell, in stages, maybe seventy feet below them, maybe a hundred. The sun reflected from the ice which sheathed the trees that overhung the waterfall basin. The churning noise as the water crashed and fell filled the air.

'Where are we?' asked Shadow.

'Where you were last time,' said Whiskey Jack. 'My place. You planning on holding on to my Bud till it warms up? They aren't good like that.'

Shadow stood up and passed him the can of beer. 'You didn't have a waterfall outside your place last time I was here,' he said.

Whiskey Jack said nothing. He popped the top of the Bud, and drank half the can in one long slow swallow. Then he said, 'You remember my nephew? Henry Bluejay? The poet? He traded his Buick for your Winnebago. Remember?'

'Sure. I didn't know he was a poet.'

Whiskey Jack raised his chin and looked proud. 'Best damn poet in America,' he said.

He drained the rest of his can of beer, belched, and got another can, while Shadow popped open his own can of beer, and the two men sat outside on a rock, by the pale green ferns, in the morning sun, and they watched the falling water and they drank their beer. There was still snow on the ground, in the places where the shadows never lifted.

The earth was muddy and wet.

'Henry was diabetic,' continued Whiskey Jack. 'It happens. Too much. You people came to America, you take our sugar cane, potatoes and corn, then you sell us potato chips and caramel popcorn, and we're the ones who get sick.' He sipped his beer, reflecting. 'He'd won a couple of prizes for his poetry. There were people in Minnesota who wanted to put his poems into a book. He was driving to Minnesota in a sports car to talk to them. He had traded your 'Bago for a yellow Miata. The doctors said they think he went into a coma while he was driving, went off the road, ran the car into one of your road signs. Too lazy to look at where you are, to read the mountains and the clouds, you people need road signs everywhere. And so Henry Bluejay went away forever, went to live with brother wolf. So I said, nothing keeping me there any longer. I came north. Good fishing up here.'

'I'm sorry about your nephew.'

'Me too. So now I'm living here in the north. Long way from white man's diseases. White man's roads. White man's road signs. White man's yellow Miatas. White man's caramel popcorn.'

'White man's beer?'

Whiskey Jack looked at the can. 'When you people finally give up and go home, you can leave us the Budweiser breweries,' he said.

'Where are we?' asked Shadow. 'Am I on the tree? Am I dead? Am I here? I thought everything was finished. What's real?'

'Yes,' said Whiskey Jack.

'Yes? What kind of an answer is *Yes*?'

'It's a good answer. True answer, too.'

Shadow said, 'Are you a god as well?'

Whiskey Jack shook his head. 'I'm a culture hero,' he said. 'We do the same shit gods do, we just screw up more and nobody worships us. They tell stories about us, but they tell the ones which make us look bad along with the ones where we came out fairly okay.'

'I see,' said Shadow. And he did see, more or less.

'Look,' said Whiskey Jack. 'This is not a good country for gods. My people figured that out early on. There are creator spirits who found the earth or made it or shit it out, but you think about it: who's going to worship Coyote? He made love to Porcupine Woman and got his dick shot through with more needles than a pincushion. He'd argue with rocks and the rocks would win.

'So, yeah, my people figured that maybe there's something at the back of it all, a creator, a great spirit, and so we say thank you to it, because it's always good to say thank you. But we never built churches. We didn't need to. The land was the church. The land was the religion. The land was older and wiser than the people who walked on it. It gave us salmon and corn and buffalo and passenger pigeons. It gave us wild rice and walleye. It gave us melon and squash and turkey. And we were the children of the land, just like the porcupine and the skunk and the blue jay.'

He finished his second beer and gestured toward the river at the bottom of the waterfall. 'You follow that river for a way, you'll get to the lakes where the wild rice grows. In wild rice time, you go out in your canoe with a friend, and you knock the wild rice into your canoe, and cook it, and store it, and it will keep you for a long time. Different places grow different foods. Go far enough south there are orange trees, lemon trees, and those squashy green guys, look like pears—'

'Avocados.'

'Avocados,' agreed Whiskey Jack. 'That's them. They don't grow up this way. This is wild rice country. Moose country. What I'm trying to say is that America is like that. It's not good growing country for gods. They don't grow well here.

They're like avocados trying to grow in wild rice country.'

'They may not grow well,' said Shadow, remembering, 'but they're going to war.'

That was the only time he ever saw Whiskey Jack laugh. It was almost a bark, and it had little humor in it. 'Hey Shadow,' said Whiskey Jack. 'If all your friends jumped off a cliff, would you jump off too?'

'Maybe.' Shadow felt good. He didn't think it was just the beer. He couldn't remember the last time he had felt so alive, and so together.

'It's not going to be a war.'

'Then what is it?'

Whiskey Jack crushed the beer can between his hands, pressing it until it was flat. 'Look,' he said, and pointed to the waterfall. The sun was high enough that it caught the waterfall spray: a rainbow nimbus hung in the air. Shadow thought it was the most beautiful thing he had ever seen.

'It's going to be a bloodbath,' said Whiskey Jack, flatly.

Shadow saw it then. He saw it all, stark in its simplicity. He shook his head, then he began to chuckle, and he shook his head some more, and the chuckle became a full-throated laugh.

'You okay?'

'I'm fine,' said Shadow. 'I just saw the hidden Indians. Not all of them. But I saw them anyhow.'

'Probably Ho Chunk, then. Those guys never could hide worth a damn.' He looked up at the sun. 'Time to go back,' he said. He stood up.

'It's a two-man con,' said Shadow. 'It's not a war at all, is it?'

Whiskey Jack patted Shadow's arm. 'You're not so dumb,' he said.

They walked back to Whiskey Jack's shack. He opened the door. Shadow hesitated. 'I wish I could stay here with you,' he said. 'This seems like a good place.'

'There are a lot of good places,' said Whiskey Jack. 'That's kind of the point. Listen, gods die when they are forgotten. People too. But the land's still here. The good places, and the bad. The land isn't going anywhere. And neither am I.'

Shadow closed the door. Something was pulling at him. He was alone in the darkness once more, but the darkness became brighter and brighter until it was burning like the sun.

And then the pain began.

***

There was a woman who walked through a meadow, and spring flowers blossomed where she had passed. In this place and at this time, she called herself Easter.

She passed a place where, long ago, a farmhouse had stood. Even today several walls were still standing, jutting out of the weeds and the meadow-grass like rotten teeth. A thin rain was falling. The clouds were dark and low, and it was cold.

A little way beyond the place where the farmhouse had been there was a tree, a huge silver-gray tree, winter-dead to all appearances, and leafless, and in front of the tree, on the grass, were frayed clumps of colorless fabric. The woman stopped at the fabric, and bent down, and picked up something brownish-white: it was a much-gnawed fragment of bone which might, once, have been a part of a human skull. She tossed it back down onto the grass.

Then she looked at the man on the tree and she smiled wryly. 'They just aren't as interesting naked,' she said. 'It's the unwrapping that's half the fun. Like with gifts, and eggs.'

The hawk-headed man who walked beside her looked down at his penis and seemed, for the first time, to become aware of his own nakedness. He said, 'I can look at the sun without even blinking.'

'That's very clever of you,' Easter told him, reassuringly. 'Now, let's get him down from there.'

The wet ropes that held Shadow to the tree had long ago weathered and rotted, and they parted easily as the two people pulled on them. The body on the tree slipped and slid down toward the roots. They caught him as he fell, and they took him up, carrying him easily, although he was a very big man, and they put him down in the gray meadow.

The body on the grass was cold, and it did not breathe. There was a patch of dried black blood on its side, as if it had been stabbed with a spear.

'What now?'

'Now,' she said, 'we warm him. You know what you have to do.'

'I know. I cannot.'

'If you are not willing to help, then you should not have called me here.'

'But it has been too long.'

'It has been too long for all of us.'

'And I am quite mad.'

'I know.' She reached out a white hand to Horus, and she touched his black hair. He blinked at her, intently. Then he shimmered, as if in a heat haze.

The hawk eye that faced her glinted orange, as if a flame had just been kindled inside it; a flame that had been long extinguished.

The hawk took to the air, and it swung upward, circling and ascending in a rising gyre, circling the place in the gray clouds where the sun might conceivably be, and as the hawk rose and it became first a dot and then a speck, and then, to the naked eye, nothing at all, something that could only be imagined. The clouds began to thin and to evaporate, creating a patch of blue sky through which the sun glared. The single bright sunbeam penetrating the clouds and bathing the meadow was beautiful, but the image faded as more clouds vanished. Soon the morning sun was blazing down on that meadow like a summer sun at noon, burning the water vapor from the morning's rain into mists and burning the mist off into nothing at all.

The golden sun bathed the body on the floor of the meadow with its radiance and its heat. Shades of pink and of warm brown, touched the dead thing.

The woman dragged the fingers of her right hand lightly across the body's chest. She imagined she could feel a shiver in his breast – something that was not a heartbeat, but still . . . She let her hand remain there, on his chest, just above his heart.

She lowered her lips to Shadow's lips, and she breathed into his lungs, a gentle in and out, and then the breath became a kiss. Her kiss was gentle, and it tasted of spring rains and meadow flowers.

The wound in his side began to flow with liquid blood once more – a scarlet blood, which oozed like liquid rubies in the sunlight, and then the bleeding stopped.

She kissed his cheek and his forehead. 'Come on,' she said. 'Time to get up. It's all happening. You don't want to miss it.'

His eyes fluttered, and then they opened, two eyes of a gray so deep it was colorless, the gray of evening, and he looked at her.

She smiled, and then she removed her hand from his chest.

He said, 'You called me back.' He said it slowly, as if he had forgotten how to speak English. There was hurt in his voice, and puzzlement.

'Yes.'

'I was done. I was judged. It was over. You called me back. You dared.'

'I'm sorry.'

'Yes.'

He sat up, slowly. He winced, and touched his side. Then he looked puzzled: there was a beading of wet blood there, but there was no wound beneath it.

He reached out a hand, and she put her arm around him and helped him to his feet. He looked across the meadow as if he was trying to remember the names of the things he was looking at: the flowers in the long grass, the ruins of the farmhouse, the haze of green buds that fogged the branches of the huge silver tree.

'Do you remember?' she asked. 'Do you remember what you learned?'

'Yes. It will fade though. Like a dream. I know that. I lost my name, and I lost my heart. And you brought me back.'

'I'm sorry,' she said, for the second time. 'They are going to fight, soon. The old gods and the new ones.'

'You want me to fight for you? You wasted your time.'

'I brought you back because that was what I had to do,' she said. 'It's what I can do. It's what I'm best at. What you do now is whatever you have to do. Your call. I did my part.'

Suddenly, she became aware of his nakedness, and she blushed a burning scarlet flush, and she looked down and away.

***

In the rain and the cloud, shadows moved up the side of the mountain, up to the rock pathways.

White foxes padded up the hill in company with red-haired men in green jackets. There was a bull-headed minotaur walking beside an iron-fingered dactyl. A pig, a monkey, and a sharp-toothed ghoul clambered up the hillside, in company with a blue-skinned man holding a flaming bow, a bear with flowers twined into its fur, and a man in golden chain mail holding his sword of eyes.

Beautiful Antinous, who was the lover of Hadrian, walked up the hillside at the head of a company of leather queens, their arms and chests steroid-swollen and sculpted into perfect shapes.

A gray-skinned man, his one cyclopean eye a huge

cabochon emerald, walked stiffly up the hill, ahead of several squat and swarthy men, their impassive faces as regular as Aztec carvings: they knew the secrets that the jungles had swallowed.

A sniper at the top of the hill took careful aim at a white fox, and fired. There was an explosion, and a puff of cordite, gunpowder scent on the wet air. The corpse was a young Japanese woman with her stomach blown away, and her face all bloody. Slowly, the corpse began to fade.

The people continued up the hill, on two legs, on four legs, on no legs at all.

* * *

The drive through the Tennessee mountain country had been startlingly beautiful whenever the storm had eased, and nerve-wracking whenever the rain had pelted down. Town and Laura had talked and talked and talked the whole way. He was so glad he had met her. It was like meeting an old friend, a really good old friend you'd simply never met before. They talked history and movies and music, and she turned out to be the *only* person, and I mean the only other person he had ever met who had seen a foreign film (Mr Town was sure it was Spanish, while Laura was just as certain it was Polish) from the sixties called *The Manuscript Found in Saragossa*, a film he had been starting to believe he had hallucinated.

When Laura pointed out the first SEE ROCK CITY barn to him he chuckled and admitted that that was where he was headed. She said that was so cool. She always wanted to visit those kinds of places, but she never made the time, and always regretted it later. That was why she was on the road right now. She was having an adventure.

She was a travel agent, she told him. Separated from her husband. She admitted that she didn't think they could ever get back together, and said it was her fault.

'I can't believe that.'

She sighed. 'It's true, Mack. I'm just not the woman he married anymore.'

Well, he told her, people change, and before he could think he was telling her everything he *could* tell her about his life, he was even telling her about Woody and Stoner, how the three of them were the three musketeers, and the two of them were killed, you think you'd get hardened to that kind of thing in government work, but you never did. It never happened.

And she reached out one hand – it was cold enough that he turned up the car's heating – and squeezed his hand tightly in hers.

Lunchtime, they ate bad Japanese food while a thunderstorm lowered on Knoxville, and Town didn't care that the food was late, that the miso soup was cold, or that the sushi was warm.

He loved the fact that she was out, with him, having an adventure.

'Well,' confided Laura, 'I hated the idea of getting stale. I was just rotting away where I was. So I set off without my car and without my credit cards. I'm just relying on the kindness of strangers. And I've had the best time. People have been so good to me.'

'Aren't you scared?' he asked. 'I mean, you could be stranded, you could be mugged, you could starve.'

She shook her head. Then she said, with a hesitant smile, 'I met you, didn't I?' and he couldn't find anything to say.

When the meal was over they ran through the storm to his car holding Japanese-language newspapers to cover their heads, and they laughed as they ran, like schoolchildren in the rain.

'How far can I take you?' he asked, when they made it back into the car.

'I'll go as far as you're going, Mack,' she told him, shyly.

He was glad he hadn't used the Big Mack line. This

woman wasn't a bar-room one nighter, Mr Town knew that in
his soul. It might have taken him fifty years to find her, but
this was finally it, this was the one, this wild, magical
woman with the long dark hair.

This was love.

'Look,' he said, as they approached Chattanooga. The
wipers slooshed the rain across the windshield, blurring the
gray of the city. 'How about I find a motel for you tonight? I'll
pay for it. And once I make my delivery, we can. Well, we
can take a hot bath together, for a start. Warm you up.'

'That sounds wonderful,' said Laura. 'What are you
delivering?'

'That stick,' he told her, and chuckled. 'The one on the
back seat.'

'Okay,' she said, humoring him. 'Then don't tell me, Mister
Mysterious.'

He told her it would be best if she waited in the car in
the Rock City parking lot while he made his delivery. He
drove up the side of Lookout Mountain in the driving rain,
never breaking thirty miles per hour, with his headlights
burning.

They parked at the back of the parking lot. He turned off
the engine.

'Hey. Mack. Before you get out of the car, don't I get a hug?'
asked Laura with a smile.

'You surely do,' said Mr Town, and he put his arms around
her, and she snuggled close to him while the rain pattered a
tattoo on the roof of the Ford Explorer. He could smell her
hair. There was a faintly unpleasant scent beneath the smell
of the perfume. Travel would do it, every time. That bath, he
decided, was a real must for both of them. He wondered if
there was anyplace in Chattanooga where he could get those
scented bath bombs his first wife had loved so much. Laura
raised her head against his, and her hand stroked the line of
his neck, absently.

'Mack . . . I keep thinking. You must really want to know

what happened to those friends of yours?' she asked. 'Woody and Stone. Do you?'

'Yeah,' he said, moving his lips down to hers, for their first kiss. 'Sure I do.'

So she showed him.

***

Shadow walked the meadow, making his own slow circles around the trunk of the tree, gradually widening his circle. Sometimes he would stop and pick something up: a flower, or a leaf, or a pebble, or a twig, or a blade of grass. He would examine it minutely, as if concentrating entirely on the *twigness* of the twig, the *leafness* of the leaf, as if he were seeing it for the first time.

Easter found herself reminded of the gaze of a baby, at the point where it learns to focus.

She did not dare to talk to him. At that moment, it would have been sacrilegious. She watched him, exhausted as she was, and she wondered.

About twenty feet out from the base of the tree, half-overgrown with long meadow-grass and dead creepers, he found a canvas bag. Shadow picked it up, untied the knots at the top of the bag, loosened the drawstring.

The clothes he pulled out were his own. They were old, but still serviceable. He turned the shoes over in his hands. He stroked the fabric of the shirt, the wool of the sweater, stared at them as if he were looking at them across a million years.

For some time he looked at them, then, one by one, he put them on.

He put his hands into his pockets, and looked puzzled as he pulled one hand out holding what looked to Easter like a white and gray marble.

He said, 'No coins.' It was the first thing he had said in several hours.

'No coins?' echoed Easter.

He shook his head. 'It was good to have the coins,' he said. 'They gave me something to do with my hands.' He bent down to pull on his shoes.

Once he was dressed, he looked more normal. Grave, though. She wondered how far he had traveled, and what it had cost him to return. He was not the first whose return she had initiated, and she knew that, soon enough, the million-year stare would fade, and the memories and the dreams that he had brought back from the tree would be elided by the world of things you could touch. That was the way it always went.

She led their way to the rear of the meadow. Her mount waited in the trees.

'It can't carry both of us,' she told him. 'I'll make my own way home.'

Shadow nodded. He seemed to be trying to remember something. Then he opened his mouth, and he screeched a cry of welcome and of joy.

The thunderbird opened its cruel beak, and it screeched a welcome back at him.

Superficially, at least, it resembled a condor. Its feathers were black, with a purplish sheen, and its neck was banded with white. Its beak was black and cruel: a raptor's beak, made for tearing. At rest, on the ground, with its wings folded away, it was the size of a black bear, and its head was on a level with Shadow's own.

Horus said, proudly, 'I brought him. They live in the mountains.'

Shadow nodded. 'I had a dream of thunderbirds once,' he said. 'Damndest dream I ever had.'

The thunderbird opened its beak and made a surprisingly gentle noise, *crawroo*? 'You heard my dream too?' asked Shadow.

He reached out a hand and rubbed it gently against the bird's head. The thunderbird pushed up against him like an affectionate pony. He scratched it behind where the ears must have been.

Shadow turned to Easter. 'You rode him here?'

'Yes,' she said. 'You can ride him back, if he lets you.'

'How do you ride him?'

'It's easy,' she said. 'If you don't fall. Like riding the lightning.'

'Will I see you back there?'

She shook her head. 'I'm done, honey,' she told him. 'You go do what you need to do. I'm tired. Bringing you back like that . . . it took a lot out of me. I need to rest, to save up my energies until my festival begins. I'm sorry. Good luck.'

Shadow nodded. 'Whiskey Jack. I saw him. After I passed on. He came and found me. We drank beer together.'

'Yes,' she said. 'I'm sure you did.'

'Will I ever see you again?' asked Shadow.

She looked at him with eyes the green of ripening corn. She said nothing. Then, abruptly, she shook her head. 'I doubt it,' she said.

Shadow clambered awkwardly onto the thunderbird's back. He felt like a mouse on the back of a hawk. There was an ozone taste in his mouth, metallic and blue. Something crackled. The thunderbird extended its wings, and began to flap them, hard.

As the ground fell away beneath them, Shadow clung on, his heart pounding in his chest like a wild thing.

It was exactly like riding the lightning.

***

Laura took the stick from the back seat of the car. She left Mr Town in the front seat of the Ford Explorer, and climbed out of the car, and walked through the rain to Rock City. The ticket office was closed. The door to the gift shop was not locked and she walked through it, past the rock candy and the display of SEE ROCK CITY birdhouses, into the Eighth Wonder of the World.

Nobody challenged her, although she passed several men and women on the path, in the rain. Many of them looked faintly artificial; several of them were translucent. She walked across a swinging rope bridge. She passed the white deer gardens, and pushed herself through the Fat Man's Squeeze, where the path ran between two rock walls.

And, in the end, she stepped over a chain, with a sign on it telling her that this part of the attraction was closed, and she went into a cavern, and she saw a man sitting on a plastic chair, in front of a diorama of drunken gnomes. He was reading the *Washington Post* by the light of a small electric lantern. When he saw her he folded the paper and placed it beneath his chair. He stood up, a tall man with close-cropped orange hair in an expensive raincoat, and he gave her a small bow.

'I shall assume that Mister Town is dead,' he said. 'Welcome, spear-carrier.'

'Thank you. I'm sorry about Mack,' she said. 'Were you friends?'

'Not at all. He should have kept himself alive, if he wanted to keep his job. But you brought his stick.' He looked her up and down with eyes that glimmered like the orange embers of a dying fire. 'I am afraid you have the advantage of me. They call me Mister World, here at the top of the hill.'

'I'm Shadow's wife.'

'Of course. The lovely Laura,' he said. 'I should have recognized you. He had several photographs of you up above his bed, in the cell that once we shared. And, if you don't mind my saying so, you are looking lovelier than you have any right to look. Shouldn't you be further along on the whole road to rot and ruin business by now?'

'I was,' she said simply. 'I was much further along. I'm not sure what changed. I know when I started feeling better. It was this morning. Those women, in the farm, they gave me water from their well.'

An eyebrow raised. 'Urd's Well? Surely not.'

She pointed to herself. Her skin was pale, and her eye-sockets were dark, but she was manifestly whole: if she was indeed a walking corpse, she was freshly dead.

'It won't last,' said Mr World. 'The Norns gave you a little taste of the past. It will dissolve into the present soon enough, and then those pretty blue eyes will roll out of their sockets and ooze down those pretty cheeks, which will, by then, of course, no longer be so pretty. By the way, you have my stick. Can I have it, please?'

He pulled out a pack of Lucky Strikes, took a cigarette, lit it with a disposable black Bic.

She said, 'Can I have one of those?'

'Sure. I'll give you a cigarette if you give me my stick.'

'No,' she said. 'If you want it, it's worth more than just a cigarette.'

He said nothing.

She said, 'I want answers. I want to know things.'

He lit a cigarette and passed it to her. She took it and inhaled. Then she blinked. 'I can almost taste this one,' she said. 'I think maybe I can.' She smiled. 'Mm. Nicotine.'

'Yes,' he said. 'Why did you go to the women in the farm-house?'

'Shadow told me to go to them,' she said. 'He said to ask them for water.'

'I wonder if he knew what it would do. Probably not. Still, that's the good thing about having him dead on his tree. I know where he is at all times, now. He's off the board.'

'You set up my husband,' she said. 'You set him up all the way, you people. He has a good heart, you know that?'

'Yes,' said Mr World. 'I know.'

'Why did you want him?'

'Patterns, and distraction,' said Mr World. 'When this is all done with, I guess I'll sharpen a stick of mistletoe and go

down to the ash tree, and ram it through his eye. That's what
those morons fighting out there have never been able to
grasp. It's never a matter of old and new. It's only about
patterns. Now. My stick, please.'

'Why do you want it?'

'It's a souvenir of this whole sorry mess,' said Mr World.
'Don't worry, it's not mistletoe.' He flashed a grin. 'It symbolizes
a spear, and in this sorry world, the symbol is the thing.'

The noises from outside grew louder.

'Which side are you on?' she asked.

'It's not about sides,' he told her. 'But since you asked, I'm
on the winning side. Always. That's what I do best.'

She nodded, and she did not let go of the stick. 'I can see
that,' she said.

She turned away from him, and looked out of the cavern
door. Far below her, in the rocks, she could see something
that glowed and pulsed. It wrapped itself around a thin,
mauve-faced bearded man, who was beating at it with a
squeegee stick, the kind of squeegee that people like him use
to smear across car windshields at traffic lights. There was a
scream, and they both disappeared from view.

'Okay. I'll give you the stick,' she said

Mr World's voice came from behind her. 'Good girl,' he
said reassuringly, in a way that struck her as being both
patronizing and indefinably male. It made her skin crawl.

She waited in the rock doorway until she could hear his
breath in her ear. She had to wait until he got close enough.
She had that much figured out.

***

The ride was more than exhilarating; it was electric.

They swept through the storm like jagged bolts of
lightning, flashing from cloud to cloud; they moved like the
thunder's roar, like the swell and rip of the hurricane. It was
a crackling, impossible journey, and Shadow forgot to be

scared almost immediately. You cannot be afraid when you ride the thunderbird. There is no fear: only the power of the storm, unstoppable and all-consuming, and the joy of the flight.

Shadow dug his fingers into the thunderbird's feathers, feeling the static prickle on his skin. Blue sparks writhed across his hands like tiny snakes. Rain washed his face.

'This is the best,' he shouted, over the roar of the storm.

As if it understood him, the bird began to rise higher, every wing-beat a clap of thunder, and it swooped and dove and tumbled through the dark clouds.

'In my dream, I was hunting you,' said Shadow, his words ripped away by the wind. 'In my dream. I had to bring back a feather.'

Yes. The word was a static crackle in the radio of his mind. *They came to us for feathers, to prove that they were men; and they came to us to cut the stones from our heads, to give their dead our lives.*

An image filled his mind then: of a thunderbird – a female, he assumed, for her plumage was brown, not black – lying freshly-dead on the side of a mountain. Beside it was a woman. She was breaking open its skull with a knob of flint. She picked through the wet shards of bone and the brains until she found a smooth clear stone the tawny color of garnet, opalescent fires flickering in its depths. *Eagle stones*, thought Shadow. She was going to take it to her infant son, dead these last three nights, and she would lay it on his cold breast. By the next sunrise the boy would be alive and laughing, and the jewel would be gray and clouded and, like the bird it had been stolen from, quite dead.

'I understand,' he said to the bird.

The bird threw back its head and crowed, and its cry was the thunder.

The world beneath them flashed past in one strange dream.

***

Laura adjusted her grip on the stick, and she waited for the man she knew as Mr World to come to her. She was facing away from him, looking out at the storm, and the dark green hills below.

In this sorry world, she thought, *the symbol is the thing. Yes.*

She felt his hand close softly onto her right shoulder.

Good, she thought. *He does not want to alarm me. He is scared that I will throw his stick out into the storm, that it will tumble down the mountainside, and he will lose it.*

She leaned back, just a little, until she was touching his chest with her back. His left arm curved around her. It was an intimate gesture. His left hand was open in front of her. She closed both of her hands around the top of the stick, exhaled, concentrated.

'Please. My stick,' he said, in her ears.

'Yes,' she said. 'It's yours.' And then, not knowing if it would mean anything, she said, 'I dedicate this death to Shadow,' and she stabbed the stick into her chest, just below the breastbone, felt it writhe and change in her hands as the stick became a spear.

The boundary between sensation and pain had diffused since she had died. She felt the spear head penetrate her chest, felt it push out through her back. A moment's resistance – she pushed harder – and the spear pushed into Mr World. She could feel the warm breath of him on the cool skin of her neck, as he wailed in hurt and surprise, impaled on the spear.

She did not recognize the words he spoke, nor the language he said them in. She pushed the shaft of the spear further in, forcing it through her body, into and through his.

She could feel his hot blood spurting onto her back.

'Bitch,' he said, in English. 'You fucking bitch.' There was a wet gurgling quality to his voice. She guessed that the blade of the spear must have sliced a lung. Mr World was moving now, or trying to move, and every move he made rocked her too: they were joined by the pole, impaled together like two fish on a single spear. He now had a knife in one hand, she saw, and he stabbed her chest and breasts randomly and wildly with the knife, unable to see what he was doing.

She did not care. What are knife-cuts to a corpse?

She brought her fist down, hard, on his waving wrist, and the knife went flying to the floor of the cavern. She kicked it away.

And now he was crying and wailing. She could feel him pushing against her, his hands fumbling at her back, his hot tears on her neck. His blood was soaking her back, spurting down the back of her legs.

'This must look so undignified,' she said, in a dead whisper which was not without a certain dark amusement.

She felt Mr World stumble behind her, and she stumbled too, and then she slipped in the blood – all of it his – that was puddling on the floor of the cave, and they both went down.

***

The thunderbird landed in the Rock City parking lot. Rain was falling in sheets. Shadow could barely see a dozen feet in front of his face. He let go of the thunderbird's feathers and half-slipped, half-tumbled to the wet tarmac.

The bird looked at him. Lightning flashed, and the bird was gone.

Shadow climbed to his feet.

The parking lot was three-quarters empty. Shadow started toward the entrance. He passed a brown Ford Explorer, parked against a rock wall. There was something deeply familiar about the car, and he glanced up at it curiously, noticing the man inside the car, slumped over the steering wheel as if asleep.

Shadow pulled open the driver's door.

He had last seen Mr Town standing outside the motel in the center of America. The expression on his face was one of surprise. His neck had been expertly broken. Shadow touched the man's face. Still warm.

Shadow could smell a scent on the air in the car; it was faint, like the perfume of someone who left a room years before, but Shadow would have known it anywhere. He slammed the door of the Explorer and made his way across the parking lot.

As he walked he felt a twinge in his side, a sharp, jabbing pain that must have only existed in his head, as it lasted for only a second, or less, and then it was gone.

There was nobody in the gift shop, nobody selling tickets. He walked through the building and out into the gardens of Rock City.

Thunder rumbled, and it rattled the branches of the trees and shook deep inside the huge rocks, and the rain fell with cold violence. It was late afternoon, but it was dark as night.

A trail of lightning speared across the clouds, and Shadow wondered if that was the thunderbird returning to its high crags, or just an atmospheric discharge, or whether the two ideas were, on some level, the same thing.

And of course they were. That was the point, after all.

Somewhere a man's voice called out. Shadow heard it. The only words he recognized or thought he recognized were '. . . to *Odin!*'

Shadow hurried across Seven States Flag Court, the flagstones now running fast with a dangerous amount of rainwater. Once he slipped on the slick stone. There was a thick layer of cloud surrounding the mountain, and in the gloom and the storm beyond the courtyard he could see no states at all.

There was no sound. The place seemed utterly abandoned.

He called out, and imagined he heard something

answering. He walked toward the place from which he thought the sound had come.

Nobody. Nothing. Just a chain marking the entrance to a cave as off-limits to guests.

Shadow stepped over the chain.

He looked around, peering into the darkness.

His skin prickled.

A voice from behind him, in the shadows, said, very quietly, 'You have never disappointed me.'

Shadow did not turn. 'That's weird,' he said. 'I disappointed myself all the way. Every time.'

'Not at all,' chuckled the voice. 'You did everything you were meant to do, and more. You took everybody's attention, so they never looked at the hand with the coin in it. It's called misdirection. And there's power in the sacrifice of a son – power enough, and more than enough, to get the whole ball rolling. To tell the truth, I'm proud of you.'

'It was crooked,' said Shadow. 'All of it. None of it was for real. It was just a set-up for a massacre.'

'Exactly,' said Wednesday's voice from the shadows. 'It was crooked. But it was the only game in town.'

'I want Laura,' said Shadow. 'I want Loki. Where are they?'

There was only silence. A spray of rain gusted at him. Thunder rumbled somewhere close at hand.

He walked further in.

Loki Lie-Smith sat on the ground with his back to a metal cage. Inside the cage, drunken pixies tended their still. He was covered with a blanket. Only his face showed, and his hands, white and long, came around the blanket. An electric lantern sat on a chair beside him. The lantern's batteries were close to failing, and the light it cast was faint and yellow.

He looked pale, and he looked rough.

His eyes, though. His eyes were still fiery, and they glared at Shadow as he walked through the cavern.

When Shadow was several paces from Loki, he stopped.

'You are too late,' said Loki. His voice was raspy and wet. 'I have thrown the spear. I have dedicated the battle. It has begun.'

'No shit,' said Shadow.

'No shit,' said Loki. 'It does not matter what you do any more. It is too late.'

'Okay,' said Shadow. He stopped and thought. Then he said, 'You say there's some spear you had to throw to kick off the battle. Like the whole Uppsala thing. This is the battle you'll be feeding on. Am I right?'

Silence. He could hear Loki breathing, a ghastly rattling inhalation.

'I figured it out,' said Shadow. 'Kind of. I'm not sure when I figured it out. Maybe when I was hanging on the tree. Maybe before. It was from something Wednesday said to me, at Christmas.'

Loki just stared at him, saying nothing.

'It's just a two-man con,' said Shadow. 'Like the bishop and the diamond necklace and the cop. Like the guy with the fiddle, and the guy who wants to buy the fiddle, and the poor sap in between them who pays for the fiddle. Two men, who appear to be on opposite sides, playing the same game.'

Loki whispered, 'You are ridiculous.'

'Why? I liked what you did at the motel. That was smart. You needed to be there, to make sure that everything went according to plan. I saw you. I even realized who you were. And I still never twigged that you were their Mister World. Or maybe I did, somewhere down deep. I knew I knew your voice, anyway.'

Shadow raised his voice. 'You can come out,' he said, to the cavern. 'Wherever you are. Show yourself.'

The wind howled in the opening of the cavern, and it drove a spray of rainwater in toward them. Shadow shivered.

'I'm tired of being played for a sucker,' said Shadow. 'Show yourself. Let me see you.'

There was a change in the shadows at the back of the cave.

Something became more solid; something shifted. 'You know too damned much, m'boy,' said Wednesday's familiar rumble.

'So they didn't kill you.'

'They killed me,' said Wednesday, from the shadows. 'None of this would have worked if they hadn't.' His voice was faint – not actually quiet, but there was a quality to it that made Shadow think of an old radio not quite tuned in to a distant station. 'If I hadn't died for real, we could never have got them here,' said Wednesday. 'Kali and the Morrigan and the Loa and the fucking Albanians and – well, you've seen them all. It was my death that drew them all together. I was the sacrificial lamb.'

'No,' said Shadow. 'You were the Judas Goat.'

The wraith-shape in the shadows swirled and shifted. 'Not at all. That implies that I was betraying the old gods for the new. Which was not what we were doing.'

'Not at all,' whispered Loki.

'I can see that,' said Shadow. 'You two weren't betraying either side. You were betraying both sides.'

'I guess we were at that,' said Wednesday. He sounded pleased with himself.

'You wanted a massacre. You needed a blood sacrifice. A sacrifice of gods.'

The wind grew stronger; the howl across the cave door became a screech, as if of something immeasurably huge in pain.

'And why the hell not? I've been trapped in this damned land for almost twelve hundred years. My blood is thin. I'm hungry.'

'And you two feed on death,' said Shadow.

He thought he could see Wednesday, now, standing in the shadows. Behind him – through him – were the bars of a cage which held what looked like plastic leprechauns. He was a shape made of darkness, who became more real the more Shadow looked away from him, allowed him to take shape in his peripheral vision.

'I feed on death that is dedicated to me,' said Wednesday.

'Like my death on the tree,' said Shadow.

'That,' said Wednesday, 'was special.'

'And do you also feed on death?' asked Shadow, looking at Loki.

Loki shook his head, wearily.

'No, of course not,' said Shadow. '*You* feed on chaos.'

Loki smiled at that, a brief pained smile, and orange flames danced in his eyes, and flickered like burning lace beneath his pale skin.

'We couldn't have done it without you,' said Wednesday, from the corner of Shadow's eye. 'I'd been with so many women . . .'

'You needed a son,' said Shadow.

Wednesday's ghost-voice echoed. 'I needed you, my boy. Yes. My own boy. I knew that you had been conceived, but your mother left the country. It took us so long to find you. And when we did find you, you were in prison. We needed to find out what made you tick.What buttons we could press to make you move. Who you were.' Loki looked, moment-arily, pleased with himself. Shadow wanted to hit him. 'And you had a wife to go back home to. It was unfortunate. Not insurmountable.'

'She was no good for you,' whispered Loki. 'You were better off without her.'

'If it could have been any other way,' said Wednesday, and this time Shadow knew what he meant.

'And if she'd had – the grace – to stay dead,' panted Loki. 'Wood and Stone – were good men. You were going – to be allowed to escape – when the train crossed the Dakotas . . .'

'Where is she?' asked Shadow.

Loki reached a pale arm, and pointed to the back of the cavern.

'She went that-a-way,' he said. Then, without warning, he tipped forward, his body collapsing onto the rock floor.

Shadow saw what the blanket had hidden from him; the

pool of blood, the hole through Loki's back, the fawn raincoat soaked black with blood. 'What happened?' he said.

Loki said nothing.

Shadow did not think he would be saying anything any more.

'Your wife happened to him, m'boy,' said Wednesday's distant voice. He had become harder to see, as if he was fading back into the ether. 'But the battle will bring him back. As the battle will bring me back for good. I'm a ghost, and he's a corpse, but we've still won. The game was rigged.'

'Rigged games,' said Shadow, remembering, 'are the easiest to beat.'

There was no answer. Nothing moved in the shadows.

Shadow said, 'Goodbye,' and then he said, 'Father.' But by then there was no trace of anybody else in the cavern. Nobody at all.

Shadow walked back up to the Seven States Flag Court, but saw nobody, and heard nothing but the crack and whip of the flags in the storm-wind. There were no people with swords at the Thousand Ton Balanced Rock, no defenders of the Swing-a-Long bridge. He was alone.

There was nothing to see. The place was deserted. It was an empty battlefield.

No. Not deserted. Not exactly.

He was just in the wrong place.

This was Rock City. It had been a place of awe and worship for thousands of years; today the millions of tourists who walked through the gardens and swung their way across the Swing-a-Long bridge had the same effect as water turning a million prayer wheels. Reality was thin here. And Shadow knew where the battle must be taking place.

With that, he began to walk. He remembered how he had felt on the carousel, tried to feel like that, but in a new moment of time . . .

He remembered turning the Winnebago, shifting it at right angles to *everything*. He tried to capture that sensation—

And then, easily and perfectly, it happened.

It was like pushing through a membrane, like plunging up from deep water into air. With one step he had moved from the tourist path on the mountain to . . .

To somewhere real. He was Backstage.

He was still on the top of a mountain. That much remained the same. But it was so much more than that. This mountaintop was the quintessence of place, the heart of things as they were. Compared to it, the Lookout Mountain he had left was a painting on a backdrop, or a papier-mâché model seen on a TV screen – merely a representation of the thing, not the thing itself.

This was the true place.

The rock walls formed a natural amphitheatre. Paths of stone that wound around and across it, forming twisty natural bridges that Eschered through and across the rock walls.

And the sky . . .

The sky was dark. It was lit, and the world beneath it was illuminated by a burning greenish-white streak, brighter than the sun, which forked crazily across the sky from end to end, like a white rip in the darkened sky.

It was lightning, Shadow realized. Lightning held in one frozen moment that stretched into forever. The light it cast was harsh and unforgiving: it washed out faces, hollowed eyes into dark pits.

This was the moment of the storm.

The paradigms were shifting. He could feel it. The old world, a world of infinite vastness and illimitable resources and future was being confronted by something else – a web of energy, of opinions, of gulfs.

People believe, thought Shadow. It's what people do. They believe. And then they will not take responsibility for their beliefs; they conjure things, and do not trust the conjurations. People populate the darkness; with ghosts, with gods, with electrons, with tales. People imagine, and people believe: and it is that belief, that rock-solid belief, that makes things happen.

The mountain-top was an arena; he saw that immediately. And on each side of the arena he could see them arrayed.

They were too big. Everything was too big in that place.

There were old gods in that place: gods with skins the brown of old mushrooms, the pink of chicken-flesh, the yellow of autumn leaves. Some were crazy and some were sane. Shadow recognized the old gods. He'd met them already, or he'd met others like them. There were ifrits and piskies, giants and dwarfs. He saw the woman he had met in the darkened bedroom in Rhode Island, saw the writhing green snake-coils of her hair. He saw Mama-ji, from the carousel, and there was blood on her hands and a smile on her face. He knew them all.

He recognized the new ones, too.

There was somebody who had to be a railroad baron, in an antique suit, his watch-chain stretched across his vest. He had the air of one who had seen better days. His forehead twitched.

There were the great gray gods of the airplanes, heirs to all the dreams of heavier-than-air travel.

There were car gods there: a powerful, serious-faced con- tingent, with blood on their black gloves and on their chrome teeth: recipients of human sacrifice on a scale undreamed-of since the Aztecs. Even they looked uncom- fortable. Worlds change.

Others had faces of smudged phosphors; they glowed gently, as if they existed in their own light.

Shadow felt sorry for them all.

There was an arrogance to the new ones. Shadow could see that. But there was also a fear.

They were afraid that unless they kept pace with a changing world, unless they remade and redrew and rebuilt the world in their image, their time would already be over.

Each side faced the other with bravery. To each side, the

opposition were the demons, the monsters, the damned.

Shadow could see an initial skirmish had taken place. There was already blood on the rocks.

They were readying themselves for the real battle; for the real war. It was now or never, he thought. If he did not move now, it would be too late.

In America everything goes on forever, said a voice in the back of his head. *The 1950s lasted for a thousand years. You have all the time in the world.*

Shadow walked in something that was half a stroll, half controlled stumble, into the center of the arena.

He could feel eyes on him, eyes and things that were not eyes. He shivered.

The buffalo voice said, *You are doing just fine.*

Shadow thought, *Damn right. I came back from the dead this morning. After that, everything else should be a piece of cake.*

'You know,' said Shadow, to the air, in a conversational voice, 'This is not a war. This was never intended to be a war. And if any of you think this is a war, you are deluding yourselves.' He heard grumbling noises from both sides. He had impressed nobody.

'We are fighting for our survival,' lowed a minotaur from one side of the arena.

'We are fighting for our existence,' shouted a mouth in a pillar of glittering smoke, from the other.

'This is a bad land for Gods,' said Shadow. As an opening statement it wasn't *Friends, Romans, Countrymen*, but it would do. 'You've probably all learned that, in your own way. The old gods are ignored. The new gods are as quickly taken up as they are abandoned, cast aside for the next big thing. Either you've been forgotten, or you're scared you're going to be rendered obsolete, or maybe you're just getting tired of existing on the whim of people.'

The grumbles were fewer now. He had said something they agreed with. Now, while they were listening, he had to tell them the story.

'There was a god who came here from a far land, and whose power and influence waned as belief in him faded. He was a god who took his power from sacrifice, and from death, and especially from war. He would have deaths of those who fell in war dedicated to him – whole battlefields which, in the Old Country, gave him power and sustenance.

'Now he was old. He made his living as a grifter, working with another god from his pantheon, a god of chaos and deceit. Together they rooked the gullible. Together they took people for all they'd got.

'Somewhere in there – maybe fifty years ago, maybe a hundred, they put a plan into motion, a plan to create a reserve of power they could both tap into. Something that would make them stronger than they had ever been. After all, what could be more powerful than a battlefield covered with dead gods? The game they played was called "Let's You and Him Fight".

'Do you see?

'The battle you're here to fight isn't something that any of you can win or lose. The winning and the losing are unimportant to him, to them. What matters is that enough of you die. Each of you that falls in battle gives him power. Every one of you that dies, feeds him. Do you understand?'

The roaring, *whoompf*ing sound of something catching on fire echoed across the arena. Shadow looked to the place the noise came from. An enormous man, his skin the deep brown of mahogany, his chest naked, wearing a top hat, cigar sticking rakishly from his mouth, spoke in a voice as deep as the grave. Baron Samedi said, 'Okay. But Odin. He *died*. At the peace talks. Motherfuckers killed him. He died. I *know* death. Nobody goin' to fool me about death.'

Shadow said, 'Obviously. He had to die for real. He sacrificed his physical body to make this war happen. After the battle he would have been more powerful than he had ever been.'

Somebody called, 'Who are you?'

'I am – I was – I am his son.'

One of the new gods – Shadow suspected it was a drug from the way it smiled and spangled and shivered – said, 'But Mister World said . . .'

'There *was* no Mister World. There never was. He was just another one of you bastards trying to feed on the chaos he created.' He could see that they believed him, and he could see the hurt in their eyes.

Shadow shook his head. 'You know,' he said. 'I think I would rather be a man than a god. We don't need anyone to believe in us. We just keep going anyhow. It's what we do.'

There was silence, in the high place.

And then, with a shocking crack, the lightning bolt frozen in the sky crashed to the mountaintop, and the arena went entirely dark.

They glowed, many of those presences, in the darkness.

Shadow wondered if they were going to argue with him, to attack him, to try to kill him. He waited for some kind of response.

And then Shadow realized that the lights were going out. The gods were leaving that place, first in handfuls, and then by scores, and finally in their hundreds.

A spider the size of a rottweiler scuttled heavily toward him, on seven legs; its cluster of eyes glowed faintly.

Shadow held his ground, although he felt faintly sick.

When the spider got close enough, it said, in Mr Nancy's voice, 'That was a good job. Proud of you. You done good, kid.'

'Thank you,' said Shadow.

'We should get you back. Too long in this place is goin' to mess you up.' It rested one brown-haired spider-leg on Shadow's shoulder . . .

***

. . . and, back on Seven States Flag Court, Mr Nancy coughed. His right hand rested on Shadow's shoulder. The rain had stopped. Mr Nancy held his left hand across his side, as if it hurt. Shadow asked if he was okay.

'I'm tough as old nails,' said Mr Nancy. 'Tougher.' He did not sound happy. He sounded like an old man in pain.

There were dozens of them, standing or sitting on the ground or on the benches. Some of them looked badly injured.

Shadow could hear a rattling noise in the sky, approaching from the south. He looked at Mr Nancy. 'Helicopters?'

Mr Nancy nodded. 'Don't you worry about them. Not any more. They'll just clean up the mess, and leave. They're good at it.'

'Got it.'

Shadow knew that there was one part of the mess he wanted to see for himself, before it was cleaned up. He borrowed a flashlight from a gray-haired man who looked like a retired news anchor and began to hunt.

He found Laura stretched out on the ground in a side-cavern, beside a diorama of mining gnomes straight out of Snow White. The floor beneath her was sticky with blood. She was on her side, where Loki must have dropped her after he had pulled the spear out of them both.

One of Laura's hands clutched her chest. She looked dreadfully vulnerable. She looked dead, but then Shadow was almost used to that by now.

Shadow squatted beside her, and he touched her cheek with his hand, and he said her name. Her eyes opened, and she lifted her head and turned it until she was looking at him.

'Hello, puppy,' she said. Her voice was thin.

'Hi, Laura. What happened here?'

'Nothing,' she said. 'Just stuff. Did they win?'

'I don't know,' said Shadow. 'I think these things are kind of relative. But I stopped the battle they were trying to start.'

'My clever puppy,' she said. 'That man, Mister World, he said he was going to put a stick through your eye. I didn't like him at all.'

'He's dead. You killed him, hon.'

She nodded. She said, 'That's good.'

Her eyes closed. Shadow's hand found her cold hand, and he held it in his. In time she opened her eyes again.

'Did you ever figure out how to bring me back from the dead?' she asked.

'I guess,' he said. 'I know one way, anyway.'

'That's good,' she said. She squeezed his hand with her cold hand. And then she said, 'And the opposite? What about that?'

'The opposite?'

'Yes,' she whispered. 'I think I must have earned it.'

'I don't want to do that.'

She said nothing. She simply waited.

Shadow said, 'Okay.' Then he took his hand from hers and put it to her neck.

She said, 'That's my husband.' She said it proudly.

'I love you, babes,' said Shadow.

'Love you, puppy,' she whispered.

He closed his hand around the golden coin that hung around her neck. He tugged, hard, at the chain, which snapped easily. Then he took the gold coin between his finger and thumb, and blew on it, and opened his hand wide.

The coin was gone.

Her eyes were still open, but they did not move.

He bent down then, and kissed her, gently, on her cold cheek, but she did not respond. He did not expect her to. Then he got up and walked out of the cavern, to stare into the night.

The storms had cleared. The air felt fresh and clean and new once more.

Tomorrow, he had no doubt, would be one hell of a beautiful day.

Part Four
EPILOGUE:
SOMETHING THAT THE DEAD
ARE KEEPING BACK

Chapter Nineteen

One describes a tale best by telling the tale. You see? The way one describes a story, to oneself or to the world, is by telling the story. It is a balancing act and it is a dream. The more accurate the map, the more it resembles the territory. The most accurate map possible would be the territory, and thus would be perfectly accurate and perfectly useless.

The tale is the map which is the territory.

You must remember this.

— From the Notebooks of Mr Ibis

The two of them were driving the VW bus down to Florida on I-75. They'd been driving since dawn, or rather, Shadow had driven, and Mr Nancy had sat up front in the passenger seat and, from time to time, and with a pained expression on his face, offered to drive. Shadow always said no.

'Are you happy?' asked Mr Nancy, suddenly. He had been staring at Shadow for several hours. Whenever Shadow glanced over to his right, Mr Nancy was looking at him with his earth-brown eyes.

'Not really,' said Shadow. 'But I'm not dead yet.'

'Huh?'

'*Call no man happy until he is dead*. Herodotus.'

Mr Nancy raised a white eyebrow, and he said, '*I'm* not dead yet, and, mostly *because* I'm not dead yet, I'm happy as a clamboy.'

'The Herodotus thing. It doesn't mean that the dead are happy,' said Shadow. 'It means that you can't judge the shape of someone's life until it's over and done.'

'I don't even judge then,' said Mr Nancy. 'And as for happiness, there's a lot of different kinds of happiness, just as there's a hell of a lot of different kinds of dead. Me, I'll just take what I can get when I can get it.'

Shadow changed the subject. 'Those helicopters,' he said. 'The ones that took away the bodies, and the injured.'

'What about them?'

'Who sent them? Where did they come from?'

'You shouldn't worry yourself about that. They're like valkyries or buzzards. They come because they have to come.'

'If you say so.'

'The dead and the wounded will be taken care of. You ask me, old Jacquel's going to be very busy for the next month or so. Tell me somethin', Shadow-boy.'

'Okay.'

'You learn anythin' from all this?'

Shadow shrugged. 'I don't know. Most of what I learned on the tree I've already forgotten,' he said. 'I think I met some people. But I'm not certain of anything any more. It's like one of those dreams that changes you. You keep some of the dream forever, and you know things down deep inside yourself, because it happened to you, but when you go looking for details they kind of just slip out of your head.'

'Yeah,' said Mr Nancy. And then he said, grudgingly, 'You're not so dumb.'

'Maybe not,' said Shadow. 'But I wish I could have kept

more of what passed through my hands, since I got out of prison. I was given so many things, and I lost them again.'

'Maybe,' said Mr Nancy, 'you kept more than you think.'

'No,' said Shadow.

They crossed the border into Florida, and Shadow saw his first palm tree. He wondered if they'd planted it there on purpose, at the border, just so that you knew you were in Florida now.

Mr Nancy began to snore, and Shadow glanced over at him. The old man still looked very gray, and his breath was rasping. Shadow wondered, not for the first time, if he had sustained some kind of chest or lung injury in the fight. Nancy had refused any medical attention.

Florida went on for longer than Shadow had imagined, and it was late by the time he pulled up outside a small, one story wooden house, its windows tightly shuttered, on the outskirts of Fort Pierce. Nancy, who had directed him through the last five miles, invited him to stay the night.

'I can get a room in a motel,' said Shadow. 'It's not a problem.'

'You *could* do that, and I'd be hurt. Obviously I wouldn't say anythin'. But I'd be real hurt, real bad,' said Mr Nancy. 'So you better stay here, and I'll make you a bed up on the couch.'

Mr Nancy unlocked the hurricane shutters, and pulled open the windows. The house smelled musty and damp, and a little sweet, as if it were haunted by the ghosts of long-dead cookies.

Shadow agreed, reluctantly, to stay the night there, just as he agreed, even more reluctantly, to walk with Mr Nancy to the bar at the end of the road, for just one late night drink while the house aired out.

'Did you see Czernobog?' asked Nancy, as they strolled through the muggy Floridian night. The air was alive with whirring palmetto bugs and the ground crawled with creatures that scuttled and clicked. Mr Nancy lit a cigarillo,

and coughed and choked on it. Still, he kept right on
smoking.

'He was gone when I came out of the cave.'

'He will have headed home. He'll be waitin' for you there,
you know.'

'Yes.'

They walked in silence to the end of the road. It wasn't
much of a bar, but it was open.

'I'll buy the first beers,' said Mr Nancy.

'We're only having one beer, remember,' said Shadow.

'What are you,' asked Mr Nancy. 'Some kind of
cheapskate?'

Mr Nancy bought them their first beers, and Shadow
bought the second round. He stared in horror as Mr Nancy
talked the barman into turning on the karaoke machine, and
then watched in fascinated embarrassment as the old man
belted his way through 'What's New, Pussycat?' before crooning out a moving, tuneful version of 'The Way You Look
Tonight'. He had a fine voice, and by the end the handful of
people still in the bar were cheering and applauding him.

When he came back to Shadow at the bar he was looking
brighter. The whites of his eyes were clear, and the gray
pallor that had touched his skin was gone. 'Your turn,' he
said.

'Absolutely not,' said Shadow.

But Mr Nancy had ordered more beers and was handing
Shadow a stained printout of songs from which to choose.
'Just pick a song you know the words to.'

'This is not funny,' said Shadow. The world was beginning
to swim, a little, but he couldn't muster the energy to argue,
and then Mr Nancy was putting on the backing tape to 'Don't
Let Me Be Misunderstood', and pushing – literally *pushing* –
Shadow up onto the tiny makeshift stage at the end of the
bar.

Shadow held the mike as if it was probably live, and then
the backing music started and he croaked out the initial

'*Baby . . .*' Nobody in the bar threw anything in his direction. And it felt good. '*Can you understand me now?*' His voice was rough but melodic, and rough suited the song just fine. '*Sometimes I feel a little mad. Don't you know that no one alive can always be an angel . . .*'

And he was still singing it as they walked home through the busy Florida night, the old man and the young, stumbling and happy.

'*I'm just a soul whose intentions are good,*' he sang to the crabs and the spiders and the palmetto beetles and the lizards and the night. '*Oh lord, please don't let me be misunderstood.*'

Mr Nancy showed him to the couch. It was much smaller than Shadow, who decided to sleep on the floor, but by the time he had finished deciding to sleep on the floor he was already fast asleep, half-sitting, half lying, on the tiny sofa.

At first, he did not dream. There was just the comforting darkness. And then he saw a fire burning in the darkness and he walked toward it.

'You did well,' whispered the buffalo man without moving his lips.

'I don't know what I did,' said Shadow.

'You made peace,' said the buffalo man. 'You took our words and made them your own. They never understood that *they* were here – and the people who worshiped them were here – because it suits us that they are here. But we can change our minds. And perhaps we will.'

'Are you a god?' asked Shadow.

The buffalo-headed man shook his head. Shadow thought, for a moment, that the creature was amused. 'I am the land,' he said.

And if there was more to that dream then Shadow did not remember it.

He heard something sizzling. His head was aching, and there was a pounding behind his eyes.

Mr Nancy was already cooking breakfast: a pile of

pancakes, sizzling bacon, perfect eggs, and coffee. He looked in the peak of health.

'My head hurts,' said Shadow.

'You get a good breakfast inside you, you'll feel like a new man.'

'I'd rather feel like the same man, just with a different head,' said Shadow.

'Eat,' said Mr Nancy.

Shadow ate.

'How do you feel now?'

'Like I've got a headache, only now I've got some food in my stomach and I think I'm going to throw up.'

'Come with me.' Beside the sofa, on which Shadow had spent the night, covered with an African blanket, was a trunk, made of some dark wood, which looked like an undersized pirate chest. Mr Nancy undid the padlock, and opened the lid. Inside the trunk there were a number of boxes. Nancy rummaged among the boxes. 'It's an ancient African herbal remedy,' he said. 'It's made of ground willow bark, things like that.'

'Like aspirin?'

'Yup,' said Mr Nancy. 'Just like that.' From the bottom of the trunk he produced a giant economy-sized bottle of generic aspirin. He unscrewed the top, and shook out a couple of white pills. 'Here.'

'Nice trunk,' said Shadow. He took the bitter pills, swallowed them with a glass of water.

'My son sent it to me,' said Mr Nancy. 'He's a good boy. I don't see him as much as I'd like.'

'I miss Wednesday,' said Shadow. 'Despite everything he did. I keep expecting to see him. But I look up and he's not there.' He kept staring at the pirate trunk, trying to figure out what it reminded him of.

You will lose many things. Do not lose this. Who said that?

'You miss him? After what he put you through? Put us all through?'

'Yes,' said Shadow. 'I guess I do. Do you think he'll be back?'

'I think,' said Mr Nancy, 'that wherever two men are gathered together to sell a third man a twenty dollar violin for ten thousand dollars, he will be there in spirit.'

'Yes, but—'

'We should get back into the kitchen,' said Mr Nancy, his expression becoming stony. 'Those pans won't wash themselves.'

Mr Nancy washed the pans and the dishes. Shadow dried them, and put them away. Somewhere in there the headache began to ease. They went back into the sitting room. Shadow stared at the old trunk some more, willing himself to remember. 'If I don't go to see Czernobog,' he said, 'what would happen?'

'You'll see him,' said Mr Nancy flatly. 'Maybe he'll find you. Or maybe he'll bring you to him. But one way or another, you'll see him.'

Shadow nodded. Something started to fall into place. 'Hey,' he said. 'Is there a god with an elephant's head?'

'Ganesh? He's a Hindu god. He removes obstacles and makes journeys easier. Good cook, too.'

Shadow looked up. '. . . *it's in the trunk*,' he said. 'I knew it was important, but I didn't know why. I thought maybe it meant the trunk of the tree. But he wasn't talking about that at all, was he?'

Mr Nancy frowned. 'You lost me.'

'It's in the trunk,' said Shadow. He knew it was true. He did not know why it should be true, not quite. But of that he was completely certain.

He got to his feet. 'I got to go,' he said. 'I'm sorry.'

Mr Nancy raised an eyebrow. 'Why the hurry?'

'Because,' said Shadow, simply, 'the ice is melting.'

Chapter Twenty

it's
   spring
   and
      the
         goat-footed
balloonMan whistles
   far
   and
   wee

                                    – e.e. cummings

Shadow was driving a rental, and he came out of the
forest slowly, about 8:30 in the morning, drove down the
hill doing under forty-five miles per hour, and entered
the town of Lakeside three weeks after he was certain he had
left it for good.

He drove through the city, surprised at how little it had
changed in the last few weeks, which were a lifetime, and he
parked halfway down the driveway that led to the lake. Then
he got out of the car.

There were no more ice-fishing huts on the frozen lake
any longer, no SUVs, no men sitting at a fishing hole with a
line and a twelve-pack. The lake was dark: no longer covered
with a blind white layer of snow, now there were reflective
patches of water on the surface of the ice, and the water
beneath the ice was dark, and the ice itself was clear enough
that the darkness beneath showed through. The sky was
gray, but the icy lake was dark and empty.

Almost empty.

There was one car remaining on the ice, parked out on the
frozen lake almost beneath the bridge, so that anyone driving
through the town, anyone crossing the town, could not help
but see it. It was a dirty green in color; the sort of car that
people abandon in parking lots, the kind that they just park
and leave because it's just not worth coming back for. It had
no engine. It was a symbol of a wager, waiting for the ice to
become rotten enough, and soft enough, and dangerous
enough to allow the lake to take it forever.

There was a chain across the short driveway that led down
to the lake, and a warning sign forbidding entrance to people
or to vehicles. *Thin ice*, it said. Beneath it was a hand-
painted sequence of pictograms with lines through them: no
cars, no pedestrians, no snowmobiles. *Danger*.

Shadow ignored the warnings and scrambled down the
bank. It was slippery – the snow had already melted, turning
the earth to mud under his feet, and the brown grass barely
offered traction. He skidded and slid down to the lake and
walked, carefully, out onto a short wooden jetty, and from
there he stepped down onto the ice.

The layer of water on the ice, made up of melted ice and
melted snow, was deeper than it had looked from above, and
the ice beneath the water was slicker and more slippery than
any skating rink, so that Shadow was forced to fight to keep
his footing. He splashed through the water, as it covered his
boots to the laces and seeped inside. Ice water. It numbed
where it touched. He felt strangely distant as he trudged

across the frozen lake, as if he were watching himself on a movie screen – a movie in which he was the hero, a detective, perhaps: there was a feeling of inevitability, now, as if everything that was going to happen would play itself out, and there was nothing he could have done to change a moment of it.

He walked toward the klunker, painfully aware that the ice was too rotten for this, and that the water beneath the ice was as cold as water could be without freezing. He felt very exposed, out on the ice alone. He kept walking, and he slipped and slid. Several times he fell.

He passed empty beer bottles and cans left to litter the ice, and he passed circular holes cut into the ice, for fishing, holes that had not frozen again, each hole filled with black water.

The klunker seemed further away than it had looked from the road. He heard a loud crack from the south of the lake, like a stick breaking, followed by the sound of something huge thrumming, as if a bass string the size of a lake was vibrating. Massively, the ice creaked and groaned, like an old door protesting being opened. Shadow kept walking, as steadily as he could.

This is suicide, whispered a sane voice in the back of his mind. *Can't you just let it go?*

'No,' he said, aloud. 'I have to *know*.' And he kept right on walking.

He arrived at the klunker, and even before he reached it he knew that he had been right. There was a miasma that hung about the car, something that was at the same time a faint, foul smell and was also a bad taste in the back of his throat. He walked around the car, looking inside. The seats were stained, and ripped. The car was obviously empty. He tried the doors. They were locked. He tried the trunk. Also locked.

He wished that he had brought a crowbar.

He made a fist of his hand inside his glove. He counted to

three, then smashed his hand, hard, against the driver's side window-glass.

His hand hurt. The side-window was undamaged.

He thought about running at it – he could kick the window in, he was certain, if he didn't skid and fall on the wet ice. But the last thing he wanted to do was to disturb the klunker enough that the ice beneath it would crack.

He looked at the car. Then he reached for the radio antenna – it was the kind which was meant to go up and down, but which had stopped going down a decade ago, and had remained in the up position ever since – and, with a little waggling, he broke it off at the base. He took the thin end of the antenna – it had once had a metal button on the end, but that was lost in time, and, with strong fingers, he bent it back up into a makeshift hook.

Then he rammed the extended metal antenna down between the rubber and the glass of the front window, deep into the mechanism of the door. He fished in the mechanism, twisting, moving, pushing the metal antenna about until it caught: and then he pulled up.

He felt the improvised hook sliding from the lock, uselessly.

He sighed. Fished again, slower, more carefully. He could imagine the ice grumbling beneath his feet as he shifted his weight. And slow . . . and . . .

He *had* it. He pulled up on the aerial and the front door locking mechanism popped up. Shadow reached down one gloved hand and took the door handle, pressed the button, and pulled. The door did not open.

It's stuck, he thought, iced up. *That's all*.

He tugged, sliding on the ice, and suddenly the door of the klunker flew open, ice scattering everywhere.

The miasma was worse inside the car, a stench of rot and illness. Shadow felt sick.

He reached under the dashboard, found the black plastic handle that opened the trunk, and tugged on it, hard.

There was a thunk from behind him as the trunk door released.

Shadow walked out onto the ice, slipped and splashed around the car, holding on to the side of it as he went.

It's in the trunk, he thought.

The trunk was open an inch. He reached down and opened it the rest of the way, pulling it up.

The smell was bad, but it could have been much worse: the bottom of the trunk was filled with an inch or so of half-melted ice. There was a girl in the trunk. She wore a scarlet snowsuit, now stained, and her mousy hair was long and her mouth was closed, so Shadow could not see the blue rubber-band braces, but he knew that they were there. The cold had preserved her, kept her as fresh as if she had been in a freezer.

Her eyes were wide open, and she looked as if she had been crying when she died, and the tears that had frozen on her cheeks had still not melted. Her gloves were bright green.

'You were here all the time,' said Shadow to Alison McGovern's corpse. 'Every single person who drove over that bridge saw you. Everyone who drove through the town saw you. The ice fishermen walked past you every day. And nobody knew.' And then he realized how foolish that was.

Somebody knew.

Somebody had put her here.

He reached in to the trunk – to see if he could pull her out. He had found her, after all. Now he had to get her out. He put his weight on the car, as he leaned in. Perhaps that was what did it.

The ice beneath the front wheels went at that moment, perhaps from his movements, perhaps not. The front of the car lurched downward several feet into the dark water of the lake. Water began to pour into the car through the open driver's door. Water splashed about Shadow's ankles, although the ice he stood on was still solid. He looked around urgently, wondering how to get away – and then it was too late, and the ice tipped precipitously, throwing him against the car and the dead girl in the trunk; and the back of the car went down, and Shadow went down with it, into the cold waters of the lake. It was ten past nine in the morning, on March the twenty-third.

He took a deep breath before he went under, closing his eyes, but the cold of the lake water hit him like a wall, knocking the breath from his body.

He tumbled downward, into the murky ice water, pulled down by the car.

He was under the lake, down in the darkness and the cold, weighed down by his clothes and his gloves and his boots, trapped and swathed in his coat which seemed to have become heavier and bulkier than he could have imagined.

He was falling, still. He tried to push away from the car, but it was pulling him with it, and then there was a bang which he could hear with his whole body, not his ears, and his left foot was wrenched at the ankle, the foot twisted and trapped beneath the car as it settled on the lake bottom, and panic took him.

He opened his eyes.

He knew it was dark down there: rationally, he knew it was too dark to see anything, but still, he could see; he could see everything. He could see Alison McGovern's white face staring at him from the open trunk. He could see other cars as well – the klunkers of bygone years, rotten hulk shapes in the darkness, half-buried in the lake mud. *And what else would they have dragged out onto the lake, thought Shadow, before there were cars?*

Each one, he knew, without any question, had a dead child in the trunk. There were scores of them down there. Each had sat out on the ice, in front of the eyes of the world, all through the cold winter. Each had tumbled into the cold waters of the lake, when the winter was done.

This was where they rested: Lemmi Hautala and Jessie

Lovat and Sandy Olsen and Jo Ming and Sarah Lindquist and all the rest of them. Down where it was silent and cold . . .

He pulled at his foot. It was stuck fast, and the pressure in his lungs was becoming unbearable. There was a sharp, terrible, hurt in his ears. He exhaled slowly, and the air bubbled around his face.

Soon, he thought, soon I'll have to breathe. *Or I'll choke.*

He reached down, put both hands around the bumper of the klunker, and pushed, with everything he had, leaning into it. Nothing happened.

It's only the shell of a car, he told himself. *They took out the engine. That's the heaviest part of the car. You can do it. Just keep pushing.*

He pushed.

Agonizingly slowly, a fraction of an inch at a time, the car slipped forward in the mud, and Shadow pulled his foot from the mud beneath the car, and kicked, and tried to push himself out into the cold lake water. He didn't move. *The coat*, he told himself. *It's the coat. It's stuck, or caught on something.* He pulled his arms from his coat, fumbled with numb fingers at the frozen zipper. Then he pulled both hands on each side of the zipper, felt the coat give and rend. Hastily, he freed himself from its embrace, and pushed upward, away from the car.

There was a rushing sensation but no sense of up, no sense of down, and he was choking and the pain in his chest and in his head was too much to bear, so that he was certain that he was going to have to inhale, to breathe in the cold water, to die. And then his head hit something solid.

Ice. He was pushing against the ice on the top of the lake. He hammered at it with his fists, but there was no strength left in his arms, nothing to hold onto, nothing to push against. The world had dissolved into the chill blackness beneath the lake. There was nothing left but cold.

This is ridiculous, he thought. And he thought, remembering some old Tony Curtis film he'd seen as a kid, *I should roll onto my back and push the ice upward and press my face to it, and find some air, I could breathe again, there's air there somewhere,* but he was just floating and freezing and he could no longer move a muscle, not if his life depended on it, which it did.

The cold became bearable. Became warm. And he thought, *I'm dying.* There was anger there this time, a deep fury, and he took the pain and the anger and reached with it, flailed, forced muscles to move that were resigned never to move again.

He pushed up with his hand, and felt it scrape the edge of the ice and move up into the air. He flailed for a grip, and felt another hand take his own, and pull.

His head banged against the ice, his face scraped the underneath of the ice, and then his head was up in the air, and he could see that he was coming up through a hole in the ice, and for a moment all he could do was breathe, and let the black lake water run from his nose and his mouth, and blink his eyes, which could see nothing more than a blinding daylight, and shapes, and someone was pulling him, now, forcing him out of the water, saying something about how he'd freeze to death, so come on, man, *pull*, and Shadow wriggled and shook like a bull seal coming ashore, shaking and coughing and shuddering.

He breathed deep gasps of air, stretched flat out on the creaking ice, and even that would not hold for long, he knew, but it was no good. His thoughts were coming with difficulty, treacle-slow.

'Just leave me,' he tried to say. 'I'll be fine.' His words were a slur, and everything was drawing to a halt.

He just needed to rest for a moment, that was all, just rest, and then he would get up and move on, for obviously he could not just lie there forever.

There was a jerk; water splashed his face. His head was lifted up. Shadow felt himself being hauled across the ice, sliding on his back across the slick surface, and he wanted to protest, to explain that he just needed a little rest – maybe a little sleep, was that asking for so much? – and he would be just fine. If they just left him alone.

He did not believe that he had fallen asleep, but he was standing on a vast plain, and there was a man there with the head and shoulders of a buffalo, and a woman with the head of an enormous condor, and there was Whiskey Jack standing between them, looking at him sadly, shaking his head.

Whiskey Jack turned and walked slowly away from Shadow. The Buffalo man walked away beside him. The thunderbird woman also walked, and then she ducked and kicked and she was gliding out into the skies.

Shadow felt a sense of loss. He wanted to call to them, to plead with them to come back, not to give up on him, but everything was becoming formless and devoid of shape: they were gone, and the plains were fading, and everything became void.

* * *

The pain was intense: it was if every cell in his body, every nerve, was melting and waking and advertising its presence by burning him and hurting him.

There was a hand at the back of his head, gripping it by the hair, and another hand beneath his chin. He opened his eyes, expecting to find himself in some kind of hospital.

His feet were bare. He was wearing jeans. He was naked from the waist up. There was steam in the air. He could see a shaving mirror on the wall facing him, and a small basin, and a blue toothbrush in a toothpaste-stained glass.

Information was processed slowly, one datum at a time.

His fingers burned. His toes burned.

He began to whimper from the pain.

'Easy now, Mike. Easy there,' said a voice he knew.

'What?' he said, or tried to say. 'What's happening?' It
sounded strained and strange to his ears.

He was in a bathtub. The water was hot. He thought the
water was hot, although he could not be certain. The water
was up to his neck.

'Dumbest thing you can do with a fellow freezing to death
is to put him in front of a fire. The second dumbest thing you
can do is to wrap him in blankets – especially if he's in cold
wet clothes already. Blankets insulate him – keep the cold in.
The third dumbest thing – and this is my private opinion –
is to take the fellow's blood out, warm it up, and put it back.
That's what doctors do these days. Complicated, expensive.
Dumb.' The voice was coming from above and behind his
head.

'The smartest, quickest thing you can do is what sailors
have done to men overboard for hundreds of years. You put
the fellow in hot water. Not too hot. Just hot. Now, just so
you know, you were basically dead, when I found you on the
ice back there. How are you feeling now, Houdini?'

'It hurts,' said Shadow. 'Everything hurts. You saved my
life.'

'I guess maybe I did, at that. Can you hold your head up
on your own now?'

'Maybe.'

'I'm going to let you go. If you start sinking below the
water I'll pull you back up again.'

The hands released their grip on his head.

He felt himself sliding forward in the bathtub. He put out
his hands, pressed them against the side of the tub, and
leaned back. The bathroom was small. The tub was metal,
and the enamel was stained and scratched.

An old man moved into his field of vision. He looked
concerned.

'Feeling better?' asked Hinzelmann. 'You just lay back and
relax. I've got the den nice and warm, You tell me when
you're ready, I got a robe you can wear, and I can throw your

jeans into the dryer with the rest of your clothes. Sound good, Mike?'

'That's not my name.'

'If you say so.' The old man's goblin face twisted into an expression of discomfort.

Shadow had no real sense of time: he lay in the bath until the burning stopped and his toes and fingers flexed without real discomfort. Hinzelmann helped Shadow to his feet and let out the warm water. Shadow sat on the side of the bath and together they pulled off his jeans.

He squeezed, without much difficulty, into a terrycloth robe too small for him, and, leaning on the old man, he went through to the den, and flopped down on an ancient sofa. He was tired and weak: deeply fatigued, but alive. A log fire burned in the fireplace. A handful of surprised-looking deer heads peered down dustily from around the walls, where they jostled for space with several large varnished fish.

Hinzelmann went away with Shadow's jeans, and from the room next door Shadow could hear a brief pause in the rattle of a clothes dryer, before it resumed. The old man returned with a steaming mug.

'It's coffee,' he said, 'which is a stimulant. And I splashed a little schnapps into it. Just a little. That's what we always did in the old days. A doctor wouldn't recommend it.'

Shadow took the coffee with both hands. On the side of the mug was a picture of a mosquito and the message, *Give Blood – Visit Wisconsin!!*

'Thanks,' he said.

'It's what friends are for,' said Hinzelmann. 'One day, you can save my life. For now, forget about it.'

Shadow sipped the coffee. 'I thought I was dead.'

'You were lucky. I was up on the bridge – I'd pretty much figured that today was going to be the big day, you get a feel for it, when you get to my age – so I was up there with my old pocket watch, and I saw you heading out onto the lake. I shouted, but I sure as heck don't think you coulda heard me.

I saw the car go down, and I saw you go down with it, and I thought I'd lost you, so I went out onto the ice. Gave me the heeby jeebies. You must have been under the water for the best part of two minutes. Then I saw your hand come up through the place where the car went down – it was like seeing a ghost, seeing you there . . .' He trailed off. 'We were both damn lucky that the ice took our weight as I dragged you back to the shore.'

Shadow nodded.

'You did a good thing,' he told Hinzelmann, and the old man beamed all over his goblin face.

Somewhere in the house, Shadow heard a door close. He sipped at his coffee.

Now that he was able to think clearly, he was starting to ask himself questions.

He wondered how an old man, a man half his height and perhaps a third his weight, had been able to drag him, unconscious, across the ice, or get him up the bank to a car. He wondered how Hinzelmann had gotten Shadow into the house and the bath.

Hinzelmann walked over to the fire, picked up the tongs and placed a thin log, carefully, onto the blazing fire.

'Do you want to know what I was doing out on the ice?'

Hinzelmann shrugged. 'None of my business.'

'You know what I don't understand . . .' said Shadow. He hesitated, putting his thoughts in order. 'I don't understand why you saved my life.'

'Well,' said Hinzelmann, 'the way I was brought up, if you see another fellow in trouble—'

'No,' said Shadow. 'That's not what I mean. I mean, you killed all those kids. Every winter. I was the only one to have figured it out. You must have seen me open the trunk. Why didn't you just let me drown?'

Hinzelmann tipped his head on one side. He scratched his nose, thoughtfully, rocked back and forth as if he were thinking. 'Well,' he said. 'That's a good question. I guess it's because I owed a certain party a debt. And I'm good for my debts.'

'Wednesday?'

'That's the fellow.'

'There was a reason he hid me in Lakeside, wasn't there? There was a reason nobody should have been able to find me here.'

Hinzelmann said nothing. He unhooked a heavy black poker from its place on the wall, and he prodded at the fire with it, sending up a cloud of orange sparks and smoke. 'This is my home,' he said, petulantly. 'It's a *good* town.'

Shadow finished his coffee. He put the cup down on the floor. The effort was exhausting. 'How long have you been here?'

'Long enough.'

'And you made the lake?'

Hinzelmann peered at him, surprised. 'Yes,' he said. 'I made the lake. They were calling it a lake when I got here, but it weren't nothing more than a spring and a mill pond and a creek.' He paused. 'I figured that this country is hell on my kind of folk. It eats us. I didn't want to be eaten. So I made a deal. I gave them a lake, and I gave them prosperity . . .'

'And all it cost them was one child every winter.'

'Good kids,' said Hinzelmann, shaking his old head, slowly. 'They were all good kids. I'd only pick ones I liked. Except for Charlie Nelligan. He was a bad seed, that one. He was, what, 1924? 1925? Yeah. That was the deal.'

'The people of the town,' said Shadow. 'Mabel. Marguerite. Chad Mulligan. Do they *know*?'

Hinzelmann said nothing. He pulled the poker from the fire: the first six inches at the tip glowed a dull orange. Shadow knew that the handle of the poker must be too hot to hold, but it did not seem to bother Hinzelmann, and he prodded the fire again. He put the poker back into the fire, tip first, and left it there. Then he said, 'They know that they live in a good place. While every other town and city in this county, heck, in this part of the state, is crumbling into nothing. They know that.'

'And that's your doing?'

'This town,' said Hinzelmann. 'I care for it. Nothing happens here that I don't want to happen. You understand that? Nobody comes here that I don't want to come here. That was why your father sent you here. He didn't want you out there in the world, attracting attention. That's all.'

'And you betrayed him.'

'I did no such thing. He was a crook. But I always pay my debts.'

'I don't believe you,' said Shadow.

Hinzelmann looked offended. One hand tugged at the clump of white hair at his temple. 'I keep my word.'

'No. You don't. Laura came here. She said something was calling her here. And what about the coincidence that brought Sam Black Crow and Audrey Burton here, on the same night? I don't believe in coincidence any more.

'Sam Black Crow and Audrey Burton. Two people who both knew who I really was, and that there were people out there looking for me. I guess if one of them failed, there was always the other. And if all of them had failed, who else was on their way to Lakeside, Hinzelmann? My old prison warden, up here for a weekend's ice fishing? Laura's mother?' Shadow realized that he was angry. 'You wanted me out of your town. You just didn't want to have to tell Wednesday that was what you were doing.'

In the firelight, Hinzelmann seemed more like a gargoyle than an imp. 'This is a good town,' he said. Without his smile he looked waxen and corpse-like. 'You could have attracted too much attention. Not good for the town.'

'You should have left me back there on the ice,' said Shadow. 'You should have left me in the lake. I opened the trunk of the klunker. Right now Alison is still iced into the trunk. But the ice will melt, and her body'll float out and up to the surface. And then they'll go down and look and see what else they can find down there. Find your whole stash of kids. I guess some of those bodies are pretty well preserved.'

Hinzelmann reached down and picked up the poker. He made no pretense of stirring the fire with it any longer; he held it like a sword, or a baton, the glowing orange-white tip of it waving in the air. It smoked. Shadow was very aware that he was next-to-naked, and he was still tired, and clumsy, and far from able to defend himself.

'You want to kill me?' said Shadow. 'Go ahead. Do it. I'm a dead man anyway. I know you own this town – it's your little world. But if you think no one's going to come looking for me, you're living in a dream world. It's over, Hinzelmann. One way or another, it's done.'

Hinzelmann pushed himself to his feet, using the poker as a walking stick. The carpet charred and smoked where he rested the red-hot tip as he got up. He looked at Shadow and there were tears in his pale blue eyes. 'I love this town,' he said. 'I really like being a cranky old man, and telling my stories and driving Tessie and ice fishing. Remember what I told you, it's not the fish you bring home from a day's fishing. It's the peace of mind.'

He extended the tip of the poker in Shadow's direction: Shadow could feel the heat of it from a foot away.

'I could kill you,' said Hinzelmann, 'I could fix it. I've done it before. You're not the first to figure it out. Chad Mulligan's father, he figured it out. I fixed him. I can fix you.'

'Maybe,' said Shadow. 'But for how long, Hinzelmann? Another year? Another decade? They have computers. They aren't stupid. They pick up on patterns. Every year a kid's going to vanish. They'll come sniffing about here. Just like they'll come looking for me. Tell me – how old *are* you?' He curled his fingers around a sofa cushion, and prepared to pull it over his head: it would deflect a first blow.

Hinzelmann's face was expressionless. 'They were giving

their children to me before the Romans came to the Black
Forest,' he said. 'I was a god before ever I was a kobold.'

'Maybe it's time to move on,' said Shadow. He wondered
what a kobold was.

Hinzelmann stared at him. Then he took the poker, and
pushed the tip of it back into the burning embers. 'Maybe it
is, at that,' he said. 'But it's not that simple. What makes you
think I can leave this town, even if I want to, Shadow? I'm
part of this town. You going to make me go, Shadow? You
ready to kill me? So I can leave?'

Shadow looked down at the floor. There were still
glimmers and sparks in the carpet, where the poker-tip had
rested. Hinzelmann followed the look with his own, and
crushed the embers out with his foot, twisting. In Shadow's
mind came, unbidden, children, hundreds of them, staring
at him with bone-blind eyes, the hair twisting slowly around
their faces like fronds of seaweed. They were looking at him
reproachfully.

He knew that he was letting them down. He just didn't
know what else to do.

Shadow said, 'I can't kill you. You saved my life.'

He shook his head. He felt like crap, in every way he could
feel like crap. He didn't feel like a hero or a detective any
more – just another fucking sell-out, waving a stern finger at
the darkness before turning his back on it.

'You want to know a secret?' asked Hinzelmann.

'Sure,' said Shadow, with a heavy heart. He was ready to
be done with secrets.

'Watch this.'

Where Hinzelmann had been standing stood a male child,
no more than five years old. His hair was dark brown, and
long. He was perfectly naked, save for a worn leather band
around his neck. He was pierced with two swords, one of
them going through his chest, the other entering at his
shoulder, with the point coming out beneath the ribcage.
Blood flowed through the wounds without stopping and ran

down the child's body to pool and puddle on the floor. The swords looked unimaginably old.

The little boy stared up at Shadow with eyes that held only pain.

And Shadow thought to himself, *of course*. That's as good a way as any other of making a tribal god. He did not have to be told. He knew.

You take a baby and you bring it up in the darkness, letting it see no one, touch no one, and you feed it well as the years pass, feed it better than any of the village's other children, and then, five winters on, when the night is at its longest, you drag the terrified child out of its hut and into the circle of bonfires, and you pierce it with blades of iron and of bronze. Then you smoke the small body over charcoal fires until it is properly dried, and you wrap it in furs and carry it with you from encampment to encampment, deep in the Black Forest, sacrificing animals and children to it, making it the luck of the tribe. When, eventually, the thing falls apart from age, you place its fragile bones in a box, and you worship the box; until one day the bones are scattered and forgotten, and the tribes who worshiped the child-god of the box are long gone; and the child-god, the luck of the village, will be barely remembered, save as a ghost or a brownie, a kobold.

Shadow wondered which of the people who had come to northern Wisconsin a hundred and fifty years ago, a woodcutter, perhaps, or a mapmaker, had crossed the Atlantic with Hinzelmann living in his head.

And then the bloody child was gone, and the blood, and there was only an old man with a fluff of white hair and a goblin smile, his sweater-sleeves still soaked from putting Shadow into the bath that had saved his life.

'Hinzelmann?' the voice came from the doorway of the den.

Hinzelmann turned. Shadow turned too.

'I came over to tell you,' said Chad Mulligan, and his voice was strained, 'that the klunker went through the ice. I saw it had gone down when I drove over that way, and thought I'd come over and let you know, in case you'd missed it.'

He was holding his gun. It was pointed at the floor.

'Hey Chad,' said Shadow.

'Hey pal,' said Chad Mulligan. 'They sent me a note said you'd died in custody. Heart attack.'

'How about that?' said Shadow. 'Seems like I'm dying all over the place.'

'He came down here, Chad,' said Hinzelmann. 'He threatened me.'

'No,' said Chad Mulligan. 'He didn't. I've been here for the last ten minutes, Hinzelmann. I heard everything you said. About my old man. About the lake.' He walked further into the den. He did not raise the gun. 'I mean, Jesus, Hinzelmann. You can't drive through this town without seeing that goddamned lake. It's at the center of everything. So what the hell am I supposed to do?'

'You got to arrest him. He said he was going to kill me,' said Hinzelmann, a scared old man in a dusty den. 'Chad, I'm pleased you're here.'

'No,' said Chad Mulligan. 'You're not.'

Hinzelmann sighed. He bent down, as if resigned, and he pulled the poker out from the fire. The tip of it was burning bright orange.

'Put that down, Hinzelmann. Just put it down slowly, keep your hands in the air where I can see them, and turn and face the wall.'

There was an expression of pure fear on the old man's face, and Shadow would have felt sorry for him, but he remembered the frozen tears on the cheeks of Alison McGovern, and could not feel anything. Hinzelmann did not move. He did not put down the poker. He did not turn to the wall. Shadow was about to reach for Hinzelmann, to try to take the poker away from him, when the old man threw the burning poker at Chad Mulligan.

Hinzelmann threw it awkwardly, lobbing it across the room as if for form's sake, and as he threw it he was already hurrying for the door.

The poker glanced off Chad's left arm.

The noise of the shot, in the close quarters of the old man's room, was deafening.

One shot to the head, and that was all.

Mulligan said, 'Better get your clothes on.' His voice was dull and dead.

Shadow nodded. He walked to the room next door, opened the door of the clothes dryer and pulled out his clothes. The jeans were still damp. He put them on anyway. By the time he got back to the den, fully dressed – except for his coat, which was somewhere deep in the freezing mud of the lake, and his boots, which he could not find – Mulligan had already hauled several smoldering logs out from the fireplace.

Mulligan said, 'It's a bad day for a cop when he has to commit arson, just to cover up a murder.' Then he looked up at Shadow. 'You need boots,' he said.

'I don't know where he put them,' said Shadow.

'Hell,' said Mulligan. Then he said, 'Sorry about this, Hinzelmann,' and he picked the old man up by the collar and by the belt buckle, and he swung him forward, dropped the body with its head resting in the open fireplace. The white hair crackled and flared, and the room began to fill with the smell of charring flesh.

'It wasn't murder. It was self-defense,' said Shadow.

'I know what it was,' said Mulligan, flatly. He had already turned his attention to the smoking logs he had scattered about the room. He pushed one of them to the edge of the sofa, picked up an old copy of the *Lakeside News* and pulled it into its component pages, which he crumpled up and dropped onto the log. The newspaper pages browned and then burst into flame.

'Get outside,' said Chad Mulligan.

He opened the windows as they walked out of the house, and he sprang the lock on the front door to lock it before he closed it.

Shadow followed him out to the police car in his bare feet. Mulligan opened the front passenger door for him, and Shadow got in and wiped his feet off on the mat. Then he put on his socks, which were pretty much dry by now.

'We can get you some boots at Henning's Farm and Home,' said Chad Mulligan.

'How much did you hear in there?' asked Shadow.

'Enough,' said Mulligan. Then he said, 'Too much.'

They drove to Henning's Farm and Home in silence. When they got there the police chief said, 'What size feet?'

Shadow told him.

Mulligan walked into the store. He returned with a pair of thick woolen socks, and a pair of leather farm boots. 'All they had left in your size,' he said. 'Unless you wanted gumboots. I figured you didn't.'

Shadow pulled on the socks and the boots. They fitted fine. 'Thanks,' he said.

'You got a car?' asked Mulligan.

'It's parked by the road down to the lake. Near the bridge.'

Mulligan started the car and pulled out of the Henning's parking lot.

'What happened to Audrey?' asked Shadow.

'Day after they took you away, she said she liked me as a friend, but it would never work out between us, us being family and all, and she went back to Eagle Point. Broke my gosh-darn heart.'

'Makes sense,' said Shadow. 'And it wasn't personal. Hinzelmann didn't need her here any more.'

They drove back past Hinzelmann's house. A thick plume of white smoke was coming up from the chimney.

'She only came to town because he wanted her here. She was something to help him to get me out of town. I was bringing attention he didn't need.'

'I thought she liked me.'

They pulled up beside Shadow's rental car. 'What are you going to do now?' asked Shadow.

'I don't know,' said Mulligan, his normally harassed face was starting to look more alive than it had at any point since Hinzelmann's den. It also looked more troubled. 'I figure, I got a couple of choices. Either I'll . . .' and he made a gun of his first two fingers, and put the fingertips into his open mouth, and removed them, '. . . put a bullet through my brain. Or I'll wait another couple of days until the ice is mostly gone, and tie a concrete block to my leg and jump off the bridge. Or pills. Sheesh. Maybe I should just drive a while, out to one of the forests. Take pills out there. I don't want to make one of my guys have to do the clean up. Leave it for the county, huh?' He sighed, and shook his head.

'You didn't kill Hinzelmann, Chad. He died a long time ago, a long way from here.'

'Thanks for saying that, Mike. But I killed him. I shot a man in cold blood, and I covered it up. And if you asked me why I did it, why I really did it, I'm darned if I could tell you.'

Shadow put out a hand, touched Mulligan on the arm. 'Hinzelmann owned this town,' he said. 'I don't think you had a lot of choice about what happened back there. I think he brought you there. He wanted you to hear what you heard. He set you up. I guess it was the only way he could leave.'

Mulligan's miserable expression did not change. Shadow could see that the police chief had barely heard anything that he had said. He had killed Hinzelmann and built him a pyre, and now, obeying the last of Hinzelmann's desires, or simply because it was the only thing he could do to live with himself, he would commit suicide.

Shadow closed his eyes, remembering the place in his head that he had gone when Wednesday had told him to make snow: that place that pushed, mind to mind, and he smiled a smile he did not feel and he said, 'Chad. Let it go.'

There was a cloud in the man's mind, a dark, oppressive cloud, and Shadow could almost see it and, concentrating on it, imagined it fading away like a fog in the morning. 'Chad,' he said, fiercely, trying to penetrate the cloud, 'this town is going to change now. It's not going to be the only good town in a depressed region any more. It's going to be a lot more like the rest of this part of the world. There's going to be a lot more trouble. People out of work. People out of their heads. More people getting hurt. More bad shit going down. They are going to need a police chief with experience. The town needs you.' And then he said, 'Marguerite needs you.'

Something shifted in the storm cloud that filled the man's head. Shadow could feel it change. He *pushed* then, envisioning Marguerite Olsen's practical brown hands and her dark eyes, and her long, long black hair. He pictured the way she tipped her head on one side and half-smiled when she was amused. 'She's waiting for you,' said Shadow, and he knew it was true as he said it.

'Margie?' said Chad Mulligan.

And at that moment, although he could never tell you how he had done it, and he doubted that he could ever do it again, Shadow reached in to Chad Mulligan's mind, easy as anything, and he plucked the events of that afternoon from it as precisely and dispassionately as a raven picking an eye from roadkill.

The creases in Chad's forehead smoothed, and he blinked, sleepily.

'Go see Margie,' said Shadow. 'It's been good seeing you, Chad. Take care of yourself.'

'Sure,' yawned Chad Mulligan.

A message crackled over the police radio, and Chad reached out for the handset. Shadow got out of the car.

Shadow walked over to his rental car. He could see the gray flatness of the lake at the center of the town. He thought of the dead children who waited at the bottom of the water.

Soon, Alison would float to the surface . . .

As Shadow drove past Hinzelmann's place he could see the plume of smoke had already turned into a blaze. He could hear a siren wail.

He drove south, heading for Highway 51. He was on his way to keep his final appointment. But before that, he thought, he would stop off in Madison, for one last goodbye.

* * *

Best of everything, Samantha Black Crow liked closing up the Coffee House at night. It was a perfectly calming thing to do: it gave her a feeling that she was putting order back into the world. She would put on an Indigo Girls CD, and she would do her final chores of the night at her own pace and in her own way. First, she would clean the espresso machine. Then she would do the final rounds, ensuring that any missed cups or plates were deposited back in the kitchen, and that the newspapers that were always scattered around the Coffee House by the end of each day were collected together and piled neatly by the front door, all ready for recycling.

She loved the Coffee House. She'd gone there as a customer for six months before she talked Jeff, the manager, into giving her a job. It was a long, winding series of rooms filled with armchairs and sofas and low tables, on a street lined with second-hand bookstores.

She covered the leftover slices of cheesecake and put them into the large refrigerator for the night, then she took a cloth and wiped the last of the crumbs away. She enjoyed being alone.

As she worked she would sing along with the Indigo Girls. Sometimes she would break into a dance for a step or two, before catching herself, and stopping, smiling wryly at herself.

A tapping on the window jerked her attention from her chores back to the real world. She went to the door, opened it, to admit a woman of about Sam's age, with pigtailed magenta hair. Her name was Natalie.

'Hello,' said Natalie. She went up on tiptoes and kissed Sam, depositing the kiss snugly between Sam's cheek and the corner of her mouth. You can say a lot of things with a kiss like that. 'You done?'

'Nearly.'

'You want to see a movie?'

'Sure. Love to. I've got a good five minutes left here, though. Why don't you sit and read the *Onion*?'

'I saw this week's already.' She sat on a chair near the door, ruffled through the pile of newspapers put aside for recycling until she found something, and she read it, while Sam bagged up the last of the money in the till and put it in the safe.

They had been sleeping together for a week now. Sam wondered if this was it, the relationship she'd been waiting for all her life. She told herself that it was just brain chemicals and pheromones that made her happy when she saw Natalie, and perhaps that was what it was; still, all she knew for sure was that she smiled when she saw Natalie, and that when they were together she felt comfortable and comforted.

'This paper,' said Natalie, 'has another one of those articles in it. "Is America Changing?"'

'Well, is it?'

'They don't say. They say that maybe it is, but they don't know how and they don't know why, and maybe it isn't happening at all.'

Sam smiled broadly. 'Well,' she said, 'That covers every option, doesn't it?'

'I guess.' Natalie's brow creased and she went back to her newspaper.

Sam washed the dishcloth and folded it. 'I think it's just that, despite the government and whatever, everything just feels suddenly good right now. Maybe it's just spring coming a little early. It was a long winter, and I'm glad it's over.'

'Me, too.' A pause. 'It says in the article that lots of people have been reporting weird dreams. I haven't really had any weird dreams. Nothing weirder than normal.'

Sam looked around to see if there was anything she had missed. Nope. It was a good job well done. She took off her apron, hung it back in the kitchen. Then she came back and started to turn off the lights. 'I've had some weird dreams recently,' she said. 'They got weird enough that I actually started keeping a dream journal. They seem to mean so much while I'm dreaming them. I write them down when I wake up. And then when I read them, they don't mean anything at all.'

She put on her street coat, and her one-size-fits-all gloves.

'I did some dream work,' said Natalie. Natalie had done a little of everything, from arcano self-defense disciplines and sweat lodges to feng shui and jazz dancing. 'Tell me. I'll tell you what they mean.'

'Okay.' Sam unlocked the door and turned the last of the lights off. She let Natalie out, and she walked out onto the street and locked the door to the Coffee House firmly behind her. 'Sometimes I have been dreaming of people who fell from the sky. Sometimes I'm underground, talking to a woman with a buffalo head. And sometimes I dream about this guy I kissed once in a bar.'

Natalie made a noise. 'Something you should have told me about?'

'Maybe. But not like that. It was a Fuck-Off Kiss.'

'You were telling him to fuck off?'

'No, I was telling everyone else they could fuck off. You had to be there, I guess.'

Natalie's shoes clicked down the sidewalk. Sam padded on next to her. 'He owns my car,' said Sam.

'That purple thing you got at your sister's?'

'Yup.'

'What happened to him? Why doesn't he want his car?'

'I don't know. Maybe he's in prison. Maybe he's dead.'

'Dead?'

'I guess.' Sam hesitated. 'A few weeks back, I was certain he was dead. ESP. Or whatever. Like, I knew. But then, I started to think maybe he wasn't. I don't know. I guess my ESP isn't that hot.'

'How long are you going to keep his car?'

'Until someone comes for it. I think it's what he would have wanted.'

Natalie looked at Sam, then she looked again. Then she said, 'Where did you get *those* from?'

'What?'

'The flowers. The ones you're *holding*, Sam. Where did they come from? Did you have them when we left the Coffee House? I would have seen them.'

Sam looked down. Then she grinned. 'You are so sweet. I should have said something when you gave them to me, shouldn't I?' she said. 'They are lovely. Thank you so much. But wouldn't red have been more appropriate?'

They were roses, their stems wrapped in paper. Six of them, and white.

'I didn't give them to you,' said Natalie, her lips firming.

And neither of them said another word until they reached the movie theatre.

When she got home that night Sam put the roses in an improvised vase. Later, she cast them in bronze, and she kept to herself the tale of how she got them, although she told Caroline, who came after Natalie, the story of the ghost-roses one night when they were both very drunk, and Caroline agreed with Sam that it was a really, really strange and a spooky story, and, deep down, did not actually believe a word of it, so that was all right.

. ***

Shadow had parked near the Capitol building, and walked slowly around the square, stretching his legs after the long drive. His clothes were uncomfortable, although they had dried on his body, and the new boots were still tight. He passed a pay phone. He called information, and they gave him the number.

No, he was told. She isn't here. She's not back yet. She's probably still at the Coffee House.

He stopped on the way to the Coffee House to buy flowers.

He found the Coffee House, then he crossed the road and stood in the doorway of a used bookstore, and waited, and watched.

The place closed at eight, and at ten past eight Shadow saw Sam Black Crow walk out of the Coffee House in the company of a smaller woman whose pigtailed hair was a peculiar shade of red. They were holding hands tightly, as if simply holding hands could keep the world at bay, and they were talking – or rather, Sam was doing most of the talking while her friend listened. Shadow wondered what Sam was saying. She smiled as she talked.

The two women crossed the road, and they walked past the place where Shadow was standing. The pigtailed girl passed within a foot of him; he could have reached out and touched her, and they didn't see him at all.

He watched them walking away from him down the street, and felt a pang, like a minor chord being played inside him.

It had been a good kiss, Shadow reflected, but Sam had never looked at him the way she was looking at the pigtailed girl, and she never would.

'What the hell. We'll always have Peru,' he said, under his breath, as Sam walked away from him. 'And El Paso. We'll always have that.'

Then he ran after her, and put the flowers into Sam's hands. He hurried away, so she could not give them back.

Then he walked up the hill to the Capitol building, walked around it until he found his car, and he took Highway 90 south to Chicago. He drove at or slightly under the speed limit.

It was the last thing he had to do.

He was in no hurry.

***

He spent the night in a Motel 6. He got up the next morning, and realized his clothes still smelled like the bottom of the lake. He put them on anyway. He figured he wouldn't need them much longer.

Shadow paid his bill. He drove to the brownstone apartment building. He found it without any difficulty. It was smaller than he remembered.

He walked up the stairs steadily, not fast, that would have meant he was eager to go to his death, and not slow, that would have meant he was afraid. Someone had cleaned the stairwell: the black garbage bags had gone. The place smelled of the chlorine-smell of bleach, no longer of rotting vegetables.

The red-painted door at the top of the stairs was wide open: the smell of old meals hung in the air. Shadow hesitated, then he pressed the doorbell.

'I come!' called a woman's voice, and, dwarf-small and dazzlingly blonde, Zorya Utrennyaya came out of the kitchen and bustled towards him, wiping her hands on her apron. She looked different, Shadow realized. She looked happy. Her cheeks were rouged red, and there was a sparkle in her old eyes. When she saw him her mouth became an O and she called out 'Shadow? You came back to us?' and she hurried toward him with her arms outstretched. He bent down and embraced her, and she kissed his cheek. 'So good to see you!' she said. 'Now you must go away.'

Shadow stepped into the apartment. All the doors in the apartment (except, unsurprisingly, Zorya Polunochnaya's) were wide open, and all the windows he could see were open as well. A gentle breeze blew fitfully through the corridor.

'You're spring cleaning,' he said to Zorya Utrennyaya.

'We have a guest coming,' she told him. 'Now, you must go away. First, you want coffee?'

'I came to see Czernobog,' said Shadow. 'It's time.'

Zorya Utrennyaya shook her head violently. 'No, no,' she said. 'You *don't* want to see him. Not a good idea.'

'I know,' said Shadow. 'But you know, the only thing I've really learned about dealing with gods is that if you make a deal, you keep it. They get to break all the rules they want. We don't. Even if I tried to walk out of here, my feet would just bring me back.'

She pushed up her bottom lip, then said, 'Is true. But go today. Come back tomorrow. He will be gone then.'

'Who is it?' called a woman's voice, from further down the corridor. 'Zorya Utrennyaya, to who are you talking? This mattress, I cannot turn on my own, you know.'

Shadow walked down the corridor, and said 'Good morning, Zorya Vechernyaya. Can I help?' which made the woman in the room squeak with surprise and drop her corner of the mattress.

The bedroom was thick with dust: it covered every surface, the wood and the glass, and motes of it floated and danced through the beams of sunshine coming through the open window, disturbed by occasional breezes and the lazy flapping of the yellowed lace curtains.

He remembered this room. This was the room they had given to Wednesday, that night. Bielebog's room.

Zorya Vechernyaya eyed him uncertainly. 'The mattress,' she said. 'It needs to be turned.'

'Not a problem,' said Shadow. He reached out and took the mattress, lifted it with ease and turned it over. It was an old wooden bed, and the feather mattress weighed almost as much as a man. Dust flew and swirled as the mattress went down.

'Why are you here?' asked Zorya Vechernyaya. It was not a friendly question, the way she asked it.

'I'm here,' said Shadow, 'because back in December a young man played a game of checkers with an old god, and he lost.'

The old woman's gray hair was up on the top of her head in a tight bun. She pursed her lips. 'Come back tomorrow,' said Zorya Vechernyaya.

'I can't,' he said, simply.

'Is your funeral. Now, you go and sit down. Zorya Utrennyaya will bring you coffee. Czernobog will be back soon.'

Shadow walked along the corridor to the sitting room. It was just as he remembered, although now the window was open. The gray cat slept on the arm of the sofa. It opened an eye as Shadow came in and then, unimpressed, it went back to sleep.

This was where he had played checkers with Czernobog; this was where he had wagered his life to get the old man to join them on Wednesday's last doomed grift. The fresh air blew in through the open window, blowing the stale air away.

Zorya Utrennyaya came in with a red wooden tray. A small enameled cup of steaming black coffee sat on the tray, beside a saucer filled with small chocolate-chip cookies. She put it down on the table in front of him.

'I saw Zorya Polunochnaya again,' he said. 'She came to me under the world, and she gave me the moon to light my way. And she took something from me. But I don't remember what.'

'She likes you,' said Zorya Utrennyaya. 'She dreams so much. And she guards us all. She is so brave.'

'Where's Czernobog?'

'He says the spring-cleaning makes him uncomfortable. He goes out to buy newspaper, sit in the park. Buy cigarettes. Perhaps he will not come back today. You do not have to wait. Why don't you go? Come back tomorrow.'

'I'll wait,' said Shadow. This was no *geas*, forcing him to wait, he knew that. This was *him*. It was one last thing that needed to happen, and if it was *the* last thing that happened, well, he was going there of his own volition. After this there would be no more obligations, no more mysteries, no more ghosts.

He sipped the hot coffee, as black and as sweet as he remembered.

He heard a deep male voice in the corridor, and he sat up straighter. He was pleased to see that his hand was not trembling. The door opened.

'Shadow?'

'Hi,' said Shadow. He stayed sitting down.

Czernobog walked into the room. He was carrying a folded copy of the *Chicago Sun-Times*, which he put down on the coffee table. He stared at Shadow, then he put his hand out, tentatively. The two men shook hands.

'I came,' said Shadow. 'Our deal. You came through with your part of it. This is my part.'

Czernobog nodded. His brow creased. The sunlight glinted on his gray hair and moustache, making them appear almost golden. 'Is . . .,' he frowned. 'Is not . . .' He broke off. 'Maybe you should go. Is not a good time.'

'Take as long as you need,' said Shadow. 'I'm ready.'

Czernobog sighed. 'You are a very stupid boy. You know that?'

'I guess.'

'You are a stupid boy. And on the mountain top, you did a very good thing.'

'I did what I had to do.'

'Perhaps.'

Czernobog walked to the old wooden sideboard, and, bending down, pulled an attaché case from underneath it. He flipped the catches on the case. Each one sprang back with a satisfying thump. He opened the case. He took a hammer out, and hefted it, experimentally. The hammer looked like a scaled-down sledgehammer; its wooden haft was stained.

Then he stood up. He said, 'I owe you much. More than you know. Because of you, things are changing. This is spring time. The true spring.'

'I know what I did,' said Shadow. 'I didn't have a lot of choice.'

Czernobog nodded. There was a look in his eyes that Shadow did not remember seeing before. 'Did I ever tell you about my brother?'

'Bielebog?' Shadow walked to the center of the ash-stained carpet. He went down on his knees. 'You said you hadn't seen him in a long time.'

'Yes,' said the old man, raising the hammer. 'It has been a long winter, boy. A very long winter. But the winter is ending, now.' And he shook his head, slowly, as if he were remembering something. And he said, 'Close your eyes.'

Shadow closed his eyes and raised his head, and he waited.

The head of the sledgehammer was cold, icy cold, and it touched his forehead as gently as a kiss.

'*Pock*! There,' said Czernobog. 'Is done.' There was a smile on his face that Shadow had never seen before, an easy, comfortable smile, like sunshine on a summer's day. The old man walked over to the case, and he put the hammer away, and closed the bag, and pushed it back under the sideboard.

'Czernobog?' asked Shadow. Then, '*Are* you Czernobog?'

'Yes. For today,' said the old man. 'By tomorrow, it will all be Bielebog. But today, is still Czernobog.'

'Then why? Why didn't you kill me when you could?'

The old man took out an unfiltered cigarette from a pack in his pocket. He took a large box of matches from the mantelpiece and lit the cigarette with a match. He seemed deep in thought. 'Because,' said the old man, after some time, 'there is blood. But there is also gratitude. And it has been a long, long winter.'

Shadow got to his feet. There were dusty patches on the knees of his jeans, where he had knelt, and he brushed the dust away.

'Thanks,' he said.

'You're welcome,' said the old man. 'Next time you want to play checkers, you know where to find me. *This* time, I play white.'

'Thanks. Maybe I will,' said Shadow. 'But not for a while.' He looked into the old man's twinkling eyes, and he wondered if they had always been that cornflower shade of blue. They shook hands, and neither of them said goodbye.

Shadow kissed Zorya Utrennyaya on the cheek on his way out, and he kissed Zorya Vechernyaya on the back of her hand, and he took the stairs out of that place two at a time.

Postscript

Reykjavik in Iceland is a strange city, even for those who have seen many strange cities. It is a volcanic city – the heat for the city comes from deep underground.

There are tourists, but not as many of them as you might expect, not even in early July. The sun was shining, as it had shone for weeks now: it ceased shining for an hour or two in the small hours. There would be a dusky dawn of sorts between two and three in the morning, and then the day would begin once more.

The big tourist had walked most of Reykjavik that morning, listening to people talk in a language that had changed little in a thousand years. The natives here could read the ancient sagas as easily as they could read a newspaper. There was a sense of continuity on this island that scared him, and that he found desperately reassuring. He was very tired: the unending daylight had made sleep almost impossible, and he had sat in his hotel room through the whole long nightless night alternately reading a guidebook and *Bleak House*, a novel he had bought in an airport in the last few weeks, but which airport he could no longer remember. Sometimes, he had stared out of the window.

Finally the clock as well as the sun proclaimed it morning.

He bought a bar of chocolate at one of the many candy stores, walked the sidewalk, occasionally finding himself reminded of the volcanic nature of Iceland: he would turn a corner and notice, for a moment, a sulphurous quality to the air. It put him in mind not of Hades but of rotten eggs.

Many of the women he passed were very beautiful: slender and pale. The kind of women that Wednesday had liked. Shadow wondered what could have attracted Wednesday to Shadow's mother, who had been beautiful but had been neither of those things.

Shadow smiled at the pretty women, because they made him feel pleasantly male, and he smiled at the other women too, because he was having a good time.

He was not sure when he became aware that he was being observed. Somewhere on his walk through Reykjavik he realized that someone was watching him. He would turn, from time to time, trying to get a glimpse of who it was, and he would stare into store windows and out at the reflected street behind him, but he saw no one out of the ordinary, no one who seemed to be observing him.

He went into a small restaurant, where he ate smoked puffin and cloudberries and arctic char and boiled potatoes, and he drank Coca-Cola, which tasted sweeter, more sugary than he remembered it tasting back in the States.

The waiter brought his bill – the meal was more expensive than Shadow had expected, but that seemed to be true of meals in every place on Shadow's wandering. As the waiter put the bill down on the table, he said, 'Excuse me. You are American?'

'Yes.'

'Then, happy Fourth of July,' said the waiter. He looked pleased with himself.

Shadow had not realized that it was the Fourth. Independence Day. Yes. He liked the idea of independence. He left the money and a tip on the table, and walked outside. There was a cool breeze coming in off the Atlantic, and he buttoned up his coat.

He sat down on a grassy bank and looked at the city that surrounded him, and thought, one day he would have to go home. And one day he would have to make a home to go back to. He wondered whether home was a thing that happened to a place after a while, or if it was something that you found in the end, if you simply walked and waited and willed it long enough.

He pulled out his book.

An old man came striding across the hillside toward him: he wore a dark gray cloak, ragged at the bottom, as if he had done a lot of traveling, and he wore a broad-brimmed blue hat, with a seagull feather tucked into the band, at a jaunty angle. He looked like an aging hippie, thought Shadow. Or a long-retired gunfighter. The old man was ridiculously tall.

The man squatted beside Shadow on the hillside. He nodded, curtly, to Shadow. He had a piratical black eye patch over one eye, and a jutting white chin-beard. Shadow wondered if the man was going to hit him up for a cigarette.

'Hvernig gengur? Manst pú eftir mér?' said the old man.

'I'm sorry,' said Shadow. 'I don't speak Icelandic.' Then he said, awkwardly, the phrase he had learned from his phrase book in the daylight of the small hours of that morning: 'Ég tala bara ensku.' I speak only English. 'American.'

The old man nodded slowly. He said, 'My people went from here to America a long time ago. They went there, and then they returned to Iceland. They said it was a good place for men, but a bad place for gods. And without their gods they felt too . . . alone.' His English was fluent, but the pauses and the beats of the sentence were strange. Shadow looked at him: close-up, the man seemed older than Shadow had imagined possible. His skin was lined with tiny wrinkles and cracks, like the cracks in granite.

The old man said, 'I do know you, boy.'

'You do?'

'You and I, we have walked the same path. I also hung on the tree for nine days, a sacrifice of myself to myself. I am the lord of the Aes. I am the god of the gallows.'

'You are Odin,' said Shadow.

The man nodded thoughtfully, as if weighing up the name. 'They call me many things, but, yes, I am Odin, Bor's son,' he said.

'I saw you die,' said Shadow. 'I stood vigil for your body. You tried to destroy so much, for power. You would have sacrificed so much for yourself. You did that.'

'I did not do that.'

'Wednesday did. He was you.'

'He was me, yes. But I am not him.'

The man scratched the side of his nose. His gull-feather bobbed.

'Will you go back?' asked the Lord of the Gallows. 'To America?'

'Nothing to go back for,' said Shadow, and as he said it he knew it was a lie.

'Things wait for you there,' said the old man. 'But they will wait until you return.'

A white butterfly flew crookedly past them. Shadow said nothing. He had had enough of gods and their ways to last him several lifetimes. He would take the bus to the airport, he decided, and change his ticket. Get a plane to somewhere he had never been. He would keep moving.

'Hey,' said Shadow. 'I have something for you.' His hand dipped into his pocket, and palmed the object he needed. 'Hold your hand out,' he said.

Odin looked at him strangely and seriously. Then he shrugged, and extended his right hand, palm down. Shadow reached over and turned it so the palm was upward.

He opened his own hands, showed them, one after the other, to be completely empty. Then he pushed the glass eye into the leathery palm of the old man's hand and left it there.

'How did you do that?'

'Magic,' said Shadow, without smiling.

The old man grinned and laughed and clapped his hands together. He looked at the eye, holding it between finger and thumb, and nodded, as if he knew exactly what it was, and then he slipped it into a leather bag that hung by his waist. '*Takk kærlega*. I shall take care of this.'

'You're welcome,' said Shadow. He stood up, brushed the grass from his jeans. He closed the book, put it back into the side-pocket of his backpack.

'Again,' said the Lord of Asgard, with an imperious motion of his head, his voice deep and commanding. 'More. Do again.'

'You people,' said Shadow. 'You're never satisfied. Okay. This is one I learned from a guy who's dead now.'

He reached into nowhere, and took a gold coin from the air. It was a normal sort of gold coin. It couldn't bring back the dead or heal the sick, but it was a gold coin sure enough. 'And that's all there is,' he said, displaying it between finger and thumb. 'That's all she wrote.'

He tossed the coin into the air with a flick of his thumb. It spun golden at the top of its arc, in the sunlight, and it glittered and glinted and hung there in the mid-summer sky as if it was never going to come down. Maybe it never would. Shadow didn't wait to see. He walked away and he kept on walking.

Acknowledgments

I t's been a long book, and a long journey, and I owe many people a great deal.

Mrs Hawley lent me her Florida house to write in, and all I had to do in return was scare away the vultures. She lent me her Irish house to finish it in and cautioned me not to scare away the ghosts. My thanks to her and Mr Hawley for all their kindness and generosity. Jonathan and Jane lent me their house and hammock to write in, and all I had to do was fish the occasional peculiar Floridian beastie out of the lizard pool. I'm very grateful to them all.

Dan Johnson, MD gave me medical information whenever I needed it, pointed out stray and unintentional anglicisms (everybody else did this as well), answered the oddest questions, and, on one July day, even flew me around northern Wisconsin in a tiny plane. In addition to keeping my life going by proxy while I wrote this book, my assistant, the fabulous Lorraine Garland, became very blasé about finding out the population of small American towns for me; I'm still not sure quite how she did it. (She's part of a band called The Flash Girls: buy their new record, *Play Each Morning, Wild Queen* and make her happy.) Terry Pratchett helped unlock a knotty plot point for me on the train to Gothenburg. Eric Edelman answered my diplomatic questions. Anna Sunshine Ison unearthed a bunch of stuff for me on the west coast Japanese internment camps, which will have to wait for another book to be written for it never quite fitted into this one. I stole the best line of dialogue in the epilogue from Gene Wolfe, to whom, my thanks. Sergeant Kathy Ertz graciously answered even my weirdest police procedural questions and Deputy Sheriff Marshall Multhauf took me on a drive-along. Pete Clark submitted to some ridiculously personal questioning with grace and good humor. Dale Robertson was the book's consulting hydrologist. I appreciated Dr Jim Miller's comments about people, language and fish, as I did the linguistic help of Margret Rodas. Jamy Ian Swiss made sure that the coin magic was magical. Any mistakes in the book are mine, not theirs.

Many good people read the manuscript and offered valuable suggestions, corrections, encouragement, and information. I am especially grateful to Colin Greenland and Susanna Clarke, John Clute and Samuel R. Delany. I'd also like to thank Owl Goingback (who really does have the world's coolest name), Iselin Røsjø Evensen, Peter Straub, Jonathan Carroll, Kelli Bickman, Dianna Graf, Lenny Henry, Pete Atkins, Amy Horsting, Chris Ewen, Teller, Kelly Link, Barb Gilly, Will Shetterly, Connie Zastoupil, Rantz Hoseley, Diana Schutz, Steve Brust, Kelly Sue DeConnick, Roz Kaveney, Ian McDowell, Karen Berger, Wendy Japhet, Terje Nordberg, Gwenda Bond, Therese Littleton, Lou Aronica, Hy Bender, Mark Askwith, Alan Moore (who also graciously lent me *Litvinoff's Book*), and the original Joe Sanders. Thanks also to Rebecca Wilson; and particular thanks to Stacy Weiss, for her insight. After she read the first draft, Diana Wynne Jones warned me what kind of book this was, and the perils I risked writing it, and she's been right on every count so far.

I wish Professor Frank McConnell were still with us. I think he would have enjoyed this one.

Once I'd written the first draft I realized that a number of other people had tackled these themes before ever I got to them: in particular my favorite unfashionable author, James Branch Cabell, the late Roger Zelazny, and, of course, the inimitable Harlan Ellison, whose collection *Deathbird Stories* burned itself onto the back of my head when I was still of an age where a book could change me forever.

I can never quite see the point of noting down for posterity the music you listened to while writing a book, and there was an awful lot of music listened to while I was writing this. Still, without Greg Brown's *Dream Café* and the Magnetic Field's *69 Love Songs* it would have been a different book, so thanks to Greg and to Stephin. And I feel it my duty to tell you that you can experience the music of the House on the Rock on tape or CD, including that of the Mikado machine and of the World's Largest Carousel. It's unlike, although certainly not better than, anything else you've heard. Write to: The House on the Rock, Spring Green, WI 53588 USA, or call 1-608-935-3639.

My agents – Merrilee Heifetz at Writers House, Jon Levin and Erin Culley La Chapelle at CAA – were invaluable as sounding boards and pillars of wisdom.

Many people, who were waiting for things I had promised them just as soon as I finished writing this book, were astonishingly patient. I'd like to thank the good folk at Warner Brothers pictures (particularly Kevin McCormick and Lorenzo di Bonaventura), at Village Roadshow, at Sunbow, and at Miramax; and Shelly Bond, who put up with a lot.

The two people without whom: Jennifer Hershey at HarperCollins in the US and Doug Young at Hodder Headline in the UK. I'm lucky to have good editors, and these are two of the best editors I've known. Not to mention two of the most uncomplaining, patient, and, as the deadlines whirled past us like dry leaves in a gust of wind, positively stoic.

Bill Massey came in at the end, at Headline, and lent the book his editorial eagle eye. Kelly Notaras helped shepherd it through production with grace and polish.

Lastly, I want to thank my family, Mary, Mike, Holly, and Maddy, who were the most patient of all, who loved me, and who, for long periods during the writing of this book, put up with my going away both to write and to find America – which, turned out, when I eventually found it, to have been in America all along.

Neil Gaiman
near Kinsale, County Cork.
15 January 2001.

Exclusive Material

Contents

1. An Interview with Neil Gaiman

2. Reading-group Discussion Questions

Bonus Material

1. How Dare You?
   An essay by Neil Gaiman on *American Gods*

2. 'The Monarch of the Glen'
   An *American Gods* novella

An Interview with Neil Gaiman

Which god-like powers would you like to posses?

I want to make time stretchier. I would like much more rubbery days, and I just wish that you could lean on a week, and sort of push the walls out a bit, and suddenly about nineteen extra days would rush in to fill the vacuum.

There is not enough time, and I wind up just wanting to do things that I don't have time for. There are so many things that I'd love to do, and I have to put off, or that it's a matter of me choosing, when really I'd love to do both. And if only time were infinitely stretchy, I could.

As an Englishman in America, do you see yourself as an immigrant or an ex-pat, or something in between?

I think I'm slightly more of an ex-pat than an immigrant. I've lived in America more than anywhere else for the last thirteen years, and when I went over there I figured it would probably be a three-year stay and then we'd come back. These days I know that I'm stuck there at least for another eight years until my youngest daughter finishes high school.

But I've never felt that I was a permanent addition to continental America. I've always felt like somebody who would eventually fly away, or possibly get the boat and go away. Or just walk off.

What's your favourite roadside attraction?

The House on the Rock in *American Gods* actually is real. Most people think I made it up, whereas in actual fact I just toned it down a bit so that people would believe it. Because being a real place it has no obligation to be likely. So I left out the 120 piece robot orchestra and other stuff.

I remember, the first time I went to The House on the Rock, thinking, I just don't believe this place, and the second time I went to The House on the Rock still not believing this place. Then I had to go back for *Entertainment Weekly* to take my photograph standing beside the largest carousel in the world.

It was the single loudest photo session I've ever had because they actually pitch the volume of the mechanical instruments in that room in order to keep people moving through. You're not really meant to linger too long by the largest carousel in the world.

The photo session went on for several hours and the photographer was communicating with me entirely by hand gestures. He would tap his chin and point up so that I'd know to look up a bit.

How did you find out about it?

Like most roadside attractions in America, they have signposts for it that start about 300 miles away, and imply it's just round the corner. I'd seen all these signs saying 'The

House on the Rock', and thought it was very near where I lived, and eventually discovered it was 250 miles away.

On the other hand, Rock City, which is also in *American Gods*, is worse, because I saw my first signpost to 'See Rock City, the World's Wonder' driving through mountainous Tennessee or Kentucky or somewhere, and again assumed it was just around the corner, and then drove for the greater part of a day.

And then of course, because it's almost impossible to get to once you're there, I drove straight past it. Then I drove back and checked it out, and decided it was going to be in my book.

Do you think this is one of the big differences between England and America, in that you could drive from London to Scotland in the time it takes to follow the signs to Rock City?

I think the biggest difference between England and America is that England has history, and America has geography. In England, you can find whatever you need as long as you're willing to go back far enough, or go and find out when it happened. In America you can find whatever you need just as long as you're prepared to drive far enough.

Also I get fascinated by the difference between England and America whereby places in England are all about time – the time it takes you to get there. And getting to places which would be five minutes away in America would take three or four hours sometimes. Not to mention Scotland, which gets positively fractal. You have these infinitely wiggly roads. Fractally wiggly roads.

What was your strangest plane journey?

The trouble with plane journeys is you start folding them all together. I do remember one which was not necessarily my strangest plane journey, but had something I've never seen happen before or since.

I'd just been served with a large cup of apple juice and the plane hit one of those air pockets and dropped several hundred feet. It didn't bother any of us because we were all seatbelted in, but my apple juice shot straight out of my cup. The cup remained in the same place, but the contents made a slow and incredibly graceful arc across the cabin and landed in a businessman's lap half an aeroplane away.

I was with Dave McKean at the time on a Mr Punch signing tour and we tried to pretend it wasn't us. At least they knew we hadn't actually thrown it; it was the apple juice that made a mad leap for freedom.

What's your favourite coin trick?

The favourite coin trick I've ever done was when I started work on *American Gods* and I had a large notebook, a fountain pen, and a copy of Bobo's *Modern Coin Magic*.

I went from one to the other and I spent days practising my French Drop and my Downs Palm and all of those things because I knew Shadow was going to be into coin magic and I felt that I had to be able to write about it reasonably convincingly. I'd never done any magic before but I decided I had to now.

I was actually on a train across America, going to San Diego, and there was a ten-year-old girl traveling with her mother. We'd all been on this train now for about three days so we all knew each other, and I disappeared a coin for her rather unexpectedly and reappeared it from her ear. I don't think anybody had ever done anything like that for her and seeing the expression on her face left me understanding why people become magicians.

I of course have never become a magician, but I get to hang around with the Penn and Tellers and the Derren Browns of this world, who are all very, very good people and who will humour me and treat me like one of their own although they know that really I'm not.

Favourite con artist or con trick?

Ponzi, who created the Ponzi scheme. The thing that people laugh at in terms of confidence tricks is somebody selling you the Brooklyn Bridge, or in England somebody selling you London Bridge, or in France somebody selling you the Eiffel Tower.

Ponzi sold the Eiffel Tower by going to all the major scrap metal agents in France, presenting himself as a representative of the French government, and explaining that the Eiffel Tower had become unsafe and they were going to be scrapping it, but they needed somebody who could handle the dismantling of the tower and the volume of metal that this would generate. He also implied that the French government was going to be so grateful that there would probably be all sorts of decorations involved for anybody who took this on.

And then he explained to each of them in turn that it was a sealed envelope bid, so there was no possibility for corruption. So they went off to prepare their bids, and he privately got in touch with each of these gentlemen and explained that he could be bribed. And each of them gave him vast sums of money in order to buy the Eiffel Tower. And that, I feel, is still my favourite con.

Did you enjoy making up the con tricks in AMERICAN GODS?

I did enjoy making up the con tricks very much, although I have to say I found myself rather baffled. The one that I thought you could actually do I tried to sort of fuzz the edges of a bit, so the reader can't actually figure out exactly how things work with Mr Wednesday and the credit cards. What he did is doable but I fuzzed the edges so that the reader can't do it.

But I was very proud of myself for coming up with the ATM card-night deposit con. I made that up, and I thought it was really funny until the phone rang about eighteen months ago and it was a reporter from Canada letting me know that somebody who was a fan of the book had just done it and was now on the run, having taken local merchants for $30,000.

You don't expect your readers to go, 'Ah, this book's not just a fine work of literary whatsisname, but also a get-rich-quick scheme,' to be followed shortly afterwards by a go-to-prison-quick scheme, which I believe he did.

Are there any myths you would like to dispel?

I have my journal over at www.neilgaiman.com, and one of the reasons for having it, apart from the fact that it's incredibly useful to have an immediate plug-in to your readers, is that I used to turn up at signings and people would expect me to be characters that I'd created. Particularly the Sandman.

So I'd turn up to the signing and see the disappointment on people's faces because I wasn't tall and pale and beautiful and very morbid. They expected me to speak in gnomic gothic sentences and possibly iambic pentameter, or triolets or something.

I like the blog because it undercuts and dispels that. I don't think you can imagine somebody as a beautiful gothic figure if they've just written about clearing up cat vomit from the floor at three o'clock in the morning.

It's now a few years since AMERICAN GODS came out. Do you have any thoughts on the novel?

People were incredibly nice about *American Gods*. I never expected all the awards that it won, particularly when it won the Hugo, and the Nebula, and the Bram Stoker award – that was delightful. And Americans were terribly nice about it. Nobody actually did the whole 'How dare you, being English, write about America?', which I thought was kind of them.

The thing I found really amusing was about some places in the middle where people are talking in the way they talk in Wisconsin and Minnesota: occasionally I would have New Yorkers and Los Angelenos accusing me of lapsing into Briticisms there, mostly I think because people have no idea what people talk like in the rest of their country.

Reading-group Discussion Questions

1. *American Gods* is an epic novel dealing with many big themes, including sacrifice, loyalty, betrayal, love and faith. Which theme affected you most strongly, and why?

2. Shadow begins the novel as a convict, and ends it a different man. How does the novel exploit the idea of America as a place where immigrants and exiles, both physical and emotional, can reinvent themselves? What makes Shadow himself so compelling and complex?

3. *American Gods* is partly a road trip through small-town America, where Shadow can see the darker side of life that other people ignore. What does the novel say about what people will accept in order to maintain a sense of normality?

4. The old gods expect sacrifice, violence and worship. How have they adapted to the modern world? What does this say about the nature of divinity? How and why have Americans transferred their devotion to the new technological and material gods from the old spiritual gods? What comment is being made about modern cultural values?

5. What is the significance of the illusions, cons and magic tricks that occur throughout the novel? *American Gods* is a novel where magic, myth and the divine coexist with the normal, mundane and human in a way that is utterly believable. How is this illusion maintained?

6. How does the rick background description increase the power of the narrative? What do the secondary characters, particularly the gods whose lives and deaths we are given a brief insight into, add to the novel?

How Dare You?

Nobody's asked the question I've been dreading, so far, the question I have been hoping that no one would ask. So I'm going to ask it myself, and try to answer it myself, in the hopes that, like the airline passenger scared of being hijacked who always smuggles her own bomb on to the plane, my doing it increases the odds against someone else doing it.

And the question is this: *How dare you?*

Or, in its expanded form: 'How dare you, an Englishman, try and write a book about America, about American myths and the American soul? How dare you try and write about what makes America special, as a country, as a nation, as an idea?'

And, being English, my immediate impulse is to shrug my shoulders and promise it won't happen again.

But then, I did dare, in my novel *American Gods*, and it took an odd sort of hubris to write it.

As a young man, I wrote a comic-book about dreams and stories called *Sandman* (collected, and still in print, in ten graphic novels, and you should read it if you haven't). I got a similar question all the time, back then: 'You live in England. How can you set so much of this story in America?'

And I would point out that, in media terms, the UK was practically the 51st state. We get American films, watch American TV. 'I might not write a Seattle that would satisfy an inhabitant,' I used to say, 'but I'll write one as good as a New Yorker who's never been to Seattle.'

I was, of course, wrong. I didn't do that at all. What I did instead was, in retrospect, much more interesting: I created an America that was entirely imaginary, in which *Sandman* could take place. A delirious, unlikely place out beyond the edge of the real.

And that satisfied me until, following my American wife and my desire for an Addams Family-style house, I came to live in America.

Slowly – and it took a while – I realized both that the America I'd been writing was wholly fictional, and that the real America, the one underneath the what-you-see-is-what-you-get surface, was much more interesting than the fictions.

The immigrant experience is, I suspect, a universal one (even if you're the kind of immigrant, like me, who holds on tightly, almost superstitiously, to his UK Citizenship, long after his accent has become rather dodgy). On the one hand, there's you, and on the other hand, there's America. It's bigger than you are. So you try and make sense of it. You try to figure it out – something which it resists. It's big enough, and contains enough contradictions, that it is perfectly happy not to be figured out, and somewhere in there you realise that the very best you can hope for is to be like one of the blind men in the fable who each grasped the elephant by its trunk, its leg, its side, its tail, and who each decided that an elephant was like a snake, a tree, a wall, a rope. As a writer all I could do was to describe a small part of the whole.

And it was too big to see.

I didn't really know what kind of book I wanted to write

until, in the summer of 1998, I found myself spending 48 hours in Reykjavik, in Iceland, and in the middle of that stay I knew what my next book was. A bunch of fragments of plot, an unwieldy assortment of characters, and something faintly resembling a structure came together in my head. Maybe it was because I was far enough away from America to see it clearly, maybe it was just that its time had come. It would be a thriller, and a murder mystery, and a romance, and a road trip. It would be about the immigrant experience, about what people believed in when they came to America. And about what happened to the things that they believed. I'm English. I like being English. I've kept my passport. I've as much of my accent as I could. And I'd lived in the US for almost nine years. Long enough to know that everything I'd learned about it from the movies was wrong.

I wanted to write about myths. I wanted to write about America as a mythic place.

I went back to my hotel room and wrote a three-page-long rough outline – more of a loose description of the book I had in my head. I tried calling it *Magic America* (after the Blur song), and that didn't seem right. I tried calling it *King of America* (after the Elvis Costello album) and that didn't seem right either. So I wrote *American Gods* (not after anything) at the top of the first page of the outline, and figured I'd come up with a better title sooner or later.

I'd not started writing the novel by the time the publisher sent me the cover. It showed a road and a lightning bolt and, in large letters, a title: *American Gods*. There seemed no point in fighting it – to be honest, I was starting to like it – and I started to write.

It's a big book, but then, America's a big country, and trying to fit it into a book was hard enough.

American Gods is the story of a man called Shadow, and the job he is offered when he gets out of prison. It is the story of a road trip. It tells the story of a small Midwestern town, and the disappearances that occur there every winter. I discovered, as I wrote it, why roadside attractions are the most sacred places in America. I learned a lot about gods, and about secret organizations, and wars. I discovered many other strange by-ways and moments. Some of them delighted me. A few scared me. Some of them amazed me.

When it was almost done, when all that remained was to pull together all the diverse strands, I left the country again, holed up in a huge, cold, old house in Ireland, and typed all that was left to type, shivering, beside a peat fire.

And then the book was done, and I stopped. Looking back on it, it wasn't really that I'd dared, rather that I had had no choice.

This is an expanded version of the essay written for the Borders website in March 2001, and which appears on www.neilgaiman.com and was published in *The View from the Cheap Seats* in 2016.

The Monarch
of the Glen

An *American Gods*

Novella

> 'She herself is a haunted house. She does not possess
> herself; her ancestors sometimes come and peer out of
> the windows of her eyes and that is very frightening.'
> Angela Carter, 'The Lady of the House of Love'

I f you ask me,' said the little man to Shadow, 'you're
something of a monster. Am I right?'
They were the only two people, apart from the
barmaid, in the bar of a hotel in a town on the north coast
of Scotland. Shadow had been sitting there on his own,
drinking a lager, when the man came over and sat at his
table. It was late summer, and it seemed to Shadow that
everything was cold, and small, and damp. He had a
small book of Pleasant Local Walks in front of him, and
was studying the walk he planned to do tomorrow, along
the coast, towards Cape Wrath.

He closed the book.

'I'm American,' said Shadow. 'If that's what you mean.'

The little man cocked his head to one side, and he winked, theatrically. He had steel-grey hair, and a grey face, and a grey coat, and he looked like a small-town lawyer. 'Well, perhaps that is what I mean, at that,' he said.

Shadow had had problems understanding Scottish accents in his short time in the country, all rich burrs and strange words and trills, but he had no trouble understanding this man. Everything the little man said was small and crisp, each word so perfectly enunciated that it made Shadow feel like he himself was talking with a mouthful of oatmeal.

The little man sipped his drink and said, 'So you're American. Oversexed, overpaid and over here. Eh? D'you work on the rigs?'

'Sorry?'

'An oilman? Out on the big metal platforms. We get oil people up here, from time to time.'

'No. I'm not from the rigs.'

The little man took out a pipe from his pocket, and a small penknife, and began to remove the dottle from the bowl. Then he tapped it out into the ashtray. 'They have oil in Texas, you know,' he said, after a while, as if he were confiding a great secret. 'That's in America.'

'Yes,' said Shadow. He thought about saying something about Texans believing that Texas was actually in Texas, but he suspected that he'd have to start explaining what he meant, so he said nothing.

Shadow had been away from America for the better part of two years. He had been away when the towers fell. He told himself sometimes that he did not care if he ever went back, and sometimes he almost came close to believing himself. He had reached the Scottish mainland two days ago, landed in Thurso on the ferry from the Orkneys, and had travelled to the town he was staying in by bus.

The little man was talking. 'So there's a Texas oilman, down in Aberdeen, he's talking to an old fellow he meets in a pub, much like you and me meeting, actually, and they get talking, and the Texan, he says, "Back in Texas I get up in the morning, I get into my car" – I won't try to do the accent, if you don't mind – "I'll turn the key in the ignition, and put my foot down on the accelerator", what you call the, the—'

'Gas pedal,' said Shadow, helpfully.

'Right. "Put my foot down on the gas pedal at breakfast, and by lunchtime I still won't have reached the edge of my property." And the canny old Scot, he just nods and says, "Aye, well, I used to have a car like that myself." '

The little man laughed raucously, to show that the joke was done. Shadow smiled, and nodded, to show that he knew it was a joke.

'What are you drinking? Lager? Same again over here, Jennie love. Mine's a Lagavulin.' The little man tamped tobacco from a pouch into his pipe. 'Did you know that Scotland's bigger than America?'

There had been no one in the hotel bar when Shadow came downstairs that evening, just the thin barmaid, reading a newspaper and smoking her cigarette. He'd come down to sit by the open fire, as his bedroom was cold, and the metal radiators on the bedroom wall were colder than the room. He hadn't expected company.

'No,' said Shadow, always willing to play straight man. 'I didn't. How'd you reckon that?'

'It's all fractal,' said the little man. 'The smaller you look, the more things unpack. It could take you as long to drive across America as it would to drive across Scotland, if you did it the right way. It's like, you look on a map, and the coastlines are solid lines. But when you walk them, they're all over the place. I saw a whole programme on it on the telly the other night. Great stuff.'

'Okay,' said Shadow.

The little man's pipe-lighter flamed, and he sucked and puffed and sucked and puffed until he was satisfied that the pipe was burning well, then he put the lighter, the pouch and the penknife back into his coat pocket.

'Anyway, anyway,' said the little man. 'I believe you're planning on staying here through the weekend.'

'Yes,' said Shadow. 'Do you ... are you with the hotel?'

'No, no. Truth to tell, I was standing in the hall when you arrived. I heard you talking to Gordon on the reception desk.'

Shadow nodded. He had thought that he had been alone in the reception hall when he had registered, but it was possible that the little man had passed through. But still ... there was a wrongness to this conversation. There was a wrongness to everything.

Jennie the barmaid put their drinks on to the bar. 'Five pounds twenty,' she said. She picked up her newspaper, and started to read once more. The little man went to the bar, paid, and brought back the drinks.

'So how long are you in Scotland?' asked the little man.

Shadow shrugged. 'I wanted to see what it was like. Take

some walks. See the sights. Maybe a week. Maybe a month.'

Jennie put down her newspaper. 'It's the arse-end of nowhere up here,' she said, cheerfully. 'You should go somewhere interesting.'

'That's where you're wrong,' said the little man. 'It's only the arse-end of nowhere if you look at it wrong. See that map, laddie?' He pointed to a fly-specked map of northern Scotland on the opposite wall of the bar. 'You know what's wrong with it?'

'No.'

'It's upside-down!' the man said, triumphantly. 'North's at the top. It's saying to the world that this is where things stop. Go no further. The world ends here. But, you see, that's not how it was. This wasn't the north of Scotland. This was the southernmost tip of the Viking world. You know what the second most northern county in Scotland is called?'

Shadow glanced at the map, but it was too far away to read. He shook his head.

'Sutherland!' said the little man. He showed his teeth. 'The South Land. Not to anyone else in the world it wasn't, but it was to the Vikings.'

Jennie the barmaid walked over to them. 'I won't be gone long,' she said. 'Call the front desk if you need anything before I get back.' She put a log on the fire, then she went out into the hall.

'Are you a historian?' Shadow asked.

'Good one,' said the little man. 'You may be a monster, but you're funny. I'll give you that.'

'I'm not a monster,' said Shadow.

'Aye, that's what monsters always say,' said the little man. 'I was a specialist once. In St Andrews. Now I'm in general practice. Well, I was. I'm semi-retired. Go into the surgery a couple of days a week, just to keep my hand in.'

'Why do you say I'm a monster?' asked Shadow.

'Because,' said the little man, lifting his whisky glass with the air of one making an irrefutable point, 'I am something of a monster myself. Like calls to like. We are all monsters, are we not? Glorious monsters, shambling through the swamps of unreason . . .' He sipped his whisky, then said, 'Tell me, a big man like you, have you ever been a bouncer? "Sorry mate, I'm afraid you can't come in here tonight, private function going on, sling your hook and get on out of it", all that?'

'No,' said Shadow.

'But you must have done something like that?'

'Yes,' said Shadow, who had been a bodyguard once, to an old god; but that was in another country.

'You, uh, you'll pardon me for asking, don't take this the wrong way, but do you need money?'

'Everyone needs money. But I'm okay.' This was not entirely true; but it was a truth that, when Shadow needed money, the world seemed to go out of its way to provide it.

'Would you like to make a wee bit of spending money? Being a bouncer? It's a piece of piss. Money for old rope.'

'At a disco?'

'Not exactly. A private party. They rent a big old house near here, come in from all over at the end of the summer. So last year, everybody's having a grand old time, champagne out of doors, all that, and there was some trouble. A bad lot. Out to ruin everybody's weekend.'

'These were locals?'

'I don't think so.'

'Was it political?' asked Shadow. He did not want to be drawn into local politics.

'Not a bit of it. Yobs and hairies and idiots. Anyway. They probably won't come back this year. Probably off in the wilds of nowhere demonstrating against international capitalism. But just to be on the safe side, the folk up at the house've asked me to look out for someone who could do a spot of intimidating. You're a big lad, and that's what they want.'

'How much?' asked Shadow.

'Can you handle yourself in a fight, if it came down to it?' asked the man.

Shadow didn't say anything. The little man looked Shadow up and down, and then he grinned again, showing tobacco-stained teeth. 'Fifteen hundred pounds, for a long weekend's work. That's good money. And it's cash. Nothing you'd ever need to report to the taxman.'

'This weekend coming?' said Shadow.

'Starting Friday morning. It's a big old house. Part of it used to be a castle. West of Cape Wrath.'

'I don't know,' said Shadow.

'If you do it,' said the little grey man, 'you'll get a fantastic weekend in a historical house, and I can guarantee you'll get to meet all kinds of interesting people. Perfect holiday job. I just wish I was younger. And, uh, a great deal taller, actually.'

Shadow said, 'Okay,' and, as soon as he said it, wondered if he would regret it.

'Good man. I'll get you more details as and when.' The little grey man stood up, and gave Shadow's shoulder a gentle pat as he walked past. Then he went out, leaving Shadow in the bar on his own.

II

Shadow had been on the road for about eighteen months. He had backpacked across Europe and down into northern Africa. He had picked olives, and fished for sardines, and driven a truck, and sold wine from the side of a road. Finally, several months ago, he had hitchhiked his way back to Norway, to Oslo, where he had been born thirty-five years before.

He was not sure what he had been looking for. He only knew that he had not found it, although there were moments, in the high ground, in the crags and waterfalls, when he was certain that whatever he needed was just around the corner: behind a jut of granite, or in the nearest pinewood.

Still, it was a deeply unsatisfactory visit, and when, in Bergen, he was asked if he would be half of the crew of a motor-yacht, on its way to meet its owner in Cannes, he said yes.

They had sailed from Bergen to the Shetlands, and then to the Orkneys, where they spent the night in a bed and breakfast in Stromness. Next morning, leaving the harbour, the engines had failed, ultimately and irrevocably, and the boat had been towed back to port.

Bjorn, who was the captain and the other half of the crew, stayed with the boat, to talk to the insurers and field the angry calls from the boat's owner. Shadow saw no reason to stay: he took the ferry to Thurso, on the north coast of Scotland.

He was restless. At night he dreamed of freeways, of entering the neon edges of a city where the people spoke English. Sometimes it was in the Midwest, sometimes it was in Florida, sometimes on the East Coast, sometimes on the West.

When he got off the ferry he bought a book of scenic walks, and picked up a bus timetable, and he set off into the world.

Jennie the barmaid came back, and started to wipe all the surfaces with a cloth. Her hair was so blonde it was almost white, and it was tied up at the back in a bun.

'So what is it people do around here for fun?' asked Shadow.

'They drink. They wait to die,' she said. 'Or they go south. That pretty much exhausts your options.'

'You sure?'

'Well, think about it. There's nothing up here but sheep and hills. We feed off the tourists, of course, but there's never really enough of you. Sad, isn't it?'

Shadow shrugged.

'Are you from New York?' she asked.

'Chicago, originally. But I came here from Norway.'

'You speak Norwegian?'

'A little.'

'There's somebody you should meet,' she said, suddenly. Then she looked at her watch. 'Somebody who came here from Norway, a long time ago. Come on.'

She put her cleaning cloth down, turned off the bar-lights, and walked over to the door. 'Come on,' she said, again.

'Can you do that?' asked Shadow.

'I can do whatever I want,' she said. 'It's a free country, isn't it?'

'I guess.'

She locked the bar with a brass key. They walked into the reception hall. 'Wait here,' she said. She went through a door marked PRIVATE, and reappeared several minutes later, wearing a long brown coat. 'Okay. Follow me.'

They walked out into the street. 'So, is this a village or a small town?' asked Shadow.

'It's a fucking graveyard,' she said. 'Up this way. Come on.'

They walked up a narrow road. The moon was huge and a yellowish brown. Shadow could hear the sea, although he could not yet see it. 'You're Jennie?' he said.

'That's right. And you?'

'Shadow.'

'Is that your real name?'

'It's what they call me.'

'Come on, then, Shadow,' she said.

At the top of the hill, they stopped. They were on the edge of the village, and there was a grey stone cottage. Jennie opened the gate, and led Shadow up a path to the front door. He brushed a small bush at the side of the path, and the air filled with the scent of sweet lavender. There were no lights on in the cottage.

'Whose house is this?' asked Shadow. 'It looks empty.'

'Don't worry,' said Jennie. 'She'll be home in a second.'

She pushed open the unlocked front door, and they went inside. She turned on the light switch by the door. Most of the inside of the cottage was taken up by a kitchen-sitting room. There was a tiny staircase leading up to what Shadow presumed was an attic bedroom. A CD-player sat on the pine counter.

'This is your house,' said Shadow.

'Home sweet home,' she agreed. 'You want coffee? Or something to drink?'

'Neither,' said Shadow. He wondered what Jennie wanted. She had barely looked at him, hadn't even smiled at him.

'Did I hear right? Was Doctor Gaskell asking you to help look after a party on the weekend?'

'I guess.'

'So what are you doing tomorrow and Friday?'

'Walking,' said Shadow. 'I've got a book. There are some beautiful walks.'

'Some of them are beautiful. Some of them are treacherous,' she told him. 'You can still find winter snow here, in the shadows, in the summer. Things last a long time, in the shadows.'

'I'll be careful,' he told her.

'That was what the Vikings said,' she said, and she smiled. She took off her coat and dropped it on the bright purple sofa. 'Maybe I'll see you out there. I like to go for walks.' She pulled at the bun at the back of her head, and her pale hair fell free. It was longer than Shadow had thought it would be.

'Do you live here alone?'

She took a cigarette from a packet on the counter, lit it with a match. 'What's it to you?' she asked. 'You won't be staying the night, will you?'

Shadow shook his head.

'The hotel's at the bottom of the hill,' she told him. 'You can't miss it. Thanks for walking me home.'

Shadow said good-night, and walked back, through the lavender night, out to the lane. He stood there for a little while, staring at the moon on the sea, puzzled. Then he walked down the hill until he got to the hotel. She was right: you couldn't miss it. He walked up the stairs, unlocked his room with a key attached to a short stick, and went inside. The room was colder than the corridor.

He took off his shoes, and stretched out on the bed in the dark.

III

The ship was made of the fingernails of dead men, and it lurched through the mist, bucking and rolling hugely and unsteadily on the choppy sea.

There were shadowy shapes on the deck, men as big as hills or houses, and as Shadow got closer he could see their faces: proud men and tall, each one of them. They seemed to ignore the ship's motion, each man waiting on the deck as if frozen in place.

One of them stepped forward, and he grasped Shadow's hand with his own huge hand. Shadow stepped on to the grey deck.

'Well come to this accursed place,' said the man holding Shadow's hand, in a deep, gravel voice.

'Hail!' called the men on the deck. 'Hail sun-bringer! Hail Baldur!'

The name on Shadow's birth certificate was Balder Moon, but he shook his head. 'I am not him,' he told them. 'I am not the one you are waiting for.'

'We are dying here,' said the gravel-voiced man, not letting go of Shadow's hand.

It was cold in the misty place between the worlds of waking and the grave. Salt spray crashed on the bows of the grey ship, and Shadow was drenched to the skin.

'Bring us back,' said the man holding his hand. 'Bring us back or let us go.'

Shadow said, 'I don't know how.'

At that, the men on the deck began to wail and howl. Some of them crashed the hafts of their spears against the deck, others struck the flats of their short swords against the brass bowls at the centre of their leather shields, setting up a rhythmic din accompanied by cries that moved from sorrow to a full-throated berserker ululation . . .

A seagull was screaming in the early morning air. The bedroom window had blown open in the night, and was banging in the wind. Shadow was lying on the top of his bed in his narrow hotel room. His skin was damp, perhaps with sweat.

Another cold day at the end of the summer had begun.

The hotel packed him a Tupperware box containing several chicken sandwiches, a hard-boiled egg, a small packet of cheese-and-onion crisps, and an apple. Gordon on the reception desk, who handed him the box, asked when he'd be back, explaining that if he was more than a couple of hours late they'd call out the rescue services, and asking for the number of Shadow's mobile phone.

Shadow did not have a mobile phone.

He set off on the walk, heading towards the coast. It was beautiful, a desolate beauty that chimed and echoed with the empty places inside Shadow. He had imagined Scotland as being a soft place, all gentle heathery hills, but here on the north coast everything seemed sharp and jutting, even the grey clouds that scudded across the pale blue sky. It was as if the bones of the world showed through. He followed the route in his book, across scrubby meadows and past splashing burns, up rocky hills and down.

Sometimes he imagined that he was standing still and the world was moving underneath him, that he was simply pushing it past with his legs.

The route was more tiring than he had expected. He had planned to eat at one o'clock, but by midday his legs were tired and he wanted a break. He followed his path to the side of a hill, where a boulder provided a convenient windbreak, and he crouched to eat his lunch. In the distance, ahead of him, he could see the Atlantic.

He had thought himself alone.

She said, 'Will you give me your apple?'

It was Jennie, the barmaid from the hotel. Her too-fair hair gusted about her head.

'Hello, Jennie,' said Shadow. He passed her his apple.

She pulled a clasp-knife from the pocket of her brown coat, and sat beside him. 'Thanks,' she said.

'So,' said Shadow, 'from your accent, you must have come from Norway when you were a kid. I mean, you sound like a local to me.'

'Did I say that I came from Norway?'

'Well, didn't you?'

She speared an apple slice, and ate it, fastidiously, from the tip of the knife blade, only touching it with her teeth. She glanced at him. 'It was a long time ago.'

'Family?'

She moved her shoulders in a shrug, as if any answer she could give him was beneath her.

'So you like it here?'

She looked at him and shook her head. 'I feel like a *hulder*.'

He'd heard the word before, in Norway. 'Aren't they a kind of troll?'

'No. They are mountain creatures, like the trolls, but they come from the woods, and they are very beautiful. Like me.' She grinned as she said it, as if she knew that she was too pallid, too sulky and too thin ever to be beautiful. 'They fall in love with farmers.'

'Why?'

'Damned if I know,' she said. 'But they do. Sometimes the farmer realises that he is talking to a *hulder* woman, because she has a cow's tail hanging down behind, or worse, sometimes from behind there is nothing there, she is just hollow and empty, like a shell. Then the farmer says a prayer, or runs away, flees back to his mother or his farm.

'But sometimes the farmers do not run. Sometimes they throw a knife over her shoulder, or just smile, and they marry the *huldra* woman. Then her tail falls off. But she is still stronger than any human woman could ever be. And she still pines for her home in the forests and the mountains. She will never be truly happy. She will never be human.'

'What happens to her then?' asked Shadow. 'Does she age and die with her farmer?'

She had sliced the apple down to the core. Now, with a flick of the wrist, she sent the apple core arcing off the side of the hill. 'When her man dies . . . I think she goes back to the hills and the woods.' She stared out at the hillside. 'There's a story about one of them who was married to a farmer who didn't treat her well. He shouted at her, wouldn't help around the farm, he came home from the village drunk and angry. Sometimes he beat her.

'Now, one day she's in the farmhouse, making up the morning's fire, and he comes in and starts shouting at her, for his food is not ready, and he is angry, nothing she does is right, he doesn't know why he married her, and she listens to him for a while, and then, saying nothing, she reaches down to the fireplace, and she picks up the poker. A heavy black iron jobbie. She takes that poker and, without an effort, she bends it into a perfect circle, just like her wedding ring. She doesn't grunt or sweat, she just bends it, like you'd bend a reed. And her farmer sees this and he goes white as a sheet, and doesn't say anything else about his breakfast. He's seen what she did to the poker and he knows that at any time in the last five years she could have done the same to him. And until he died, he never laid another finger on her, never said one harsh word. Now, you tell me something, Mister everybody-calls-you-Shadow, if she could do that, why did she let him beat her in the first place? Why would she want to be with someone like that? You tell me.'

'Maybe,' said Shadow, 'maybe she was lonely.'

She wiped the blade of the knife on her jeans.

'Dr Gaskell kept saying you were a monster,' she said. 'Is it true?'

'I don't think so,' said Shadow.

'Pity,' she said. 'You know where you are with monsters, don't you?'

'You do?'

'Absolutely. At the end of the day, you're going to be dinner. Talking about which, I'll show you something.' She stood up, and led him to the top of the hill. 'See. Over there? On the far side of that hill, where it drops into the glen, you can just see the house you'll be working at this weekend. Do you see it, over there?'

'No.'

'Look. I'll point. Follow the line of my finger.' She stood close to him, held out her hand and pointed to the side of a distant ridge. He could see the overhead sun glinting off something he supposed was a lake – or a loch, he corrected himself, he was in Scotland after all – and above that a grey outcropping on the side of a hill. He had taken it for rocks, but it was too regular to be anything but a building.

'That's the castle?'

'I'd not call it that. Just a big house in the glen.'

'Have you been to one of the parties there?'

'They don't invite locals,' she said. 'And they wouldn't ask me. You shouldn't do it, anyway. You should say no.'

'They're paying good money,' he told her.

She touched him then, for the first time, placed her pale fingers on the back of his dark hand. 'And what good is money to a monster?' she asked, and smiled, and Shadow was damned if he didn't think that maybe she *was* beautiful, at that.

And then she put down her hand and backed away. 'Well?' she said. 'Shouldn't you be off on your walk? You've not got much longer before you'll have to start heading back again. The light goes fast when it goes, this time of year.'

And she stood and watched him as he hefted his rucksack, and began to walk down the hill. He turned around when he reached the bottom and looked up. She was still looking at him. He waved, and she waved back.

The next time he looked back she was gone.

He took the little ferry across the kyle to the cape, and walked up to the lighthouse. There was a minibus from the lighthouse back to the ferry, and he took it.

He got back to the hotel at eight that night, exhausted but feeling satisfied. It had rained once, in the late afternoon, but he had taken shelter in a tumbledown bothy, and read a five-year-old newspaper while the rain drummed against the roof. It had ended after half an hour, but Shadow had been glad that he had good boots, for the earth had turned to mud.

He was starving. He went into the hotel restaurant. It was empty. Shadow said, 'Hello?'

An elderly woman came to the door between the restaurant and the kitchen and said, 'Aye?'

'Are you still serving dinner?'

'Aye.' She looked at him disapprovingly, from his muddy boots to his tousled hair. 'Are you a guest?'

'Yes. I'm in room eleven.'

'Well . . . you'll probably want to change before dinner,' she said. 'It's kinder to the other diners.'

'So you *are* serving.'

'Aye.'

He went up to his room, dropped his rucksack on the bed, and took off his boots. He put on his sneakers, ran a comb through his hair, and went back downstairs.

The dining room was no longer empty. Two people were sitting at a table in the corner, two people who seemed different in every way that people could be different: a small woman who looked to be in her late fifties, hunched and birdlike at the table, and a young man, big and awkward and perfectly bald. Shadow decided that they were mother and son.

He sat down at a table in the centre of the room.

The elderly waitress came in with a tray. She gave both of the other diners a bowl of soup. The man began to blow on his soup, to cool it; his mother tapped him, hard, on the back of his hand, with her spoon. 'Stop that,' she said. She began to spoon the soup into her mouth, slurping it noisily.

The bald man looked around the room sadly. He caught Shadow's eye, and Shadow nodded at him. The man sighed, and returned to his steaming soup.

Shadow scanned the menu without enthusiasm. He was ready to order, but the waitress had vanished again.

A flash of grey; Dr Gaskell peered in at the door of the restaurant. He walked into the room, came over to Shadow's table. 'Do you mind if I join you?'

'Not at all. Please. Sit down.'

He sat down, opposite Shadow. 'Have a good day?'

'Very good. I walked.'

'Best way to work up an appetite. So. First thing tomorrow they're sending a car out here to pick you up. Bring your things. They'll take you out to the house. Show you the ropes.'

'And the money?' asked Shadow.

'They'll sort that out. Half at the beginning, half at the end. Anything else you want to know?'

The waitress stood at the edge of the room, watching them, making no move to approach. 'Yeah. What do I have to do to get some food around here?'

'What do you want? I recommend the lamb chops. The lamb's local.'

'Sounds good.'

Gaskell said loudly, 'Excuse me, Maura. Sorry to trouble you, but could we both have the lamb chops?'

She pursed her lips, and went back to the kitchen.

'Thanks,' said Shadow.

'Don't mention it. Anything else I can help you with?'

'Yeah. These folk coming in for the party. Why don't they hire their own security? Why hire me?'

'They'll be doing that too, I have no doubt,' said Gaskell. 'Bringing in their own people. But it's good to have local talent.'

'Even if the local talent is a foreign tourist?'

'Just so.'

Maura brought two bowls of soup, put them down in front of Shadow and the doctor. 'They come with the meal,' she said. The soup was too hot, and it tasted faintly of reconstituted tomatoes and vinegar. Shadow was hungry enough that he'd finished most of the bowl off before he realised that he did not like it.

'You said I was a monster,' said Shadow, to the steel-grey man.

'I did?'

'You did.'

'Well, there's a lot of monsters in this part of the world.' He tipped his head towards the couple in the corner. The little woman had picked up her napkin, dipped it into her water-glass, and was dabbing vigorously with it at the spots of crimson soup on her son's mouth and chin. He looked embarrassed. 'It's remote. We don't get into the news unless a hiker or a climber gets lost, or starves to death. Most people forget we're here.'

The lamb chops arrived, on a plate with overboiled potatoes, underboiled carrots, and something brown and wet that Shadow thought might have started life as spinach. He started to cut at the chops with his knife. The doctor picked his up in his fingers, and began to chew.

'You've been inside,' said the doctor.

'Inside?'

'Prison. You've been in prison.' It wasn't a question.

'Yes.'

'So you know how to fight. You could hurt someone, if you had to.'

Shadow said, 'If you need someone to hurt people, I'm probably not the guy you're looking for.'

The little man grinned, with greasy grey lips. 'I'm sure you are. I was just asking. You can't give a man a hard time for asking. Anyway. *He*'s a monster,' he said, gesturing across the room with a mostly chewed lamb chop. The bald man was eating some kind of white pudding with a spoon. 'So's his mother.'

'They don't look like monsters to me,' said Shadow.

'I'm teasing you, I'm afraid. Local sense of humour. They should warn you about mine when you enter the village. Warning, loony old doctor at work. Talking about monsters. Forgive an old man. You mustn't listen to a word I say.' A flash of tobacco-stained teeth. He wiped his hands and mouth on his napkin. 'Maura, we'll be needing the bill over here. The young man's dinner is on me.'

'Yes, Doctor Gaskell.'

'Remember,' said the doctor to Shadow. 'Eight fifteen tomorrow morning, be in the lobby. No later. They're busy people. If you aren't there, they'll just move on, and you'll have missed out on fifteen hundred pounds, for a weekend's work. A bonus, if they're happy.'

Shadow decided to have his after-dinner coffee in the bar. There was a log fire there, after all. He hoped it would take the chill from his bones.

Gordon from Reception was working behind the bar. 'Jennie's night off?' asked Shadow.

'What? No, she was just helping out. She'll do it if we're busy, sometimes.'

'Mind if I put another log on the fire?'

'Help yourself.'

If this is how the Scots treat their summers, thought Shadow, remembering something Oscar Wilde had once said, *they don't deserve to have any.*

The bald young man came in. He nodded a nervous greeting to Shadow. Shadow nodded back. The man had no hair that Shadow could see: no eyebrows, no eyelashes. It made him look babyish, and unformed. Shadow wondered if it was a disease, or if it was perhaps a side-effect of chemotherapy. He smelled of damp.

'I heard what he said,' stammered the bald man. 'He said I was a monster. He said my ma was a monster too. I've got good ears on me. I don't miss much.'

He did have good ears on him. They were a translucent pink, and they stuck out from the side of his head like the fins of some huge fish.

'You've got great ears,' said Shadow.

'You taking the mickey?' The bald man's tone was aggrieved. He looked like he was ready to fight. He was only a little shorter than Shadow, and Shadow was a big man.

'If that means what I think it does, not at all.'

The bald man nodded. 'That's good,' he said. He swallowed, and hesitated. Shadow wondered if he should say something conciliatory, but the bald man continued, 'It's not my fault. Making all that noise. I mean, people come up here to get away from the noise. And the people. Too many damned people up here anyway. Why don't you just go back to where you came from and stop making all that bluidy noise?'

The man's mother appeared in the doorway. She smiled nervously at Shadow, then walked hurriedly over to her son. She pulled at his sleeve. 'Now then,' she said. 'Don't you get yourself all worked up over nothing. Everything's all right.' She looked up at Shadow, bird-like, placatory. 'I'm sorry. I'm sure he didn't mean it.' She had a length of toilet paper sticking to the bottom of her shoe, and she hadn't noticed yet.

'Everything's all right,' said Shadow. 'It's good to meet people.'

She nodded. 'That's all right, then,' she said. Her son looked relieved. He's scared of her, thought Shadow.

'Come on, pet,' said the woman to her son. She pulled at his sleeve, and he followed her to the door.

Then he stopped, obstinately, and turned. 'You tell them,' said the bald young man, 'not to make so much noise.'

'I'll tell them,' said Shadow.

'It's just that I can hear everything.'

'Don't worry about it,' said Shadow.

'He really is a good boy,' said the bald young man's mother, and she led her son by the sleeve, into the corridor and away, trailing a tag of toilet paper.

Shadow walked out into the hall. 'Excuse me,' he said.

They turned, the man and his mother.

'You've got something on your shoe,' said Shadow.

She looked down. Then she stepped on the strip of paper with her other shoe, and lifted her foot, freeing it. She nodded at Shadow, approvingly, and walked away.

Shadow went to the reception desk. 'Gordon, have you got a good local map?'

'Like an Ordnance Survey? Absolutely. I'll bring it into the lounge for you.'

Shadow went back into the bar and finished his coffee. Gordon brought in a map. Shadow was impressed by the detail: it seemed to show every goat-track. He inspected it closely, tracing his walk. He found the hill where he had stopped and eaten his lunch. He ran his finger south-west. 'There aren't any castles around here, are there?'

'I'm afraid not. There are some to the east. I've got a guide to the castles of Scotland I could let you look at—'

'No, no. That's fine. Are there any big houses in this area? The kind people would call castles? Or big estates?'

'Well, there's the Cape Wrath Hotel, just over here,' and he pointed to it on the map. 'But it's a fairly empty area. Technically, for human occupation, what do they call it?, for population density, it's a desert up here. Not even any interesting ruins, I'm afraid. Not that you could walk to.'

Shadow thanked him, then asked him for an early-morning alarm call. He wished he had been able to find the house he had seen from the hill on the map, but perhaps he had been looking in the wrong place. It wouldn't be the first time.

The couple in the room next door were fighting, or making love. Shadow could not tell, but each time he began to drift off to sleep raised voices or cries would jerk him awake.

Later, he was never certain if it had really happened, if she had really come to him, or if it had been the first of that night's dreams, but in truth or in dreams, shortly before midnight by the bedside clock-radio, there was a knock on his bedroom door. He got up. Called, 'Who is it?'

'Jennie.'

He opened the door, winced at the light in the hall.

She was wrapped in her brown coat, and she looked up at him hesitantly.

'Yes?' said Shadow.

'You'll be going to the house tomorrow,' she said.

'Yes.'

'I thought I should say goodbye,' she said. 'In case I don't get a chance to see you again. And if you don't come back to the hotel. And you just go on somewhere. And I never see you.'

'Well, goodbye, then,' said Shadow.

She looked him up and down, examining the T-shirt and the boxers he slept in, at his bare feet, then up at his face. She seemed worried. 'You know where I live,' she said at last. 'Call me if you need me.'

She reached her index finger out and touched it gently to his lips. Her finger was very cold. Then she took a step back into the corridor and just stood there, facing him, making no move to go.

Shadow closed the hotel-room door, and he heard her footsteps walking away down the corridor. He climbed back into bed.

He was sure that the next dream was a dream, though. It was his life, jumbled and twisted: one moment he was in prison, teaching himself coin tricks and telling himself that his love for his wife would get him through this. Then Laura was dead, and he was out of prison; he was working as a bodyguard to an old grifter who had told Shadow to call him Wednesday. And then his dream was filled with gods: old, forgotten gods, unloved and abandoned, and new gods, transient scared things, duped and confused. It was a tangle of improbabilities, a cat's cradle that became a web that became a net that became a skein as big as a world . . .

In his dream he died on the tree.

In his dream he came back from the dead.

And after that there was darkness.

IV

The telephone beside the bed shrilled at seven. He showered, shaved, dressed, packed his world into his backpack. Then he went down to the restaurant for breakfast: salty porridge, limp bacon and oily fried eggs. The coffee, though, was surprisingly good.

At ten past eight he was in the lobby, waiting.

At fourteen minutes past eight, a man came in, wearing a sheepskin coat. He was sucking on a hand-rolled cigarette. The man stuck out his hand, cheerfully. 'You'll be Mister Moon,' he said. 'My name's Smith. I'm your lift out to the big house.' The man's grip was firm. 'You *are* a big feller, aren't you?'

Unspoken was 'But I could take you,' although Shadow knew that it was there.

Shadow said, 'So they tell me. You aren't Scottish.'

'Not me, matey. Just up for the week to make sure that everything runs like it's s'posed to. I'm a London boy.' A flash of teeth in a hatchet-blade face. Shadow guessed that the man was in his mid-forties. 'Come on out to the car. I can bring you up to speed on the way. Is that your bag?'

Shadow carried his backpack out to the car, a muddy Land-Rover, its engine still running. He dropped his bag in the back, climbed into the passenger seat. Smith pulled one final drag on his cigarette, now little more than a rolled stub of white paper, and threw it out of the open driver's-side window into the road.

They drove out of the village.

'So how do I pronounce your name?' asked Smith. 'Balder or Borl-der, or something else? Like Cholmondeley is actually pronounced Chumley.'

'Shadow,' said Shadow. 'People call me Shadow.'

'Right.'

Silence.

'So,' said Smith. 'Shadow. I don't know how much old Gaskell told you about the party this weekend.'

'A little.'

'Right, well, the most important thing to know is this. Anything that happens, you keep shtum about. Right? Whatever you see, people having a little bit of fun, you don't say nothing to anybody, even if you recognise them, if you take my meaning.'

'I don't recognise people,' said Shadow.

'That's the spirit. We're just here to make sure that everyone has a good time without being disturbed. They've come a long way for a nice weekend.'

'Got it,' said Shadow.

They reached the ferry to the cape. Smith parked the Land-Rover beside the road, took their bags, and locked the car.

On the other side of the ferry crossing, an identical Land-Rover waited. Smith unlocked it, threw their bags into the back, and started the car along the dirt track.

They turned off before they reached the lighthouse, drove for a while in silence down a dirt road that rapidly turned into a sheep track. Several times Shadow had to get out and open gates; he waited while the Land-Rover drove through, closed the gates behind them.

There were ravens in the fields and on the low stone walls, huge black birds that stared at Shadow with implacable eyes.

'So you were in the nick?' said Smith, suddenly.

'Sorry?'

'Prison. Pokey. Porridge. Other words beginning with a P, indicating poor food, no nightlife, inadequate toilet facilities and limited opportunities for travel.'

'Yeah.'

'You're not very chatty, are you?'

'I thought that was a virtue.'

'Point taken. Just conversation. The silence was getting on my nerves. You like it up here?'

'I guess. I've only been here for a few days.'

'Gives me the fucking willies. Too remote. I've been to parts of Siberia that felt more welcoming. You been to London yet? No? When you come down south I'll show you around. Great pubs. Real food. And there's all that tourist stuff you Americans like. Traffic's hell, though. At least up here we can drive. No bloody traffic-lights. There's this traffic-light at the bottom of Regent Street, I swear, you sit there for five minutes on a red light, then you get about ten seconds on a green light. Two cars max. Sodding ridiculous. They say it's the price we pay for progress. Right?'

'Yeah,' said Shadow. 'I guess.'

They were well off-road now, thumping and bumping along a scrubby valley, between two high hills. 'Your party guests,' said Shadow. 'Are they coming in by Land-Rover?'

'Nah. We've got helicopters. They'll be in in time for dinner tonight. Choppers in, then choppers out on Sunday evening'.

'Like living on an island.'

'I wish we were living on an island. Wouldn't get loony locals causing problems, would we? Nobody complains about the noise coming from the island next door.'

'You make a lot of noise at your party?'

'It's not my party, chum. I'm just a facilitator. Making sure that everything runs smoothly. But, yes, I understand that they can make a lot of noise when they put their minds to it.'

The grassy valley became a sheep path, the sheep path became a driveway running almost straight up a hill. A bend in the road, a sudden turn, and they were driving towards a house that Shadow recognised. Jennie had pointed to it yesterday, at lunch.

The house was old. He could see that at a glance. Parts of it seemed older than others: there was a wall on one wing of the building built out of grey rocks and stones, heavy and hard. That wall jutted into another, built of brown bricks. The roof, which covered the whole building, both wings, was a dark grey slate. The house looked out on to a gravel drive, and then down the hill on to the loch. Shadow climbed out of the Land-Rover. He looked at the house and felt small. He felt as though he were coming home, and it was not a good feeling.

There were several other four-wheel-drive vehicles parked on the gravel. 'The keys to the cars are hanging in the pantry, in case you need to take one out. I'll show you as we go past.'

Through a large wooden door, and now they were in a central courtyard, partly paved. There was a small fountain in the middle of the courtyard, and a plot of grass, a ragged green, viperous swath bounded by grey flagstones.

'This is where the Saturday-night action will be,' said Smith. 'I'll show you where you'll be staying.'

Into the smaller wing through an unimposing door, past a room hung with keys on hooks, each key marked with a paper tag, and another room filled with empty shelves. Down a dingy hall, and up some stairs. There was no carpeting on the stairs, nothing but whitewash on the walls. ('Well, this is the servants' quarters, innit? They never spent any money on it.') It was cold, in a way that Shadow was starting to become familiar with: colder inside the building than out. He wondered how they did that, if it was a British building secret.

Smith led Shadow to the top of the house, and showed him into a dark room containing an antique wardrobe, an iron-framed single bed that Shadow could see at a glance would be smaller than he was, an ancient washstand, and a small window that looked out on to the inner courtyard.

'There's a loo at the end of the hall,' said Smith. 'The servants' bathroom's on the next floor down. Two baths, one for men, one for women, no showers. The supplies of hot water on this wing of the house are distinctly limited, I'm afraid. Your monkey-suit's hanging in the wardrobe. Try it on now, see if it all fits, then leave it off until this evening, when the guests come in. Limited dry-cleaning facilities. We might as well be on Mars. I'll be down in the kitchen if you need me. It's not as cold down there, if the Aga's working. Bottom of the stairs and left, then right, then yell if you're lost. Don't go into the other wing unless you're told to.'

He left Shadow alone.

Shadow tried on the black tuxedo jacket, the white dress shirt, the black tie. There were highly polished black shoes as well. It all fitted, as if it had been tailored for him. He hung everything back in the wardrobe.

He walked down the stairs, found Smith on the landing, stabbing angrily at a small silver mobile phone. 'No bloody reception. The thing rang, now I'm trying to call back it won't give me a signal. It's the bloody stone age up here. How was your suit? All right?'

'Perfect.'

'That's my boy. Never use five words if you can get away with one, eh? I've known dead men talk more than you do.'

'Really?'

'Nah. Figure of speech. Come on. Fancy some lunch?'

'Sure. Thank you.'

'Right. Follow me. It's a bit of a warren, but you'll get the hang of it soon enough.'

They ate in the huge, empty kitchen: Shadow and Smith piled enamelled tin plates with slices of translucent orange smoked salmon on crusty white bread, and slices of sharp cheese, accompanied by mugs of strong, sweet tea. The Aga was, Shadow discovered, a big metal box, part oven, part water-heater. Smith opened one of the many doors on its side and shovelled in several large scoops of coal.

'So where's the rest of the food? And the waiters, and the cooks?' asked Shadow. 'It can't just be us.'

'Well spotted. Everything's coming up from Edinburgh. It'll run like clockwork. Food and party workers will be here at three, and unpack. Guests get brought in at six. Buffet dinner is served at eight. Talk a lot, eat, have a bit of a laugh, nothing too strenuous. Tomorrow there's breakfast from seven to midday. Guests get to go for walks, scenic views and all that in the afternoon. Bonfires are built in the courtyard. Then in the evening the bonfires are lit, everybody has a wild Saturday night in the north, hopefully without being bothered by our neighbours.

Sunday morning we tiptoe around, out of respect for everybody's hangover, Sunday afternoon the choppers land and we wave everybody on their way. You collect your pay packet, and I'll drive you back to the hotel, or you can ride south with me, if you fancy a change. Sounds good?'

'Sounds just dandy,' said Shadow. 'And the folks who may show up on the Saturday night?'

'Just killjoys. Locals out to ruin everybody's good time.'

'What locals?' asked Shadow. 'There's nothing but sheep for miles.'

'Locals. They're all over the place,' said Smith. 'You just don't see them. Tuck themselves away like Sawney Beane and his family.'

Shadow said, 'I think I've heard of him. The name rings a bell . . .'

'He's *historical*,' said Smith. He slurped his tea, and leaned back in his chair. 'This was, what?, six hundred years back – after the Vikings had buggered off back to Scandinavia, or intermarried and converted until they were just another bunch of Scots, but before Queen Elizabeth died and James came down from Scotland to rule both countries. Somewhere in there.' He took a swig of his tea. 'So. Travellers in Scotland kept vanishing. It wasn't that unusual. I mean, if you set out on a long journey back then, you didn't always get home. Sometimes it would be months before anyone knew you weren't coming home again, and they'd blame the wolves or the weather, and resolve to travel in groups, and only in the summer.

'One traveller, though, he was riding with a bunch of companions through a glen, and there came over the hill, dropped from the trees, up from the ground, a swarm, a flock, a pack of children, armed with daggers and knives and bone clubs and stout sticks, and they pulled the travellers off their horses, and fell on them, and finished them off. All but this one geezer, and he was riding a little behind the others, and he got away. He was the only one, but it only takes one, doesn't it? He made it to the nearest town, and raised the hue and cry, and they gather a troop of townsfolk and soldiers and they go back there, with dogs.

'It takes them days to find the hideout, they're ready to give up when, at the mouth of a cave by the seashore, the dogs start to howl. And they go down.

'Turns out there's caves, under the ground, and in the biggest and deepest of the caves is old Sawney Beane and his brood, and carcases, hanging from hooks, smoked and slow-roast. Legs, arms, thighs, hands and feet of men, women and children are hung up in rows, like dried pork. There are limbs pickled in brine, like salt beef. There's money in heaps, gold and silver, with watches, rings, swords, pistols and clothes, riches beyond imagining, as they never spent a single penny of it. Just stayed in their caves, and ate, and bred, and hated.

'He'd been living there for years. King of his own little kingdom, was old Sawney, him and his wife, and their children and grandchildren, and some of those grandchildren were also their children. An incestuous little bunch.'

'Did this really happen?'

'So I'm told. There are court records. They took the family to Leith to be tried. The court decision was interesting – they decided that Sawney Beane, by virtue of his acts, had removed himself from the human race. So they sentenced him as an animal. They didn't hang him or behead him. They just got a big fire going and threw the Beanies on to it, to burn to death.'

'All of his family?'

'I don't remember. They may have burned the little kids, or they may not. Probably did. They tend to deal very efficiently with monsters in this part of the world.'

Smith washed their plates and mugs in the sink, left them in a rack to dry. The two men walked out into the courtyard. Smith rolled himself a cigarette expertly. He licked the paper, smoothed it with his fingers, lit the finished tube with a Zippo. 'Let's see. What d'you need to know for tonight? Well, basics are easy: speak when you're spoken to – not that you're going to find that one a problem, eh?'

Shadow said nothing.

'Right. If one of the guests asks you for something, do your best to provide it, ask me if you're in any doubt, but do what the guests ask as long as it doesn't take you off what you're doing, or violate the prime directive.'

'Which is?'

'Don't. Shag. The posh totty. There's sure to be some young ladies who'll take it into their heads, after half a bottle of wine, that what they really need is a bit of rough. And if that happens, you do a *Sunday People*.'

'I have no idea what you're talking about.'

'*Our reporter made his excuses and left*. Yes? You can look, but you can't touch. Got it?'

'Got it.'

'Smart boy.'

Shadow found himself starting to like Smith. He told

himself that liking this man was not a sensible thing to do. He had met people like Smith before, people without consciences, without scruples, without hearts, and they were uniformly as dangerous as they were likeable.

In the early afternoon the servants arrived, brought in by a helicopter that looked like a troop carrier; they unpacked boxes of wine and crates of food, hampers and containers with astonishing efficiency. There were boxes filled with napkins and with tablecloths. There were cooks and waiters, waitresses and chambermaids.

But first off the helicopter there were the security guards: big, solid men with earpieces and what Shadow had no doubt were gun-bulges beneath their jackets. They reported one by one to Smith, who set them to inspecting the house and the grounds.

Shadow was helping out, carrying boxes filled with vegetables from the chopper to the kitchen. He could carry twice as much as anyone else. The next time he passed Smith he stopped and said, 'So, if you've got all these security guys, what am I here for?'

Smith smiled affably. 'Look, son. There's people coming to this do who're worth more than you or I will ever see in a lifetime. They need to be sure they'll be looked after. Kidnappings happen. People have enemies. Lots of things happen. Only with those lads around, they won't. But having them deal with grumpy locals, it's like setting a landmine to stop trespassers. Yeah?'

'Right,' said Shadow. He went back to the chopper, picked up another box marked 'baby aubergines' and filled with small black eggplants, put it on top of a crate of cabbages and carried them both to the kitchen, certain now that he was being lied to. Smith's reply was reasonable. It was even convincing. It simply wasn't true. There was no reason for him to be there, or if there was it wasn't the reason he'd been given.

He chewed it over, trying to figure out why he was in that house, and hoped that he was showing nothing on the surface. Shadow kept it all on the inside. It was safer there.

V

More helicopters came down in the early evening, as the sky was turning pink, and a score or more of smart people clambered out. Several of them were smiling and laughing. Most of them were in their thirties and forties. Shadow recognised none of them.

Smith moved casually but smoothly from person to person, greeting them confidently. 'Right, now you go through there and turn left, and wait in the main hall. Lovely big log fire there. Someone'll come and take you up to your room. Your luggage should be waiting for you there. You call me if it's not, but it will be. 'Ullo, your ladyship, you do look a treat – shall I 'ave someone carry your 'andbag? Looking forward to termorrer? Aren't we all.'

Shadow watched, fascinated, as Smith dealt with each of the guests, his manner an expert mixture of familiarity and deference, of amiability and Cockney charm: aitches, consonants and vowel sounds came and went and transformed according to who he was talking to.

A woman with short dark hair, very pretty, smiled at Shadow as he carried her bags inside. 'Posh totty,' muttered Smith, as he went past. 'Hands off.'

A portly man, whom Shadow estimated to be in his

early sixties, was the last person off the chopper. He walked over to Smith, leaned on a cheap wooden walking-stick, said something in a low voice. Smith replied in the same fashion.

He's in charge, thought Shadow. It was there in the body language. Smith was no longer smiling, no longer cajoling. He was reporting, efficiently and quietly, telling the old man everything he should know.

Smith crooked a finger at Shadow, who walked quickly over to them.

'Shadow,' said Smith, 'this is Mister Alice.'

Mr Alice put out his hand, shook Shadow's big, dark hand with his pink, pudgy one. 'Great pleasure to meet you,' he said. 'Heard good things about you.'

'Good to meet you,' said Shadow.

'Well,' said Mr Alice, 'carry on.'

Smith nodded at Shadow, a gesture of dismissal.

'If it's okay by you,' said Shadow to Smith, 'I'd like to take a look around while there's still some light. Get a sense of where the locals could come from.'

'Don't go too far,' said Smith. He picked up Mr Alice's briefcase, and led the older man into the building.

Shadow walked the outside perimeter of the house. He had been set up. He did not know why, but he knew he was right. There was too much that didn't add up. Why hire a drifter to do security, while bringing in real security guards? It made no sense, no more than Smith introducing him to Mr Alice, after two dozen other people had treated Shadow as no more human than a decorative ornament.

There was a low stone wall in front of the house. Behind the house, a hill that was almost a small mountain; in front of it, a gentle slope down to the loch. Off to the side was the track by which he had arrived that morning. He walked to the far side of the house, and found what seemed to be a kitchen garden, with a high stone wall and wilderness beyond. He took a step down into the kitchen garden, and walked over to inspect the wall.

'You doing a recce, then?' said one of the security guards, in his black tuxedo. Shadow had not seen him there, which meant, he supposed, that he was very good at his job. Like most of the servants, his accent was Scottish.

'Just having a look around.'

'Get the lay of the land, very wise. Don't you worry about this side of the house. A hundred yards that way there's a river leads down to the loch, and beyond that just wet rocks for a hundred feet or so, straight down. Absolutely treacherous.'

'Oh. So the locals, the ones who come and complain, where do they come from?'

'I wouldnae have a clue.'

'I should head on over there and take a look at it,' said Shadow. 'See if I can figure out the ways in and out.'

'I wouldnae do that,' said the guard. 'Not if I were you. It's really treacherous. You go poking around over there, one slip, you'll be crashing down the rocks into the loch. They'll never find your body, if you head out that way.'

'I see,' said Shadow, who did.

He kept walking around the house. He spotted five other security guards, now that he was looking for them. He was sure there were others that he had missed.

In the main wing of the house he could see, through the french windows, a huge, wood-panelled dining room, and the guests seated around a table, talking and laughing.

He walked back into the servants' wing. As each course was done with, the serving plates were put out on a sideboard, and the staff helped themselves, piling food high on paper plates. Smith was sitting at the wooden kitchen table, tucking into a plate of salad and rare beef.

'There's caviar over there,' he said to Shadow. 'It's Golden Osetra, top quality, very special. What the party officials used to keep for themselves in the old days. I've never been a fan of the stuff, but help yourself.'

Shadow put a little of the caviar on the side of his plate, to be polite. He took some tiny boiled eggs, some pasta and some chicken. He sat next to Smith, and started to eat. 'I don't see where your locals are going to come from,' he said. 'Your men have the drive sealed off. Anyone who wants to come here would have to come over the loch.'

'You had a good poke around, then?'

'Yes,' said Shadow.

'You met some of my boys?'

'Yes.'

'What did you think?'

'I wouldn't want to mess with them.'

Smith smirked. 'Big fellow like you? You could take care of yourself.'

'They're killers,' said Shadow, simply.

'Only when they need to be,' said Smith. He was no longer smiling. 'Why don't you stay up in your room? I'll give you a shout when I need you.'

'Sure,' said Shadow. 'And if you don't need me, this is going to be a very easy weekend.'

Smith stared at him. 'You'll earn your money,' he said.

Shadow went up the back stairs to the long corridor at the top of the house. He went into his room. He could hear party noises, and looked out of the small window. The french windows opposite were wide open, and the party-goers, now wearing coats and gloves, holding their glasses of wine, had spilled out into the inner courtyard. He could hear fragments of conversations that transformed and reshaped themselves; the noises were clear but the words and the sense were lost. An occasional phrase would break free of the susurrus. A man said, 'I told him, judges like you, I don't own, I sell . . .' Shadow heard a woman say, 'It's a monster, darling. An absolute monster. Well, what can you do?' and another woman saying, 'Well, if only I could say the same about my boyfriend's!' and a bray of laughter.

He had two alternatives. He could stay, or he could try to go.

'I'll stay,' he said, aloud.

VI

It was a night of dangerous dreams.

In Shadow's first dream he was back in America, standing beneath a streetlight. He walked up some steps, pushed through a glass door, and stepped into a diner, the kind that had once been a dining car on a train. He could hear an old man singing, in a deep gravelly voice, to the tune of 'My Bonnie Lies Over the Ocean':

'My grandpa sells condoms to sailors,
He punctures the tips with a pin,
My grandma does back-street abortions,
My God how the money rolls in.'

Shadow walked along the length of the dining car. At a

table at the end of the car, a grizzled man was sitting, holding a beer bottle, and singing, 'Rolls in, rolls in, my God how the money rolls in'. When he caught sight of Shadow his face split into a huge monkey grin, and he gestured with the beer bottle. 'Sit down, sit down,' he said.

Shadow sat down opposite the man he had known as Wednesday.

'So what's the trouble?' asked Wednesday, dead for almost two years, or as dead as his kind of creature was going to get. 'I'd offer you a beer, but the service here stinks.'

Shadow said that was okay. He didn't want a beer.

'Well?' asked Wednesday, scratching his beard.

'I'm in a big house in Scotland with a shitload of really rich folks, and they have an agenda. I'm in trouble, and I don't know what kind of trouble I'm in. But I think it's pretty bad trouble.'

Wednesday took a swig of his beer. 'The rich are different, m'boy,' he said, after a while.

'What the hell does *that* mean?'

'Well,' said Wednesday, 'for a start, most of them are probably mortal. Not something *you* have to worry about.'

'Don't give me that shit.'

'But you *aren't* mortal,' said Wednesday. 'You died on the tree, Shadow. You died and you came back.'

'So? I don't even remember how I did that. If they kill me this time, I'll still be dead.'

Wednesday finished his beer. Then he waved his beer bottle around, as if he were conducting an invisible orchestra with it, and sang another verse:

'My brother's a missionary worker,
He saves fallen women from sin,
For five bucks he'll save you a redhead,
My God how the money rolls in.'

'You aren't helping,' said Shadow. The diner was a train carriage now, rattling through a snowy night.

Wednesday put down his beer bottle, and he fixed Shadow with his real eye, the one that wasn't glass. 'It's patterns,' he said. 'If they think you're a hero, they're wrong. After you die, you don't get to be Beowulf or Perseus or Rama any more. Whole different set of rules. Chess, not checkers. *Go*, not chess. You understand?'

'Not even a little,' said Shadow, frustrated.

People, in the corridor of the big house, moving loudly and drunkenly, shushing each other as they stumbled and giggled their way down the hall.

Shadow wondered if they were servants, or if they were strays from the other wing, slumming. And the dreams took him once again . . .

Now he was back in the bothy where he had sheltered from the rain the day before. There was a body on the floor: a boy, no more than five years old. Naked, on his back, limbs spread. There was a flash of intense light, and someone pushed through Shadow as if he was not there and rearranged the position of the boy's arms. Another flash of light.

Shadow knew the man taking the photographs. It was Dr Gaskell, the little steel-haired man from the hotel bar.

Gaskell took a white-paper bag from his pocket, and fished about in it for something that he popped into his mouth. 'Dolly mixtures,' he said to the child on the stone floor. 'Yum yum. Your favourites.' He smiled and crouched down, and took another photograph of the dead boy.

Shadow pushed through the stone wall of the cottage, flowing through the cracks in the stones like the wind. He flowed down to the seashore. The waves crashed on the rocks and Shadow kept moving across the water, through grey seas, up the swells and down again, towards the ship made of dead men's nails.

The ship was far away, out at sea, and Shadow passed across the surface of the water like the shadow of a cloud.

The ship was huge. He had not understood before how huge it was. A hand reached down and grasped his hand, pulled him up from the sea on to the deck.

'Bring us back,' said a voice as loud as the crashing of the sea, urgent and fierce. 'Bring us back, or let us go.' Only one eye burned in that bearded face.

'I'm not keeping you here.'

They were giants, on that ship, huge men made of shadows and frozen sea-spray, creatures of dream and foam.

One of them, huger than all the rest, red-bearded, stepped forward. 'We cannot land,' he boomed. 'We cannot leave.'

'Go home,' said Shadow.

'We came with our people to this southern country,' said the one-eyed man. 'But they left us. They sought other, tamer gods, and they renounced us in their hearts, and gave us over.'

'Go home,' repeated Shadow.

'Too much time has passed,' said the red-bearded man.

By the hammer at his side, Shadow knew him. 'Too much blood has been spilled. You are of our blood, Baldur. Set us free.'

And Shadow wanted to say that he was not theirs, was not anybody's, but the thin blanket had slipped from the bed, and his feet stuck out at the bottom, and thin moonlight filled the attic room.

There was silence, now, in that huge house. Something howled in the hills, and Shadow shivered.

He lay in a bed that was too small for him, and imagined time as something that pooled and puddled, wondered if there were places where time hung heavy, places where it was heaped and held – cities, he thought, must be filled with time: all the places where people congregated, where they came and brought time with them.

And if that were true, Shadow mused, then there could be other places, where the people were thin on the ground, and the land waited, bitter and granite, and a thousand years was an eyeblink to the hills – a scudding of clouds, a wavering of rushes, and nothing more, in the places where time was as thin on the ground as the people . . .

'They are going to kill you,' whispered Jennie, the barmaid.

Shadow sat beside her now, on the hill, in the moonlight. 'Why would they want to do that?' he asked. 'I don't matter.'

'It's what they do to monsters,' she said. 'It's what they have to do. It's what they've always done.'

He reached out to touch her, but she turned away from him. From behind, she was empty and hollow. She turned again, so she was facing him. 'Come away,' she whispered.

'You can come to me,' he said.

'I can't,' she said. 'There are things in the way. The way there is hard, and it is guarded. But you can call. If you call me, I'll come.'

Then dawn came, and with it a cloud of midges from the boggy land at the foot of the hill. Jennie flicked at them with her tail, but it was no use: they descended on Shadow like a cloud, until he was breathing midges, his nose and mouth filling with the tiny crawling stinging things, and he was choking on the darkness . . .

He wrenched himself back into his bed and his body and his life, into wakefulness, his heart pounding in his chest, gulping for breath.

VII

Breakfast was kippers, grilled tomatoes, scrambled eggs, toast, two stubby, thumb-like sausages and slices of something dark and round and flat that Shadow didn't recognise.

'What's this?' asked Shadow.

'Black pudden,' said the man sitting next to him. He was one of the security guards, and was reading a copy of yesterday's *Sun* as he ate. 'Blood and herbs. They cook the blood until it congeals into a sort of a dark, herby scab.' He forked some eggs on to his toast, ate it with his fingers. 'I don't know. What is it they say, you should never see anyone making sausages or the law? Something like that.'

Shadow ate the rest of the breakfast, but he left the black pudding alone.

There was a pot of real coffee, now, and he drank a mug of it, hot and black, to wake him up and to clear his head.

Smith walked in. 'Shadow-man. Can I borrow you for five minutes?'

'You're paying,' said Shadow. They walked out into the corridor.

'It's Mister Alice,' said Smith. 'He wants a quick word.' They crossed from the dismal whitewashed servants' wing into the wood-panelled vastness of the old house. They walked up the huge wooden staircase, and into a library. No one was there.

'He'll just be a minute,' said Smith. 'I'll make sure he knows you're waiting.'

The books in the library were protected from mice and dust and people by locked doors of glass and wire mesh. There was a painting of a stag on the wall, and Shadow walked over to look at it. The stag was haughty, and superior; behind it a valley filled with mist.

'*The Monarch of the Glen*,' said Mr Alice, walking in slowly, leaning on his stick. 'The most reproduced picture of Victorian times. That's not the original, but it was done by Landseer in the late 1850s as a copy of his own painting. I love it, although I'm sure I shouldn't. He did the lions in Trafalgar Square, Landseer. Same bloke.'

He walked over to the bay window, and Shadow walked with him. Below them, in the courtyard, servants were putting out chairs and tables. By the pond in the centre of the courtyard other people, party guests Shadow could see, were building bonfires out of logs and wood.

'Why don't they have the servants build the fires?' asked Shadow.

'Why should *they* have the fun?' said Mr Alice. 'It'd be like sending your man out into the rough some afternoon to shoot pheasants for you. There's something about building a bonfire, when you've hauled over the wood, and put it down in the perfect place, that's special. Or so they tell me. I've not done it myself.' He turned away from the window. 'Take a seat,' he said. 'I'll get a crick in my neck looking up at you.'

Shadow sat down.

'I've heard a lot about you,' said Mr Alice. 'Been wanting to meet you for a while. They said you were a smart young man who was going places. That's what they said.'

'So you didn't just hire a tourist to keep the neighbours away from your party?'

'Well, yes and no. We had a few other candidates, obviously. It's just you were perfect for the job. And when I realised who you were – well, a gift from the gods, really, weren't you?'

'I don't know. Was I?'

'Absolutely. You see, this party goes back a very long way. Almost a thousand years, they've been having it. Never missed a single year. And every year there's a fight, between our man and their man. And our man wins. This year, our man is you.'

'Who . . .' said Shadow. 'Who are *they*? And who are *you*?'

'I am your host,' said Mr Alice. 'I suppose . . .' He stopped, for a moment, tapped his walking-stick against the wooden floor. '*They* are the ones who lost, a long time ago. *We* won. We were the knights, and they were the dragons, we were the giant-killers, they were the ogres. We were the men and they were the monsters. And *we won*. They know their place now. And tonight is all about not letting them forget it. It's humanity you'll be fighting for tonight. We can't let them get the upper hand. Not even a little. Us versus them.'

'Doctor Gaskell said that I was a monster,' said Shadow.

'Doctor Gaskell?' said Mr Alice. 'Friend of yours?'

'No,' said Shadow. 'He works for you. Or for the people who work for you. I think he kills children, and takes pictures of them.'

Mr Alice dropped his walking-stick. He bent down, awkwardly, to pick it up. Then he said, 'Well, I don't think you're a monster, Shadow. I think you're a hero.'

No, thought Shadow. *You think I'm a monster. But you think I'm your monster.*

'Now, you do well tonight,' said Mr Alice, 'and I know you will, and you can name your price. You ever wondered why some people were film stars, or famous, or rich? Bet you think, He's got no talent. What's he got that I haven't got? Well, sometimes the answer is, he's got someone like me on his side.'

'Are you a god?' asked Shadow.

Mr Alice laughed then, a deep, full-throated chuckle. 'Nice one, Mister Moon. Not at all. I'm just a boy from Streatham who's done well for himself.'

'So who do I fight?' asked Shadow.

'You'll meet him tonight,' said Mr Alice. 'Now, there's stuff needs to come down from the attic. Why don't you lend Smithie a hand? Big lad like you, it'll be a doddle.'

The audience was over and, as if on cue, Smith walked in.

'I was just saying,' said Mr Alice, 'that our boy here would help you bring the stuff down from the attic.'

'Triffic,' said Smith. 'Come on, Shadow. Let's wend our way upwards.'

They went up, through the house, up a dark wooden stairway, to a padlocked door, which Smith unlocked, into a dusty wooden attic, piled high with what looked like . . .

'Drums?' said Shadow.

'Drums,' said Smith. They were made of wood and of animal skins. Each drum was a different size. 'Right, let's take them down.'

They carried the drums downstairs. Smith carried one at a time, holding it as if it was precious. Shadow carried two.

'So what really happens tonight?' asked Shadow, on their third trip, or perhaps their fourth.

'Well,' said Smith, 'most of it, as I understand, you're best off figuring out on your own. As it happens.'

'And you and Mister Alice. What part do you play in this?'

Smith gave him a sharp look. They put the drums down at the foot of the stairs, in the great hall. There were several men there, talking in front of the fire.

When they were back up the stairs again, and out of earshot of the guests, Smith said, 'Mister Alice will be leaving us late this afternoon. I'll stick around.'

'He's leaving? Isn't he part of this?'

Smith looked offended. 'He's the host,' he said. 'But.' He stopped. Shadow understood. Smith didn't talk about his employer. They carried more drums down the stairs. When they had brought down all the drums, they carried down heavy leather bags.

'What's in these?' asked Shadow.

'Drumsticks,' said Smith.

Smith continued, 'They're old families. That lot downstairs. Very old money. They know who's boss, but that doesn't make him one of them. See? They're the only ones who'll be at tonight's party. They'd not want Mister Alice. See?'

And Shadow did see. He wished that Smith hadn't spoken to him about Mr Alice. He didn't think Smith would have said anything to anyone he thought would live to talk about it.

But all he said was, 'Heavy drumsticks.'

VIII

A small helicopter took Mr Alice away late that afternoon. Land-Rovers took away the staff. Smith drove the last one. Only Shadow was left behind, and the guests, with their smart clothes, and their smiles.

They stared at Shadow as if he were a captive lion who had been brought for their amusement, but they did not talk to him.

The dark-haired woman, the one who had smiled at Shadow as she had arrived, brought him food to eat: a steak, almost rare. She brought it to him on a plate, without cutlery, as if she expected him to eat it with his fingers and his teeth, and he was hungry, and he did.

'I am not your hero,' he told them, but they would not meet his gaze. Nobody spoke to him, not directly. He felt like an animal.

And then it was dusk. They led Shadow to the inner courtyard, by the rusty fountain, and they stripped him naked, at gunpoint, and the women smeared his body with some kind of thick yellow grease, rubbing it in.

They put a knife on the grass in front of him. A gesture with a gun, and Shadow picked the knife up. The hilt was black metal, rough and easy to hold. The blade looked sharp.

Then they threw open the great door, from the inner courtyard to the world outside, and two of the men lit the two high bonfires: they crackled and blazed.

They opened the leather bags, and each of the guests took out a single carved black stick, like a cudgel, knobbly and heavy. Shadow found himself thinking of Sawney Beane's children, swarming up from the darkness holding clubs made of human thigh-bones . . .

Then the guests arranged themselves around the edge of the courtyard and they began to beat the drums with the sticks.

They started slow, and they started quietly, a deep, throbbing pounding, like a heartbeat. Then they began to crash and slam into strange rhythms, staccato beats that wove and wound, louder and louder, until they filled Shadow's mind and his world. It seemed to him that the firelight flickered to the rhythms of the drums.

And then, from outside the house, the howling began.

There was pain in the howling, and anguish, and it echoed across the hills above the drumbeats, a wail of pain and loss and hate.

The figure that stumbled through the doorway to the courtyard was clutching its head, covering its ears, as if to stop the pounding of the drumbeats.

The firelight caught it.

It was huge, now, bigger than Shadow, and naked. It was perfectly hairless, and dripping wet.

It lowered its hands from its ears, and it stared around, its face twisted into a mad grimace. 'Stop it!' it screamed. 'Stop making all that noise!'

And the people in their pretty clothes beat their drums harder, and faster, and the noise filled Shadow's head and chest.

The monster stepped into the centre of the courtyard. It looked at Shadow. 'You,' it said. 'I told you. I told you about the noise,' and it howled, a deep throaty howl of hatred and challenge.

The creature edged closer to Shadow. It saw the knife, and stopped. 'Fight me!' it shouted. 'Fight me fair! Not with cold iron! Fight me!'

'I don't want to fight you,' said Shadow. He dropped the knife on to the grass, raised his hands to show them empty.

'Too late,' said the bald thing that was not a man. 'Too late for that.'

And it launched itself at Shadow.

Later, when Shadow thought of that fight, he remembered only fragments: he remembered being slammed to the ground, and throwing himself out of the way. He remembered the pounding of the drums, and the expressions on the faces of the drummers as they stared, hungrily, between the bonfires, at the two men in the firelight.

They fought, wrestling and pounding each other.

Salt tears ran down the monster's face as it wrestled with Shadow. They were equally matched, it seemed to Shadow.

The monster slammed its arm into Shadow's face, and Shadow tasted his own blood. He could feel his own anger beginning to rise, like a red wall of hate.

He swung a leg out, hooking the monster behind the knee, and as it stumbled back Shadow's fist crashed into its gut, making it cry out and roar with anger and pain.

A glance at the guests: Shadow saw the blood-lust on the faces of the drummers.

There was a cold wind, a sea-wind, and it seemed to Shadow that there were huge shadows in the sky, vast figures that he had seen on a ship made of the fingernails of dead men, and that they were staring down at him, that this fight was what was keeping them frozen on their ship, unable to land, unable to leave.

This fight was old, Shadow thought, older than even Mr Alice knew, and he was thinking that even as the creature's talons raked his chest. It was the fight of man against monster, and it was as old as time: it was Theseus battling the Minotaur, it was Beowulf and Grendel, it was every hero who had ever stood between the firelight and the darkness and wiped the blood of something inhuman from his sword.

The bonfires burned, and the drums pounded and throbbed and pulsed like the beating of a thousand hearts.

Shadow slipped on the damp grass, as the monster came at him, and he was down. The creature's fingers were around Shadow's neck, and it was squeezing; Shadow could feel everything starting to thin, to become distant.

He closed his hand around a patch of grass, and pulled at it, dug his fingers deep, grabbing a handful of grass and clammy earth, and he smashed the clod of dirt into the monster's face, momentarily blinding it.

He pushed up, and was on top of the creature, now. He rammed his knee hard into its groin, and it doubled into a foetal position, and howled, and sobbed.

Shadow realised that the drumming had stopped, and he looked up.

The guests had put down their drums.

They were all approaching him, in a circle, men and women, still holding their drumsticks, but holding them like cudgels. They were not looking at Shadow, though: they were staring at the monster on the ground, and they raised their black sticks and moved towards it in the light of the twin fires.

Shadow said, 'Stop!'

The first club-blow came down on the creature's head. It wailed and twisted, raising an arm to ward off the next blow.

Shadow threw himself in front of it, shielding it with his body. The dark-haired woman who had smiled at him before now brought down her club on his shoulder, dispassionately, and another club, from a man this time, hit him a numbing blow in the leg, and third struck him on his side.

They'll kill us both, he thought. *Him first, then me. That's what they do. That's what they always do.* And then, *She said she would come. If I called her.*

Shadow whispered, 'Jennie?'

There was no reply. Everything was happening so slowly. Another club was coming down, this one aimed at his hand. Shadow rolled out of the way awkwardly, watched the heavy wood smash into the turf.

'Jennie,' he said, picturing her too-fair hair in his mind, her thin face, her smile. 'I call you. Come now. *Please.*'

A gust of cold wind.

The dark-haired woman had raised her club high, and brought it down now, fast, hard, aiming for Shadow's face.

The blow never landed. A small hand caught the heavy stick as if it were a twig.

Fair hair blew about her head, in the cold wind. He could not have told you what she was wearing.

She looked at him. Shadow thought that she looked disappointed.

One of the men aimed a cudgel-blow at the back of her head. It never connected. She turned . . .

A rending sound, as if something was tearing itself apart . . .

And then the bonfires exploded. That was how it seemed. There was blazing wood all over the courtyard, even in the house. And the people were screaming in the bitter wind.

Shadow staggered to his feet.

The monster lay on the ground, bloodied and twisted. Shadow did not know if it was alive or not. He picked it up, hauled it over his shoulder, and staggered out of the courtyard with it.

He stumbled out on to the gravel forecourt, as the massive wooden doors slammed closed behind them. Nobody else would be coming out. Shadow kept moving down the slope, one step at a time, down towards the loch.

When he reached the water's edge he stopped, and sank to his knees, and let the bald man down on to the grass as gently as he could.

He heard something crash, and looked back up the hill. The house was burning.

'How is he?' said a woman's voice.

Shadow turned. She was knee deep in the water, the creature's mother, wading towards the shore.

'I don't know,' said Shadow. 'He's hurt.'

'You're both hurt,' she said. 'You're all bluid and bruises.'

'Yes,' said Shadow.

'Still,' she said, 'he's not dead. And that makes a nice change.'

She had reached the shore now. She sat on the bank, with her son's head in her lap. She took a packet of tissues from her handbag, and spat on a tissue, and began fiercely to scrub at her son's face with it, rubbing away the blood.

The house on the hill was roaring now. Shadow had not imagined that a burning house would make so much noise.

The old woman looked up at the sky. She made a noise in the back of her throat, a clucking noise, and then she shook her head. 'You know,' she said, 'you've let them in. They'd been bound for so long, and you've let them in.'

'Is that a good thing?' asked Shadow.

'I don't know, love,' said the little woman, and she shook her head again. She crooned to her son as if he were still her baby, and dabbed at his wounds with her spit.

Shadow was naked, at the edge of the loch, but the heat from the burning building kept him warm. He watched the reflected flames in the glassy water of the loch. A yellow moon was rising.

He was starting to hurt. Tomorrow, he knew, he would hurt much worse.

Footsteps on the grass behind him. He looked up. 'Hello, Smithie,' said Shadow.

Smith looked down at the three of them. 'Shadow,' he said, shaking his head. 'Shadow, Shadow, Shadow, Shadow, Shadow. This was not how things were meant to turn out.'

'Sorry,' said Shadow.

'This will cause real embarrassment to Mister Alice,' said Smith. 'Those people were his guests.'

'They were animals,' said Shadow.

'If they were,' said Smith, 'they were rich and important animals. There'll be widows and orphans and God knows what to take care of. Mister Alice will not be pleased.' He said it like a judge pronouncing a death sentence.

'Are you threatening him?' asked the old lady.

'I don't threaten,' said Smith, flatly.

She smiled. 'Ah,' she said. 'Well, I do. And if you or that fat bastard you work for hurt this young man, it'll be the worse for both of you.' She smiled then, with sharp teeth, and Shadow felt the hairs on the back of his neck prickle. 'There's worse things than dying,' she said. 'And I know most of them. I'm not young, and I'm not one for idle talk. So if I were you,' she said, with a sniff, 'I'd look after this lad.'

She picked up her son with one arm, as if he were a child's doll, and she clutched her handbag close to her with the other.

Then she nodded to Shadow, and walked away, into the glass-dark water, and soon she and her son were gone beneath the surface of the loch.

'Fuck,' muttered Smith.

Shadow didn't say anything.

Smith fumbled in his pocket. He pulled out the pouch of tobacco, and rolled himself a cigarette. Then he lit it. 'Right,' he said.

'Right?' said Shadow.

'We better get you cleaned up, and find you some clothes. You'll catch your death, otherwise. You heard what she said.'

IX

They had the best room waiting for Shadow, that night, back at the hotel. And, less than an hour after Shadow returned, Gordon on the front desk brought up a new backpack for him, a box of new clothes, even new boots. He asked no questions.

There was a large envelope on top of the pile of clothes.

Shadow ripped it open. It contained his passport, slightly scorched, his wallet, and money: several bundles of new fifty-pound notes, wrapped in rubber bands. *My God, how the money rolls in*, he thought, without pleasure, and tried, without success, to remember where he had heard that song before.

He took a long bath, to soak away the pain.

And then he slept.

In the morning he dressed, and walked up the lane next to the hotel that led up the hill and out of the village. There had been a cottage at the top of the hill, he was sure of it, with lavender in the garden, a stripped pine counter-top and a purple sofa, but no matter where he looked there was no cottage on the hill, nor any evidence that there ever had been anything there but grass and a hawthorn tree.

He called her name, but there was no reply, only the wind coming in off the sea, bringing with it the first promises of winter.

Still, she was waiting for him, when he got back to the hotel room. She was sitting on the bed, wearing her old brown coat, inspecting her fingernails. She did not look up when he unlocked the door and walked in.

'Hello, Jennie,' he said.

'Hello,' she said. Her voice was very quiet.

'Thank you,' he said. 'You saved my life.'

'You called,' she said dully. 'I came.'

He said, 'What's wrong?'

She looked at him, then. 'I could have been yours,' she

said, and there were tears in her eyes. 'I thought you would love me. Perhaps. One day.'

'Well,' he said, 'maybe we could find out. We could take a walk tomorrow together, maybe. Not a long one, I'm afraid, I'm a bit of a mess physically.'

She shook her head.

The strangest thing, Shadow thought, was that she did not look human any longer: she now looked like what she was, a wild thing, a forest thing. Her tail twitched on the bed, under her coat. She was very beautiful, and, he realised, he wanted her, very badly.

'The hardest thing about being a *hulder*,' said Jennie, 'even a *hulder* very far from home, is that, if you don't want to be lonely, you have to love a man.'

'So love me. Stay with me,' said Shadow. 'Please.'

'You,' she said, sadly and finally, 'are not a man.'

She stood up.

'Still,' she said, 'everything's changing. Maybe I can go home again now. After a thousand years I don't even know if I remember any *norsk*.'

She took his hands in her small hands, which could bend iron bars, which could crush rocks to sand, and she squeezed his fingers very gently. And she was gone.

He stayed another day in that hotel, and then he caught the bus to Thurso, and the train from Thurso to Inverness.

He dozed on the train, although he did not dream.

When he woke, there was a man on the seat next to him. A hatchet-faced man, reading a paperback book. He closed the book when he saw that Shadow was awake. Shadow looked down at the cover: Jean Cocteau's *The Difficulty of Being*. 'Good book?' asked Shadow.

'Yeah, all right,' said Smith. 'It's all essays. They're

meant to be personal, but you feel that every time he looks up innocently and says, "This is me," it's some kind of double-bluff. I liked *Belle et la Bête*, though. I felt closer to him watching that than through any of these essays.'

'It's all on the cover,' said Shadow.

'How d'you mean?'

'The difficulty of being Jean Cocteau.'

Smith scratched his nose.

'Here,' he said. He passed Shadow a copy of the *Scotsman*. 'Page nine.'

At the bottom of page nine was a small story: retired doctor kills himself. Gaskell's body had been found in his car, parked in a picnic spot on the coast road. He had swallowed quite a cocktail of painkillers, washed down with most of a bottle of Lagavulin.

'Mister Alice hates being lied to,' said Smith. 'Especially by the hired help.'

'Is there anything in there about the fire?' asked Shadow.

'What fire?'

'Oh. Right.'

'It wouldn't surprise me if there wasn't a terrible run of luck for the great and the good over the next couple of months, though. Car crashes. Train crash. Maybe a plane'll go down. Grieving widows and orphans and boyfriends. Very sad.'

Shadow nodded.

'You know,' said Smith, 'Mister Alice is very concerned about your health. He worries. I worry too.'

'Yeah?' said Shadow.

'Absolutely. I mean, if something happens to you while you're in the country. Maybe you look the wrong way crossing the road. Flash a wad of cash in the wrong pub. I dunno. The point is, if you got hurt, then whatsername, Grendel's mum, might take it the wrong way.'

'So?'

'So we think you should leave the UK. Be safer for everyone, wouldn't it?'

Shadow said nothing for a while. The train began to slow.

'Okay,' said Shadow.

'This is my stop,' said Smith. 'I'm getting out here. We'll arrange the ticket, first class, of course, to anywhere you're heading. One-way ticket. You just have to tell me where you want to go.'

Shadow rubbed the bruise on his cheek. There was something about the pain that was almost comforting.

The train came to a complete stop. It was a small station, seemingly in the middle of nowhere. There was a large black car parked by the building, in the thin sunshine. The windows were tinted, and Shadow could not see inside.

Smith pushed down the train window, reached outside to open the carriage door, and he stepped out on to the platform. He looked back in at Shadow through the open window. 'Well?'

'I think,' said Shadow, 'that I'll spend a couple of weeks looking around the UK. And you'll just have to pray that I look the right way when I cross your roads.'

'And then?'

Shadow knew it, then. Perhaps he had known it all along.

'Chicago,' he said to Smith, as the train gave a jerk, and began to move away from the station. He felt older, as he said it. But he could not put it off for ever.

And then he said, so quietly that only he could have heard it, 'I guess I'm going home.'

Soon afterwards it began to rain: huge, pelting drops that rattled against the windows and blurred the world into greys and greens. Deep rumbles of thunder accompanied Shadow on his journey south: the storm grumbled, the wind howled and the lightning made huge shadows across the sky, and in their company Shadow slowly began to feel less alone.

Neil Gaiman is the author of over thirty acclaimed books and graphic novels for adults and children, including *American Gods*, *Neverwhere*, *Stardust*, *Coraline*, *The Graveyard Book* and *Trigger Warning: Short Fictions and Disturbances*, His most recent novel for adults, *The Ocean at the End of the Lane*, was highly acclaimed, appeared on the hardback and paperback *Sunday Times* bestseller lists and won several awards, including being voted Book of the Year at the National Book Awards 2013: 'Some books you read. Some books you enjoy. But some books just swallow you up, heart and soul' Joanne Harris.

The recipient of numerous literary honours, Neil Gaiman's work has been adapted for film, television and radio. He has written scripts for *Doctor Who*, collaborated with authors and illustrators including Terry Pratchett, Dave McKean and Chris Riddell, and *The Sandman* is established as one of the classic graphic novels. As George R. R. Martin says: 'There's no one quite like Neil Gaiman.'

Originally from England, Neil Gaiman now lives in America.

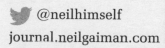 @neilhimself

journal.neilgaiman.com